INFINITE DIMENSIONS

(SUPERHEROES FROM WALL STREET)

INFINITE DIMENSIONS

(SUPERHEROES FROM WALL STREET)

J.A. SEBASTIN

If you have any questions regarding the trademark, copyright or content,
please email the author @ Author@jasebastin.com

Book cover designer: Joseph Meloy
Book interior designer: David Moratto

Publisher : Create Space (Print on Demand) powered by Amazon.

For readers' comments and feedback please email @ readers@jasebastin.com
Also, visit us at www.jasebastin.com for additional details about the book.

Paperback : ISBN-13: 978-0-9898675-9-7
Hardcover : ISBN-13: 978-0-9898675-5-9

Library of Congress Control Number (LCCN) : 2013916170

Dedicated to my loved ones,
Oliver Frank Sebastin, Rev. Sam,
Latouchmi Narayanan and Liga Pabrukle.

My heartfelt thanks to all the souls below,
who did an outstanding job copy editing and proof reading.
Tamara Hellgren
Joyce Glimour
Laurel Robinson
John Sully
Nowick Gray
Laura Bush
Paula Plantier

Special thanks to my book cover designer.
Joseph Meloy

ACKNOWLEDGEMENTS

When I heard a voice from *Infinite Dimensions*, ten happy kids walked into my mind and said, "You are the only chosen one to write this true message of the universe, and you are a true, ready-born writer; write everything that comes from your mind, for your name shall be exalted beyond time and space." I searched my entire life for signs of my purpose, and I found that I love art and creativity. I realized one fact about myself: As far back as I could remember, I wanted to be a writer and movie director. I would love to now thank all of the souls who encouraged me along the way. When I first came up with the idea about this novel, I shared it with my friends Michael Lo and Latouchmi Narayanan. They appreciated it and blessed me, saying, "You are going to be one good writer; just go for it." I didn't know which city to pick in this country, and after much debating, my Scottish best friend Kris Craig said "Wisconsin, Milwaukee, will be the best place to start." I pondered this for days, and realized that the great Midwest would indeed be an interesting place to start my novel. I therefore thank every living soul residing in the American Midwest.

My special thanks to my beloved and noble friend, Divna Duke, who agreed to hang out for a full day while I was telling her about my novel. We discussed various aspects of life and shared our wisdom, which reassured me that I have the greatest message to tell this world. Also, my love and kisses to my sweet godchild Victoria, daughter of Divna, who revived me constantly with the innocence and high energy that all children carry with them. After I started writing, I had serious doubts about my language and grammar. At this juncture, I met Tamara Hellgren, who volunteered to be my copy editor and encouraged me a great deal. She was the first copy editor of my life as a novelist, and my heart will always thank and appreciate her for her confident and compassionate words.

If someone were to ask me: "Who is a real, talented person in all aspects of life here in NYC?" I wouldn't think twice: it is my man Frank Jones. He was very enthusiastic when I shared my novel, and said only one thing to me always: "This novel is for people with cerebrum, mind and wisdom, for people who are looking for radical change" and that "this will be a book for the future." He told me that my approach to my idea was outstanding, and that the world wanted to read a book like this.

Now let's talk about blunders: while writing I made a pretty big mistake in the novel; due to a mental block, I miswrote the name "Judah" as "Juan," one of the ten kids. I thank my two buddies, my first best American woman, Alisha Frank (Hawrylyszyn), and her best friend, Stephanie Rosenberg, for correcting this error. Simple words of appreciation don't suffice, but I will always be grateful for how they motivated me and gave me lots of positive vibrations.

I could write an encyclopedia about all the characters, imaginations, and personalities I met while I wrote this novel. To keep the list short, I will simply give my thanks to all the living souls who motivated and appreciated my novel; without you beauties, this day would not have been possible.

CONTENTS

Chapter 1
A New Way

ONE DAY, I WILL FLY LIKE A BIRD WITH NO LIMITS, SOARING ACROSS THE universe, smelling the scent of the Milky Way. First, my hope in myself needs to be strengthened and my WORD will make it happen. My inspirations and passions are like those of every human who dreamed to be immortal. Every soul has died trying to be a genius, an aberrant, a mystical legend, a superhero; to be rich, to have eternal happiness, or to be efficacious, a celebrity in movies, hailed as glorious by the world, for all ages and for all time. Yet all of these desires waned when I realized that I am still a human with faded flesh, a broken spirit, and a weak heart. But it is not my fault, being the product of this world's fragile knowledge and teachings.

My search started at a very young age. I asked myself why a common man, with his mighty strength, couldn't be a superhero. Since then, I have been in a constant search to make sci-fi characters real in this world. I am on a search to perform miracles, such as those heard of only in myths, and to lead an exemplary life with no failures. I am on a search to make philosophy a part of life for prosaic people. To begin, I am called Oliver J. Oscar, named after the great Oscar Shrine family. I was born in Milwaukee, Wisconsin. My father was a general in the U.S. Marines. He died a hero in the Gulf War. He fought for his country and saved countless innocent lives before he died. Did you hear what I said? He was a real hero; he believed that being a Marine was a burden and he placed his life in the hands of the galaxy. He is my superhero, now and forever.

My father was a big fan of Superman. He was also the one who influenced me and taught me to be brave, powerful and compassionate like a real Superman. We would sit up late at night, with his green teacup in his hand and he tucked me in my furry white blanket, talking about superheroes. We would discuss their adventures, missions, mighty strengths, powers, blessings and curses for hours. We watched superhero movies, and he read me all the superhero comics he could find. I enjoyed each and every discussion. We often had debates over certain aspects of being a superhero, and he patiently listened to my doubts and answered my never-ending questions. All of my father's teachings made me feel active and alive, like there was a special purpose in life for me. I loved my father so much, and because of him, I started to explore the origins of the lives of superheroes. I then started to uncover the truth about them.

After my father's death, my mother raised me. She was a really wonderful lady and the best mom that one could ever hope for. But she was not like my father and me. She didn't believe in superheroes, and she was very religious — a true Christian. Her superheroes were God and Jesus. She went to church every day and conducted Bible studies during the week with her friends. She wanted to steer me away from the fantasy of a superhero search and the craziness she thought it would lead to in my mind. She spent all of her time trying to make me religious. I do believe in God, but I didn't agree with the way she viewed the world. My mother was not named after a Greek god, like Aphrodite, Athena, or Hera; she was just called Olivia Oscar. My mom is the messenger of light and prays for me every day so that I may be enlightened to walk in God's way. With her soft hands on my head, she asks God to shower me with his wisdom, and I do feel something running through me when she touches my head, but I can't wholly accept her view. Every day I search for a way to make a mortal man into a superhero, and this is often the only thought running through my mind. I often just sit and think about this very deeply. But with my thoughts wandering, I would find myself ending up critiquing and analyzing the characters of 'superheroes' characters, such as why didn't they teach common men and women how to be strong and become the master of one's own fate? Were they jealous? Is that why they kept all the secrets to themselves?

Well, at this time you might be wondering where I am now. I am sitting in an office on Wall Street, the very place where the concept of money was born and nursed. My superhero suit, which I made for myself, is a chairman and CEO suit. There is no cape or mask or wings or frills. It's just a blue suit and blue shirt with a tie wagging around my neck like a dog's tail, telling the world that I dress for success. My life has changed now and I know the rules. I sometimes bend them, but I never break them. I have made a difference to the people around me and they are also learning, practicing, mastering, and living the lessons and truth I have learned in my life and tried to pass on to them.

It takes only a little time, even less than a second, to understand who you are, why you are here, the very purpose of life. But in order to understand the concept of life in less than a second, we have to first open our eyes, ears, minds, and listen, observe and think. If we do this, we will find wisdom, and all the answers will appear.

I see the world differently now. I see all the waves passing around me, the electromagnetic fields, the patterns of light and all of the energy that exists in this hyperspace. At this moment, everyone can experience one singular idea and concept: the truth, which exists in the superhero realm. Unfortunately, the realm has been misunderstood throughout the years due to philosophical doctrines, religions, cults, fantasy stories, scientific theories, evolutionary misconceptions, cultural and patriotic practices. But my goal is to make every son and daughter, all made of atoms and molecules, a better race, a singular race filled with happiness, peace, immortality and abundance. That is the goal in life. I believe that, at this point in my life, I have found it in myself and now is the time to share the good message. When did this actually begin? How did I find it? What inspired me? Who pointed me in the right direction towards the single answer that could define our existence?

It all started when I was a child. Every kid should have a city and state name and I do. Yes, I was born in Milwaukee, Wisconsin. It is a beautiful city filled with fresh air that filled me with wondrous thoughts. Fresh air is very important, because it is harder to get these days due to our environmental pollution. My street name is called Wall Street, but it's not the financial capital or international money-laundering center; it's a street in a neighborhood filled with families who believed in the idea of superheroes and dreamed to one day be like them. They veered away from other ideas the world tried to teach us; ours was a fun fantasy neighborhood. My father's family grew up here and our house name is called 'Krypton'. This is the home where I was born. My mom is from a different neighborhood, where they believed in God and the values of this country, a heavenly neighborhood filled with angels' voices to give directions and church bells chiming to tell the time. My dad always teases mom about her neighborhood, because she did not use the wall clock in our home to check the time, but rather depended on the rusted church bells ringing.

The church bells in my life mean a lot, because on my parents wedding day, the bell ringer was so drunk that he forgot to ring the bell. He had fallen asleep in the bell room, with his pants around his ankles, and did not ring the bell as my father took out the wedding ring and was about to place it on my mother's hand. My father didn't know the rules of church bell practices, so as he was pulling my mother's hand to put the ring on her finger, she was pulling back from him. My father was in a panic because he assumed she didn't like him, and his face grew pale as he asked her, "Olivia, why are you doing this to me now?" The people in the congregation started to whisper, and the priest peeped out over his glasses and, looking at my father, said, "Son, have patience. We are working on it." The priest ordered the altar boys to check the bell ringer, and my mom explained through her tears, "They have to ring the bell for us to exchange rings." My father gave a deep sigh of relief as he realized that he hadn't lost my mother after all. He said wittily, "If by chance I take you on a honeymoon to Paris, don't put the church bell in your pockets and carry the bell ringer in your luggage."

They found the bell ringer, who was drunk and had locked the bell room from the inside so no one could get in. My father's friends decided to shoot bullets in the air instead of the traditional church bell. Standing outside of the church, his friends began shooting and bullets flew up into the air like fire tongues. My mother and father exchanged rings and the priest, who was angry about the chaos the bell ringer had caused, said, "Amen to this wonderful couple." My father's first words to my mother after the wedding were, "When God's children make a mistake, only a Superman can fix it." Bing! This, of course, made my mother's face pale as she asked him to stop. My mother was a gentle woman, but when faced with conflictions regarding her faith, she would become very upset.

Seriously, what happened to the bell ringer? He had fallen asleep in the bell room, like a little baby. How did they wake him? They broke down the room and woke him with a water hose. They showered him for ages like a great waterfall, with strong jets of water. The priest was disappointed with the bell ringer, because not only did he forget to do his job and turn up drunk during a wedding ceremony, but this time he had gotten himself high on cocaine and moonshine.

So, my parents' married life started with a funny bell-ringing story, and beliefs were put on trial. Nevertheless, they were the happiest couple I've ever known. They loved each other so much. The one thing that tied them together was their common belief: they loved good and hated evil, in the same way that Superman and Jesus acted upon good and evil. But Jesus forgave the people who committed crimes, while Superman reprimanded them. My whole family believed in a supernatural world, one with both God and superheroes in it, with divine power that could create and protect the good while crushing evil. So I am a product of superheroes and God combined: two book-ends of the world's hyper-beliefs.

My parents started their life together in my father's home on Wall Street. My father got time off from the Marines and worked as an assistant manager at a local bank while my mother stayed at home and took care of the household. Accepting of their differences in beliefs, they were very happy. When my father came home late after work, with his shirt and pants disheveled and wrinkled, he would sit quietly on our brown couch and not move from there. My mom would return from church with a sense of rejuvenation about her. She would mix fresh drinks for my father, all the while sharing her experiences and revelations from her time at church. My father would patiently listen to her talk while waiting for her to finish his drink. He would drink a few sips and say, "Olivia, you have been going to church your entire life. Why don't any of your Gods—say, Jesus, his father, the Holy Spirit, or at least Jesus's disciples—come and visit you?" My mother, bending down and removing my father's shoes, would say, "Why don't any of your fantasy heroes—say, Superman, Spider-man, Batman, Thor, or at least Iron Man with that metal suit—come and knock at our door?"

Father responded, "Well, an eye for an eye. Why don't you believe that superheroes exist, Olivia?"

"They don't exist, it's just a myth!" was my mother's reply.

"It's the same as God. No one has seen him, but people believe in him," my father would snap back.

"Why don't you call yourself a superhero? You're always reading these comics and watching movies about them, just like a kid."

"Why should I call myself one?" My father sounded resigned, as though he didn't believe he deserved the title.

"You served and protected the country from our enemies. In my eyes, you are a superhero," my mother said warmly.

"Yes, true, you could call me a hero, but not a superhero," my father conceded.

At that point, my father didn't know how to answer my mother because his thoughts were hanging in limbo. I am not like my father. I do have answers for all questions; to me, a person who does good deeds should be called a god. A superhero is defined as an extraordinary person with powers such as flying, stopping a train, or being able to climb a building like a monkey. These individuals are able to do unexpected things at unexpected times, and essentially they are indestructible.

Though my parents loved to debate and talk a lot about their different perspectives, they spent their nights surrounded with love. If my dad had really had the strength of a superhero, he would have killed my mom by the morning with his strength while making love. But she woke up every day, unharmed. My father really was just a human under the sun and grounded by gravitational force.

During their time together, they continued their debates, arguing their beliefs. One day, my mother asked my father what he found inspiring about superheroes.

Father: In this world of injustice, evil and pain, I knew there had to be people who could help. That's when I started to believe in superheroes. I chose to follow Superman, my personal icon and hero, and I started to explore more about him in books, comics and movies.

Mother: Why don't you believe in God?

Father: No one has seen him. He has never helped anyone; he just watches people dying. I am better than God. In times of war I saved innocent people. I was able to help my friends.

Mother: How about Moses? He saved his people from the Egyptians.

Father: That may be true—a cult created by some fancy rabbi who wanted their fringes to be longer and shinier than other clans and people. Even if it did happen, Moses only saved his people once, and the story has been in the wind for about three thousand years, so why did the same God or Moses not save the Jews from the Holocaust? It was the Russians and Americans who went and put an end to the Nazis. Why isn't Moses considered a superhero?

Mother: That is the revelation, that we are the soldiers of God, to help the just when in need. Moses wasn't the only one to do things like that. There was Joshua, Elijah, and many others. But I would I love it, James, if you called Moses a superhero.

Father: Where are they now? I haven't heard of anyone in our day and age creating miracles. They're only in fairy tales.

Mother: These stories are documented in different forms of literature from different kinds of religions. There must be some truth in it.

Hearing all the debates from my mother and father I could tell one thing: they could not find a way to connect the dots. In the old days, superheroes were called angels, prophets, mystics, gods and magicians. In modern days we also call them superheroes. In our age, superheroes do exist in the form of Superman, Spider-Man, He-Man, Batman, and all types of *-man*. These people are not called angels, prophets, or gods, but rather they are characters of someone's imagination. Their costumes and outfits are different from the heroes of the past, the heroes from thousands of years ago. Our superheroes wear either pants or vests? We made superheroes look civilized and made them a part of our popular history. Our modern-day superheroes were invented around the eighteenth century. That is the time when pants started to become more popular, but the actual origin of superheroes dates back to around five thousand years ago, when we were still covering our bodies with leaves, mud and animal skins. The question is, did all these superheroes exist in our universe or in a parallel universe? How do we know what outfits they used, when we took so much time to upgrade them ourselves? Are these all man-made myths to make superheroes look better? Well, perhaps superheroes had their outfits upgraded so they could be proper twenty-first-century men. We always create images of ourselves with better skills than we have, yet we never claim that they are our ideals. We have created these ideal humans in all ages and in all aspects of life, from adventure, religion, fantasy stories, movies, cartoons, and so on.

Days passed by, and my parents made love often. They wanted to invent me, to have a by-product. It's time for the church bell to ring again for my anointing, and everyone hopes that this time the bell ringer does his job and does not get drunk. Right now I am communicating with you from my mother's womb. Yes, she's is pregnant and I am three months old in her womb. I can hear the world, but I can't see anything. I can hear my mother and father, the things that move around my mother and me. In fact, my search started when I was three months old inside my mother's womb.

When my mother and father have their heated discussions, I listen and try moving in the womb. My mom misunderstood this as a sign of my discomfort, as I moved inside and kicked her. She would tell my father, "James, we should stop it. He is not comfortable and is unhappy. He's rolling inside and kicking me while we argue." Yet, I was very comfortable as I moved. I just wanted to express myself, but she thought I was upset. My father would apologize and say, "I'm sorry, Olivia." He would press his ear to her belly and feel me, his boy, moving inside and say to my mom, "I think he is listening." He would then say to me, "I know he will follow my ways and become a fan of superheroes." My mother would get angry and say no. Then she would say that I would become a good Christian.

Nine months had passed and I was still an unborn child in my mother's womb. The Halloween party was around the corner, and I was preparing myself for that night as I listened to the discussion between my mother and father about the upcoming Halloween party. The teenagers in my neighborhood went crazy every Halloween, yelling and screaming in the street, and I couldn't take a good nap because of it. I was trying to roll from this side to that side, but I couldn't get any rest. There was a big celebration going on in my home, and my dad was dressed like Superman and all his friends came to visit him with their children. My mom cooked dinner for everyone, but she didn't like the Halloween party. My dad had convinced her to wear a costume, so she dressed as a pregnant angel. I loved the Halloween party and was trying to talk to everybody, but my voice was less than one decibel, so no one could hear me, and I felt sad. I couldn't even say "Hi" to anyone. Before I went to bed, I found out something strange, that people have dress codes and outfits for all occasions, from church to going to the cemetery, from citizens to Presidents, from sailors to astronauts, from chefs to dishwashers, from Halloween to Santa Claus, and so on. But why doesn't anyone want to wear an outfit of truth and wisdom? I wondered. And how does that outfit really look, anyway? Do we hide our inner minds from all the outfits and costumes that we wear?

After nine months in my mother's womb, searching for all the facts around me, listening to my dad's agnostic ways and my mother's religious ways, it is high time for me to come out and explore more facts about this world. So, I finally come out of my mother's womb and say, "Hi" to this world. I was born during a cold winter in December of 1992. I was born in a wonderful way, a magical push from my mother as I came upside down into this world. My mother was crying in pain. I never understood why pain had to create new life. I would not wish labor pains on any woman.

The nurse greeted me with her wide opened lips, and whispered, "Hi, sweetie. Welcome to Earth." I spoke to myself, "I know it is Earth and not Krypton." I was crying and asked her, "Do you have some candies for me, Nathalie?" I saw her name on her name tag. I was crying and talking, but she didn't understand me, saying, "Shhh, don't cry, sweetheart. You are fine. We are here." She wrapped me in a towel and started showing my male organ to all the other nurses in the room, saying, "It is a beautiful boy." Yet, all I said to myself was, "Stop showing my little package to everyone. I feel shy." I was crying so loud for a while because I could see surgical knives, blades, and other sharp objects in the room.

Nurse Nathalie washed me in warm water and cleaned me. She held me to her breast and wrapped me in a cloth. Then she brought me to my mother, who was sleeping after my painful birth.

I heard Nathalie whispering to my mother, but my mother could hardly listen, as she was drowsy and sleepy. My dad rushed into the room, wearing his suit and holding flowers in his hand. The nurse saw my dad and said, "It is a boy!" My dad very happily smiled and said, "I know." He hugged the nurse and said, "Thanks very much," then took a bar of chocolate from his pocket and gave it to her. She thanked my dad and walked out of the room. He was so excited to see me and was full of joy. "My son, Oliver Oscar: the great-grandson of Oliver Shrine, the one who will make a difference and reveal the secret from the swallows." I couldn't see his face, as my eyes were not opened, but with my mind I saw his face for the first time. He looked very handsome with blue eyes and blond hair, and his face was filled with love and honesty.

It was my day, and everyone around me was happy. My grandparents, cousins, uncles, aunts, and family friends soon arrived with hugs and kisses. Even my dad's friend who fired bullets at the wedding and the priest visited us. After my mom and I got out of the hospital, there was a celebration at our home on the Seventh day. Everyone brought presents. All my dad's friends from the neighborhood brought me presents. There were toys, comic books, T-shirts, and diapers with cartoons. My mother's religious friends brought us expensive things like scented candles, holy crosses, fragrances, oils, and different types of Bibles. My father's friend, "Uncle" Tim, gave us a check for $20,000 for my education. When I looked at all the gifts, I knew that my Uncle Tim's gift was the best. Education is the most essential thing for a child to have. I appreciated all of the other gifts, but when you give someone a gift, it is important to make sure it is something they need. It doesn't have to be expensive. It just has to be useful. If you give an electrician a gift, you buy him a tool kit, not a bottle of champagne.

Am I criticizing everyone too often? No. Sometimes we just don't know how to approach our problems and solve them with simple solutions. If we don't pay attention to all the little things we do in our life, like give gifts, then how can we all work together as a human race to lead our lives as successful, happy, and peaceful people? There is a saying: "An answer to the greatest quest comes from the little things that we do in life."

The party went on for hours and lasted until midnight. So many different types of people were there—people from different backgrounds, hierarchies of wealth, mental states and belief systems. I could feel that not all of them were wholeheartedly happy, but they were happy to see me, and I could tell that they cared about me. I am just seven days old, and all I can see of myself is that I was born clueless and innocent. I am helpless and can barely even move. I needed someone to give me milk and someone to clean me. But my mind was working and searching for something I was looking for, yet I didn't know how to clearly explain myself at this tiny age. Maybe I wanted everyone to be successful, rich, healthy, and peaceful. Or maybe I wanted everyone to live in a society without crime, pain, sorrows, regrets, or failures. All of this untold knowledge and unexpressed feelings enveloped me as a baby.

The party was over at midnight and everyone left. My mom and dad took me into the bedroom and I was fully awake. They put me in the middle of the bed and started to unwrap all the gifts I had received. There were lots of toys of different cartoon characters. And my dad, being a Superman fan, found there were quite a few Superman toys. He kept those toys close to me and often played with those toys with me. I felt that he wanted me to be Superman one day and save the world.

I am not comfortable with my father's idea that I may change or save the world. If all men were equally created or evolved, then how could I change or save anyone's existence? There have been many people throughout history who thought their purpose in life was to save the world, and all wound up creating more problems than they solved. They perhaps brought some temporary changes in people's lives, but I am looking for a radical and permanent change forever. Change should happen within oneself. Violence in any form is not a method of change, as violence only fuels and creates more problems. Do you know why? If we try eliminating evil through violence, it only spurs more violence, since violence is a product of evil.

As a child, I grew up with many questions and spent my time listening to all of the debates between my mother and father, and the people who were around me. I enjoyed the tender love of my parents. Each person expressed their own ideas and views, and my own search for the truth began at a very young age. I wanted to know how to improve human life and restore one's own true identity. As an infant, I didn't know whether my search or thoughts were correct or not, but I continued searching with humbleness and meekness, so eventually one day I would find an answer to all the questions I was looking for. All I know is that a seed is planted within me, and I am watering and feeding it. That seed of search is growing in me now, every day and in everything I do: eat, walk, run, talk and read.

Chapter 2
MY EARLY DAYS

THE EARLY DAYS OF MY CHILDHOOD, SPENT WITH MY FATHER, WERE splendid. He was so involved with his beliefs about superheroes that he considered himself almost like Jor-El and me as Kal-El. My father wanted only the best for me in this world. His wish for me was that I would grow into a man who would make a difference in this world and restore peace. He talked to me about it constantly, and I wondered, "Why can't he do it? Why is he waiting for me?" Now I understand that he wanted me to take the credit. He wanted me to experience true success. He would call me his "Only Great Boy" or his "Rock." But the fact is, he never had a real nickname for me until reality knocked on his door one evening as he was filling out my play school application form.

On a winter evening, wearing a T-shirt and night pants, a glass of wine on the table next to him, my father carefully filled out my application for preschool. He sipped wine every time he filled in a column on the form, and when he came across the column labeled "Nickname," he put down his wine and stared at it hard, thinking very deeply. He had no idea what to write and slowly took his eyes from the form and asked my mother for help. My mother was in the kitchen, busy making a potpie and soup, but upon hearing this, she stopped working on dinner and came to help my father. She was also confounded by the question, and after a few minutes she suggested names like "Honey," "Sweetie," or "Teddy." My father closed his eyes and shook his head a couple of times, then took a deep breath and told her, "Those are words for girls, puppies, or homemade fancy-pants boys." It was then that my father realized the importance of a name and a nickname, knowing it would create a harbinger effect. He decided that evening that I should have the best one.

Yet my father did not know what to do. He is not a linguistic specialist, but he chose the best nickname in this world for me. He wrote down the name Kal-El. He drank the whole glass of wine in one gulp, called my mother in from the kitchen, and told her that he had found their son's nickname. My mom was excited and rushed over to check the form. That's when she saw the name. Her face grew red and hotter than the potpie in the oven—and she said, "There are a billion words in this world. Why did you pick this one?" My father got up to retrieve some wine from the cellar and, before heading downstairs, said, "It is true, Kal-El is not from this Earth. He was picked far from this galaxy, so this is what is best. It is the best a father can do for his son." I was in the bedroom watching cartoons, and mom started on her dogma and thesis about names and their meanings. My father filled his glass with wine, as he was enjoying their conversation. He grinned at her and then proceeded to ask my mother if he could question her on her ideas.

Mother: What is that, James? I am sorry I was pushing you on this.

Father: Don't be, dear. I love you. (He kissed her lips gently.) I am very curious about the attitude of religious people. When I asked you your opinion about a nickname, you couldn't think of one. You could have told me something like Moses, Abram, or Joshua. Alas, you didn't know and that is fair enough. But when I came up with a name using my limited intellectual powers, you're immediately arguing over it.

Mother: I'm very much impressed that you know the characters from the Bible.

My father smiled and said, "I've heard these characters' names a million times, again and again, and it's recorded in my deepest memory. Thanks for also knowing the name Kal-El."

My mother understood and smiled at my father. Superman is well known as Superman or Clark Kent, but only very few know his real name as Kal-El.

For a while I thought that their arguments and debates were pointless, but now I realize that they listened to each other while they were talking. They not only loved each other a lot, but also respected one another, and neither of them was fully biased with their beliefs; they were both looking for eternal truth. My mother and father searching for eternal truth caused my own acumen to grow.

I began my preschool, which was a few blocks from my home. I never cried about going to preschool because I played with lots of kids and they were very nice to each other. My first friend was a boy named Judah. Since Judah's father was best friends with my father, we all spent lots of time together. We would play games like hide-and-seek; red light, green light; and many others. Judah was a good friend and very carefree. I admired him and wanted to be like him. I couldn't be, as I had too many thoughts on my mind and half the time I was disconnected from this world. Throughout my life, even when I am searching within myself, I don't express it in my face, I am clueless to everyone. The search in me runs deep and is multiplying so fast that it could occupy this universe.

I can still remember all the good times I had with Judah. He is still my best friend; forgiving, compassionate, trustworthy, and possesses great foresight. We were closer than the other kids in school. Everyone wanted to be like us.

The first girl I met as a child also impacted me deeply. She was beautiful, cute, and lovable, and her name was Madison. She breezed into my life as a wind, and I can still remember the first conversation I had with her. At the time, I considered her to be just a friend. When I saw her wearing a pink hat and pink dress, tiny rose lips, and a look of innocence filled her face, I couldn't resist, and I looked into her eyes. Suddenly I was swimming in oceans of her thoughts. She smiled with her tiny lips and said, "Hi. I'm Madison. What are your names?" Judah was standing next to me, and I wanted to answer before him, so I jumped up quickly, before Judah did, and said, "My name is Oliver, Oliver J. Oscar."

Madison: "Sorry, I didn't hear that."

Me: "Oh, I am Oliver."

She smiled at me and we shook hands. Judah slowly introduced himself. We told her that Judah and I were best friends and lived in the neighborhood. Madison liked us from the very first day and asked us to be her friend. We didn't hesitate and accepted her friendship.

Very soon the three of us became really close. We would sing, play, share snacks, and paint pictures together. We were the "Three Musketeers". When our friendship started, Madison's parents became friends with my parents and with Judah's family. We all became one big neighborhood family.

Both Madison's parents loved superheroes and appreciated my father's ideas very much. Madison's family was a typical crazy family, much like the other families in the neighborhood who believed in superheroes. This made our family gatherings much more intense and frequent. Judah's family was on my mother's side: they were a very religious and a philosophical family and understood my mother's views. Our three families talked and shared ideas and discussed the world and its existence. Madison and Judah were not very interested in these conversations, so I would tune out our parents when we were together so I could play with my friends and have moments of normal reality.

Yet the isolation from our parents' conversations was only for Judah and Madison, not for me. Even when we were playing, I tried to stay close to where they were talking, whichever room they were in, or on the porch, always trying to listen to them. Their conversations were very energetic and constructive, and every day I learned something new; as facts and ideas were filling my mind, my search continued to grow. All parents should discuss ideas, as that is what makes kids interested and motivated so they will always stay connected to you, even when they are far away. If your conversation is folly, they will start to move inch by inch away from you, and one day in their lives when they are faced with isolation of place or state, they will either change to form a newfound intelligence or form the foundation of a flagitious mind. I enjoyed Judah and Madison company at school, where our parents were at a distance, so I was able to put my full mind and soul into our friendship and be happy in the way children are happy, rather than having to think about the conversations taking place around me.

I learned about the basics of philosophy from Madison's father, who was a renowned professor. He was an expert on many interesting subjects, like the purpose of life, evolution, and the world's interconnectivity. There were too many ideas always floating, an ocean of doctrines, theories, and viewpoints constantly pouring out of him. Yet none of his theories gave me an answer, and I am continually searching for knowledge and truth, not just abstraction, hypothesis and presuppositions.

Our preschool life flew by quickly, and before I realized it, I was in kindergarten. All of the kids in school were from various backgrounds. I remember studying the kids around me and thinking that they looked like preprogrammed and predestined robots, always talking about cartoons, movies, zoo animals, birds, ice cream, or junk food. Judah sat next to me and we both sat in the back row, while Madison sat up front. I often felt bored and lonely in the classroom, as they taught very basic stuff that I didn't care about. Instead I would research how to be a superhero and how to make myself as strong as a superman, and ponder all the conversations that I listened to my parents have. The only happiness I found in the classroom was that I could see Madison's cute short hair swaying from left to right like a pendulum. Sometimes kids would talk to me about Superman, Batman, Spider-man, and every possible fictional character they ever saw on television or in the movies. I listened to them very carefully and realized that most of these kids were very selfish, that they wanted to be like their favorite superheroes but never thought of making all the humans on this planet like them. I tried to stay away from them and to stay with Madison and Judah. Most of the kids had their favorite superhero and would play-fight each other to prove that their superhero was the best.

Every single day after school, my friends and I would watch kids wrestle with each other, usually in friendly fights. With my crazy neighborhood and the youngsters around us, I had a very interesting childhood. But out of all the kids in the school, I liked two in particular, Nelek and Urson. These two boys did not fight with each other, but rather talked about interesting topics and I would listen to their conversations with endless fascination. They always had the best arguments. Nelek would always defend Superman and Urson would take the side of Spider-man. Nelek argued that Superman flies and circles around the Earth, almost reaching the stars. His argument was that Spider-man could never do anything like that. Urson would reply by saying that Spider-man moved quickly in populated areas, whereas Superman wasted his time going to places where no one lives. Nelek sided with Superman's strength and Urson with Spider-man's agility. This argument happened time and time again.

Some kids would fight each other at school and it was brutal, as they were set on claiming that their superhero was stronger and mightier. We would all have to be pulled apart, someone would have to stop them from fighting. It would then get reported to the teachers and their parents would be called into school. I would feel so embarrassed about these kids because they followed all the great superheroes but put great shame on their parents by fighting with each other and not displaying discipline. I realized then that it is not your outfit or role model that makes you a great person; it is your very thoughts, actions, personality, and above all, endurance that will make you a better person.

I continued searching for answers, sometimes to the point that I thought I was too judgmental. But I convinced myself when I got this thought that I was not judging anyone by words; rather I stayed away from all silliness. For instance, the first Halloween after I started school, I felt strange in my Superman costume. My father bought me a new Superman costume and dressed me up for Halloween. He took lots of pictures of me in that suit. I went into my room to look into the mirror and I saw myself, noticing that the underwear was worn on the outside. Though I had many toys and pictures, and had watched all the Superman movies, I felt weird. I asked myself, "Was this how they dressed on Krypton? If yes, what am I doing with this Superman costume on our planet? We should be better than Superman, hiding our underwear inside our pants." I thought I looked like an upside-down superhero, and I felt that something was wrong. But I calmed down and went out with my mom and dad for trick-or-treating. My dad, with his white silk shirt, blue jeans, and Texas-style cowboy hat, looked like a movie star. He held my hand with great pride as he walked with me down the street. My mom was dressed traditionally and spent the evening talking with her friends. Every soul on the street wished my mom a good evening, and my dad lifted his hat each time. He proudly introduced me to everyone, "My boy Oliver, the superman!" I could see that his eyes were filled with happiness because he felt he possessed the right heir.

Our neighborhood was covered in lights and pumpkins. I heard music from teenage kids who were having parties, and even adults were dressed in Halloween costumes. As we walked, Judah and Madison and their families joined us. Judah was dressed like a rabbi, with long hair on the sides, and Madison was dressed as Supergirl. My dad liked Madison's attitude and her good manners, and she immediately made a good impression on him. Seeing Madison's Halloween costume, he said, "Wonderful, beautiful, brilliant" a thousand times that night. He held Madison's other hand and walked us through the neighborhood. After my concern over wearing my underwear on the outside, I looked at Madison's costume and suddenly felt like Krypton made men look like clowns and women look normal. Yes, she had a shirt and looked very normal, but on me everything was upside down from my regular life, and I decided that I would never wear this funny costume again. Every time I turned and looked at her and smiled she smiled back and looked at my mid-riff, I felt shy.

As we collected chocolates and candies in our bag, we saw a gentleman in a grey suit and with a leather bag in his right hand. He had a very pious expression on his face and was telling everyone that Jesus could save the world from a major catastrophe. As he stood there, he also handed out flyers to people who were walking by. He spoke in a soft voice, "Do not celebrate. It is unclean in the Lord's eyes, and all your evil actions will follow you to the final judgment." He handed one to each of us. The flyer said: "HALLOWEEN IS A DEMON FESTIVAL AND IMPURE TO THE LORD. STAY AWAY FROM EVIL."

That flyer lit up the parents. They began intense discussions with each other. They discussed religion and Halloween while we were trick-or-treating. In the discussion, Madison's father said that the history of Halloween dated back to Ireland. Madison's mother said it was a religious day and linked to All Souls Day. My father said nothing and was quiet, he simply remarked in a very casual tone, "Everyone is happy and having fun, regardless of what day it is." My mom could not stand with my dad's opinion and said, "Happiness only comes from God." My dad's statement upset my mom, and he placed both his hands on my mom's shoulders and kissed her and said, "If happiness only comes from God and not from demons, then I think I have a problem with your God. Your God should be a maniac and jealous, as God always pretends to be good and says that all good deeds originate from him." This upset my mother and Judah's parents. Judah's father explained how people acted crazy on Halloween and how people drank too much and defiled each other.

My father replied, "Are you saying people don't do that at Christmas? Or at a Jewish wedding or at Easter?" Judah's father ignored the question my father asked and started talking about how bad Halloween is and that it was not approved by the Lord, and finally he said that all parents celebrated it because of their children. My father quietly listened to him and replied slowly, "You didn't answer my question. Are you saying that, as long as God approves, then we can sin? All we need is permission?"

My father made sense. Evil exists during all holidays. And although they argued constantly and debated to no end, we all considered ourselves as one big family and loved each other, even with many differences in thoughts. After these heated debates, we all became calm again and started appreciating diverse thoughts, there were no grudges or feeling of guilt or disrespect. This neutral feeling and calmness that we all experienced after the tempestuous debates is what we called "Absolute Being."

As we walked around our neighborhood on that Halloween, I ran into a friend from school, Nikifor, and his family. My mom knew his father well, and they greeted each other and began talking. Nikifor's costume was Captain America. Being a veteran himself, my dad appreciated his costume. He told Nikifor that maybe he would be a real Captain America one day and protect our country from danger. Nikifor was a second-generation Russian American. Being a Russian in blood, and America being his homeland, he dressed up as Captain America and his parents never stopped him. If Halloween was "demon's day," according to religious people, the question that I had in my mind was, "If Halloween made Niki the Cossack wear a Captain America suit, how come I never saw a traditional Jew wearing a Santa Claus costume on Christmas Day?" It's all one world, but we have created so many differences and useless rules, and all these were created to make man a slave of the system.

I also realized that some "facts" are not actually based in truth and instead were created by a society with blind vision and narrow thoughts. It became clear to me that Halloween day, demon's day, at least was able to unite an American and a Russian, yet Christmas had no impact on uniting a Christian and a Jew.

I started to see things very differently, and I started to adjust searching with my rationale mind but with an open heart and free spirit, so that one day I would find ways to make everyone immortal and imperishable. My understanding grew, and I learned to correlate all of the events that happened around me. I was an average student in my class, and my mom wanted me to be an engineer. My dad, however, wanted me to be a commander in the Marines. I knew that either of these goals would take a lot of work. My goal was different, though.

My father inspired all of the crazy concepts of superheroes and their good deeds, but my father's life was always different from that which he believed. He was stuck between dreams and reality, but for me, they were the same thing. He assumed joining the Marines was an act of patriotism. With all his feeble-mind, using up all his strength and exhausted energy, he thought he could protect his country in a limitless universe with endless ideas. But my father is not Superman, and he could not handle all his enemies by himself. I knew that was why he wanted me to be a Marine, his patriotism had blinded him.

At my young age, my ideas and thoughts were not clouded by uncertainty. My search was not like that of all great people in history, searching for an answer and creating more trouble in this world with their current answers. This is not what I am doing. I am searching this universe with my limitless thoughts.

Chapter 3

SCHOOL LIFE

With my new friends Judah, Madison, and a few others, the early grades of school passed quickly. I learned about the alphabet, letters and numbers, and every day when I woke up, even before brushing my teeth, I would run and pick up the newspaper and try reading it. My dad always bought lots of magazines, and I would sit with him in the evening, putting my head on his lap and looking at the pictures in the magazines. My mom didn't read any magazines or newspapers, but she would watch TV for news, and read church articles, religious-related books, and books about the "The Revelation". I was not interested in her subjects, but she would kiss me and hold my shoulder, coaxing me to take a look at her taste in books. I didn't read her books, but the pictures attracted me and pulled me in, so I often pretended that I was interested. Certain Hebrew names didn't form easily in my mouth, so I asked my mom how to say them, and she would be very pleased as she helped me say them correctly. Actually, the words didn't make me curious but rather the meanings behind the words. Names will change people's lives, so we have to be careful when we name our child, or when we give nicknames; name businesses, pets and shops; and even when we make up passwords.

One time when I was reading one of mom's church articles, I came across the name Judah, and I was excited that my best friend's name was there in the book. I asked my mom what *Judah* meant and she said it meant "praise." But my mom went on to tell me many other meanings of that one word - *Judah,* such as "confess," "sin," and so on . That was the last time I ever asked her because she took three hours to tell me the inner meaning of the word. After three hours, I started to fall sleep. My mom woke me and said, "Am I boring you, honey?" With my eyes half opened, I looked at her and said, "So *Judah* means 'praise,' right, mom?" She smiled and rubbed my head and said, "You didn't hear anything I said after 'praise.'" I leaned on her breast and said, "You are the best teacher I've ever known. For one word, you gave me a three hour lecture." She laughed and said, "You are the sweetest kid I've ever known." If my mom is one thing, she is a character.

My dad buys comics for me to read and I understand all the characters in them so well. I really came to enjoy reading them. There were lots of pictures in all the comics and few words and sentences to read. The pictures were catchy and innovative, and I marveled at the ideas of all the creators. Most inspiring was Superman, with his blue outfit and red wings. I enjoyed all the books yet I found I couldn't fully understand and interpret what I was reading. But I could visualize the words in my mind and this helped me understand better. When I asked something about the comic, my dad also offered explanations that would last for hours, only I never fell asleep when my dad was explaining. He used his face and hands to express himself, his explanations were interesting to me, so I never slept. My reading skills and analyzing power helped me to become one of the better students in my class. I started to do my homework regularly and to answer the questions that my teacher asked me. Along with searching how to be a superhero and create a perfect world, I also started concentrating on my academics. My teacher really started to like me, and I moved from being a mediocre student to an intelligent student.

My teacher met my mother and father at a parents-teacher meeting and shared her ideas about me. They were happy when they heard such good feedback about me.

My teacher (Rhoda): Oliver is doing great these days; he always does his homework and answers most of the questions during class time.

Father: On certain subjects or all subjects?

My teacher (Rhoda): He is doing excellent in all the subjects. I think he is showing lots of interest in learning and is very attentive.

Mother: That is awesome!

My teacher (Rhoda): But I have some interesting news, too, about things I didn't realize Oliver was missing.

Mother and Father: What things, Rhoda?

My teacher (Rhoda): He didn't score very well on his exams. His grades are only average.

Mother: Really? Why is that?

My teacher (Rhoda): I don't know. I assume because he becomes very nervous during exams.

Mother (turning to me): Why is that, Oliver?

I didn't answer I stayed quiet and then looked at my mom and then responded.

Me: I know I did well, mom, but the total didn't add up well.

My teacher (Rhoda): The total didn't add up well? What's the joke Oliver? (She starts to laugh upon hearing me.)

Both my mom and dad joined my teacher and laughed loudly, and told me I was a very funny boy. I don't know why they said I was funny, since I told them the truth; I knew they did not really understand what I meant. I know if I get good grades, it will make me look like an intellectual student. So what is the big deal? My grades never answer my quest, which is what I was looking for. Good grades will help me go to the best colleges in the country, help me obtain a good job, and find a successful career. Yet that was not the life I was looking for, with good grades, colleges, jobs, and careers. Those things don't exist for people like me. So, then why do I answer all the questions that the teacher asks me in class? It was because I wanted to test myself on how good my listening and reading skills were, and now I know they are outstanding. So then, why do I fall back on my exams? It is because when I start taking my exams, I get lost in my thoughts; I start searching for the life beyond this realm. I feel myself sitting at that moment in the exam, answering the questions before me, and I start judging myself on the ignorance of my knowledge. Why does this happen especially when I sit for an exam? I don't know, but all I felt was that I didn't want to be tested with these idiotic questions. When all these ideas started to show up, I definitely held back in the exam, and I know these exam results don't make sense. They exist in a system to create fake experts and geniuses. I knew that I didn't want to be a victim of this system anymore. So then what scale of grades do I use to measure my knowledge? I have my own scale of measurement, which is my consciousness and self-realization, which may be standardized one day by this world. My scale of grades is better than US or British metrics standardization. The only grade on my scale is "NIL"—yes, that is exactly the scale grade I use. Why? If the world is filled with experts, geniuses, and legends, then why do we need different grades to measure their potential? There should only be one. Everyone is equal and everyone should be a genius, expert, and legend, and there should be no scale of measuring their knowledge.

As I continued on in school, I started to make new friends. I became better friends with Nikifor from kindergarten. He was a very cool kid, and he really wanted to be friends with Judah and Madison as well. All four of us became fast friends and we talked about different movies, made fun of our teachers, talked about our favorite foods, exchanged juvenile stories and jokes, and had a great time. We started to hang out on weekends, as we all stayed in the same neighborhood, so we played in the little park that was near our home. It was a lovely park, with lush grass and lots of great equipment. We spent most of our time playing there trying out lots of new games. There was no competition between us while we played. No arguments, no fights, no disappointments and no envy. I started to believe that I had some friends who cared about me as much as my mother and father. All four of us became close, like the Fantastic Four. I was always the one who was lost in thoughts, but I tried to co-exist with them when we were together. My dilemma has always been that physically my body is there, yet I travel with my search to find a better place beyond the world I live in, to remove pain, depression, and agony from what all humans are going through. I always feel this desire and I am not well connected to the realm I am in. I feel I am lost and not enjoying life's moments. But I am at peace because I know I am searching for the truth, which means searching for happiness for everyone, a real world with absolute peace.

Before I go further into my childhood, I have to first apologize for not introducing my best mentor and friend, Nathalie, who was the midwife for me as well as for Madison, Judah, and Nikifor. We all considered her the one noble woman we all knew better than our parents. She was from a wealthy family, really wealthy, but she lost her family, both children and her husband, in an accident. She wanted to compensate for her losses, as she was not in a good mental condition for years and later decided to become a midwife. She felt she could be happy when new babies were born. It was a way to focus on the beginning of new life instead of grieving for the lost ones. Nathalie was from the Strass family, a very noble family that lived for generations in America. They had a big house in our neighborhood and both her kids were born in the same house. It was her ancestors' property, which she treasured dearly. It was the most expensive house in our neighborhood and was worth more than $22 million.

Nathalie made the right decision in becoming a midwife, and she believed that she had to be the midwife to all newborns in my neighborhood, as her family believed that babies should be born at home. Her job didn't end at the birth, either. She visited the children she helped birth every day until we were well into our childhood. She would bring us chocolates, milk, candies, cakes, cream pies, and many other treats. She sold all her property and started this godly job, which was incomparable to any other profession, in my opinion. I remember some days, even when she was sick, she still visited without changing her schedule. One time she had a severe cold, and she wore a brown jacket and a yellow shawl wrapped around her neck. She still visited me, but she didn't come in. My mom greeted her and asked her in, but she said that she was sick. Mom didn't care for Nathalie, but she said, "No, Olivia, he should always be fit and healthy, because he is the one who can change the world for the better." It was like somehow Nathalie was able to read my mind and understand me better than anyone else on the planet, including my parents.

She was a noble woman. She showed very special interest in the four of us, even more than other kids. When we played in the park in the evening after school, Nathalie would also play with us. My heart felt blissful whenever I was with her. Nathalie is an even stronger presence in my life than my mother and father, because my parents care about me, love me, and will even die for me, because I am of their own blood. Nathalie is not my blood, yet she would do the same for me, and I think that is the best love that anyone could show another person.

As we moved from the early grades to the upper grades, there was one interesting new friend who became our fifth compatriot, Ejaz. Ejaz's family moved to the neighborhood after his father got a job in my father's bank. He joined our school, and was different from all of us, in color and in the way he spoke. At first no one wanted to talk to him, as he did not look like a European or African-American. He looked Middle Eastern, with fair skin, straight hair, and a thin body. But there was some very interesting aspect about him that really fascinated me. I still remember how we were first introduced.

Me: Hey, dude.

Ejaz: Hi

Me: What's your name?

Ejaz: Ejaz.

Me: Oh, my name is Oliver. (I shake hands with him.)How well do you speak English? (I was trying to be smart but not wishing to hurt his feelings.)

Ejaz: Pretty well. (He smiled and retorted.) How well do you understand me?

Me: Very well, as we are able to talk to each other. So, who is your favorite superhero?

Ejaz: Genghis Khan.

Me: I've heard about him but don't know a great deal regarding his life. But he is not a superhero; he was a conqueror and invader, Ejaz.

Ejaz: He is a superhero. Why don't you agree, Oliver?

Me: He doesn't fly, stop trains or jump from one building to the other. He doesn't do any super stunts, like Superman does.

Ejaz: A superhero does not need to be like that. If you think someone is extraordinary and can save your life from danger, they will be your superhero. Your mind is in limbo, Oliver.

Me: You mean he saved a lot of people?

Ejaz: He protected our people and destroyed our enemies, and my father insists that he was a savior and superhero for our people.

Ejaz opened my mind to the possibility because he was right; a superhero shouldn't necessarily have to do a juggling circus act. Anyone who saves someone's life, protects them, takes care of them, sacrifices, and performs good deeds is definitely a superhero. Ejaz was a prophet for me on that day. He delivered a good message, and my thoughts and search started to widen and become more focused on how humans can be superheroes. I mean, it is the mind that drives these various levels of energy and definitions of how one should look and should not look. That's why we say that a superhero should do this or that and so on. But Ejaz's statement was, don't look at what they are taught to do, look with your own eyes. Remove your lens of false teachings and ideas and look!

Energies are different and definitions change. Ejaz made me think in a new way, and that's why I started to like him very much. That's why he is our fifth partner. I still felt that Genghis Khan is not a true superhero, since some facts were missing and his explanation did not make me fully accept Genghis Khan as a superhero. Yet that is me again, always continuing my search. In this case, I was trying to reconcile that Genghis Khan killed civilians and lots of them but is also viewed as a hero to many. He killed and massacred almost 50 million people, according to the history and data. Yes, he was a superhero for his people, but not for others. Why is it that he should have carried humanity and righteousness with him but not to his enemies also? He was a challenging warrior, and some benefited from his actions and others were victims. Benefactors and followers called him a superhero and victims called him a murderer, a bad guy. To my mind, a real superhero will never kill anyone in war; he just makes the enemies surrender and keeps them from the gates of the city, as he knows he is fighting a mortal man and will never take pride in killing anyone. As a superhero he is immortal and cannot be killed, and has endless power, with which he can protect his people from danger. I may be wrong about this, but my search or quest is just and honest, however I may change my view later.

You may ask this question yourself: "Why does God kill so many people in history, as engineered by many religions?" It was a punishment for human wickedness, to remove evil from good, and yet all religious people have one basic theory: "free will." So removing evil from good makes good prevail. I never thought about evil, as I know it exists everywhere and make me unhappy and fearful; hence I strive to remove the evilness in my search and understanding. As I am agnostic, I accept that I don't know whether God exists or not, but upon thinking about the miseries that happen to everyone in this world, I do expect God to save us if he exists. If someone thinks God is a superhero (as I always felt), then God should die one day. How can you face death and be immortal?

Ejaz's statement started to make me change my views, but at some point in time humans would be able to fly, to be immortal, undefeated, powerful, and perfect. That is what I am searching for. I started to look at everyone as a superhero: cops, veterans, parents, doctors, even the farmers, because they all protect us from dying. I knew that Nathalie would be our first superhero, as she was a mid-wife; she made sure I was born into this world safely.

I introduced Ejaz to Madison, Judah, and Nikifor. Ejaz liked all of us and we formed a close friendship. Ejaz always brought lots of Mediterranean food and we enjoyed his lunches. We would eat all his food and only leave him a little. He was a big fan of American food, and slowly he started to taste our food and like it a lot. Every month all the families in our neighborhood held a family gathering in each of our homes. As Ejaz is Islamic, both his mother and father were strictly devoted to their God, Allah, and believed in their culture. My mother and Ejaz's parents got on well, since they shared many of the same beliefs. The Torah was a common point of discussion between them, as they felt their God was from the Middle East and that he is the only powerful God who created Heaven and Earth and protects all people. They discussed different faiths they believed in and various historical events related to the different charters in their religious books. Though they were all good to each other, my mother and Judah's parents had a sort of difference and separation from Ejaz's parents. My mother always tried to force that her way to Jesus was correct and would take them to eternal salvation. But there was some internal difference between my mother and Judah's family. Yes, Judah was a Jew, and Judah's family believed in the Torah, similar to Ejaz's family. Yet the friction between Ejaz's family and Judah's family was that both believed in different ideologies. The difference was, "Who is the right heir of Abraham?" Three different sects of believers and all of their origins were from the Torah, yet each has their own theory of how they will be saved on Judgment Day.

Though all these people were good to each other and very helpful, they drew a line of indifference that made them feel that their faith was better than the others', and by these lines they believe that they glorify God. In my assumption, these three religions are the ones that have caused major bloodshed and war in human history and continue to do so. As we children grow in this world of terror and pain, there is no government that promises us peace and happiness. When we read and try to understand the Torah, it seems that it was given to us for some good purposes by their God, but the ambassadors and interpreters have ineptly conveyed the true message and have added more burdens and problems to all these religious cult followers. My search is always inclined towards religion, as the major religions have impacted human history and most powerful countries are still centered on core religious beliefs.

As for my understanding now, looking at Judah's family, Ejaz's family, and my family, they were united, and though there were some clear differences between them, there was not a single trace of violence between them. They only differed in faith and the way they saw things. But we always hear news about the bombings and homicides that happen in countries like Iran, Iraq, Syria, Israel, and their neighbors. From a view of 20,000 feet above the Earth, it looks like all the common people in the world are good and love each other, like Ejaz's and Judah's families. It is only the politics, religious leaders, governments, and selfish individuals who cause all the major destruction and suffering in society. To cover all their faults, they blame one another's faith, and their vengeance against others is transferred from generation to generation.

In my own life, things were pretty simple for a long time. My friends and I all turned into seven-year-olds, and suddenly we wanted to ride our bikes. All five of us planned to buy different brands of bikes because we wanted to ride each other's bikes for fun. There were lots of brands available, such as Swing, Wiley, Schwinn, GT, Super Sun, Rasta, Mongoose, Dahon Folding Bikes, Firmstrong, Biria, to name a few. Some of our choices were the same, so to decide who would get which bike, we decided to hold a race. The only thing was, we chose to race during a rainstorm! We were all wearing shorts and T-shirts, and had raincoats with us. We decided to race, and we chose a big banyan tree that was close to the park in our neighborhood as the winning pole. The first one to reach the tree chose the bike brand he wanted, then the second one chose a second brand, and so on, but obviously the bike brand couldn't be the same.

So there we were, all standing with raincoats on, each one a different color. As time passed, everybody grew nervous watching the sky. The dark clouds started moving in and we were all waiting for the first drop to hit our faces. That raindrop was the whistle sound we used for us to start the race. As soon as the first raindrop hit our faces, we started running toward the tree. The race was almost a half mile from the place we started. I was the first one, next was Ejaz, then Nikifor, followed by Judah, and finally Madison. I really wanted to be the first, so I held my breath and used all my energy to win the race. Everyone was using all their energy, and I could see the same feeling on everyone's faces. The bike was some dream, since it is the first time we are having a real bike. And it was the perfect time for us to buy and choose our first bike. Then I had a thought, that something bad was going to happen, and I started to slow down and finally I stopped. Nikifor, Ejaz, and Judah were still running at full-throttle and quickly passed me. The other three passed me and screamed and, still running, cried, "Oliver, come on, you little boy!" I turned and looked for Madison. She had tripped and fallen down on the road, and her head had hit the ground and she was lying flat. There was no movement from her legs or hands or body. I panicked and cried out, "Madison, Madison, wake up!" I started running toward her, feeling so nervous, my body was shaking. The rain started to pour hard on us. I went quickly toward her and slid next to her. Hearing my voice, all three stopped and turned toward us. They waved their hands and all screamed, "Oliver, Madison, run faster, run, run. . . ." Thunder was cracking in the sky heavily and loud, which frightened everyone, and the other three didn't know what had happened to us because the rain was so heavy, they couldn't see us, except for my red raincoat and Madison's yellow raincoat.

Judah was the first one who started to run towards us. Then, seeing Judah running towards us, Ejaz and Nikifor also started advancing. We saw there was a small cut on Madison's forehead and it was bleeding. We all surrounded Madison, shouting, screaming and crying, we wanted her to wake up. She was unconscious and we carried her and began running towards the tree to find shelter. We carried her, holding both her shoulders and legs, her face was facing the sky. I had a small towel in my pocket, and I covered her face with the towel to protect her from the rain and the lightning. We gently set her down next to the tree trunk and removed the towel, and started cleaning her face with a hanky. Her whole face was covered in a mixture of blood and mud. She was still unconscious. I placed her head on my thigh. Everyone was talking to her—"Madison, wake up, wake up"—but she didn't wake up. We were all scared and our faces were red with anguish. She didn't respond to us, and after ten minutes, the other three started blaming each other for what had happened to Madison. I tried calming them down, and they moved away from Madison to give her some fresh air. Something occurred to me at that moment, and I remembered the very first thing I had felt for Madison, at an age when I didn't know how to define it. It was love; there was no beating around the bush about the words I should use. I kissed her forehead and said in a soft voice, "Madison, we need you, we love you, wake up." A miracle happened, and she opened her eyes slowly, and her lips were dry. She started to cry, and said, "Oscar, I love you. Thanks for coming." Then more tears started rolling from my eyes, and I hugged her close to my chest. The other three saw that Madison had woken up and were happy to see her eyes opened and that she was talking. Judah shouted happily, "She's alive!" After a few minutes, while we were talking to Madison, we saw that a big bolt of lightning had struck the same place where Madison had fallen down. We became scared and all went silent for a while. We could see flames and smoke coming from the ground. . We were sure there would be a deep hole in the road, and no one dared go near to see it. We were so quiet and so close to each other, as we all felt troubled in our hearts. Since it was a rainy day, no one was walking on that side of the road, and we all stayed under the tree till evening, sitting in great silence as we waited for the rain to stop.

While we sat under the tree, my mind was completely disturbed and I felt a lot of pressure on me. We were all great friends, and when we saw Madison down on the ground, we didn't think about winning the game. We all gave up and wanted to save our friend from danger. I call this "the moment of true passion and love," because we didn't intervene and try understanding the future that lightning was going to strike the same place where Madison had fallen. We all thought about our friend and our only goal at that moment was to save her. I felt happy that I had good friends with me, and we were ready to die for each other. And though we wanted to race, we didn't have any ego or ill feelings toward one another. Even if the race would have gone on without this unfortunate incident, I am pretty sure that we would have respected each other's choice of bicycle and completely accepted each other's preferences.

That's how our friendship started and continued. I also started to love nature at this time in my life. Even after the incident with the lightning, I understood that nature didn't want to hurt us. It moved to hit the ground and landed in the same place where Madison was lying when she fell. It reminded me that nature loves us and protects us from disasters. But my other question was, why did nature have to be cruel to humans at times, even if unintentionally? A lot of people have been killed by lightning. If nature was the source of human existence, then lightning shouldn't kill anyone. People have a theory that lightning on the ground brings minerals and feeds the earth with energy, and though it may be true, the force that helps and protects us should never kill anyone while on duty. Was lightning created to kill evil men and women, and does it have intellectual judgment, knowing good and bad? Is that why some superheroes and gods use it as their weapon, not knowing it is the right tool? These threats of nature created more gods in history than more humans ever lived. That's how the thunder god came into existence. We need Thesla back to create one for us, so we can strike back nature's thunder when it runs amok and kills some of us for no reason.

After the incident, we didn't see Madison for a month, as she was injured. Her parents did not allow her to hang out, and she also skipped school for a week. The only messenger was Nathalie, and we would send some chocolates and candies and little gifts every day with a note saying, "We miss you, Madison." We all signed our names to it. She in turn sent the same message. Her parents were worried about the incident. They eventually got over it and understood it was not our fault. They were confident we were good kids and we would take care of her. After a month I saw Madison again, out of school, and was so delighted. We all took her to a flower shop and asked her to pick the flowers of her choice. She insisted that I pick out her flowers, and she didn't care what color they were. I picked beautiful purple tulips for her. She liked them very much, and thanked me. We were all united again and happy moments started to flow again in our hearts.

A few weeks after being reunited, we had a discussion and agreed who should buy which specific brand of bike. We approached our parents and conveyed our ideas about the bikes. Due to Madison's incident, they denied our requests. We started to nag them about this, and eventually all our parents decided to meet and discuss it. Initially they started with a more negative discussion focused on why they were not getting bikes for us. Then, as we started to express our views and thoughts, they slowly started to change their "no" decision to a "yes". But they insisted on certain stipulations: we were not to ride our bikes on the highway; we were not to ride outside of our neighborhood; we were not to race with each other; there would be no circus stunts; and other such rules. Eventually we memorized all the rules and made the joke that we could pedal our bikes, but only in the locked position. In seriousness, we promised to listen to our parents' requests and our parents bought the bikes for us, each of them buying the brand that we asked for. The only rule we had a hard time following was racing, which we couldn't resist. We didn't race on the roads, but we did on the playgrounds. We had learned our lesson from Madison's accident and became much more careful.

For some reason during this time, I no longer missed my mother and father. They knew I had very good friends and they knew all my friends and their families. There is one important fact about friends: always make sure that your family knows them. It will be better if they know your friends' families also. Sometimes their critique and judgment may be right about your friend, in which you could be warned in some way about the danger that is ahead of you. Since our neighborhood was small and all my friends lived close by, it was easy for our parents to keep track of us. But I started to have the feeling that both my mother and father's spirits were always with me: when I was outside the home, they guarded me, watched me, and protected me. I shared this particular feeling with all of my friends, and they said the same. A sort of vibration connected us all. It was not an incident or random event that united us as good friends, but rather we shared the same vibe. There were lots of other kids in the neighborhood and they also existed in groups, as we did, but they were often up to bad and evil deeds. They screamed, made fun of old people, stole cookies and candies in the grocery stores, threw tomatoes and eggs at windows, caused chaos , had foul mouths, and got into all sorts of mischief. We didn't do any of those things, feeling that was nonsense and ignorant. Our group was well respected in the neighborhood and everyone admired us.

There were five of us and we got bored with bicycles and wanted to learn how to swim and wanted to go for lessons on the weekends. We approached our parents and they all approved. So, we all went to swimming classes in our neighborhood called Stretch. Our trainer was Mike Tyler, who was a very good swimmer and had won three Olympic gold medals one for the 1,500-meter freestyle, one for the 200-meter breaststroke and one for the 200-meter butterfly. He visited Milwaukee for a two-month vacation in the summer and wanted to train the kids in town. He was an outstanding swimmer and wanted all the kids to be like him. Initially we had some problems in the water and lost our breath quickly, but our trainer taught us all the small tricks that are involved in being a good swimmer. We all did a good job and within a month we became good swimmers. Of all of us, Nikifor was the champion. We were only able to do forward style and a little backstroke, but Nikifor picked up new skills very quickly and soon he could swim using all the various styles. The trainer liked Nikifor and showed more interest in him, and soon he started training him to be a swimming champion.

Nikifor was so good at swimming that Mike started to place bets on him as the surefire winner.

One weekend near the end of fall, just before the shivering cold set in, we walked across a bridge over a small lake near our homes. It was a small lake, about twenty feet deep. Usually there were lots of people near the lake, families and kids in boats, some swimming near the shore, others having barbecues or campfires at night. As we passed over the bridge, we thought it was unusual that nobody was around, but we figured it was because it was chilly and the lake water was cold. We noticed a current in the lake and thought the water looked scary. We saw two girls on the other side of the bridge, near the shore, chatting with each other. Nikifor, being an undeclared champion at this point, wanted to take a dive into the lake. He wanted to swim in the chilly weather, nonstop for fifteen minutes, to prove his endurance. Initially we stopped him, as it was not safe because his trainer was not around and there were no lifeguards. But Nikifor was overly confident and wanted to dive in. We didn't stop him, since we knew that he learned a lot from his swimming classes and we didn't doubt his skills. He asked us to join, but all four of us said no, since the weather was cold and we had never tried swimming in a lake before. Nikifor removed his pants and shirt. We asked him to swim in his shirt, because it was chilly, but he didn't listen to us. In his black underwear, he stood on the edge of the bridge and shouted loudly, looking at the sky, "The champ is diving!" His loud voice got the attention of the two girls toward us and they looked at us in disbelief. We all became excited that he was going to swim in the lake, which was a new experience for all of us.

He dived into the lake like a real champ, with hands forward and his body straightened, ninety degrees perpendicular to the water. The bridge was twenty-five to thirty feet high above the water, and he glided into the water. After ten seconds he reappeared from the water and started floating with his head above the water, waving his hands at us. We didn't know what he was doing. Madison called out, "Hey, Niki, are you alright?" We watched and saw that as he was floating, he couldn't balance himself. He started to lose control and drift away from the bridge. Slowly, he started drowning. Niki started to shout, "Help, help me!" We were all in a panic, and shouted, "Nikifor, come on, swim back!" He replied, "Help me, Oliver!" We knew that if we dived in and tried to save him, our lives would also be in danger. Judah and I quickly needed to find some rope or a life jacket, but Madison and Ejaz started crying and shouting, "Someone save Nikifor!" The two girls who were sitting on the other side of the bridge were observing all of this, and both quickly jumped into the water to save him. As soon as Judah and I heard the splash, we thought that Madison and Ejaz had jumped in to save Nikifor. We started to rush to the bridge, but they were standing on the bridge, and we saw these two girls, swimming fast toward Nikifor, and at that time he was almost under the water. He had completely lost control and his head started to sink. One girl grabbed his hair and the other got hold of his leg and started swimming towards the shore.

Then we all rushed from the bridge to the shore to see Nikifor, and we were all in shock. We went to grab him but he was unconscious, and pleading with him to wake up. He didn't respond. Madison and Judah thanked the girls for helping us. It seemed Nikifor had swallowed a lot of water. We started rubbing his hands and feet to warm him up. We didn't know what to do next and we had forgotten all our first aid lessons. One girl quickly opened Nikifor's mouth and started to suck water out of his lungs, and water started slowly coming out of his mouth. The other girl was gently pressing his stomach to help the water come out. We were all very alarmed that Nikifor was still unconscious. Then after a few minutes he started coughing and started to cough up water. We all slowly regained our breath and were relieved that he was back, and he slowly started to breathe. We could see his eyes were happy to see us again, and we all hugged him. Then he asked us who saved him? We told him what happened and introduced the girls to him.

One girl was named Aika and the other was Shu. Aika was wearing a green sweater and jeans, and Shu was wearing a blue jacket with pants. We asked who they were. They lived near our neighborhood and their families had moved from Boston. We learned from them that their parents were running a grocery store and they were going to one of the schools in our neighborhood. We thanked them over and over again for their help, and told them that Nikifor, by this time, would have died if it hadn't been for them. The evening was getting darker and we wrapped Nikifor in a towel that the girls had given to us. We wanted him to get some hot water and food, and some warmth. Due to the cold and being wet, he was shivering. We didn't want to go home because we knew our parents would freak out. Nikifor was concerned about the incident, it was disturbing him. We comforted him and tried to encourage him and he slowly regained his composure. The two girls said that we could go with them to their home and get some hot soup for him. We initially didn't want to go to their home, but they insisted and they seemed to be very considerate and genuine. We accepted their generous offer. Madison and I asked the girls not to tell their parents or anyone, because this would cause a big problem for us with our families. They promised not to tell their parents and they took us to their home. As we started our trek, Ejaz and I held Niki up by his sides. We learned on our walk that Aika was Japanese and Shu was Chinese. Shu's family ran the grocery store and Aika's father was an electrical engineer working for IEEE (Institute of Electrical and Electronics Engineers). Both families had been friends for many years and they moved together to Milwaukee. We went to Aika's home, which was a lovely house with a tended lawn and a cedar tree in the front yard. Aika's parents came out in surprise at seeing five strange kids in front of their house. Aika's mom was wearing a white sweater and a blouse, pale blue jeans and socks and sandals. She looked very elegant, and without even asking anything of Aika, she invited us inside their home. We were surprised and we walked inside. We removed the towel from Niki and asked Niki to try and pretend that he was feeling normal again. We met Aika's father, who respectfully greeted us and we all sat on the couch. Her parents were very nice people. Her mother asked in Japanese who we were, and they said they met us near the lake. Aika asked her mother to prepare some hot soup, as Nikifor was not feeling well. She asked, "What happened to him?" She lied to her mom, as we had asked her to do, and said that he got a cold from sitting outside all day. Aika's mother said that she had some good miso and corn soup for him. She also offered him some Japanese medicine that would relieve him from his cold. Niki was playing smart and took some of the pills. Aika said they had really good medicine that would help him recover faster than traditional Western medicine. Nikifor agreed to take the pills, but first made the comment, "Well, you want to challenge our medicine with yours, so if your medicine doesn't work, you owe me ten dollars." Hearing that, both Aika's mother and father laughed, but we felt enraged toward Niki, because it was not polite to say that, especially under our circumstances. Aika's mother politely replied, "All medicines are good. It depends upon how each type of medicine will work on specific bodies. It is based upon the metabolism. Our medicine is made of organic and natural ingredients, which will heal, clean, and strengthen the body. All unnatural medicines will heal temporarily, but always affect the immune system." I felt those were words of wisdom and neutrality, since she didn't respond that Japanese medicine was superior. This showed me that the family was genuine and generous, and I started to gain more confidence that we were in good hands.

Aika's mother went to the kitchen to prepare the miso and corn soup, and Aika's father continued talking to us. Aika's father spoke to us kindly, and he had a soft voice that I responded to very positively. He asked where we were from, which school we attended, where we lived, and so on. Meanwhile, Shu went next door to bring her mother to meet us. Shu's family lived next to Aika's house. Shu returned bringing her mother to meet us. Shu's mother dressed and looked simple and resembled Shu. She respectfully greeted us and it seemed like she was not fluent in English, but she was polite and asked how we were doing, which school we went to, and so on. It seemed that Shu had explained that Nikifor was sick and had a cold. Her mother also brought some herbal medicine to help build up his resistance so that in the future he might avoid catching colds and help protect his immune system. Shu's mother explained how good the medicine was and how it would help him. I felt that Shu and her family were also some of the nicer, honest, and simple-living people on this Earth.

Aika's mom wound up preparing miso, corn, and chicken soup for all of us, including Shu's mother. We were stunned by their hospitality and kindness. We were not comfortable taking the soup, but their kindness somehow made us agree without any fuss. They took all of us to the table, and we sat at the table and started drinking the miso soup. Before even finishing the miso soup, Aika's mother brought corn soup. We said we should go home to eat dinner, and Aika's mother, with her gentle face said, "Well, this is also home." They were so kind and nice to us. The soup was good and we drank it heartily. Then she brought chicken soup. Now our stomachs were becoming full and we struggled to continue eating. Madison asked, "You said you had only miso and corn soup. Where did you get the chicken soup?" Aika's father very wittily answered, "We got the chicken soup from chicken!" We all laughed and Madison felt a little bad, and asked them, "Well, I never said you got it from the meat shop, but two soups are more than good for us!" Aika's mother answered, "I had two soups prepared and since Niki had a cold, I made the chicken soup, which will be a better remedy for a cold." Ejaz was eating the crackers, and asked, "Then why did you give the miso soup first? You should have given the chicken soup first, at least to Niki."

Aika's mother replied, "I gave Niki chicken soup first and the rest of you miso soup first." Niki was feeling better by this time and his eyes were half closed. Upon hearing what Aika's mother said, he replied, "Did you give me chicken soup? I thought it was miso soup." Then Aika's mother asked Niki, "Don't you know the difference between chicken and miso soup, my son?" Niki answered, "Well, I know, but I never had miso soup, so I thought miso is called chicken in Japanese."

Hearing that, we all started to laugh, and Madison, frowning at Niki, said, "What kind of a boy are you?" We all had the chicken soup and chatted while we were eating. The chicken soup was delicious and we were hungry, and we all craved more. To be polite, we pretended that we were full, but Ejaz couldn't stop himself and jumped up and asked Aika's mother, "Aunty, could we have one more bowl?" We all said no for Ejaz and I kicked Ejaz's leg, and whispered, "We already had three bowls!" Ejaz quietly whispered, "Sorry, Oliver." Aika's mother noticed and gave him another bowl. After the soup, Aika's family insisted that we stay for dinner, but we said we had to go, as our parents would be looking for us. Then Aika's mother gave some medicine to Nikifor. It was some powder mixed into water, but tasted sweet. Shu's mother gave him a small bottle and asked him to take it once a day for a week, so that his resistance would improve.

They showed so much friendship to us, and both families walked us to the gate, and we all thanked them for their help and kindness. Aika and Shu said they would walk with us for one block, and while walking, Aika and Shu said that they had never lied to their parents before, not even once in their life, and today they had because of us. I could see the bond and trust that they started to have with us, and later understood this was called "Love for strangers, the repercussion of confidants." We apologized and told them we wanted to be their friends. Without any hesitation we all said yes, all seven of us should be best friends for life. On that day, we seven became continents. So we got Aika and Shu's phone numbers and said that they could hang out with us from then on.

The following week we invited Aika and Shu's families to our usual monthly gathering, which was happening at Nikifor's house. They gladly accepted our invitation and came for the party. We introduced Aika and Shu and their parents to our families. They were happy to meet our families and they quickly got to know each other better. It was a delightful night, and Nikifor's mom was a great cook, so she made a very delicious meal for everyone. Her specialty was making cupcakes of different varieties, chocolate orange, red velvet, latte, and strawberry. She also made pasta, crab, salad, sandwiches, artichoke dip, and grilled fish. We were all enjoying our meal when the moment of turbulence started. Aika's mother asked Nikifor's mother how his cold was, and if her herbs and pills were working.

Nikifor's mother: What cold are you talking about?

Aika's mother: The first time they came to our home, Nikifor was sick and had a cold and had been taking pills for a while, and his recovery was slow.

Nikifor's mother: And you gave him medicine?

Niki was enjoying a cupcake, and hearing the question from his mother, he became anxious. Not thinking, grabbed his head with the icing in his hand. His hair was red and white with the colors of the cream. Then Aika's mother took a quick look at Aika's and Shu's faces. They both appeared nervous, and she understood the situation and predicted that the issue was completely different. She turned slowly and looked at Nikifor's mother.

Aika's: Oh, I know Nikifor is a great swimmer, so I wanted to keep him from getting a cold because he spends most of his time in the water, so I gave him some herbal pills to help him stay healthy.

Nikifor's mother: Oh God, I was confused for a minute. You are wonderful for doing that. Thank you. (She hugged and kissed Aika's mother on her cheek. Then she turned to Nikifor.) You should always tell me everything. I am happy that you've got great friends and people around you.

Nikifor had no clue what to say, and just said, "I am sorry, mom. I didn't say anything because I thought it was a nourishing pill, not a sick pill." Then we all looked at him, not for the lie he told but because of his sweet face, and icing in his hair and his innocent expression. Everyone laughed after hearing what Nikifor said and they couldn't stop and control themselves, and for the rest of the party, we all repeated, "It is a nourishing pill, not a sick pill." The gathering went well and everyone seemed to become one big happy family.

The following evening, Aika told us what happened after the party with her parents. They asked what happened and they were sad that she had lied to them. Then Aika explained exactly what happened, how she saved Nikifor from drowning. After listening to her explanation they understood why she had lied and they were proud of what she had done. They appreciated her brave actions and the courage she had. But they didn't understand why she had lied.

Aika's mother: Oh sweetie, you have done a great deed and we are proud of you.

Aika's father: You are a special girl and you've made your parents proud today. But why did you lie to us? You always speak the truth, no matter what the situation.

Aika: They requested that we not tell you, so I didn't.

Aika's father: (With a smile) They requested and you didn't. You've known us for a very long time and you just met them for the first time that day.

Aika: I didn't want to lie, dad. I felt so bad about it in my heart. I wanted to make them feel better and didn't want to lose their friendship. I've only had one friend, Shu, for a very long time, and now I have five angels descended from the sky, reciprocating my friendship and love.

Hearing this puzzled philosophy about her new friendship, her parents felt bad that they had asked her the wrong question. Both Aika's mother and father were glad that she had found new friends who were noble and genuine. The same happened at Shu's home, and the outcome was the same. They all liked us and didn't judge us; rather they wanted to be close to us, despite our initial mistake of lying.

After hearing about Aika's experience with her parents and Niki's accident, I pondered what had happened and wondered if I could interpret it. I was lying in my bed one night with the night-light on, looking through the window, and I saw the moon and asked myself, "Is my search over?" Yet I knew it was not. It was still there in my mind and I was still walking through it. A pain and depression washed over me because I knew I still had a long road ahead in order to find an answer to my search. All these incidents and moments that I encountered in my life made me think in a new direction, and I felt that maybe the answers could be within ourselves. I knew that my life was very blessed, as I had a good family and great friends. I thought about the Nikifor incident, and was still shocked about it and surprised by the new friends who were willing to risk their lives for another person. What happens to the message "The moment of friendship and brotherhood" when you see your friend or your brother drowning in the lake? Any of us should have jumped in to save him and not just stood-by aimlessly. It was not our fault, as for blame, it seemed to point towards our swimming trainer Mike Tyler, "Great champ."

On the very first day of our training lesson, and with his expensive suit and tons of medals around his neck, he said loudly:

"I want to make sure these are the rules that you keep close to your heart and mind, and if you do, then you will never die in the water.

"Rule one: Do not jump into the water if you don't know how to swim.

"Rule two: Again, do not jump into the water if you don't know how to swim, because you don't know how deep the water is.

"Rule three: Jump into the water if you know how to swim.

"Rule four: Do not jump into the water if you know how to swim and feel you don't want to.

"Rule five: Jump into the water to save someone only if you have an escape plan or you know you can help."

After stating the five rules, he showed his palm with five fingers opened and said: "These five rules work as perfectly as the five fingers work together like a machine." Then he folded his palm together and pointed his index finger into his temple and said, "Listen to your mind, to what it says" and he moved his finger to his heart and said, "Obey your heart, and your instincts." The five rules appeared very similar, since we couldn't distinguish one from the other. It took me months to understand how these rules worked. I half figured it out when Nikifor jumped into the water. For Nikifor, rule one and rule two disappeared, rule three penetrated his mind deeply, and he did exactly what Mr. Tyler said: "Listen to your mind, to what it says, and obey your heart, as it talks." My best friend applied the rules perfectly and jumped in, but it was neither our trainer's nor Nikifor's fault, because our trainer said many times that it would be a different experience swimming in a lake, river, intercostal waterway, or sea, rather than what we did in still water. Niki blindly followed the rules because he assumed Mike Tyler was the "godfather" of all swimmers. Yet we always needed to expand the rules and find all the pros and cons, then apply our logic, which was eventually what I did. This, I learned, is important in understanding and eliminating failures throughout life.

When I thought about Niki almost drowning, I realized that all of us only followed rule four. Why? He was our best friend and we also knew how to swim. So, what happened? We assumed that he was the best swimmer, and even though we saw that he was drowning, we couldn't match his swimming skills. We thought, how could we help him with our skills? Negative thoughts entered our minds. Now what happened to the best student and the focus that was showed to him? All is in jeopardy now? No, what our trainer did was right. Nikifor liked swimming and he practiced hard every day, and then the trainer started showing more interest and seemed to want to promote him to become a champion. The trainer also said there was a difference in the type of waters to swim in. Niki wanted to give it a shot and paid for it. My frustration was that there were some teachers who picked and chose their students as though they were prized deer. Such teachers placed all their time and money into investing in this deer, even though their deer was not a deer, but a donkey. We need a world of minds, weak and strong working together, to make the weak stronger and the stronger even stronger. We have to live together, both the weak and strong, and we should help each other in times of need, so one day everyone can be a genius. But the system is flawed intelligent students go to an intellectual college, and the weaker go to a moderate college. I believe the weaker should go to the intellectual college, but then we should remove the moderate college from the system. Then what is left in this world? Intellectual colleges for all!

Obviously, those who followed rule number five from the class, saving strangers, were Aika and Shu. They didn't get trained by an Olympic swimming champion. Their parents taught them to swim and they didn't start from still waters and progress to moving waters. They started in moving waters, and that's why their minds were not stuck in the idea that they could only swim in still waters. Their parents had let knowledge and wisdom flow in interminable ways. The second search I had concerning Niki's incident was about how Aika felt she had lost her morality and the trust her parents had forged with her for so many years, just because of our selfishness. Surely Aika and Shu would be my friends for eternity. I was also impressed by Aika's and Shu's parents' reaction when discussing Niki and for playing along with his dubious story. They didn't expose our faults to anyone at the gathering, and kept a low profile and helped us with the situation. They took their daughters aside later and inquired about the incident, which is the way every parent should deal with such circumstances. This applies to all inquiries and investigations, which should be dealt with in a way that will help everyone understand the situation and fix the problem. I had a new view after this whole experience, examining different circumstances of human reactions and application of knowledge, senses and responses that helped me understand humanity better before I went on to experience the predefined limits carved out by ignorant humans.

Chapter 4
MORE NEW FRIENDS

WE TURNED EIGHT, MY PARENTS WERE BEATIFIC THAT I HAD GOOD friends.But my father's passion for superheroes and their legacy, and the heated discussions between my parents, were still a part of my life. We still watched superhero movies, but the interest and passion for watching those movies was becoming diluted in me, not because our relationship as father and son was waning, but because we were both maturing. Maturity for my father, as well as me, was a definite reality. Though my dad was a middle-aged man and he was trained to be a veteran who often sounded tough in the war field, he was really gentle in real life. As I grew older, my ideas and discussions were changing him a lot, and he started to think differently about this world, too. We started watching lots of action and comedy movies along with superhero films. But the craziness about superheroes never vanished, and when new fictional superhero movies came out in the theaters, we were always the first ones to see them. But the fact is, these days I hang out with my friends a lot. I stay either at school or with my friends, and spend less and less time in my home.

When I am in my home, I talked to my father every day about everything. I never hid any experience or incident from him, and he even knew about Nikifor's drowning event. The reason I don't hide anything from him is that I trust my father so much, and I knew he would never discourage me; he knows that I am an invincible kid. He always tells me that I would "change the scene of this world." He believed in me a lot, and by sharing my experiences with him, I feel less burdened. He never judged or took advantage of my sharing with him. That is the key to sharing ideas and experiences with anyone. So, be careful with whom you talk and share your thoughts and experiences, because your destiny will be in trouble if you are dealing with jackals.

My mom knows that I am a blessed and chosen child, but she did not think I was invincible as my father did. Maybe too many religious ideas made her think like this. She has always been a very generous lady because she knows that I share all my experiences and rarely keep secrets from my dad. Yet she never asked, even once, "Why don't you share with me, Oliver?" She knows why I don't, because the one time I shared a very personal secret, she judged me! The secret I shared was that, a couple of years back when I was six years old; Madison and I were sitting alone waiting for the rest of the gang to join us. Madison was talking about something regarding helping her mom cook dinner. She explained how she washed the vegetables, opened the cans, and stirred the food, and so on. She said that her mom appreciated her being so helpful and smart, and described the daughter-and-mother bond that they had.

Throughout the conversation, while she was talking to me, I was mesmerized, watching her pale rose cheeks and small rosy lips while they moved up and down, left and right, in all directions, together. I jumped up and kissed her cheek, and she didn't move; she was in shock. She looked away, and stared at the street. She was embarrassed and got very angry with me, and after a while she turned to me and said, "Oscar, and why did you do that?" I couldn't answer her question. I was feeling very embarrassed about what I had done, and without looking at her face, said, "I kissed you." She was very angry now, her face went from pale rose to bright red in color, and she asked, "I know that, but why did you do that, Oscar?" She was the only one in this whole world who called me Oscar and not by my first name. She does it when she needs to convey something important, but this time it was because she was very upset. I didn't know how to deal with this situation, so I quickly gave up, like a weasel, and said, "I am very sorry for what I have done, and I'll never do it again." A few moments of silence passed and then she calmed down. She understood that I felt bad. Madison turned and looked at me and I looked at her out of the corner of my eye, my head down. She raised her eyebrows and put her hand on my shoulder and asked, "Oscar, are you feeling good now?" I replied my head still down, "Maybe." She saw that I was embarrassed. She noticed my face was also pale, and started to move her hands from my shoulder. She pulled my hands from my knee and grasped them. I felt so comfortable and this was my first time feeling comfort from a woman aside from my mother; this was the first romance I experienced in my life. She held my hands for a while and calmed down. This was one of the only incidents I didn't feel the need to search and ponder over, because I knew this was a necessary feeling and our actions were totally normal. I knew this was love and I've learned that there are mistakes that we all make to be united as one.

So, now comes the fun part. I went home, whistling and dancing, because that was the first time I'd ever kissed a girl, even if it was only on the cheek, which was great fun for me at the age of six. I first told my father, as he was always my "dear-diary parent" and while he was happy for me, he also looked at me like a morality teacher and asked, "Why did you do that?" It sounded like an echo of what Madison had asked me. I looked at my father but tried to stay confident this time and said, "Dad, Madison asked me the same question?" My father started laughing loudly and could not control himself. I didn't know what was so funny about what I'd said. He finally stopped laughing and asked me, "What did you tell Madison?" I replied, "I didn't respond." My father then asked me, "Are you guys still friends?" I remembered the moment when she grasped my hands and held them so tightly, and with this pleasant memory I replied to my father, "We are even better friends than before!" Hearing my answer, my father understood what I meant and just patted my head, kissed my head, and said, "Take care, Oliver, and stop blushing" and left my room. He understood I was having feelings for Madison and he wanted me to be ecstatic, rather than bothering me with questions. My father is a man of great understanding, and I learned a lot from him that day.

After an hour, my mother walked into my room to tell me dinner was ready. She saw me sitting quietly, relaxed and blushing. It was very strange for her, seeing me with an unusual expression on my face. I was sitting near my window, looking out over the garden. She slowly walked to me and looked at me lovingly and asked, "Is my honey good?" I didn't hear her. After a few seconds I realized someone was talking to me, and I turned and looked at her and said, "Yes, Mom." She came closer and looked at me, hoping I would talk to her. After a few minutes I turned to her and said, "I have to tell you what happened today. Will you tell me if it feels right or wrong?" My mom became curious about what I'd said, and she replied, "You can always tell me anything, Oliver. I am your mom. I care for you." Then I started to tell her everything that happened with Madison. My mom's face began to show signs of confusion and she asked me, "Why did you do that?" I was so annoyed because she asked me the same question that Madison and my father had asked me.

Well, the real fun began when she started explaining every idea from the Gospel and from the church, repeatedly. Of all the pieces of advice she gave me, all I heard again and again was, "You are God's children, and you cannot sin to make him unhappy." For Christ's sake, I thought, she should stop! She stopped by telling me to say the "Our father" prayer twenty-five times and the Apostle's Creed twenty times before I went to bed. And that day at the dinner table my father was relaxed and didn't let on that he knew about my silly behavior. But my mom was watching me all through dinner with her judgmental eyes. She also used my confiding in her to take advantage of the situation and tell me to stop spending my time with my father indulging in movies, comics, and superhero stuff and started making me go to church and be on my best behavior. I did not feel this was necessary, because I didn't think I needed to repent for kissing Madison; those "Our fathers" and Apostle's Creeds are real sins against other human beings, not for me. If God exists according to an immoral thesis, then he was the one who created man and woman, and why? So they could kiss their loved ones. My dad was right when he said that

Madison is my Lois Lane. This incident made me learn one great lesson: I will never share my secrets with mom.

The seven continents, ruled in the neighborhood. We studied in the evenings together, worked on our homework, played music at our family gatherings, sang songs, and danced, and we also started playing football. Aika and Shu impressed us more and more, and they wanted to move from their school to ours so that we could be together all the time.

Aika: Hey, Niki and Oliver, we want to move to your school.

Nikifor: Sure, please, we want to be together all the time, even in school.

Aika: Should we ask our mom and dad about this?

Nikifor: What a silly question, Aika! You should. It's the end of the school term and probably it's a good time to move.

Ejaz: I heard the school fee is a little more. Is that fine with your dad?

Shu and Aika: What? More fees! I don't know anything about that.

Ejaz: I know. When I moved here, my father complained about it. He said, "Ejaz, I'm sending you to an expensive school. It's better than the other school in Boston." So, he wanted me to study well. He also said he is spending some of his savings for the school. He wants me to be a good student and become a doctor or engineer.

All: Whoo!!!

Shu: Should we still talk to our parents regarding this?

Nikifor: It won't be a problem.

Shu and Aika: Okay, we will talk to them and let you know.

Both Aika and Shu talked to their parents about changing schools. At first they were happy that they would be joining our school. Aika's parents were comfortable with it, since her father was an engineer and well-established, so they quickly accepted her wish. It seemed they had these thoughts even before Aika asked. However, this was not the case with Shu, as Shu's father was running a small grocery store and wasn't as economically well off. Shu once said that her uncle had financed the grocery store and they had to share the profits with their uncle until the debt was paid off. So Shu asked them about the school and they quickly said yes because they didn't want their daughter to know about their financial situation. This quick response surprised Shu, and she assumed her parents had money. However, that same night, Shu's mother and father had a heated conversation about Shu's school transfer request.

Shu's father: I know you're well aware of our financial situation. I don't know what to do.

Shu's mother: Yes, I know very well. Then why did you say yes to Shu?

Shu father: She is just a child, and I don't want her to know how hard it is for us to make money and to keep our family active and living well.

Shu's mother: You should have explained it. I think you made a mistake. If you could have explained it, then she would know about our situation. She will understand, honey.

Shu's father: This is the first time in her life that she's asked me for something. From the time she was a baby, she's never asked for anything from us. Do you agree?

Shu's mother: Yes, you're correct. I don't know what to say now.

Shu's father: Well, she asked for a better education, and I am not going to deny her that. She has to go to that school, and she believes her friends are the greatest. I don't want her to feel depressed because she can't be with her best friends.

Shu's mother: Yes, that makes a lot of sense, and since Aika's parents approved it, if we don't do it, Shu will feel awful. We should make her feel proud.

Shu's father: Yes, definitely, we should make her feel proud. I have a plan. Let me ask my brother about it. He'll help us.

Shu's mother: That sounds like a good plan, but do you think he will help us?

Shu's father: Yes, he will. If I explain it is for Shu's education, he will never deny us.

Shu's mother: But even if he says yes, how are we going to repay him?

Shu's father: Well, I will cut my expenses, work hard, and work even harder.

Shu's mother: What expenses are you going to cut? Gambling?

Shu's father: Yes. I am not going there anymore.

Shu's father sometimes gambled a little with his friends on the weekends. It was part of Chinese tradition, but he didn't waste much money on it; it was chump change. He had a few friends in Chinatown, whom he had known for years, and that was his only guilty pleasure, spending a few hours on the weekend. He decided that what he was going to do from that point on was work more and more every extra hour he could, and repay his debts.

The next day, Shu's father called his brother, who lived in Boston. He explained the exact situation, and Shu's uncle agreed with his proposal and said that he would transfer money within a couple of days. After two days passed, there was no money transferred. Shu's father started to check his account every five minutes to see if the money had come through. After two days, he called his brother to check on what had happened. He left many voice messages, but there was no response. Shu's father was not worried about the money anymore, but he was very much concerned about what had happened to his brother. So the next day he planned to visit his brother in Boston, and asked Shu's mother to take care of the grocery store for a few days while he was gone.

Shu's father rode a bus all the way to Boston to check on his brother. As he walked through his old neighborhood, he was happy to see a few old friends and greeted them happily on his way to his brother's home. He began to inquire about his brother, and all of his friends said that he was doing well; some even said they had seen him yesterday at his store. This caused Shu's father more suspicion about what was happening. Shu's uncle was very wealthy and enjoyed a 'rich-lifestyle'. Shu's father tried to remain positive about his brother, thinking that maybe he just didn't always answer his phone. As he neared his brother's home, his brother's wife spotted him and opened the door and stood in front of him, not moving. He was excited to see his brother's wife and walked quickly to open the gates. He greeted her with a friendly "Hi!" But she was not happy to see him, and with a pensive look she said "Hi" to him.

Brother's wife: Why are you here?

Shu's father: I came to see my brother.

Brother's wife: Not us?

Shu's father: No, I meant everyone.

Brother's wife: He is not here. He's away on business.

While the whole conversation was going on, she didn't invite him inside and kept him standing outside. He was treated like stranger. What Shu's father didn't realize was that while they were talking, his brother was inside and heard the conversation and walked to the door to see what was happening. At this point he saw his brother, and rushed to hug him and kiss him on the cheek. He invited Shu's father inside, and at this point Shu's father guessed what was going on. He took his brother aside and they sat on the couch and started talking. He gave him some apple juice to drink, and Shu's father was so thirsty that he drank the whole glass in one gulp. He poured more juice, and Shu's father finished off two full glasses. Shu's father explained that he had tried reaching him for two days, and since there was no answer, he came to see him.

Brother: I saw your call and I am very sorry for not picking it up.

Shu's father: You saw my call and didn't pick it up? Why? I was so worried about you!

Brother: I don't want to lie to you anymore. I cannot give you any more money.

Shu's father: Are you doing fine? Is business good? If not, sorry for bothering you.

Brother: Yes, I am doing very well and my business, too. But my wife said no.

Shu's father was surprised and also felt dejected.

Shu's father: Why is that?

Brother: You know, my family doesn't want you to come here, and I cannot give you any more money. She also knows that I help you run your grocery store, and I am in big trouble.

Shu's father: You told your wife? Did you tell her that I am paying back the money every month?

Brother, *his eyes filling with tears:* Forgive me, please. I lied to you. No one knew until you called me two days ago. And my wife listened to our phone conversation.

Shu's father: You were helping me without your family's knowledge?

Brother: Yes, because you are my brother, but this time I can't. But don't worry, I have one of my best friends who could definitely help you. I will give you his number.

Shu's father: Fine. I can handle it.

Brother, *holding Shu's father's hands:* I apologize for all this.

Shu's father, *his eyes filled with great sorrow:* You are my brother. You have helped me a lot. It's me who cannot help you.

Brother: I have to ask you one more thing. Could you accept it?

Shu's father: What is that?

Brother: Could you please pay me the interest also for the money I loaned you for the grocery store? It was not from me. They learned I helped you in building your life and business. Now they are asking for the loan and interest payments also.

Shu's father: You also agreed to ask me?

Brother: I have no choice, you know. I asked to pay back the money without interest so that you'd think that my family was happy to help you. I kept this as a secret, making you think that my wife and family are supporting this, because you are a very sensitive man. And if you had known my family was not involved, you would have refused the money. I care about you and want you to build a new life.

Shu's father: I know you do, brother. You've always been my mentor and guardian. You have taken care of me for all these years as a mother and father, and I am proud of you. I will pay back your money with interest. Give me some time and I will do it.

Shu's father stood up, his legs started to shake and he tried to balance himself and hug his brother. "Take care of your family, brother. Buddha will protect you. Bye for now." He walked out of the room, and he could see his brother's wife and children standing to the side, he saw his little niece. He touched her head and said, "You look like your mother, so beautiful. You remind me of when Shu was little," and he left the house swiftly. On the way back home, with deep sorrow, and kept thinking of how he could feed his family. He had gone to his brother for some help and ended up having to pay interest. He came home very sad. Shu's mother asked him about the trip, but then noticed that his face looked agonized filled with sorrow. He tentatively explained all that had happened with his brother. She also felt very sad and asked him, "What can we do?" He was very confident and said, "We will overcome all these problems. Buddha will help us. He is on our side and now I will begin to master my life."

Eventually we learned about Shu's family and the problems they were going through.

Shu's father is Chinese and very strict, he is also very sensitive. Shu's mother is Japanese, and this is the predicament. We were surprised to hear that Shu's father and brother were from a wealthy family, and while Shu's father was dating her mother, there were lots of problems and conflicts in the family. It was all about color, race, and historical conflict; it was rooted in the Chinese and Japanese fight clubs, the ninjas versus kung fu. The problem reached its peak when they got married. Shu's father's family abandoned him and didn't give him his share of the wealth or any money for living, and they threw him out of their family. But, Shu's uncle loved him a lot, and he helped him by giving him money without disclosing it to his family. He did this so that Shu's father could start a new life. But, his brother lied to him, saying that his wife knew that he was helping him. His brother's wife is also from a wealthy family and both their business got merged together. It's become one big family business. Now at this point he cannot rebuke his family and people, because of Shu's father, which will put his life in jeopardy. And moreover, his brother is the oldest one and has six kids, so eventually he could not take any risks in his life.

Shu's mother requested help from Aika's father and Shu's father refused it. Why? We were astonished to hear that, because Aika's mother and Shu's mother were sisters. Yes, they were sisters from the same very rich family. The same rule of abandonment also applied to Shu's mother; they banished her from their family. The sisters loved each other very much and they moved together to Milwaukee from Boston, as Aika's mother wanted to take care of her sister. Both Shu's mother and father were abandoned by their families, and the only friendship and family they had was Aika's mother and father. After marriage, Shu's father and Aika's father became best friends, but he didn't want to get any help from him, as Shu's father still considered him his wife's sister's family. Since all their family ignored them, getting help from his best friend, he considered as betraying himself. Yes, betraying himself, he made an oath that he would not get help from either Shu's mother's family or his family. He was very confident that he would be very successful in his life one day, and would make Shu's mother and his kids live in a palace and fulfill all their needs and desires. The only person who was helping all these years was his brother, because he considered him his own flesh and blood. Now he has been rejected by his loving brother and his heart is broken. He feels he has also gone too far.

What could Shu's father do now? Shu's mother said it is a question of pride and honor for them to ask for help from Aika's father.

Shu's father: Why do you say that?

Shu's mother: At least for Shu's education, it will never be a problem.

Shu's father: I am not able to follow you.

Shu's mother: Could you think for a while, and remove all the principles that are driving your life? Please, honey, give up your ego for your daughter, please.

Shu's father: I am honestly not following you.

Shu's mother: Why do Aika and Shu have to go to the same school if Aika's family is able to afford for their daughter to go to a better school?

This statement struck Shu's father and he started to think about what she had said. He said to his wife, "Because they shouldn't find any difference in them." She agreed, as they were cousins and grew together, and neither set of parents wanted the girls to feel any difference between them. Aika's parents had sacrificed their child's education, and made their child go to the same school where Shu went. Shu's father felt very bad and started to gain more inward respect for his friend Aika's mother and father. Shu's father was not a racist and he didn't feel any guilt about getting help from somebody who was Japanese, or else he would not have accepted his friendship. After his recent experience with his brother, his mind was opened like a child, and he was able to see all the positive forces helping him. He started crying like a baby, holding Shu's mother's hands. He rested his face on her hands and said, "Let me wash away your toil with my tears, and forgive me for what I have done." Shu's mother was moved by his words, and she cried and put her face on Shu's father's head and said, "I will wash you and keep you clean with all my tears, honey. Be strong." They then started convincing each other, and they finally agreed to ask for help from Aika's family.

The next evening both of Shu's parents went to Aika's home. They didn't feel as confident as usual. They stumbled and swerved as they walked. A heavy burden was holding them down, and they walked very slowly. They rang the bell. Aika's father opened the door and saw Shu's mother and father looking down, which was very unusual. Aika's father asked, "Is everything all right?" Shu's father said, "I apologize for being so stubborn for all these years." Aika's father didn't understand what he meant. He welcomed them both inside and they sat down. Aika's father was confused and said, "I don't understand." Shu's mother and father were very quiet, and Shu's mother explained everything that had happened. Aika's father felt very bad about what had happened to Shu's father and family. Aika's father wanted to encourage him, and said to Shu's father, "I've always liked your zeal and prestigious mind, and not letting your oath fail. You are a man with principles. China should be very proud of you, and I've always seen you as my master of hope." These words penetrated Shu's father, and he started to see this world full of living souls who wanted to help, support, and give him an opportunity to start his life in a better way. Shu's father explained his side of events with his brother, and how he now felt deserted. But Aika's father said "We will take care of Shu's new school fees and give back the money with interest to your brother. You can repay us when you have it." These supportive words made him happy, and he felt at ease both in body and mind. "I have to thank you very much for the help that you've given me, and I will repay it very soon, with a great gift," Shu's father humbly replied.

After a week, Shu shared all of this with us, and it was the first time many of us had heard about such family drama. In our minds, one man was the hero, and it was Shu's father, Wang. Wang left everything in his life for the sake of love and thought it was a noble principle not to go back to his family and to the people who insulted him. I awarded the same respect for Shu's mother, Kew, who left and followed Wang to build a happy family together.

"Where are you now, Oliver?" My soul was asking and I replied, "Yes, I am still here. I am perplexed. My new superheroes are Wang and Kew." After hearing this story, my search started again for the greatest love story I had ever heard from the soils of Asia. Why? He left behind everything they had for one reason: love, a "Chin-Jap affair," as it was called. I realized that Wang is a man with great principles and exercised his life by what he believed. Yet his principles were often blinded by stubbornness, because he always saw Aika's family as Kew's family who had abandoned them. It is complicated why he saw them that way, as it was because they were Japanese. He accepted Aika as his daughter's best friend but had trouble asking his own friends for help. He was getting help from his brother, who he thought loved him the most from his family and was his own flesh. But the more he thought about it, why couldn't his wife get help in the same way from her sister, Aika's mother? Kew had the same feeling, and she thought that her sister was the one she loved the most from her family and was also her own blood. Was it so called male ego or brotherly-in-law conflict that they found themselves always competing?

As Kew was willing to make herself vulnerable to help her daughter, she is my first superheroine, and she taught me that women could also be superheroes. It felt to me that the Japanese-Chinese theology and all the false teachings that have been inserted in the minds of the Chinese and Japanese people by their ancestors were at fault for Shu's parents' problems; one day I vowed to enact vengeance on all those who perpetrate injustice for what they have done. On the other hand, I didn't check what was in Wang's blood, whether it was in his DNA to be wary of Japanese people or not. Either way, he was blinded and mentally blocked by certain beliefs, like a blunt arrow still flying in the air with no direction.

Now his mind is cleared, and he accepted the change, which is very important for a man and woman to grow. The day you accept your failures, weaknesses, and faults, there will be drastic change in your life, and it can bring everlasting happiness and peace, which Wang has earned.

But the reality is, who saved them? Who helped in times of need? Was it Chinese tradition or Japanese tradition? No, it was neither one of them. It was only Aika's mother and father's sacrifice and love for their sister that saved them. I started to see them as glorious and noble couples, and I valued them more and more. Yukio and Noa, who are Aika's mother and father, sacrificed a great deal so their daughter could go to a school that they didn't want her to go to. Both of them were highly educated and Aika's father was an engineer and scientist in IEEE. I used to think to myself, how can one sacrifice their daughter's education and future for the sake of friendship and family? I guessed Aika's father knew one golden rule, which was, "Popular, top ten, or best schools don't produce legends. Legends are born by themselves." This proverb should change the mind of the educational cult in this world. The rich, smart, inherited are chosen to go to the best schools, while the poor, weak, forsaken, and underserved go to inferior schools. I started to like Aika's father's idea, and he began to seem like a revolutionary to me.

What school are, Aika and Shu going to? To the public school that is near our neighborhood, which is a pretty rough place. I have a question for this world: We are all patriots of this great America, right? Of the people, by the people, and for the people. If public school is aided by the government and we love this country so much, then why don't we have only public schools in this country? Do private schools mean that the government-funded education is not sufficient? I think the kids from public schools make better citizens than the private school kids. Public schools were built for education for all, for the uncared-for and poor along with the wealthy.

Hearing about Shu's father's troubles and the problems in this world for poor kids and their education system, I wanted to change this system and decided to start working on it. What would have happened if Aika and Shu had never met us? Would they have stayed in their school, worked hard, moved to a better college, and lived a better life, or would they have become drug addicts, alcoholics, and lived a bad life? Some might blame the big singular theory called "choice." But since we became friends, Aika and Shu wanted to join us and attend our school, so what does it mean? The probability of using drugs, alcohol, and having a bad life are lessened. So the whole point is that if we have one school system, and if all wealthy children go to the same school, and if anyone sells drugs or liquor in the school, what happens? Then wealthy parents use all their influence and power, take the easy way out. This disparity is problematic to me, as my whole search is to make a perfect world for all.

Did Aika and Shu only want a better education? Not really. They are my best buddies, and truthfully, they just wanted to be with us and not because public schools failed them. Both Aika and Shu are princesses, and definitely it was the public school system that produced them. To all the public schools I give honor, applause and praise. Why? Because those two superheroes, Aika and Shu, are the ones who saved Nikifor's life, without any second thought, and we are the ones who watched it.

The school we all attended is called Wisinf. A very strange name, it means "Infinite Wisdom," but is abbreviated and written the opposite way. Everyone on this planet asks this question, when they hear that it is only wisdom that travels and reaches infinity, not that through infinity we find wisdom. The intended meaning is that wisdom has different levels, and the purpose of this school is to train everyone to reach infinite wisdom. All I see is a very good marketing pitch that they have designed. My only thought about the name of my school, Wisinf, is, how do you write a dollar? We write $1, but we say "one dollar." My school name and the dollar expression are the same. No matter what the reason, it is really only money that counts. You can't buy wisdom, and that is how I see my school. To add more prestige and more pride to our school, one of our nation's presidents studied here: Alan Squash, our honorable president of the United States of America. We were very proud to study here, because the nation believes that he is our elitist, a source of pride, and a legend. We explained about Aika's and Shu's family and the hardship that they went through in their life and the school transfer problem to our parents. They were amazed by their sacrifice and family relationship, of how they valued family, which is a diluted value in American society. So what could we do to honor our new superheroes, Wang, Kew, Yukio, and Noa, the Fantastic Four? We decided to celebrate the Chinese New Year together at Aika's and Shu's homes.

Ejaz came up with an idea of getting a gift for all four. We discussed this and decided to get a splendid gift for them. Each one came up with an idea, and that was one of the funniest moments, when we started talking and asking each other about our ideas.

Ejaz: I always have great ideas—a gold locket for Aika's and Shu's mothers.

All: Whoo! That is wonderful.

Judah: That will be expensive, dude.

Ejaz: You said splendid gift. That's why I said it, or else I would have said a cookie.

Judah: Cookie, you said "cookie." Ejaz, you're a nut!

Ejaz: You said "nut cookies." That also sounds interesting. (Ejaz's first language was not English, and he always had problems understanding us, but he was a sweetheart.) If not a cookie, I will say it should be a golden locket.

Nikifor: An expensive swimsuit, with silver trimming on the edges.

Aika, *her face turning red:* You want to buy a bikini for my mom?

Shu: Niki, we don't do that in our culture.

Nikifor: What is the problem with that? If they want to swim, what do they wear, pants and shirts? You guys wore them when you saved me. You guys are screaming at me for nothing. I see Chinese and Japanese people wearing swimsuits in the Olympics.

Aika and Shu: Yes, but father once said our culture doesn't give exotic gifts, and that includes bikinis and swimsuits.

Nikifor: Whatever. Forgive me, guys.

Madison: Maybe a nice red dress. That would be good.

All: Hmm! That sounds awesome.

Judah: But clothes get worn out after some time. We should give them something that will last forever.

Madison: What are you thinking of, Judah?

Judah: A silver lamp would be awesome! It brings light and happiness into the home.

Madison: That's interesting! Oscar, what amazing idea do you have?

Me: I'll stick with Ejaz's choice. That will be a magnificent gift.

Judah, *with surprise on his face:* You too, Oliver! I thought Ejaz had no clue, but I think I'm wrong. Sorry, Ejaz.

Me: You don't have to say sorry, Judah. Ejaz is a genius! He was right to say that a gift that will last long and always looks precious in body and soul is a gold locket.

Madison, *after listening to the conversation and seeing the expression between Judah and me:* Is that what you think is a good gift for them, Oscar?

Me: It is just my opinion. If anyone has a better choice, we could go for it. A sliver lamp also sounds good to me. What do you say, Judah?

Judah: A gold locket makes more sense, and Oliver might agree.

Me: What about you guys? Niki, Aika, and Shu?

Aika, Shu: It's perfect. Both our parents love gold, and they would be very impressed if we gave them that.

Niki: Better than a bikini, Oliver!

All, *laughing:* You are very funny, Niki.

Madison: What could we get for Uncle Wang and Yuiko?

Then again there was silence among us. Nikifor was the first to jump in with an idea.

Nikifor: We should get them gold watches.

Ejaz: That will be super-expensive, Niki.

Nikifor: More than a gold locket?

Ejaz: Yes, I think so.

Nikifor: How much do you think it would cost us?

Ejaz: Maybe ten grand.

Nikifor: Wow. Do we have that much money?

Madison: Don't know. Hmm!

Judah: We could get a ring that would be reasonable, and it would be a better gift than a watch.

Ejaz: You are a genius, Judah. I love you.

All: Whoo!!!

Madison: That sounds cool.

Nikifor: Perfect gift. Good job, Judah.

Me: Do we all agree with it, guys?

All: Yes, Oliver.

Now we needed money to buy two golden lockets and two rings. First we went to the store to ask about prices. There was a jewelry store in our neighborhood called Glittering Ammos. It was one of the best jewelry stores in the state, and it was owned by Judah's relatives. The owner of the store was Tziyon, who was a family relative and an "Uncle" of Judah and a good friend to Judah's father. He was one of the very wealthiest bankers and gold merchants in the world. He ran a bank in Israel's Gaza and a gold business in America. They carried more pride in their hearts and felt very special about themselves because of their wealth. Yet Judah didn't like Tziyon and his family, as they were the head of the Jewish community and bossed his family around all the time. Judah loved simplicity and honesty in people instead of those who showed off their wealth. That's why he always stayed with us. Since he doesn't like them, he never even mentioned any gold gifts, and I understood what he was feeling inside when Ejaz mentioned it. But I supported Ejaz's idea, and that is why Judah said, "You too, Oliver." I knew he didn't like to go there and get discounts, but we had no other choice to go to another jewelry shop, as it would cause an ego problem between Judah's family and Tziyon's family. Discounts and rebate coupons are some of the best things on Earth, and we knew we could negotiate a discount because of Judah. But Judah didn't want to approach his uncle. Why? Judah's father was a doctor and a surgeon and came from a wealthy family. He ran his own hospital in our neighborhood. Judah's father was well respected, because he was a successful, humble and generous man, and all the Jewish people and others believed he was a man of great character.

What about the discount? Judah knows that if he goes there to buy our gifts, he will get a great discount. Judah didn't feel right about accepting a discount from filthy hands, as Tziyon's family collects more interest from their own people and from anyone who's borrowed money from them. Judah's mother once told Judah about all the different personalities in their community. Why a huge discount only for Judah? Tziyon has blood pressure and heart problems, so every week he consults with Judah's father and makes sure he is in good shape. He doesn't even bill his friends or poor people a penny for his work. Tziyon wants to make Judah happy, so he could give a discount so Judah will give some positive feedback about Tziyon being a very good "Uncle", and in turn he could get more favors from his father. Tziyon is a man with limited brain powers. Even if Judah says he is a bad guy, his father will never buy that; he is still going to be a good friend and treat him like other patients.

Later on I will introduce Judah's father, who is one more superhero in our life. He saves lives as a doctor. He is one of a kind in this world, and he does a real life service and has dedicated his life to this profession. He never overbills anyone, and for everyone he charges a fair amount of money; he never goes over their budget. For very poor people who don't have insurance coverage, he doesn't bill them at all. If they wish to give whatever they have, he takes it. All the indigent and moneyless in other neighborhoods think Judah's father is a messenger. Judah's father is named Dr. Enoch, a great, inspiring, and noble man in the medical field. Our whole neighborhood has great respect for Dr. Enoch, and he is the doctor for all of us.

His wife, Judah's mother, is also a doctor, and she is a child specialist. She runs her own hospital, and that's where Madison, Judah, Nikifor, and I were born. That's why Judah is special to all of us and especially to me. Judah's mother is an angel, a benevolent lady, and she is the same as her husband, a great contributor to the medical field. She is deeply involved and committed to the medical profession. All the children's parents in the neighborhood choose her hospital, and people from far away cities and towns travel here for their delivery. She must be a lucky star, as any child who is born in her hospital will be a successful and accomplished child. She has a great reputation, but it's one that she lives for, and this makes a difference between what is gained and what is lived. For additional compliments and thanksgiving for Judah's mother, it is known that she donates 50 percent of her earnings to charity and most of the money goes to a charity organization called The Uncared and Deserted—TUAD—a charity for homeless and elderly people in need. TUAD was a charity organization started by our former president Alan Squash, to help create a society where everyone is cared for and someone is there for you when you cry. It is a home for the homeless, a place to care for the forsaken ones, a better place than paradise. And Judah's mother is very much involved with it. I don't want to diminish her great deeds, but every six months she also flies to Third World countries like Africa, India, and countries in Asia Minor, as well as Russia and war-torn regions to offer free medical services for all the poor and injured people. She works with the UN and WHO and spends one month in these places. You would be inspired now to know her name: she is Dr. Ruth Enoch. She is an extraordinary lady whom everyone should know and try to follow as an example.

With such great honor and family values, Judah's reputation is secure, and it was time to go to the Glittering Ammos shop. We didn't have a choice, since everyone knows us and Judah's uncle Tziyon has a monopoly. We figured he would either try putting Judah in an awkward situation by twisting his words and predicament, or things would become awkward if we didn't see his uncle and then his dad started asking him why he didn't go to Tziyon's place. Dr. Enoch doesn't want anyone to get hurt feelings. So, because of these possibilities, Judah and I agreed to go to his uncle Tziyon's shop. We needed money and we didn't have a part-time job yet and were dependent on our parents' money. So, what could we do now? Yes, we all have small piggybanks. We were all very good kids. We saved our pocket money, and we didn't buy many chocolates, candies, ice cream, cakes, or fancy, unworthy products like other kids. The golden lockets cost $2,500 and the rings were $1,250, and the total was $3,750. We checked some of the flyers from Glittering Ammos for rates and picked the ones that matched our rates and budget. We all had saved quite a bit of money. Each of us had almost $500, and in total we had $3,500. Now we needed $250 and at least another $250 for the tax.

We were about $500 short, so Judah saved more money, and eventually he had $500. How was he able to save it? It's a deal that he has with his mom. Judah is a very smart businessman, so every six months when his mom goes for medical services to other countries, he makes a deal that she needs to pay him $50 each time and bring him a gift from the place where she goes. Though his dad will take care of him and he has lots of maids at home to take care of him, this is a deal he made with his mom. So he had saved $500 over five years. He made this deal so that his mother would not worry about him when she was out of town, always thinking he would be happy with his father until she returned. So, when we were short of money, he volunteered that he had an extra $500, and we were all surprised and asked how it was possible. Judah explained his $50 foreign trip deal.

Once we had the money, we shared our idea with our parents, and they approved of it. They were happy and surprised to know what our gift was, and they appreciated all our efforts. They too became excited and were eagerly awaiting the Chinese New Year celebration. Except Aika and Shu, didn't say a word about this surprise gift to their parents. In addition to our contribution, all our parents wanted to buy a gift for them. Our parents decided to buy a gift in the same price range, so that no one spent more money than the other. They had their own choice of selecting the gift and made sure no one's gift was the same.

On the day we went to buy the gifts, we decided that Ejaz, the responsible accountant in our group, should hold on to the money. He had all the money with him, $4,000. On a Sunday afternoon, we decided to go to the jewelry shop. Ejaz went and picked up Aika and Shu, and then they went and picked up Judah. Madison, Nikifor, and I were waiting at my house for them to come and join us. On the way, they were whistling and dancing. They took a shortcut through the alley and it was a pretty lonely place. A man who was covered with a hood and a ski mask walked towards them. It was very weird, because they couldn't see his face. Ejaz spotted the man, and while the others were dancing and talking to each other, he slowed and made signs to Judah quickly. Judah saw Ejaz's signs and turned and spotted the man heading toward them. As soon as Ejaz and Judah slowed down, Aika and Shu stopped dancing and started observing the guy walking toward them. Because it was wintertime here, the weather was in the 40s. All four had on a sweater and coat, but it was not so cold of a day to have a hood and a mask covering the face. This alerted them that something was wrong with the guy.

When he was about twenty feet away, he started to walk quickly toward them. They were all in a panic and stood still, because no one knew whether he was walking toward them to talk or to hurt them. As he started to walk faster, he pulled something from his pocket. All four didn't know what it was, but as he pulled it out, they saw it was a handgun. He ran and pushed all four one by one to the ground. Shu was hurt badly; she hit her hand on the ground so that it was twisted and fractured. Then he turned and asked them, "Where is the money? Give me the money. I am going to shoot you and take the money, but I don't want to kill anyone today." All four were on the ground and Shu was screaming in pain, and Aika started to cry. Judah pleaded with the man in the hood, "Please don't shoot us." Ejaz was terrified and crawling backward with his hands. The man with the hood said, "If you give me the money, I will let you live."

The man in the hood continued to threaten them and they started to scream, "Don't shoot us, please don't shoot us!" and they begged him many times. The man in the hood started to grow angrier as they started screaming for help. Ejaz was watching Shu, as she was badly hurt and really crying loudly for help. Then the stranger shot one bullet on the ground, to make them stop screaming. Since it was a lonely alley, no one was there and no one even heard the gunshot. He trapped my friends knowingly near this alley that was isolated most of the time, and the situation looked bad for my friends. The man in the hood said, "Hey, kids, who has the money, and who is Ejaz?" He turned toward Ejaz and looked at him very sharply in his eyes. Ejaz slowly said to him, "I am Ejaz and I have the money." He shook his head twice to confirm it and the man in the hood told Ejaz, "Give me the money now, or else I will blow your brains out." Ejaz was scared and took all the money from his pocket and kept it in his hand. Then the stranger asked, "Is it all there $4,000?" They were all shocked that he knew Ejaz's name and the exact amount of money.

Shu was sobbing and holding her hand, as she was in terrible pain. With all her pain she was listening to the man and was shocked that he knew about Ejaz and the money. They all became very aware that he knew about us and that someone had tipped him off. Then Judah boldly asked the stranger, "How do you know Ejaz's name and the money we have?" He said, "Shut up," and said to Ejaz, "Come here and give me the money." Ejaz didn't hesitate for a second. He started to get up and walked slowly toward him. He was ten feet away from the man and he walked inch by inch and was really scared, because no one knew what he would do after getting the money.

As he was walking toward him and was a few feet away, there was someone standing near the corner of the alley. As all three on the ground spotted the person while Ejaz was walking toward the man, the man saw that they were looking in the other direction, since their sight got deflected from him. They were all before him, each one at different angles, and he turned back to see what they were looking at and saw a boy. Their eyes were filled with fear. The boy had a sling in his hand pointed toward his head. The stranger took the gun to shoot him, but the boy was so fast, he released the sling, and a stone came fast like a light. Before he positioned his gun to shoot the boy, the stone struck his head. The man in the hood was about six and a half feet tall and muscular, and when the stone struck his forehead, they heard a noise like brick crashing into a wall. As soon as it hit his head, the man lost control, his head was knocked back, and he dropped the gun to the ground. Then the boy started to run toward them and shouted at them, "Take the gun, take the gun." As the man lost complete control, he kneeled down and saw the boy was running toward him, shouting at them, "Take the gun." The man in the hood, was trying to focus, but there was blood spilling from his forehead and his right eye was filled with blood. He picked the gun up from the ground again. The boy was so brave. He had one more stone pointed at the man's face and ran toward them. He hit him with one more stone, and it hit the same spot on his forehead. He was knocked out and dropped the gun on the ground. Shu started to move herself with her fractured hand by dragging herself on the ground. Shu took the gun from the ground and started to move away.

The man had lost all consciousness and had fallen over, his chest hitting the ground, his face covered in dirt. Quickly, Aika grabbed onto Shu, and pulled her hard as they tried moving away from the stranger. Then Ejaz put the money in his pocket, and he rushed to the stranger and started kicking him in his face. Then Judah quickly rushed over and started to kick him on the back of the chest. While he was kicking and yelling at him, Ejaz was saying, "You hurt all my friends, and broke my sweetheart's hand, and made our day really bad, and I am going to kill you." Judah quickly stopped him after hearing him say "kill."

Then the boy came running towards them and started to pull Ejaz away from kicking the man. Ejaz became so violent, he seemed to turn aggressive and cruel, and he broke the hooded man's jaw. Ejaz pushed the boy who was helping them. Ejaz grew insane, and Judah rushed and tried to pull him off. The boy also joined Judah and helped to pull him off, but Ejaz became even more aggressive. Then the boy said, "Sir, he will be dead if you keep kicking him!" But they couldn't control him. Seeing that Ejaz had turned into a wild beast now, Aika left Shu on the ground and ran and started to help control him. All three had a tough time controlling him. Judah said, "Stop it! We have to leave here and take Shu to the hospital now. Please stop it, Ejaz!" Upon hearing these words he started to calm down and turned and looked at Shu. He ran toward her and kissed her forehead and asked her if she was okay. He really liked Shu. I think he had the same feelings for her that I had for Madison.

The four of them picked Shu up and quickly started running down the street to my house, which was closer. Everyone on the street was in a panic about what had happened, since they saw them carrying Shu, who was now unconscious. When they got about fifty feet away from my house, they noticed there was a cop standing on the street and we started screaming, "Help us and help Shu!" The cop looked up, and the boy and Aika explained that they had been hurt by a stranger who was trying to rob them. The cop reacted quickly and started asking them for details, like where the man was and what he looked like. He also called an ambulance and the precinct for additional cops. All the people who had been out on the street started rushing toward them to inquire what had happened. And hearing the commotion in the streets, Madison, Nikifor, my mom and dad, and I all rushed outside.

We saw Shu had been hurt, and Ejaz, Aika, and Judah's clothes were covered in dirt and mud. We completely lost our minds, and Nikifor and I rushed to Judah to check out what had happened. The boy and Aika explained what had happened to my parents and the cops. For some reason the officer was able to recognize the boy and started to take note of all he said, but he gave little importance to Aika, because she was panicking and mumbling her words. The boy was not panicking and gave the exact information about the place where it happened and what had happened. Then two cop cars came to the scene, and they took Aika, Ejaz, and the boy to the crime scene. . The stranger who tried to rob us was still lying down on the ground, and the three cops walked toward him and saw there was blood on the ground near his face. It was Ejaz who had broken his jaw when he kicked him, and I thought that our boy seemed to be a tough guy. One cop held a gun at the stranger and two cops cuffed his hands behind his back. One of the officer's removed the hood from the stranger and took his mask off. He was a black man with a tattoo on his neck that looked like a scorpion. Very quickly the cop was able to identify him, as he was a well-known thief who mugged people in the city. He had been to prison at least six times and sentenced a couple of times for two years for mugging and bag snatching. He was involved in one of the most famous bank robberies in the state, knocked off a local state bank, and was sentenced to ten years. The court was able to recover only half of the money he stole from the bank but not the rest. The stranger's name was Kevin Burner, - the thief who had caused all of these problems.

Meanwhile, the ambulance took Shu to the hospital, and we called Shu's parents and asked them to come to our house so we could tell them what had happened. My dad and Nikifor's father went to the hospital with Shu and asked the rest of us to stay home. After all this commotion our families gathered at my home, and we explained what had happened to Shu. Shu's parents grieved and started to cry. They wanted to go to the hospital, but my dad had told everyone to stay in our home until it was the right time. My father's intention was to keep Shu's parents from the hospital, as he knew it would make them sad, looking at their daughter. We all comforted them and chatted with the boy who saved us. We thanked him for his brave actions and the way that he saved us from danger that afternoon. My mom cooked lunch for everyone and we had lunch together. Shu's mother and father were too upset to eat anything and just had some orange juice.

My father called home after two hours and asked Shu's mother and father to come to the hospital. Everyone wanted to see Shu and they all rushed to the hospital, including my friends and the boy who saved us. I was not feeling well, so I stayed back, and my friends asked me why. I told them I was staying back to help them if they needed anything from our house. Everyone believed what I said, and they left me alone in my home. I lied to everybody, and after they left, I felt a headache coming on. In my mind I could see Shu's pain and in my ears I could hear her cry. I didn't know what was happening to me, and my search began as I pondered what had happened to Shu and all the events that had happened before. We were trying to do good things, so why did all these scary things happen? What was happening in this world?

I went to my bedroom, locked my room from the inside, sat by my study table and turned on my AC, and started to search again, trying to find out where this pain came from and what all this meant to me. I wanted to observe and understand all the events that had started from the moment we decided to buy gifts for Aika's and Shu's parents. It was like, when we decided to buy a gift, we started to open up a discussion about what gift we should buy. After much debate, it was decided that we would give a gift that they could always use. I thought about offering Shu's parents a piece of land, a small factory, or some physical properties that are imperishable, but my friends and I don't have that much money and had done the best we could. The rule I learned was to give anything to anyone that is imperishable.

Then my search shifted and I started to think about our insatiable and false leader Tziyon, and why he was so greedy. He never gave money to help anyone, but doubled his profits when he sold jewels, gold, and ornaments. But he gave one-tenth to the temple as part of his custom. Yeah, I mean, he gives to God as part of his religious practice. I don't know—either if his God is poor, or he asks for money from us and we make God wealthy. God takes our money and gives it to some good projects or poor and helpless people, all in the name of religion. If we are the ones who are helping the poor and the needy, why do the poor and the needy thank God, when they receive help from us? They should thank us, and ideally we should be a god. The giver is the god and the receiver is the servant. I like it.

If Tziyon is donating one-tenth to the temple, I don't know why he spat at a beggar on the road when he asked him for some money, a poor beggar. Yes, one time Judah, Madison, and I were playing near the Shalom temple where Tziyon goes to worship. He found a non-Jewish beggar who was begging for money. He was handicapped, as he'd lost a leg, and was begging in front of the temple. It was the first day of the month—not in our calendar, but in the Jewish calendar—and Tziyon went to the temple to give his portion of earnings, which is one-tenth, as a check to the rabbi in the synagogue. As he was coming out, with his fringes dangling and a hat on his head, the beggar addressed him, "King Solomon, the chosen one, lend me some money. I am hungry." In turn, without acknowledging a portion of his greeting, Tziyon smiled and said, "You Gentile filthy dog, no money. Earn it. Don't beg!"

Tziyon was a coward, so he said it in Hebrew, not in English. Judah was the one who translated for us what Tziyon said. If he had said it in English, the beggar would have spat on him and several fallacious words would have traveled through the air, tearing the temple into pieces. The beggar, though, knew something about Christianity, about King Solomon and other rich people from the Bible. He didn't realize Jesus died for him to be rich, but was honored to be a beggar and have little self-esteem. The beggar couldn't understand the Hebrew words, but he could see the deceitful smile on Tziyon when he cursed him, and he very gently replied, "No problem, sir, next time. God bless you." I was looking for a fistfight, but sometimes it doesn't work the way you think it will. The same God is the God that the beggar and Tziyon believe. Some are the chosen ones, but one knows it and the other ignores it.

Now you know why we don't like Tziyon. We have a fair reason not to like someone. Tziyon spotted Judah, who was standing with us, and quickly walked to him with the same sly mouth. "Shalom Aleichem," he said, and our tough guy didn't respond to him. Tziyon again greeted us, "Shalom Aleichem!" Judah gave him a small smile, and Tziyon got a little pissed off and greeted us for a third time: "Shalom Aleichem." Then our smart guy Judah with his right hand pointed to his mouth with his index finger shook his head, saying no. Tziyon became delighted, hugged him and kissed him on his cheek, and said, "That is so good to know that you fast so hard, not talking for the whole day. Sheh-Hashem Yivarech Otcha." The last words mean "God bless you." Tziyon is one of the real fools I know, and couldn't even properly understand a kid's simple psychology, but I don't know how God blessed him with so much. If God really exists, and he believes in God and claims he gave all this, I think God didn't do this. I think with his wickedness and evilness he is able to multiply all his wealth. Yet if that is the case, then why does he give one-tenth of the portion to God? To bribe God and keep him quiet. He even pretends to God that he is good and follows all his ordinances. Sometimes I wanted to believe in God and follow him, but looking at Tziyon, I feel that even God could be bribed, so now I think the very definition of God is in question. Judah reacted very correctly, with his mouth he cursed a poor innocent man for no reason, and even the word was still in the air, and with the same foul mouth, he greeted Judah "Shalom Aleichem," and Judah cannot take it.

So I sound like a person lashing out at Jewish people, but no, I am not. As you know, I am searching. Dr. Enoch and Dr. Ruth Enoch, who are also Jewish, are people I respect and love the same as my mom and dad. Why? There is very calculated reasoning for this; you decide whether I am right or wrong. Let us take Judah's mom's dedication and contribution to our society. As I said, she gives 50 percent of her earnings to the TUAD foundation, not to the temple, where 50 percent stands before 10 percent. This is called a goodwill offering. She is also a Jew, where she learned moral rituals from, yet what she knows better than others and especially Tziyon are the differences between the words *conscious* and *subconscious* and *necessary* and *unnecessary*. Yes, I got this new idea about the conscious human soul and I am exploring it and have some ideas about it, but I will be able to explain and understand clearly and precisely very soon. She has a morally conscious soul, though she is part of the Jewish community; she has a counter-effect on religion and it's false ideas. She offers free medical services, flying to third-world cities and villages and helping the sick and oppressed. If Tziyon cannot help people who are before him and cannot acknowledge a greeting by the poor man, will his senses work if someone is crying and suffering from a third-world country?

Dr. Enoch, our friend Judah's father, does the same service, and sacrifices and contributes to people in society. But he helps with economic development and creating programs in the insurance world. He never fills in the papers for the maximum capacity of anyone's insurance; he bills just 50 percent of the insurance-allowed claim, and in his case the insurance company never argues and reimburses his exact claimed amount. He saves 50 percent for the insurance company and does not rip off the patient. He is not concerned with the net profit for the insurance company being 15 percent every year, no matter how much the claim is. His contribution is outstanding and the medical world's lust for money must be put to an end. Dr. Enoch represents the beginning for the medical field, because they cure disease and ailments as a temporary fix in a very short span of a human life, compared to the universe's lifetime; if they could fix death, then I could agree with their lust for money, not for worn-out soul, fading blood and flesh that we humans have now. Yes, Judah's family inspired me to start thinking about how to stop death.

Finally, what about Judah's extra $500 agreement with his mom? His mom sacrificed her visit for overseas medical services for a couple of years when Judah was born. Once he started to go to school, where we met, he started to gain my friendship, and slowly Madison walked into our lives. His mom saw that he was more comfortable with us and started to forget his mom's thoughts, and she started with the overseas services. She would be out of town for a month. Though he had several maids to take care of him, he often stayed with me for the month. This went on for a couple of years, and as he started to grow, his mom was the one who made a statement confirming her motherhood to him, and said, "Judah, I know you love me a lot, but do you really miss me when I am out for a month?" He said he did but that he loved spending time with his friends most. His mom's eyes started to water and filled like an ocean, and she was happy to hear that her son was happy and that there were people who really cared for him. She kissed him and asked, "So you never asked me if you need some gifts when I go on a trip." Judah replied, "You never asked me, mom, what I want, and you give me everything I need. I know you go for a very good reason, and all I wish is that you will come home safe. You need to come home safe, mom."

His mom was emotional and started to cry because of his love and the unexplained wisdom that he had at this age. So at this time Judah asked his mom for $50 each time she left. He explained that he would make sure to save it and that it would be his way to wait for her to come home safely. He saved all this money over the years to buy a good gift for his mom, to honor her noble work for poor and abandoned people. But when we all needed some extra money, he didn't hesitate to give it to us, and he gave it under one thought: that he wanted to honor Aika's and Shu's parents for their genuine and heartfelt affection and love for their families and themselves. Judah's family is an admirable Jewish family, and nowhere are Tziyon and his family even worthy to untie the laces of their shoes. Now I am trying to understand the chosen-one cult. If anyone claims they are the chosen one, then it means their God was also chosen from the product of this nature with a higher visibility. This is a clear example of both Tziyon's family and Judah's family being in the same boat, the evil and good in the boat where evil dominance could sink the good and where the good ones go unnoticed. As an old man once said, "If you ever found a nice Jew, you would be the best explorer in the world."

Back to our gift. How did we all have the same amount of money, $500 each? Our parents were all friends, so they gave the same amount every day as others. We maintained the same savings because we were equals in our group, and no one should carry more weight in their pockets. If our parents decided to give an equal amount of money so that there was no difference among us, then we would have a better way and answer more efficiently to show we are responsible. If by chance someone had extra money, then we would divide it and give it to the beggar that Tziyon insulted. He is the only beggar in our neighborhood and we always take care of him. Now you understand why Judah doesn't like his uncle, and we all had the same thoughts, same feelings, same love, same friendship, and same amount of money. We probably sound like communists living in a capitalist country.

Now, where did the stranger with the gun come from? The well-known proverb "Walls have ears" offers an answer. We had the whole discussion about the gift, the money, and our plans in the park. This man was somewhere close to us, listening to the whole conversation. None of us could remember how we didn't notice him, but we could remember only some shadow infiltrating into our conversation. He is a thief, but during the whole scene I referred to him as a stranger, because I don't know what his background is, and because he was a black man, I don't want to discriminate by saying a black man attacked us. In a free country with so many choices, I don't know why he decided to be a mugger and a thief. So, equal rights for black men—right to vote, right for politics, right for a seat on the bus, right for this, right for that, and they got it. And now what are they doing? Mugging, stealing, raping, selling drugs, and many things. Was the attitude of black men the same before the Emancipation Proclamation? I think not, they were the nicest people in America. Freedom with no education is like a bow without an arrow. Before declaring freedom, educate and liberate them, so they know the difference between good and evil.

But I have to appreciate the stranger. Except for fracturing Shu's hand, he didn't shoot my friends—just a warning bullet into the ground. But Ejaz broke his jaw, which should not have happened, and I hope he'll be a better person when he comes out of jail. The only lesson that we learned was never discuss something that is related to money, treasures, jewels, or a secret out in the open like we did, as there will always be someone listening and waiting for their chance to get to us.

Another question people had was, who was the brave boy who saved us? He is Benjamin, our new superhero, and he deserves the Medal of Honor. How was he so brave? Who could bring a six-and-a-half-foot, muscled man down? He is the son of Captain Kadin Gail, the most respected, feared-by-criminals law protector from the department of police. He is the role model for most police officers in America. He is in charge of the province and lives in a different neighborhood, and Benjamin was visiting his grandparents, who live in our neighborhood. He saw the stranger with the hood and mask, with hands in his pockets, and followed him. His dad trained him to be a perfect cop, and he always carried a sling and a knife in his pocket for self-defense. He is so good at using the sling and pocketknife, that's how he ended up saving us. Most of the police officers know him very well, and respect and admire him.

CHAPTER 5
CELEBRATIONS AND SORROWS

THE PHONE WAS RINGING AT HOME, BUT I WAS SO COMPLETELY LOST IN MY "search world" that I didn't answer. They called a few times and I didn't respond. Then my dad drove back home to check on me. He knocked the door, but I was in very deep thought, searching for answers. I didn't hear him and he started to bang on the door. I eventually snapped out of my trance and opened the door. My hair was messy and my face was stressed out, and I was very disturbed. My dad was upset to see me like that and asked me, "Are you all right, my son?" I hugged my dad and said, "Why are all these bad things happening in this world? Why did Shu break her hand, and why did someone try to rob us?" My dad figured out that I was a little disturbed by Shu's incident and said, "These days all events are random, and evil has different faces and shapes. Be happy, my boy, that Shu is safe."

On the way to the hospital, I had a comforting feeling that we had made a valuable new friend in Benjamin. My dad told me that Shu's fracture was only a minor one, which also made me feel better. After the police arrested the stranger, my four friends had to fill-in the FIR (First Information Report) report of the incident. So in the whole process of the police inquiry, the events had to be explained without any alterations; Ejaz had been carrying $4,000 and had to say why he had so much money. At this point we had to explain about the gifts and the jewelry shop.

We reached the hospital, our "Champ" and healer, Dr. Enoch, was treating Shu's facture. He believed all of us were his own family. He instructed all the nurses and other doctors to give extra attention and care to Shu. He had other doctors in his hospital, including a famous specialist orthopedic doctor, Dr. Victor Klaus. Judah's father instructed him to take Shu's case. Judah's father said that he would take care of Shu and asked us to go home and prepare a meal and a gathering. He said to all of us to be happy and rejoice, because it was a day of celebration, and that we had escaped from danger and shouldn't be mourning today. He added that this is the moment of experience that would unite us when we are in deep sorrow and pain, so we are all there to help each other. He comforted Shu's mother and father and told them to be happy and steadfast, but Shu's parents were still grieving in their hearts.

Dr. Enoch saw that they were very sad, because Shu was their only child and they looked at her as the answer to their problems. Dr. Enoch understood the situation and gave a stern but kind warning to them: "If you keep crying here, you don't accept me as your brother, and since you don't accept me as your brother, you can take Shu to a different hospital." Within moments they stopped crying and realized Shu was doing better and Dr. Enoch wanted them to stay calm and relaxed. Dr. Enoch called himself Wang's brother and said Shu was his own daughter. We all were surprised he said that, because till now they were good family friends, but since they had been abandoned by their own families and Shu was hurt, he wanted to be nicer to them. After Dr. Enoch addressed Wang as a brother, they felt that there were more people to care and love them.

At this point a few police officers came to the hospital to get some paperwork filled out. As the officer was explaining the situation to them in more detail, they came to learn about the surprise gift, and now they rejoiced and all the sorrows about Shu's injury disappeared. For us, it was not good, because the details of the surprise were disclosed. But anyway, we had to change our philosophy for our own comfort in this situation. How could we do that? We understood that if this incident had not happened and we had given the gift to them, they would have had a moment of great happiness. Yet after this incident and disclosing the surprise, they moved from a moment of sorrow to a moment of internal bliss. Yes, they moved beyond to a world of glee. An object is not what makes a person happy, but the moment and intention of what we were trying to do is what filled their hearts with joy. The gift was not of such value to them, but the care and love that was wrapped around it was very important. And now we didn't have to hold this secret until Chinese New Year, so the pressure of excitement, surprise, and anxiety was transferred from us to them. Ha-ha: I am convincing myself and changing the patterns of this universal space with my needs and favors. This is what I call living better when failing.

There was excitement and joy in their eyes, but I could see too many sentiments being manifested. We all went to my home, and my mom and all my friends' moms started preparing dinner. We had been united again for a gathering, and our new friend Benjamin and his mother and father also joined us. A feeling of contentment filled the party that night.

Even though we were rejoicing together, all of us were filled with thoughts of Shu and eagerly waiting for her to come home. Very late in the evening, Judah's father brought Shu home. Shu was excited to see us again. Shu had a minor crack above the left wrist and she had a bandage on her hand and a sling over her neck. She said she had some pain, but more than pain she felt fearful. After a few moments she put her head on Madison's shoulder and started to cry. We asked her if her hand hurt, but she said that she was scared of the gun's sound. We all offered her encouragement, and slowly her fear began to disappear.

To add to the excitement of Shu's return, there was some romance between Shu and Ejaz. At one point we couldn't find Ejaz, and we started asking everyone where he was, but no one knew. When he finally reappeared, he was carrying three beautiful red roses. He walked into my room like a romantic hero. Apparently he had gone home to shower and get dressed up in his finest clothes. So he walked and handed the roses to Shu. This was unusual for him, and we could see he was nervous, because he was blushing as he handed her the flowers. Nikifor and Judah giggled at each other, but I didn't understand what was happening at first. I figured we were not even teenagers, so I was a little surprised at his emotions and feelings at this age, but I did know that he was interested in Shu. She was happy and excited to get the flowers, and he gave her a kiss on the cheek.

Another kid we were all happy to have with us was Benjamin. We all appreciated what he'd done for us, and we gave him a few gifts as tokens of gratitude for his great help. We also invited his family for a gathering to celebrate the Chinese New Year at Aika and Shu's home, so that we could start to learn more about him and his family. This decision was made not only by us, but with the help of our families. They were surprised to see all of our families and seemed to appreciate the bond that we had all created.

Benjamin liked all of us and wanted to be our friend. With open hearts, we invited him to be the eighth wonder of our group. We decided he was definitely the Messiah and savior of our group, the one who had saved our friends that very day. We told him about the gifts for Aika's and Shu's families for Chinese New Year. He was very interested to join the party, even after knowing us for only a few hours, and offered to contribute $500 for the gift. Initially we refused to take it, but he insisted. We felt we had no choice but to accept his share for the gift, and we all remarked what a great person he was. He saved our $4,000, risked his own safety for us, and still wanted to give a contribution of $500 towards the gift.

I've heard other sides of this story—that when someone helps, they will demand something in exchange, like money—but in our case we felt we should be giving $1,000 to him. My more cynical side wondered why he gave $500 to us so quickly, as though it was a membership fee to join our club, so my thought had become negative for a while, forgive me. Judah got his $500 back and now the cost of our gift was equally divided among all of us, and now we were ready to buy it.

The whole night we were talking about the incident again and again, and everyone had different versions of telling the same story. Have you guys ever experienced that effect? Yes, while in our room, we spoke about it nearly forty times. I counted, eight of us, each one asking five times. Then our parents called us down to talk about the incident, and how many of them were there? It should be sixteen—all of our parents—but there were actually seventeen, including Nathalie. She had heard about Shu, and everyone took their turn asking the same question in different ways: "Tell me, guys, what happened?" "Do you know what time it happened?" "Who saw the stranger first?" "Who fell down first?" and so on. However, the answers as you could imagine, were not all the same. Every time they asked, my buddies told the story from the beginning, and there was never the same version. It was a thrilling story and people never get bored when we told it, but sometimes you have to fall back from knowledge and just enjoy the thrill of a good story, which will train you to be a better friend, because you are listening when they are talking.

It was a great night because we also had good food, and all the parents shared wine and beer and cherished their time together, and it was like we were one big family now. That night, all my friends stayed over in my room. The four girls slept on my king-sized bed, which I have because my dad refused to buy me a kid's bed, as he always saw me as a king. Ejaz and I slept on an air mattress on the floor, Judah always likes the closet, and Nikifor slept on my study table. The whole night no one slept except Shu, because she had taken some pills for her pain. We were all watching Shu and her fractured hand and felt very sorry for her. We looked at each other every few hours, until about three in the morning, when we couldn't stay awake any longer and finally slept. After a day of problems, hard times, and stress, we slept for only five hours and we all woke up at eight o'clock. Even though it was only a five-hour night of sleep, I'll never forget it. It was like the best sleep I ever had. I could finally understand how workers who do physical work every day, from morning to evening, are so exhausted when they go to bed at night.

Since Shu's injury was minor, she recovered faster than we expected. For the first week she didn't go to school, and every day we'd all go to her home and spend a couple of hours with her, talking and playing. The romance between her and Ejaz flourished. Every day he brought her flowers when we went to see her. I wanted to do that for Madison, but Madison was not hurt or sad or injured, so I thought that Ejaz was the lucky one in our group.

After a week, Shu returned to school. We all decided to buy gifts from the jewelry shop for her. The only downside was that we had to face Tziyon. Unlike most stores, his shop was not open on Saturday, so we went on a Sunday for the purchase. But the rules never changed: Ejaz is our accountant and holds all of our cash. We made a different approach this time. We all went to Ejaz's home to pick him up, and then we went to the jewelry shop. We carried weapons with us this time: Benjamin had his sling; Nikifor and I had baseball bats; Aika and Shu had some smoke bombs and tear gas, also called pepper spray; Madison carried a small foldable hand knife; and Judah had small scissors. We carried these dangerous weapons in our hands and went to Ejaz's home to pick him up. We wanted to make sure we didn't make the same mistake this time. But our family, wanted to drive us or at least walk with us. It was a challenge for us to go by ourselves, but we thought we didn't need any help from anyone. Once we reached Ejaz's house, his father asked us, "Do you guys want me to walk with you?" Without looking at each other, we just shook our heads from left to right 'No thanks' we all repeated. He saw that we were confident and was proud of us and said, "Allah be on your way. Fight well if you encounter a problem, and win the battle."

Then we left Ejaz's home and walked to Tziyon's shop, Glittering Ammos. Everyone we walked past knew what had happened and saw us in a different light this time. We all had our hands inside our pockets. Ejaz was in the center, Judah on the left with the scissors, and I was on the right with my baseball bat. Nikifor was in front of Ejaz with his bat, and in the front were Aika and Shu, with their pepper spray; Madison walked behind Ejaz, and at the very front was our leader, Benjamin, with his sling. It was just like walking in to a war zone. Our eyes were opened and we scanned the streets, buildings, and every person who walked past us. We probably looked crazy, because no one in our neighborhood had ever seen us like this; we had completely changed the whole groups appearance.

Finally we reached Tziyon's shop. Everyone who worked in the shop was Jewish. They were easily noticeable: they wore a Yamaka and their hair resembled twisted ringlets, just like a doll. They wore black pants and white shirts, and the women wore special outfits. But Judah was in his T-shirt, with a sweater and jeans, and they identified him and greeted him in Hebrew with a huge grin, while the rest of us just got a smile. I was wondering, how could they know Judah was Jewish? I thought maybe it was his rose skin color, his curly hair, some scent from his body, or his facial expression. I don't know. Maybe a chip is installed in all these people and beeps when they see their own kind. The really funny thing was, we were walking with our weapons inside the jewelry shop, and no one knew, even though we were dressed casually and neatly, we were children, they didn't mind us.

Once inside the shop, we took our hands from our pockets, and Nikifor and I were holding the bat in a way to show that we were coming back from a game. Besides us, there were businessmen, elders, and young people purchasing ornaments. We could see on everyone's face a sarcastic look that said, "Don't send a kid to do a man's job." It was a big jewelry store with five floors filled with gold, silver, and diamonds, like sand on the beach. At the reception a very pretty lady who dressed like a flight attendant in a grey suit, greeted and asked us what we needed to buy. We replied that we needed gold rings and lockets. I wanted to describe her again and again. She was really hot, and we could see her cleavage in perfect symmetry not too low or too high. We, all five boys in our group misbehaved that day. We couldn't resist. Our eyes didn't move, and we looked at her the whole time. Aika and Madison were talking to her, and when Madison saw that I was lost in her beauty, she hit me on the shoulder and said, "Oscar, stop it!" I realized that I was staring very blatantly, and Madison said that next time I should bring my sunglasses. It happened with Ejaz also. Shu's right hand tapped Ejaz's shoulder. I could guess what was going on between Ejaz and Shu, but Aika stared at Nikifor—I have no idea why—this happened. I knew that Nikifor was alive because of Aika and Shu, but as it turned out, from that day on Nikifor started to have a crush on Aika, and started talking about her to me at times when we were alone, but I didn't pay much attention to it. Judah and Benjamin were the priests and monks in our group, as they weren't staring at the saleswoman. We realized it was not a good sign, but they could check out all the women, since they didn't have their loved one next to them.

I thought to myself, if I become rich, I will definitely come here every day and buy gold to show this hot woman my money power. I really mean I want to impress her. Everyone there was a Jew, and I wondered why she dressed differently from the other women in the store. Maybe she was a modern Jewish woman, but it didn't matter to me because she was very sexy. Lucky for Tziyon, he had all this money and hot women working for him. The whole point here is, they have all the beautiful women at the front desk to attract the customers, and these beautiful women deceive customers. It is always the same rule: the opposite sex attracts customers no matter what their age is.

She took us to the ring section, for Aika's and Shu's mothers' gifts, and there were lots of models working there and the rings were all very expensive. The hot woman left us, handing us over to a specialist in that section. We explained this was a gift to our friends' mothers for Chinese New Year. She showed us lots of designs, and since we had less money, we told her the price range we were looking for. We liked almost everything, and due to our budget problem, we had some problems in making decisions, but finally we picked a ring with a little butterfly on it for $800 each. It was a small ring but we all liked the design and agreed to buy two of them—one with a red butterfly and the other one purple.

Now she was asking the size of the ring and no one had any idea what the size was. Benjamin had an idea. He said she looked exactly like the lady who had brought us in here. He meant the pretty lady who had walked with us from the front desk. The salesperson told us her name was Sharon. She called Sharon to come back and check the ring size. The three of us—Nikifor, Ejaz, and I—couldn't do anything, and Judah was on his best behavior, because they all knew his father. Lucky boy, it was Benjamin's day. Sharon tried wearing rings of different sizes on her finger and checked them. Then quickly Benjamin asked Sharon, "Can I help you?" and Sharon replied, "Yes, please." He began rubbing her finger and hand back and forth, probably feeling aroused by her and finally, after all the massaging, she found one ring that fitted best and gave it to the lady who was helping us.

Then they packed two rings for us, but Benjamin didn't want Sharon to leave his sight. He asked her to take us to the locket section, and she gladly agreed. She ran her fingers through Benjamin's hair before saying, "Please follow me." All the way to the locket section the three girls' eyes were on us—Madison on me, Shu on Ejaz, and Aika on Nikifor. We had to control our emotions and feelings and keep our heads down while we walked to prove that we were good guys. As we bent our heads down, the three of us spotted her back while she was walking. It went zigzag from left to right, like a pendulum clock. I enjoyed the view, and Niki and Ejaz noticed I was focused on something. Ejaz tapped me on my hand and asked, "What are you looking at?" Then I nodded at Sharon's back, and quickly the smart guys understood and started to follow my lead. It took exactly seven minutes to the locket section, and we were enjoying the trip. But Benjamin was the luckiest of all because she was holding his hand all the way. We were going to be teenagers soon, so we didn't judge each other over our feelings of temptation.

Once we were in the locket section, there was an agent who showed us different types of lockets in our price range. The man was polite and Sharon was very helpful, modeling all the lockets in our price range and showing us a few pieces on sale. We finally picked out a locket that we all liked. It was an oval-shaped one from one of the famous brands, Phil Brothers, and on the locket, they could carve any image. We decided to have a dragon carved on it. They didn't charge any extra money for the image, because that is the Phil Brothers credo: the carving of any image is absolutely free.

While we were waiting for our items, Tziyon came to the locket section. Someone had informed him that Judah was here, and he came and greeted us saying "Shalom Aleichem" and hugged Judah. Judah replied "Aleichem Shalom." He was happy this time that Judah replied, and he jokingly asked, "Are you not fasting today, Rabbi?" Judah answered by looking straight into his eyes. "No, Rabbi." He laughed and said, "I am so happy that you have chosen my place to buy gifts." Judah was a little suspicious now, wondering how he knew that we were buying gifts, and in turn he asked, "What gift do you mean, "Uncle" Tziyon?" He replied, "Gifts for your friends Aika's and Shu's parents." We all were shocked, thinking, how does this guy know? Then Tziyon said, "It was in the papers."

We could now understand what he was trying to do. Then he added, "The belief and myth is that anybody who buys gold from my shop will have good luck, and it is a good investment and will never be a waste of money." We couldn't understand what he said, but it sounded very scary, like he was doing something behind our backs. I knew at that moment that I needed to figure out what all this was about. Quickly Judah saw I had grown impatient, and in the meantime workers at the store started bringing us juices, ice creams, and treats. Tziyon said, "This is all for you. We greet and respect our customers with juices and ice cream!" There were so many refreshments from good-quality brands like Hersely, Movenpick, and Valio before us that we could have gorged ourselves for at least three days.

On the one hand, we were tempted to consume the goodies, but we didn't want to fall prey to his deceitful ways. Everyone looked at Judah and then at me, trying to figure out whether we could eat. My motionless silence understood to mean no. We had to somehow convince Tziyon that we were not ignoring it. Aika was smart enough to start eating, saying, "Thanks, "Uncle", but it is winter, and my mom advised me not to take any cold stuff, especially ice cream." Good start, Aika. Then we all followed in the same way and had the right reason. Then Tziyon said, "Oh, sorry. That's right—I should have served hot beverages and hot snacks. You guys are so right. For winter we should change the menu." He quickly told his assistant to have an alternative menu of hot beverages, soups, and crackers, and the assistant replied, "Yes, sir; consider it done." Again he told us, "We have some hot coffee, tea, and chocolate beverages. Would you like some?" We all glanced at each other when we realized he was not going to leave us, and Judah replied, "We said no, we had some when we left home, and we all have to go for lunch. So nice of you, though, "Uncle" Tziyon."

Tziyon said, "I cannot send Dr. Enoch's son and his mates home empty handed. I have to do something nice, so do you guys want to go for lunch? I will take you to the Inordinate Cope. It is a five-star hotel and they have a great restaurant." We have been there a few times, and the only thing we know is that it is where rich people go. Judah quickly responded, "Our parents are waiting and we have a small gathering in

Ejaz's house, so the meal is ready. Definitely next time I will join you, "Uncle"." He was convinced and said, "Judah, at least consider the purchase that you made to be on me. You don't need to pay. It is a gift from "Uncle" Tziyon." Judah already knew this would happen, and we had a little mock response that we had practiced before we came in. Judah replied, "Thank you very much, "Uncle" Tziyon. This is my first marketing attempt for your business. I wanted to show my friends, to bring them here, and I will do lots of marketing and references for your shop to everyone. Make sure you give me my cut for the reference; that's how we should develop business. If you want to show some respect and honor me, I will come by myself to buy what I need. At that time, please give me the jewelry as a gift, okay?"

Hearing this, Tziyon was surprised and everyone around was astonished, and Tziyon again hugged Judah and said, "Oh, you clever Yiddish boy. I am proud of you, Judah. You should be a good businessman like "Uncle" Tziyon." He did not let him go, and then he asked one of his assistants, "How much is the bill?" They calculated and said, "It is $3,950." Tziyon said, "I give 3 percent for the reference that makes $115 discount Judah." Judah smartly answered, "Let the first fruit be for Elohim, so give it to some poor people that you find on the streets. Don't give it to the temple, because you already donate. You are representing me for the first fruit, so go ahead with my choice." Then Tziyon was enlightened and could understand partially what Judah said, but he couldn't completely get the whole meaning and replied to Judah, "Yes, little master. As you say so; I will follow it."

Tziyon walked us to the counter, where we all paid the full bill and said goodbye to him. We were about to leave the shop when Tziyon stopped Judah and said, "You refused everything I offered, but you are carrying some gold with you. Last time you did that, you and your friends had some problems. Could I give you a ride home in my car?" Shu, who was standing next to Judah, quickly jumped in and said, "Yes, "Uncle", please." Judah turned and smiled at Shu, because she was able to read that Judah's answer would have been the same. Since Tziyon had three cars outside his shop, he was able to drive us to Ejaz's house. When we got out and Tziyon said goodbye to all of us, we thanked him and said, "Thank you very much for coming down." We all saw some changes in his eyes; it was love, peace, and forgiveness. After that we started to appreciate him more.

We were still waiting for Chinese Year to come, and before we knew it, it was two weeks until we were going to give our gifts. The preparation started in both Aika's and Shu's home's a week before the celebration. They had to buy a lot of groceries and decorate their homes, and they needed someone to help them. Shu's father was tied up at the grocery store and Aika's father couldn't take a break from his job, so both Aika's and Shu's mothers were hard at work. We offered to help them, and for one week after school, we helped both families get ready for the New Year. Nikifor and Ejaz were more than happy to do work for their parents, because they wanted to impress their families and were doubly energized and active all those days. We helped them buy groceries, arrange, and clean their home. We also decorated, organized the backyard, and made their homes look like grand party palaces.

They served us wonderful home cooked Chinese and Japanese food, and it was delicious. Not like the food from Chinese or Japanese take-out joints. We had all tried sushi and raw fish a few times, but that week at their home, we started to love sushi, and each night there was some kind of sushi as part of the meal. We loved the dumplings, soups, vegetables, and noodles. It looked like we were only eating and not helping them, but it turned out to be more work for Aika's and Shu's moms to prepare food every day for dinner, because we were six extra people. They enjoyed cooking for us.

We were finally ready for the Chinese New Year, and our parents also brought gifts for them. They all brought gold chains for Yukio and Wang, Aika's father and Shu's father, and gold bracelets for Kew, Shu's mother, and Noa, Aika's mother. On the day of Chinese New Year, we all got dressed very elegantly. Benjamin, Judah, and I dressed in a suit and tie. Madison wore a short black dress and looked adorable. Our handsome friends Ejaz and Nikifor were in their tuxedos and had a flower pinned in their lapels and a red hanky in another pocket. Their hair was oiled with hair gel and fully combed back; they looked like the Italian mafia. They looked so different, and at first we were blown away by their appearance. Later we found out that they wanted to impress Aika and Shu and their families.

We all went to their home together with our gifts and, on the way, everyone in our neighborhood complimented us on how great we looked. We reached Aika and Shu's home, and they were waiting at the front door for us to come. We saw both of them in their red traditional Chinese QiPao dresses, and I have to admit, with their light red lipstick, Chinese rose powder, and red nail polish, they looked beautiful and gorgeous. Nikifor and Ejaz gave red roses to their loved ones, and somehow they knew the girls would be in red dresses and they brought red roses that perfectly matched their dresses. We went inside for the party, and all our parents joined us later.

As soon as our parents arrived, we decided it was time to give our gifts. Aika's parents and Shu's parents opened their gifts and were pleased upon seeing the gold chain and bracelet. They thanked us a hundred times that day and were happy to get such treasured gifts from their daughters' best friends. Then we gave them their surprise gifts, which were the gold lockets and gold rings. They were very excited and hugged and kissed all of us, and they also took a lot of photos. They had invited all their neighbors, which was surprising for us. We asked Aika and Shu about this, and they said it was Chinese custom to invite neighbors and share their food. Nathalie was also there and we were always glad to see her. She knew that we had brought gold lockets and rings for them, so she gave each of them, including Aika and Shu, a pearl. Nathalie was always so nice, and she loved giving presents. Since she had lots of family jewelry, she had begun giving us and our families some of her jewelry collection as presents.

The party was also memorable because of the food. There were lots of special foods prepared, like meat, soup, desserts, and cookies. We enjoyed everything and were thankful for their hospitality. During the party we took many photos, and in addition they had hired a photographer to capture the event. The eight of us took photos with Nathalie as well, since she was our guest of honor. There was much fun to be had, and excitement flowed throughout the party. We ate so much that we felt like we would need to fast for the next week.

At that point our life was fine, with schools and in general, but I was still searching for ways to be a better person. The concept of being a superhero was part of me now, even though I was mostly involved with my friends and having a good time. Yet inside I was still the same. Even though I am with them half the time, I am always just a bit disconnected, and my search always rules my life. During this time, my dad got promoted at the bank and became a senior manager. Also, my dad had two new businesses that had begun to grow, so we were making a lot of money. Even though I spent less time with dad, I still valued my daily reporting to him. My mom was very happy that I was not going crazy with my dad's global fantasy ideas about superheroes, and my dad began talking to me about becoming a cop or joining the Marines.

My mom still didn't understand one concept that emerged during this time. My dad's talk about superheroes had become an ingrained concept in me, and my search continued to grow and expand even faster. Also at this age, my mom and dad started to really like Madison and wanted me to be her best friend for life. They also told me they would accept us if we wanted to date in the future. We were also all delighted for Ejaz's father, who had been promoted to assistant manager at the bank.

At school, we had quite an exciting experience when we played football. We had good times in the field playing football, and sometimes we played baseball, bicycled, or skated around in the neighborhood. For some reason Benjamin invited all of us to his neighborhood to play football. Benjamin didn't like anyone in his neighborhood. We all made sure we were not playing too rough with Shu because she had just recovered. But Shu was smart and took advantage of this situation and wound up scoring more points than anyone else. We had no choice here, and she completely took over the points scoring and strived to win the game.

Then suddenly we had a really challenging moment. Madison was trying to throw the ball to Nikifor, but he missed it and the ball accidentally hit a kid who was a little older than us. He was tall and heavy, had fair skin with freckles and curly hair, and looked very intimidating. When the ball hit him on the head, he turned and saw Madison and walked over to her. As he approached, we all walked and stood close to Madison. Madison quickly said, "Sorry, dude, it was a mistake. I apologize." Then the big boy and his crew stood before us and, staring at her, he said, "Little girl, you should go to the park or zoo and stay away from the boys' ground." Madison grew very angry when he addressed her like that and she couldn't control herself. "Well, why don't you go to kindergarten or play school and change some diapers!" she yelled back.

It turned into a messy situation after that. It seemed that Benjamin knew all these guys, and he said, "Ambrose, you'd better leave right now! We don't want to fight with you." The big boy was named Ambrose and he sneered back at us, "I want to smack this little piece of rat down!" He was about to raise his hand to hit Madison, but Benjamin and Nikifor quickly grabbed his hand, and I pushed him back. Then their gang got angry, and everyone looked like they were about to fight. Then quickly Aika said to Ambrose, "If you have the guts, beat us in football. If you win, we will never, ever come to this playground for the rest of our lives and you can call us cowards whenever you see us, and vice versa." Everyone stopped pointing their fists, and Ambrose said, "That sounds interesting, you Chinese pony."

We all realized this guy was nothing more than a brazen idiot, as were his friends, because they couldn't tell the difference between Chinese and Japanese. We all agreed to accept this challenge, but we grew nervous because Ambrose's group had almost fourteen kids, while we had only eight. We decided to play eight-a-side football, but they had six extra players left outside and could swap players when they wanted to and keep the players active and energetic. That was not the case for us.

For their team, Ambrose was the captain. We needed to have a captain for our team, but we didn't know whom to pick. We finally agreed upon Madison as our team captain. The reason Nikifor suggested her was that Ambrose picked a fight with her and we wanted to teach him a lesson, but Judah, Ejaz, and the others wanted either Benjamin or Nikifor to be the captain. In the end, it was our friend Madison's reputation that won her the spot. At first she was scared and said no, but Ambrose and his crew kept making fun of her, and she got angry and decided to be captain. No one on our team had much experience playing football except Benjamin and Nikifor. Still it was a great challenge for us, and we gave it our best shot.

We started playing the game, and right away it was clear that Ambrose's team was much more professional. They got a touchdown in the first five minutes of the game. In the first twenty minutes they scored twenty-two points and we didn't score any. Then we had a break and Benjamin was trying to explain how to be united and play this game in a condescending way. We noticed there were two girls sitting and watching the whole game. One girl had hazel-colored hair and fair skin, and the other girl looked Hispanic. They were also dressed in football pants and shirts, and they approached us.

We looked at the two girls as they walked toward us and said, "Do you need some help?" Benjamin replied, "No, thanks, we're good." Then Benjamin started to talk about the game. The two girls were standing and listening, and we didn't understand what they were trying to do. Then Madison said, "We didn't say we don't need any help," and the Hispanic girl said, "We know a little football. We'd like to join your team, and we can play really well." We didn't know who these girls were, so Judah asked, "Do you guys live around here?" The fair-skinned girl said that they did, and then Judah asked, "How come you are with Ambrose and his team?" The Hispanic girl replied, "That is a long story." She took her hand and shook Judah's and said, "I am Sadie" and Judah quickly replied, "Oh, I am Judah." Ejaz was rolling his eyes at all of us and said, "These girls look cool. Maybe we should make a ten-player team?" Ejaz turned and looked at me, but I was looking at the girls, thinking that they looked special to me and were about the same age. I found some shining quality in them and asked their names. The fair-skinned girl replied, "I am Fay." We all made quick introductions, and we told Ambrose that we would have a ten-man team. Ambrose saw both the girls and was pissed off and said, "You moths are going to die with them."

We don't know why he was angry with the girls. We thought maybe they wanted to help us and he just hated anyone who wanted to help us. We started the game again, and the first touchdown for our team was made by Fay. We couldn't believe we had made seven points and all carried Fay on our shoulders. Ambrose's team was very angry. Ambrose said, "It is a long road there, dogs. Better gear up to get beaten soon." Those two girls, Fay and Sadie, knew more about football than Ambrose, and they were in high spirits. Niki also teamed up with the two girls, and they scored three more touchdowns and Ambrose's team lost the ball twice. We had twenty-seven and Ambrose's team had twenty-one.

The game started to become harder and harder. Ambrose's team couldn't believe they were losing, and they started to play foul. We started to punch each other, and it started to become a real football game. Both our teams started to have hand fights because the game was not fair anymore. We decided we needed a referee, and Ambrose said that one of his buddies would be the referee, but we declined, because it would not be fair. There was a cleaner, who cleaned up garbage, standing and watching the game. I was observing him the whole time and I said to everyone, "Why can't we take the man who is standing there as a referee?" One of Ambrose's friends said, "A cleaning man? He stinks, like you guys. No way." Then there was an argument concerning whether to take him, and finally we didn't have any choice, because except for us and the garbage man, there was no one around. We asked him to be our referee, and he was very interested in the game and became the referee. He was a tall, well-muscled man, and he quickly took the place of a referee and the game started again. We wrestled, pushed, blocked, kicked, banged, gave all our strength, and played the game.

We were leading and Ambrose got upset that he might lose the game. Ambrose even pulled the referee aside and tried to bribe him with a hundred dollars, but the referee slapped his face and said, "I am a street cleaner and a garbage man and I work very hard to fill my hours. I am very proud of my job, and I clean the streets of peoples waste, but I am clean and pure. Don't ever try to bribe me and make me stink like other people, you little devil. You should be in Africa, India, or Mexico. Don't spoil the pride of this nation." We heard his wisdom and we all laughed, because he held Ambrose by his collar and warned him, and Ambrose was squeezed like a little cockroach. He was scared and almost shat his pants. But we appreciated the referee's thoughts and his pride in his job.

At this point we were getting tired and both teams started scoring. The final score was Ambrose's team, thirty-nine, and our team, fifty-three. Yes, we won the match, and we shouted for joy and lapped the field in celebration. We thanked the cleaning man for his help, and he shook hands with all of us. With our thanks we gave him all the snacks that we had in our bag. He took them and went home very happy.

Ambrose and his team were extremely disappointed, because they not only lost, but lost against a team with girls. Also they were really mad at us, especially Madison, because they thought she was the one who started everything. Now we had more responsibility to always make sure Madison was safe. Our job was to protect her. Fay and Sadie liked us a lot, and I had a very positive feeling about them, that they would be in our group and become our friends. We decided that we would never again go to Benjamin's neighborhood to play, and we also wanted to make sure that Ambrose and his crew didn't come to our neighborhood and try to create problems for us.

Fay and Sadie had a lot of dislike for Ambrose and his crew because Ambrose and his friends acted like delinquent boys and got up to all sorts of mischief, caused mayhem, broke common civil laws, and terrorized other kids in their neighborhood. Fay and Sadie didn't want to be in their company and waited for four years, hoping that someone would walk into their neighborhood and kick them out. According to their belief, it was a great day for them. We all became resilient and strengthened in ourselves because we didn't want to let our fierce captain Madison down since she had been so brave.

Fay and Sadie had to go to school with Ambrose since they lived in the same neighborhood. Their life was in more trouble because they had to see those punks every day at school and there were only two of them, whereas Ambrose's group was quite big: there were nearly two dozen of them. I am not sure how they would coexist now with Ambrose. Did they really want to help us because they saw some vibration in us, or did they just want to put down Ambrose's group? Either way, every friendship needs a start, so there are always risks, losses, and displacement from their momentary state, but time and energy drive new bonds of friendship. I could see that they were honest and righteous kids, and that they would grow with us.

After the game, we took Fay and Sadie to Madison's house. When Madison's mom and dad saw two more new girls with us, they were surprised, because they had never seen them in the neighborhood. We explained what had happened with the game and said that Madison was the captain of the team, and they both were very proud of their brave daughter and appreciated our accomplishments. Madison's mother was very pleased, and thanked and greeted our friends with a gentle kiss on Fay's and Sadie's foreheads. Madison's parents were astonished by Fay and Sadie's contribution, because though they were new to us, they still volunteered to join our crew and help us. Madison's mother was happy and invited all of us to stay for dinner, and we all did. Madison's mom took me aside and thanked me for always taking care of Madison. In turn I said, "Aunt, we all did." She in turn looked into my eyes very deeply and said, "No, Oliver, you always stay close to her. Promise me that you will continue to do so." I didn't know what exactly she was asking of me, and my first thought went to the incident when I kissed her. I felt a little uncomfortable and wanted to get out of this scenario with her mother, so I made a promise to her quickly, without asking her to explain what she meant.

I made the first promise to Madison's mother that I would always stay close to Madison. I know Madison's mom is a very genuine lady, but in her eyes I saw some strange emotions, like wanting me to be with

Madison, and thinking only I could keep life safe. But deep down I loved Madison and had an unexplained feeling at my age. Even without the promise to her mom, I knew I would always stay and take care of her.

That day we had a wonderful dinner at Madison's house and ate delicious food. Fay and Sadie enjoyed our company, and our friendship grew. Madison's parents asked to have a gathering with Fay and Sadie's families, and they agreed to do so. We all agreed to meet for Easter and have a big feast.

Benjamin started to bring Fay and Sadie with him to visit our neighborhood. We all had a lot of fun playing and hanging out during the week. Fay and Sadie were great girls, and we started to practice and play football better because of their company and because Benjamin became our coach. We started to play some hard-core games after our previous experience with Ambrose and his gang. Things changed somewhat after that experience because we decided to learn football and get stronger in body and mind. Shu was also fully recovered now, and she became the one who practiced more than any of us. Our friendship also grew more deeply with Fay, Sadie, and Benjamin, and they decided they were not happy anymore at their school. Because Ambrose and his friends tried to create more problems, they began to feel vulnerable.

Fay: Niki, could we join your school after summer? We are not comfortable anymore going to our school.

Niki: Why? Because of Ambrose?

Fay and Sadie: Yes.

Niki: Benjamin is there; you should be alright.

Benjamin: Hey, Niki, they outnumber us at school and have lots of punks with them, and I only have a couple of other friends, Lauzo and Alroy, with me. I shouldn't have taken you guys there. It is my fault all this has happened.

Shu: Relax, Benjamin, we have to straighten out this situation.

Ejaz: Why don't you guys join our school? Leave all the punks there and come with us.

Judah: Well said, Ejaz. I think that sounds like a plan. What do you say, Oliver?

Me: I think it is a great plan. Our school has better education and teachers. I know your school ranks third in the city, but the kids are wild there—that's the problem.

Madison: If they leave the school like that, won't they make fun of them and call them cowards?

Aika: They may, but they are not going to see them very often—maybe once or twice, here and there—so it shouldn't be a problem.

Madison: We have to teach them a lesson! We will go and challenge them to a fight and show our strength.

Niki: Just stop Madison! What is happening to you? The best way to solve this is to get rid of the problem. Till now they are the ones who are defeated, not us. Let us keep the same feelings. Fay, Sadie, and Benjamin, please leave your school and join our school.

Judah: Good idea, Niki; you should do it.

Sadie: How could we talk to our parents about this?

Me: We are getting together for a feast on Easter in a week, and we have to make sure we impress your parents. We have to be exceptionally good and disciplined kids. We should make sure that we don't mention the topic about a school transfer to your parents. And let us make sure no one knows about the football game, Ambrose, or anything else that happened.

We all agreed to meet at the party and roll the dice. We prepared ourselves to stage this drama, with no room for error. We made sure that when anyone asked Benjamin, Fay, and Sadie about their school—how is it, how are the classes, the campus, friends, and so on—that they would always say it was a wonderful school and they really liked it. There should be nothing said that was negative. Within a week, Easter was here and all ten families and a few other friends gathered together. A very important person also joined us this year: Nathalie. We told Nathalie about our new friends Fay and Sadie, and she was excited to see them and their families. When we all saw Nathalie, the noblest person we ever knew, we ran and hugged her, as it was the same affection and love we felt for our parents. We had some tasty cookies and chocolates that we brought for Nathalie for Easter, and we all presented them to her. When she saw Fay and Sadie, she was happy and said to both of them that they were beautiful, like princesses. That was a very true compliment.

The party started and as usual we had good music, ballet dance, drinks, food, and lots of fun. We behaved so nicely; Fay and Sadie's parents started to like us and our families. Everybody treated them as royal guests, and they could see all our parents in one place. The best moment of that day was when all ten of us took a photo with Nathalie. The picture was awesome—all of us in our suits and the girls in their frocks, with Nathalie sitting in the middle and us all surrounding her. The reason we liked it so much was that Nathalie cared about us like our parents. Before she left the party, she called all ten of us together and said, "Always be united." And she blessed us all and left the party.

Even though I continued to meet new people and have fun, my search for a perfect life never stopped. After the Easter party everyone left and I was exhausted. I went to my bedroom to rest, but I couldn't sleep and was tossing and turning. Suddenly I felt lonely in my bed, and I went to the living room and slept on the couch. My mom and dad went to bed, and my search started to kick in. What about all these football games? We were good kids, with no violence in our history, yet we had turned into street cats that day. What was happening around us?

Then I started to wonder why Fay and Sadie, though they were strangers, still volunteered to help us. They should have been with Ambrose and his group. Why did they help us instead? They didn't have any good thoughts or opinions about Ambrose and his friends, but why did they join us before they knew us? To take vengeance against Ambrose's team because of the few times they had fights? Did they find the right opportunity to get back at them using us? Or did they find something in our group that they hadn't found before? I think they found a superior bond and friendship in us than with Ambrose and his crew. They didn't like them because they were troublesome and mean. I thought they made the right decision, because they seemed to follow their sixth sense to choose between right and wrong.

Ambrose and his buddies were corrupt, and Fay and Sadie didn't want to partake in their wrongdoing. But they also wanted to take a stand this time and it seemed like we gave them the right opportunity to take revenge against them. Everyone has vengeance toward someone in their mind, body, and soul, and everywhere in them. Getting revenge can calm a restless mind, but there will be a risk and an outcome that will always follow you long after you get revenge. For us, it didn't stop with Fay and Sadie, because all ten of us became victims of revenge, since Ambrose and his friends were looking for us. We learned that revenge may involve everyone—even the ones who shouldn't be part of it. I don't judge Fay and Sadie. They joined us for their own reasons, but their intent was to fight against evil, which to my mind is a noble cause. Let me try to find an answer whether their intentions were right or wrong, in conclusion. If vengeance against evil was the solution, then we all have to die, because we are all evil.

Talking about vengeance and Fay and Sadie, we had one mole among us, and it was Madison. She also wanted revenge because she got insulted and wanted to pay them back. We call it payback, but it is well known as vengeance in an uncivilized world. The second reason I couldn't sleep was Easter itself. I went to church that morning and the priest said, "Jesus is resurrected. Hallelujah, hallelujah, hallelujah." I am very interested about his resurrection. How can a dead man come alive, as a man and not a zombie? Does he have super natural powers, if we all live in the same density and space of this universe? Is nature unfair in giving power to some people and not to others? But the priest also added, "He died for us, and washed away our sins." Why should he die for us, to stop our death, because through sin we all die, and he washed away our sins, but billions of people died after Jesus died. Still I cannot understand why he should die for us.

My mom always said, "Jesus is our Lord and God." If so, how come God can die? If he dies, he is not God. This concept and religion were there for ages with so many contradictions and so much confusion. But one fact I was interested in was that this man Jesus gave the same powers of healing, miracles, and authority to all who believed in him. Some perform good deeds in Jesus's name, and it works. I was deeply pondering about transformation of energy from one person to another and passing authority from one to another. All I could understand is that we could be doing better and become more powerful in this world. There is somewhere in this world where lots of power and energy are stored, and it could be transferred to humans, like Jesus did for his people; it will make all of us god like superheroes. Now my search is profound, but I will find answers to my search. I was thinking deeply and intensely and didn't fall asleep until early in the morning.

A week passed by after Easter and the following Sunday morning at six o'clock we heard lots of noise and people talking loudly and a few women and children crying. We got up and my dad rushed to open the door to see what was happening. I opened my bedroom window and saw a cloud of dust as everyone was rushing and walking fast. A few people were running around in bare feet without any shoes or flip-flops on.

We saw Ejaz's father, who came rushing to our home and opened the gates. My father stepped out of our house, walking faster to the gate and asked, "What happened?" Ejaz's father whispered and I watched the whole scene through my window. It was the first time I saw my father cry, and tears started rolling. My mom rushed out of our house and asked, "What's going on?" My father put his hand on my mom's shoulder and looked very sadly at her face, and Ejaz's father continued talking to my mom. My mom looked shocked and started to cry. While watching all this I was panicking about what was going on. Then I saw Nikifor and Madison approaching my house, and that's when I realized something was really wrong. I hurried and left my room and went running to ask Nikifor and Madison what had happened. Nikifor said, trying not to cry, "Nathalie died this morning." For a minute I could not comprehend what Niki had said. Madison added, "Nathalie died and left us." Then I understood what was going on, but honestly I didn't understand the meaning of death. This was the first time I heard the local church bell ringing in different patterns. I asked my father, "Why is the bell ringing in a different pattern?" My father's eyes were red and his face was wet with tears. He couldn't look at me, and he said, "It is the mourning bell. It rings when someone from the neighborhood is dead."

My mom told me to get dressed because we were going to Nathalie's house. When we arrived, I was amazed that Nathalie's home was so big and beautiful, and there were even a couple of maids. Though we all were sad and in mourning, we were impressed by the pristine beauty of her home. We learned from her family that Nathalie had died early in the morning; before the sun came to smile on the Earth, Nathalie's smile was removed from us. She had chest pains and couldn't move from the bed and rang the bell to call the maids. They woke up hearing the bell ringing from her room and came rushing in, but by the time they reached her, she was dead. All this happened within five to ten minutes. That is how quickly she left us.

After we paid our respects to her family, my father and all our friends started to work on preparing for the funeral. She had a few relatives in Germany, London, and New Zealand, and a lot of friends outside our state. Everyone in the neighborhood sent faxes, telegrams, and e-mails, and telephone calls. They decided to keep her body for five days, and then bury her. Those five days were a period of mourning in our neighborhood. Everyone was sad and depressed, and some seemed completely lost without her. Though Nathalie was not anyone's blood relative, we saw her like our godmother, and everyone held her friendship and love close to their heart. Surprisingly, our school was even closed for a week because of Nathalie's death. She was the midwife for all of us in the neighborhood and for most kids in our school. Though she was very rich, the job she chose and the way she presented herself was so meaningful that she made an incredible impact on many in our neighborhood. Even Benjamin, Fay, and Sadie and their families joined us for these sad times. Though they were not Nathalie's descendants and didn't know much about her, they had all met her at the Easter party, and she was nice to all of them and showered her love on everyone. She was the mother of our neighborhood, but alas, no longer with us.

The day came for her funeral, and it was the first time I saw everyone in black suits, black shirts, and black dresses: everything was black. The whole neighborhood was weeping in pain and agony, and we took Nathalie's body to the church for the final Mass and then for burial. The priest talked about how death entered this world and we could be in Christ in the future. He was talking about hope. I was very depressed at this point, and couldn't really focus on the sermon or my own search. I halted the search in my mind and was only focused on Nathalie's death. After the church service, we took her to the cemetery. It was a Friday evening, and a chilly wind blew on our faces. There were hundreds of people in the cemetery—all the local people, and her relatives and friends from foreign countries and outside the state. We never knew Nathalie knew so many people or friends outside our neighborhood.

The sun was no longer with us. It slowly became dark, and the priest came and said a few prayers and sprinkled water around her coffin and blessed it and asked to put it in the ground. We all had flowers and slowly threw them into the pit on top of the coffin. And a few people slowly moved and put the coffin in the ground, and started to roll a stone on top of it. The sun dropped down in the sky and it was now dark. Everyone left for home and we all went to Ejaz's house. This was the first time we all gathered not for a dinner or happy times, but for a very sad moment.

Ejaz's mother said we should all have food, but everyone refused it. Because for five days we hadn't eaten proper food, we could only eat small snacks or sandwiches here and there. On the day of the funeral we had only liquids from the morning and no solid food, so we were all quite weak. Our throats were dry and we had no energy to swallow food. Ejaz's mom said she was going to prepare a meal and said, "If Nathalie were alive now, she would feel very bad and sorry for all of you starving like this." She added, "If we want to remember, and have good memories about Nathalie, first we need to be alive, and for that we should eat first." The other adults agreed with his mother, and a group of neighbors helped Ejaz's mother prepare the dinner.

We started talking about Nathalie and her personality and the services that she did, and we kept talking about her for almost three hours. Around 9:00 p.m., the meal was ready and a few of us sat in the dining room and a few in the hall, and everywhere in the house small groups gathered and ate quietly. I saw everyone eating so quietly; no one spoke to each other. But the meal was a wonderful Mediterranean feast, and we enjoyed it, as we were hungry after our long, sad week. We continued talking to each other about our sadness or problems or memories of Nathalie until one o'clock in the morning.

For the next month many of us were still in shock and still sad about Nathalie's death. I continued to see my friends all the time, but the talk was always about Nathalie, and even in school and at home, Nathalie was the example discussed in all our classes. The only topic on the street, in our homes, and in our neighborhood was Nathalie.

What could I say about all the incidents that started near Easter and led up to Nathalie's death? After all this turmoil, my search began again. Easter was a very interesting occasion for me. Though all ten of our families come from different backgrounds, we all celebrated and enjoyed the day without conflict. We were all so united that everyone happily took part in Easter. Though Ejaz, Aika, and Shu were from a non-Christian background, they enjoyed all the moments of Easter day. Yet I wondered: supposedly on Easter, Christ won over death and crushed Satan's head. So, if he could conquer death, why couldn't Nathalie do that? I waited for three days for Nathalie to come back and she didn't, so what about Easter? Is it myth, a fantasy, or something unexplained?

I know Jesus was a very good person, the same as Nathalie. She was a holy and noble woman—sin was not a problem for her—so why couldn't she come out of her grave on the third day? Maybe I should have helped by moving the stone from her grave to help her come back? I thought for a second, and then was scared to go to the graveyard by myself or even talk about it with my friends. I heard the priest say at the funeral that she would be united with Christ after death. We needed Nathalie here to care for us and be with us. What was Christ going to do with her in heaven? There are so many good people in heaven, I thought, and we needed Nathalie here, as there are more bad and evil people here on Earth.

Her death made me think terrible thoughts; because this was the first time I heard and felt what death means. The word *death* is a unique term that is unpredictable and the most dangerous word ever to have evolved in human life. When kids are born and start to grow, they learn every different aspect of life, about nature and the world around us, always having one common thought: they are invincible, and knowledge always expands. But the first time they encounter the word *death* and see someone whom they know dead, all the analysis and searching that they have started becomes very controlled. The boundary is closed and fear about exploring this universe just stops and fades. For me, I had the same experience for a month, but I recovered. As my father always says, I am a special child and my stand has already begun, and now my conflict is with the human enemy "death." I will face it like a man and a warrior, and death will evade. At this point my search reached a higher space as I started exploring how to defeat it and stop humans from dying. My search shifted to finding a way to have everlasting life.

Chapter 6
MEMORIES WITH MY FATHER

AFTER NATHALIE'S DEATH, OUR SORROW LINGERED IN THE NEIGHBORHOOD for months. No one was there to take Nathalie's role, because she was one in a billion. I learned one fact: sometimes you just have to move on—just move. The default principle built into this universe is to mourn for the dead and move on, to live and to die. The next generation does the same; it is a cycle.

We started our regular life again, and everything was restored to normal in our lives and families. The good news was that both Fay and Sadie moved to our neighborhood and would be starting at our school that year. Both families sold their houses for good prices and bought new houses in our neighborhood that were even bigger than their old homes. Their new friendship helped us focus on the bright side of life again. Nathalie's last wish for all ten of us was to be together all the time and be best friends forever and it was fulfilled. When they shared this with us—that they had been waiting for quite a long time to buy the homes of their dreams—they said it was through our new friendship that their dreams were accomplished. Thus they created a positive atmosphere of trust and transformation in their hearts when they started to know us.

Everyone in our neighborhood started to envy us. We started to have barbecues and family dinners every week at each other's houses. My dad got promoted again, this time to director of the bank. To celebrate the promotion he threw a grand party in one of the best hotels in the city and invited all his friends, coworkers and relatives. The party lasted for two days one weekend, and everyone brought lots of gifts and treats. The happiest person among the ten families was Ejaz's father, because he was best friends with my father. He brought him a diamond watch, which was worth almost $80,000. My father was so surprised that he asked Ejaz's father, "Why did you present such an expensive gift?" He replied, "James, I not only see my friend, but always think of you as my own brother and my family. I will be very trustworthy toward you and your family, Oliver and Olivia." My dad appreciated these words, since Ejaz's father was one of the key people for my father's growth and this very promotion. My father was impressed and moved by his words and said to him, "I know you will be the guardian of my family when I have passed on. Take care of my wife and my only son, Oliver." The people near them couldn't understand exactly what my father said, but they could feel the bond and friendship between them.

The party was awesome. My dad's salary increased by 35 percent, and he had more stocks and investments and was able to buy a new BMW. My mom and I were proud of him and were very happy with how he was proceeding in his career. My life was moving in a positive direction, and I felt that the same was happening for all my friends and their families.

Since becoming the director for the bank, my dad could make business loans to his friends and family up to a certain amount without any review required from the bank assessment team. He always had Shu's father in mind, as he wanted to lend him money for his supermarket business. Aika's father had given him some money to pay off his loans. As usual, Shu's father didn't have any intention of asking my father for help, but my father didn't need a request to help a friend. My father also felt a bond with Shu's father because they were both veterans. Shu's father had the ambition to enjoy a military career, but everything changed when he met Shu's mother. I was always impressed with Shu's father for being such a generous man, and although he was facing many financial and family troubles, there was never a trace of jealousy or envy in his eyes when he heard about my father's accomplishments.

Once my father received his promotion, he told Shu's father that he could offer him a loan at very low interest up to $200,000 for his supermarket business. At first he said, "No, thanks, James. I don't need it, and I am good at what I am doing." Then my father told him that he wanted to see him become the most successful businessman in town. My father even added, "I know you had some differences in borrowing money from Aika's father, but I am your friend, and this is not my personal money. It is from the bank, and I am entitled to use it and give it to the right people. And I am positive that you are the right man." My father finally convinced him, and he finally accepted it. He was happy and said, "I will definitely repay it, and I will always show my gratitude and loyalty to you and your family." My father knew that Wang was a man of his word and that he would work hard to repay the loan. We were all growing together as one big family.

Things continued to be very positive for a long time—until something weird and unusual happened. It was a Wednesday evening around seven o'clock. Everyone was home, and my father came in after work. I came in from playing with friends, and my mom came back from church. We were all watching TV when we had a phone call from Ejaz's mother. My father was the one who answered. At first Ejaz's mother was crying and couldn't speak at all. My father understood it was Ejaz's mother. He was nervous and then panicked and asked her, "Farah, are you all right?

Is there a problem?" She started to cry even more, and for a few moments she couldn't talk. He realized maybe my mom could help her, so we all gathered around the phone and my mom took the receiver and asked, "Farah, this is Olivia. Are you all right?" Finally Farah calmed down and said, "Homeland Security arrested Mukhlis ten minutes ago. They accused him of terrorist activity." My mom frightened and turned to my father and said, "Mukhlis was arrested by Homeland Security." My father grew very angry, because Ejaz's father was his best friend. He took the phone and said to Ejaz's mom, "Hang on, dear, and don't worry. I will send Olivia and Oliver to your home. They will be there in a few minutes. I will make a few calls to my influential friends and talk to my lawyer. Don't panic. We are here to help you." She now felt a little more comfortable, and said to my father, "My brother, I don't know many people, and I trust you alone. Please help us." My father replied, "Yes, I will help you."

My mom and I hurried to Ejaz's home, but before we left, my dad pulled me aside and said, "Oliver, don't go calling and telling all your friends about this. Stay with mom and Ejaz. Will you do that, my son? Promise me?" My father never asked promises of me, because he always trusted and believed in me to make the right choice. Now I realized that the situation was very bad. We went to Ejaz's home and saw that his mother was still crying. When Ejaz saw me, he rushed over and shouted, "Oliver, they took my father away!" I felt very bad, as his face was distraught and pale. I saw tears rolling down his face, and his T-shirt was wet with tears. My mom went to comfort Ejaz's mother.

In the meantime my father called his lawyer and explained everything that had happened. He also contacted Benjamin's father, who was the police captain. It seemed that Benjamin's father didn't know anything about it, as this was Homeland Security business. Benjamin's father was also surprised by what happened, as he knew Ejaz's father well. He said, "I know this is not true. We know Mukhlis very well. Something went wrong, and we should save him. I will be there soon. In the meantime, let me talk to some of my contacts at Homeland Security." My father thanked Benjamin's father, and started calling all his most influential contacts.

My mom called Judah's father and informed him. She shouldn't have done that, but all that went through her mind was that Judah's father was an influential Jewish person and well connected, and he could help Ejaz's family. Judah's father felt very bad about what had happened to Mukhlis and he promised to check with all his contacts. Within half an hour after Ejaz's mother called, both Benjamin's father and Judah's father started to work on fixing the problem. Benjamin's father came to Ejaz's home and asked Ejaz and his mother what exactly had happened. Ejaz's mother replied, "There were three Homeland Security vans with almost twenty agents. They rang the bell, and Ejaz opened the door. They said they were looking for Mukhlis, and Ejaz replied, 'That is my father.' The homeland guard asked him, 'Is he home, kid?' and Ejaz replied, 'Yes.' They rushed inside. Ejaz's father was sitting in his office doing some work, and they asked him, 'Are you Mukhlis?' He replied calmly with a confused face, and they arrested him and charged him with carrying out terrorism in the United States of America and cuffed him and took him away!" After listening to this, Benjamin's father asked Ejaz's mother a genuine question: "Do you have any thoughts about this, and if yes, could you please share them?" Ejaz's mother replied, "I know that he would never, ever do such a thing—I promise." Benjamin's father said, "I am just looking for answers—that is all I want. I am leaving now and going to the Homeland Security office to check on what is happening."

My father rushed into Ejaz's home with our family's lawyer, Riley Tree. Riley Tree was one of the top ten criminal attorneys in the country. Everyone's faces looked very solemn and confused. Benjamin greeted my father. "James, I am going to the Homeland Security office. Could you and your attorney join me?"

"Sure, we will drive with you," my dad replied without hesitation. The three left to check on Ejaz's father, and later Benjamin and his mother came to Ejaz's home, as did Judah and his mother and father. Everyone was clueless about what was happening. We were all comforting Ejaz and his mother, and they started to feel better as they knew that we would never leave Ejaz's father, Mukhlis, to deal with such a problem on his own. Judah's father told Ejaz's mother that one of his best friends was the head of Homeland Security in Wisconsin. He said he had explained the situation to his friend and that there must have been a misunderstanding. The head of Homeland Security took the information very seriously, and promised he would provide justice for his friend.

Benjamin's father, our attorney, and my father arrived at the Homeland Security office. Seeing Benjamin's father, some of the guards greeted him with great respect, shaking his hand. A few greeted him, "My man, Kadin," because Benjamin's father was a well-known officer in the state. Then Benjamin's father asked one of the guards about Ejaz's father, Mukhlis. "Did you guys arrest a man named Mukhlis an hour ago, near Wall Street?" One of the guards replied, "Yes, Chief, we did. We have a report that he is involved with terrorism, and we got a message from D.C. and did our job." Benjamin's father asked him, "Is he in here?" The guard replied, "Yes, he is. He's in the interrogation room. Hey, Chief, do you know him?" Benjamin's father replied, "Yes, he is my good friend, and I want to make sure that we are doing the right thing here." The guard was very positive and knew about Benjamin's father's reputation. "Oops, something is wrong here, sir. Hey, get in and check in with the head officer—see what he says about it."

Benjamin's father and our attorney went inside and met with the head of Homeland Security and asked what happened to Mukhlis and why he was arrested. Seeing both Benjamin and Riley Tree, the head asked them, "Do you know Mukhlis?" and Benjamin's father replied, "He is my good friend, and I am here to find out what happened to him." The head of Homeland Security began thinking as Judah's father spoke to him about Mukhlis. The head officer asked Benjamin's father if they were friends, and Benjamin's father replied that they were. The head officer promised to take a close look at the case and help as much as he could. The head officer and Benjamin's father discussed the possibility that a mistake had been made in the arrest, and Benjamin's father assured the head of Homeland Security that Mukhlis was a good man, not a terrorist. The head of Homeland Security replied, "I don't know what to tell you. We got a call from D.C., and they said it was critical that we arrest Mukhlis Jin. They said he stole $150 million from the bank where he worked and transferred the money to the most dangerous terrorist organization, Al-Sayyid Ifrit." Hearing this from the head officer of Homeland Security, Benjamin's father was stunned. He looked into the officer's eyes. "Is it true?" The officer showed him all the papers pertaining to the theft and the account number, passwords, e-mail, IP address, and office login records, as well as a pile of documentation. Though Benjamin's father had known Mukhlis for only six months, he believed he was innocent, despite the damning evidence.

Benjamin's father asked the man, "Did Mukhlis say anything about the case while you were investigating?" The Homeland Security head said, "No. He says he has no idea what is happening, and colleagues say he is not cooperating." The head officer also said, "If he cooperates, we could reduce his punishment, and at this juncture I assume that something may be going on. Kadin, you are a very esteemed and honest law enforcer, and you have risked your name for Mukhlis. If he were a real criminal, you would not be here. This makes me question whether he really is not aware of anything that happened or is happening."

The security head asked Benjamin's father for ideas about what may have caused this arrest if he was innocent. Benjamin's father offered to speak with James Oscar, who was the head of the bank and also the suspect's best friend. The head officer said, "That sounds good, but it can only be in the interrogation room, and the conversation should be recorded." Benjamin's father said, "That should be the process, so let it be." Benjamin's father thanked the security officer for helping them. He then took my father aside and explained the situation, and said they needed to ask him some questions in the interrogation room. My father thanked Benjamin's father and the Homeland Security officer for their help. He willingly entered the interrogation room, where he saw Ejaz's father sitting with his hands cuffed and his head down. He gave a weary smile to my father as he entered the room. There were two chairs and a table surrounded by glass and recording equipment. Everyone was standing outside listening and watching the conversation and the entire conversation was recorded. My father sat across from Ejaz's father and coughed; he was speechless and couldn't stand to see his friend in such a situation. Everyone was nervous as they waited to see what would happen. Neither of them seemed to know how to start the conversation, but eventually Ejaz's father spoke.

Mukhlis: Thanks for coming down, James.

My father (James): It is my duty and you are my friend. I can't turn my back. Do you know what happened? I know you're not involved, but this whole thing could ruin me.

Mukhlis: I don't know what is happening. All they say is that I stole money from our bank, around $150 million, and transferred it to Al-Sayyid Ifrit to promote terrorist activity in America.

James: Do you know that organization?

Mukhlis: Yes, I do.

James (a little shocked): How do you know about it?

Mukhlis: Through my younger brother.

James: Hmm. I am very sorry to ask this, Mukhlis, and I hope you don't mind. Where did you get the money to buy me such an expensive watch?

Mukhlis: It was my brother's gift, and I gave it to you.

James: You told me that you only had one sister and she lives in Texas, and now you say that you have a brother? Did you lie to me, Mukhlis, or are you hiding something from us?

Mukhlis: It hurts me, James that you ask me if I lied. I have never lied in my life, and I would never lie to you.

James: Not even a white lie? Did you lie to me for a good reason, because you felt like you had to?

Mukhlis: Do you want the truth, James, about the watch and Al-Sayyid Ifrit?

Everyone behind the glass mirror and my father were really anxious. Their hearts were pounding, and no one knew what was going on.

James: Could you explain to us so that we can help you?

Mukhlis: My family moved to America thirty-five years ago, and I have a younger brother and a younger sister. Everything was fine in our life, and my younger brother, Purdhil Jin, was a chemical engineer and a great hacker. He was doing great until he met someone from the Al-Sayyid Ifrit organization. They deceived him, talking about jihad, and offered him a lot of money to work in Afghanistan to make weapons for them. He was fooled and came to me and said he was going to join the force. I tried convincing him, but he didn't listen to me. He earned a lot of money and saved money right from when he was a kid, so he had $80,000 of hard-earned, real money that he wanted to use for the right purpose. He bought me this watch and gave it to me for my wedding and left.

James (stunned): Then why did you give me the watch, Mukhlis?

Mukhlis: You are an honest man and a veteran, and you protected this country from bad guys and terrorists. My brother is very wrong, killing innocent people and taking their lives for no reason. I admired you and wanted to thank you for the great service that you have done for this country.

James (his eyes filled with tears): So you love this country more than your people who want war with us and want to destroy us?

Mukhlis: Yes. I see the bright side of life and I value it. My brother, Purdhil, is doing wrong and you, my brother James, are doing right.

James: We have been close friends for a while, so why didn't you say anything about this?

Mukhlis: I was ashamed to say that I have a brother who seeks to kill innocent people. Look, James, would you tell someone if you had a brother who is a terrorist?

James: No, I understand. What about the phone calls that was made from the office, and the money that was transferred from your computer?

Mukhlis: I don't know, James. I promise I don't know.

James: Did your brother do those things?

Mukhlis: Though he left us and joined the wrong organization, he would never, ever involve me.

James: Then how did these things happen? There are a few calls from your home that you received from Afghanistan.

Mukhlis: My brother calls me sometimes at my home to check on my family and to see how Ejaz is doing. Every time he calls, I try to advise him not to call us. I know, James, this is America, and I have the right to have family conversations with my brother, even though he is a terrorist.

James: Okay, okay, then how about the calls from the office?

Mukhlis: I don't know anything about that.

James: I trust you, Mukhlis. I know something happened behind our backs. I will get you out.

My father got up from the chair and was about to leave when he said to Mukhlis with great confidence, "Take care, and thanks for the watch. I promise, I will get you out." And with those words he left the room.

All the officers and everyone who was standing outside the room were shocked by this discussion and started to feel Mukhlis was a good man and innocent. The Homeland Security head, Benjamin's father, and my father discussed what to do next. My father asked for the phone call reports, the Internet reports, and the evidence they had from the office.

By this point it was almost eleven o'clock at night, and my father agreed to review all the logs from the bank and report back on his findings. Benjamin's father and my father thanked the security head officer for his support and flexibility. Before they left, the security head said, "We have three days to interrogate and keep him here, and then we have to take him to Washington, D.C. Make sure you find something for us to use as evidence in his support. We will involve the CIA in this as well, and they will start the investigation for us tomorrow morning." Benjamin's father thanked the security head for his help.

We returned to Ejaz's house. His mother rushed toward us and asked what happened. My father replied, "Everything is fine. It seems there is some misunderstanding that caused his arrest, but he will be out in a couple of days." Ejaz's mother's face lit up, and she thanked everyone profusely for their help. My father said firmly that my mother and I were to stay with Ejaz and his mother while he went to work on the case. Benjamin wanted to stay with us, so his father let him stay, and we spent the evening comforting Ejaz. He was still very sad, but we encouraged him, and slowly he understood that we were all with him. We had dinner at Ejaz's, but few words were exchanged.

My mother took care of Ejaz's mom and they chatted the whole night. While Ejaz and Benjamin were fast asleep, I stayed up and listened to their conversation. I heard Ejaz's mother speak about Purdhil, his uncle, and about the watch and his involvement with terrorism. I could tell that my mom was shocked. As I listened, I was amazed about the facts and all the hidden stories of people's lives. My mom was nice to Ejaz's mother and said to her, "Christ will save us from all injustice." Ejaz's mother replied, "I completely believe it." Around four in the morning they both went to bed, and I was tired and went to sleep at the same time. My dad, however, spent the entire night at the bank pulling all the papers, log entries, phone call records, Internet logs, and everything he could find on everyone who worked under him at the bank. He started reviewing all of these documents and comparing them with the Homeland Security papers line by line.

The following day we went home for a quick shower and some food, but when we entered our house, we were hit with the smell of cigar smoke. My mom and I looked at each other, not sure where it was coming from. We went to my father's room and knocked on the door. "Come in," he called. We opened the door, and the cigar smell was so strong, it choked both of us. My dad looked at us and slowly opened the window, and the smell started to fade. My father was smoking a cigar, which I had never seen him do before. He had his reading glasses on, piles of papers in front of him, and a cigar in his hand. When I looked into his eyes, he looked like Sherlock Holmes. My mom was just staring at him. "Where is my love?" she asked him tenderly, and father replied, "It is always with you." Then my mom asked, "What happened to the promises before we got married?" My father replied, "I am already tired, so why do you throw riddles at me now?" My mom answered, "You said you would never smoke in your life. You promised." My father put down his cigar and said to mom, "I am sorry. Please forgive me. I was thinking about Mukhlis and got nervous. I need something to calm me. I've only got two days left to find out the truth and save him."

My mom sat down next to my dad and held his hand. "Sorry, honey. I know everything about it. Farah told me. I didn't know how deeply you felt." My father asked my mom, "How do you know that I know the same thing as you?" She replied, "I could see it in your eyes. I can see everything, James and you are lost now." My dad said, "We have to save him, Olivia." My mom said, "You could smoke for a couple of days—I permit you. Let the promises wait for two days." My dad smiled. "You permit me. So you permit me to sin now. Is there a vacation break to commit sins in your religion?" My mom laughed and my dad kissed her, and I left the room because I knew they wanted to be alone.

That same day I took breakfast to my father's room and he was smoking. Usually he hugs me when he sees me, but this time he only nodded his head when I set down his breakfast. I moved closer to him and he touched my shoulder and said, "Could I ask a question of you, Oliver? Will you do the same thing that I am doing when your friend's life is in danger?" I looked into his eyes and said, "I have nine of them, dad, and being your son, I am proud of you and would lose my life for the sake of saving my friends." My dad said, "I know you would, Oliver. Always remember, you should be prudent and loyal to your friends. The truth will save you, your soul and body." He returned to his work.

I didn't want go to school that day. I wanted to be with my father and help him. I'd only had a few hours of sleep the night before, and I was tired. I decided to stay home and went back to sleep until the afternoon. I took lunch to my dad, and when I walked close to him and whispered "Dad," he saw me with complete inner blindness and didn't say anything for two minutes. For the first time in his life he was thinking, *who is this?* As he was completely involved in the investigation. He shook his head and said, "Hey, Oliver" and removed his glasses. He touched my face and rubbed my head softly. Then he asked me, "What are you doing here? Didn't you go to school?" I told him I had stayed home to help him. He smiled with uncertainty and said, "Thanks, my son, but I have no idea when I'm checking all the logs. All the evidence points to Mukhlis, and I don't have any clue how to find the truth." I said, "You will do it, dad. I know for sure," and my dad replied, "Thanks, Oliver, for the vote of confidence." Then I said, "You should rest. Maybe that will refresh your mind." I asked my dad to take a walk with me and he agreed, thinking it might clear his mind.

We walked for about an hour, and although my dad was walking and talking with me, I could tell his mind was completely tied up with the investigation. We mostly talked about the investigation and his plans. He could see only Mukhlis's imprints on all the phone access, account access, and e-mails that were sent from his inbox, and all the Internet logs were from his PC. Though I could only understand a few things, he explained everything in detail, assuming that I was an experienced investigator. I responded with things like, "Yes, dad," "Sure," "Okay," "Hmm," and looked into his eyes to make him feel that I was involved in the conversation. I hoped this would also encourage him to talk about all he knew so I could find the missing pieces of the equation.

After our walk, we went home and he said, "Bye, Oliver. Please bring my dinner tonight. Thanks, Oliver. I have more energy now. Let me see how it goes from here." There were thirty-six hours left before Mukhlis was moved to Washington, D.C., so he went to his room and closed the door to continue his work. I went to Ejaz's home to check how he and his mom were doing. When I got to his house, he was lying down on his mom's lap, they were both depressed. As soon as he saw me at the front door, he was happy and ran to me. "Oliver thanks for coming back!" My mother had prepared some shrimp pasta and chicken potpie for them, which I brought over. Ejaz's mom's eyes filled with tears. She hugged me and said, "You will always be my son, Oliver," and I replied, "I will always be your son." We had lunch together that day, and really enjoyed it. Ejaz always liked chicken potpie and was happy that I had brought him that.

We chatted all evening, and he asked, "Where are the others, Oliver?" I explained that they were in school, and he asked why they hadn't come to see him. "I think they don't like me anymore, since now I am the son of an accused thief and terrorist. Only you are still with me. I have no one else, Oliver." I was really mad to hear that and could see he was desperate. I said, "How do you know they think you are a terrorist and such things? Who said that to you?" He replied, "I was listening to the whole conversation between your mom and my mom. I didn't sleep, Oliver, and I know it." I thought I was the only one listening to their conversation, but it seemed he was also awake. I said to him, "Ejaz, your dad is a very good man and you should be proud of him. The rest of our friends don't know about this because my dad wanted it to stay on the down-low."

"Really, Oliver?" he asked, seeming relieved.

"Even if your father is convicted for a crime he has not committed, we will never leave you, Ejaz. You are our best friend." This made him feel more confident, and he thanked me. I said, "I told you a few times that we are here to change this world's thinking and to save it from all traditional practices and their clutches." He replied, "Yes, I do remember, Oliver. We will do it."

Later that day we saw the rest of our team walking together to Ejaz's home. We saw them all coming, so Ejaz and I ran to open the door. The sight of them when we opened the door, I will never forget. Except Benjamin and Judah, all of them were staring at both of us. Their faces were pale and I could see lots of anger in them. They were standing on the porch, and no one wanted to come inside the house. Madison and Shu were looking very agitated. Ejaz and I looked at each other with some surprise at the unusual scene and unexpected reaction from our best friends. We told them to come inside. They were quiet and just stood there looking at us like we were aliens, or demons, or some strange animal with no legs.

For a long while we all just stared at each other without speaking, and then finally Ejaz said, "Do you want to come in or not?" Niki said, "Oh, you want us to leave, huh?" Ejaz replied, "I didn't mean it. It looks like you guys are moody." Madison yelled back, "You both changed in two days! We were all together and never lied to each other, but it looks like you have ignored us." Ejaz replied, "We never lied or hid anything from you. Why are you picking on us, Madison? Are you looking for a fight?"

Then Benjamin jumped into the conversation. "Guys, guys, please, please, please, we are all friends. Why should we have this argument?" Ejaz smiled at Niki and Madison, and they slowly smiled at Ejaz with compassion. Finally, they both shouted "Ejaz, my friend!" and hugged him. Madison kissed him on the head. The rest followed, and everyone hugged and kissed him. They were all in tears. Sadie asked Ejaz, "Why didn't you tell us, Ejaz? We would all have been here." Ejaz's face looked angelic, and he was really happy. He turned to me and said, "Guys, you should thank Oliver. He was taking care of me." Madison looked at me intensely and came towards me. "And you could have told me, Oliver!" I explained what my dad had told me to do, and then everyone understood what had happened. Benjamin and I explained the whole story and everything that was connected and how Ejaz's father was being blamed as both a bank robber and a terrorist. They were all surprised, and I said my dad was working on finding evidence that would clear him before they took Ejaz's dad to Washington, D.C.

Later that night, my friends wanted to see my dad to thank him. I also wanted to go home to bring him dinner. I took all of my friends except Ejaz, because he and his mom needed to stay home, as Homeland Security was keeping them under curfew. Once our friends' families heard the news, everyone came to meet Ejaz and his mom. After comforting them they all came to my home, and on the way Fay said that we should buy my dad some nice snacks since he was working so hard. I said that was not required, but everyone wanted to. We went to the convenience store nearby and bought water, energy drinks and bars, chips, cookies, some almond cakes, some fruit, and ice cream.

We went home where mom was waiting for me, and as soon as she saw me and my friends, she was happy and greeted everyone. She saw all our bags and asked what was in them. We replied, "It is for dad." She smiled and said, "Thank you. You guys are the best!" They all wanted to see my father, so I first went to his room with dinner and all my friends waited in the hall. The room was still heavy with cigar smoke, and my dad was so busy with his investigation, he didn't even notice me come in. I placed the dinner on the table and slowly walked over and looked at him. He shook his head and said, "Hey, Oliver. Whazz up, my boy?"

"I brought your dinner," I replied, and he thanked me. I added, "All my friends are waiting to see you and say hi." My dad seemed surprised and replied, "Really? Why?" I explained that they wanted to thank him for his effort, and my dad came with me to see my buddies, who were all sitting in the hall waiting. As soon as they saw my father, they stood and greeted him. "Hello, Uncle!" My dad replied, "Hi guys. Thanks for coming down." Sadie said, "We are very proud of you, Uncle, putting all your energy and efforts into saving your friend." Everyone started showing their appreciation, thanking my father and hugged him. At that moment I was so proud of my father and so proud to be his son. My dad was really touched by all of my friends, and he was moved by all the little deeds and actions that we showed him. He told us we were rock stars and he was honored that his son had such gifted friends. My father added, "I am a little tired, guys, and want to take a walk. Could you all join me?" He decided to take us to the Australian restaurant Hobart for dinner, which was a nice casual neighborhood restaurant with great steaks, seafood, and very good ice cream.

On the way to the restaurant I asked my dad if we were taking him away from his work. My dad replied, "My mind is very much frozen right now, Oliver, and I need some rest. I hope when I am with you guys, I will get refreshed and think clearer." We were not really in the mood to eat because we were all so anxious about our friend Ejaz, but we all wanted to make sure my dad had a nice time out so that he could work more efficiently. We all shared a seafood appetizer and a few good fish entrées and steaks, and while we were eating, my dad shared his experience regarding the investigation. We were all very quiet and asked a few questions here and there. He answered our questions and made us understand how banks and audits worked and all the different pieces involved in this case. We all began to understand an overall idea of how banking worked. After the meal we shared ice cream, but Ejaz was never far from our minds, because he was the missing member of our group. Benjamin offered, "Shouldn't we get some food for Ejaz and his mother?" My dad thought that was a great idea and bought a bounty of food to take to their house.

When we left the restaurant, we had a lot of food and were all carrying boxes like delivery workers. My dad took Benjamin and Niki in his car and all the food, and drove us to Ejaz's home. That night, Madison, Shu, and Judah stayed over at my home, and the rest of our friends went to Ejaz's home and stayed with him. My dad was on a regular schedule, so he went back to his workroom and continued his investigation.

The next day the news was leaked and Ejaz's father was all over the newspapers. The headlines read, "Greatest Bank Robbery in Recent History" and some newspaper claimed, "Terrorist Working in a Milwaukee Bank." It was all over the news and even in the top daily papers like the *New York Times*, the *Washington Post*, *LA Times*, and many others. We were all shocked that the rumor was the talk of the country, and we all felt very bad about it. No one went to school, as we also knew it was the last day for Ejaz's father to stay close to home before being moved to Washington, D.C., for further investigation. We knew that was going to be a mess and it would take forever to prove him innocent.

My father's last day to prove him innocent was upon us, and early that morning Benjamin's father came home and met my father and asked if there had been any break in the case. My father said, "There is nothing I could find, and all the traces lead to Mukhlis." But Benjamin's father replied, "James, you have more time. Twenty-four hours is a lot of time. I know you can do something. Relax, man—stay focused and don't get despondent. I will be back this evening to see how it's going." That morning I went to Ejaz's house again, and as soon as I walked in, I saw the news on TV and his name printed in the newspapers. I spent that morning with him, and all ten of us were there by the afternoon. Ejaz was depressed when he saw his father's name and photo on the news channel as a robber and terrorist, along with all the false accusations. His mother was out of control, crying in her bedroom from morning till night, and all the women from our families took turns comforting her.

Around noon we were all feeling pretty low, and something in me told me to go home and serve lunch to my father. The voice inside me was faint yet strong. At first I neglected it, but it was hovering in my inner thoughts. I decided to go home, but it was hard because Ejaz was crying and saying, "Don't leave me, Oliver." I replied, "I will be back in an hour." He repeated, "Please don't go, Oliver!" He was asking and begging me, and I turned and said sternly, "Ejaz, I will come back with good news if you let me go. Stop crying! Everything is fine now, okay?"

Everyone looked at me with a strange face and didn't understand why I had told him that. I looked at everyone and said, "Take care of Ejaz. I will come back with good news." Madison walked me to the door and said, "I know you will, Oliver." She held my hand and said, "We will be waiting for you, Oliver. Go now."

I left Ejaz's house and went home. My mom was in the kitchen preparing lunch. She said, "Hey, Oliver, you're back?" I replied, "Mom, I heard a voice in my conscious saying that I had to come home and get lunch for dad." My mom looked at me and said, "Was the voice faint and strong?" I told her it was, and my mom said, "That is the word of God and the Holy Spirit who spoke to you." I replied softly, "I don't know, mom. I am here because something drives me."

I took the lunch and walked to my father's room which was very messy. The usual smoke was hanging in the room, papers were scattered on the floor, and bottles were strewn throughout. The room was also colder because he'd closed the door and the window, and the air conditioner was running non-stop. I tried moving all the cans and bottles, picking up the papers, and organizing a little bit, but because he was so busy, he didn't notice me. After ten minutes he slowly noticed that I was in the room cleaning and called to me, "Oliver, I thought you were in school." I replied, "I am home now; I came from Ejaz's house and just brought you some lunch." My father replied, "I didn't know you were here. I thought you were at school on the weekdays." I replied, "No problem. I took a couple of days off to help you, dad. No one can be in two places, at school and at home. I wish I had that gift like the old mythical legends, so I could stay home all the time."

My dad's eyes started to sparkle and he asked me, "What did you say?" I thought I had made some mistake in answering and replied, "Sorry, dad. I was kidding." He became curious and asked me again, "What did you say?" I was a little uncomfortable and said, "Dad, sorry, I was joking." Then in a higher voice he asked me again, "Oliver, could you tell me what you said about home and school?" I became anxious at this moment; I trembled as I answered him. "I said I wish I could be in two places at the same time, in school and at home." I swallowed the rest of my words because I thought he was really upset.

Then my father said, "How could I be in two places?" He started to say it to himself many times, shaking his head, and his voice grew louder as he said the same sentence: "How could I be in two places?" He stood up from his chair and started to walk, saying the same sentence, and I became scared. I went to the corner of the room, leaning toward the wall to get some support, because I was worried at this moment by the way he was acting. He paced up and down in the room and completely forgot I was there.

Then he screamed, "Yes, I've got it, I've got it!" He became elated, and he rushed back to his seat. He took a file and started looking at it, and I now understood the situation—that his reaction was because he was thinking so deeply. I sat in a chair near the small dining table in his office. I was looking at him, and he was turning and referring to all the papers on his table and searching for something on the computer. I watched him for almost an hour. Then he screamed loudly, declaring, "I found it! Yes! I did it!" Hearing such a loud scream, my mom rushed into my father's room and looked at him. For the first time in days he looked happy and excited. He rushed over to me and carried me and kissed me and started to dance with me. Then he kissed my mother and lifted her so high, I thought she was going to hit her head on the ceiling. My mom was touching the ceiling and she was scared that he would drop her. "What is it, James? Don't drop me!" My dad let her down and then rushed and opened the fridge in his room. He grabbed a beer, opened it, and drank half of it, pouring the rest on himself. He took another beer can and threw it to my mother, and then took a can, opened it, and asked me to drink with him. My mother had no idea what he was up to, but after they had a few sips, I finally asked my dad, "What is this, dad? Did you find the culprit?" My dad replied, "I almost did," and my mom asked him, "What do you mean by 'almost?'"

Then my dad started to explain what he had found, but before that, he thanked me, saying, "Oliver, my boy, you enlightened me! Without you I wouldn't ever have found this." I replied "Dad, did I help you? How?" He smiled at me and said, "You said to me, 'I wish I could be in two places at the same time, in school and at home' and it clicked in my mind to check all the logs of Mukhlis's holiday and vacation schedule and compare them with the logs of Homeland Security on the days the money transactions and phone calls occurred. It seems that last winter Mukhlis was on vacation for a week and went to California to meet one of his old friends. One day during his vacation $300,000 was transferred using his account ID and a phone call was made to Afghanistan. I checked the remote network access account to the bank, and I saw that he didn't log in remotely. Someone else inside the bank made this transaction." We were stunned at his explanation and I said, "Dad that is fantastic. What are you going to do now?" My mom added, "Please call Kadin and tell him. Do you have a clue who would have done this inside the bank?" father replied, "I don't know, Olivia; it could be anyone in the bank. Let me call Kadin first."

My dad called Benjamin's father and explained what he had found, and he replied that he would be over in fifteen minutes. When he got to our house, dad showed him all his findings. He was very impressed by my dad's work and said, "Well done, James. I am very proud of you. The

Marines should be happy to have you there, and this country owes you a lot." Benjamin's father said, "We should hurry and go to the Homeland Security office and inform them about the findings so they can offer some directions on how we should proceed." My father and Benjamin's father hurried to the Homeland Security office. They met with the head officer and explained their findings. At this point the officer was convinced there was more to the story, and they wanted to help my father prove his case. They called the CIA staff who were directly involved in the investigation, and they came to the Homeland Security office.

Now there was a team made up of my dad, representing the bank; Benjamin's father, representing the police force; and a small team from the CIA. They explained what they had found from the paper trail and how it showed that Ejaz's father was not in the office when a call and money transaction went through. It was determined that there was a culprit in the office who had made these transactions. The CIA started performing technology forensics on the phone lines, electronic data, logs from databases, server logs, voice pattern recognition, and so on. At this time, Homeland Security contacted officials in Washington, D.C., explaining that they had found some leads to the actual person who committed these crimes and needed more time before they sent Mukhlis there. Their proposal was accepted, and the best part was that Mukhlis was not moved to Washington, D.C.

Once the CIA became directly involved, they started to turn over all the records in the bank's transactions and details about all the employees who worked for the bank, even those who had since quit. They were looking for all possible attacks on Ejaz's father's computer and phones, but initially they couldn't find anything. Then they tried to locate information for the days Ejaz's father was on vacation, and they found some random IP address that was used on his computer and phone lines. They started to check the IP allotment for the users and found that it was linked to an employee called Jay Mons. They started to investigate this man more and found out Jay Mons was a security and network manager at the bank and maintained the IT systems for them. He had resigned six months earlier, saying that he was moving to New Jersey with his father's family. There had been no reason to suspect him till now, but everyone in the bank and in his neighborhood gave a testimony about him, and almost everyone said, "He was greedy." This gave some sign of his personality, but on further investigation the CIA found that his father-in-law had some problems in his business and needed money to recover his losses. Since he was so committed, Jay Mons decided to help him, and he needed almost $3 million to recover. So, the CIA started to focus on him and trace his phone call history, and they found a lot of incoming and outgoing calls made from his home phone to Afghanistan and other

Middle Eastern countries. At this point everyone concluded that he was the correct suspect, and it was confirmed when it was discovered that he hadn't moved to New Jersey. He and his family had left the country and gone to Kenya. He was now living in Kenya with his father and family, while his father-in-law still lived in New Jersey.

Now there was enough evidence to prove his crime, but they needed more reasons and records to prove that all the transactions occurred through him. With more intelligence forensics experts on the scene, they traced Ejaz's father's computer logs and found that Jay Mons had hacked his computer and was using it and the phone lines as a zombie and making illegal transactions. The CIA still needed to understand how the Al-Sayyid Ifrit terrorist organization was connected to Jay Mons. This was the toughest part of the puzzle yet to be solved. However, they had recently arrested one of the key financiers, Jinnah, in Iraq, and when they interviewed him; he supplied information about the connection.

As it turned out, Purdhil Jin, Mukhils's brother, called once a month to check on his brother and see how his family was doing. But no one in Al-Sayyid Ifrit knew that Purdhil Jin's brother was working in a bank, since Purdhil never talked about his family and he didn't involve his brother in his business. But somehow Al-Sayyid Ifrit traced Purdhil's phone calls and found that he called his brother every month. They tapped and listened and understood that his brother was working in a bank, where he was a respectable key person. They decided to rob the bank and wanted a vulnerable person in the bank, so they found Jay Mons, and the bad guys started to run a check on him. They found out he was greedy and needed money desperately, which was sufficient for them to make a move. They also found that his father-in-law had many problems in business, and they used both weaknesses to make a deal with them.

Jay Mons had negotiated for a high price, around 25 percent of the deal. So he took his cut for almost $35 million and vanished in the wind to Kenya. Al-Sayyid Ifrit contacted Jay Mons. At first he acted like a patriot. Then they convinced him by making sure they gave him a big cut of almost 25 percent, but the basic idea was that stolen money could be negotiated at any price. Jay was too dumb to understand that he was the one who ran the risk. They knew the scapegoat from the beginning, and they knew that to persuade anyone to commit a robbery, you always pick the right scapegoat and then talk about the cut. This whole event had happened close to three years before, and they slowly started moving the money, like hundreds of thousands of dollars, every four to five days, eventually stealing almost $50 million. The final amount was $100 million, for which Jay Mons planted a logic bomb virus in their network to continue doing the job after he left the company. This surplus amount of $100 million was the total loss. The logic bomb was a bomb with no real brains. It transferred $300,000 when Mukhils was on vacation. The very strange part of the whole operation was that they used Purdhil, Mukhils's brother, to hack into the bank's network. Purdhil didn't know that he was helping Jay Mons, who was working with his brother, but the head of Al-Sayyid Ifrit tricked Purdhil and told him that they were hacking into the Federal Bank of the United States to bring down the country.

Al-Sayyid Ifrit also planned to kill Purdhil after this operation, because once he was caught, Purdhil could turn against them. But Purdhil was a very smart man, and he escaped once he heard his brother was arrested and realized that the organization needed money, not him, because there were millions of men like Purdhil out there. Purdhil accepted his crime in helping the terrorist organization against America and surrendered to the American government. Jay Mons used the situation and weaknesses around him for this operation and made Ejaz's father the scapegoat. The American government contacted the Kenyan government and informed them about Jay Mons's crime, and the Kenyan police arrested him and brought him to Washington, D.C., for trial. They also seized his father-in-law's business, and Jay Mons's family was brought back to America.

Our great hero, Ejaz's father, was released. On the day of his release we all went to greet him. When he came out of the Homeland Security office, he shouted loudly, "I am innocent, I am innocent!" Everyone could understand his intense emotions after all that he had been through and justice was finally on his side. Ejaz was so happy; he ran and hugged his father. Ejaz's father then walked to my father and shook his hand. They hugged each other, and Ejaz's father said, "You believed me. Thanks, James." My father replied, "I always did."

That day there was a big feast at Ejaz's home. This time we were not enjoying food among just our ten families; we also distributed chocolates and cakes to everyone in our neighborhood, and the response was amazing. Everyone from our neighborhood came to Ejaz's home. They appreciated his patriotism to America and felt terrible about the unjust treatment that had happened to him. Ejaz's father was moved by everyone's support. All the elders in our families wanted to buy him a gift, so they brought him a gold chain with an American eagle as a locket. He was so glad to receive it. Both Benjamin's father and my father honored him by placing the chain around his neck. The greatest cop in American history and the best veteran honored Ejaz's father, and he felt very happy in this moment.

That day we listened to music and danced, and all the families danced the night away. Many members of the police force also joined the party, but the best guests that day were the Homeland Security head and his friends, who also joined us for the feast. It was one of the most splendid days I've ever experienced, and for the first time after Natalie's death, many people in our neighborhood joined us for a joyful feast. On that day Madison and I joined in and danced the tango together, and I felt how much love I had for her. My dad noticed the way Madison and I spoke and danced together, and later in the party he took Madison aside to talk more privately. My dad asked Madison, "Do you love Oliver?" She replied, "I love Oscar," and my dad said, "I said Oliver, not Oscar." She in turn replied, "Yes. I call him Oscar." My dad smiled and said to Madison, "No matter what you call him in your life, never forsake Oliver. Stay with him always. He needs you. Could you promise me that?" Without even thinking, Madison said, "I promise I will, Uncle." My father smiled and thanked her. I don't know why my father did that, but it was the same thing Madison's mother said to me. I couldn't understand it then, but later it would become clear to me.

The party was joyful, and our sorrows seemed to disappear. Everyone was finally able to return to a normal life. We all went home early in the morning after the party. I couldn't sleep because of all that had happened, and my search started to kick in. I wondered what had happened here, with all the strange events and experiences in my life. Where could one start the whole search for bliss, and how could I interpret these events to improve my knowledge? I started with my dad's promotion: My dad was very sincere and a hardworking, smart person. The man behind my father's success was Ejaz's father. He was my father's confidant and trusted him very much, with good cause, as he deserved to be trusted. To be successful in work you needed to be a confident person and to have a good confidant. Ejaz's father was a friend and colleague. My father knew it was tricky to mix his personal and professional life, but in spite of this, he became close friends with his work colleague, Ejaz's father. You will always have a weak spot in life, and that's how people get into trouble. Still, people have friends from work in their personal life. Everything will appear fine when there is no problem, but when things start to go wrong, the consequences remind people why there is such a thing as work etiquette. My father is a genius and knew how to handle difficult situations, so if you are like my father, then do it. Imagine if Ejaz's father had been the real bad guy. It would have been easier for him to include my father's name with this problem; then both would have been seeing the world from behind bars.

I then started to think about Ejaz's father and how he got into that terrible situation. I thought about Mukhlis's brother, who knew the difference between right and wrong but still chose the wrong path. Mukhlis's brother, Purdhil, knew the difference between hard-earned money and blood money, so I am sure he had a good soul and thoughts, and one day he will walk in the path of the righteousness. One day he will promote peace, because the seed of difference between good and bad is sown in him already. That is the reason he escaped from their camp when they tried to kill him, rather than taking vengeance and going against them. If Purdhil changes his ways, he could be a very reasonable superhero now. But Mukhlis, I've decided, is the greatest American patriot next to George Washington. Though he was an immigrant, he respected American values. More than that, he had great love for humanity. That's why he gave a precious gift from his brother to the person he valued the most, who would be a better person to get it, my father, James Oscar. The value of the diamond watch is not its cost, but in the value behind the gift: the thoughts, friendship, brotherhood, respect, gratitude, and so on. A gift of such value was passed from Purdhil to Ejaz's father and from Ejaz's father to my father.

Now I started thinking deeply about the robbery itself, how Homeland Security didn't have a second chance to think about events and decided to arrest someone before conducting a thorough investigation. All they heard was the word *terrorist* and they reacted like handpicked monkeys. One keyword, *terrorism* will make good people bad and bad people good. Yes, someone may be a reputedly bad person, but if he says "war on terrorism," the very next day he turns into a good person. The word *terrorism* didn't exist in most people's vocabulary until recently, but it was there for a very long time. My mom always says Simon, one of the disciples of Jesus, was a "terrorist." There were Jewish "terrorists" who existed in my century called "Zionists." There is transformation in which the world changes these terms; first they are called "rebels," then "terrorists," then "freedom fighters," and every country and war monger benefits in this name-changing game. But any crime, war or injustice that is committed in the name of Judaism and Christianity, the name transformation hastens, which means the religion that is in power gets this transformation and the weaker ones have to watch and die. Ejaz's father was the easiest scapegoat, because he was Islamic, and the world, especially Americans, can be biased and discriminate based on false ideas. Good and evil exists everywhere, but we should not be judgmental by statements. We Americans had ears to listen to the IRA, so why not Islamic terrorism? All things boil down to religion and untold cults. I also wondered what compensation the government would give to the falsely accused Mukhlis.

I thought about how much of this was caused by Mukhlis not telling my father, his dear friend, the whole truth about his family. The key fact I learned is that even the best friend in your life will always have secrets you don't know. The secrets between my dad and Ejaz's father were like those of the mob, gangsters, and drug dealers, who never talk about their families, friends, wives, or children, because it will hurt them later. Ejaz's father was unintentionally acting like a mobster who didn't want to share information about his notorious brother, but he made one mistake, which was talking to him once a month. That decision was used in the case against him. It wasn't Ejaz's father's fault, because Purdhil was the one calling him. I also realized that Ejaz didn't lie to me about not having an uncle, because only Ejaz's father hid the facts from my father. It seemed like when you had such a bad rat in your family, you had to either talk to everyone about it or no one.

Then I thought about the master of crime, Jay Mons, our phony hero. He thought he was smart, but in the end he was caught and put in jail for a long time. He was a greedy man who was only out for money. He even married his wife because his father-in-law was a wealthy person. But to shatter his greediness, his father-in-law went broke and lost his business. In his predicament he needed $3 million to settle all his debts. Ideally, Jay Mons should have negotiated only $3 to $6 million with Al-Sayyid Ifrit, but instead he negotiated 25 percent with them—such a smart businessman. That was the end of that greedy and unpatriotic person. His greed drove him to steal money from his own country and give it to our enemies to kill us. The best part of his idiocy in this robbery is that he thought he picked the right scapegoat in Ejaz's father but never realized the real scapegoat chosen by Al-Sayyid Ifrit was both Ejaz's father and Jay Mons, as they are the ones who were controlling and playing the game. The biggest blunder he made was the logic bomb one single call and single transaction when Ejaz's father was out of the office. With this one mistake he dug his own grave. Jay Mons's whole family was also greedy, and they were corrupt. They didn't even question where he got his money or why they moved to Kenya. As a result, his wife and father-in-law were sentenced to ten years. He had a boy and a girl who were seven and five, and sadly, they were sent to foster homes.

My search for understanding goes on and on, and I have many things to think about regarding these incidents. Eventually I got a headache, so I calmed my thoughts, because we were back to normal and were in peace, and all our friends and families were united and able to share the love and affection we have for each other. It felt like the world was on our side. The wind, the light, the rain, and all the energy was working for us and it felt like the world was mine. Days passed by and everything was normal, and I had a great time with friends and family.

Then, out of nowhere, something happened. It was the end of fall, and one evening my dad and I were playing chess and mom was watching TV. I had beaten my dad twice that day, but during the third game, I was about to lose, and he was in a good position and had most of the pieces on the board. Suddenly we heard someone ringing the bell. My mom saw there was a telegram addressed to my father. My mother called father to open it. After reading the message, he was bothered and worried, and he went and sat on the couch, scratching his head. My mom asked dad what was going on, and dad replied, "Yes, everything is okay, but I am sorry." Mom asked, "Sorry for what?" and dad replied, "I have to leave." My mom moved closer to him and kneeled before him and asked, "Leave for where, honey?" Dad replied, "I have to go and serve in the war in Iraq." Mom became upset and started to cry, "No, no, no, you are not going!" My father replied quietly, "I'm sorry. I have no choice. I have to go."

Mom asked my dad if he could get out of serving, but he replied, "No, we cannot, because the order comes directly from the Secretary of Defense. I have to do it." My mom asked how long he would be gone and my dad said it was a two-year tour. I asked him when he had to leave, and he told us in two days. Then my mom said, "Two days? That is insane," but my dad said, "It is critical and they are impatient." That whole night my whole home was in silence. We didn't even eat dinner. Each one of us was looking at the ceiling, to find some answers, comfort, and support. It was the first time I saw my dad truly depressed, because he didn't want to leave us.

The night passed and it was the next day, and I didn't want to go to school because my dad was leaving us in two days. I wanted to help him. That morning I called Judah and explained about my dad. He felt very bad and said they would all come and visit that evening after school. My dad seemed happier the next day. He called mom and me over and said, "Cheer up, guys. I will be back in two years, maybe less, and I am always here with you." My mom said, "Less than two years?" and he replied, "Yes, if everything is in control and I can ask my chief to relieve me from duty." Now we got our hopes up and assumed that he would be coming back very soon. My dad said that there would be a get-together the next day before he left, with all his friends and their families. He called all his friends and informed them about his duty to the Marines, and arranged to have Chef Helder, one of the best chefs in the region, cater his going-away party.

He started to pack his stuff and I helped him. I could see my father was not happy at all, but he pretended to be busy and focused on his duties. He took all that is required for personal needs, which he could use when he was there. He took lots of music—CDs, cassettes, an MP3 player—some books, good shirts, skin cream, cologne, reading glasses, underwear, movies, and so on. While I was helping my dad, my mom walked over to us and said to my father, "I need you to take only one thing that I am giving you. Please don't say no." Dad replied, "I will never say no. I will take it." My mom gave him her favorite Bible, and my dad, without say anything, took it and kissed her and said, "Thanks very much. I will keep it with me." Mom and I were surprised he didn't debate anything. He put the Bible in his bag and then looked at me and said, "Oliver, what do you have for me?" I said to him, "Give me some time, dad, before you leave. I will give you something you really like." My dad said, "You need time to think about the best gift you could give? Mom didn't even think anything and gave me a Bible. It seems her mind is programmed that the Bible will always be the best gift for my life." Mom said, "No, James, you need it. It will save you." My father replied, "Maybe, but if I am in a war field, I am pretty sure that two types of bullets will save me. One is my bullet, and the other is a missed bullet shot by my enemy." Mom and I were quiet after he said this; we had no answers. Mom said only two sentences: "Christ is with you. You will be fine."

I was helping dad the whole day, and in the evening all my friends came to see us. My father was excited to see my friends, and they started asking the regular questions: "When are you leaving?" "What will you do in Iraq?" "When will you come back?" and so on. He patiently answered everything. It was eight o'clock in the evening and he was leaving the next day, so I asked my friends if we could go out to eat at a restaurant. My dad booked a reservation at a Montenegro restaurant called Zabljak, which served some of the finest southeastern European cuisine. We all went to the restaurant. The whole evening was an awesome experience. It was the first time my dad talked about his life experiences with my friends. He explained why he joined the marines and what he had accomplished for his country. He was motivated by George Washington, the only reason he joined the Marines. My father highlighted one single philosophical phrase about George Washington: "pride and courage." He used the same words when he proved himself and the same words when he denied himself. My father meant the incident when Washington marched against the British and when he stepped out of his presidency. All my friends, plus my mom and I, were astonished about the way he was talking about facts and facts only. That night we all listened to my father's greatest sermon, words of wisdom, courage, bravery, and how to focus in life. He was in high spirits, and the clock adjusted so well that all he had to say to us was completed without a single word left for us to share. We were in the restaurant until one thirty in the morning. Then we left and went home, this time not only with food, but a great deal of new knowledge.

The next day was my father's last day with us before he left for the war. He had packed his bags himself and was arranging his send-off party. He picked a unique hall from one of his Latvian friends. The hall was called Miers, which means "peace." It was strange that my father picked this restaurant, because there he was, going to war in Iraq, yet he picked this restaurant named "Peace" in Latvian. I didn't ask him about it. The chef was a Portuguese man called Helder, an old high school friend of my dad's. Everyone came for the send-off party, they were not convinced about my father going back to war and being gone for two years. It was so generous that everybody brought lots of gifts with them. My father gave a talk to all his friends and their families about the pride of America and why he was going to Iraq. He spoke about how patriotism works and is the contribution of every citizen in this country. For me, personally, it sounded like the president's speech, and everyone admired it.

After the speech, all the elders grabbed drinks and we had some fresh juices. Then the dancing started. We all danced and tried to be in good mood, but in everyone's minds we had one thought: James is leaving us for a while. Still, dad maintained his humor by cracking jokes, distracting their minds with random talk, and didn't allow anyone to be carried away by emotional thoughts. We all had a fine dinner that night, the food was delicious, and everyone ate to their heart's content. I saw dad talking to Madison, but I didn't know what was going on. Again, he was asking Madison to take care of me and be with me all the time, and he got a promise from her. I don't know why dad did it the second time, but one thing was for sure: Madison loved my father and respected him very deeply. My father treats and looks at her like his daughter, and they somehow have a deep bond between them. My father was one of the reasons Madison loves me and thinks I am special to her.

The party ended and everyone thanked my dad and us. Judah's father wanted to contribute to the party and pulled out his wallet. My dad stopped him from doing it, but Judah's father was a real smooth talker and convinced my father that he would pay the whole party's bill. My dad thanked him for his generosity, and Judah's father paid the bill because of Judah; Judah was the one who influenced his father to pay.

That night was the last night with my dad, and after dinner we were lying on the couch and talking about the party. I opened my mouth and asked, "Why do you always tell Madison to take care of me and be with me?" My dad looked at me. "Did she say that to you?" I replied, "Yes. She will never hide anything." My dad smiled. "She is a very special girl, and she is blessed. She is the right fit for you. Never disappoint her at any point in your life, will you promise me, Oliver?" I nodded my head.

Then we went to bed, and in the morning he had to leave. He got all his belongings ready. He was dressed in his Marine uniform and looked great and bright, with all his medals hanging on his coat. The flight was at ten o'clock, and we went with him to the airport. Surprisingly, all my friends and their families also joined us at the airport. My mom and dad and I were happy to see everyone, and he thanked everyone individually for coming down. We took a group photo with my dad in his uniform, and we each took a photo with him. He said goodbye to everyone, hugged my mother tightly, and said, "Take care. I will be fine." He walked over to me and smiled, and pulled my cheeks. "Be strong, Oliver, and you will find the answer one day." I looked at my father and asked, "What answer, dad?" He replied, "The one you have been searching for in your mind." I was totally shocked that he knew about that, and I asked, "How do you know about it, dad?" He replied, "I did the same and gave up. I know you are carrying on from where I left off. You will find it, but stay focused on your career, and your answers will follow in your life as you grow." I was heartbroken and my eyes started to fill with tears. I said, "I will! Dad" and I kissed and hugged him. Everyone in the airport saw us, and Fay's mother said, "I have never seen someone like Oliver and his father, being so affectionate." Everyone joined and said, "They love each other like father and son." My father said goodbye to everyone, checked into the airport, waved to all of us, and left for duty.

I experienced great loneliness without my father, and he knew all the time that I was searching for an answer to "a better life for everyone." I was ignorant all those days, assuming that he didn't know what I was thinking inside, but it seems he was also searching. For some reason he gave up, yet I don't know why. Days passed by, and I still felt lonely. When I came home, I looked out the window to see if my dad was returning. When I am with my friends, everywhere—at school, the playground, in the garden, at a restaurant, even in the bathroom—I think about my dad. A few months passed, and my home felt silent and empty. Mom had the same feeling. I had to thank my friends, as they understood that I missed my father and they always tried to improve my mood. My friends and their families always came over, talked to my mom, and took care of her. A life without a father is a life without direction, and I felt that I didn't have any direction. I just lived, just breathed, just ate. I could only "just" do everything.

One day I was home, drinking orange juice and watching TV. I had a feeling inside me that something was not right. I took my orange juice and went near the window and was watching the street. There came a car, and two men in military uniforms got out. I thought my dad was back. I screamed at the top of my voice, "Daddy is back!" Mom was in the bedroom, she heard my voice, and I ran to open the front door. Mom followed me and there were two gentlemen standing there. They asked me, "Is this General James Oscar's home?" I replied, "Yes, it is. He is my dad." After I responded, he didn't look at me. He looked at my mother. There were a couple of women in uniform behind these two gentlemen. Mom looked at him and he said, "Can we come in?" Mom said of course they could, and they came inside.

The man said, "Sorry, ma'am. We are sorry to tell you that we lost James Oscar in the line of duty." They both took an American flag and gave it to my mom. She started crying and I also was in tears. The two ladies came and comforted my mother while the two gentlemen were trying to talk to me and comfort me. My mother asked them what happened, and they said, "He was shot dead in combat. A bomb in the building exploded, and we couldn't find his body." He added, "You should be very proud. He saved three thousand children's lives." The president declared he would give General James Oscar the Medal of Honor. He was brave and saved three thousand innocent souls. They spent the whole day trying to talk about my dad's accomplishments, bravery, and patriotism, and how great a man he was. The whole time they were talking, I was thinking we didn't get my dad's body, because it was blown to pieces. The only thing we got from him was his luggage, which he carried with him. They left in the evening, telling us to be strong. My mom and I were in the greatest agony of our lives.

After they left, mom and I held each other's hands and cried. We didn't sleep that night. No food, no water—it was like our throats were blocked with a knife. We were in great pain, but we didn't call anyone to tell them, because we didn't have the guts or courage to say it. We lay in bed. We had both lost everything; we had both lost the best person in our lives. The night was depressing, and we felt like we didn't want to live anymore, and that moment it felt right, because we had no purpose for living any more. The joy, the happiness, the debates, and my dad's vision about superheroes, my daily confessions, my spiritual renewal with my father, it all was washed away in a minute. We both thought, *who will care for us now? No one.* We didn't fall asleep until six in the morning, and then we slept, not because we had to rest, but because we were tired of crying and had no energy left. I didn't call it sleep; it was partial death for both of us. All of my senses were shut down, and I could not think anymore. Time would heal us, but I knew that right now I had to take care of mom and myself.

Chapter 7
A New Career

HOW COULD I START MY LIFE WITHOUT MY FATHER? WHY DID HE LEAVE us? How did he die? The officers were talking about this on the day they were there. We heard that he saved three thousand children's lives and that no piece of his body was found. I didn't go to school the next day. My dad was all over the news, and slowly the message of his death reached everyone. My mom didn't call anyone, even her family and my dad's family—not anyone. The news started to come out and spread like wildfire, and soon everyone, both those who knew us personally and the people, who didn't know us, were aware that he was dead.

Everyone came to our home as soon as they heard about my dad's death. By morning, everyone was there, including my friends. Everyone around only added more sorrow because of their tearful condolences. My friends and family didn't know what to say, and they had always been my greatest comforters and my light. They felt terrible and they all held my hands tightly. I could still feel there was hope for my life, that my father is not truly dead. He is no more with us in this world, and I had to accept that for the time being, as there was nothing more I could do.

At my worst moment of distress and sorrow, a woman's hug, with my face pressed close to her heart, made me feel better. Madison did that for me. She took my face and kept it close to her heart. It felt good to be comforted by her, and hope started to grow in me. I felt the heartbeat of Madison, and the rhythm of her heartbeat said, "I care for you, I am always with you, and I love you, Oscar." Yes, even in her heartbeat she calls me Oscar. That was the first joke I could think of after my father's death.

At first, the news about my father's death was clear, depending on the source, but after a week we understood exactly what had happened. There was a children's yearly gathering in Iraq near Baiji in a town hall, and almost three thousand children had joined. The hall was a four-storey building with an auditorium inside. There were endless conflicts between the Shiites and Sunnis, and all the kids at the celebration were from the Sunni tribe. The Shiites had planted a bomb in the building the day of the gathering. My dad was in charge of the Baiji conflict zone, as it was a very problematic city. The US Marines got information that there was a bomb in the building and that it would detonate in an hour. They had limited time and informed the Iraqi police of the situation. My dad and his unit of almost twenty soldiers arrived on the scene. My dad called for additional troops as a backup and a bomb squad, but they were almost 100 miles away from Baiji, and it was going to require more time to reach the scene.

My dad and his crew rushed to the town hall where the gathering was taking place. The building was equipped with electronic doors. The terrorists very smartly hacked and locked down the building doors and exits. The local Iraqi cops and my dad's unit arrived on the scene and had only forty-five minutes to rescue all the kids. When they tried to enter the building, all the doors were locked and the phone lines were down, so at the moment, no one inside the building knew there was a bomb inside, and all the guards had been shot dead.

My dad had a few hackers in his unit, and when they started to unlock the main electronic door of the building, one of my dad's men, who were opening the door, was hit by a bullet from a Shiite sniper and died on the spot. Blood splashed on all the walls and on to the electric circuit of the doors. When my dad's troops saw this, they went on alert and checked to see who fired the shot, but they could see no one. Then one more troop was shot in the chest and died instantly. There were snipers around the building, and my dad's team couldn't see any of them. He quickly instructed ten of his troops to split up and keep an eye on each building. My dad and his eight men and Iraqi cops started firing bullets in the air, which gave off so much sound that all the children and their teachers began rushing toward the exits of the building.

There were three windows that were not closed, and they started shooting one foot away from the window. One sniper showed up and started to fire back. They figured out where he was and shot him in the head. In the meantime, my dad engaged a couple of men to work on getting the doors open, and all the kids in the building started to panic. They moved away from the windows and lay on the floor, but they still didn't know there was a bomb in the building. That was the smartest move my dad made, because he knew they would start to panic and react badly. While the men worked to open the door, one more sniper appeared from another window and wanted to shoot the guys who were trying to open the main door. My dad just put a bullet in his head. It was so lucky that the main door's electric circuit was filled with blood, and didn't fuse or jam the circuit.

There was a window left open, and my dad's unit started shooting near the window. Lots of bullets flew, and no one appeared after that. After a few minutes they thought there was no one in that room, and the men opened the front door, and there was a surprise attack. There were two Hummers and a truck with a terrorist ready to open fire at my dad and his troops. At this point they had only thirty minutes left before the building would blow up. The Iraqi cops fled when they saw the group of terrorists, and immediately bullets started flying back and forth. Dad took a stand and all his men fought in this deadly combat. Men faced death from both sides; all the combatants were killed, and my dad was left with only two of his soldiers.

There were fifteen minutes left to get all the people out of the building. My dad had one soldier enter the building with him while he left one behind, guarding the front door. They quickly opened all the doors, and then they went to the second floor where the auditorium was. They saw all the children and hundreds of elders and teachers. They directed all the kids, elders, and teachers to leave as fast as they could. Everybody panicked and the kids' eyes were filled with fear and tears. No one wanted to leave, because they didn't believe there was a bomb in the building. They were more worried about the guns firing in the street, and they felt safer inside the building.

Then in one of the windows across the building where snipers were hiding, a man appeared out of nowhere. He was bleeding and held a rocket launcher in his hands, which he aimed at the soldier standing in front of the building. He pulled the rocket, and in an instant the soldier was blown to pieces. My dad and the other soldier rushed in and saw there was a guy with a rocket launcher bleeding and standing near the window, aiming it at the second floor. My dad shot him with a grenade launcher. Once the people inside saw this happen, the elders realized the building was wired with bombs, because there was no other reason the terrorist would be attacking these men but not entering the building.

At this point there were only ten minutes left and everyone started to rush out, my dad stopped them and gave quick instructions. He told them to move quickly but in an orderly way, because there shouldn't be a stampede, and he knew that ten minutes was plenty of time to evacuate if everyone moved in an orderly fashion. People followed my dad's instructions, and when they were out of the building, they started to run toward open ground that was a hundred meters away. Dad and the other soldier were now standing outside the building, and at this point my dad realized that two bullets had struck the sides of his body and blood was gushing from his wounds.

There were five minutes left, and they heard a voice from the building. A kid was crying, "Save me! Please save me!" It was a young boy's voice, and my dad and the other soldier rushed in to check on it. They found a boy who had fallen out of his wheelchair. My dad picked him up and started running out of the building. He handed the child to the other soldier and asked him to run away from the building. Dad said, "I will quickly check to see if anyone else is inside, and then I will be out." The other soldier said, "I will go in, sir" but my dad replied, "No, I will go."

The other soldier tried stopping him, but dad said to him, "It is an order: take the kid and run away from the building!"

Now my dad had only two minutes, and he assumed he could do the search in ninety seconds and leave before the thirty-second mark, but it didn't work. The building exploded, and the other soldier saw that his boss hadn't made it out. He screamed in horror, "General James!" The explosion was so loud that everyone within a three-mile radius could hear it. All the bricks and stones from the building were in pieces. There was no way my dad could have survived; he was not even in pieces, but had melted with the fire. The other soldier's eyes were filled with tears and pain, and he knelt down to the ground and cried loudly. And every single soul they saved came close to him felt pity as he put his face on the ground He was crying loudly and saying, "I should have been in there and been killed, not you, James, not you, sir. No, sir, you have a family and a child. I am still single and my mom has three more boys."

Everyone was in a panic and running and searching the bombed buildings, to find survivors. A few children were standing next to the solider. The children who had been saved bent down to the soldier, like angels, and said, "You saved our lives. You shouldn't be putting your face in the ground and getting dirty." One little girl had some roses in her hands, and she plucked all the petals and threw them on his dusty head. On seeing this, the other children who had flowers in their hands did the same. Seeing the flowers he took his face from the ground and saw the sweet and innocent faces of the children and said "Thank you, I saved some innocent souls today".

After all this combat and mayhem, the backup and bomb squads arrived on the scene and saw the burnt out building. The only soldier left was a Bolivian-American named Moise Boti. He was left behind to tell the press about everything that had happened and to report on my father's death. Moise Boti, the other soldier, visited us after two weeks and shared all that had happened. He said my dad was brave, smart, and never wavered in combat, and that he saved three thousand innocent children's lives. My dad knew him personally as a good friend, and he took care of everyone in his unit, treating them like brothers and sons. Moise told us how much my dad talked about how much he loved his family, his great wife and his smart son.

When Moise came to visit, he brought his family, his mom, and three brothers, and they brought us gifts. They spent a couple of days in our home, and they liked us a lot. Every time Moise was there, he spoke about my father, sometimes his eyes was shaken and sometimes with tears. The unit that was in combat that day was all Moise's friends. My father, being a general, would have stayed back and sent lower-ranking troops inside, but he was very committed and motivated to save lives.

Moise lost all his military friends in that combat, and now he wanted to retire and go back home and farm the land. Despite her grieving, my mom still prepared a wonderful meal for Moise and his family, since he was not only a friend of her husband, but a man who went to combat to save the lives of innocent children and risked his life and was the last living witness my father ever shared with the world.

Before Moise left, he took me to my room and said, "Your dad wanted you to be an IT engineer and wanted you to be an anti-hacker—that's what he told me all the time." He added, "He always said that you had to be an anti-hacker and save this country from enemies." I replied, "I swear I will be, Moise. I will fulfill my dad's last wish." Moise and his family thanked us and invited us to Utah for a vacation to spend time with them. I was proud to hear about all the great things my father did, and mom was also delighted to hear such good things about him.

It had been a month, and mom seemed to start recovering from the sorrow and pain of losing my dad, but I couldn't. My search for knowledge, truth, and wisdom had all but disappeared for the past month, but it seemed I was getting it back. My search was working, and I was angry now and a little biased because I had lost my father. I began to show my anger toward the silly and hateful people who were involved in his death. Let me start with Saddam Hussein, the real "dirt bag" who started this problem by conquering Kuwait and creating war and trouble for the whole world. He was a ruthless murderer who bombed and killed lots of innocent people, posing as a dictator and involving everyone in combat.

Those terrorists, or the so-called doltish rebel tribes, the Shiite and Sunni, I don't understand how they could knowingly kill innocent children. How could they even do it? I heard a saying, "Even a monster walks away when he sees a child." These are supposedly humans, not even monsters, so where is their humanity? They are in two divisions, Shiite and Sunni, because they have different understandings of one book, the Quran. One book with two sets of ideas means two sets of views, not two sets of bullets, bombs, and shells. I could understand how these guys wound up fighting each other—that's what happens when people can't see eye to eye—and I could explain this in one simple sentence: "You have a book and many interpretations around it, so stay with the one you believe and never bother with the other one."

This same concept applies to Catholics and Protestants. Three-fourths of the time they say the other one is wrong, so when are they going to talk about the right thing to do? One book, the Bible, so many wars and views, and still they call it one source and say it is from God and return to it for everything to solve all their problems.

I feel the one-book concept is really the dictionary of all troubles, since there is a constant battle over who is correct. That's why the single nuclei in the big bang theory abolishes these people's ideas and destroys their views, since that is how the universe was really formed. Now we are in the big nuclei of the universe, and still so many concepts and ideas flow without basic structure. I wanted to see how long all these evil happenings would go on for. If this continues, the universe consciousness has to make some hasty decisions.

The Shiites planted the bomb in the building, they hacked the electronic door and shut it down, they killed the guards and the people at the front desk; they were also watching from the building across the street as their bomb blew everything up. Why didn't they go into the building and gun down all the children, elders, and teachers? Maybe they had some humanity and could not watch the kids die in front of their eyes. That's why they chose to bomb it. Or maybe they just wanted everyone to disintegrate so that no bodies could be found and they couldn't be charged with an act of terror. Or maybe they just didn't want to waste bullets, like the Japanese built a sand tunnel in World War II so they wouldn't waste bullets. Or maybe the Shiites were scared that some children could counterattack and chase them away, cowards that they were. No matter what the reason, they are psychos, because they set the timer on a bomb and waited for it to go off, then the screaming on the streets, panic, pain, and blood. They were prepared to enjoy it and say to themselves, "I accomplished it, praise to Allah."

What could I say about the combat? There were two sets of people: one was the American troops and the other was the Iraqi cops. We fought the bad guys to save these innocent souls, but the Iraqi police just fled like cowards. It is their own country that they have to protect, but they failed, and we all died for their people. Not even one cop was dead, except us, the US military. I will never bad-mouth the Iraqi cops. Why? Their same people were the rebels, and everyone fought and died and the cops just ran away, because the cops were not motivated in the same way as the rebels and terrorists, who were motivated by their religious zeal. So maybe I should start a religion for all the cops in the world, so that they could fight against all these rebels and terrorists. What religion could it be for the cops, and who will be the God? Yes, a religion where Serpico or Benjamin's father, Kadin Gail, should be God and their life story, filled with combat, miracles, and experience in the field, would be the content of the book. The book's name is *"The Cop's Diary"* and the religion is called Top Cops.

All the soldiers who worked under my father were brave. They didn't run away, which means they were motivated by some cause or they worked under his leadership because he was a friend and a good man, and they didn't want to let him down. Maybe some were motivated by patriotism, which is fine, but patriotism shouldn't be a religion, because religion is a blinded animal. Yet all these dutiful troops died, and they died for one cause: to save children. Did they know these children? No. So then why would they risk their own lives? It is a common emotion for most humans to take risks to help children, and most will try saving a child if they are in danger, because if you could stand to watch a child die, then you are not human. We are inclined so much to help children because they are innocent and helpless, and everyone who dies for them, including my father, is fully human, and for that I am glad.

After my father's death, the focus of my search was on my dad. My father was a general, and he should have stayed in the camp and sent his troops to fight, but he tried helping others by taking care of them. Sadly, in doing that, he wound up leaving us behind with no one to help or care for us. If you are an authority, just make others do the work. Don't micromanage things; if it is combat or a war zone, you know what to do. He shouldn't have gone into the building the second time. That was his fateful mistake: trying too hard to save everyone. He assumed he would have ninety seconds to search for survivors, but his only thought was that there shouldn't be anyone left inside, and he lost track of time. Two minutes was not enough time in general, but he was focused on searching for anyone who could have been left behind. I could only think he was searching for me in that building, because he loved me so much. His love became his greatest point of weakness.

He taught me everything about superheroes, yet no superheroes came to save my father; his best friend was Superman, but Superman didn't save him. My father once said, "Superman dies in his real comics, but in the movies he lives forever." Therefore, I can't blame Superman for it, because he was a good hero and is dead now, too, so the universe now needs to conceive of and create a new superhero for us. We are in need of a superhero to save good souls. Though he was a general, my father was very kind to his troops, and Moise spoke of this often. Although I miss my dad more than words can express, I am comforted that he is not alone. Nineteen of his friends are with him now, and I know they will take care of him.

The beginning of my turning point to want to fulfill my dad's dream changed my focus, and I started training to become an anti-hacker and a top guy in technology. I had seen with my own eyes how Ejaz's father was tripped up by hacking, and I wanted to protect the good from the bad. I decided that I would be a savior of this digital universe. I would embody the bits and codes for all software on this planet, and decided I was not going to cry again for my father. I knew he still lived in me, and I wanted to make his dream come true. I made an oath to myself to be the best anti-hacker I could be. I was not going to hang out as much with my friends anymore because I needed to focus on helping the world.

In this sense, I really grew up after my father died. Because my mom is a religious person, she was comforted by all the priests, so-called servants of God, who convinced her that she would meet my father again in Heaven or paradise. She was truly convinced of this and it gave her great comfort, as she believed that since my father was a good man, he is now in Heaven with God. Since he is happy now in Heaven, she felt that his wish was for us to be happy on Earth. I thought these were very nice concepts, except I could not accept her version of events. The main difference between my mom's recovery and mine is that for my mom, my dad is dead and lives in Heaven. For me, he is not dead. He lives in me and I will one day find him. He is my first superhero. On the same day I made my resolution to focus on my career, I went to my mom to share this.

Me: Mom, I want to talk to you about something important.

Mom: Sure, honey, what is it?

Me: I have decided to focus more on my studies.

Mom: You are already focused and you're a good student, Oliver.

Me: Well, I want to be even more focused on it, mom. I want to fulfill dad's dream. I want to be an anti-hacker.

Mom: Yes, dad spoke about it many times, and even before his death he said to his friends in Iraq that he wanted you to do that. I am proud if you want to make your dad happy and help his soul rest in peace.

Me: I know, mom. I am going to be very serious about my career, and I am not going to hang out with my friends anymore.

My mom felt that something had happened to me. Her face changed quickly and she looked concerned.

Mom: Are you all right, Oliver? Why don't you want to hang out with your friends? They love you so much! You could study and still hang out with them, you know.

Me: Okay, let me try it. Mom, can you guide me and help me to achieve entry so that I can go to MIT to study engineering?

Mom: Yes, I can do that, Oliver. I will give you all the support you need. I will try to give you what dad gave us.

Me: Thanks, mom. (I hugged mom and kissed her.) I love you, mom.

This was the first time I saw that my mom was starting to have more confidence in me. She felt that I had become responsible in my life. The usual expectation for any widow is to want their kids to be okay after a father leaves the family. My dad still had mortgages on our house and a new condo, as well as a car payment. Those were two major purchases my dad made when he got promoted as bank director. The government and the bank paid a very large amount of money for my father's death, because he died in the line of duty, and with that money we settled the car and the condo loan. After settling all the debts, we still had $200,000, which was quite helpful for us to start living without my father.

In the long run we would need more money to live, and since I was only twelve years old, my mom was relieved she would not have to send me to work. My mom had finished only her high school degree and hadn't gone to college. She had no work experience, but the bank offered her a job because of my father. They offered her a clerical position with a very low salary. Ejaz's father was the manager, so he pushed certain people to give my mom a good salary, and he helped us a lot, too. Ejaz's father is a great man. He is the only one who took care of my mom by finding her work, and he remained loyal to my family.

Once I made my decision about my future, I wanted to share my news with my friends. Before my father's death, I would talk things over with them first, before telling my mom and dad. This time it was just the reverse, as I had learned something that I needed to talk about with my mom before anyone else. I learned I had to fulfill my father's dream. It was at a weekend gathering near the football grounds in our neighborhood when I told them my plans. They all showed me sympathy and were very nice to me. They showed more kindness to me because I was now fatherless. They were right to show sympathy toward me, but I did not even want to feel comforted at this time in my life, because I was so focused on my mission.

Me: Hey guys, I have to talk to you about something important.

Benjamin: What? Do you want to play football with someone?

Me: Hmm.

Fay: It seems Oliver has something to say to us. Let's listen.

Niki: One more fan for Oliver! Ha.

Shu: Come on, guys. Go ahead, Oliver.

Me: My father's dream was for me to aspire in the technology field, and he wanted me to become an anti-hacker. I want to be this in my life, to make his dream come true.

Madison: That's awesome. We're happy for you, Oliver.

Me: But the thing is, I need to stay focused.

Shu: You should, Oliver. Could we do something to help?

Oliver: No, no, I am good, but I cannot hang out with you as often as we did before. Now I have to be a career-oriented person. I feel responsibility on my shoulders.

Everybody became silent. Their faces changed like a camel when brought to the Arctic Circle. They became tense and all their eyes were on me, I didn't really care what they were thinking. Everything after my father's death changed, including my expression and attitudes. There was a long silence, minutes passed. No one knew how to start the conversation. Eventually Judah responded.

Judah: That is a good decision, Oliver. You should be very happy, and we are proud of you, that you are our friend.

Madison got mad and turned to Judah.

Madison: You, you, you little shrimp, you always say yes to Oliver. Are you out of your mind, Judah?

Me: Judah is right. Thanks, Judah, for understanding me.

Judah understands me better than any of my other friends. Madison loses her brains sometimes when it comes to me, because, because, because she loves me.

Ejaz: So you don't like us anymore?

Me: I love you guys like family, but now I feel responsible and want to do what my father wished me to do.

Benjamin: Oliver, that's fine, man, but what is the problem in hanging out? Are we stopping you from becoming what you have to be?

Me: We could hang out—I never said no—but it can only be once in a while and only a few hours. I just can't spend all my time with you guys anymore.

Fay: It looks like we are irresponsible, Oliver. Why don't we join you to do something like you? We shouldn't be waiting for any of our parents to die to talk about dreams and missions.

Saide: Fay, you're being rude! Stop it.

Me: No, Fay is absolutely right. She is not rude. She said exactly what I had in mind, but I couldn't say it because I may look selfish, but she said it for me.

Aika: So what are you telling us, Oliver, that you want us to be anti-hackers as well?

Me: I didn't say that. We could all be very successful in life and choose things we are capable of doing well and stay focused on our careers.

Aika: Sounds good. Do you have any suggestions about what each of us has to be in life?

Me: Ask yourself, guys, what are you good at? Figure that out and start building it.

Judah: You never spoke of anything like this before. You really have changed. I think this change didn't happen yesterday. Is there something on your mind? Tell us, Oliver.

Me: Bingo! You hit the spot, Judah. I never shared this message and my ideas with any of you. I want to change the world and make it a better place for everyone. That is my only goal in life. My father said before he left, 'Focus on your career, and be successful and answers will follow and you can do it.' So, the first thing is to be successful, and the way to be successful is to just stay focused on a career. If we are successful, we can help other people who are in trouble, oppressed, innocent, poor, and so on.

Judah: You never said anything like this to us before, Oliver, not even to me.

Me: Hey, hey, don't take it personally. The reason I love you guys and wanted to be good friends is that you have good energy, and you will be with me all the time. Now I've arrived at the moment of truth, and I need to face it. Our parents already love us very much, and the decisions that we make today will change our lives and everyone around us in the future. Our parents will be proud of us if we make the right choices.

Madison: But we don't know what we have to do in our life, Oliver.

Me: I am not pushing you, Madison. Take your time, think and only think about what you are thinking, and you will have answers. Then proceed with the answer and never turn back, no matter what difficulties you're faced with while pursuing it. Work hard and every step will take you from great to the greatest.

Benjamin: Got it, Chief. We will work on that.

Me: It is the beginning of a new revolution, and I am glad that you wanted to be a part of it with me. We will meet next weekend. So please, work on what we agreed. Even if you don't have answers next week, that is fine. Take your time, and never make hasty decisions. I'll see you guys later.

Everybody looked at me in a new way. I have no words to express what the look was, but I could see a light inside of them that started to shine through. We all went home, and the moment of seriousness started in our life. We were no longer kids playing in the street and having no cares. We were growing up and wanted to make a change in this world.

I didn't know how to start a career as an anti-hacker, but my mom reminded me that one of my dad's friends was a college professor. His name was Simula Jones, and he was from Andorra but was now settled in America. He was a well-known IT professor for the college and had taught at many prestigious universities, like Stanford, MIT, Harvard, and Yale. I got an appointment with him, and he remembered my father very well. I told him about my father's dream for me to become an anti-hacker. He was happy to help me, and recommended some books on programming languages, networking, and operating systems, and a few basic hacking manuals. He gave me lots of input on how to be a good hacker. The thing I remember most was one golden statement: "If you want to be a good hacker, you should know everything about technology." He gave me a few books on hacking and was very impressed with my passion. He gave me his blessing and told me I could talk to him anytime if I had any doubts.

I'd had a computer in my home since I could remember, but I used it only for playing video games and chatting with my friends. After I made my resolution, I started to use it as a study tool. I installed operating systems, software, and even some hacking tools. My mom bought me three new computers from "Best Buy" and at that point I decided I needed to build a lab. I didn't want to use my room and wanted to have a separate room dedicated to my work. I decided to use my dad's office because I wanted his energy to be with me as I continued my studies. I remembered when he was investigating Ejaz's father's case, and how he shut himself in that room for days. He was a very positive man with good energy, and I needed to be the same. I bought new routers and switches for my lab, and a technician in my neighborhood helped me install everything.

The lab was just built, but I had no idea how each piece worked. There was a pile of books stacked on the desk like a pyramid, and initially I had no idea what I was doing; it all looked like a puzzle to me. I slowly started to study all the books that the professor gave me. I didn't see any of my friends for a month, except a few phone calls to chat once in a while. My friends were still deciding what they wanted to become. After a month they started to visit on the weekends, and we would have little chats and catch up. They were impressed with my lab and all the books that I'd started to read. I motivated them, and we decided to meet for dinner on a weekend.

One Saturday evening, we all met at a local "burger joint" for dinner, and everyone chatted over cheeseburgers, fries, and juice. We started to talk about different things that we hadn't shared for a month, and they all appreciated my efforts in working toward my goals. My friends took more than a month to decide about their own goals—not because they are not smart, but because they wanted to be accurate in their decisions. I was very happy for my friends about their decisions, and each one started to explain what he or she wanted to become.

Judah said he wanted to be a doctor, because his mother and father were doctors. This made absolute sense to all of us, and we were confident that he would be the best doctor because his parents would motivate him. Madison loved creativity and wanted to be a fashion designer and artist. Since Madison's uncle is a top designer, we knew that he would definitely guide her in her goal. Benjamin wanted to become a commissioner of the police force, like his dad. We knew he would also make this his life goal because his father's reputation preceded him.

Our favorite news came from Ejaz, who said he wanted to be a banker like his dad. Ejaz's father was a very smart banker, and his dad always admired Ejaz's business skills, so he got support for fulfilling his dreams. Shu wanted to be a successful businessperson, and she was very much influenced by Chinese business techniques and had learned many skills from her father. Lately she had started running the grocery store in her father's absence, which had given her useful experience. Aika wanted to be an electronics scientist. She was very good in electronics, always building electronic kits, and her father is also an engineer and scientist at IEEE (Institute of Electrical and Electronics Engineers), so she was influenced by him.

Our tough guy, Nikifor, wanted to be a chemical and nuclear physicist. He was good at chemistry and his father's family back in Russia owned a chemical factory. His whole family is made up of chemists, so they were very supportive of him. Fay wanted to do research in biology and wildlife, and to find new species and life forms. Fay's parents worked as directors and board members of National Geographic. Sadie wanted to earn a doctorate in religion and philosophy, since she was influenced by her father, a successful professor who teaches philosophy at Oxford University. Her uncle is also a priest and theologian, so she was very educated on these topics and was also the most religious person in our group.

We all shared our views and ideas about why we wanted to have our specific careers and what motivated us to choose them. The reason we did this was that if there is no motivation, we cannot reach our goals. We all encouraged one another, which helped to build our confidence. We all understood the purpose of life now and wanted to fulfill this purpose. After a while we had all gotten together and shared our joy and happiness since my father's death. We spent the whole night chatting, and I completely forgot about my work. I was too busy sailing in the moment of bliss. We agreed to meet only once a week on Saturdays to hang out and have fun. The rest of the week we would dedicate to our studies and work hard for the professions we had chosen. We left the restaurant happily that night, and everyone started to build their plans to achieve their dreams.

Simula Jones, the professor, showed me some ways to work with IT systems and opened my eyes to possibilities. I started to work hard to understand computers and technology. Initially it was tough for me and I couldn't understand many concepts. I kept trying, though, and Professor Simula Jones helped me learn and taught me the easiest way to understand concepts. I have to personally thank him for all his efforts.

A year flew by quickly, and before I knew it, I was turning thirteen. I was constantly busy with my studies, and my friends were also busy with their career goals. We couldn't make our meeting once a week; slowly it became every two weeks, and then we met only once a month.

It took me a whole year to understand what a computer is and the very basics of how it works. My fundamental knowledge was very strong, which I knew was the key to becoming a rock star in any field. I made very good progress in school and was earning A's all the time. My teachers, my mom—everyone was happy with me. During this time mom also started to work, which she had never done before? She was toiling both in the office and at home. I have to thank Ejaz's father, who was promoted to my father's old job of director and made sure she was not overloaded with work and was always back home by six o'clock.

Another event that happened was that Shu's father opened one more grocery store in a different town. His business picked up, and I heard from my mom that he had repaid half of the loan. All of my friends' families started to become very successful, except for us, as we were living like survivors: eating, drinking, no vacation, just breathing. No more parties and gatherings, though all of our families did meet every month, taking a turn in each family's home. We didn't have that much money anymore, but that was okay because our friends understood and wanted to help us. We did not want to get help from them. Why? We were sensitive, and I had decided that I had the desire to become very rich. Without my father, I started to feel the pain of how one's life could be when they became poor and broken, but I was determined to beat the cycle once I got older.

Though our group met only once a month, Madison came to see me every week to check in with me. I was always happy to see her, and I always made a few hours for her. She was happy that I was doing better and learning lots of new stuff. At this point in my life I was trying to learn. Sometimes I became discouraged and felt like I could not achieve this dream, but the zeal in me motivated me to try again and again. I started to code simple programs and learn networking and some Web design here and there, but in all aspects I was still reasonably inept in the computer field. Professor Jones was a really good man and continued to teach me, but something was missing in him. Over time I figured out what was missing: it was the ability to teach to the soul and spirit. He taught like a regular professor who reached the mind but never entered the soul or spirit.

I shared my feelings with my friends about how difficult it was for me to build my career, and they all encouraged me. They, too, shared the same problems and didn't know where to start exactly, and we convinced each other to keep building on the little knowledge we had. The only thing that made me really happy was to hear them say they were trying, and not being lazy. Ejaz, however, revealed some strange things to me that really shook me up. "Oliver, my buddy, you could do it. One day a miracle will knock on your door and everything will come together, and you will be the best hacker in history." I replied, "I don't believe in miracles, Ejaz. I believe in hard work, and my hard work will bring me success." In turn Ejaz said, "Wait and see. You will have the greatest turning point in your life," and I said, "If you say so, Ejaz, I believe you."

It was a Sunday evening and mom and I were at home. My mom had just finished her Bible studies with her friends and we were watching a movie. There was a knock at our front door, but our TV was loud, and we couldn't hear it. After a few minutes we heard someone knocking on the door and asking for my father. "Is James Oscar home?" the voice yelled through the door. The voice was new to us, and we didn't know who it was. Mom got up from the couch and walked slowly to the door. "On a Sunday, who would be visiting us?" she said to me in a confused tone before she opened the door. There was a man dressed in a suit, sharp and very handsome, with a slight beard. He looked Mediterranean. My mom asked him, "You look familiar. Do I know you?" I went to see who was at the door. I too thought he looked familiar, but I couldn't place him. He said his name was Purdhil Jin and he asked, "Is James Oscar home?" Mom asked him, "Are you Mukhlis's brother?" and he said, "Yes, I am!"

My mom was not comfortable with him at her door, and she ushered him inside with weariness because of all the problems Ejaz's family went through because of him. He walked into the front room, and he looked at me and smiled before taking a seat. For a while he was quiet. I also was not comfortable with him, but he looked different from how I thought he would, not as intimidating as I had pictured him.

Finally, my mom asked him, "Everyone thought you were in prison. Are you out?" and he said, "I got released six months ago." My mom then asked him, "What are you doing now, and why did you come here?" He replied, "I am working for the NSA. My training is over, and I came to thank your family for the help James gave our family and saving my life." and we couldn't believe it and asked, "Do you work for the NSA?" He said he did, we were both shocked. We had heard that Purdhil had surrendered to the American Army, but he told us the whole story and filled us in with the details.

Purdhil had joined Al-Sayyid Ifrit, and while there he designed many missiles and automatic bombs, hacked American government computers, and was the "brains" behind Al-Sayyid Ifrit's success. He explained that the organization learned that he knew of things that had happened to his brother and now, they wanted to assassinate him. He told us that his brother had moved to America when he was a kid, and they wanted to assassinate him because any American citizen they hired would be "used and terminated," including Purdhil. He also said that he thought they would be fighting the American military but was shocked when he learned they wanted to kill innocent civilians; he was not interested in doing that. He continually refused when they asked him to plot some bombings of public spaces, and he had many arguments with his boss. They were not comfortable with him in many ways.

Luckily, he learned that they were planning to assassinate him, and he was able to escape from the camp. He hid for a month in Uzbekistan and Kyrgyzstan with help from some of his friends. He told us that now he didn't have any country to live in. During that one month he was in exile, he became very angry and wanted to take revenge against Al-Sayyid Ifrit. He also felt terrible about what he had done to his brother and his brother's family. He wanted revenge, and he knew that he could surrender to the American Army, and they could help him bring Al-Sayyid Ifrit down. He knew their hideouts, weapons purchases, future plans, funders, bunker locations, and specific details. He knew everything about them, because he sneaked into all their meetings, tapped their phone communications, copied their files, and so on.

"I started the project to mask all data with the random information to mask the original records, in case the CIA or American government ceased the files," he said. "The project started with my brother. They masked the data, such as a client's name, changing 'James' to 'Bob,' for instance, changing an address from Florida to California, and so on. They changed everything to cover their tracks, but he was smart and kept copies of their old records." The new records for his brother, to which only the chief of Al-Sayyid Ifrit had a key, I learned was 4096-bit encrypted, and only he had access to it.

He told us how he worked for days on end to find the key to the database, because some fishy thoughts were hovering in his soul, that these guys were not good. He built the logic bomb and all the hacking tools that Jay Mons used in the bank, because he didn't realize that he was plotting against his own blood. Purdhil credited Allah for helping him, because the day he broke the key was the same day his brother was arrested. He took all the new data, which was masked, and escaped from the camp on the same day.

He decided to surrender to the enemies, the Americans, so he contacted them and made a deal that they were not to kill him and that they would clean his records and allow him to have a normal civilian life. If they did that for him, he would give them all the information. They didn't argue and accepted his proposal, but they did want to negotiate the terms of the agreement. They met in Tajikistan, a country covered with mountains and glaciers and ice. Al-Sayyid Ifrit didn't have much control over Tajikistan territory, and it was easy for Americans to come over and reach him.

He surrendered to the American Army and gave them all his documents. They took him from Tajikistan and moved him to CIA headquarters for investigations. My mom asked, "Why didn't you surrender to the Russians?" Purdhil replied, "I cannot trust them. They are corrupt and favor Al-Sayyid Ifrit, and they would have killed me." Then Purdhil continued, "I was in prison for six months—that was part of the deal—and a miracle that changed my life." My mom and I both said, "A miracle? What was it?" He replied, "Yes, a miracle. It changed my life." My religious mother, of course, asked him if he had a vision or saw angels. Purdhil replied, "I met some humans, real humans," and my mom asked him, "You mean a man?" He continued to say that the prison he was in housed people from many different countries, like Nicaragua, Nigeria, Nauru, Guinea-Bissau, Guinea, and Cuba, and he interacted with all these people. Yet in that context, everyone was the same: they all needed justice and vengeance, and bloodshed was guaranteed.

The man who changed Purdhil was from Nepal. He was a Buddhist named Devak, and he was influenced by Gandhi's teachings. He was a very pious and religious man and a follower of Gandhi. Devak was an innocent man who was arrested near the borders of Nepal for terrorist activity, and since he was a very poor, no one was there to help him. Purdhil started interacting with him and asked him how he wound up in jail. He said the locals didn't like him because he was comparing Hinduism and Buddhism. He also claimed and proved that Buddhism was a better religion than Hinduism, and that the methodology of Hinduism was not followed correctly. He had many disputes with the powerful Nepalese people because of his stance on Hinduism and Buddhism.

Devak liked Gandhi's teaching and set him as an example of the perfect Hindu. At one point in time, he conveyed that Gandhi was the modern Buddha, and wanted to start his own, new religion, which would have been a mix of Hinduism, Buddhism, and Gandhi's teachings. Some people feared his ideas, but there were many people from Tibet, India, China, and Pakistan who started to visit him and follow his teaching. The powerful people plotted against him and linked him to a terrorist act by framing him for smuggling weapons to Afghanistan and Pakistan. They also used his efforts to start a new religion, called Maha-Buddha, which is a mix of ideas from Hinduism, Buddhism, and Gandhi's teachings, against him. They claimed he wanted to cause terrorism activity under the name of his new religion. Since there were lots of people who were convinced of his teachings, they didn't want a civil war inside the country, so they handed him over to the American government. Purdhil knew that Devak was a good and noble man and saw that he didn't collect even a single penny from anyone. He lived in a hut and preached his ideas. Yet they still framed the case and found a way to make him into a culprit.

Purdhil became friends with him, and they spent their time in prison together. Purdhil opened his mind and told him everything about himself. He wanted to have peace in his life, but before that, he wanted to get revenge on Al-Sayyid Ifrit for his problems. Devak gave him a book about Ahimsa Satyagraha, by Gandhi, and asked him to read it. For two months, Purdhil read the book many times, day and night, and his life slowly changed. His desire for revenge slowly diminished, and he started to believe in nonviolence and connected it to Gandhi's teachings. After six months in prison he was converted, and now, though his faith was in Islam, he had started to view the Quran in a different way because he read with the eyes and vision of Gandhi. At one point he asked Devak, "When you get out of this prison, will you seek revenge against all the people who framed you for this crime?" Devak replied, "Do not fight evil. Allow it to pass and be patient. Evil will die. Evil is in the mind, not in the body."

Devak added, "You want to avenge the body, but the body doesn't deserve the punishment, because the mind influences it. How could you avenge the mind when you kill the body?" Devak went on and on about teaching the art of life and how to be at peace and forgive others. These talks changed Purdhil's life, and after six months he became a new man, unbound from the chains of evil and negative forces. He became a free spirit with no chains to curse anything.

He went on to say that some of the workers from the CIA saw that there was a drastic change in him and found he would be very helpful for the American government. The American government gave him a couple of options: either join the Delta team to fight against Al-Sayyid Ifrit or become a civilian. Initially they didn't realize the change in him was for nonviolence and to promote Gandhi's teaching about Ahimsa Satyagraha. He disclosed how his life had changed and they were surprised, and he denied joining their forces. He gave them a proposal to join the NSA as a hacker, but initially they were not comfortable with it and said they needed to review his proposal. They took three months to review it and then offered him a job in the NSA. He had joined the NSA the previous month. He heard that James was the one who saved his brother's life and the lives of his brother's family, and he had saved his life also, which was why he came to our home.

My mom and I were deeply moved and touched by his experience, and in his eyes we saw absolute peace and calmness. My mom said, "Thanks for coming down. I'm happy your life changed. God works in a miraculous way." She then said, "If you don't mind, could you join us for dinner?" He said he would be honored to dine in the Oscar household, and for the first time since my father's death, my mom was excited to cook for a new guest. In the past year we had mostly gone to gatherings with sad hearts. We had also had one gathering in our home with all my friends, but mom didn't cook. Instead, all my friends worked and prepared the meal, because they wanted her to rest. They wanted to treat her well and take care of her.

I asked Purdhil if he liked working for the NSA. He replied, "Yes, very much—no blood and vengeance, just finding the bad guys." Then he looked at me and asked, "Your name is Oliver, right?" I nodded and Purdhil said, "Ejaz really loves you. He said you are his best friend." I was flattered and replied, "Yeah, I love Ejaz. He is cool and very smart." Purdhil then asked what I was interested in, and I replied, "I go to school and work in my lab." Purdhil asked me about my lab and I explained my setup with multiple computers and servers. I told him about my father's dream and how I was influenced by it, and about my mission to be an anti-hacker. Purdhil was interested and asked, "Are you sure you want to be a anti-hacker?" I nodded, and Purdhil asked me to show him my lab.

I took Purdhil to my lab and showed him all the computers, equipment, and books that I'd read. I explained that this was my dad's office, where dad had done his work, and even where he found the culprit of the bank robberies, Jay Mons. Purdhil said, "So this is your dad's workshop and you are breathing in his air in here, huh?" Proudly, I replied, "Yes, I am." Purdhil then asked me how good I was at computers. I replied, "I know the basics, but it is very hard for me to pick it up, although I am working hard to perfect myself." He looked into my eyes and said, "No one is born a perfect hacker; they need skill and luck to do it. Do you have a professor, a teacher, or a guru to teach you?" I told him about Simula Jones and how he was mentoring me to be a good hacker. The next question he asked was "Does he teach you well?" and I replied, "He is the best professor for teaching computer science and IT, but I have a feeling I am missing something from him." He said, "You are missing something. Though he may be the best, you may be looking for something he doesn't have." I agreed.

He was checking the books in my lab and I was checking my computer. He looked at me and said, "You want to be a real legend in hacking, huh?" I answered him, "Yes, certainly." He turned and crossed his legs and said, "I could open your eyes, and you are the one who should walk to the door. Do you have any objection to learning from me?" I was shocked that he asked me, because I knew Purdhil was the smartest guy and he lived for hacking. "Will I be a burden for you, because you would be busy at the NSA?" He had a pen in his hand and was tapping the table. "No way, Oliver," he said. "You will be my first student, and a real student. I could show gratitude and respect to your family and father by helping you build your career and life, and you should be by yourself after the training and travel with your dream." I was so excited by the prospect of learning from him, and I asked him when I could start training. He said he was moving to Wisconsin and that in the next week, he would be living in our neighborhood to be close to his brother, Mukhils, and his family. He promised me that he would help me in the evenings. I thanked him for his generosity.

By this time my mom had prepared dinner, and we went to the dining table. I told her Purdhil would be teaching me about computers and hacking. My mom was surprised and thanked him for the offer, and we had a tasty dinner. After a long time since my father had left us, I enjoyed the meal and dinner table conversation. I was very impressed by Purdhil's knowledge and all his life experience. It seemed like he was a reasonable man like his brother, Mukhils, and that after all he'd been through, he wanted to restore peace in this world. He had a living soul, and after a period of self-realization he understood the difference between good and bad and chose the right track for his life.

We all enjoyed the dinner that night, and before he left, he took an envelope from his pocket and gave it to my mom. "What is this?" she asked, looking surprised. "A small gift," he said, looking into her eyes with concern. My mom slowly opened the envelope and saw $100 bills. "Why are you giving us this money?" she asked, completely stunned. He replied, "This is my first month's salary from the NSA. I thought a token of appreciation and respect was necessary, so I'm giving this to you." My mom tried to hand back the envelope, and even told him to take the money to a church, but Purdhil replied, "I am not supporting violence anymore." Hearing that, my mom's face changed, as she was shocked by his answer.

He said goodbye to us and gave me his contact address and phone number before he left. I walked him to the gate, and he said, "We will change the world, Oliver Oscar. It was a pleasure to meet you." We shook hands and he walked down the street, and I watched him, noticing how he walked with confidence and purpose. I realized that he impressed me. After he left, my mom said to me, "He is a noble and great man, and the only man I've met who compares to your father. Let the Lord be with him and he shall have a peaceful life."

In that past year I had been so focused on my work, I had stopped pondering life's greater questions, but hearing Purdhil's story, my mind started racing again. I saw joy in myself and hope in my life, and as I was lying in my bed that night, I started to think about everything that had happened. I thought about Purdhil and the data masking project he created to hide data and that only the chief could have real data. I thought that was a brilliant idea, and was surprised no one in America did it. I was also amazed by Purdhil's story of fate and how he listened to his instincts when something didn't feel right with the people from the terrorist organization. I learned from his story that if I ever felt fear at a place where I worked and the fear came from deep inside me, I needed to move on.

I also noted the importance of gathering information as evidence, looking for whether information was legal or illegal, and making sure to stay relaxed and to never give a clue about what you're doing. Though the data was masked with 4096 bits, an encryption that is impossible to break down in the physical world, Purdhil is the man who broke it. The moment he found the data, he didn't take a second chance of going and talking to his chief about his loyalty or commitment, he departed. He didn't turn back. He made the smartest move to surrender to the Americans, because Russia and China were supporting Al-Sayyid Ifrit and he believed in the right of free speech in America, which meant that he could defend himself.

His transformation is a very interesting story that was new to me. Though he was Islamic, he was influenced by Buddhism and Gandhi's teachings. Devak, the Nepalese teacher who was Buddhist, became influenced by Gandhi's teaching and practiced nonviolence. I thought it was inspiring to hear how Devak was not satisfied with any mainstream religion, so he tried to create a new sect that combined the best of other teachings. Though Devak was framed for terrorism, he didn't seek vengeance. Even Devak's own people couldn't understand his true intention and ideas, Purdhil, a man far from the fundamental theses of Hinduism and Buddhism, was enlightened in the ways of Devak. I wondered if spending time and being mentored by Devak made Purdhil want to be my mentor for hacking, since he volunteered to help me.

Everything worked in mysterious ways, as my father wanted to find the bad guys who linked his best friend Ejaz's father in a crime and the leader of the terrorist organization made Purdhil to plan, who he did not know that he was plotting against his own brother. Finally, Purdhil was considered a terrorist and clothed himself with violence, but he became a good recovered citizen and a master in nonviolence, and now I wanted him to be my mentor. This made me think how the world was functioning in such a complex way, and I wondered if we could make the future simpler, and then maybe it would become less judgmental. Ejaz's prophecy came true, as he had said to me, "One day a miracle will knock on your door and you will be doing well after that, and you will be the best hacker in history." Do I believe in *prophecy*? I don't know, whether it is a *prophecy* or not, because I checked with Ejaz after Purdhil left us, and he said he was the one who recommended his uncle that he acts as my mentor. So ideally Ejaz knew about his uncle and may even have sent him to my home. He prophesied and it came true, because he knew the patterns that were happening around him. According to my estimations, he helped me, which I cannot call a prophecy.

Now, the other way, I have to admit he actually did have a prophecy, because when Purdhil was in college, he took an oath when he wanted to be a hacker that he would not teach anyone about hacking. He always believed the future should be peaceful, and he wouldn't share his ideas and knowledge to anyone. Purdhil was a confident, tough guy, and he claimed he would never teach anyone, even Ejaz. Yet, the first time he met his nephew Ejaz, he felt a sense of love for him, and when Ejaz asked his uncle, "Will you teach my best friend Oliver about hacking and be his mentor?" Purdhil's face changed, and he asked Ejaz about his friend. Ejaz replied, "He is my best friend. He is James's son. His father saved my dad and you."

But now he is a new man with understanding and realization. He broke the oath, because that oath was taken when he was a bad man with no feelings for humanity. He didn't hesitate to make a promise and broke his oath and said to Ejaz, "As peace lives in me and as it should always abide in me, and upon my peace I promise, I shall teach Oliver and be his mentor." So I should consider that a prophecy and prophecies do exist. This - I started to believe.

The only piece left in my search was the statement that Purdhil made before he left my home: "I am not supporting violence anymore," which is a very good concept. To be simple, if a religion spends money on violence, we shouldn't give our money to support it.

I was happy now that I had a good mentor to teach me hacking and make my father's dream come true. Purdhil moved to our neighborhood a week later and lived next to his brother's home. I didn't want to bother him the same day he moved in, but he was interested in my life. So, on the day he moved in, he called me to come to his house and meet him. I was very happy to hear from him. I asked my mom to make Swedish meatballs with mashed potatoes and greens, because he had just moved in and should eat some good homemade food and experience real hospitality. It looked like he was more interested in teaching me than I was in learning. I went to Ejaz's home and picked him up, and we went to Purdhil's house. We entered his home, and in the front room we found furniture all around and just two suitcases. He was unpacking on the couch and we started to help him. We fixed the couch and Purdhil thanked us and asked us to sit down. He looked at Ejaz and said, "Is he your best friend?" Ejaz replied, "Yes, Uncle." He looked at me and asked, "So how are you, Oliver, and how are your studies going?" I replied, "I am good and looking for more knowledge," and he gave me a sparkling smile. Then he looked at Ejaz and asked him, "Do you have a goal and mission like Oliver does, Ejaz?" Ejaz replied, "Yeah, I want to be a banker, a very important banker." Purdhil said, "You want to be a billionaire, huh?" Ejaz replied, "Not like that. I want to be successful, that's it, and help the poor." Purdhil said, "Not bad. My nephew wants to be a new king, and create a new control, and feed all his citizens." We both looked at him and didn't answer him. Ejaz was a little clueless, but I knew exactly what he was saying. He said to me, "Oliver, I just want to see you and check what you are doing. You could come tomorrow evening and we will start work."

I didn't want to leave him, because I wanted to help him arrange his house. I asked him, "Uncle Purdhil, could I help you in getting this all organized?" He said of course I could, but that I needed to stop calling him "Uncle." I looked at him. "I wouldn't have done it, but I heard Ejaz address you as Uncle." He replied, "Ejaz wants to make me look old, but Oliver, you could help me look young. Do we have a deal now?" Ejaz got a little insulted and said to Purdhil, "That's what my mom asked me to call you." He said to Ejaz, "Relax, big boy, I was kidding. You should call me Uncle. That's for Oliver, because he is my friend." I was happy when Purdhil addressed me as his friend.

As we were helping him, we didn't find much personal stuff like video games, CDs, tapes, books, and so on. He opened his suitcase and showed us that he had five suits, dress shirts, and pants, some underwear shorts, T-shirts, two books, and a couple of framed photos: one with his brother and another of Gandhi. He took the two books and photos and placed them on his office table. He kept the Quran and a book about Satyagraha side by side. On the left was the Quran and on the right was the Satyagraha book, and in the middle, between his brother's photo and to the right of the Satyagraha book, he kept Gandhi's photo. Ejaz and I were surprised and the first question I asked him, apart from one about the clothes, was "You only have these four pieces?" Purdhil replied, "What do you expect from an absconded terrorist and prisoner? I have the most inner-valued things in this world, the Quran and Gandhi's Satyagraha book, which mean more to me than the gold and silver with which many people fill their homes but have no inner meaning, only monetary value."

I asked him, "When you absconded from Al-Sayyid Ifrit, what did you take with you?" Purdhil replied, "My life, only my life." Then I asked him, "Didn't you take any other stuff, even your brother's photo, or the Quran?" Purdhil replied, "I was not so foolish as to have my brother's photo in my pocket when I worked there. If they were not able to nick me, they wouldn't find my brother." I asked him, "Without a photo, how could you remember your brother's face?" He told me his brother was always in his eyes. I then asked him, "You didn't even take the Quran with you when you left?" Purdhil replied, "No, it is in my heart and misinterpreted wrongly for all these days due to bad influences, and my search is to have a better world. I knew Allah would show me the right way, and he did."

I was stunned at his answers, and we worked the whole evening until eleven at night, chatting and fixing almost all the stuff in his home. After working we had dinner. We chatted about our experiences and shared a few jokes. I had a wonderful time with Purdhil, as he was not only a smart guy, but a very social person and very funny. Purdhil recounted a lot about himself and his brother when they were kids and teenagers, and told us all the silly stuff they did. We learned that he has a fine attachment with his family and loves his brother more than anybody in this world. He said to Ejaz, "Whenever I see you, Ejaz, it reminds me of your father when he was a child. He looks just like you."

I was honored that at my age I was chatting with one of the top intelligence guys from the NSA, who was also an ex-terrorist and a modern follower of Gandhi. After a very good dinner, we took a walk to a great ice cream parlor owned by some people from Côte d'Ivoire and stayed there talking until one o'clock in the morning. He then walked Ejaz and me home. Before he left, he shook my hand and said, "It was an honor to meet you, Oliver." I was surprised by his words and said to him, "No, Purdhil, the honor is mine." He smiled and said, "The honor will always be mine."

I was happy that night, thinking about all the events that had happened from the time Purdhil called me, and my search kicked in again. Usually people who had a high status or older people did not take the time to engage with younger people, but this was not my case, I needed help from him. I wanted to be a reasonable kid, so I decided to wait for three days before calling him, thinking he would be busy with his new apartment. But it happened the other way around; he called me to check on our lessons and start on the same day. This analogy works for life in general: don't wait for the person to call you. You be the initiator. Just make a call and take a risk. See what happens. If you get a bad response, that means they are not the right person for you, and you are still in a better place.

The strange fact is that Purdhil knew what I wanted to be, but he didn't know about the ambition of his own nephew, and when he asked and Ejaz said he wanted to be a banker, I liked his response: "My nephew wants to be a new king, and create new control, and feed all his citizens." His response means a lot and I understood what he meant, that there would be one king making laws and rules, and feeding all the citizens with his own money and hardship. Yet my goal was to make everyone king in their own right, with self-esteem and pride and with no ego, and Purdhil also wanted the same. That answer impressed me a lot, and I had a feeling that he could sense my energy and that we were very similar in that way.

When I called Purdhil, he told me not to call him "Uncle," and his reply was funny: "Ejaz wants me to look old." We need to know all these little tricks to help others and to know whether they want respect or to appear youthful. I also realized I was silly to ask him why he had so little luggage. Never ask this question of anyone who is moving. It hurts them, because they want to start a new life and may not want to be reminded of the past. Purdhil is a very clever guy, and was smart not to keep his brother's photo when he was working with the terrorist cell, because he knew that it might harm his brother's family in some way. However, he remembered his brother by keeping his image before his eyes. When I thought about it, what did people do before photography? They kept a clear image before their eyes, which is a better way to remember them and the love you have for them. The best camera in the world is your eyes, and the best photo is your memory. When he ran and tried escaping from the camp, he didn't even take the most important book of his life, the Quran, because that was in his soul, the religious preachers had misguided him. But for me, when you are running for your life, just run. Don't try grabbing your certificates, gold, money, and precious gifts from precious people, just run, because your life is more valuable than any belongings in this entire universe. Yes, a single life is more valuable than this physical universe, because you are the universe.

I was tired by this point and had to go to bed, grateful to have met such a great man from whom many people would learn so much and enable them to change their lives.

CHAPTER 8
CYBER TRAINING

THE NEXT EVENING I WENT TO PURDHIL'S HOME TO START LEARNING ABOUT hacking. He was glad to see me and he made some coffee for himself and a chocolate drink for me. We were chatting outside about my learning, and then Purdhil asked me to take a walk. I had a pen and a small notebook in my jacket, as I was very curious to learn anything I could from Purdhil.

As we walked, he was looking at all the trees and houses in the neighborhood and enjoying the scenery. We were quiet for some time, and finally he said, "It's a beautiful day outside. So what do you want me to teach you exactly, Oliver?" I replied, "Yes, it is a lovely day. I want to learn everything about hacking, so that I can stop bad guys from hacking." Purdhil said, "Before being a cop, you should know the mind of a thief." He then asked, "I know that you have been working very hard and studying for a year. So, tell me, what do you know about the essentials of becoming a hacker?" I replied, "Well, if one wants to be a good hacker, one should be good at programming, scripting, networking, understanding all protocols, and encryption. One should know all the security products—pretty much everything." Purdhil said, "Fair enough—a good collection of subjects, but Oliver, will all this knowledge really help you to be a good hacker?" I said I thought it would, and Purdhil asked, "Did you know that you missed three important things?" I asked him to tell me what I had missed. Purdhil stopped walking, and with his hands in his pockets, he said, "You should know philosophy, then you should have a vision, and lastly you should be able to see time, space, and patterns."

This was mind-blowing stuff for me. I never knew these were the important concepts for hacking. Purdhil said, "You need to know this before you jump into studying hacking, though I will take some time in teaching you about philosophy, vision, seeing time, space, and patterns. When your mind is opened, you will understand zero and one better than anyone, and you will be faster and smarter than the zeroes and ones."

Purdhil continued, "Oliver, everyone is a decent hacker. The difference between you and everyone else is that your legacy is in understanding time and space. You need to know the methodology of how this universe functions in terms of time and space. If you understand that well, then you are good to go and you will be a rock star. Before going into those details, I'd like to ask you, Oliver, do you know what philosophy is exactly?" I looked at him for a moment, not with curiosity, but because I wanted to give him the right answers. I replied, "Philosophy means wisdom or love of wisdom." Purdhil replied with a smile, "Good, Oliver, I am glad you know the meaning of philosophy."

"Yes, I know," I said, "but I don't know what you mean by the inner meaning." We started to talk about that as we continued walking in our neighborhood.

Purdhil: I like the way you think, Oliver. I feel your energy now, so when you say philosophy is love of wisdom, then what is wisdom itself?

Me: Wisdom is applying knowledge and a vision.

Purdhil: Some forms of wisdom use knowledge, deeper understanding, experience, common sense, and intelligence in order to see the full aspects of everything. Sometimes without all these, you can still see using intuition and revelation. It doesn't matter whether you have all the building elements of wisdom or not. When you can predict something and it happens the same way you predicted, and then on the whole you have wisdom.

Me: Wow that is a very good explanation. So what is philosophy?

Purdhil: Philosophy is reasoning, pursuits, and questioning wisdom. So, Oliver, now I ask you, what is wisdom?

Me: Well, wisdom is the use of knowledge. (I used my hand to count.) Deeper understanding. (Then Purdhil started to help me recite the list, and I repeated after him.)

Purdhil: Oliver, there are many definitions of philosophy, and this singular word *philosophy* answers many questions about reality, but in reality there is no one single definition of philosophy, because philosophy works in the mind as thought, and defining *mind* and *thought* is very complex. There are zillions of thoughts in this world on a single day. The very first rule one needs to know about philosophy: never argue or debate about the word *philosophy* itself. When you hear a new definition, if you want to accept it, just accept it or else append the new idea to your older definition. Or remove your older definition completely, or go with your previous idea about philosophy.

Me: Hmm, a very precise definition, Purdhil. I appreciate that. As far as I know, *philosophy* is a Greek word that means "love of wisdom." If we love something, then why should we use reasoning, pursuit, and questions? Is philosophy used to doubt?

Purdhil (laughing): You are a brilliant boy, Oliver, and that was a damn good question. Philosophy is the study of broad and fundamental problems. When you love someone, and there is no problem in what you are doing, you don't need philosophy.

Me: I am sorry to ask this question, Purdhil, but I thought you would be teaching me some computer and hacking technique, but we are discussing philosophy.

Purdhil: Do you enjoy our conversations, Oliver?

Me: Yes, Purdhil, I love them, but I'm curious if there is any link between studying hacking and philosophy.

Purdhil: Good point, Oliver. You need to know what a brick is, and then you can build a palace. You need to know what water is before you swim. You need to know what is around you before you really understand it.

His answer was in riddles and I started to convince myself of whatever he said.

Me: Oh, okay, thanks for the clarification.

Since this was our first class, he took me to an Azerbaijan café named Awwal, which was the best café in our neighborhood, and we started to chat about other subjects. I enjoyed some very tasty tea and snacks. When we were finished, he walked me home. I thanked him for teaching me, and he said that he would meet me the next day. This was the first day and I could sense that my eyes were opening now, because he was talking about wisdom and philosophy. I knew them only as terms, but had never understood their inner meanings.

While my search started to work that evening after he left, I came up with this one great philosophy: if you know the inner meaning of any one word, it will make you understand all the languages in this universe. Yes, I think it is very true, because my mind started to clear some doubts that I had about computers. I was able to find peace of mind for the questions I had about hacking. I wanted to see Purdhil again and again because I felt a great energy wave from him, and he got me to think on a bigger scale. I wanted to learn from him. I realized that I was blessed to know him and have him as a great teacher. I called Ejaz and thanked him and shared my experience with him, which he was very happy to hear about. He wished me success and told me to keep going with my goal, and that night I slept very well, like a wise prince who had first encountered the words *wisdom* and *philosophy*.

The next day I awoke, and as soon as I opened my eyes, I felt that my inner eyes were opened with wisdom. I had had only one class with Purdhil and had only learned about the definition of philosophy, but that discussion impacted everything I saw around me. This approach was so different from the searches I had done all my life. My search had always been about different events that had happened in my life, but now my search started to reflect broader questions.

As soon as I got up, I started asking questions and reasoning with myself. What is the first thing a man does when he gets out of bed? Why should I brush my teeth, if animals don't? Why should I use napkins to wipe my ass when half of the world uses their hand? Why do I have to take a shower every day with soap and shampoo, rather than just rub my body with my hand? Why do I need to wear underwear? Why should I tuck in my shirt? Why should I wear a tie? Why didn't the world ask Einstein to brush his hair and yet they ask me to? Why should I use socks for my shoes, if shoes protect my feet? Why should I use a fork and spoon if I have fingers? People hate vampires because they drink blood, so why do we drink cows' milk? Why is breakfast the most important meal of the day? What time is the best time to take a shit? Why do I need a school bag that is heavier than me? If I am intellectual, why should I go to school? I say "goodbye" to my mom every day before I leave, but how could an ethicist say "goodbye"? If we have cops in the town, why do we lock our homes? If I pay money to go to school, then why should I go to school at a certain time?

I was sitting in class, but my mind was all over the place, and in the afternoon I got a headache and decided not to reason over anything. But my mind was full of excitement to meet Purdhil in the evening. The first day when I stepped into the shoes of the philosopher, I knew why they are the most hated, because they make people think a hundred times before they swallow their food. I was just waiting for the day to be over because I wanted to meet Purdhil and learn more. His teachings were more interesting than the boring teachers in my class. After school I stood outside waiting for Purdhil, and I used that time to chat with my friends.

In the midst of my philosophical classes, I was happy to see Madison, and we had a little chat. Everyone was happy to hear that I was learning about philosophy and that Purdhil was teaching me about hacking. This was the first time everyone had been together since we met Purdhil, and Ejaz and I introduced him to our friends. They all shook hands with him, and all my friends were honored to see him. Purdhil is a man of great thought, and invited all of us out for dinner. Everyone was surprised that he asked us and gave us a choice about where we would go. We said it was his choice, and he said we should go to a Barbados-inspired restaurant called Night and Black.

It was typical Caribbean-style food—hot, colorful, and spicy, but delicious. It was also an expensive place where some of the top pop stars ate when they had a concert in town. Purdhil knew about all the different food varieties and ordered the best dishes. He knew a few people working there and got first-class treatment, and we had a good time. All my friends asked him about his adventures and experiences while he was working for Al-Sayyid Ifrit. My friends never judged him as a Mr. Ex-something, but they saw him as one of us, since he was very social and interesting and he calmly answered all their questions.

This was the first time my friends were exposed to Gandhi's teachings, and they started to like Eastern philosophy. Everyone was envious that he had such a wonderful Uncle and they didn't have one quite as cool as Purdhil. Purdhil always addressed us as his good friends and his nephews and nieces, but we all hesitated to call him Uncle, because of my previous experiences.

After dinner he walked Ejaz and me home, and on the way he looked at me and asked, "Are you disappointed that we wasted time with your friends, rather than learning?" I smiled and replied, "Time is never wasted with my friends." He said to me, "I wanted you to take a rest, Oliver, and stop running those ideas of philosophy in your mind. I wanted you to take a break, and that is why I took it easy today." I was really surprised. "How did you know, Purdhil, that I was thinking about philosophy all day?" He wittily answered, "I was a student at one time, and I had the same feelings." He then added, "Before I leave, I will tell you one good philosophy: a real philosopher will never look for an answer, but rather, answers search for him."

"When can I be a real philosopher?" I asked him, and he replied, "Very soon." We said good night to each other and parted ways.

The second day I slowed myself down in thinking and reasoning about philosophy, and that night it was quiet; I had a good sleep. The next day I followed the same routine. I went to my school, but I couldn't wait to see Purdhil. This time I made sure that my friends were not around me and I was away from them, because I really wanted another lesson. I knew my friends understood the situation. Purdhil left his office, changed into track apparel, and came by to pick me up. Purdhil asked me, "So, Oliver, did you understand what philosophy and wisdom are? Do you have any questions?" I replied, "I have the fundamentals down, but as you said, philosophy is the study of broad and fundamental human problems, so what do you mean by problems, Purdhil?"

Purdhil: Well, Oliver, when you say *fundamental problem,* it means everything, such as God, reality, emotions, existence, knowledge, fate, values, reason, war, death, the mind, and language—anything. When there is a fundamental problem, we humans should have answers, and most of the time we don't. Did I answer your question, Oliver?

Me: Yes. So we are trying to find answers to all the fundamental problems that we have in society. It seems like philosophy is a religion, is that right?

Purdhil: Bingo! I was expecting you to ask this question and you did, Oliver. There are lots of explanations regarding this concept, and I wanted to be precise and accurate. We use philosophy to evaluate everything when we feel it is not good for us. *Everything* means religion also, and we can use philosophy in all disciplines in our life.

Me: So when was philosophy formed?

Purdhil: Well, it was formed when humans became a victim of everything and ignorance and superstition shadowed their lives. It goes back to 600 BC, to a Greek philosopher called Thales, who was the first to engage in Western philosophy.

Me: Thales was the first philosopher, so what fundamental problem did he solve?

Purdhil: You read his history: he was a mathematician and a very poor man, and no one accepted him in society. He said that the origin of all matter is water, which was an insane idea at the time. But in a way, he was right, because today's science proves the largest element is hydrogen, which makes two of the three atoms in water (H2O). But his philosophy was barely recognized, although the world has since accepted him as the first philosopher.

Me: So was he a mathematician and also a philosopher?

Purdhil: Mathematics, philosophy, and science were closely related in the works of the early Greek philosophers.

Me: You said Western philosophy, so does it mean we have Eastern philosophy also? If yes, is it different from Western philosophy?

Purdhil: There are many Eastern philosophies, like Chinese, Korean, Indian, Japanese, Iranian/Persian, and so on.

Me: So what is the difference between Western and Eastern philosophy?

Purdhil: Western philosophy is mainly focused on cause and effect, and thereby understanding the logic behind it. Western philosophy is much more inclined to focus on science and mathematics, but of course there are many aspects of nature, religion, culture, and language that are also factors. Eastern philosophies mainly focus on religion and God. They primarily deal with life, control, and death.

Me: So you say Western philosophy is what contributed to modern technology's development?

Purdhil: Hmm, in many ways the answer is yes. Arabs, Egyptians, and Indians are well known for their mathematics and have contributed many ideas to this world, but the majorities come from the Western world.

Me: What philosophy do you prefer?

Purdhil: Me? Both.

Me: I thought for a long time that engineers, researchers, scientists, and mathematicians were the ones who formed this modern world. Is that true?

Purdhil: Everything you see, Oliver, from governments, to health, computers, transportation, communication, banking, politics, law—they all have roots in philosophy.

Me: Whoo! That is an interesting piece of information. So the question is, are all scientists philosophers?

He smiled and was very excited, when I asked that question.

Purdhil: No, sir.

Me: Then what is the difference between a philosopher and a scientist?

Purdhil: That is a very important question. A scientist is the one who does experiments and understands the trial-and-error method. A philosopher never does experiments, but creates a theory by logic, and through cause and effect.

Me: I am sorry, Purdhil, it is confusing, because it seems a philosopher is just a person who talks about anything, like, "Why can't I grab the star in the sky in my hands?" It seems philosophers are people who just talk about the thoughts that run through their minds, and as per your statement, scientists are the ones who work hard to make sure we grab the stars in our hands, if that's possible.

Purdhil: That is a very fair comment, but you didn't apply the philosophical method, my friend.

Me: I didn't apply the method, Purdhil? What do you mean?

Purdhil: You know philosophy is used when there is a problem. An example is that once people feared the massive wind, and everyone worshipped it. Now we have a problem with what?

Me: The wind.

Purdhil: No, with people.

Me: What?

Purdhil: Yes, in this problem a philosopher says, "Why don't we use this massive wind for our benefit, rather than fearing it?" So, the windmill was invented.

My eyes were opened wide now, and I looked him in the eyes.

Me: I got it!

Purdhil: So you've got the idea now, Oliver. Always remember this singular truth: all scientists are philosophers, but they deny it because philosophy is food to all humans every single minute in their life, and they don't know they have been fed. So, let me ask another question. People feared the flood and started worshipping it. Now, you are the philosopher, Oliver. What will you say with your intuition and revelation in the midst of this problem?

Me: We have a flood now, so we need a dam for it to store water.

Purdhil: You got it, my son. You are now a philosopher.

Me: Is that the right answer, Purdhil?

Purdhil: You said it correctly. Now you understand the difference. A philosopher will open the door, and a scientist walks through it to complete the revelation.

Me: I thought a scientist's job was difficult, but it seems like it's the other way around.

Purdhil: Yes, a philosopher's job is definitely difficult.

Now I understood the basics of philosophy. It seemed like God's job, where they create objects and dream nothing. Predication and vision are the key points; we needed to have more revelation, to predict this. But my question was, where do we get this revelation? How do we build the knowledge so that everyone can do it? Or was it that only chosen people could do it? Slowly I started to use my philosophical mind in every problem I faced every day. After two days of classes, Purdhil was busy for a week with his new job. A week later he came to my school to pick me up and started to teach me again.

Purdhil: So do you understand how philosophy works, Oliver?

Me: Yes, I do, but this question was on my mind for a week, Purdhil, and I don't know how to phrase it.

Purdhil: Shoot, my boy. Don't hesitate.

Me: I came to you to learn hacking, but you are teaching me philosophy. Do you want me to be a philosopher and not a hacker?

Purdhil: I knew you would ask me such a question. Tell me in what era or world we live in.

Me: I don't know.

Purdhil: We live in a world of technology, and it is a technology era. From humans we became techno-humans, from Homo sapiens to Homo technologicus.

Me: So why do we learn philosophy instead of technology?

Purdhil: Because you need to know the basics, the fundamental subjects and objects in this universe. This knowledge will help you in technology.

Me: Really?

Purdhil: Yes. In today's world we have many hackers and they are good at what they do, but they are bonded slaves to their own knowledge. The difference you are going to make first is that you shouldn't be a slave to your own knowledge. That will allow you to become the best hacker of all time.

Me: Slave of their own knowledge—what do you mean by that?

Purdhil: Imagine you are the best in your business and very successful at what you are doing, but you don't know what is around you, and you have no self-realization. Tell me exactly what you are doing.

Me: Just working to put bread on the table and quenching the thirst of my soul.

Purdhil: More or less, but you don't know the cause and consequences of the work that you are doing.

Me: Oh, I got it. So where do we start now?

Purdhil: First we will start with general philosophy, starting from Socrates and Plato, because we have a past, and we should learn and understand it.

Me: Do you want me to read any books?

Purdhil: Let me give an introduction to the subject we are going to deal with, and then, for additional information, start reading the books that I tell you to read and ask me any questions you may have. We should meet on alternate days, so that you will have time to read yourself and have ideas for us to discuss.

Me: Sounds like a plan. Thank you very much, sir, for your generosity in helping me to shape my path.

Purdhil (smiling): Anytime, Oliver.

That was how I started to learn about philosophy; at first I didn't realize there were many core divisions in philosophy, such as metaphysics, epistemology, logic, aesthetics, ethics, and politics. I started my study with Plato. I learned that Plato was a family man, and I liked him because he talked about the relationship between father and son, which is a recurrent theme in philosophy. I reflected on his thoughts because I loved my own father very much, and I could derive only one thought from my mind: *A real father will always love his son, and a real son will never hate his father.* Here, the father is the universe itself and sons are humans in his kingdom. I realized myself as a part of Platonism. I love the singular concept of deny thyself. I denied myself everything. I denied becoming the best hacker; I just removed the words *the best,* but *hacker* still remains. This was necessary because I was self-improving to be the best hacker, yet in real life, I could not see myself as the best hacker in this world of senses. As Socrates and Plato said, "Reality is unavailable to those who use their senses," but I could see a reality in my future using my wisdom. I saw that I was guaranteed to be the best hacker. Yet, until I reached that higher level of wisdom, I should deny myself the notion of the best hacker of all time.

Plato was the central philosophical soul of minds, while my mom with her Bible class in my home once quoted Jesus as saying, "If anyone would come after me, he must deny himself and take up his cross and follow me." I even asked Purdhil how there was a match of ideas between two extremes of teaching: Plato and Christ. He gave the best answer, which was "Anyone's mind with greater wisdom will at some point coincide with another's at the same level." The basic tenant of Plato's idea is the theory of ideas, and I learned different aspects of Plato's philosophy by reading *The Republic* (facts about government and politics), knowledge, and beliefs, theory of forms (the sensible world and the intelligible world), all thirty-six of his dialogues, and thirteen letters.

Purdhil helped teach me all the different aspects and teachings of Plato and showed me how different scholars had different views about

Plato's philosophy. I started to learn about other great philosophers as well, from Aristotle, to Confucius, St. Thomas Aquinas, Emerson, Kant, Nietzsche, Descartes, and Marx. Purdhil helped me see the world without time and space, and his knowledge about this universe was vast. He taught me about Eastern philosophy as well, but I didn't read as many books about it. It felt like a long time that I went through this learning process to obtain adequate knowledge. Since my wisdom was expanding in an exponential way, I got an A+ grade in eight classes. I could read and understand any script, not only schoolbooks. I applied this thought to the cause, the outcome, using why/where/when, the state, the mind involved in it, its relationship to us, its reality, and its future. I applied wisdom to the problems I saw, felt, encountered, and classified, and I understood the inner meanings of things.

I looked at myself in the morning and saw Plato's boy. I had a feeling that Oliver Oscar was becoming a modern Greek god of wisdom, since my spirits were high. That year I saw my friends only once a month outside of school, and a few times we all hung out with Purdhil. Everyone liked Purdhil, and I could see a big difference in myself after spending time with him. Before, my wisdom expanded in the horizon, and I could see only a shadow following me. But now, I see that my spirit walks with me. I could see two personalities in me: one was my body from this sensual world of life and destruction, and the other was my spirit, which was from an intelligible world of universal, eternal, and invisible realities. I am no more alone since my father died. When my father was alive, I shared all my incidents, thoughts, and experiences with him every day. Now he is not with me, so these days I meditate and confess myself of all my daily incidents, thoughts, and experience in spirit with my father. My spirit makes me stronger and realistic.

My mother is overjoyed with my new life, but for my mom, philosophy contradicts Christianity, and she still tries to make me learn the Bible. I even convinced her that the church also uses philosophy and there are lots of theologians from the church working in the field of philosophy. I realized that I have wisdom now, and I attended a few meetings and Bible studies with my mother. When I attend the meeting, I start asking questions with my philosophical ideas. The people get embarrassed because they cannot answer my questions or reason with me.

All my friends were also busy with their careers and goals, so we lost the continuous moments of friendship that we had before my father left us. Yet our friendship was still very strong, and we spent time together in school—just not outside of school. We also didn't talk as much about our goals while in school because there were lots of envious souls, spies and spiteful hearts. We started to be more attentive in our classes and work hard on our schoolwork, so that when we were out of school, we could focus on dreams and goals.

Regarding my learning about hacking, it still improved a lot, because I started to reason about what I was doing and started to build confidence. Purdhil had never even taught me a single hacking technique, because he wanted me to concentrate on philosophy. If I was to become strong in IT, then the rest was assured. Once I understood the philosophies of this universe and its principles, and Purdhil was satisfied with my understanding, he wanted to teach me something new. We met over the weekend to talk about something new, and this time, he took me to a small river near my neighborhood. We sat near the sandbanks and started to talk. The sun was setting and there was a beautiful horizon of orange, blue, and yellow colors. We looked at the sky as we talked.

Me: For the past year I've learned many aspects of philosophy, from Plato to Karl Marx. Is this enough for me to go and explore technology and hacking?

Purdhil: No, you need to learn more, Oliver.

Me: You said that you will teach me something new. Is that why we are starting new classes today?

Purdhil: Yes, very much so, Oliver. I wanted to teach you something about technology. Before that, let me ask you a question. So, the philosophy you have learned, was it traditional or modern?

Me (I answered, feeling slightly unsure): It is both.

Purdhil: It is traditional. Did you ever realize that you could apply the philosophy you've learned to modern technology?

Me: Yes. I did, and I was completely unsatisfied with my answers.

Purdhil: Why?

Me: I found some sort of emptiness in me.

Purdhil: The feeling of emptiness is from beginning new concepts, and I'm glad you have emptiness in you.

Me: So is there a new philosophy of modern technology?

Purdhil: Bingo! You got it, Oliver. I wanted you to first understand traditional philosophy, how it evolved, and the pros and cons of it. We took a year to share different ideas about purpose, reasoning, knowledge, governments, emotions, reality, and so on. Now you know the physical universe very well. The philosophy we are now going to learn is very important for your goal in hacking. It is the philosophy of modern technology. In short, we call it PMT (Philosophy of modern technology).

Me: Philosophy of modern technology. Does that vary a lot from traditional technology?

Purdhil: Yes, definitely. But before comparisons and learning about PMT (Philosophy of modern technology), I wanted you first to understand the general question, "What is technology?"

Me: Yeah, I know. Technology is when machines replace man, and technology is the result of science.

Purdhil: Well, close answer for a layman, but not for a philosopher. You need to understand in-depth exactly what technology is.

Then Purdhil started explaining technology to me. Just like when we started discussing philosophy and wisdom, he clearly explained the differences and the inner meanings. The same process was required now because I found the term *technology* vague and confusing. There is a great saying by PMT (Philosophy of modern technology) users, and clarity of the term is important because it is the beginning of philosophical speculation of modern technology. It is a saying by Seneca: "When the words are corrupt, the mind is also."

Purdhil: So what does technology mean? The first idea is a "collection of artifacts," which means it is an expression of human brilliance in accomplishing tasks using artifacts.

Me: Artifacts—you mean man-made objects?

Purdhil: Yes, man-made objects for societies use, like the watch, car, bus, and so on.

Me: So anything that we use in our day-to-day life that involves technology is an artifact?

Purdhil: Yes, exactly. The second definition of technology is "transformation or manipulation of nature," meaning we use nature to satisfy human desires and needs. This one is dangerous because this is an expression of human power over nature.

Me: What do you mean by nature? Like an atom bomb?

Purdhil: The answers are in you, Oliver; you should find them.

Me: Well, I know what you are saying. Let me meditate on it.

Purdhil: The third definition of technology is "extension of human capacities," when many tasks need to be performed. When individual humans cannot perform them, the final outcome is that we need superior systems for direct action, including both quantitatively and qualitatively.

Me: Something like a truck, goods wagon, Xerox machine, and things like this?

Purdhil: Exactly.

Me: So, what about an elevator? Someone is using it to go to the third floor, rather than taking the stairs.

Purdhil: Well, that is laziness. (We both laughed.)

We laughed for a while and talked about some nonsense, and then we were back to the subject.

Me: Do you have more definitions of technology?

Purdhil: Yes, Oliver, they are coming. The fourth definition is "purposeful form of human activity." This definition is linked and concerned with the design and transformation of objects.

Me: What do you mean by "design and transformation of objects"?

Purdhil: *Design* means the adaption of materials with some newly preconceived end, and *transformation* means the skill to change the matter and mold it into a new form. But remember, both designing and transforming involve the one who designs and transforms it.

Me: But do you have a monopoly on technology?

Purdhil: You got it, Oliver. It is the expansion of human will. Technology expands the human will, but the will was chosen or inserted. Remember that technology is a "value-laden enterprise" and not a neutral activity.

Me: That makes sense.

Purdhil: There are other definitions for technology: from Aristotle, the distinction between action and production; technological activities belong to the latter category. Hans Jonas referred to technology as "the process of their creation and utilization, an abstract system function that acts through them." This implies direct and free intervention of human beings who choose a course of action. There is another philosopher, Stephen J. Kline, who says technology is a "socio-technical system of manufacture." This includes all the material things needed to produce objects: the machinery, resources, processes, people, legal economic means, and the political and physical environments. You got it, Oliver.

Me: Yes, I am getting it and thinking about it.

Purdhil: You need to know the difference between technique and technology. Do you know it?

Me: Yes, technique is a method and technology is the application of science.

Purdhil: Good explanation. Oliver, never confuse the terms and their inner meanings. If you have some doubt to the inner meaning go to it's origin. Say for instance in our case technique and technology, the Greek word of technique, is derived from the Greek word "techne". The word "techne" meaning in Greek, means "craft knowledge" or "craftsmanship". The great Greek philosopher Aristotle well said that "techne" is the knowledge that brings an output, but he didn't mean technology. One of the best philosophers of our modern days, took the insight concept of Aristotle's defined technique, is not technology, as what we see in today's world, like the machines, computers, communications or industries. Technique is a procedure or process for reaching an end to a problem, with logical collection of methods of ideas and principles, and having total control, knowledge and efficiency in every field of human activity.

Me: Wow, so much to learn, Purdhil.

Purdhil: I hope you understood the basics that I am trying to teach you.

Me: It is always enlightening for me to learn from you. I understood what you said and will think about it more tonight.

PMT (Philosophy of modern technology) became the main topic to enrich my knowledge and help me reach my goal of perfecting my hacking skills. I didn't realize that the word *technology* had so many inner meanings. Looking at this world there are lots of engineers, and I am not sure how many of them truly know the actual inner meaning of *technology.* When Purdhil was explaining the meaning of *technology,* he defined it as transformation or manipulation of nature, and I gave the answer of an atom bomb, and he said the answers are within me. While I was thinking and searching, why did he say the answers were within me?

In my research later, I found a very fascinating fact about nature. According to the big bang theory, after the initial expansion from a singular realm, the universe cooled to convert energy into electrons, protons, and neutrons. If nature took the time to create the fundamental elements, what is the problem in splitting the nuclei to create an atom bomb? We were not challenging nature; we were applying the same principle as nature. Someone created fear about nature, and this fear stays in human minds. There is some control in this world and the control itself doesn't exist without us, so it needs us to be fearful. That is how there is some limitation that seems to be a blocking factor for human development.

I also learned the difference between ancient, traditional, and modern technology. Ancient technology was a mere "possession" and a "state" in the hands of human beings. It was always within the power of humans to control or direct employment. While traditional technology was used to improve the general standard of human living, it was the "means" cleverly employed to achieve specific human "ends." Yet modern technology has an inner dynamism, so the "means" and the "ends" are always shifting. This means we create and even impose "new ends" that were never conceived of; there is a "fluidity of ends" in modern technology. After learning from Purdhil, I became enriched with all these valuable ideas and understood that technology is a human activity and an expression of human will and creativity.

While I was going through my training with Purdhil, I was constantly trying to figure out how I would repay him. Money, a car, a private plane—but really I felt I owed him my life. I looked at myself as a man with a great debt to someone who gave me fresh air, a new mind, and a refreshed soul. A change in our relationship occurred, however, once Purdhil started to come every day to pick me up after school. Since he had only been coming every other day, I wondered if something was going on. He also started wearing his office clothes, with a tie and polished shoes, whereas before, he would always change into his athletic gear. To add to the mystery, he started showing up at my school about a half hour earlier every day.

After a week I asked him, "Purdhil, you are coming every day to pick me up for classes. Are you bored at the office?" He swallowed his words and replied, "No, it's just that, you know, Oliver you need to learn a lot of stuff, and we are running out of time." I doubted his answer, because I knew Purdhil now, and could tell he was hiding something from me. So one day I decided to check what exactly was on his mind. He came to school early as usual, but I didn't meet him. Instead I hid in the front building on the third floor and observed him from above. He looked nervous and desperate, after ten minutes I saw his eyes follow a lady. He was constantly looking at her as she walked. Purdhil didn't move, and his eyes stayed on this woman until she left his sight.

It took exactly five minutes for her to disappear from his sight, and after that he breathed heavily and smiled to himself. I smiled too, because I could guess exactly what was happening, but I didn't want to judge him because he was my mentor. I left the building and walked to meet him. I pretended I didn't notice anything and said "Hi," and he replied, "Hi, Oliver. You are late!" I said, "I just caught up with one of the teachers —sorry, Purdhil." He replied, "That's fine. Can we walk?" We started walking and we both seemed quiet.

Usually I started with a ton of questions, but I didn't on this day, and he either didn't speak because his mind was caught up with the thought of some lady. He said, "Well, I wanted to teach you more about PMT (Philosophy of modern technology) the different philosophers we should focus on." I looked at his eyes and replied, "When there is a problem, we have to use philosophy, right, Purdhil?" He agreed, so I asked him, "But I don't have a problem, I have a question about something you know." He looked surprised and said, "What question, Oliver?" I took a deep breath and asked him, "Be honest; I am your friend. Why do you come early every day?" He looked at me and said, "Do you doubt me, Oliver?" I replied, "No. If anything, I could help you. I could be a better friend." Purdhil then told me the truth, that he had met a woman who works in our school while he came to see me. For almost a year he had noticed her and she had created a warm feeling in him, a week earlier, he had met this lady at a party. He had a chance to talk to her and they chatted for a while, but no one exchanged any telephone numbers. I asked him why he didn't get her number, and he said he was nervous and didn't want to make a mistake. We were in the same boat, because I couldn't express my love to Madison and tell her how much I care for her.

The beautiful woman who had caught his eye was He-Ran, our Korean teacher. I understood why Purdhil had fallen for her. She is a lovely woman, and everyone in our school watches her with our mouths and eyes wide open when she passes by. She makes you feel like a tender breeze is passing over you, like a snowflake falling on your fore-head very softly. Purdhil also said to me that she is the woman for his life and she is the chosen one for him. I knew that we could help Purdhil because

Aika and He-Ran were very close, and she knew Aika's family very well. We had someone who could talk to her about Purdhil's crush, so I asked Purdhil, "Do you need some help?" He said to me, "I trust you, Oliver; you are my wing man." This was a more complicated situation and different from regular American dating, where he could walk in and ask her to take a long walk or go to dinner. He-Ran lives with her family, and there was no way Purdhil could try any Western techniques. We needed to use Eastern philosophy, which I was not as strong in. I didn't want to carry a billet-doux, like a carrier pigeon, because I felt I would get a solid slap, be stuck standing outside the principal's office, or would wind up in church confessing to God. I gathered my nine friends together for this matter and we started to work on a scheme to get these two hearts together. We finally decided to have a party at Aika's home and to invite He-Ran. We also told our families to be there, as everyone knew about Purdhil's crush on He-Ran and they all wanted to help him. We knew that he had started a new life and everyone had come to think of him as their own brother and loved him. We knew he did not feel like a complete man because he was not married, and we wanted to help fill the emptiness he felt inside.

The very highlight of this whole arrangement was that everyone would spend the evening talking about Purdhil and his genius mind and what an accomplished man he was, how nice he was, such a gentleman, and so on. The day came and we arranged for a couple of chefs to prepare Moroccan and Japanese food, because we knew from Aika that she liked both these types of cuisine. As soon as she walked into the party, I thought she looked like a princess with her straight hair, small red lips, and perfect body, which made everyone turn to look at her. One thing I observed in men, including myself, was that every man at the party was hedging their bets in their minds every time they saw her. Everyone was introduced and she was very soft spoken, so all the women from the families tried to make her feel more comfortable. He-Ran recognized Purdhil as soon as he walked into the party, and they quickly began chatting. We all did our best to talk about Purdhil, his job in the CIA, how he was mentoring Oliver, and how all we cared for him. I did my best as a wing man, and talked to He-Ran about how Purdhil was shaping me to be an advance hacker and teaching me about PMT (Philosophy of modern technology), the future of philosophy, and so on. We made sure to let her know that Purdhil was single and an accomplished person. He-Ran's family was also there, and they seemed very impressed with Purdhil. She seemed interested in what we were saying, but it seemed like it was something Purdhil said that really captured her interest. He mentioned that he was influenced by Gandhi's teachings and had started to learn about Buddhism. He-Ran was a devout Buddhist and a believer in nonviolence, and she was also influenced by Gandhi's teaching, so the math worked very well. We all had a great time that evening, eating good food and dancing, and for the first time since my father's death, our neighborhood felt restored to happiness.

The best moment of the party, from my perspective, was seeing Purdhil and He-Ran holding hands as Purdhil took her for a spin on the dance floor. I didn't know Purdhil knew how to dance, but they danced salsa and we all clapped and cheered for them. I had never seen any couple dance that well in real time, and in my mind I wanted that to be Madison and me dancing together. We were all happy that they got together and started to know each other. He-Ran wanted to leave earlier, so Purdhil walked with her, and took her home. Later he stopped by Aika's home, and he seemed very happy and everyone was teasing him. This was the first time I saw him hold his head down and look shy. Everyone left the party and I decided to walk with Purdhil, but all my friends decided to walk with him too. He was happy and speechless. While walking, I asked him, "What connected you and He-Ran?" He replied to us, "Well, I think she is really into Buddhism and Gandhi's teachings, so basically she values nonviolence, which I deeply appreciate." I asked Purdhil, "Did you talk about this tonight or the first time you met her at your friend's party?" He was quiet for some time and then we all started to ask him for an answer. He slowly opened his mouth and said, "Well, guys, I didn't want to talk about religion or the moral ways of my life, which I guessed wouldn't be a good start."

Fay asked him, "So what were you guys chatting about when you first met?" He replied, "I played a very safe game. I talked about my job, my accomplishments, my visions. I sounded like a jerk at first, because I didn't bother to ask her what she was doing and what she wants to do. Then when I walked her home tonight, I asked her what she felt the first time she met me, and she answered that I seemed like other men. I asked her what she meant by that, and she replied, 'Telling me how successful, smart, rich, invincible you are.' I smiled to myself, and with some hesitation I asked her what made her change her mind. She told me it was seeing how much all you kids liked me, and seeing what a great family I had, and also hearing me talk about being influenced by Buddhism and Gandhi's teachings. She admired that and asked why I didn't bring it up when we first met. I told her I did not think it was a good way to start a conversation with anyone. Talking to her tonight taught me one lesson. I guess I'd call it the philosophy of women, because she said, 'That's why you should always ask questions of the woman and never answer any of their questions,—that's how you know what they like and don't like, so you can answer them in a way they like.' So I learned something from her, and she said something to me that I felt was very convincing. She said, 'So you didn't know this simple trick with women. That means you don't know many women and are not a womanizer.' I jumped in and said, 'No, I know how to talk to women and impress them,' and she replied, 'Purdhil, I meant you are not a game player.'"

Hearing him talk, I realized I had something I could do in return for Purdhil's help in shaping my life. The following week, Purdhil came to school at his usual time. But this time I arranged for He-Ran to come with us on our walk. As we walked, Purdhil and I talked about PMT (Philosophy of modern technology). Purdhil asked me, "What is actual PMT?" I replied, "I am not yet clear," and Purdhil started to teach me. I learned that PMT is a systematic science of recent origin. It is still in the process of evolving into a recognized branch of academic philosophy. But an impressive diversity of approaches to it has already been developed. PMT is a very slow-growing branch, and recognition of it in the field has been delayed for many reasons. The term *philosophy* itself is looked at like "a way of looking at life" or "a set of belief systems." Technology itself looks very innocent, because we can control it anytime, and we humans take good ideas from a certain philosophy and ignore the rest.

Me : Why do we need to learn PMT (Philosophy of modern technology)?

Purdhil : Oliver, technology is an art, where a human's mind, will and creativity is involved. Since it is involved with mind and will, it can improve human status or degrade human dignity.

Me : So PMT is like a master with a stick.

Purdhil : Something like that. Since science and technology are involved in all aspects of life, we need to have a discipline and morality. It is like rules in sports, or in a game. To provide discipline and morality, we use different methods such as anthropology, cosmology, epistemology, transcendent metaphysics, and more . . .

Me : Let me see whether I am getting it correct; we are applying different methods of philosophies to technology to have some control over it.

Purdhil : It is not control, it is balance that we need to create between humans and the material world.

Me : Very interesting. But does PMT really help me in hacking?

Purdhil : Yes definitely. With PMT we could predict the technological development and it's outcome from different perspectives. And also, PMT could be used as a tool to unlock the true nature of science and technology with human reasoning. Though you have thousands of hacking tools, PMT has only one, the tool of reasoning. This is the most powerful that one could use to explore science and technology to their cores.

Me : When, if I know the true nature of science and technology, could I play a "Godlike" role in this world?

Purdhil : There you go; the longest dream and desire of humans to become GOD through technology. But the question that derives here is: do we want everyone on this earth to become gods and immortal? Or do we want to create a singular vacuum for one man to be a God?

Me : That is not fair; that is evil; everyone should be God.

Purdhil : Bingo, Oliver! To do that, we not only need scientific or mathematical knowledge to attain the end, but we need to evaluative accurate knowledge. So we need PMT for it.

I had learned about PMT and why I should use it. After a couple of days I realized that Purdhil and He-Ran needed some privacy because they were officially dating. I said to Purdhil, "Maybe you guys should walk together, and I will join you later." Purdhil replied, "No, no, Oliver, we are fine. She loves all our conversations, and she is enjoying learning from us." I replied to Purdhil, "This is love and not philosophy. Focus on it, Purdhil. I am cool." Purdhil asked me, "Then when do you want to have your lesson? I will walk her home and come back and pick you up later, probably in an hour." I told him that was fine, and this became our routine.

Every day he walked He-Ran to her home after school, and they had time to understand each other better, and their dating was going well. After a while Purdhil started driving her to school in the mornings and walking with her in the evenings. I was very happy about the relationship between them, because they loved each other a lot.

Another benefit of their relationship was that He-Ran became one of our dear friends, too, and we invited her to all the family gatherings. Everyone in our neighborhood knew that they were dating and that very soon they would be engaged. I also learned a lot about PMT during this time. There were so many new philosophers to study, such as Francis Bacon, Rene Descartes, Martin Heidegger, Hans Jonas, and Jacques Ellul. Francis Bacon became a major source of inspiration for me, and his work truly enriched my knowledge of PMT.

I became immersed in the ancient Greek philosophy of "reason" in terms of "understanding" and contemplating the world, which never jeopardized the *object* of understanding and contemplation. The physical, or natural, world remained intact, even though it was utilized by humans for their essential and nonessential ends. But Francis Bacon redefined *reason,* whereby reason is no more a guiding principle of human existence. Rather, reason has become a tool of manipulation. With "reason" humans only gained power over the natural world, but we needed to have "knowing," which was a way of overcoming and exploiting the natural world to the fullest extent. So, Francis Bacon's declaration, "knowledge is power," pushed today's technological advancement ahead of certain anthropological and metaphysical principles. In *The New Organon,* Bacon also said that "Wisdom, which we have derived principally from the Greeks, is but the boyhood of knowledge." I took this to mean that we should discard ancient wisdom, because it was the dawn of new knowledge.

His thoughts caused a big revolution in my mind, as I had always thought the Greeks were the greatest intellectuals, but I had greatly expanded my knowledge base. Francis Bacon's idea about knowledge equaling power changed the scientific world in the sixteenth and seventeenth centuries and changed people's ways of thinking. So, knowledge is the path that will help us overcome all the limitations that we have in today's technology. I needed to have knowledge, which, in a way, I had been missing throughout my life as most of my time I was only reasoning through all the events that were happening in my life.

Uncle Purdhil recommended that I watch a few Sci-Fi movies, where the machines took over humanity. I watched a lot of them and they spooked me. I shared my thoughts with uncle Purdhil, and he said that if we play the game of mind-matter, then one day the matter will take over the mind. I was puzzled at his statement and asked, "Does this have something to do with philosophy?" and he smiled and replied, "Welcome to Rene Descartes' matter world of disposable and exploitation game." I was not certain who Rene Descartes was and wanted to learn more about him. Purdhil explained to me about Rene Descartes, who was a prominent philosopher in history. His theory was called Cartesian Dualism, and according to him the world was classified into the world of mind (Res Cogitans) and the world of matter (Res Extensa). In his theory mind-matter, mind is superior to matter. This very definition gave a world where anyone can dispose matter at will, and he made the matter as a slave and servant to the mind. Purdhil requested me to respect the matter and never exploit it. Hearing that I felt bad about myself, I kick the fence at my house every time, while I am thinking deeply. On that day I went home and I apologized to the fence and stopped kicking it.

On a summer evening Uncle Purdhil and I were sitting in the backyard and enjoying the weather. Uncle Purdhil was checking me, for how well I had learnt all the concepts. During the chat I asked him, "There are so many philosophers who contributed to the PMT, who will be the ones who really inspired you"? He just looked at the sky and said, "From the skies the wisdom bestowed upon the men who changed my life and many others, and they are the trinity of legends of our ages and forever". Hearing that I smiled and, shaking my head, said, "You have become a poet," and uncle Purdhil said, "That was a greeting and acknowledgement to Martin Heidegger, Hans Jonas, and Jacques Ellul. Well, there will be a different list for everybody, but these people's ideas governed me and made me think radically."

Me : Oh whoo, those three are your mentors?'

Purdhil : You could say that.

Me : How did they change your views of life, uncle?

Purdhil : Let's start with the most powerful twentieth-century philosopher, Martin Heidegger. He proclaimed that technology is a form of truth and revealing. He believes that energy in nature can be independently stored and transmitted at will. According to Martin Heidegger "What is unlocked is transformed, regulated, and ordered. For instance, imagine you have a clock. Why do you need a clock in the daytime when you could use the sun as the metric? But at night, we need to know the time, and that is why we have a clock; it is a backup."

Me : So you mean, technology is backup. What happens if we have sunlight day and night?

Purdhil : We have to break the sphere shape of the earth and make it flat

Me : You are funny uncle.

Purdhil : It is not funny Oliver; it is the "question of Being." Martin Heidegger explained very well about "Being" in his book Being and Time. It will help you to understand more about his work.

Mc : So what in short is the book Being and Time about?

Purdhil : I am glad that you asked me this question. It is a small book, but the content in it was so extensive and deep, many people have done their theses just based upon picking a line in that book. In simple words, to know about something, where something is called a being, you need to have clear and true knowledge of the being that is explored. How do you attain true and clear knowledge? Always reference your being in question to the other being that is random, and remember, time will play an important role in your question and understanding.

Me : Well, let me see whether I grasped it. So, you are asking me to compare and reference two beings, to find an answer.

Purdhil : Very good, Oliver, as a start, yes you are correct. Just read the book one time, and don't think too much; pick the points that you like and work on it. I'd like to tell you a small story about how people get addicted to concepts and ideas in life. They read a book or watch a movie about it again and again, and their minds create more ideas than the original content in the book or movie. They believe there are more in-depth knowledge concepts in the book, but on the ideal reality, the original content of the creator is only one dimensional, and the reader takes it into higher dimensions, and the sad part is: the credit goes to the creator, while the real creator of the idea is the reader. One example I would like to tell you about is, "Sally had a red hog; she felt deserted and lost and was struggling to find a way." If you really observe and meditate on that one line, you could build a whole outstanding book out of it. Say for example, who was Sally? Was she Jewish, Irish, Scottish, Mexican?

Was Sally a boy or a girl? Was Sally a real name or nickname? Was Sally a prince or princess? If she is, what is she doing with a red hog? Where is she lost? Eastern Texas, some countryside, or is she on another planet? Why is she struggling to find a way? If the red hog was her friend, why did she feel deserted? You can build an encyclopedia about it. With this small story always remember this Oliver, as time changes, ideas, knowledge, and wisdom changes, but the eternal truth will never change, and you are on a mission to find eternal truth.

Me : That was a splendid story and you have opened my mind about how to approach the ideas of this world, I got it, will do.

Purdhil : Let's talk about another philosopher, Hans Jonas. He mainly focuses on ethics and the responsibility of technology. By this time how technology could be used to perpetuate evil. Like my brother who was a victim of the evil forces that misuse technology. Technology didn't affect individual's lives, for instance my brother, but rather it has given rise to "Universal Catastrophes," that is, effects like nuclear wastes causing radioactive emissions, global warming, environmental pollution, endangered species, lead and mercury content in seafood and many others. Will you be responsible, Oliver?

Me : Yes I am master, like Superman.

Purdhil : Very good, Oliver, Hans Jonas said "One must act so that the effects of your action are compatible with the permanence of genuine human life, and never compromise the conditions for an indefinite continuation of humanity."

Me : So my actions in technology affect mankind in the future also.

Purdhil : With knowledge comes power, and with power comes responsibility. You should be like a Superman in Hacking; think and calculate all your actions when handling zeros and ones.

Me : I promise Purdhil, I will never let humanity fall into the hands of the evil.

Purdhil : My boy, do you have fear, Oliver?

Me : I do, but I hide it.

Purdhil : Me too; with all knowledge, wisdom, power, responsibility, you need to have spiritual fear, which is the salt of actions. You would have heard 'Kill the fear, before the fear kills you,' but Hans Jonas said, 'Everyone should deliberately cultivate spiritual fear, it will alert us to possible disasters.' I say to you the same thing, Oliver. Build a spiritual fear both in your personal and technological life. You will always have the awakening."

Me : That is interesting, I am learning so much today; I will build spiritual fear in me from now on.

Purdhil : Do you know why I made an oath to myself that I would never share the knowledge I gained and which falsely guided me to take down the world in the name of Islam?

Me : Not really, but you had built a philosophy in your mind, which drove you.

Purdhil : Yeah, I built my own demonic philosophy, I got it from Jacques Ellul. He is the last one on my list. Jacques Ellul said, 'A technique is anything used to attain a particular end.' You see, "anything" is the word that caught my eye, I would do anything in the name of technology: build bombs, hack networks, anything to fulfill Allah's plan on this earth. With that false idea in mind, I know, we live in a technological civilization, where ends become means, and means become ends. My original plan was to destroy everybody who rebelled against Allah, and when I would have achieved my ends, I didn't want technology in Allah's kingship. So, I decided not to share with anyone, and I wanted to keep it to myself. Life is awesome, Oliver. Now I am a new man in the mercy of Allah.

Me : I don't know what to say, Purdhil; you are a rock star. I have a question. Are you anti-technology sometimes, Purdhil?

Purdhil : We all are imperfect, Oliver. In today's world we need technology. You have to realize that technology is a method of delivery and necessity. We need technology for food and goods, for agriculture, home appliances, communication, transportation, medicine, banking and financing, and many other things.

Me : Well, that makes sense. What happens when someone is against technology?

Purdhil : Anyone or any country that blocks technological growth will be considered outdated, traditional morons or anti-scientific. So, if a nation or a community is violating the improvement of technology, they will be pushed aside or forced to modernize their societies. This is one of the causes of the third world countries lack of development. Though they have so many cultural and historical values, in the name of marching towards a technological universe, all their inner ideas are considered obsolete and dying. Also, the nations that are encumbered by science and technology, while failing to consider 'human values,' can spell disaster to their own people.

Me : I have another opinion on it, Purdhil. It is a choice. They want to stay close with nature, and they believe that technology is evil. So we shouldn't push them. And since it would not be wise, in the name of science and technological progress, the super powers shouldn't do it.

Purdhil : Valid point taken, Mr. Oliver. Modern technology is Pandora's Box and, in a way, it is true, it is evil. Do you know how precisely it is evil?

Me : Hmm, I know bits and pieces, but not precisely.

Purdhil : We know modern technology has also caused much good and much destruction to humankind. To anyone who possesses the power of science and technology, the future of humanity is at his mercy.

So it will be in the hands of governments, scientists, and technologists, either nations or just individual's.

Me : So you say that America as a government spends the most money to build technology in order to enslave humanity? That is why you rebelled Purdhil?

Purdhil : That may be one reason, Oliver, I will explain it to you later. We need to approach technology with neutrality and responsibility, with a sense of moderation in the development and progress of science and technology.

Me : Definitely we need responsibility.

Purdhil : Yes, we need responsibility. I will ask you a question. Who has given power to gangsters, mobs, and drug dealers?

Me : Maybe the cops.

Purdhil : In some cases, but if you really look, to keep gangsters, mobs, and drug dealers in power it is the government servants, accountants, and common people who help them.

Me : Oh whoo! How does it relate to my question?

Purdhil : It is responsibility, personal responsibility. This is my last point Oliver and you must make and must listen like you've never listened before. No one should give any science and technological power to a government, a nation, a community, or an individual, and be in their shadows for protection. Nor the development of sciences and technology should be monitored, counter checked, examined by some experts or governing bodies. It is your personal responsibility and everyone's responsibility that we use technology sensibly and productively. As a personal responsibility we are urged to know the difference between needs and desires. And when personnel moves to a scientific community, they should know the various differences between "Quest of knowledge," "Pursuit for solutions" and "Passion for accomplishments."

Me : Makes perfect sense, it starts from an individual, and they are the one who gives the total power to the system of science and technology.

Purdhil : There is no escapism from anyone. So with personal responsibility as the moral thought, we should admit that science and technology are the future, and we are indivisible from its potential. We should use PMT as a weapon to safeguard from all disasters of science and technology.

Me : We should balance the machine world and our world.

Purdhil : Well said Oliver. So back to the first question I asked you when we started this training. What is wisdom?

Me : Well, we have the Greeks, French, Germans and English, all with different thoughts and approaches. At this point with all controversy and rivalry ideas, I don't know what is wisdom is.

Purdhil : The state you are in now is called "The birth of wisdom." Bacon said "Wisdom which we have derived principally from the Greeks is but the boyhood of knowledge."

Me : What did you say Purdhil? You meant Plato and Greek wisdom in their infancy.

Purdhil : I didn't say that, Bacon said it. There is one co-relation in ancient Greek and PMT. It is consequences, danger and fear. As I taught you, when you encounter a situation in technology, what will you do Oliver?

Me : Use it for our benefit, rather than fearing it, just tame it, as we did to the forces of nature wind and water with PMT.

Purdhil : That's my boy Oliver, you've got the insight. Always remember we cannot completely ignore old-school ideas, as they often win in very complicated situations.

I was still happy to be Plato's boy, as I have always believed his philosophy and worked to keep it alive, and technology is always a friend to humans, but it should not be viewed as our creator. I thanked Purdhil for all the information he shared with me, as he was my next mentor after my dad, who first taught me the essentials of life. I owe my breath and life to him, and without him my life would not be filled with any real reasoning, knowledge, or wisdom.

CHAPTER 9
LAND OF GENIUS MINDS

THE DAY OF MY SIXTEENTH BIRTHDAY, I FELT MYSELF FILLED WITH KNOWLEDGE and wisdom. I sounded like an ageing gray-haired philosopher with missing teeth. I had matured greatly and thought I had quenched my thirst for understanding, but still an emptiness lingered in my heart, and I always felt that something was missing in myself. Over the past three years I had made every effort to shape myself to perfection to fit into the shoes of a philosopher. I tried, practiced, and improved myself all the time, yet I still saw myself in a hollow world of darkness.

But in the quest for this knowledge, I didn't spend much time with my friends, and our friendship looked like a long-distance vibration, though we all lived in the neighborhood and studied at the same school. We were still united on a deep level and very close to each other. I was excited to share my news with them, that this young philosopher had gained admission into MIT, in Boston, to study electrical engineering and computer science. For the past three years my grades were A+, and I scored 2400 on my SATs. Purdhil was the one who influenced me to go for MIT, and he brought me lots of SAT study books. Although I was admitted into MIT, Princeton, Stanford, and Carnegie Mellon, Purdhil suggested that I go to MIT. Because he is my mentor and has always had my best interests at heart, I followed his advice, even when the other universities came through with better offers. My mom was in leap of joy and proud of me. I had started my life as an average student, most of the time thinking and reasoning about different aspects of life, that is, until I met Purdhil and my whole life changed. He opened my inner conscience. His teaching about philosophy and wisdom enriched me to crank all the exams and studies, like pulling a speck from my blinded eye to make my vision clearer and have great clarity.

I had two months left in my neighborhood before going to Boston. I finally had time now for my friends. They were the happiest people in this world to know about my success, especially because I was so young. I had skipped my junior year and was going directly to MIT for engineering studies. I also broke a record in my city for being the first person with such high grades to go to an esteemed college like MIT at only sixteen. The day I received the confirmation from MIT, we had a party at a restaurant called Antidote. This time it was only my nine best friends and Purdhil and He-Ran. We were all young and single, including Purdhil and He-Ran. I'd never seen Purdhil drink before, as he always sat with either his apple or orange juice. This time he had four glasses of whiskey because he was very happy and proud of me. Usually he was very diplomatic and polite when we were out with my friends, but he was so excited for me that he was sharing some of his little secrets and how creepy he used to be when he was a teenager. He told us he used to smoke weed, stole money from his father's pocket, watched porn videos with his friends, played pranks with his friends and neighbors, tried to impress his lady teachers, stole goods from convenience stores, stole money from the candy machines, hacked his neighbors' phones, and so on. It was the exact opposite of the person I saw him as today, but I did not make a single judgment regarding his actions. Everybody makes mistakes in their life, but in a perfect world, you missed all these fun times.

Purdhil wanted to smoke a cigar, which he did on rare occasions. He had a Cohiba Behike cigar, and he asked me to walk out of the restaurant with him. So it was Purdhil and me who went outside while he smoked. He lit his cigar and looked at me and said, "I am pleased, Oliver, and this is the best day of my life." He smiled. "Before I started to drink, I was raptured, because you are going to study at MIT at this very early age and you mastered philosophy, but after two glasses of whiskey, I am feeling light as a feather because I am drunk." I replied, "So you are somehow gratified, and I feel happy for you." We were silent, and then I asked, "I heard you and He-Ran are going to get engaged next month. Is that true, Purdhil?" Purdhil replied, "Yes, that's true. The first week of next month we are getting engaged, and within a couple of weeks is my wedding, my man." I was so thrilled and stretched out my arms to give him a hug. We hugged, and I whispered in his ear, "You have the best woman and I have the best man, and we are all the best. Congrats, Purdhil." He replied, "Thank you Oliver."

Purdhil wanted to make sure I was coming to both of his occasions. I said I wouldn't miss them, and I had two months to prepare for college. Purdhil replied, "People change with time, Oliver, when money, success, and fame follow them. My only advice to you, Oliver, is to be the same man you were when I first met you. Never forget the good memories, and don't remember the bad memories at all."

"Is that a philosophy of advice, Purdhil, or some frustration in your life that you want to tell me?" I asked. Purdhil laughed and said, "Both, Oliver. Never forget any of your good friends and people in your life. It will guide you to eternal happiness." I replied, "I never have, and you have renewed my mind. I will never forget it."

Then I asked him a weird question, which embarrassed him. "Do you mind me asking you something?" Purdhil replied, "Are you going to tell me something bad? You asked for a confession, so please proceed, sir."

Me: You guys didn't move in and live together, so how can you get married?

Purdhil: Well, I'd love to. My brother is next door, and He-Ran's family will not allow her to move in.

Me: Is it a part of your culture, something called arranged marriage?

Purdhil: Something like that.

Me: But you guys have known each other for three years. You found and chose He-Ran—and you still call it an arranged marriage?

Purdhil: Yes, very true. I chose her. Arranged marriage is very strict. Your parents choose for you, or in some situations you share your thoughts with your parents and then they go meet the girl's parents and propose your opinion. Either way, parents look for you or you look for someone who they will approve of, if it is within their boundaries. Mine is different. I saw her, loved her, and wanted to marry her, and I expressed my decision, and they all confirmed it.

Me: It's pretty confusing, Purdhil, but I'll try to understand.

Purdhil: Well, the same term is used for different situations. When your parents look for a girl for you, it is called arranged marriage. But if either one or both parties are in disagreement, it is called forced marriage. If you fall in love with a girl, then the marriage is called regular marriage. But if it's none of the three, then it is called limbo marriage.

Me: So you are in limbo marriage?

Purdhil: Spot on.

Me: Why do you say so?

Purdhil: Some disagreement, doubts, different ideas, understanding and complexities.

Me: Did Ejaz's father approve of it?

Purdhil: He is my lovely brother, and I had no single problem with him, but my sister and parents—they never said no, but they are not completely satisfied.

Me: Still you might disappoint them if you get married to He-Ran?

Purdhil: The best compliment a man could ever give to a woman is that she is noble and has great values, trust, and respect. And I have all four of those thoughts about her. Do you want me to lose such a woman?

Me: No, no, no, I didn't mean that. I wanted to know if you are able to deny the facts and thoughts of your parents and family; then you should have something greater with her.

Purdhil: Yes, I do, Oliver.

Me: The original question, in a very specific way: did you guys ever hook up, or have you guys had sex before?

Purdhil: I was thinking that would be your actual question, but you were beating around the bush. The simple answer is no.

I was perplexed by his answer and became quiet.

Purdhil: What made you ask this question?

Me: I was reading some magazine about how marriage works in Asian cultures. Sorry, Purdhil. I didn't ask you to embarrass you. I am sorry.

Purdhil: You don't need to be sorry, but I have a question for you, Oliver. Do you think it is good or bad?

Me: I don't get the question, Purdhil.

Purdhil: Do you think it is good or bad to have sex before marriage?

He lit a cigar, and I was passively smoking with him. My mind usually bounces back and forth a million times, after the passive smoke my mind was steady and focused and I looked at him.

Me: Do you want my opinion or my judgment?

Purdhil: Doesn't matter. Say something—whatever you think.

Me: As a man I could say to men who are dating, don't use or cheat on women. Knowing someone sexually is not the true and real understanding, but you could create a better bond with your partner through sex. Always the mind is the key. Date the mind and not the body. Sex before or after marriage is still called sex, but the pleasure in it varies according to time and pressure. Time and pressure are the keys; they create an illusion in the mind. It always takes time to understand anyone, because humans are complex. Rather than trying to understand someone better, just start to love. That is the easiest expression given to anyone without any questions on different levels. And in the end you just love them, rather than saying I understand him or her better.

Purdhil: Oh boy, Plato should have been alive today. You would have puffed on a cigar with him in Greece.

Me: Was I right or mistaken?

Purdhil: That is wisdom and truth—no one would deny it. You got the answers, Oliver. No matter what the facts are about sex before or after marriage, it is still the same person you love. Time and pressure create the illusion, and it is your mind, that will be the judge and master of your understanding.

Me: Well said, Purdhil. So where are you guys going to get married? In a mosque or in a hall?

Purdhil: In a Buddhist temple—you know the one called Vihara in our city. It is a small temple, but a pretty nice place.

My: Why not in a mosque?

Purdhil: Well, a wedding is a very auspicious occasion for both a man and a woman, and something that should be common between them. You know we have only Buddhism in common, so I prefer to get married in a Buddhist temple.

Me: Will they allow you to get married in a mosque?

Purdhil: No way. I can't do it, Oliver. According to Ahl al-Kitāb I cannot marry a non-Muslim woman.

Me: That is ridiculously insane. This is America. You could do it in the mosque if she agrees.

Purdhil: Yes, we are free in America—we can go do anything we want—but the orders for Islam come from Mecca and Asia, not America.

Me: That is true. Are you happy getting married in a Buddhist temple? Will all your family come?

Purdhil: Except my brother and his wife and Ejaz, no one will come, because it is undecided before the Lord Allah, according to them.

Me: Sorry to hear that, Purdhil. Why not convert to Buddhism? Why are you still hanging between Islam and Buddhism?

Purdhil: I love Allah and he is the true God and the one and only God. But I like the teachings of Buddha and Gandhi, and I am learning more about love and peace from them, transferring all their inferred thoughts to my belief in Allah and the Quran.

Me: Why? Don't you find anything about love and peace in the Quran?

Purdhil: Yes, we do.

Me: Then why do you need other concepts, if you claim he is the only true God? You never learnt anything about love and peace before encountering Buddha and Gandhi.

Purdhil gave me a smile. He looked like a man who had been misguided from the truth for a long time. Then he answered me.

Purdhil: They never thought.

Me: Thought what?

Purdhil: About love and peace for everyone in any situation. My eyes are opened now; I'm now erasing from my brain and heart all the misleading teachings that I was exposed to for a long time. I have so much misinformation. It is taking so much time for me to get the actual essence of the teaching of Allah back. Now I have the eyes of Allah and read it in the way he asks me to read rather than my own eyes the way I wanted to read.

Me: One book with two sets of eyes: one from God and the other from the demigod, huh?

Purdhil: You called me a demigod. Very funny, Oliver.

Me: Anyone from God should be a demigod, and then why do religious folks call themselves servants, friends, sons, children, or slaves.

Purdhil: Valid thoughts—no arguments.

Me: Who is your best man for the wedding, Purdhil?

Purdhil: Take a guess; you know me better. Guess three names, Oliver.

Me: You said your best friend is from kindergarten, so is it Nadir?

Purdhil: No.

Me: Is it your Argentinian friend in your office, Meddy?

Purdhil: Hmm. You're not good at guessing are you? Oliver.

Me: I got it! Devak, the Nepalese friend you met in prison.

Purdhil: Very close, but wrong answer.

Me: I give up. Tell me, Purdhil.

Purdhil: I will give you a hint. It's a man who will save the world, a chosen one, a messenger from Allah.

Me: I can only think of Prophet Muhammad. He is your best man? You're kidding!

Purdhil: It is you, Oliver, not Prophet Muhammad.

Me: You said I'm the chosen one, a messenger, saving this world. I mean, I am the best man? Really?

Purdhil: Yes, sir.

I went speechless for a moment, because he said such flattering things.

Me: But why me?

Purdhil: I am a philosopher and a religious genius, and I know you are the one, Oliver. It was my honor and pleasure to meet you. I didn't say this to anyone, but I wanted to reveal the truth now.

Me: What is that?

Purdhil: Do you remember when my brother was arrested for the robbery? On the previous night when I was in Afghanistan, I had a sense that something was wrong with the Al-Sayyid Ifrit organization. I had a dream where a messenger of Allah appeared to me and said, "You have to go back to America to help a boy who is close to your brother's family."

Me: Do you mean an angel appeared in your dream?

Purdhil: Yes.

Me: Then you left the camp?

Purdhil: I got up from my sleep, disturbed. How could I go to America when I was taught that Allah's message was to bring American down? It was the opposite now. But I wanted to see the encrypted list of victims. I tried many times and I failed. I was also running a code to break the ciphers, but it would take another month to get the key.

Me: So what did you do? How did you see your brother's file when you were not able to break the encryption?

Purdhil: Always a miracle, Oliver. The files were in chronological order-listing dates and targeted victims. My brother's name was the first on that list. Somehow when we encrypted, the first file was missed. Before I left, I found my brother's file in a folder, and it was not encrypted. When I found it, I became angry. I made up my mind that I had to leave the camp, because I got a feeling they would kill me, so I planted malware in their mainframes and hacked their database. I found all the records, and my brother's name was first on the list there also. So there my brother's file was in two places, encrypted and non-encrypted. I was shocked by this simple miracle—one set of data in two places—and it reconfirmed that the message was truly from Allah.

Oliver: So after this you left the camp?

Purdhil: Yes, I left and surrendered to the Americans. I heard about your father when I was in jail. I saw Ejaz and asked him who his best friend was, and he said your name. I even asked my brother, "Who do you think your friend's best friend is?" He replied "Your name".

Me: Did they say it was me?

Purdhil: You doubt their friendship?

Me: Never—it's just a question of confirmation.

Purdhil: My dream matched the boy and it was you. When I first met you, I had no doubt it was you, and when I started to teach you and hang out with you, I felt that you are a special kid. I prefer you to be my best man because you are a messenger from Allah.

I hesitated, overwhelmed that someone was calling me the chosen one and the messenger and such bullshit. Everyone is the chosen one; I am not the special one.

Me: Thanks, Purdhil. I don't want to be rude to you in my reply, but I don't like someone calling me that.

Purdhil: I know you, Oliver. I think you still need time to know yourself.

The whole conversation between Purdhil and me lasted an hour. I had to deny it, but he had found me. The prophecy may or may not be true, but he opened the door to a new world of wisdom, so I had to respect his prophecy. Time is an illusion and will answer me one day, but my search is always there, and I will never give up. Since we'd been gone for an hour, He-Ran came out of the restaurant to check on us. "Are you guys all right?" she asked. Purdhil replied, "Yes, we are fine, honey. We will be there in a minute." She went inside the restaurant, and Purdhil and I followed. We had a very good dinner and it was fun and everyone appreciated and congratulated me on my success. They all shared their comments and praised me for my good deeds, my friendship, respect, and so on. I was the first one in our group to achieve the dream that we had mapped out years before. They were all proud of me, how I was successful even though I was a fatherless boy. I knew my father was somewhere watching me and was happy to know that I was fulfilling his dream. I should correct that: He was not somewhere; he was in me. He was happy inside me, and I could feel it.

I had two months left before college, and I hung out with my friends all the time. We went to different movies and shows, and started to play football again. It was so much fun now. I was back where I had started. I was always with my friends, and I needed them and they needed me. But this time the caring and friendship was different, because it seemed like a severed friendship. I was going to leave my friends and my lovely neighborhood behind. Everyone was there with me, and although my father was not with me physically, I kept thinking all the time about his teachings, encouragement, friendship, love, and care. After almost three years I was having thoughts of Nathalie and how I missed her a lot because she was the most genuine woman I ever knew. Sometimes I'd have dreams about Nathalie bringing me chocolates, cookies, and cakes. She would say that she missed me and all my friends and the kids in the neighborhood. Maybe I was getting a little depressed. This was the first time in my life I was leaving everything behind and concentrating on my future. My mom was a little upset because I spent most of my time with my friends and not with her. So I made sure I spent at least two hours with her in the evenings. But she understands me, and she knows that I love my friends a lot and they love me in return.

Of all these simple, innocent moments with my family and friends, I really treasured preparing for Purdhil's engagement. The engagement party was going to take place in a local hall, and we were busy decorating it. The hall belonged to Judah's family and it was only used for their family celebrations, but Judah's father wanted Purdhil's engagement to be in his hall. Judah's father's relatives and his community complained about it because Purdhil was a Muslim and He-Ran was a Buddhist. They tried to stop it, telling Judah's father that he was defiling his family's values and the community orders by giving their traditional wedding hall to a non-Jewish couple. They pressured Judah's father, but Judah's father didn't care and said to all of them, "I am a better and chipper, when I am with my friends rather than with your community." We took three weeks to decorate the hall because we decorated it inch by inch and not foot by foot. We arranged everything, curly ribbons, helium balloons on the ceiling, flowers in vases, photos of us with Purdhil and He-Ran, reed diffusers, tableware, napkins, tablecloths, utensils, games, chairs, and so on. Since it was a Buddhist engagement, there was some confusion about whether the food should be vegetarian or not. Purdhil and He-Ran came to the conclusion that the engagement would be vegetarian food and the wedding would be non-vegetarian. So, for the engagement we had a variety of Malaysian and Thai-style food.

The engagement day drew near, and we were so busy getting prepared for it that before we knew it, the day was upon us. All the boys were dressed in blue suits, and the girls wore contemporary dresses and gowns. Purdhil had on a gray suit and He-Ran wore a contemporary red dress. Our families were all there that day, but no one from Purdhil's family came except Ejaz's family. There were, however, lots of Purdhil's friends, including people from the CIA office. The engagement included Buddhist rituals, and there were two priests doing the rituals, which included burning incense sticks. This was also the first time in my life we had vegetarian cuisine at a party, and we enjoyed it a lot. No one complained except Fay, who thought that fish and eggs were vegetarian and should have been included on the menu. After the party, Purdhil took us out to a seafood restaurant called Sea Universe because he wanted to treat us for the efforts we had made to prepare his party. We had a great time that night, and Purdhil and He-Ran thanked all of us personally. They were so moved that He-Ran started to cry out of joy, touched that our families were so nice to her. We spent that night in the restaurant, and Purdhil was so delighted, he had seven bottles of beer. We all ate several varieties of fish. After filling myself to the brim, I wondered if there were any fish left in the ocean. I could almost feel the fish swimming in my belly.

The day of the wedding came and the ceremony took place in a Buddhist temple, Vihara. The temple itself was at the edge of Milwaukee, and the reception was in the same hall belonging to Judah's father. He insisted on having the reception in the same hall because he thought of Purdhil as his brother. He again met a lot of resistance for allowing a non-Jewish wedding. Somehow people were able to forgive the engagement, but not this. They said if this wedding happened in the hall, there would not be even one Jewish wedding there in the future. They also decided to cast him out from the Jewish community, but they couldn't do that, because he was very influential and had a lot of money. This was the first wedding of a non-Jewish couple, and Judah's father decided that in the future he would donate the use of the hall to anyone who wanted to get married. The hall would be completely free. Anyone could donate whatever money they wished for its maintenance.

This shocked his community, because the hall, called El Elyon, was famous. It was 1.4 million square feet and was very important for all the Jewish people in the Midwest and in the South, including Wisconsin, because their traditional festivals always took place there. It had been their hall for more than 100 years, and for generations Judah's family owned it and rented it out for free to the Jewish community. The hall was maintained by a trust managed by Judah's family, and Jewish people from different backgrounds, poor or rich, held their festivals and weddings there. The rich Jewish people also didn't pay for using it. He insisted that anyone who was rich and well off should give the cost of a wedding, so they would spend money on the hall. Then he could use the money to build a small community hall for non-Jewish people. But these guys had never given any money to him, and Judah's father kept on asking them, begging them, and no one wanted to give money. They used the hall for free and didn't spend any of their money; they only wanted to save it. It came to a point when he wanted to use this hall for one of his good friends, but they said no because of traditional values. They made some bad comment about Purdhil being Islamic and the child of a slave, as per some old Torah hereditary clash, which he felt very bad about. That is why Judah's father decided to give it all to charity and made an agreement that it should be used only for the poor, both Jewish and non-Jewish. Still he had authority over the hall. Ejaz and Fay's father said to Judah's father, "If this is the case, then poor Jewish people will also be affected, as they don't want to have their wedding in a non-Jewish place; they think it is polluted." Judah's father, the wise man, gave the right answer: "You are already poor, so why do you still carry inhumanity, vengeance and stubbornness with you?" He also said, "'Poor' will also include middle-class people. I still consider middle-class people poor, because a poor person cannot sustain himself a month without wages, and a middle-class person cannot sustain himself six months without wages. Only the rich can sustain themselves for years and years." He knew how society worked and wanted to be fair to everyone, and that is the reason he is blessed with all this goodness.

Leading up to the wedding, we and our parents worked hard to make the day blissful for Purdhil and He-Ran. On that day Purdhil presented me with a Rolex watch that cost $8,000, which was expensive, and was a little big for my wrist. He also bought all the suits and dresses for all our friends. Time went fast, and the wedding day was before our eyes. We had the sun coming up on the wedding day from the east for us to the ring of wedding bells to start the wedding. The wedding was in the evening, and we were all in the temple per their rituals. Once they were married, they exchanged rings and there were grand fireworks. We had almost a thousand helium balloons that we released into the air, and a hundred doves. We threw rose petals and confetti at the couple, too. We had the reception and the food was of two varieties: from Singapore and Yemen. The wedding was unforgettable, and I had a great time being Purdhil's best man. I stayed near him and he introduced me to everyone who came for the wedding as the best man. I received all the gifts that were given to Purdhil.

This wedding was unique because once they exchanged their rings, Judah's father had a glass wrapped, and he stamped it to break it and shouted, "Mazel tov!" A few people knew what that meant and shouted, "Mazel tov!" Then everyone at the wedding started to shout, "Mazel tov," which means "Congratulations!" in Hebrew. My mom and her friends from the church choir sang a few songs from the psalms and praised the couple for the blessing that God showed them. It was a surprise and honor for me to meet Devak, the man who changed Purdhil's life, as he came for the wedding. He performed some Hindu practices by having the couple join hands, which is called "Hasta Melap," and the couple performed some vows to the divine power, thanking it for all the gifts, and made a wish to have love, sympathy, compassion, and respect, and to be righteous. Then they did some rituals with a copper plate and some fruits and camphor with fire, circling their faces a few times in both directions. Since the wedding was done in the Buddhist style, Ejaz's father didn't have a chance to do the Nikah, which is an Islamic tradition. However, he did the Dukhlah, a procession of the couple in public. We did the procession in a limousine with the top opened as we drove through our neighborhood. It was so much fun for this wedding rally with all our friends and families in their cars following the limousine.

Purdhil wanted me to share my thoughts and philosophy about marriage on their wedding day, so I took a chance to address everyone at the wedding. I had ever talked to a big crowd, and I was a little nervous about what to say, but I made it very precise. As per Socrates, "By all means marry: If you get a good wife, you'll become happy; if you get a bad one, you'll become a philosopher," but my philosophy is "Purdhil is being a very good philosopher, so what could be left in this world that is better than a philosopher?" And everyone at the wedding stood up and raised their hands and clapped.

It was the first best wedding I had ever attended, as all souls from different backgrounds joined together to make two hearts and souls united. We saw how a wedding of different beliefs could be there in one place: a Jewish way, the Christian faith, an Islamic procession, a Hindu blessing, a Buddhist ceremony, and a philosopher's statement from an agnostic intellectual who had an atheist father who lived inside of him. The third day after the wedding, all our family arranged a party for Purdhil and He-Ran. We decided to pick a unique restaurant from Vanuatu, called Pleach. The restaurant only allows their customers to hold family gatherings, celebrations, and functions, not for regular dining. We had dinner with Purdhil, He-Ran and her parents, and all our families. It was a delightful night because the next day He-Ran would officially move into Purdhil's house as his wife.

Time flew by too fast, and suddenly my time came to leave for college.

It should be mentioned that I was very grateful to Fay and her father because they got me a scholarship. Fay's father worked at National Geographic, and he was also a board member on HSA (Helix Sigma Axis), a large funding company. Though we were not broke, and my mom earned a decent salary from the bank, Fay's father wanted to help us by getting me a scholarship so that I would not be a burden to my mother. The scholarship covered my college fees, room and board, books, computers, vacation benefits for fifteen days, commuting expenses, car insurance and college-related supplies. I was so relieved that I wouldn't burden my mother or have to waste my time doing some part-time job rather than studying.

Suddenly it was the week before I was leaving my neighborhood. I started to pack my luggage books, clothes, skateboard, convertible bicycle, superhero movies (my father's favorites), and many other items. I took a couple of photos such as a family photo of my dad, mom, and me and the photo of all ten of us with Nathalie. When I was packing my luggage, my heart started to ache with pain and loss. I realized I was leaving behind everything and going for my dream, which I wanted to do, but I still felt sadness. I had a hovering spirit in me saying, "Your life's journey has started. When you become old, you will come here where you started." Yes, it was a journey to a new world with many ideas. It was like I was in a pit visualizing the whole world with my knowledge, not knowing how the real world looked, how it could feel, and how it would react to me.

My mom wanted to drive me to Boston, which was crazy, because it was almost 1,100 miles from Wisconsin. I said we could fly, but she wanted me to take my father's BMW, and I couldn't say no, because I had never taken a long road trip in my entire life. It took two days and we wanted to leave three days in advance. The day before I left, all my friends and their families wanted to throw a grand send-off party for me, but Sadie's father wanted to host it this time. We decided and agreed on Spanish-style food, so he booked a famous chef, Ulfrido Sancho, who is the ultimate cook of Spanish dishes. We had the send-off party in Judah's father's hall. I invited everyone from my school, most of my neighborhood, my friends and their families, and both my dad's and my mom's families. It was a great gathering in our neighborhood, and everyone was happy for me. Everyone brought gifts, and my school collected money from everyone and bought me a very expensive laptop with high configuration in it. I was pleased with their gifts, and all my teachers gave a speech about me. This is the first time I ever knew that they had such great regard and respect for me. They praised me for being gentle, reasonable, polite, respectful, shrewd and intellectual. Some teachers shared that they had never seen a student like me, and others had tears after they talked. I didn't realize I had had such a big impact on my teachers. All my friends gave talks about me, and it was inspiring as they shared all their opinions, how much they loved me, cared for me, and valued my friendship. There wasn't one negative comment or remark about me, which made me very happy.

They asked me to give a talk and I was happy to give it. I said how much I loved this neighborhood and everybody in it, my school, my teachers, my friends' families, my friends, and Nathalie, and how much I was going to miss them. I was inspired and said philosophically, "Great and genius minds travel to learn and deliver. When mind becomes motionless, it will settle down expecting a transformation." I finished my talk with "My mind is in a quest of searching, my body lives where I dwell, but my soul and spirit are always in this neighborhood." Everyone was moved and speechless, and they stood and clapped, and a few kids whistled loudly out of joy.

My party was the first time I had seen everyone gathered for a celebration in a hall and I could see all the school kids and my family together in one place. We had many dishes: appetizers, fish, roasted chicken, turkey, pork soup, beef, fried calamari, shrimp, empanadas, kipes, and desserts, especially flan, which everyone loved. There was a cocktail party going on for the adults, and everyone cherished the event. Purdhil was also drinking and was in the heights of ecstasy. We all danced to different music, like salsa, belly dancing, break dancing, Drobushki, ballroom, and house dancing. I never knew the kids from my school had so many talents. I liked the ballroom dance the best because I did that with Madison. All my favorite friends—Nikifor, Ejaz, Benjamin, and Judah—picked out beautiful girls from school who they were longing for and danced with them. It was interesting to watch the kids' reactions to who was dancing. Aika was staring at Nikifor, Shu at Ejaz, Fay at Benjamin, and Sadie at our favorite boy, Judah. Benjamin was the only one who seemed to understand that a girl liked him, so rather than make a big fuss about it, he just went and asked Fay for a dance and pretended nothing bad had happened. He was a cool guy. It was great being on the dance floor with my best friends. We had all been friends, and we started to realize that we had crushes and desires for the girls in our group.

Early Thursday morning, the day after the party, we woke up and started to pack and get ready for the road trip. My mom was busy getting the car ready and packing her luggage. I was busy with packing and saw the Superman toy sitting on my desk. It was the first gift that my dad gave me when I was a kid, and I wrapped it in paper and a velvet cloth and put it in the middle of my suitcase. That toy reminded me of my dad, how crazy he was about superheroes, and his influence on me. I had grown now and had developed great wisdom, but his gift was a very valuable memento to me. Quickly I went to his room and looked at his desk. Being in there reminded me of him, the way he smoked and worked. I started touching the walls and his desk and moving my fingers over them. I felt that he was still living with us.

Then I heard Madison's voice talking to my mom on the ground floor, and I quickly went and greeted her. It was unusual for her to come to our house at six o'clock. We were going to leave at ten in the morning, but all my friends said they would be there at eight to help me move my luggage. She said she would help me out, and she came to my room and we started to pack stuff. She was sad and her face had dried tears on it. I asked her, "Are you all right?" Through her tears she said, "'I'm fine." I asked her again, "Madison, is there something wrong. What is it?" She held my hand and asked, "Will you forget me, Oliver?" I replied, "What? What are you talking about, Madison? You are the best!" She then asked me, "Could you promise me that you will never forget me?"

I knew that she thought she was losing me, and I promised her I would never forget her. Then something happened. We started kissing for the first time—I mean a real adult's kiss on her lips. Though we were sixteen, I didn't have sex with her. All this time I had been too busy and hardly found time for her. I felt that I was in paradise while we were kissing, and there were angels around me and a peaceful silence came over me. I didn't know whether she made the move or I did—we both did. For the first time I felt angels or Cupid around me. I felt some consummate energy around me. It lasted for about an hour. I didn't look at the clock while kissing. All I knew was that we stopped at seven, and I knew she had come to my house at six. After we kissed, I felt my lips were wet. I had heard that a good kiss is when our lips get wet, and my first kiss was wet. We sat on the bed for a while in silence, and she rested her head on my chest and I stroked her head. My mother came to my room and knocked on the door a few times and we didn't respond. She opened the door and saw us, and smiled. She wanted to distract us so she coughed a couple of times. We realized someone was in the room and got off the bed. I looked at her and she smiled very gently. Her smile signified, *Oliver, you have a girl in your life.* But Madison was really shy. She partially looked at my mom, and after a minute she rushed out of my room. My mom was smart. She didn't ask what had happened but rather asked me, "Have you finished packing?" I replied, "Nearly, Mom."

It was a quarter to eight, and Judah came first and started helping me. Around eight all my friends were there. Everyone started helping me move my luggage. I had four big suitcases: three were in the car's trunk and one we put in the back of the car. Even on this busy day, my mom prepared breakfast for all our friends. She sliced some bagels, fried eggs, squeezed orange juice, and made salad. We ate breakfast, talking to each other and trying to stay upbeat, but everyone was heartbroken about my leaving. Still, everyone maintained the mood and acted very cool. It was a quarter after nine and all my friends' families came to say goodbye, including Purdhil and He-Ran. The time was moving both faster and slower. The clock was deceptive; it was suddenly 10:00 a.m.

We had to leave. My mom had a small bag and her handbag. Everyone hugged and said bye. It was a heartbreaking feeling for me, and all my friends' eyes were red with tears. Then we got into the car and Benjamin's father asked my mom through the window if they could all drive with us. My mom replied, "No, thank you. You are all so kind!" Benjamin's father asked me, "Are you sure, Oliver?" I replied, "Thanks, Uncle, we will be fine." My mom started the car, and all my friends were on the other side with me near the window, holding their hands. Mom said bye to everyone, and the car slowly started to move. I could see everyone behind the car waving their hands. But my friends started walking with the car and followed us to the end of the road. Finally my mom stopped the car and said, "Guys, Oliver is still with us. Only a momentary distance separates us. You should go now." Sadie understood and started to move everyone from the car, and my mom accelerated. I turned and looked back and saw all my buddies. They looked like people who were lost in the desert and didn't know which direction to move. I watched them until they vanished from sight. The view grew fainter and fainter, and finally I saw an image like an insect, and I could only see the skies above them. And then they were gone.

As we left the neighborhood, I saw my school and thought, *Thank you for making me successful.* I saw the park, the football ground, and all the restaurants, one by one. They reminded me of the great occasions we had had. I saw Tziyon's jewelry shop, and we even passed by our competitor's Ambrose's neighborhood, and the tree where Madison fell when we were little kids. I saw Purdhil's office, my dad's bank, the Buddhist temple, Nathalie's castle, the cemetery—I couldn't forget that—the Homeland security office, and my mom's church. Outside my mind I started to see a new world with new neighborhoods. It was an exciting experience for me, and I couldn't believe I was sixteen years old living in my neighborhood and my mom also stayed with me, except my father who went outside. We hit the highway and I saw trees, bushes, many cars and trucks on the road, and different lanes, tolls, and road dividers. My mom was looking at me while she was driving. My face was excited and my eyes were bright with colors and scenery. I felt meek and humble inside when I saw the beauty of this universe outside my neighborhood. I was speechless for an hour. My mom enjoyed looking at me, and I knew what she was feeling: *There will be twice as many moments of joy if you look into the eyes of your loved ones when they enjoy watching something.* My father used to do it, when he took me to see fireworks. I enjoyed looking at the sky, but my father never looked at the sky; he looked into my eyes instead, and enjoyed both the fireworks and my happiness. After an hour's drive my mom pulled the car over. I looked at her and asked why she had stopped. She said, "Do you want to take the wheel?" I had a driver's license, but I was sixteen and had never driven in my entire life, except for the driving test. I replied, "You're kidding me. I got my license last month, I have never driven, and you are asking me to drive on a highway? That could be deadly mom, or even and suicidal."

My mom encouraged me and finally convinced me to take the wheel. I started the car a few times and stopped, unable to move more than a foot. I was resisting my mom. I thought I couldn't do it, and life she was pushing me. I had a hard time with my mom and didn't know why she was doing this to me now. My mom asked one question, and I regained all my confidence. Guess what it was? I assume no man on this Earth would ever guess what she said to make me confident, including Plato, my master. I will tell you what she said: "Oliver, will you make the same fuss and not be confident when Madison is sitting next to you in this car?" I was a little angry that her question had nothing to do with the current situation. "Mom, stop it, please." And my mom replied, "I didn't mean the romance in your room. I mean, don't you want to impress your love by driving the car for her?" I realized then what she meant, and my anger disappeared.

Now I wanted to overcome my ignorance, because Madison drives her car so well; she always drives from her home to mine with her mom. For a second I felt the cumulative love of these years, and I hugged and kissed her and said, "Thank you, Mom." For the first time she didn't use God to give some encouragement, telling me, "God will help you drive and protect you all through your journey." She spoke of her impressions this time, instead of talking about God, saying things like, "Madison will be impressed when you drive." Now it would be the other way around: Madison would be watching me and enjoying the way I drive; it wouldn't be like my mom was watching to see how I enjoyed the highway.

I started with great confidence and started to move the car, driving slowly in the right lane. My mom liked the way I was driving the car, but at first I applied the brakes a lot, and my mom gave me instructions constantly. Then after a few hours, I started to gain more momentum and more confidence. I started to move from the slowest right lane to the next lane, and to drive a little faster. I enjoyed switching lanes and shouted "Yeah!" and she was clapping and saying, "My boy, Oliver!" It was a fun trip, but all of a sudden I remembered my dad, and said to my mom, "It would have been better if Dad was here now." Mom was silent and answered, "Yes, Oliver, we miss him. Things will change." I saw a few tears in her eyes and stopped talking about him, because we were both becoming emotional.

We stopped for food, and tried to race past slow cars on the highway, and I felt better about myself. We played music all the way, including my mom's favorite rock music: Aerosmith, The Beatles, the Beach Boys, Michael Jackson, Billy Joel, Elton John, and Elvis Presley. We danced while I drove, and smiled and waved at kids, young couples, and old people. In return, most greeted us with a wave of their hands and a "Hi!" But some looked at us like we were insane. This was the first time I had been out, and I was behaving like a kid—a teenager—though I am a teenager now, but filled with philosophy and wisdom in my mind; I was Plato's boy, and if Plato had been there, he would have said, "You are still a kid." I even speed up to 120 mph at one point, and luckily wasn't caught on the police radar.

We stayed the night in Cleveland at a very good four-star hotel. It was a king-size room and was very big. We had a grand dinner in the same hotel that was delicious. This was the first time I had stayed outside my neighborhood, and it was a different experience. I could see lots of people from different states. The ambience was quite different from my regular home environment. I could tell a lot of the patrons were consumed by business and money. As I watched all the fancy people, I had one philosophy running through my mind: There is no greater place to sleep but in a home, where the bricks are made with love, not with business.

The whole journey to Boston was awesome, and I enjoyed every moment with complete acceptance with all my soul, mind, and spirit. I even developed a philosophy about road travel, whether you know your path or don't know your path: "The Earth is straight; just follow the road ahead." If you understand this simple idea, you will never get lost. Having been a cheese head from Wisconsin for sixteen years, I was entering the land of genius minds, Boston. Around midday on Saturday we reached Boston, and as soon as we had our feet in the city, I could feel intellectual waves reaching me. Hundreds of geniuses were educated here and became some of the most inspiring people in history; it was a place of inspiring wisdom and teachings. It is undeniably the land of genius minds, and I was here to improve, learn and excel.

I had gotten a one-bedroom apartment on Porter Street, and we drove there so I could unpack. It was fully furnished and included all utilities, so there was everything from frying pans to an oven, from wineglasses to a bottle opener, from an air conditioner to a garage. My mom and I arranged all my boxes and luggage, which took us the whole day. On Saturday evening we took a walk around my new neighborhood. Everything was new for me, and I didn't have any friends here. I was holding my mom's shoulder as we walked, and everyone thought we were friends. My mom is still young and very beautiful, and some people were asking us if my mother and me were a couple and had moved together. The combination in my mind is that I am very young and my mom is still young, but different eyes reach different conclusions. We had our dinner in a Slovakian restaurant that night, and the food was completely different from Wisconsin. Even the way the waitress interacted with us was different. We had never been exposed to this. At least my mom had traveled to a few places before I was born, so she knew more than I did, but I had much to learn.

We slept that night in my new apartment, but we were restless, because the place was new, and we chatted until two in the morning. The next day, mom wanted to go to her Sunday service, and she found a church around my neighborhood. She convinced me to take her, and I didn't fuss much because I would be staying far away from my mom and I wanted to make her happy. So I walked with her to the church and attended the service, but all I was doing while I was there was watching people. It was unique to me, because there were many young college students from everywhere. Maybe everyone trusted in God, or maybe they were looking to pick up some girl from the church—it was none of my business.

After Mass we had breakfast and shopped for a few grocery items, but in the evening she had to leave. As she was about to leave, she had her bag in her hand and handed me the car keys. I was confused and asked her, "Mom, you should drive back. Why are you giving the keys to me?" She said she was flying home. I asked her, "What am I going to do with the car? I cannot drive. I need someone next to me always." My mom replied, "I know that. Find some friends and they will help you."

"So what are you going to do?" I asked. She replied, "I will use the GMC Chevrolet."

"That's an old car, Mom," I said. "How could you use that?"

"I don't go very far," she said. "I drive from our home to the office. You need it more, Oliver." I asked her, "Then why didn't we drive the old car here to Boston and you could use the BMW?" My mom got a little aggravated and asked me, "What is your point, Oliver?"

"Mom, I am still in college and I don't need a car, and I don't want you to drive our old car in our neighborhood."

"You want me not to drive our old car or not to drive our old car in our neighborhood?" she asked.

"What is the difference, Mom?" I was aggravated at this point. My mom said, "A lot—Don't you want me to be seen in our old car? Will our friends and families judge me?" I replied, "Mom, my friends are the best. We never judge each other by how rich and successful we are. I am talking about other people in the neighborhood." I added, "Our father left us, but it doesn't mean anyone should criticize our way of living. We have to maintain our dad's reputation." My mom held my hand and said, "Everyone knows who your dad was. If you want to honor him, study well and fulfill his dreams."

I didn't want to argue with her, because she wanted to do something nice for me. She never understood what I was telling her. I had one philosophy and thought in mind, which I was trying to explain to her, but she never understood. "You could have a torn jacket in a foreign land, but not even torn underwear on your own soil." But people dispute this thought. They think we should look good in foreign lands, because it signifies where you come from and what values you have, but it is not your problem. If you look poor, then it is a shame for the people who accepted you in their land. But you should be majestic on your own soil. You should be proud before your people, because of one simple fact: they know you.

My mom was very smart. She had already purchased a plane ticket, and I took her in a cab and dropped her off at the airport. I thanked her for all the great things she had done for me. It was a heartbreaking moment, because she was leaving me in this new place and I didn't know how to start my life without all my closet people around me. After she left, I realized that she had left me with the last item my father purchased: the BMW. She knew that I loved my father very much, and she wanted the car to be with me.

On Monday morning, my first day of college began. I got up early and dressed myself in a black suit and white shirt. I was not sure whether I should have a tie, so I put a tie in my pocket. I had a car but could not drive myself; I needed someone for that, so I had to take the subway to my classes. I noticed one great thing: Boston people were nice and friendly, and everyone was very educated, polite and diplomatic. I was walking toward the college, and as soon as I entered the campus, my heart was exuberant and humbled to see the palace of the geniuses. The first day was our orientation. I was the only person who was sixteen; everyone else was older than me. I had never been a high school junior or senior, and everyone was looking at me very strangely. I could remember only Professor Gavin Higgs from Finland, the one who had interviewed me. Professor Gavin Higgs was the head of the department of electrical engineering and computer science, a renowned and honorable man with three PhDs in the field of electrical engineering and computer science. He spotted me and quickly walked toward me and greeted me. "Welcome to MIT, Oliver." I replied, "Thank you. How are you, Gavin?"

"I am fantastic, and I am very happy to see you on this campus," he said. On the first day of orientation, we learned about MIT and its achievements, the rules of the college, their staff, the engineering program, campus life, different projects in the curriculum, and so on. After the orientation, we had a grand lunch, and I got introduced to a few students, some of whom were from my department and in my classes. After lunch we were finished, and regular classes began the next day.

On the first day of class we had introductions from Professor Gavin as head of the department. He introduced me to everybody in class and explained that I was in the tenth grade(second year in senior high school), a sophomore who had made a great journey to be at MIT at this age. Everyone stood and clapped, and all honored me. There were a few jerks looking at me disdainfully, but I was a philosopher now, so I ignored them. Those jerks looked like Ambrose and his counterparts back at home, and the one thing that scared me was that I had no friends here and was younger than the rest of the students. I wanted to ignore situations where I might be hassled.

I started to learn more in my subject area beginning from the very first day. The first week I was sleepless, because I was excited about college and the new environment I was experiencing. My first weekend in Boston by myself, I felt lonely with all my loved ones far away from me. This was the first time in my life I felt far away from Madison's love. I loved her so much, and I wanted to see her and be with her, hold hands and lie by her side. I wanted to sit in silence, not talking so that I could listen to her heart. I missed everybody, but my love affair grew to its maximum. All my friends called me every day, and we had great conversations. We spent more time on the phone, almost four hours every day. The first weekend was depressing, and I decided not to stay in my apartment. I called my mom and said I was coming home the next weekend, and she booked tickets for me.

That next Friday I flew to Wisconsin. I was happy to see my mom, and all my friends were very excited to see me back. This was the first time I had been away for two weeks, and I could see all the excitement on my friends' faces. We all had a great dinner and a good time at Fay's house. Everyone was asking about my experience in Boston, my college, any friends, the food, and so on. They were all delighted that I was doing well and enjoyed hearing about my experience.

After the dinner, Madison came over and we slept in the same bed the whole night. We were very quiet, just holding hands, and I never had any intention of having sex with her. I had this mental block in my head and fell asleep around five in the morning. I enjoyed that night with Madison because I had been so desperate to see her for a week. The weekend passed by, and I went back to Boston. I started to acquire more knowledge and got into a routine: every weekend I would go to Wisconsin, and I did that for about three months. From Monday to Friday, I studied a lot; then I went home on the weekends and had fun with my friends. After three months I got tired of what I was doing—going to my college in Boston and going to Wisconsin to meet my friends. I realized that I was missing some pieces in my life. So I didn't go to Wisconsin one weekend, and on Saturday I took a tour in Boston. I enjoyed the fascinating city and its magnificent beauty. I hung out downtown, visited the Harvard campus, went on one of the Duck Tours, and went to Boston Harbor Islands National Park.

In the evening I walked near Chelsea Street, and I found it was strange for me to see people in this neighborhood. There were lots of African kids playing together, and the thing that drew my attention was that these kids looked like they were poor. They had T-shirts and pants, some had no shoes, and they were playing soccer. I sat down on a bench on the street, and for two hours I watched them play. They were cheerful kids, very polite, but they were so poor. I decided to walk around the Chelsea neighborhood to check out who these kids were and what their lifestyle was like. It looked like it was a broken down neighborhood, with damaged buildings, dirty streets, a couple of dented cars, and some stagnant water gathered in the road. The roads had pits, and clothes were hanging out to dry on the patios. As I walked around, everyone was looking at me, and I smiled at them. They were whispering to each other, and a few of them smiled back and waved their hands. Some people were in long African outfits and looked very poor, and a few were dressed in trousers and T-shirts. The whole scene affected me, as I had never seen a very poor neighborhood in my life. I was troubled in my mind and I left for home. That night my eyes were filled with visions of their poverty, and I couldn't sleep.

The next day, early Sunday morning, I wanted to go back and see who these people were and why they were so poor. I brought some cookies and chocolates, and some snacks for the kids. I went to their neighborhood at eight in the morning with food in my bag. The kids started to play and I heard some church services going on. I was eager to see how it looked and rushed to the church. I saw a black priest in his alb, and all the people were seated in plastic chairs, rendering offerings to the Lord. At this time I realized that there were some Christians in this African community. This was the first time in my life I stepped inside a church without being prompted, and participated in the service. I did it because I wanted to be a part of them, so I could learn who these people were. After the service a gentleman named Jacob greeted me and asked who I was. I asked if we could take a walk, and we both started to talk as we walked in their neighborhood.

Me: Where are you guys from?

Jacob: We are all from Africa.

Me: All from the same country?

Jacob: We are from all parts of Africa. Do you know how many countries are in Africa?

Me: Yes, sure. There are fifty-five countries in Africa.

Jacob: Very good, man. Do you know each of their names?

Me: Is this a puzzle to check my knowledge?

Jacob: Well, I didn't mean that, sir. If you could, I would be very impressed.

Me: Okay. Sure I will. Give me some time.

We both sat on the street bench, and I pulled my paper and pen from the bag and started to write. My memory was sharp, and I wrote the countries' names in alphabetical order. It took me like ten minutes, but I was able to do it. I gave him a piece of paper with all the countries in Africa starting from A to Z listed neatly:

Algeria, Angola, Benin, Botswana, Burkina Faso, Burundi, Cameroon, Cape Verde, Central African Republic, Chad, Comoros, Congo (Democratic Republic of the Information), Congo (Republic of the Information), Cote d'Ivoire, Djibouti, Egypt, Equatorial Guinea, Eritrea, Ethiopia, Gabon, Gambia, Ghana, Guinea, Guinea-Bissau, Ivory Coast, Kenya, Lesotho, Liberia, Libya, Madagascar, Malawi, Mali, Mauritania, Mauritius, Morocco, Mozambique, Namibia, Niger, Nigeria, Rwanda, Sao Tome and Principe, Senegal, Seychelles, Sierra Leone, North Somalia and South Somalia, South Africa, Sudan, Swaziland, Tanzania, Togo, Tunisia, Uganda, Zambia, Zimbabwe.

Me: Here it is, Mr. Jacob.

He looked at the paper for a few minutes.

Jacob: You are very knowledgeable and a prudent boy. I am very impressed with your answers.

Me: Oh, thank you, sir, and also there are some debatable colonies and countries such as South Sudan, Saint Helena, Ascension and Tristan da Cunha and Réunion.

Jacob: What information are you looking for, Oliver? We are a poor and broken people. Look at those kids there: no proper education. A new school will be built in a year, but even when they build it for us, there will not be proper education.

Me: Why did you guys leave your home lands?

Jacob: There was a campaign running where they would take a thousand people from each country in Africa to go to the United States. They would give them green cards, jobs, food, education, and a better life. We believed it and sold all our possessions and came here; but the US government is not doing anything.

Me: The government promised it, so they should keep their promise.

Jacob: Yes, we believed the same thing. America was meant to be a country of freedom of expression, and laws protect the people, but it is not the case.

Me: What went wrong?

Jacob: There is some sort of argument between Democrats and Republicans, who will gain merit for sponsoring us. The campaign was about promoting "Peace in Africa," giving us the opportunity to live in their country.

Me: I don't get it: "Peace in Africa."

Jacob: Same old crap everyone does to black men and Africa.

Me: I am very sorry; what do you mean? Can you please explain?

Jacob: Stealing our assets and enslaving us. That is how Europeans came to Africa: to steal diamonds, gold, and all our minerals from us.

Me: What does America do by bringing you here?

Jacob: America wanted to have a big presence, so it wanted public support. So to play the game fairly, they started a campaign called "Peace in Africa."

Me: So you are here according to their instructions. What is the problem now?

Jacob: The election is coming next year. It has been six months and we are stuck here in this hole. The Democrats and Republicans are fighting over who will win the hearts of the American people.

Me: Did you file a petition? Do you have a green card now? You have to act, man.

Jacob: The green card is pending, not yet issued, and still our residency status here is still undecided. But we sent a petition to the US Embassy for green cards and jobs, and they are still reevaluating our cases.

Me: I didn't find any information in the newspaper or magazines about this.

Jacob: Everything is controlled by the government. They have control over the media now, so no one wants to tell the world anything about this.

Me: What happens if you protest?

Jacob: They threatened to deport us.

Me: Perhaps it's better to go back than stay here.

Jacob: We sold everything in our country and spent half our money here, hoping we will do fine. At this point we cannot return.

Me: That is bad.

I took all the food from my bag and gave it to him to give to the kids. He looked at me very surprised.

Jacob: Thank you, Lord. You are a very generous man. But we will repay this to you, man. We Africans don't receive anything free, as charity, because we were born as kings, and now we are cursed as less than a dog.

I looked at Jacob. His face was not confident and his eyes were wet.

Me: I was not trying to insult you. I was trying to help you.

Jacob: No, no, no, Oliver, not you, my man. The way the world looks at Africans, everyone takes from us and gives us nothing in return.

Me: Everything will change. *Hope* is the only word I can give you. Hang in there Jacob.

Then Jacob and I went to give the food to the kids in the neighborhood. They all thanked me for the food, and later Jacob took me to his home for lunch. Jacob introduced me to his family. He had a boy called Yohance, and his wife was Chioma. They greeted me with the utmost courtesy and happiness. They gave me a steel chair to sit on, and Jacob sat on a worn-out plastic chair with the boy Yohance on his lap. As I was looking at the house, I noticed that there were no elaborate furnishings. Most things were broken, but it was very neat and tidy. They set a meal before me, and it was an adequate nourishing meal, in my spirit, it was as rich and royal a meal as I had ever had before. They had fish, which they caught from the river, rice, vegetables, and greens. I enjoyed each mouthful, and the food satisfied all my senses. I had never had an experience before in which food could satisfy all my senses.

After lunch, Jacob, Yohance, and his wife chatted with me for a while, and then Jacob, Yohance, and I went to a playground where kids were playing soccer. Yohance introduced me to all the kids. They invited me to play soccer with them and I didn't hesitate to join them. I removed my shoes, as I saw the other kids had no shoes to play in, and I played with my bare feet. I am not a great sportsman, but I enjoyed playing with these kids and scored two goals. My team won the game. Yohance was on my team. We all removed our T-shirts and swung them in the air, both the winners and losers, shouting and dancing. After that we opened one of the water hydrants in the street and everyone played in the water.

I had fun, and I felt that I was in Africa, where the land of human civilization started. Later I got introduced to all the kids and their families and we had a group supper. After the supper, we had a campfire, and all the West Africans danced the Yoruba dance and drums were played. Later that night, I went home feeling joyous. My loneliness was gone, but I searched for reasons why these people had been placed in this situation. I started with an embarrassing idea, as Darwin states in his evolution process, that humans came from a small organism—a bacteria or whatever we call it—and went through phases, and then became perfect, well-developed humans. This bacteria and humans were first spawned in Africa, according to researchers. We all are from the soil of Africa, but we have enslaved and treated Africans as so-called black people in a very bad way for too long a time in history. Such embarrassment and humiliation caused bloodbaths of precious lives in every direction, ensuring war and enslavement of their minds, bodies, souls, and spirits. Even in America we needed to have a civil war to end slavery, with great loss of life. My saying is "Engaging fellow-men as slaves is like an act selling your own blood to prostitution and murdering humanity, with thorns and thistles."

Yet African history didn't start with slavery. There is a saying by Maya Angelou: "It takes more than a horrifying transatlantic voyage chained in the filthy hold of a slave ship to erase someone's culture." All these Europeans—Portuguese, French, British, German, Dutch, Belgian and everyone who thought they could be a better master for a humiliated slave—occupied their land, plundered their treasures, tied them in chains, broke their identities, diminished their confidence, raped their land, and showered themselves with their blood. We sucked out every good thing from them and in turn gave them nothing in return.

Now America wanted to show a different image in the minds of the world, to try promoting better politics in this country. I am a true American. I will not allow any more of these Shakespeare dramas with the same Julius Caesar story again and again. Black men will not be in the part of this Shakespeare plot. They are with us and part of us. They have the same blood, flesh, and feelings as us. That is the reason Jacob asked me to write down the names of all the countries in Africa, to know whether I really wanted to help them. When you are assigned a job, you need to know the basics very well. All the people who wanted to promote peace, liberate others from slavery, and restore justice started the journey with a notion of becoming famous and rich. The famous and rich played their part well, being famous and rich forever. When I wrote down the names of all the countries of Africa, I saw a wave of trust in Jacob's eyes. He believed me, and I am sixteen years old. According to some, I am white trash at this young age who wants to help the black man , or to say it better, I am a modern Aryan working to help an Ethiopian king.

How could I help them? I should now use the philosophy of freedom and fighting. We should use a method of nonviolence. First I had to know this philosophy for myself. There was once a well-known slogan by Emiliano Zapata: *"Prefiero morir de pie que vivir de rodillas,"* which means, "It's better to die upon your feet than to live upon your knees!" But the same slogan was said by different people at different times. I remembered this one in particular because there is a very beautiful picture of Emiliano Zapata in Sadie's mom's home, and whenever I went to her home, I looked at it as if someone was calling me to fight for justice against slavery. This slogan had been in my heart for many years, and it is the right time for me to recall it. First I have to be thankful to Sadie and her family.

The second famous saying for freedom fighting is "United we stand, divided we fall." Yes, we should be united to fight, and the more united we are, the less likely we are to fall. I knew we could be united, not only by spirit but by knowledge and wisdom. Yes, *knowledge* and *wisdom* are the key principles to make a revolution, and these people did not have as much education as I had. I wanted to teach them what I had learned in my life—the philosophy, the reasoning, and the knowledge. It would open their eyes, and then we would fight with this government and the world. We were not going to wait for the next election in a year, we want freedom right away, since they are inherited and the birthright of humans. Freedom is the air we breathe every day, and love is the blood and bones. I decided to teach others to show the world what the world is made up of and what the universe demands of us.

The next day I went to college, but my mind was unplugged from my studies. For the first time at MIT, I felt I already knew whatever they were teaching in class and that I knew it better. The best part of the class was that I could scope out the girls, but the funny part was, none of them looked exciting. I realized at this point that there were no good-looking women in technology, especially in my department. There were exceptions—some were better—but they also dressed like nerds. Lots of foreign students were in the class, and I had a feeling that I was not in an American college.

I realized what caused the emptiness in my journey to Boston: I had to teach these broken people, the people in Chelsea. I had all that time with Purdhil, for three years, learning computers and philosophy. I have a sound knowledge in computers and during my first three months in Boston I had developed my own operating system, which was faster, more stable, and more secure than any operating system in the world. Also, I developed my own encryption software that could encrypt a petabyte of data in a few minutes. Everyone comes to MIT to learn more than to teach, and even if they teach, they teach the bright ones. I wanted it to be the other way: I wanted to teach computers to these helpless, poor, and uneducated kids. So, the next evening I went back to Chelsea Street and to Jacob's home. He was sitting in his chair and listening to the radio, and as soon as he saw me, he greeted me with surprise.

Jacob: I didn't know that you would be coming today. I thought you were returning at the weekend. Welcome, my friend. Come and sit down.

Me: Oh, thanks, Jacob. I came to talk to you.

Jacob: Sure, man. Anything urgent?

Me: No, just a casual talk.

Jacob: Oh, that is fine. Want a drink? I have cane soda. Is that good for you?

Me: Sure, I love it.

Though I am not a big fan of soda, I will never say no to any of the food and drinks they offer me, because in some way it may insult them.

Jacob: What do you want, Oliver?

Me: Could we take a walk?

Jacob: Sure, please.

Me: I was thinking last night. You know the schools are going to be built in six months and your green card is in a mess. So, I have decided to teach the children here some computers, science and technology lessons. Would that be okay?

Jacob: Are you serious, man? Yes, please, Oliver. I trust you. Can you come on weekends?

Me: Thanks. Oh no, I would do it every evening from six to eight.

Jacob: You can do it anytime! Take the whole day.

Me: I have college in the morning and I have to be there. Let the kids enjoy the whole day having fun and enjoying sports, and in the evening I will teach them.

Jacob: Thank you very much.

I went forward and hugged him.

Jacob (shaking hands with me): Oliver, I am very proud of you. Your mother and father should be proud of you.

Me: Only my mom—my father died.

Jacob: Yes, but your father is still listening to you!

When he said that about my father, I was shocked. But I believe my father is alive somewhere in some form, seeing me. He is in me. Now I have to prepare myself to teach these children, to train them to be an asset to this country and this universe. I have a new mission now. I want to do it with all my strength, with all my will, and with all my heart. I am going to spend time with these people until they are liberated from all their chains. My friends will understand what I am doing, and their families also will be of great support. I have to reach my friends and share my decision, because without their support I cannot do anything. They love me, and I need them now for this mission that I have chosen.

Chapter 10
FROM AFRICA TO NEW YORK CITY

NOW I HAVE PERMISSION FROM JACOB TO EDUCATE CHILDREN. EVERYONE likes Jacob and they don't have a leader yet, but they will all lend their ears to his ideas and thoughts because they know he is a wise man. I spent the whole night before my first class thinking of how to teach the kids in a way they could understand. I decided to teach the way Purdhil started with me when he was teaching me philosophy. I knew that if I started with computers, these kids would get bored and there would be no fruitful results for all my efforts. The next day, as a routine, I went to college, but I was eager to go and meet the kids and teach. Every minute felt like a light-year, and later I realized that if my mind thinks every minute is like a light-year, then how much could I accomplish in a minute!

My last college class was over at 5:00 p.m., and I rushed to Chelsea Street to meet with my students. Jacob and the community workers arranged a classroom in the park, which was quite big with lots of open space. They arranged chairs for the kids, but there was a shortage, so some kids sat on the carpet that was placed on the grass. There were almost 3,000 kids sitting and waiting for me when I arrived. The kids were of all ages, starting from four and going to late teens. They had set up a microphone and three speakers, which were only 500 watts and not very good. They had spent most of their money to buy these accessories for me to teach the kids. I was very happy to see their response to my proposal, as I wanted these kids to have a great future and be successful in life.

The vast majority of the kids were eager to listen and learn as I started to talk. Though I was feeling hyper from excitement and nerves, I soon found a balance in me and started the very first sentence by saying, "I am very happy and glad all of you are here to learn and improve yourself. But I don't want it to always be this way. I am teaching you folks, but I want everyone to one day teach me about my ignorance." After hearing the opening statement, the kids' mouths were open and they started to whisper to each other; suddenly they hesitated to talk to me. Seeing their hesitation, I asked them, "I think you guys have some questions." Finally, one kid had the guts to stand up and ask me a question. His name was Yohance, and he was Jacob's son. He stood boldly and said, "We have heard in the church that 'a student is not above his teacher, nor a servant above his master,' and you are a master telling us to teach you one day about your ignorance." I was puzzled by his reasoning and said, "Do you have a Bible with you, Yohance?" He replied, "Yes, Master," and I said, "Give it to me." He handed it to me. I looked at the Bible in my hand, thinking that this was the first time I had ever held the Bible in my hands with curiosity, and I asked him, "Why did you carry the Bible with you to my class?" Yohance answered me, "It is the book of books, and when the world refuses to educate slaves, this is the only book that brings hope." I looked at him with great curiosity regarding his different degrees of wisdom and asked him, "Who called you slaves?" Yohance answered me, "You are the only white man who is nice to us and cares for us. I don't see anyone else being like that. They don't come here, eat with us, or smile." I replied, "You are all the chosen ones, and no one is a slave here. You are the future of this world, and I shouldn't hear anyone saying, 'I am a slave or broken, or poor.' If I see anyone doing that, I will not come here again."

Hearing this, the kids looked shocked. They were quiet for some time, and then they started to talk to each other. One kid stood up and said, "We will never ever say that in our life time, Master, and I speak on behalf of all these other kids." The kid who took the oath for everyone was again Yohance. I was happy to see that the children understood quickly and they liked me more for my knowledge; it is not that they wanted to say "I am a slave," it was that they didn't want to miss out on me coming to teach them. I looked at Yohance, and to answer his reasoning, I took to Matthew 10:24 and showed him the verse he quoted: "A student is not above his teacher, nor a servant above his master." I gave the Bible to him and asked him to read what he had said. He hesitated when I handed him the mic, but I said, "You are fine—just read it," and he gained confidence and read, "A student is not above his teacher, nor a servant above his master." I looked at him as he read the next line and he looked at me, unsure what I was asking? He read the next passage, Matthew 10:25: "It is enough for the disciple that he becomes like his teacher and the slave like his master."

I looked at Yohance and asked him, "What does that mean?" He read it a few times to really understand and said, "The teacher and the student are the same, like the slave and the master are the same." I asked him, "If the teacher and student are the same, and the slave and master are the same, then why do you call yourself a slave and call me sir and master?" His eyes grew wide and his mind started to become clear. I looked at all the kids and could see that they were gaining wisdom, because many of their eyes were filled with tears as they looked at me. Then Yohance asked me, "So if you and I are the same, then what should I call you?" I replied, "Just call me Oliver; that will be fine."

Yohance then asked me, "We are very pleased with your explanation, but you didn't answer my question." I asked him, "What question is that?" and Yohance replied, "How could we teach you one day about your ignorance?" I looked at him sternly and answered him, "You look like my mother, so you should know the Bible very well. Let me ask you to read this passage from the Bible, John 14:12." He turned to John and started reading, "Very truly I tell you, whoever believes in me will do the works I have been doing, and they will do even greater things than these, because I am going to the Father." He looked at me with more confusion, as did all the kids, who were all very confused. I started to explain. "Now, the Bible says you could do greater wonders than your master, provided you believe in the master. Why are there two sets of ideas, one says not equal and the other says greater?"

Every kid stared at me and there was absolute silence for a few moments. Then I started to talk. "Everyone is at the same level because we are all humans, and no one is the chosen one, which means under the sun we all stink. But if your inner sub-consciousness believes the one who teaches you, then you can become smarter and have more wisdom than the one who is teaching you, and you could fill the emptiness or so-called ignorance of the master." At this point, every kid started to clap, because they were happy to hear such an empowering message from me. After the class, all the kids were energized, and at eight o'clock, their parents came and picked them up from the park. Afterward I met Jacob and we reviewed the class.

Jacob: Did the children enjoy the class?

Me: It was wonderful. I enjoyed it a lot, but I have some questions for you.

Jacob: Ask me anything, man.

Me: Are all the kids Christians?

Jacob: Most of them are Christians. They are Catholic, Pentecostal, and Baptist. A few kids' parents still practice some ancient African religions, and we have some Islamic families also.

Me: Oh, I see.

Jacob: Why do you ask this, Oliver?

Me: Your son today, when I started teaching, raised a question from the Bible.

I explained everything to him that had happened. He was very happy to know that I had done a good job.

Jacob: I don't see any problem here.

Me: Yeah, there is no problem in it, but my concern is whether all the kids understood what I taught.

Jacob: Yes, they did. If they didn't, they will ask their friends, but always explain in very simple terms and they should have no problem understanding. But the best thing is that most of the kids understand English pretty well.

Me: Great! That is awesome. How is that? I just realized that I was addressing them in English and didn't know how many of the kids were non-English speakers.

Jacob: You are fine, man. They all understand English. The good thing America did was to train all of us in English for a year before we came here.

Me: That is cool. I will continue tomorrow.

That night Jacob took me to the family of one of the elders and we had supper there. Later, after chatting with them, I went home. What could I say about my first-day experience? My search started due to all these events. All the kids were eager to learn something, and I could see the passion in them to improve themselves, but there was no one to teach them. I saw the kids who live in super powerful countries or were from well-off families; they showed no interest in learning, but learned just to make their parents happy or to gain social respect. This community didn't even have enough proper chairs for the kids, and the chairs were not even the same color or style but with different designs and colors. Some kids didn't even have a chair and simply put a blanket on the ground, but they didn't mind and were still enthusiastic to learn. *That is the spirit,* I thought to myself that night. *They are real "Plato's kids." The grass was their bench and the skies were their answers.* I made Plato very proud that day. *I expanded the kids' thought much faster than the universe's expansion,* I thought to myself.

I was stunned at Yohance's answer: "It is the book of books, and when the world refuses to educate slaves, this is the only book that brings hope." A philosophy of hope, he had said. I admired and was proud to have him as my student. I had long refused to read the Bible because so many crimes had been committed in the name of religion, but I learned a noble truth of the other side of the Bible today: "The crusher uses the Bible as the source of power. The crushed also use the Bible as the destination for escape." Yohance was a genius, and I wanted to be his student. I vowed to buy myself a Bible the next morning, but of course my mom had tucked a Bible into my suitcase without my knowledge. Yet, I had to buy one myself to know what was in it.

I was surprised that I was able to counter Yohance's question with an answer from the Bible, because I had never read it even once in my life. I was even able to quote the correct passage and verse. My mother had forced me to learn it, but I had always neglected it. When my mom had her Bible studies, I always tried to sneak in and listen to what the heck they were talking about for an hour every day. I knew all the passages in the New Testament and a few from the Old Testament just from listening in to her Bible studies. One time they were talking about Matthew 10:24, and they were explaining how they are low and stupid compared with God and Jesus. But even though they read the whole chapter, they never read the next line after "It is enough for students to be like their teachers, and servants like their masters." I thought to myself how funny and silly these guys were, including my mom. After a month the Bible reading was from John 14:12, and they talked about what it meant to say they were greater than Jesus, and each one came with their answers. One said, "It means we will convert more souls than Jesus." Another said, "We can shut down skies and stars," and another said, "We can fly," and yet another said, "We can rescue more people than Jesus," and it went on and on. My mother said, "We will live longer than Jesus, probably close to ninety, but Jesus died at thirty-three." After listening to the conversations from the pseudo-intellectual Bible students, I laughed until my stomach ached. A simple piece of logic occurred to me: just read the whole sentence and paragraph and chapter and then talk about the subject and compare it when required. These people, so-called children of God, didn't know how to read a book to understand and interpret it. We were supposedly called the descendants of demons, because we know how to read a book to understand and interpret it correctly.

The reason I chose to read the Bible at this point is that these kids were very religious and I had to quote a passage every time I taught them something. I wanted to teach them religion, philosophy, science, technology, and computers. Now when I taught them I had to make sure to emphasize that all these philosophy, science, technology and computer concepts came from God; if they felt like my ideas didn't originate from God, they might choose to reject my teachings and me, and then they would never learn. But the most important thing was that there should be something in the Bible that made it unique for the ages, and this was the first time I explored this. I was happy that all the kids knew English, and although they had been treated badly by the American government, America had taught them English so that when they cursed, we Americans could understand what they were saying. *Freaking politician punks,* I thought in anger, *I had no mercy or kindness toward these people.* But I was here to help and guide them; the Bible hadn't delivered them from slavery, so I would do it. However, I would never push my agnostic/atheist ideas upon them and make these kids lose hope, because they believed, and it gave them some hope that there was a God watching over them. Let me speak the accurate truth and broaden their minds. If they still wanted to be with their religious ideas, I was fine with it, and I would still sail with them. Yet there is a truth about agnostics and atheists. They are the most liberal, freethinking, and kind-hearted people, often more so than religious people, because they are the ones who fight for equality and people's rights in the churches, streets, cities, and countries. The religious people are the ones who deny equality and people's rights in churches, streets, cities, and countries unless their views align with their religious views. Moreover, no atheist ever bombed a temple of worship in the name of God; it is the one who believes in God who does that.

I also wanted a better environment and better conditions for these children. I knew that we needed to buy good-quality chairs and enough of them for all the kids. We also needed to have a roof and blinds for the windows for the kids to be comfortable. Winter was near, and we needed a very good auditorium in the winter. A good sound system was also a requirement. If I had to list the things I required to help these people, I needed paper a mile long. But for now I needed to focus on the basic requirements. I wondered where I could go for money. I wanted some help, and I thought I could ask my friends' families. I had never asked them for help in my life, and I knew they would never say no to me. For the first time in my life, I wanted to use my friendships for enhancing these people's lives. No one ever understood what I was doing here now, so tomorrow morning I would have to call my mom and tell her. Then I needed to call my friends and explain this situation, I thought that surely they would be a great support to me.

The next day I got up at six in the morning and called my mom. I explained what I was doing here. She didn't even question me and said, "You are my son. This is the noblest project you could do for anyone. I completely understand and support you, Oliver." She said something that really caught my attention: "First you need to watch few movies, so that you can understand black people's history and their problems. It will help you be better and more responsible in helping them." I asked my mom what movies she was referring to, and she replied, "You should watch *Gone with the Wind*, Boyz n the Hood, *To Kill a Mockingbird* and *The Color Purple*." My mom is not a big movie fan, and this was the first time in my life she had talked about movies. I was surprised that she recommended them. I was glad she didn't ask me to watch *The Ten Commandments, Ben-Hur,* or *The Passion of Christ,* or any other religious-type films.

After talking to my mom I called Madison, who was very impressed about my decision. She thought I had become a revolutionary. She also said that she missed me on the weekends and was angry with me, but she understood that I was on a mission, and wanted to be a part of it. Then I called all my friends and explained what I was doing, but I never mentioned that I needed some help to improve these people's lives. I just outlined my plans, and everyone agreed that they also wanted to be a part of this mission with me. I told them I would call later that night and explain in detail.

My day started before I went to college. I wanted a Bible and rushed to a church in downtown Boston and bought a new one. Then I went to a video store to buy the movies recommended by my mom. I was very eager for the class to watch those movies, talk to friends, and teach the kids. My pulse was beating heavily, and as soon as my last class was over, I rushed to meet the kids, with the Bible in my hands for the first time. I took it from my bag and showed them that I had my Bible today, and every kid was happy and clapped their hands. Now they knew that I worked for God and not myself, and that I was part of them. After I spoke, I was thinking to myself, *If I were a politician, I would have been president of America, but me being a revolutionary I found favors in these little hearts.* Then one kid, who was eleven and had on a green T-shirt, stood and said, "My name is Imran Ali. I don't believe in the Bible. It is a white English man's book." I was stunned by his reasoning and looked at him and said, "Imran, all the kids here are black. The Bible is not a white English man's book" and the kid replied, "Oliver, let me ask a question. If it is not a white man's book, then ask the descendants of Queen Victoria's family to marry a black man or a black woman." His question caused me to think in ways I couldn't express, and I felt like this kid was one strong, stubborn kid. Yohance was standing behind him and shouted at the kid. I calmed him down. A few older people were also there. Everyone got mad and I told them to relax. I liked this kid, Imran Ali, and I asked him, "What do you want me to do? Buy a Quran for myself? Will that help you?" The kid replied gently, "You don't need one—just stop talking about the Bible. I thought you were a great man, Master Oliver, but you looked irrelevant when you carried the Bible in your hand." I realized what I was doing and said, "Let us forget about religion. I will teach you philosophy. It was my fault. I thought I wanted to be one among you." The kid looked at me and said, "You know philosophy? Do you know Plato?" I was surprised that this kid was so smart and said, "I know what I should know—I am Plato's son." The kid replied, "Then you should be more than two thousand years old. You are very funny, Master," and I said, "Wisdom is now making me look old, Imran." The kid replied, "Religion makes me look young, so that I can declare war and kill all my enemies." I was stunned by his answer and was sure about one thing: we cannot fool around with Africans anymore. Their time has come, and there are many genius minds there that are not heard. I was here to help them, and I admired this kid, Imran Ali; he had even made me stumble that day. I appreciated him so much, and we cheered him by clapping hands to encourage him. I put my Bible in my bag and said to myself, *I have to be who I am and never pretend. I am not really good at pretending anyway.*

I gave a brief introduction of philosophy to the kids, and I did the same thing that Purdhil did with me. All those kids were happy and excited to listen. I spoke about Eastern and Western philosophies. All their ears were opened with curiosity and anxiety, but only a few kids started to ask questions, and it became a very interactive course. That day the class went until nine o'clock at night and no one looked at the time. I had a very good dinner in a different house and went home earlier because I had to talk to my friends back home.

I called my friends and we held a conference call. I explained in detail my ideas and plans for this community. I needed money to build these people a small auditorium for classes, chairs, and a sound system. I asked them to ask their parents if they could do anything to help me or guide me to get this work done. They all appreciated my efforts and agreed to work on this and talk to their parents about it. After the call I wanted to watch a movie. I started with *Gone with the Wind*. It was quite long—about four hours. It was the first classic movie I had ever watched, and I learned something about the South slavery.

The next day I started with my usual routine, going to college and then on to teach the kids. After I came home from that day's mission, I had a call from Nikifor and Judah, saying that I needed to come home that weekend to meet all our families to discuss the funding we needed to raise for the kids' school. I was surprised, but they said they had already booked a ticket for me that weekend. I knew at that moment that they were my best and most honorable friends, as they got involved in this project and booked tickets in advance without even questioning me. I would miss my fun and excitement with these 3,000 kids, because I am now their caretaker and I valued all of them. Some of them were older than me, but still they were my kids. That weekend I felt like a father going far away to make money for the betterment of their lives. I was thrilled to go back to Wisconsin to meet my friends and their families, but it was a new experience for me to ask for money. In all my sixteen years I had lived a very merit-based life, and I had never asked for help from anyone. I was blessed through my father's name. The beautiful feeling about social work and charity is that you may have had all the riches in this world in your life and never accepted a penny from anyone and considered it a disgrace to ask anyone, but the moment you decide to help people and campaign to raise funds; you stretch your hands to ask everyone for money. The heart feels no limitation anymore; rather it makes your heart fill with delight that you can help the needy, and you perceive that you still have a great amount of innocence and compassion in yourself.

On Saturday evening they arranged a big gathering at Benjamin's home with all our families. When Benjamin's father saw me at the gates, he came running toward me and hugged and kissed me on my head and said, "Hail, Martin Luther King Jr. is alive." This greeting made my eyes fill with tears, because he compared me to the finest gentleman who ever lived in our country, a man who worked for equal rights and gave a new meaning and direction to the "Black Community". His words encouraged me, and as I looked into his eyes, I found one hidden factor in him. We were one big great family and no one ever knew the smell of color, he said to me, "I have black sweat in my body." And after a while I replied to him, "Thanks, Uncle, for addressing me from your inner soul as Martin Luther King, but make your thoughts clear. You will have better visibility in your eyes, and all the shades of color will be like one color." Benjamin's father said, "Yes, now I can see with my own eyes, and everything looks the same. You are the chosen one, Oliver. Let the living universe be your shield and your thoughts will be your sword." I didn't know what he meant. He too had addressed me as the chosen one, which I again refused to hear.

All our families were assembled, including my master, Purdhil. Purdhil looked at me with excitement about my exploring the world and saw me as a rebel leader. We all sat in the hall, lots of refreshments and snacks were served. There was a lot of food, but the very thought that went through my mind was *I should wrap it up and go to Boston and give it to the kids of Chelsea*. We enjoyed the snacks and refreshments, but everyone was quiet, although smiles and ebullience was noticeable on their faces. No one knew how to start the conversation, as this was an unusual occasion, but everyone was thrilled to be part of this mission of liberation. Madison, my sweetheart, finally started the conversation and gave an opening statement: "Oliver is a great person. That's why we all love him, and I love him more than anyone in this room." She is a character, always speaking from her heart and very innocent. Fay was sitting next to Madison and replied, "We all know it, Madison. We are not here for your love story." Everyone started to laugh loudly, and the room was filled with the sound of laughter. Madison felt very bad and looked at Fay. "You tricked me, Fay," she said, but Fay replied, "No, dear, I would never do that to you." Fay rubbed Madison's back, and they held hands and whispered and exchanged words, saying, "Sorry. I love you, dear" to each other. Then, slowly Sadie's father asked me, "How much money do you need, Oliver?"

Me: I don't know yet, Uncle. I need a tent, which is a bad idea, because within a couple of months winter will set in, so probably a decent auditorium for three thousand kids is what I really need, and a good sound system and seating.

Sadie's father: That will be expensive, Oliver.

Me: Definitely, yes.

Benjamin's father: Does anyone have a rough estimate?

Purdhil: Probably three million for a decent space for three thousand kids.

Benjamin's father: That's a lot of money. Oliver, let me ask you, why don't we talk to the government and the officials about this? I work for them and I have influence. We should also expose this to the world.

Me: That is a fair idea, but for now the media and politics favor and believe the government administration. We don't want to create another problem in this country.

Benjamin's father: Anyway, the school for those kids will be built in six months to a year, so it shouldn't be too long a wait.

Me: All the Chelsea people have wasted their life for a year here and it is not guaranteed that there will even be a school after an entire year. Even if they build the school, there will be no proper education for them, and they will provide third-rate teachers.

Fay's father: What do you mean by "proper education," Oliver?

Me: They will be converting the Chelsea neighborhood completely for these immigrants, and they will slowly start a school for education. After a year or more they will allot green cards, which mean they will be able to do anything in this country. Since all the parents are not educated, the government will offer very-low-paying jobs, and the kids will be placed in an education system worse than public school. After a generation that neighborhood will be crime ridden, rife with violence, drugs, and homicides, and it will become a slum or a war zone.

Fay's father: I see your point. So your initiative will really help the kids.

Me: Yes, Uncle, I will teach them about computers, technology, and philosophy, which will open their minds. When they become legal, they will be wiser, and they can go to any school and college they like. I want these kids' generation to do better. I don't want them to be working in gas stations, cleaning toilets, babysitting, cleaning houses, polishing shoes, sweeping roads, and making Boston look like a shining silver plate, with the center of the plate made up of minds of intelligence, and the outer edges of the plate made up of black men's wasted intelligence.

Benjamin's father: You are right, my son.

Ejaz's father: Before that, Oliver, do we have space to build?

Me: Yes, the park is very big and only half of the park is being used. The rest is a wasteland, so we could use the wasteland to build on.

Ejaz's father: Could we obtain the funds, guys?

Saide's father: Yes, we could—it shouldn't be a big deal.

Judah's father was quiet for the entire conversation and then proceeded to give us a different perspective.

Judah's father: Oliver, the estimate is wrong. You are focusing on three thousand kids, but how about teaching all the fifty thousand people including the kids?

Me: You mean fifty thousand people? Why them, Uncle?

Judah's father: Think of it this way, Oliver: the kids are going to benefit from it and it will take some time for them to graduate and start earning money. In the meantime, these people will still be doing low-wage jobs to support themselves and their kids.

Me: Yes, I see your point, Uncle. That is a great way of thinking, but do you mean the parents have to go to school before the kids start to grow-up?

Judah's father: No, you could enlighten with the basics, and once they have a solid foundation, they could earn a part-time degree studying from home part time while they still do their jobs. After three to five years, they'll have a degree and can apply for a decent job, and in turn the parents will also be educated. So their kids will be well trained, and within five to ten years all their lives will have changed.

Sadie's father: That is a great idea. Do you agree, Oliver?

Me: Well, I never thought in that direction, but thanks, Uncle—yes, I agree, we could do it.

Judah's father: That means we should need more than three million dollars—probably closer to six million. But do we have space for building such an auditorium there, Oliver.

Me: The wasteland will be sufficient for three thousand kids, but next to the wasteland there is an empty garage and lots of free space —probably three to five acres of land.

Judah's father: Then we're good to go. But we need to buy that piece of land from the owner.

Benjamin's father: So we should collect money, and everyone should contribute what they can. Before that, tonight we should have a grand dinner. I have arranged a different style of food from Costa Rica. Let's enjoy the night.

As usual, we had a great night with food and drinks. All the elders were talking about how much money they could raise for this project. My friends also wanted to be part of this program, and decided they would come to Boston on alternate weekends; they each wanted to teach and share their knowledge. I happily invited them, because any help would make the kids' lives better. The weekend passed and my friends' families contributed the best they could. Judah's father donated $3 million, Purdhil and He-Ran gave $200,000, Ejaz's father gave $250,000, Aika's father gave $500,000, Fay's father gave $600,000, Sadie's father gave $1 million, Benjamin's father gave $300,000, Shu's father and my mom gave $100,000 each, Nikifor's father donated $200,000, and Madison's father gave $400,000. So, altogether we had nearly $6.5 million, which meant we had an extra half million dollars. Judah's father and Benjamin's father wanted to buy the piece of land from the owner, so they worked to find the owner of the garage. They found out that the piece of land belonged to a gentleman named Vernon Paul. He was a wealthy African American who owned many buildings in Boston. He was a multimillionaire, and Benjamin and Judah's father convinced them to buy the land for a lower price.

So the following Wednesday, Judah and Benjamin came to Boston along with their fathers to see Vernon about buying the land. Vernon had a large, magnificent house in downtown Boston with fifteen servants. Everything in the house we viewed as a sign of prosperity. While we waited for him to meet us, we sat on a large couch and sipped drinks out of silver cups. Then Vernon walked into the hall and greeted everyone saying, "Hello." Vernon was more than six feet tall and wore a suit with large gold chains outside his shirt and a big gold watch with a smoking pipe in his hand.

Vernon: Welcome, everybody. What can I do for you?

Benjamin's father: I am Kadin Gail.

Vernon: Your fame precedes you. I am happy to meet you.

Judah's father: I am Dr. Enoch.

Vernon: One of the most influential men in the Jewish community.

We all introduced ourselves and greeted him.

Benjamin's father: We are here because we want to buy the piece of land that you own in Chelsea.

Vernon: Do you mean the garage that is next to the park?

Benjamin's father: Yes, sir.

Vernon: Oh, that is my family's property. I cannot sell it.

Benjamin's father: Why?

Vernon: My great-grandfather was a mechanic. He worked in that garage and was a hard worker. His boss gave it to him as a gift, as he had no children. Then my great-grandfather was smart enough to multiply his money, and he bought many properties all over Boston.

Benjamin's father: That was very great of him. But could you sell it to us to build an auditorium for the African immigrants?

Vernon: Oh, for those poor bastards?

We all looked at each other with surprise and felt a little upset by his words.

Judah's father: Yes, for those poor people, sir. Your help would be greatly appreciated.

Vernon: I don't think I can do it because it is a memorial for my family. I have to say sorry.

Judah's father: Why can't you consider our request? We beg you to give it some thought.

Vernon: Maybe I could own the land and you could build an auditorium on it?

Judah's father: That would be fine with us.

Vernon: But I need money to build on my land.

Judah's father: What? You need money? Are you crazy, man?

Vernon: Yes, it is my land. You could build on it, and I will not question or break a brick from the auditorium for three years from the day it is built. But I need ten million dollars for it.

Benjamin's father: What? Ten million dollars? Just for a short-term lease? That's too much money.

Vernon: That is how it works.

Benjamin's father: We are just asking to buy the land to help some poor people and change their lives. We are not doing business on it.

Vernon: I love the law of nature. I hate weakness; only the strong survive.

Judah's father: You sound like Adolf Hitler.

Vernon: Maybe, but I have my own principles. That is how I work.

At this point Benjamin's father was getting angry.

Benjamin's father: We should be proud to help a fellow black man. Why are you so indifferent and biased to them?

Vernon: It's not my problem. Why the hell did they leave Africa? They should have stayed there.

Benjamin's father: Our government brought them here, and now their future is in question because of the politics that are going on here, so we wanted to help them by providing them with a better education and improve their lives.

Vernon: I don't care, man. If you are born poor and stupid, that is your problem. I am a businessman, and I don't deal with any sentiments or charity crap. I am strong, and I am winning.

Benjamin's father: Let me ask you something: Did you really inherit all these properties by yourself? No, Vernon, there was a British gentleman and his wife who owned the garage, and your great-grandfather was working for him, as a free black man, for almost forty years and since they didn't have any kids, they gave your great-grandfather all their wealth. They owned not only the garage but eight buildings in the city of Boston, and they gave everything to your great-grandpa for no price. And what did your whole family do? Did you expand? No, you're still sitting with the same eight buildings and the garage and spending your life on it.

Vernon: Seems you have done a lot of research on me, Mr. Kadin Gail.

Benjamin's father: What do you think? I am a cop, and I heard that you are hard-hearted and ruthless, and I guess I had to see it with my own eyes. If those old people showed no mercy to your great-grandpa, you would be a thug in the streets today. So when and where did the law of nature affect you? Vernon was silent, and his face shrank like a bee.

Vernon: It's true: I was lucky enough to inherit someone's money.

Benjamin's father: You call it luck. I call it mercy for the weak.

Vernon: Okay, what money could you offer me?

Judah's father: Maybe two to three million.

Vernon: As I said, I will lease it for three years, and after that we can re-negotiate. So my final offer is three million dollars.

Judah's father: After three years if you want the place, what will you do with the building? We need to spend lots of money on it.

Vernon: If I want to retain it, I will pay the market price to you.

Judah's father: That is fair enough.

We left Vernon's house and rode back to my apartment. On the way, Benjamin's father asked Judah's father, "Are you crazy, man? We are spending three million just for leasing, and it's only three years?" Judah's father replied calmly, "He seems like a heartless guy who doesn't show any courtesy to anyone, but let us start working on it. We have three years. Things will change." Benjamin's father replied, "You know better, Dr. Enoch. I trust you. I didn't know this guy was worse than a demon." I asked Judah's father, "How much time will it take for us to build the auditorium" and Judah's father replied, "We are working on it and will keep you posted, Oliver."

They all left that same day, and the next day I went to teach the kids. When I arrived, I found the kids and the elders waiting for me, and I asked them why they were all there. Jacob replied, "We heard that the kids learned a lot from you and they like the way you teach. We had the same thought—that we could join with the kids and learn something every day. Of course, we will attend only if that is fine with you, Oliver." I replied, "I have no problem with it and am glad that I am helpful, but you guys will have to stand while I am teaching, and I hope you all can hear my voice, because the sound system is not loud enough to reach all the way to the back." Jacob replied, "That is fine, Oliver. We will squeeze in and stand." I taught the class that day and the kids and the elders were happy to hear and learn from me. After the class, I explained the situation about building the new auditorium, and they were excited to hear the news.

That weekend, I taught on Saturday and after the class Jacob and a few elders invited me for dinner. It was me along with six elders, but we all got along well and enjoyed each other's company. Then Jacob pulled out a bag and gave it to me, and I asked, "What is it?" Jacob replied, "Open it and see." I opened the bag and saw a pile of money bursting out. I asked him what it was and he replied quietly, "It is for you, Oliver."

"Why did you give me money?" I asked in surprise. One of the elders replied, "We are Africans."

"So?" I asked.

The elder replied, "We don't want anything free from anyone. We feel pride that we paid the money for what we received." Jacob added, "You are teaching everyone and it requires a lot of effort and your time, so we have collected some money to pay you." I looked at Jacob and saw that inside the bag were lots of bills. "There seems to be lots of money. How much is in here?" Jacob replied, "It is $250,000."

"What! Where did you get the money?"

Jacob replied, "Each member contributed five dollars each, and there's fifty thousand people here."

"It's a lot of money, Jacob. But do you guys have enough money to survive?" I said in shock. Jacob replied, "We get food rations, utilities, toiletries, medical, and fifty dollars a month stipend for expenses." I looked at all the other elders and Jacob. "Do you want me to really take it?" One of the elders replied, "If you respect and honor us, you should take it. We will be very happy if you take it. It will help you in some way."

I did not say a word. I took it and went home. I was very proud of those people. My first salary and paycheck was $250,000. I couldn't believe it. Yes, I said "salary and paycheck," but my real intention was to help them at no cost. I took the money to make them feel honored and proud. Now I had a quarter-million dollars in my home, and I didn't know what to do with it. The very first thought that came to my mind was that I had to pay my taxes. Yes, I had to pay the IRS taxes on the money that I had earned, so I decided that on Monday morning I would go visit a tax auditor and pay my taxes.

That night I couldn't sleep. What could I say about all these events that happened? My search started again. Where could I start my search? This had begun when I told all my friends and their families that I had the desire and passion to help these people, and no one said no. With my way of thinking, we are all connected to the same energy level. That is why I adored all my friends and their families very much. But the greeting from Benjamin's father was right calling me, "Hail, Martin Luther King Jr. is alive." Yet I felt that I would have helped anyone in this situation, no matter what color, race, or ethnicity they were, or what language they spoke. In any condition, I would have done the same thing. They could have been Mexican, Columbian, Jewish, German, Indian, Pakistani, Native American, Sri Lankan, Burmese—anyone in this world who is oppressed, my voice would be there. I realized that color was not the main issue; it was one set of people putting the other down. Even Jewish fair skinned people were victimized by the Germans and Russians during World War II. Rather than Benjamin's father saying, "Martin Luther King Jr. is alive," he should have said, "A real human with a good soul is alive." This greeting would have made me more comfortable.

In regard to the school, everyone gave almost all the money they could—personal savings, loaned money, they gave with their full heart. I never personally asked how they made their money or how much money was left for them after giving, because it was not an ethical question; all I knew was that they didn't steal or lie or loot. My mom gave $100,000 and I asked her how much was left for us. She replied, "I gave three-fourths of my saved money." I said, "Thanks, Mom, but what made you give all this money? We are not investing in any business, so we won't have any returns." Mom replied, "And if anyone gives even a cup of cold water to one of these little ones, because he is my disciple, I tell you the truth, he will certainly not lose his reward." I asked where she had found that phrase and she replied, "It is Matthew 10:42." I just smiled at her and said, "You gave because you know that you will have a reward" and my mom looked at me and answered, "Yes, but not money—there are better things." Her answer made me realize that she is not a materialistic person, which is why I loved her, but I wondered, *Can anyone in this world really help anybody without any expectations?* It may be money, love, land, salvation, peace, friendship, or payback. I wanted to create a world where there was no expectation attached to any deed that is done. I am not defending or breaking the law of nature, which has its own cause and effect: karma. Yet if my idea was to build a world with "a mind without expectation," then where did karma fit? I appreciated all my friends and their families' contributions, but they gave money to help somebody they didn't know, the Chelsea people. The thought behind it was that they never wanted me to feel bad and their own philosophical version of receiving. All I was looking for, and continued looking for, was a perfect body and mind.

Vernon was one of the beasts I liked to get introduced to in such an important situation, where my group was sacrificing and this guy remained greedy for money. But here with this situation Benjamin's father made the right statement: "We should be proud to help a fellow black man. Why are you cruel to them?" If you don't know the feelings of your own people with the same instincts, which is an essential attitude, how could you ever understand other people with different backgrounds? And no one ever understood what sort of person he was, yet they all knew he was greedy. But this is not the case. The general and widely adopted and practiced American attitude, "Let us hammer and exploit the newcomers." This applies not only to Vernon, but to every color and culture that comes to America: the old visitors take advantage of the new visitors. We should know in this country we are all visitors, and we should help everyone who comes to this country. All they have in their mind is *I learned the hard way, so why not them? What could I get from him? How could we use him? How could I make him toil while I relax?* Again and again, this country continues in this cycle with torpid senior citizens and generations.

The second thing about Vernon is, he is the next Michael Jackson, assuming him blessed and part of the Aryan race by changing his skin color. He behaved in a way in which he was transformed from one race to another. I am happy when people act, behave, and live with self-respect, but he pretended he was aristocratic, from a royal bloodline, a king's heir, he felt entitled because of his money, and that is the real problem. If you remove the money from him, his spirit will be weaker than a mouse. He said, "The weaker should die and the stronger will live." He thought he was smart to use philosophy "survival of the fittest," yet he and his family didn't survive because they were fit, but because an old wealthy British couple didn't have anyone to give their wealth to and gave it to one person they'd known for a long time. So honestly it should be called "survival of the transformation." When someone doesn't give to the weak, the weak would be dead, which means the earth would have no inhabitants. I thought the funny thing about Vernon was that he received eight buildings from his beneficiary and still had only the same eight old buildings, with renovations and upgrades to make them state-of-the-art. He never multiplied the wealth or increased his holdings because he doesn't deserve to be given such wealth. But I think Vernon and his family must have had some business acumen to retain their properties for so many years, because a fool with any amount of money given to him will be poor within a few years. In this way I have some respect for Vernon, as he did try to retain his wealth and lifestyle and not lose it.

To build our school, we had no choice, so we leased the land for $3 million for three years. But I am very proud of Jacob and his people. They gave me $250,000, a quarter of a million dollars, for teaching them. I didn't want to take it, but they said they would feel embarrassed to get help from me without contributing something. These people in Chelsea are classic, high-class, aristocratic, royal bloodline, and possess King's attitude. They wanted to pay so that in the future no one could say, "Because of Oliver's free teaching and hard work these people in Chelsea became rich and prosperous." No matter how much money a person has, the attitude you have toward yourself is very important. I am very proud of all the people from Africa, a very proud and respectful race. So to support their attitude and make them majestic in their looks and thoughts and when they walk to my class, they should say to themselves, "We have paid Oliver the education fees." But I vowed I wouldn't take their money every month. Each family received $50 a month, and many families had two or more kids. The lesson is, "If your intention is true, money will follow and you don't need to chase money." Now I had to pay taxes to the IRS, because I didn't want them to be chasing me, and moreover it is the law that we pay taxes. But my father once thought that if we give money for charity or social services, we should have a tax-deductible.

So I decided the best way to use my money. I could buy the kids the books that they needed, and maybe build a small library with all the essential books, at least three copies for each student. I decided to spend $100,000 on this goal. I thought this would help them and they could not ask me, "Why do you give the money back to us in books?" It was my money and I could spend it on whatever I wished. I did a calculation and after paying all the taxes and buying these books, I figured I would be left with $90,000 to $100,000. While I was thinking about what to do with this money, I had another idea. This was my first earned money, and in reality I knew I should give all the money to Purdhil, as he had done for us. What could I get him? A car—probably a Cadillac, a BMW, or some other expensive model. But he was a man with great understanding, and right now I wanted to use the money so all of my friends could fly every week to join me to teach the kids and work with the people in the community. I could use this money for their airfare. Their families had already spent a lot of money on contributions, so I knew I should help to lower the burden. We could get discount tickets for a bulk purchase for the weekends for a year for all nine of my friends. Yet even after that expense, I had enough money to buy Purdhil a $3,000 gold locket with a photo of him and He-Ran in it. When he received it, he was delighted and I explained my reasoning and apologized to him. He said I had made the right call, but I promised him that when I became successful, I would buy him a private jet, and he well deserved it.

My life looked better and better every day, and I was becoming more responsible. I knew that very soon I would make all humans on this earth become their own version of Superman. The search of my life to be a superhero hadn't been completed yet, and I knew it was one step at a time, because we lived in a complex world. We also got approval from the state government to build the building on the park's wasteland. The construction started quickly, within ten days. They built a tent on half of the space and engaged three times more workers to get the auditorium constructed. Judah's father was so smart that he hooked this project up with the charity organization TUAD, so we had lots of people volunteering to help build it. All the Chelsea people joined in and helped in building the auditorium as well. The budget went over $6.5 million, and TUAD funded more money to keep building. The whole project was a great miracle, and built within three months. The TUAD organization also contributed lots of books to the library, so now we had a mini-college library. The auditorium was well equipped with an air conditioner, heater, toilets, water supply, projector, good sound system, seating for everyone, and additional space for an extra five thousand visitors. I started this project with just a simple step, by walking into their life, and now I was building them a future, a future with light and hope.

Every weekend my friends came to help me in teaching their subject of expertise in fields like medicine, fashion design, art, law, banking and finance, business, electronics, chemical and nuclear engineering, biology, and the history of religion. We all stayed together at my home, and because I had a one-bedroom apartment I had to buy three extra beds for my friends. I was so surprised when I learned that a very special person wanted to join us in teaching: it was Purdhil. He also wanted to join us for this mission and he came alternate weeks as a guest professor. He would watch me teach and told me that he enjoyed me teaching rather than him, because a good master always enjoyed their students teaching others. Since he was the guest professor, he addressed the people for an hour, asking questions and enlightening them with different answers and making them think radically about new ideas. He appreciated my work as well, and one time said, "You teach better than I do, and these days I learn a lot from you, Oliver. I am very proud of you as my student, and I promise I will never ever get a better student than you." I replied, "Without you this day I would have been in the dark and still clouded with thoughts of uncertainty."

My car sat undriven most of the time. I cleaned it every few days, started the engine, moved between streets, and parked it in the garage. When Purdhil visited, he would take me for a drive through Boston, but that was about as much as I did with the car. It was my dad's car and I took care of it, but I wanted to drive around Boston and sometimes wanted to take Madison and my friends. But I was still only sixteen and within a few months I would be seventeen, and then I would have to wait for a year to drive myself. So, I walked most places. One cold winter evening, I was walking back from Chelsea to my home and saw a gentleman looking at me. He waved his hand and called, "Hello." I replied, saying "Hello!" He looked like a Native American, almost seven feet tall and well built. He walked toward me and said he needed to talk to me. I looked at his face, and he looked very curious and timid, but he was a stranger, and I hesitated before replying, "Yes, sure, please." Since it was cold outside, I invited him into my home. I gave him some tea and asked him why he needed to talk to me. He introduced himself as Demonthin. He told me he had been watching me for the past three months, watching as I went to college, helping the people in Chelsea and driving my car in and out of my garage. He had watched my friends come visit on the weekends and watched as we all went to Chelsea and so on. "Why are you watching me? Do you need some help?" I asked him, surprised by his revelation. He replied, "No sir, I was very inspired by your personality and I wanted to be your friend."

"Sure, Demonthin," I replied. "I am honored to be your friend." I asked him, "Do you live by yourself? Do you have a family?" Demonthin replied, "I have no family and I live by myself."

"What do you do for a living?" I asked, growing concerned for myself. He told me that he worked in a gas station close to Chelsea. I asked him if he wanted to come down and study in Chelsea, and told him he was welcome to join my classes. He replied, "Thank you very much. You seem to be a great young man. I wanted to study with the others and I have a few friends with me. Could I bring them too?" I replied "Yes, sure, please. Who are they?"

Demonthin: They are my friends and my people.

Me: What do you mean by "your people"?

Demonthin: They are Native Americans. I don't have any other friends.

Me: Why is that?

Demonthin: No one ever talks to us. We are so-called Indians, and we spend our time by ourselves.

I felt very bad for him. All I could see was that he was lonely and needed some new friends.

Me: Bring all your friends to the school and you'll have new friends among almost fifty thousand people. And all my friends from Wisconsin will also be your new friends.

He was thrilled and held my hand.

Demonthin: Sir, I am so happy. You are a true gentleman.

Me: How many friends do you have?

Demonthin: I have almost ten friends with me.

Me: Very nice—bring them all.

Demonthin: But could I return the favor somehow, because we are ethical and senstive people.

Me: You sound like the people from the Chelsea community! (I didn't want to debate him.) What could you offer me?

Demonthin: I could drive you to college and to Chelsea, and where ever you want, Master.

Me: What do you mean? A chauffeur or a driver?

Demonthin: Yes, sir.

Me: No, no, man that is not a good idea.

Demonthin: I have a driver's license, and I see you all the time. You have no one to drive you and you commute a lot. It will help you save time, and you could spend more time with the kids and their people in Chelsea.

Me: You are a very bright man, Demonthin. You made a deal with no debates. Yes, you could, but I want to make sure it doesn't impede your job.

Demonthin: I've worked at that gas station for almost twenty-five years, and they are flexible with me, taking breaks here and there. I can do anything for you, Oliver.

Now I had a chauffeur to drive the car when I came back from my day's work. In the morning he would come to my home, clean the car, drive it to my college, and drive it from my college to Chelsea. Then at night he would drive me home, like I was some kind of prince in the backseat. I was also pleased because we had ten new students in our class and I was happy to be teaching some Native Americans. I introduced Demonthin's friends to my friends, and they all got along. The people in Chelsea also liked Demonthin and his friends. Demonthin and his friends brought cookies, chocolates, and candies to the kids. I started to build a very good friendship with Demonthin, and he became almost like my caretaker. He would stay with me to have dinner in Chelsea and we would eat food from different homes every day. Sometimes Demonthin came to my home and cooked some Native American dishes and we would chat into the night.

Of the ten friends Demonthin introduced me to, three were women, and one of them was married. The other two ladies were still single, and the lady I was interested in talking to was named Quanah. I also learned that Demonthin had a crush on her. I asked Demonthin, "Do you like her and want to marry her?" He replied, "Yes, boss, I love her" but he was too shy to tell her that he loved her. Demonthin was another noble man, a gentleman and a very down-to-earth person. We helped him get together with Quanah and it worked as expected. He was now dating her. My friends and I had a very different feeling when we hung out with Demonthin and his friends because it made me aware that Native Americans should be taken care of and that they needed attention. I was on my heart's path to love and nurture these proud people. During this time I also got my first part-time job at MIT. I earned $2,500/month to work with Professor Gavin Higgs on his research project building artificial intelligence, combining databases and operating systems into one single piece of software that stored ten times more data than other databases. It was a very critical project. Meanwhile my grades were all A's and my GPA stayed at 4.0, and moreover, Gavin Higgs was very hopeful that I could assist in this project. The project was called Veleidade X, and it was for his fourth and final PhD. I was happy to take this project on, as it would give me more visibility and importance in my career. It was not much of a burden on my time because I had more flexibility in attending my regular classes. Because I was working on Gavin's project, I felt like I could do whatever I wanted at the university. I was just seventeen and I was at the best college in the world, with a prestigious part-time job, a volunteer chauffeur, best friends, great families, my accomplishing students, and, not to forget, a wonderful girlfriend.

A year passed with all my present memories and wonderful gifts that I received from everyone, and then I turned eighteen. One of the best events during this time was that Demonthin got married to Quanah. This was the first wedding that I had attended outside of Wisconsin. The wedding was in Chelsea, and our families and my friends came for the wedding. It was not traditional Native American dress and costumes; rather Demonthin wore a suit and Quanah wore a long, white gown. For the wedding, Demonthin and Quanah's families came from South Dakota. The ceremony was interesting because I never knew until that day that Demonthin and Quanah had their own religion and their own God, known as Wachabe (it means "Black Bear," which signifies a guardian, a symbol of long life, strength, and courage) and they belonged to a tribe known as Sioux-Osage. At the wedding ceremony, they exchanged rings, made a vow and said prayers to the Wachabe God. The reception was filled with music, and everyone danced a mix of traditional and contemporary dances. The wedding was very unique because the majority of the people in Chelsea, our families and friends, had no knowledge about these ceremonies and everyone seemed to enjoy them. Demonthin and Quanah and their friends and families did a Native American dance in their traditional dress, like breechcloth, and the men wore war shirts and the women wore skirts and leggings, moccasins, feathers on their heads, and pearls on their necks. The whole performance was extremely colorful. Everyone enjoyed the dance, and in turn the African people danced in their traditional costumes to welcome and praise the newly wedded couple.

One thing I cannot forget about this ceremony is that they crowned me. Yes, they crowned me. Demonthin and Quanah crowned me as the best man of the wedding with the black bear head. It was very strange and I asked them why they did it. They replied, "Once every million years Wachabe is born, and when we find him, we should honor him at the wedding as the best man and crown him with a black bear head." I asked, "How do you know it is me?" and they replied, "That is a secret and we have preserved it for years, and that secret sign has never failed us."

I honestly don't know what they meant, but they insisted on calling me Wachabe, a god or guardian, a symbol of long life, strength and courage. My other good news was that I found out all my friends had passed their senior year of school with stellar grades, and all were admitted into the finest colleges in America. Aika was going to attend Princeton University to study electronics and engineering, Nikifor was going to Stanford for chemical and nuclear physics, Judah was attending Yale for medicine, Fay was going to pursue her biology career at CalTech,

Ejaz was going to study finance at the University of Pennsylvania, and Benjamin was going to study forensics at the University of Michigan. Shu would be studying business at Columbia University in New York, and Sadie was attending Brown University for research in philosophy and religion. Madison, my love, got into Harvard for art and design. Everyone got a scholarship from Fay's father from HSA (Helix Sigma Axis). We were all very thankful for Fay's father for the expensive scholarships he got for us, and gave the cheer, "Long live Garlen!" I was raptured on this day because we declared and proclaimed that we would be successful in our life so that we could all change the world.

The third-best news was that the elections were over and all the people in Chelsea got their paperwork as permanent residents. They finally got their green cards. Now they were not stuck in this labor camp, and they were free people in America. The government showed them favors this time and it was their job to explore this country. I asked them to leave, but they said they needed a degree and needed to learn more from us. So they all found jobs with steady wages in Boston and applied for home tutoring. The government built a public school in Chelsea, and all three thousand kids attended the regular school now.

To celebrate this special day, we had a grand feast in Chelsea, since everyone lives in Chelsea, with our friends and family, Demonthin and Quanah, and all their friends and family. For the feast we had a unique style of food. It was a kind of Middle Eastern cuisine because we didn't want to choose between European and African foods. The party was wonderful, with dancing, lots of diverse conversation, traditional games and everything that we found fun. The most interesting part was the conversation with Jacob. Jacob had a few drinks and was happy that day, and he asked with great confidence about my philosophy. I asked him, "How is the food?" Jacob replied, "It's delicious, man. I never had this type of food before; this is the best feast I've ever had." I asked him, "Do you know what type of food it is?" and he said, "Is this the philosophical question you wanted to ask me, man? Oh my God, it is Middle Eastern, man." I asked him, "How many countries are there in the Middle East?" Jacob looked at me. "Is it payback time, man?" I asked again, "Do you know or not, Jacob?" Jacob replied, "I know, man. I will write it down for you." He pulled a small piece of paper from his pocket and started writing, but he wrote only a few countries: "Iran, Iraq, Palestine, Syria, United Arab Emirates, Yemen, Kuwait, Jordan, Lebanon, Oman, and Turkey." He gave it to me and I looked at it and asked, "Do you know exactly what the Middle East is, Jacob?" He replied, "Yes I do—the place where we get oil." I answered him, "Hmm, not exactly, but *Middle East* is a very misunderstood term. It is the place where Asia, Africa, and Europe's landscape meet. It is well known as Eastern Asia. But some references say that it is Eurasia and Africa and of the Mediterranean Sea and the Indian Ocean. So, in general, Middle Eastern countries consist of Bahrain, Cyprus, Dubai, Egypt, Iran, Iraq, Israel, Jordan, Kuwait, Lebanon, Oman, Palestinian, Qatar, Saudi Arabia, Syria, Turkey, United Arab Emirates, and Yemen." Jacob then declared, "Whoo! Does Egypt also fall under the Middle East countries category?" I replied, "Yes, very much, sir."

I started to explain, "Did you know that there is something called the great Middle East also?" and Jacob answered, "No, I didn't know. What does it mean?" I replied, "It is the Middle East and North Africa, Afghanistan, and Pakistan, which means usually all the Muslim countries in one big view, but some people include the territory of Central Asia and the South Caucasus, meaning other countries like Sudan, Tunisia, Morocco, Libya, Pakistan, Afghanistan, Algeria, Kazakhstan, Kyrgyzstan, Armenia, Azerbaijan, Comoros, Djibouti, Eritrea, Georgia, Western Sahara, Uzbekistan, Turkmenistan, Tunisia, Tajikistan, Sudan, Somalia, Morocco, and Mauritania." Jacob looked impressed. "You are the man! How did you know all these places?" I replied, "I am improving myself every day to know and understand about all people and culture in this world." Jacob was curious now and asked me, "What is the real point in asking me this question? I want to know." I replied, "Before answering that, could you tell me how many states are in the US and what they are? You got the green card right—you should definitely know it." Jacob shook his head and laughed. "Oh man, you are worse than the UCSIS. I just memorized this, man, but I always miss a few states, man." I answered him, "Memorizing is the beginning, but you need to contemplate what you memorized." Jacob asked, "Why did you ask me these questions? Let me grab some whiskey, man." He took a glass of whiskey and looked at me and asked, "Tell me, what is this all about?" I replied, "The philosophy of caring and love." I started explaining to him, "Jacob, you asked me this question first: 'How many countries are there in Africa?' I answered it, so you assumed that I really wanted to help you. You are a good man, Jacob but you don't know many of the neighboring countries near Africa. You should know, if you want to care for them. I brought this message to you. Rather than being the best patriot, be the normal human who cares for everybody. Now you have a green card, and I know you will start exploring and loving this country and later without any idea, claim that all the Middle Eastern countries are troublesome and terrorist. Never go with the Christian mind-set of some citizens in America, not accepting and cursing at people from the Middle East."

Jacob looked at me with some uncertainty and said, "I am beginning to understand, Oliver. Sorry, man. I never thought about my neighboring countries. I guess I was selfish all the time, telling myself I am black and

I am Christian. But now I understand the world has different colors and different beliefs. There are many people who think they are cursed, but being cursed is in the mind." I replied, "You got it, my man and you will understand it better as time progresses." Jacob then asked me, "Do you mind if I ask you a question?"

"Shoot, shoot, man," I answered and he said, "I know you love Madison a lot. Will you marry her?" I looked at him in a funny way and asked, "What's your point, Jacob?"

"She loves you too, man, and you guys will be the perfect match. Madison is a wonderful girl. I know, don't judge me, man, I know you, Oliver, and I care for you. You should have a great life." I held his hand and said, "Thanks, Jacob, I know you care for me. I love Madison, and she got admitted to Harvard. I am moving to a new two-bedroom apartment on Porter Street, and we are going to live together." Jacob shouted, "Oh my God, this is the best news the Lord could give me!" He went to look for Madison and grabbed her hands and brought her to me and asked to hold her hands. He blessed us, singing hymns and prayers and hugging both of us. Then he kissed us on the forehead and said, "I owe my whole life to both of you living together." Yes, Madison and I are going to live together. When we told our parents, they said just one thing: "It's the right thing to do. You guys shouldn't be asking our permission. You are made for each other. Go ahead, guys." I knew that Madison was my true love and would be with me always. I had to use the terms *boyfriend* and *girlfriend* now, as we were dating, but the reality was that I didn't want to know any woman other than Madison, because she was the chosen one for me.

Madison and I started to live together, and life was different in many ways because I assumed I had a family now. I felt more responsible. I had a woman who lived with me.. A year passed quickly, and everyone was doing great in their lives. But the routine stayed the same: go to college, teach the kids, friends come around on weekends, party, gathering—all our actions and deeds were very productive and fruitful. No worries. Life was flat and we had no bumps in our life until we received a call from Vernon, asking us to meet him. We were all scared, because it had been three years, and we didn't know what he was going to do with the auditorium. So Jacob (representing the people of Chelsea), Judah's father, Benjamin's father, Madison, Benjamin, Judah, and I went to his home to meet him. On our way to his home, we discussed what this crazy guy was going to say. When we got to his home, the front doors were open, and when we entered, we realized it was not the same place. It was quiet and almost looked like it was haunted. We saw a big picture of a boy and girl who were in their mid-twenties. The man looked more or less like Vernon, and the girl had pale brown skin and looked gorgeous. As we were looking at the picture and the house, a servant saw us and came rushing to us and asked, "Are you from Chelsea regarding the auditorium?" Judah's father replied to the maid, "Yes, miss" and the maid replied, "Could you all come with me to meet Vernon?" Judah's father said, "We will wait here in the hall to meet Vernon." The maid looked upset. "No sir," she replied. "Please come with me to meet in his bedroom." We all realized something was wrong with him and followed the maid to his bedroom. Nevertheless, Vernon was still a rich man, and his bedroom was twice the size of my apartment.

Vernon was lying in a double king-sized bed and as soon as he spotted us, he started to raise his body and attempted to get out of bed. But the nurse insisted that he mustn't move from his bed. He started to cough, and in a very low voice he said, "Come here, please, please, please." We were all moved and felt very sorry for him. It looked like something very serious was wrong with him. He asked the maid to give us chairs, and we all sat near his bed. He looked very swollen and grieved in his heart, and his eyes were wet with tears. He said, "I am very sorry for what I have done." Judah's father, being a doctor, went and checked his pulse and examined his eyelids and asked him, "Do you have cancer?" He replied, "Yes, I have leukemia." Judah's father asked him, "How much time have they given you?" He coughed and said, "Two weeks or less." Judah's father said, "I am very sorry to hear this, Vernon. We are very sad to see you looking like this. We will give you the money—whatever you asked us. We want the auditorium, please. The current market price is ten million, and we have it for you." Vernon said, "Your words are hurting me more than this disease." Benjamin's father said, "Sorry, pal, we didn't mean to hurt you. Probably at this time you need money. We thought it would help you. We are heavy-hearted to see you like this." Vernon replied, "That is so nice of you, Mr. Kadin. I want to confess before I die." Benjamin's father said, "You are not going to die. You will be fine," but Vernon replied, "I know my fate. Even if God gives me a chance, I don't want to live anymore. I lost everything I had."

Benjamin's father: Hey, hey what happened?

Vernon: I lost both my children in an airplane accident. My daughter and my son—they are both dead.

Judah's father: Is that the photo we saw in the hall?

Vernon: Yes, doctor.

Judah's father: No, no, no, that is terrible!

We all saw that Judah's father's eyes were filled with tears. He held Vernon's hands and was completely frozen and looking at him. All our eyes were filled with tears.

Madison: Where is your wife, Vernon?

Vernon: No, honey, she died years back, after my kids were born.

Madison: I'm very sorry.

Judah's father: What can we do for you, Vernon? We want to help you.

Vernon called one of his maids and said something to her and the maid went outside. Then Vernon asked us to wait for few minutes. Then we saw an attorney and an old man walk into the room. Vernon introduced the attorney as his personal attorney and the old man as his accountant. The attorney gave a file to Vernon, which Vernon opened. He gave a few papers to Judah's father and said, "This is the auditorium document. I have transferred it to the people in Chelsea, and now they completely own it." Hearing this we were all surprised and thanked him very much. Benjamin's father went to his bed and kneeled down and said, "I am very proud of you, Vernon. You are a good man." Then Vernon said, "Don't thank me so fast. I have more things for you guys." He took a bunch of papers and gave it to Benjamin's father and said, "I have transferred all my business properties—those eight buildings—to all the people in Chelsea for their welfare." We were all shocked and said, "You don't need to do this. Why did you do that?" Vernon replied, "By all my losses, pain, and my weakness I realized that this is the right way I should have lived." Benjamin's father asked, "Do you want us to sell all the buildings and share the proceeds with the community?" Vernon replied, "No, I have almost thirty-five thousand people working for me. Let all the buildings go to the Chelsea welfare, and whoever is from the African community is eligible to apply for jobs in my company working in those buildings." Judah's father said, "What will you do with the people who are working now?" and Vernon replied, "Almost sixty percent of my people are going to retire or leave the job soon because they know that I will no longer be here. They also know I have transferred the property to the Chelsea people, and I convinced them to stay there. I don't want to make those people's lives miserable to favor the Chelsea people. For the new jobs and to fill the vacancies of those who retire, the Chelsea people who are interested could take the jobs, and preference will always go to them. The profits that come through all these buildings will go to the welfare of the Chelsea people and to improve their neighborhood and lifestyle." Hearing all this, we all felt that he was doing something magnificent and selfless.

Not only did he take care of the people, but he returned the money that he had taken for the lease—$3 million—and also paid the construction cost of the buildings. So in very simple words, he gave back all the money that our families contributed. At first we regretted it, but he convinced us with his emotions, saying that if we didn't take this money, his soul would not rest in peace. He also gave a great deal of money to all his maids, accountants, and his friends who worked for him. Madison and all my friends, Jacob and his son, and I visited him every day for the last two weeks of his life, and he enjoyed our company very much. He was taking too many painkillers and his whole body ached, but when he saw us, all his pain vanished. Somehow he knew I was the one who started this project in Chelsea. He blessed me a lot, and he admired and wished good success for me and for all of my friends. We entertained him with jokes, movies, wheelchair excursions, playing chess, and sharing all our experiences. He said, looking at us all, "I thought I lost everyone in this world when I heard of my son and daughter's death, but when I see you guys here; I wish I could live longer, because now I have ten kids in the world." He liked to tell us this. He died like a king and everyone in Chelsea, all the people who worked under him, businessmen, our families and us, top officials from Boston, politicians, people from the church, and cops attended his funeral, and gave him a great send-off for his next journey.

The question I had in my mind was: How much money did Vernon have? He had almost $4.2 billion and all the buildings he had were very tall and large. Some were around eighty-five stories and a few of the malls and stores in those buildings belonged to Vernon as well. He was not rich, he was mega rich. On an average every month, he made profits of around $10 million from all of his assets. And all this money now went to people in Chelsea. The place that had looked like dust and rubble turned into the land of milk and honey. Now my search started again, it was always in me, but I was trying to understand all the events that happened in Boston and to Demonthin, a real good Native American. He was watching me for a while and then he volunteered to help me in some way. I saw something precious and very profound in his eyes- I knew he really wanted to help us and everyone else. He gave his time and life for me; he encouraged me. Yes, I needed some encouragement. It didn't mean I didn't get it from my family and friends, but encouragement from strangers sometimes gives us more inner bliss and a sense of reaffirming what we are doing in our life. Whenever he drove me in the car, I initially thought it was a chauffeur-and-passenger experience. But that was wrong. The experience was a Native American who knows America better than me, guiding me to know this country better and be part of it. Yes, we had to be part of them. They valued and respected nature with utmost earnestness. The nature that I saw with him is something amazing and different. When he drove the car, he talked to me and taught me to look at different things that we see every day, the birds that fly and disappear in the sky, the sun that kisses the water, the leaves that rustle in the air, the moon that is shy to look on the Earth, the stars that wink at us all the time, the Milky Way that creates bonds with ourselves, the little fish that jumps out of the water, that travels in the lines between life and death for a second, and everything that moves, stands, and smiles at you. I never thought to look into the nature around us until I met Demonthin. I used to watch tall buildings that reached the heavens, buses, trains, windows, doors, pavement, posters, paintings, and such things. He was the one who encouraged me to see and feel nature around us. I learned a lot from Demonthin. I could see him as my chauffeur, not because he drives the car for me, but because he drives my mind to be unified with nature.

We are all strangers in this country, and the real owners of this land were the Native Americans. We came and occupied their lands with wars and destruction. Then one traveler after other travelers came and settled here, claiming that now they own this soil. The worst thing is that these travelers came to America in the early days claimed themselves as son of the soil and forgot the real people whose spirits were still living in this very air, water and soil. Until Demonthin met me, he had not been confident. After he started to hang out with me, he regained his lost identity. I am Demonthin and I am Native American and I could do better in this life. After their downfall and rising of the aliens in this country, we didn't do much to them, except we kept them in reservations and preserved relics in museums. He was living with his three roommates outside Chelsea and loved this girl Quanah, but since he didn't have a proper place to live, he hesitated to even propose to her. My friends and I encouraged him in all aspects, and his confidence grew, we helped him to move to a new apartment and also spend money for a wedding. More than that, we taught him how to be confident and face this complex world. The reason he wanted to sacrifice something for me and the help he was doing not clear to him, but I knew what was driving him. He wanted people like me to walk into his people's lives and change how they live; to be an unexpressed support that he needs in his life and for everyone who needs the same. That is why he was impressed when he saw what I was doing in Chelsea, and he addressed me as Wachabe, the 'Black Bear' god, which referred to a guardian and courageous one. Demonthin is no more a stranger or an old monumental figure in this country; rather he is my friend and father from the native soil, and I was very proud to call him my father.

I will always be proud of my friends for getting into the top colleges in this country. They worked very hard to reach this goal. Apart from studies and exams, they sacrificed a lot coming down every weekend to Boston and teaching the kids in Chelsea. I thanked them every time they came in on the weekends and they realized I felt that I was burdening them. They even asked me to be honest if I felt that way, and I replied "Yes." I took this job and mission in changing the lives of the people of Chelsea, but my job and mission did not mean I had to force my friends into it. Even if my friends had told me they were not interested and didn't want to do it, I would have stayed in touch with them and I would have loved them the same way as I always loved them. But they didn't say no; one of the basic tenets of our friendship was to help somebody when they are in need. That is why I adored my friends, and why I admired Sadie when she commented about this mission. The more you share and teach others, the more ignorance you will find in yourself, and you will grow exponentially in what you are doing. They learned and studied their subjects diligently, but they were not certain if what they learned was right or wrong until they started teaching the subject. Then they became experts in their fields. I have to sincerely thank Fay's father for getting a royal sponsorship from HAS, as he was such a great man. He helped us to change not only our lives, but the lives of others as well.

I was also very proud of this country. No matter what silly and stupid things some Americans do out of ignorance, they gave out green cards in the end. That is America. I loved my country, because it was the only country that would admit and acknowledge anyone. Welcome to the land of foreign settlers. Now everyone's mission was over—yes, including mine, because now the people in Chelsea had a green card. It was their choice what they did with their life. Live a life of survival or live like a king? We all know this was the land of freethinking, where you chose which highway you wanted to go down: a highway to success and prosperity or a highway to failures and sufferings. However, the people in Chelsea were smart, and they chose the highway of success and prosperity. Yes, I was proud that I showed them the path to walk down. They all joined home tutoring to learn and earn a degree, which would be a base for them to start acquiring a better life. Now all the kids are going to public schools they have allocated and my friends and I are backing them with additional education and training. I heard a report now that the kids from Chelsea are brilliant and very competent and are getting many sponsorships for better schools in Boston. Of all the kids, my favorite one was Yohance. He is our sweet boy. Not only me but all my friends liked him, as he was like a little son to us. I really cared for him and had a very special place in my heart for him. The conversation with Jacob was very interesting because it was talk about a big list of countries. But the only point I tried highlighting to him is to care for everyone. He had an assumption that Africa is the only place continuously being victimized over a long time. Yet the reality is that everybody is a victim of something. The weaker in mind become slaves to some entity in this world. The main thing about Jacob was his ignorance, as he knew Egypt is in Africa, but he didn't realize it was also a part of the Middle East. That showed a moment of ignorance; of not knowing what you are expressing, talking about, and feeling. Rather than thinking about your problems, if you don't know your neighbors or fellow men and women, then how can you change it? The problem Jacob had was that he thought black men were the only suppressed people in this world, but there were so many millions of people who are non-black and living under suppression, like the Irish people. The lesson that I was trying to teach him was that, when you have a problem, think on a larger scale and your answer will be simple and will narrow down the exact answers.

Surprisingly, one of the nicest gentlemen I met in Boston turned out to be Vernon, and I initially called him a beast. I felt very bad about myself, as I learned one important lesson: whenever someone thinks only from his standpoint and thinks the other is evil, there is a problem. That is why I cursed him as a beast. It was my mission to help the people in Chelsea; it was in no way connected to him. At least I could force my friends to help me, but what right did I have to make Vernon dance to my music? He was a true businessman, and when you talk to a businessman, you talk business, not charity. Did I curse him? I don't know—maybe. I am trying to be honest. It hurts me now, if I would have cursed him, Vernon's realization of his mistakes should be in a simple and harmonious way and not in a negative way. But I didn't curse him so that he should get leukemia or his kids should die. I never did that, and I feel so humiliated, and I have a pain in my heart. The only thing I could do for him is to never, ever say anything negative about anybody by addressing them with inappropriate words. In reality he is the best man I have ever known, who gave everything he had. The reason is, he had family relatives, but he never gave it to anyone; rather he left it to the people in Chelsea. It doesn't mean he abandoned his own family and tried proving his point. He gave some money to his relatives who were poor and took care of them. But the majority of the money he gave to the people in Chelsea. Before he died, he was satisfied and civil to everyone in his life. But then I pondered why he had changed radically after his losses. I understood that suffering and pain always taught us lessons. It must have been how the laws of nature were built. Why does anyone want to learn a life lesson the hard way? Affliction may be the cause of this radical change, but it is not irreversible. You experience an affliction and then realize it, but it is too late to return. One great thing I saw was that Vernon had his self-realization while he was cognizant of his own transformation. That made him a perfect person, rather than having different phases of self-realization. Those final two weeks with Vernon made a lot of changes within each of us as well. We saw him dying every day and saw how he was fighting for life, although the paradox was that he saw life on a new horizon. He didn't say one wrong word against anybody. His change made us feel only one thing what is the difference between good and bad. The good sometimes becomes bad and the bad sometimes becomes good. What lies between the two is unseen and unexplained.

My own life underwent dramatic changes during this period as well, because I was officially dating and living with Madison. I was on "top of the world". I had always been lonely in my bed, thinking all the time, but now I was with a girl I loved. It was quite a new experience for me and I enjoyed it, but sometimes I wanted to be lonely, thinking and searching as I had been doing for years. But Madison understands me better than anyone and never questioned me. All she said was "I want to be near you, Oscar, and I want to feel you, touch you and love you." So these days when I come home, I know someone is waiting for me, who cares about me, who loves me, and these days I leave all my worries outside the house and enter with a fresh outlook. All I knew was that a woman helped me feel complete, but still I didn't know why I was complete.

A year flew by and I was suddenly twenty. It was my final year of college and everything was fine now. I got a job and placement in a bank in New York City called Harvest and Reap. Yes, that is the bank where I want to start my career, and they have offered me $120,000 a year, which was a pretty decent salary. But I could not take this job because Madison was still in Boston and had two years to complete her degree. Plus, all the elders in Chelsea were doing their home tutoring, and some had another year to complete and some had two years to complete their college program. I didn't want to leave in the middle and leave them hanging. I knew that if I started a job, I had to make sure that I ended the Chelsea program feeling fully satisfied. So I informed them that I needed some time to think it over and had the following conversation with Madison to check different options.

Madison: You should take that job, Oliver. What is your problem, my love?

Me: I don't want to go to New York City, leaving you and these people here.

Madison: So what are you going to do? Are you going to work with Dr. Gavin Higgs on Veleidade X?

Me: Oh, I forgot to tell you. The project Veleidade X is almost done, but Dr. Higgs wants to expand its scope and wants me to stay here.

Madison: You like to work with him, right? Will he pay you for the work?

Me: Yes, that is true, but only twenty-five hundred dollars. I don't want to make demands of him, but working on this alone doesn't make sense. You know royal sponsorship will not pay me, and I don't want to be a burden.

Madison: Okay, I got it. Forget about the money, Oliver. I could get the money from my parents and they will give it happily. If you wanted to stay here until my college is over, I could help you out.

Me: No, no, no, Madison, we shouldn't be a problem for your parents. That is not good.

Madison: I will do anything for you, Oliver. All I want is for you to be happy here, but there is another idea I have. Why can't you do your master's degree here? It will take two years to complete. By then I will be done with my college and we could both go to New York City if their offer still stands.

Me: That is an excellent idea, Madison. I need to talk to Dr. Higgs about this, but I am positive he would agree to it. I could work for him getting the money for his project, and we should get the sponsorship also.

Madison: Yes, that's a good move. I love you, Oliver, and I am glad you are staying with me.

So we both agreed for me to do my master's degree and stay in Boston for another two years. I reached out to the HR department at Harvest and Reap and they tried to negotiate some extra money, but I was adamant in my decision. Knowing my interest, the HR department gave me a deal. They said the offer was open forever and that I could join whenever I wanted. I reached out to my professor and explained my situation. He was gratified to admit me for my master's, and I enrolled with no pre-requirements. I had been honored and awarded as the top student in electrical engineering and computer science. It was the greatest honor that I could bring for my family and my friends. I reached out to Fay's father about my master's and he was very pleased to know about my plans. Without thinking a second time, he said yes, he would fund my studies. Fay's father said one great comment that I could never forget. He said, "Helping a student like you, Oliver, is like helping myself. I am very proud of you, and I wish you all the success in this universe."

The same routine started in our life. Madison continued to attend college and, just as my friends were doing, I now went to college for my master's degree in electrical engineering and computer science. Same campus, same faces, and same mainstream—nothing had changed, except I was helping Dr. Higgs, and that was the only project that made me exuberant about going to the MIT campus. Honestly, I was bored with my studies. I had reached a point where I could see everything regarding computers and technology in my life. I was not learning anything new, but repeating the same stuff. It sounded new when I listened the first time, but I had the feeling that I already knew it; it is the philosophy of minds called *Nobilis Bonum*. I know it is very rare to reach that level of thinking, but my mind had reached that level. I could not read or study more than one hour a day, because I began to get severe headaches. I thought I had overloaded my mind, and after years of rigorous training, I needed some rest. I walked through the college gates like a preprogrammed robot, knowing what the day would be like.

The best part was that I went to Chelsea every day, and everyone continued to learn a lot and I was glad for them. They were now getting $10 million a month, and all the money was spent in the right way. I watched as new buildings, houses, a big library, and a park were being erected. The streets were clean, their clothes were in good condition; they had better food, cars, and motorbikes, and everything was improving. The government was also helping fund improvements. I couldn't believe it was the same Chelsea I had walked into a few years earlier, because it started looking like Wall Street in Wisconsin—yes, my own lovely, majestic neighborhood. I was very happy for the people in Chelsea, but I was also very proud of my student Yohance, who was now eight and a fast runner. He was clocking 100 meters in 10.45 seconds, and I could not believe it. I asked him what his ambitions were, and he said that he wanted to be the best track athlete in history of 100/200/400 meters and wanted to create new world records for all three. He also wanted to be a marathon runner and wanted to set a record by running the entire continent of Africa. I took a lot of pride in being a supporter of Yohance in his track career. Fay's father knew Yohance very well and wanted to give him a sponsorship at a better school and to better his athletics career. Jacob and his wife were very happy for Yohance, and they also wanted to see him become an Olympic champion.

The two years flew by fast and one thing I noticed was that, though Madison lived with me, she looked new to me every day and our love became stronger. Madison was not like me as a student. She was very serious about going to college and wanted to learn something new every day. She sometimes envied me, saying, "Oscar, you are not studying or doing any homework; you're always having fun." I replied, "Probably you should have learned philosophy from Purdhil." Madison replied, "I learned, and whenever you teach the people in Chelsea, I listen very carefully to every word you say. I try thinking and improving myself, but I cannot be Oliver Oscar. Maybe this is where maybe we're not right for each other." I looked at Madison, "You cannot say that, Madison. We are bound by love and understanding, not knowledge. I may look like a brilliant man in everybody's eyes, but I'm like a little boy in your arms. You have to take care of me. With my brilliance and intelligence I cannot even do the simple things in life." She felt well-turned after hearing these words and she hugged and kissed me.

All my friends and Madison were busy finishing college, and I was finishing my master's degree. All the elders in Chelsea had completed the long-distance degree courses, and all their kids had improved with knowledge. I had completed the project for Dr. Higgs very successfully and he earned a Nobel Prize for the Veleidade X project in the computing field, as it was the first unique system where he integrated a database and operating system as one entity that could store a yottabyte of data in an eight-terabyte memory. I helped him complete this project and gave him a new direction to move computing in to the future. Eventually he recommended me for the Nobel Prize and made me the cofounder of Veleidade X, so now I have a Nobel Prize in my closet. The day I received it, I was honored very much, and my family and I have brought great credit to the place where I was born. My school, my teachers, my family, my college friends, people from Chelsea, every soul who knew me was in leap of joy and proud of me. My mom, Madison, and I went to Stockholm, Sweden, for the ceremony. It was the first time I had traveled outside America.

After I returned from Sweden, there was a great feast and party both in Wisconsin and in Chelsea. Dr. Higgs joined me for the party and he was excited and surprised that I knew so many people in Boston. I told him how I had started an education foundation for the people in Chelsea. He said to me, "You should have invited me for the training classes with the Chelsea people. You were quiet about it all this time, not telling me about it. Why is that, Oliver?" I replied, "I didn't know how you would react when I said I was teaching these people. You are a genius and you work very hard in the lab, so I didn't want to bother you." He said to me, "Could I tell you a story?" I nodded and he continued, "Do you know Einstein—I mean Albert Einstein?" and I replied, "Yes, I know him." He went on to tell me that Albert Einstein lived in Princeton, New Jersey, in a very modest home for two decades, doing research on the Theory of Everything. His neighbor, an old lady, brought her grandkid to Einstein. Her grandchild was in the fourth grade and was very weak in mathematics. She said to Einstein, "I heard that you are a scientist and physicist and you are a genius in mathematics. My granddaughter is very weak in mathematics. Could you teach her?" And Einstein said to the lady, "Sure, I will." The kid was learning mathematics for a year. She made a lot of progress and started to score high grades in the class. The lady came back and thanked Einstein for being so generous in teaching the kid. Einstein in turn replied to the lady, "I have to thank you, because in this one year I have learned more from your granddaughter in mathematics than she did from me." Dr. Higgs looked at me with a kind face, and said, "So, Oliver, what do you conclude from this story?" I replied, "Probably the kid was smarter than Einstein." He started to laugh and said, "It is very funny, but I didn't ask for comedy, I meant logically." I replied to him, "Ignorance always resides." He replied, "Well said, Oliver. I would have had an opportunity to find mine, but you never reached out to me." I replied, "It's not too late, Professor. I am leaving for New York City soon, and you are going to retire. Please take my torch and start running." He replied, "You are right. I am not dead yet; I still have time. I'll do it, Oliver."

I still had my original job in New York City at the Harvest and Reap bank and they negotiated almost a $300,000 a year salary as an information security architect. It was my first job, and for an architect, it was hard to do, but they gave me the title because now I had a Nobel Prize, a Medal of Honor, and a modern African hero. Yes, I also received a Medal of Honor award from our honorable president Alan Squash Jr. Also, you will be excited to hear this from me; Nelson Mandela, noble and esteemed superhero and the lion of Africa, who received more than 250 awards in his life, wanted to award me with his own award named the Nelson Mandela's Hall of Fame and Freedom Award. He wanted to engrave, "Modern African Hero Oliver Oscar" on the award. This was a unique award because it was the first one he had given to someone under his own name. This was the award I was most pleased and honored to receive from the African hero Nelson Mandela. They invited me to Johannesburg for the ceremony. I told Nelson Mandela that I needed my friends to accompany me also, because they have contributed their life to Chelsea, and he accepted the proposal. So now you understand why they gave me $300,000 a year because of such credit that I have gained in my life. I would have been happy with the salary that they initially negotiated $120,000 a year, but all these things went through my mind: if the poor people of Chelsea paid me a quarter million out of gratitude and pride, this big corporate bank could pay me more.

Once college was over for all of my friends, we decided to take a three-month trip to Africa. We were very excited, because all this time we had been seeing and listening about Africa virtually in the faces of the Chelsea people, and now we had this great chance to go to Africa. Yohance and Jacob and his wife also joined us for the trip because they know the whole continent, and it would be helpful for us to tour with people who knew the place better. We went to Johannesburg, and Purdhil recommended that I go to Pietermaritzburg and visit the train station where Gandhi was spawned as the lord of peace. I visited it with all my friends, and we had complete silence and touched Gandhi's spirit for his freedom struggle. It was so vibrant that we wanted to go to India to see all the places he walked, so at least by following that way we could learn a better way to resist evil. I felt myself as Gandhi's grandson, and I made his name shine on the face of this earth by helping all the people in Chelsea. A few days after we arrived, we had a ceremony in Johannesburg in a very big park. The ceremony was colorful with traditional African dress, and it was not only them, but all our friends wore African costume as well, except me. I wore a black suit because I had to receive the award. There were hundreds of people in attendance; rich businessmen, politicians, a few rebel leaders, professors, teachers, the rugby team, and everybody famous and important. This was the first felicitation of Nelson Mandela's award, and it was presented to me. I personally asked Nelson Mandela if the award was presented every year and he replied, "No, Oliver, it is for the chosen one, and time should support that." I asked him, "Then why did you pick me? There are thousands of volunteers working in Africa and sacrificing their lives." Nelson Mandela answered, "Yes, I agree, and I appreciate all their efforts. They help us to improve our lives, educate us, feed us, train us, care for us, and love us. We all owe our lives to them. But what you have made for the people in Chelsea is different. You named us, gave us an identity, made us confident, showered us with wisdom, and made us feel like kings. That's why I chose you, I did research about all your activities, which are outstanding and I am very impressed. You are the chosen one!"

Those words touched me because that was my aim and I could not explain what I was trying to do, but I did it spontaneously. Nelson Mandela himself took the award and gave it to me. The award was so precious and impressive. It was a map of Africa made of gold. A diamond was placed on all the countries, and the borders were filled with platinum. My name was inscribed as "Modern African Hero Oliver Oscar." It was signed by Nelson Mandela in silver. When I got the award, my heart was carried away from this universe and went to the corners of the universe's space. I felt weightless and became speechless for a few minutes. All the people in the celebration stood and clapped for almost few minutes. Nelson Mandela gave a speech for ten minutes and all I could remember is one sentence. He said, "My son Oliver is the pride of Africa." The party was fabulous, with Sub-Saharan African dances. All the dancers had bright colors, feathers, drums, shells on their necks, jewels, animal skins, and bones of animals. Everything was amazing, but it was different from the dance we saw in Chelsea. Here it was more authentic, and Jacob admitted the same. We also danced with the people there, and not to forget I was twenty-two now, so I had some vodka and Amarula. My friends also had a couple of drinks, and we danced happily that day. I will also never forget the food we had. It was like the whole savannah was on our plates, except carnivore, which was not lawful to eat.

Before we left the ceremony to begin our three-month tour of Africa, Mandela said, "I need you guys to come down before you leave Africa. If you like, we could follow the tradition." I asked him, "What do you mean, 'If you like, we could follow the tradition'?" Mandela replied, "You will know the answers when you return here." I didn't know what he meant, but he should have meant something important. I gave myself time to answer the puzzle. We went on our tour—all my friends, Jacob's family and his son Yohance, and the tour guides. These tour guides were not only guides, but ex-veterans, and they carried guns for our protection. While in South Africa we went to Table Mountain, Kruger National Park, Gandhi's museum, and Robben Island. Then we went to see the greatest monument, the pyramids, which were filled with mystery and beauty and took ages to explore. Egypt was a profound experience for us. We went to the Abu Simbel temples and monuments and the Great Pyramid of Giza; there had always been a great mystery about the pyramids. I wondered how they built such a splendid monument without machines. As I was exploring the pyramids, I was very sad, because our Twin Towers had been destroyed and had been blown to pieces, but the Giza pyramid was strong and had remained for thousands of years. Why was that? Our Twin Towers were not even one hundred years old. I thought maybe because men and women who built this pyramid, worked hard and there was a tight bond between nature and humans that held this pyramid together through all ages of chaos. But our Twin Towers were built with the help of machines. Maybe nature envied machines and it didn't have a bond with our tower and it fell into pieces. It would be devastating if nature has done these things to us, because thousands of innocent lives were lost. Oh, I am sorry, "oh nature." You have always been so kind to us; we are always rebellious. Maybe you took the innocent lives on 9/11 and give a rebirth to build a better tower and pyramid in the future, and those may be the chosen ones, you have been thinking of for ages.

During our tours, we also went on safari and loved seeing the animals in Kenya, Tanzania, Zambia, and Uganda. We saw all the animals starting from the elephant, and we thought it looked like it was kin to dinosaurs. The yellow-bodied king of the jungle was big and magnificent. We saw the spotted brothers the leopard and the cheetah. Under the water we saw water tanks of hippos and rhinos. We saw the tall skyscraper animal, which looked like it could be in New York City, but it was Africa, the giant animal was the giraffe. We were confused whether it was a bird or an alien, but it was an ostrich, the biggest bird in the world. I wanted to take that bird and fly in the air, but I learned they don't fly. I also saw snakes like the mamba, which was faster than a Ferrari and more venomous than all the rest of the snakes on this earth. I enjoyed all the birds, animals, insects, and reptiles.

The beauty of water is that it's always compared to music, because they are both fundamentals of life. We went to Victoria Falls, the beaches, Fish River Canyon, and Masai Mara. If you ask a kid, "How big do you want to be?" the first visible thing they know is the mountains, and we wanted to be like these mountains because we felt so small before them. We trekked to High Atlas Mountains, Mount Kilimanjaro, and Table Mountain. We saw nature, and while we hiked in those mountains, we met lots of foreigners, who were also hiking with us. We met different African people of various tribes with different cultures and ideas. They were the most amazing people I had ever met. Nature is their symphony, instinct is their communication, vision is their satellite, experience is their books, plants and herbs are their medicine, stone and metal are their ammunition, trees their buildings—nature is everything for them.

In the twenty-first century we call them laid-back people, or those living on the Dark Continent, but we were still trying to fit ourselves, and explore the dark energy of the universe.

Their hospitality was outstanding; the food, places to stay, camps, welcome dances, and so on was wonderful. The people in the major cities all knew me because I appeared in magazines and on TV, but when we met the people who lived in the deep forest; the guards around me introduced me and greeted me with great spirit. They were really honored to see me, but some people didn't know where America was, which really surprised us. We shopped in Africa, too, buying African cultural costumes, jewelry for our girls, African spices, leather goods, handmade scarves, dates and nuts, and wood carvings.

The trip was exciting, and Aika and Nikifor, Shu and Ejaz, Fay and Benjamin, and Sadie and Judah had all paired off, so it was a trip of young, happy couples. Every time I talked about the relationship between Madison and myself—the love, respect, attention, romance—I realized it was the same with my friends. They cared for each other as I cared for Madison. This trip made us understand more about our mates, because we were out of our country and in a different environment. One thing I noticed among all the girls was that they needed protection, because they were in a new land. They wanted us to always be with them, and felt scared when we were not around for even an hour. These were natural feelings for women, and we made sure someone stayed with them to make them comfortable.

Time flew by so fast; three months went by like a passing cloud. Before we left Africa, we went to say goodbye to Nelson Mandela. He was inquiring about the trip, and we shared all our experiences and thanked him for all the arrangements and his hospitality. Before we parted ways, he asked me one question: "Oliver, what is the most strange and overwhelming thing you observed on this tour?" I replied, "There were many, sir." He looked at me and pointed his right index finger and said, "Only one, my son." I was thinking, but one thing that came to my mind was the scars and blood covenant, and I replied to him, "The scars and the blood covenant." Nelson Mandela replied, "Bingo! You read my mind, Oliver. So what do you think about it?" I answered, "Building real promises between two individuals or groups." And he started the following conversation.

Nelson Mandela: Well said, Oliver, but don't you think it is cannibalism, to make a covenant between two people and drinking each other's blood mixed with fluids?

Me: Sort of, but we have alternatives to the blood, and the idea of a covenant is a noble and universal concept.

Nelson Mandela: Did you know about the blood covenant before meeting these people?

Me: Yes, I did. They do it in the church, and many religions still follow it, also there are animal sacrifices to gods, but I didn't realize that it existed in the twenty-first-century. I didn't know they made this blood covenant and as identification, have scars on their bodies and faces and consider the covenant as very holy and profound and die for it. In the Western world we don't use scars; we exchange wedding rings, or some form of token to keep informed and remind us of the covenant.

Nelson Mandela: So do you think this is a dark continent, Oliver?

Me: Following old rituals doesn't mean this is a dark continent. Every country on this earth is shadowed by darkness in the night. So could you call my country half-dark America? No one in this world knows the exact meaning of darkness.

Nelson Mandela: Meaning and action—sounds interesting.

Me: What is this whole conversation about, sir?

Nelson Mandela: Simple. I wanted you and your friends to do a covenant with me and my African people, that you will always fight for us, help, protect, and guide us.

Me: Do you want us to drink blood and scar ourselves?

Nelson Mandela: We live in the twenty-first century, so we could ignore those ceremonies, but in exchange we could use wine as the covenant for blood, and no scars. I represent Africans and you, Oliver, represent Americans.

Me: Hmm. Well, sure, sir.

On that day all nine friends and Nelson Mandela made a blood covenant to protect and care for the African people. We all took a cup of wine and made an oath that we would work for the benefit of improving the African people. We thanked Mandela and his team, and we left Africa and returned to Wisconsin. Yet my search was still there with me, I searched all the time, but lots of different things had happened in the past three years, and every time I thought about it, my understanding changed.

When I returned to America to start my work in New York City, I found out that I was still getting money for the project I had worked on with Professor Higgs. I was so grateful to have met Gavin Higgs, as he was a genius and master of the modern computing era. He was not like me, who knows PMT, but he was a very hard-core technical person. He was a creator, and unlike Purdhil and me, who were hackers, he was a living legend of technology who created software representing the gateway to the future. He is the father of miniature technology; he gave the infinite database that we hold in our hands. He should definitely not only be awarded the Nobel Prize, but recognized as the genius of all minds in one man's brain. I learned a lot from him, but with me he was able to accomplish his goals much sooner than he anticipated because of PMT's strength and a logical way of thinking. He motivated me and made my life happy in Boston, even though I was going through *Nobilis Bonum* in my mind.

Because of Professor Higgs, I was awarded the Nobel Prize. He was a pious and generous man and recommended me for it. The project paid for my work, and I thought there was no way I should be getting this award, but Gavin knew that I was one of the people most responsible for his success. This is what's called acknowledgment and reward; he acknowledged all my efforts and recommended me for the Nobel Prize. But the story of the Nobel Prize, I thought, was very interesting. It started as a mistake that was circulated in the news and caused great damage to a person's reputation. In this case, Alfred Nobel was addressed as a "merchant of death" by a magazine, and he changed his mind to introduce the Nobel Prize. Though there are a lot of controversies surrounding the Nobel Prize. In my one simple answer, it is humans acknowledging the good work of other humans. Is that a problem? Because humans are not always perfect and weakness exists in them, a prize like this is a way to promote humanity for the great ideas and changes that are needed in this world. I am also a victim of fame, so I didn't resist when they nominated me for it, so in that sense I was very proud to be a Nobel Prize winner. When I received the prize, I was nervous, my hands were moist, my mom was looking at me with great pride and all my friends were delighted to have me as their friend. I was in my flashy suit in the magazine, and Madison was proud that I was her boyfriend. The people in Chelsea were excited to see me on TV, and even my teachers got a boost, because their good will and my neighborhood's reputation were all lauded.

When Prof. Gavins told the Einstein story and was sort of disappointed that I had never told him about Chelsea, I felt terrible, but it also reminded me that there are good people outside my friends and family who wanted to do the same as me. So next time I want to do something like this, I will ask all the people I know; if they say yes, well, that is good, if they say no, I will wish them well. Gavins would now take over my job when I left Boston, with this prudent saying: a good master should always keep the torch fired and make sure it is always carried and burning. I handed over my duties to Gavins, and he assured me he would keep the ball rolling from where I left off. Now Chelsea has become a paradise; money was flowing in from all directions and the people's lives improved to the same standard of an average American. I never feed them with fish; rather I made them learn to fish, and that made the difference in their lives. My boy Yohance was becoming a strong athlete, and I was overjoyed for him. He had a good trainer now and was working hard these days and improving himself every single day. I wanted to see him in the Olympics and watch him win all the gold medals and make America proud.

As I said earlier, I also received the Medal of Honor from our president Alan Squash, for the contribution I had made. I was more honored by that medal than the Nobel Prize because it was the greatest honor that was introduced in America and is an esteemed American honor that every American dreams of receiving. Of course I am also happy about receiving the prize from Nelson Mandela. He is the real African lion and a man that history will never forget. Once called a terrorist, he was awarded the Nobel Prize for Peace. There are always two ends for a man while walking for revolution. Everyone in Chelsea gave us the names of their friends and relatives to contact when we went to different places. We were all treated with great hospitality and care, and they showed us only respect and love. I could never forget the food, dance, liquor, medicine, clothing, ornaments, handmade weapons, their homes, the streets, and everything we experienced. Everything was new to us, awesome and fantastic. We lived those three months in heaven, totally forgetting about America. Our dreams and everything that we had passion for before fell away. Some moments we felt like we wanted to stay back with these people and be like in the olden times, with no science or technology. Yes, sometimes ignorance also gives happiness. I don't know why learning gives cherishment while filling the gaps of ignorance. All those days in Africa I enjoyed and felt everything and I never tried in my mind to find reasons concerning why, what, or how things worked there. I was in the moment, seeing and being while subduing anxiety and curiosity in me. The only exception was when I was at the pyramids. Something happened to me, and I started to think about the Twin Towers and the pyramid itself. Maybe there were some ghosts in the pyramid, influencing me to think like that, or some positive spirit that made me think and prophesize about the future of the innocent lives that were lost on 9/11. It gave me a different direction to understand Madison, because in this poor environment I saw how deep our love felt. Is our love poor or rich? Because during those days in America, we were surrounded by a good infrastructure and everything was perfect, but in Africa it was just the opposite. Some roads were difficult, the body odor was different, there was no sanitation, there were no bathrooms and toilets, and we used our hands to wipe our asses. My question was always, does my love need environment and infrastructure? If yes, then my love is only a quarter to Madison and three-quarters is for the environment and infrastructure. But my answer was no, because in Africa we loved the same way we did while we were in America, and there wasn't any difference between us. Now I knew it was true love I had for Madison. I had known I had a true love for her before, but life gave me an opportunity to reinsure that my love was true and pure.

The final thing is the blood covenant that I noticed in Africa. It is the way people made bonds and promises with each other for several reasons. This is an amazing fact, but for me, blood covenant is like a wedding between a man and a woman. They have scars on their bodies and faces as signs of the covenant, and the great thing is that they make the scars visible, so that everyone knows the covenant they have with someone, and they respect it and are very proud of it. That is what Nelson Mandela wanted us to do with him, though it sounded old fashioned, but the real meaning is that if either party breaks it, they will be cursed to death. It is a sort of moral fear that the old society created in humans to value promises that we make with friends, relatives, business partners, and between countries, so that no one betrays the other and each of the party in the covenant feels better and stronger because of it. But the one thing I didn't like was that they made the promise through their own blood, which they mixed and drank. I simply had to deny that fact. No one should drink human blood under any circumstances, even if it is for a good reason. I had to admit that these days I had become sort of weak. I was weak in my soul, and I was thinking about why it had happened. I realized it was because my search was not as intense as it used to be. I was thinking for a while, and I knew the answer: it was Madison. I started to devote my time to her, and whenever I was away from her, she was all I thought about. I got so involved in her that I didn't have a point of separation, as everyone says only death could separate us. For me, she was in me, and we had become one soul. It is a good feeling when you are in love, living with someone, getting married. Yes, I wanted to be married now. I was twenty-two years old, and law and society would agree and support us, but I needed to reach my goals first. I wanted to be rich so that I could get all things in this world for Madison. For that reason I went to New York City to work for the Harvest and Reap bank. The time had come to make the money I needed to reach all my goals. The clock continued running at the same pace, because it was waiting for me to take a big jump in life. It was time for me to go to New York City.

Chapter 11
THE BIG APPLE

IT WAS TIME FOR ME TO GO TO NEW YORK CITY TO JOIN HARVEST AND REAP bank and begin my new journey. Harvest and Reap was one of the biggest banks in the world, and it was the next biggest bank to the World Bank. The bank had even more assets than the Swiss Bank, totaling $75 trillion. That was an empire, not a corporation. All I knew was that it was the bank of the future, and that working with such a big corporation would help me reach my dreams. I was in ecstasy to work for them, and felt it was time for me to prove myself and make money.

Madison was going with me, as she had been accepted into New York University's art and design master's program. She wanted to go to college and not work now, because she felt working would consume all her time and she could not focus on me or our relationship. All my other friends, Ejaz, Benjamin, Sadie, and Aika, had earned gold medals in their colleges, and the rest had good GPAs around 3.8 and A grades. Ejaz went on to pursue his master's in business at the same college, Benjamin went to the police academy, Sadie joined her masters in philosophy and religion, and Aika got a job at IEEE as a junior research scientist in electronics engineering. Nikifor joined NASA and was working on his master's part time. Shu went to help her father in building his business, which was doing very well, Fay joined the Department of Defense to research biochemical weapons, Judah was still in college and had a year to complete his courses, and he also had an internship in his final year. He also wanted to do his masters.

Everyone was working on their agendas, and I was working on mine. The best part was that we were all growing in a positive direction. Before going to New York City I decided to return to Wisconsin for a week to get prepared. Madison and I had vacated the apartment in Boston and given all the furniture to charity. We wanted to do weightless travel, and my company was giving me a guesthouse for three months so that we could move to an apartment after three months. All we needed to bring with us was our clothing, books, personal items and car, and the rest we would have to buy. We would be starting a new life from scratch. I knew there would be a lot of expenses but this was how we felt we should start. Always favors and luck had worked for me so very well in the past and it will in the future. We had a gathering in Wisconsin and all our families and friends came. As I looked around, I suddenly noticed how different we all looked. We were grown-ups and in our early twenties. We could drink with our parents and Purdhil now. The other side of this was that all my young families had started to grow old and have shades of grey hair and noticeable wrinkles in their faces but always the same love and affection for us. Nevertheless times had changed. They carried a professional respect toward us because we were college graduates now and had started to have a decent place in society. So I could call it a grown-up party: no fruit juice or canned drinks for us—it was all beers and vodkas straight up. All of us looked different, too. My lady friends had started to help preparing meals with our parents, and now they watched us that we didn't get too tipsy or drunk. Everything had changed now: the whole discussion about jobs, buying houses, weddings, retirements, wealth management, settling with families. All of us were now mature, responsible, and participating in adult conversations. We were sitting outside on the lawn with all the others at the party. Judah's father was drinking brandy, and he looked like he was in quite a different mood. He was asking me about my new job in NYC, taking Madison with me, and all, and it started like this.

Judah's father: Do you like your new job, Oliver?

Me: Yeah, I love it! I think that is where my future starts.

Judah's father: Did you find accommodation in NYC?

Me: No, Uncle, we will be staying in the company's guest apartment near Wall Street and have three months to move into somewhere new. Madison and I are working to find a better place that is close for both for us. I work on Wall Street and Madison is going to NYU, so we are looking for something that works for both of us.

Judah's father: Did you buy some furniture, appliances, and other stuff?

Me: We gave all we had in Boston to charity. We wanted to buy brand new stuff, so we have three months to go shopping.

Judah's father: Do you know about real estate in NYC? Let me ask you, are you buying a new apartment or renting it?

Me: Oh, come, Uncle, we are just starting a new life. We want to get a rented apartment.

Judah's father: How big an apartment? A one-bedroom or two-bedroom, or how big?

Me: I wanted to get a two-bedroom apartment in a decent neighborhood and we were checking the price and it comes to about, with electricity and cable, three to four thousand dollars. I don't want to spend more money on the rent and waste it, so this will fit our budget.

Judah's father: I heard you got a very decent offer.

Me: Yes, Uncle, I can always tell you. I got offered around three hundred thousand dollars.

Judah's father: That's good, my son. You deserve it, and you will be earning a million times more than what you are starting at.

Me: Oh, thanks for the kind words.

I don't know why he was asking me about this, because he had never done that. I knew he was distinguished man, but I was little uneasy. However, I stayed positive and tried to understand the exact situation.

Judah's father: Are you curious why I am asking such questions, Oliver? Am I embarrassing you, my son?

Me: No, no, never, Uncle.

Judah's father: Oliver, we have a family property. It is a town house on Park Avenue. If you don't mind, you could live there.

Me:That's so nice, Uncle, but it's fine. I am earning enough so that I can afford the rent. That is not required. Thanks, Uncle.

Judah's father: It would be an honor for me; you should take it, Oliver. I always see you and Judah as the same. I have great respect for your father. You could live there as long as you wanted. You could save money and use it for other purposes. I know you do that all the time.

Me: Hmm, I know you are not going to leave me alone about this. Well, I will take it. (I was a little hesitant to say that, but I looked at my mom and she nodded.) I will take it, Uncle, thank you.

Judah's father: Thanks, my son. Any questions?

Me: You said it is a town house. It's a one- or two-bedroom apartment?

Judah's father, smiling at my ignorance: It's big enough for all of us.

Me: For all of us?

Judah's father: Yeah. It is a fourteen-bedroom apartment with three big dining rooms, interior private elevators, a mezzanine library, three living rooms, four dens for entertainment, a 50 seat home movie theater, a parking garage, a private church, a swimming pool, and a gym. And guess what, Oliver? Everything is there for you.

Me: What am I going to do there? And do I need to pay the maintenance and electricity, Uncle?

Judah's father: Just live happily, and pay nothing.

Judah's father then started to tell us about the property that they had in NYC. It was one of the biggest town houses and most eyed properties in the city. It had been there for almost 100 years and they had recently renovated it to a state-of-the-art facility. It is on Seventy-Seventh Street and Park Avenue. His family's trust paid for all the taxes, utilities, and maintenance. He went on to say there were three chefs, two doormen, and four maids, and all were available 24/7 in the building. Apart from the fourteen bedrooms, all the people who worked there had their own living space in the building. We knew Judah's family was rich, but we hadn't known they were so rich that they could afford such a grand town house in Manhattan, where no one lived.

I finally had to ask Judah's father if he'd ever given it to anyone else before me, and he replied, "No, never, not anyone, because we value the house because it was the first family property that we bought." I asked him, "Is it a problem for me staying there? Because maybe your friends visit." Judah's father answered, "I initially thought when Judah was born that I wanted him to be a banker and live in Manhattan and use this house to live in, but he wanted to follow in my footsteps, so I have no use for it." He added, "And now it's yours completely, Oliver. You will have no visitors, except we will all come and visit you. Is that fine?" I replied, "Definitely! It's your house. You can come down anytime. You have fourteen rooms, Uncle, so it should be easy to invite everyone at the same time."

To add more surprise, Shu's father took me aside and gave me a wonderful going-away gift.

Shu's father: Are you taking the car with you, Oliver?

Me: Yes, Uncle, I am taking my dad's BMW with me.

Shu's father: Oh, it must be almost ten years old now.

Me:I use it because it reminds me of my dad. Madison is buying a new car in NYC, and honestly, we don't need a car in NYC, Uncle.

Shu's father: I know, Oliver, but I have a gift for you. Will you take it?

Me: Sure, Uncle, with pleasure.

He held my hand and gave me a small box with a little ribbon on it.

Shu's father: Open it.

Me: What is inside?

Shu's father: Just open it, Oliver.

I removed the ribbon and opened the box and found a car key with the Rolls-Royce symbol on it.

Me: Is it a Rolls-Royce?

Shu's father: Yes, Oliver.

Me: That's an expensive car, Uncle. Why did you do that? (I was completely numb and in shock.)

Shu's father: It is a Rolls-Royce Phantom Coupé, and it is an honor that I pay to your father, Oliver. He helped me with my business, and now I am doing very well. I wanted to be thankful to his family. It is a small gift.

Me: Small gift? Well, thank you very much. (I held his hand tightly.) Thank you very much. I will never, ever forget your kindness, I promise.

This gathering was surprising. The gifts didn't stop with Judah's father and Shu's father, but all my friends' families started to give gifts. They gave me expensive looking gifts, from suits, to ties, cuff links, shoes, watches, diamond rings, belts, laptops, bags, pens, socks, T-shirts, jeans, coolers, both casual and dress shirts, sneakers, and so on. They simply chose the best brands. They spent a lot of money on me, and I have no idea why they did. The only answer they gave was, "To honor your father and the good work that you have been doing all your life, especially in Chelsea." I had nothing to say. All my friends and their family had been so nice all my life. I accepted all their gifts as a token of respect and as a tribute they wanted to give my father. The party was splendid and the food was outstanding. I had a few beers and a few vodka shots. After the party we all walked through our neighborhood, but this time it was different. Yes, I always saw the differences in my life, even small ones. We were a little drunk, growing up, with degree symbols after our names, jobs in our hands, wealth in our pockets, and comfort and peace throughout our minds and bodies.

While walking in the streets, we recollected all the places and memories. We went to the alley where we were attacked by a mugger; we saw the small park where Madison fell down and hurt her head, our school, the path that I walked every day with Purdhil while I was learning, all the restaurants where we had eaten, my dad's bank, the church and Tziyon's jewelry store. We walked past all the places we knew. Everyone knew us, and we chatted with people and invited a few we knew well for a drink. We were going to explore the future, so this week was the last chance to enjoy it. Maybe when we retired, we would want to come back, but we would be old at that time. We went to on Irish pub, tossed back a few beers, and called Purdhil to come and meet us. Purdhil initially hesitated because He-Ran was pregnant, but she didn't mind coming to see us. Purdhil also joined the crazy midnight beer party that we were having. We bought lots of shots for everyone in the bar and tossed them back with them. We didn't usually drink this much, but that moment was a sense of freedom after all those years of hard work. We had been out to bars in a long time, but the bad part was that the bars closed at two in the morning, so we grabbed a few beers and went to the playground and just sat and looked at the moonlight and stars and talked about our lives. We all went home at six in the morning, walking straight, sober and steady.

During the last week in Wisconsin I got a call from Demonthin. He wanted to see how I was doing and said how much he missed Madison and me. I was telling him about all the gifts and the town house that Judah's father gave me and how happy I felt about it. Then Demonthin asked me, "Oliver, could you take me to New York City? I've never been there, and I could stay with you and help you." I asked him, "Demonthin replied, "Yes, sir" and I asked him, do you have a job or place to stay?"

Demonthin: No, Oliver, I could stay with you.

Me: Well, it is not my house, but I could ask Judah's father. How about a job, man?

Demonthin: I could find something,—dishwasher, cleaning cars, selling food from a cart. I will figure it out, Oliver. I do have some savings.

Me: No, Demonthin, all the time I was teaching you many things, man, you could find a better job.

Demonthin: My wife and I want to go with you and Madison. We have no one here whom we know well.

Me: Come on, Demonthin, you know everyone in Chelsea, and you should be happy staying with them.

Demonthin: I know you, Oliver, better than the people in Chelsea. Please consider it.

Me: I have no problem. I am earning a lot of money and could help you, but you have to find some work and a place to live. Let me ask Judah's father about it and I will call you back.

I actually did have some problems with Demonthin wanting to go with me. The only reason is he loves and cares for Madison and me so much, and he was my chauffeur and a bodyguard in Boston. But I had to get permission from Judah's father, because it was not my house, and we had to find a decent job for Demonthin until he found a new place to live. I went to Judah's home and spoke to Judah's father and explained to him about Demonthin, and he said that he could stay with me until he managed to find a job. Judah's father added, "We have a couple of cars in the garage and a chauffeur just quit his job. Could Demonthin take that job?" I told him that sounded great and Judah's father replied, "You have a chauffeur now, Oliver." I answered him, "No, I didn't mean that. I earn money, so I can take care of him." Judah's father said, "The trust pays his salary, so I meant he is your chauffeur and personal bodyguard." I replied, "I wanted him to have a good job and not drive cars for me, Uncle." Judah's father said, "Why do you always think a profession is connected with a better lifestyle, Oliver? He respects you, trusts you, and likes you, and he wants to be a caretaker. That is all he knows. He is helping you with that. Everyone needs a caretaker and protector in their life. He can be your protector." I answered him, "Yeah that makes sense."

Judah's father said, "Before you leave, I have to tell you something. Next time don't come and ask me anything regarding the house. It is yours, so do whatever you wish. I trust you always. If you ask me questions next time, it means you doubt my respect and affection for you.

I called Demonthin and informed him that he could join us and go to New York City. He was elated when I told him about the job and the place to live. He said that he would come to Wisconsin in three days, and that he and his wife were going to leave Wisconsin together to go to NYC. We started to have fun every day, drinking, hanging out in the neighborhood, and meeting all of our old friends. Between all the happy times, my school had arranged for me to give a keynote address to the school. They viewed me as a role model and wanted me to give words of encouragement to the students. On the day of my address, I dressed in a suit and silk tie and looked shining and handsome. I addressed all the kids in the school with a rhetorical speech, high pitched and with as much wisdom and knowledge as possible. After my speech I said to the kids, "Life is about choices, and to make choices you need to make decisions, and to make decisions you need to have wisdom, and to have wisdom we need to explore this universe with a nonpartisan mind, body, soul and spirit." The kids in the school seemed very motivated by my talk and started to think about their lives very seriously.

After my speech we began to pack for New York City, and by this time Demonthin was already helping me out. I was scheduled to start work on Monday, so we decided to start driving the previous Thursday. On Wednesday, we had a very grand gathering with our families and friends. This felt like it would be the final gathering of the beginning, because Madison and I were moving out of our hometown for good. So all the people in the neighborhood gathered for this last grand supper for our new beginning in life. We would come back and visit only a few times a year and live back here if we made more money or when we got old. The food preparation was usual but with a unique name, as the parents called it, "the smallest and greatest of the seven continents." They called the supper TSAGSC. At first we wondered what it was. It was food that was picked from each continent, of the countries that had the smallest population and smallest land area. So from Asia they picked Maldives and the Republic of Singapore, in Africa it was Seychelles, and from Europe it was Malta and Vatican City. In North America it was Saint Kitts and Nevis, and in South America it was Suriname and Antarctica and all the small islands in Oceania Australia. The grand gathering meal was prepared from each country's style using traditional cooking methods. We had a combination platter of food from Maldives, the Republic of Singapore, Seychelles, Malta, Vatican City, Saint Kitts, Nevis, and Suriname.

The dish inspired by the Vatican City was interesting because it was called "the last supper." They started with a church service and blessed us for all the kindness God had shown us, and then they had the Eucharist service. Madison and I were wearing polar-bear skins as cloaks and ornaments that were a collection of walrus teeth. Everyone in the neighborhood attended, not a single person was missing, and the gathering was the biggest party that had ever happened in my neighborhood. I chatted with everyone and thanked them for all the support they had given us over the years. This food tasted delicious, as if it had been cooked in the parallel universe. Demonthin was impressed by everyone he met and the great feast, and he said to me, "Oliver, I should have been born in this neighborhood." I understood how comfortable he felt when he was here and I said, "You are reborn here, my man." All went well, and we took Demonthin around our neighborhood that night and shared all our experiences.

Before we knew it, it was time to leave Wisconsin and start our journey toward our future. We were going to the Big Apple to build my own visions and to make the world a better place. We planned to take two cars, the Rolls-Royce and my dad's BMW. Always a surprise waited for me from my beloved friends and family. In the morning as we were getting ready to leave, my mom said she wanted to join me. I heard a car engine stop before our home. I was thinking it was Madison's family or her, but when I looked out the window, I saw Sadie's mother and father. I opened the door to invite them in and asked, "What's up, guys?" They replied, "Are we ready to leave?" I looked at them with confusion and asked them, "Did you say 'we,' Uncle?" Sadie's father replied, "Certainly, it is 'we.' We are going with you to New York City, and then we will come back." A big smile formed on my face. "What did you say, Uncle?" Sadie's mother replied, "Yes, my son, we are all going. The rest of the crew is also joining you." Then I heard lots of cars pulling up and doors opening and I saw all my friends' families walking up to my home. I looked at all of them and I asked, "Are you serious, guys? You shouldn't be doing this." They all came inside and my mom came out of her room, hearing lots of voices in the living room.

Everyone was there, and my mom said to them, "Thanks for coming down. We will be leaving in an hour. Make yourselves comfortable. I will prepare some coffee for you." Understand that they were all going with us, and Benjamin's father said, "Olivia, my dear lady, get ready quickly. We all have to leave soon, so we can enjoy the ride." My mom asked, "Are you guys going with us? You guys are just kidding with me." Everyone said in unison, and so loud that it would have made the roof come off, "Yes, Olivia." My mom became like a little girl, hearing such a big "Yes." She was shivering with excitement and said, "Okay, okay, we'll go. Thank you so much." I went to hold my mom's hands. She was emotionally moved by all their love, and her eyes were wet. I took her to her room and helped her pack.

I didn't ask why they wanted to join me in NYC, but it was definitely going to be a very constructive and positive answer. All I knew was that we were going to have a good road trip and it was going to be fun. It was almost a thousand miles to New York City, but we would not be tired because we had lots of people to take the wheel and all my friends and family were there, so it would be fun and joyful. We all started the road trip, Madison and I in the new Rolls-Royce Coupe, Demonthin and his wife in the front seat. Yes, Demonthin wanted to drive. He is my godfather and always says, "I am happy to drive a prince and princess in their chariot." In my dad's car, my mom, Madison's mom, and He-Ran drove and everyone rode with different people.

I was struck that the feeling on this journey was different from the first time I left my neighborhood. Nothing was fading in my eyes; everything was still and strong. I had a memory of my neighborhood when my memory was passing through my mind, and as I hit the highway, I felt secure instead of nervous. Madison cuddled next to me and her hand was on my chest and with her fingers she started drawing circles. She asked me, "Will we be all right in New York City?" I replied to her, "This is the final journey and somehow I know there is no point of return. My search for my life will be over, and we will come back to Wisconsin and live happily with our kids." Madison asked, "Are we going to have kids, Oscar? When is our wedding?" I replied, "Next year, maybe next decade, next century, or next millennium—who knows, Madison." She got angry and her face grew pale, and she said, "Anytime, Oscar, but I will always be with you" and I replied, "And you will always be with me."

We stopped every fifty miles for refreshments, and to exchange cars and seats. The first mile Demonthin was happy that I was in the car. Then we moved to a different car and someone else was sitting in the backseat. Demonthin murmured, "I wanted to drive Oliver." I swapped cars and got a chance to drive all the cars with all my friends and family. We stayed in a couple of resorts at night and had lots of fun. We enjoyed the trip all the way to New York City. We swam where we found water, went fishing, grabbed beers, had a few barbecues and thoroughly enjoyed our trip. I didn't plan it this way, but it seemed like my friends had planned it for a while because they had everything with them, including the grill, spices, meat in a mini-fridge, beer, snacks, wine and supplies. It was a pleasant surprise, and altogether we were a group of thirty-five people, including the little baby in He-Ran's womb. She was eight months pregnant now, and it seemed Purdhil had advised her to stay at home, but she forced herself to go. On this whole trip she was the important person, because she was like a god now. In my eyes she was a god, as she was giving a new life to this earth. We all took turns walking with her every day at least two miles in the woods, down roads, and at resorts. We fed her well, and all of our attention was on He-Ran because this was the first baby to be born in our group. I don't want to explain all the fun we had, because you are the one listening to my past, and by this time you should know the types of people around me. They were the most wonderful people I ever knew on the planet.

We entered the Big Apple, and everyone's was excited. I could feel my vision becoming stronger now. It was the greatest city in the world

—no city could be compared to NYC—and I was happy to be part of it. We saw all the big buildings, parks, different characters, subway stations, high-end stores, colorful costumes, road construction, hyper people, pedestrians' ways with red lights, honking cars—everything was new to us. We drove to our town house where a couple of people were waiting for us. The garage was so big that we could park all our cars. All the maids, chefs, and doormen were waiting to receive us.

We entered the house and there was a very big closet for hanging our jackets. The front door was very high, and the first room was the living room. This was the common living room, and it was so big, it looked like a football stadium. The room was full of paintings, antiquities, furniture, carpets, sofa, a huge chandelier, pillars, and photos of Judah's family and his great parents. They had a 120-inch TV screen with a projector. Everything was exquisite, and at first my spirit was lowered to see this grand design in the town house, but slowly I gained confidence, because I was the one who was going to live here. I thought it was only me having these feelings, but everyone's eyes were opened, and they all stood motionless. Looking at all of us, Judah's father realized what was going through our minds, and he clapped his hands three times and said, "Welcome to our home." He smiled and said, "This is where Oliver and Madison will start their lives, our son and daughter paradise. Let us welcome them with some applause." Everybody raised their hands and clapped, and all my friends walked close to me and held Madison's and my shoulders and said, "Lucky you."

It was Saturday midday and everyone made themselves comfortable. In the evening we had a grand dinner in our house. The chef prepared delicious food: a variety of beer-battered sausages, vodka pasta with red sauce, roasted garlic chicken, shoofly pie, ham rolls, shrimp cocktails, fish fillets, and many more delicious dishes. We had a very nice dinner with red wine and whiskey, and it was the first meal in my new home.

After we ate, we all took a walk in the new neighborhood. We walked to Grand Central Station and through Central Park. The neighborhood was attractive, rich, and wonderful, and we slowly learned that was how New York City looked. That night we all stayed in the house, and the following morning everyone had brunch. They all wished us good success and we had a small prayer service before everyone left. All we had left was our luggage, the Rolls-Royce, my dad's BMW, Madison, and Demonthin and his wife. The next day I had to go to my new job, so Madison and I picked out our clothes and made preparations for the grand day. Madison had two weeks left before starting college; it was only me who had to start working the next day. It was Monday morning and I got up early to prepare myself for work. I had an Italian suit, my blue dress shirt, a leather belt, cuff links, a silk tie, my watch, and a leather bag with my laptop in it. Simply put, I was sparkling that day, and since it was my first day of work, Demonthin wanted me to drive to the office. It was a new experience, so I had a little breakfast, said goodbye to all the maids, chefs, and doorman, gave Madison a kiss, and left home with Demonthin.

The office was on Wall Street and all the roads were new to us. Demonthin was also new to the city, so we used GPS to go to my office. While I was in the car, I saw how busy it was in New York City. I could see people rushing and walking, waiting for taxis, kids with their babysitters and moms, people buying the *New York Times* on the corners, carts selling breakfast, people coming out of subways, and people walking dogs. I could see that no one is lazy in the mornings in NYC. We got to the office, which was in the tallest building on Wall Street. "Harvest and Reap" was written on a signboard that was 200 feet tall. I got out of the car and asked Demonthin to leave, and asked him to pick me up in the evening after work. I walked toward the front desk, noticing the building and all that was in it. It was magnificent. Everything was grand, starting from the front door, the paintings on the walls, the high ceilings and their lights, the front desk, the uniforms, the different levels of elevators, and the signboards. I was thrilled that I was going to work for them.

I asked for Peyton Walters, who would be my manager. They asked a few questions, and I showed my ID and they let me inside the building. My office was on the fifteenth floor, where a very pretty woman with fair brown skin and chestnut hair was sitting at the front desk and greeted me. Her name was Salomeya. Her eyes were glowing, and she had a very positive vibration and high energy. She saw me and said, "Is this the same Oliver Oscar who won the Nobel Prize and many awards?" I looked at her and said, "Yes, miss." She replied, "I am honored to meet you, Oliver. Could you please sign an autograph for me?" I gave her an autograph and had a chat with her, and found out her mom was Lithuanian and her father was African American. She had a very interesting personality. Then my boss, Peyton, who was a handsome man around five foot ten, clean shaven in a suit without a tie, came and met me in the lobby and took me up to his office. As I walked, I noticed that everyone was dressed smartly, except for a few guys who were casual. I was looking unusual in my expensive suit.

Peyton took me to his office and gave me a nice introduction about the company and my job description for an hour. Then he walked me around the floor, introducing me to everyone, and everyone knew me and greeted me as if I knew them already. The one reason I could think how they've seen me was in the newspaper and on TV. I could see one thing in all their faces—that everybody liked the idea of working with me. Later, my boss took me for coffee and was asking me about the trip and my stay in NYC in the company's guesthouse. I explained to him exactly how the trip was, with all my family and friends, and also about my staying at Seventy-Seventh Street and Park Avenue. I told him about Madison also, but during the conversation I could see my boss seemed distracted while I was talking, something was on his mind. I could tell he didn't feel good about me, and I assumed at the time that maybe he had never encountered a personality like me. My first day was over. I had my own office space, which was a small room with a computer, a phone, a table with my business cards on it, a chair for myself, and two chairs for visitors. I didn't expect much because it was my first job, and I was doing very well in my life.

I went home later in the evening when Demonthin picked me from the office. Madison was waiting for me in the living room, and as soon as she heard my voice, she came rushing to me and hugged me and started to cry with joy, saying, "I felt alone and missed you all day long." I asked her if she was all right, but she was not answering me and was weeping and whispering, "Oscar, Oscar," again and again. I soothed her and asked her what had happened. She said that she was new to this city and had a bad feeling, as she didn't know anyone. I asked Madison if she should have called, Demonthin's wife, and Demonthin because they were there too. She replied, "I didn't want to bother them, as they were busy arranging their rooms, but I have a new friend." I asked her, "You have a new friend? Who?" She ran and brought back a little girl with her and said, "This is Claudia, my new friend." I asked her who Claudia was, and she said, "She is a maid's kid." Then Madison explained to me that Claudia was Colombian and her mom was a maid named Sandra. They worked here in our house; she was a maid who took care of us. Sandra had divorced her husband and lived with her daughter, Claudia. Yes, I had to agree that Claudia was charming; she looked like an angel. I was happy that Madison had found a friend in New York City. Claudia was a wonderful kid and went to kindergarten. That night I talked to Madison about the things that had happened during the day and told her about my boss.

Again I woke early and went into the office at eight in the morning. It was the second day of my orientation, and it was interesting to meet different people from different departments. It was an amazing experience. Most of the people remembered my face or at least knew my name. This was the first time I had ever experienced "My reputation precedes me." Everybody was happy to talk to me and share my experiences with my college project and the services at Chelsea. I met different personalities with different backgrounds, but I quickly made friends with two people who belonged to my team, Edgar and Nyah. Edgar and Nyah were Americans and seemed to be very reasonable and respectful people. Edgar specialized in IT security, same as me, and Nyah was a database engineer, but they were born and raised in NYC and graduated from Hunter College.

The orientation went well. I was the one with all these luxury suits, dressed like a rich man, while the rest were dressed in average suits. After the orientation I decided to tone down my attire, because in a way I had started to make others feel bad about their style. All I did was remove my tie, which was a safe trick. I carried the same idea right from college. But the suit, shirt, cuff links, shoes, and watch remained the same. I had my tie in my laptop bag, so that on demand I could restore my look.

I was assigned to help Peyton redesign the infrastructure of their Internet and Web security, for the next generation threat to the company. I started to take my job seriously and worked very hard. The job was not hard for me; it was corporate structure where people followed process and compliance. Within a year I had totally redesigned the whole infrastructure for Harvest and Reap. I resolved all the problems for them within minutes and entire IT department soon depend upon me. All my teammates and our IT group were impressed with my skills and work ethic. All credits went to Purdhil, because thanks to him, I was using the PMT (Philosophy of modern technology). I became a superstar in the company. While all my colleagues and my managers took the subway to work, my boss and all my teammates learned that Demonthin drove me to the office and picked me up every day, and they assumed that I had a chauffeur. They also knew that I lived in a fourteen-bedroom town house, and they also knew Madison was my girlfriend. They all thought I came from a very wealthy family, and I didn't want to disappoint them by explaining my real situation. I made them think my life had always been like that, which made me feel better. All the single girls and girls with boyfriends started hitting on me and trying to impress me and prove they were better than Madison. I only knew that Madison was the best woman on this earth and that I had known her long before time was invented.

After a year I began searching through my mind again with all the things around me. I felt that I had improved my status in society. For a year I was so busy, I stopped searching for some reason and I was thinking again and again, why had my search stopped? I realized that the corporate life had made me busy and that I had been adopted as one of their own. I was not anyone's slave, I was a free man and I was Oliver Oscar. I realized my true purpose in life and my coming, and my search started again. It had started the moment I said good-bye to all the people in Chelsea. I didn't mention it to anyone, even to Madison, because it was kind of a heartbreaking moment. We had a send-off party in Chelsea before leaving Boston. All our friends, Madison, Purdhil, and I were there for the send-off party. They honored all of us with a garland, and everyone got an African map that was engraved with an elephant tusk. Now the people in Chelsea were no longer impoverished, so they could give a very expensive gift to a rich person. Their life conditions had changed radically with the money from Vernon's trust, and everyone had a job, and all of them shared the wealth in equal portion. The whole neighborhood had changed and it looked better than any of America's best cities. We had a very grand dinner and party that day, and we said our good-byes to every soul in Chelsea, all fifty thousand of them and newborn babies also. The send-off was emotional and had its eye-watering moments.

Luckily, Dr. Higgs took over once I left. He found me depressed and asked me why. I told him how bad I felt about all these people after having spent six years of my life living and breathing with them. He said, "No one is dead yet. They are separated by distance and time, and your journey is to do more good things for many more people on this earth. Take your stick and bag and walk steadily as explorer and traveler to change the world." Those words gave me encouragement; it was the perfect reality of life, and his words made a lot of sense. If I wanted to come and visit them, to fly from NYC, it would be no more than an hour, so I realized I was acting silly now. And in another way, what he said was a proverb: if I am dead, then time and distance becomes infinite, so it takes me more time to find them. That is one of the reasons I wanted to stop death, but one day I will find my answers. He lived in Boston for a very long time, and his family lived there, and he decided to dedicate his life to them. Truly, though, the Chelsea people don't need any help from anyone. They could help anyone in this world. They moved from helped to helper. But Gavin would be there as a godfather, providing moral support, and he would be there like Einstein was, not teaching them, but rather learning from them. All I could say about the people from Chelsea was that they could live, walk, work, and breathe with dignity, and I was glad I had changed their lives from poverty and slavery to richness and abundance.

I was also very proud of my friends who were on their own journeys and reaching their limits. My friends got jobs at DOD, NASA, and IEEE. One was a police officer and some went for their master's degrees. Some were gold medalists in their college. At this point I didn't try to learn more about them; I knew them already. Now I have to talk about a house in Manhattan, huh? That shocked me. I was speechless and shocked when Judah's father said I could use it. Madison and I were looking for some brokers in NYC to find a decent apartment with two bedrooms, but the rent was ridiculously high. The more surprising and unaccepted part was the broker's fees. Some was a month's rent in advance and others were two months' rent in advance. I couldn't understand how that worked. The owner of the apartment rents it to me and I pay money that is worthless, whereas the middle man does no work but comes and gets a month's rent. I do understand a standard fee, say $250 to $500 for the broker, but under American law, it says the fee is equal to a month or two. Where do these people come from, the Corleone Family? Even the godfather wouldn't admit it. He paid rent to a lady who was poor. Even if the godfather won't allow such things, the brokers are definitely not gangsters or mobsters, but these people are scavengers. Yes, I love to insult them, these people who control the rental market in some way, and we have to pay these lazy people. I am not talking about myself, I could afford that money, because I am earning money; I am speaking on behalf of the people who cannot afford it. I had the same discussion with Madison, and she agreed with me. We both decided that if we pay this money as fees, we are encouraging such unnoticed crimes in society and making the lives of the poor even worse. They called the fees cumshaw, but it is bribery and extortion. We both were so angry; we thought that if this was the only channel of getting an apartment—via this crap, broker fees—we would rather stay in the streets and go to work. At least this way, the world notices: a Nobel Prize-winning young man lives in the street and goes to work on Wall Street. This will catch the world's eyes and there will be a revolution to put harmful, illegal practices to rest.

Luckily, I didn't have to live in the street while working on Wall Street. Sometimes we get noticed for what we are doing, and other times, people will think we are different and leave you in the street. I heard about some management groups that didn't deal with broker fee scams, and rented their own building, Madison and I waited for such an apartment. But time was on our side, and we were given a fourteen-bedroom apartment, and I had Judah's father to thank for it. His generosity saved me from the street. But my search is not yet over. I will find a way to stop all the venomous activities in society.

Judah's father preciously maintained that family property; he valued it a lot. He had been to Manhattan a few times and stayed there. Many friends other than us, such as his relatives, had asked him to stay there when they went to NYC or to conduct a gathering for the Jewish community service, or even to visit it. No matter what the requirement was, the answer was simply no. But such a big "NO" was not for me, and I didn't ask him about it. I realized that Dr. Enoch felt that I was his virtual son, his shadow; this shadow didn't have his own blood, but it would follow him always. That is the beauty of a shadow: it creates a perfect image of you, removing your physical characteristics. It imitates, and shows your mind and spirit—how you should look. The house and its grandness didn't depict his money, but rather his thoughts and mind. Every time I looked at that house, I saw Judah's father's heart, and I lived inside it.

How could I describe Shu's father's gift as "women love cars and men love women." So, first I have to talk about his achievement, as he had grown radically since I first met Shu. From one small store, he now owned twenty-six department stores in Wisconsin and fourteen outside of Wisconsin. He also started importing Chinese foods and groceries from China and became one of the main distributors in America. He expanded as the universe, and I marveled at his growth as he became a multimillionaire. He became so rich that he could buy his brother's family and his wife's assets with one damn single check. But he would never hurt them by doing that, because he was Mr. Wang, Shu's father, and he had no time for cruelty. Yes, that was his philosophy of life: when someone insults or betrays you, just move on and don't keep thinking about it. Work hard to overcome your situation. If you keep singing those insults and betrayals in your mind over again and again, then you cannot grow or overcome the situation you are in. But once you overcome the situation, don't go for revenge, because you will agitate the person even more. What happens when they are doubly agitated? They hunt you like vampires. A vampire is a beast and is not in control, so the total outcome is that you lose your peace and your precious life. So play the game as if there is nothing to lose. Just always acknowledge all these incidents with one small smile, and with ambition in mind.

Shu's father remembered my father's help, for the loan he gave him from the bank. He wanted to be grateful to my family always, so that is why he gave me the Rolls-Royce. Such a great gentleman is Mr. Wang. He knows that life is dictated by simple thoughts, and never forgets the people who changed his life. The good memories about the people whom you care for and friends who help you always make you feel better. He knew the laws of this nature and he respected and followed them, so he will never, ever encounter failures in his life. The car is simply an art of transportation, and having a Rolls-Royce is like having a heritage. The only thing that made me feel weird about an object with no life was that I liked to give more value to objects with life. The object with no life is the Rolls-Royce, and the object with life is me. If you remove the car from me, then I am a poor peasant just walking onto this world stage.

Now that my friends and I were grown, we started to have liquor in moderation, but one time we hung out and got completely drunk. We had never done it before, because we had been the most disciplined kids in the neighborhood. I was sure that we still were, but this time with a little wine in our minds. After having wine, our walk in the old Wisconsin neighborhood gave us a different experience, because we felt bolder and started to face things that we had been scared of at one time. We had a good time, drinking with the people we liked, and everyone shared their secrets by trusting one another. One thing I learned was that if you talk when you are drunk, you will be accountable for every wrong word you say. We know the rules, and better, we are disciplined and well organized, so after drinking we enjoyed ourselves, and our enjoyment was appreciated by everyone. I asked my friends' families why they had picked the name TSAGSC ("The smallest and greatest of the seven continents."). Was it really to remember the minority people in this world? They answered with their infinite wisdom, "Everybody is a minority in some way."

What can I say about my loyal friend Demonthin? He always said he wanted to drive me. I tried many times to convince him otherwise, but I could help him. He fixed his mind to be my personal bodyguard, and all I have to say is that he would not even let an ant bite me, so I had to take care of him. The whole car rally from Wisconsin to NYC was initiated and sponsored by Sadie's father. He is a pious and honorable gentleman who wanted to do things differently and get everyone involved. The road trip itself was a different experience, because I'd never been on a road trip with all my friends and their families. I think that is the reason Sadie's father decided to go for a road trip like this, because I shouldn't feel that I was missing my neighborhood and leaving everybody behind. It all started with the first trip to Boston when I went with my mom, and I shared my feelings with her. My mom shared this with my friends' families, and they didn't want me to feel the same way this time. So the whole neighborhood had gone with me and made me happy. My people were so pleasant, they didn't want me to be sad or depressed at any point of my life.

The house I was living in on Park Avenue was the most admired and envied house in the whole neighborhood, not because of its magnificence or its beauty, but because of its importance and because it was like a paradise that everyone desired to see. In a year I made a few friends around the neighborhood, and we had a few barbecues, watched movies, and hung out. I even invited them to my house. They all initially thought I was Judah, but after telling them my situation, they were perplexed by all the families being so united and caring for each other. I was also lucky because our families came for short vacations twice, and all our new friends were happy to meet them.

On the first day off from my job, Madison was scared, and the only reason I could think why was that it was because we were in New York City. Everybody became excited when they came to this great city because the city far exceeded their expectations. But Madison was not a city girl, she was a Midwest girl, and the feeling was very normal, and I could understand it. She had this feeling for a few months, but she overcame that feeling and became acclimated to life in a major city. She had a few friends at college and some friends she trusted. They stopped by and hung out at our house and they all liked us and always said we were the finest couple they had ever met. But on the very first day, she found her new friend, Claudia, and I like her too. She is smart, sweet and polite. We even thought that we should raise Claudia, since we both liked her so much. She comes and plays and greets us every day, and reminds us of our early life. Her mom, Sandra, is a very pleasing and honest maid. In a very simple expression, Claudia is a daughter to us, and she will be with us for a very long time.

In terms of my job, I worked for a great company, but there were still some problems. At first, everything was running smoothly and everybody had their own game going on. I always thought I should dress sharp and go to the office, but not everybody does the same as I do, so I had to lose my tie and keep it in my bag. Though we all worked for Harvest and Reap, we were all daily workers and paid if we were there. The only difference between the working class and our working in corporations was that we didn't sweat in the office and we had paid vacation to go someplace and sweat. That was the whole idea about the corporate life, and even the CEO was a highly paid worker. Since I was part of the working class, I limited myself and expressed myself like the people around me. I didn't want to show who I was, or brag about myself, but rather I just wanted to show everyone, "I am one of you."

I made three friends in the office: Edgar and Nyah, who worked in my department, and Salomeya, who worked at the front desk. I talked to them all the time, and went to lunch with them most of the time. Madison and I hung out with them a few times and both liked them. All three were really down to earth, very honest, and cultured. One thing I noticed about them was that they were unique from the rest of the people in the office. Every time I had a chat with them, they spoke very differently and talked very positively about their lives. I used to share my PMT ideas and different aspects of my life, but they never got excited about anything; they just listened and asked me some simple questions. Yet I could never answer their questions. At this time I found that something was still missing in me, and I didn't know what.

My boss, Peyton, however, was one of the negative aspects of my new job. Peyton was forty-five years old and had been in the company for almost twenty years. At first he looked like a gentleman and was always trying to help me. After a few months, he started to treat me differently, like not involving me in the meetings, not highlighting me to the management, taking my ideas and presenting them before management as if they were his ideas—all sorts of dirty little tricks. All I remember is that he was one diplomatic donkey in the office. How did I know this? Demonthin. The very first time Demonthin met him, he warned me to be careful of him. I asked him why, and he answered, "I too have intuition, Oliver." I completely trusted Demonthin because I had known him for a long time. At first I ignored his statement, but I never forgot his warning, and now after a year in this office I learned Peyton was a damn politician. The best part about my office was that I had three friends: Edgar, Nyah, and Salomeya.

After a year, it was time for my review and potential bonus. This was where the real plot started, and this became my turning point, the moment where my life's true journey started. Peyton, his boss, and the HR team had a review with me. At first there was a lot of talk about how great I was, how they appreciated all the work that I did for the company in the first year, my attitude, my team spirit, my working to meet the company's business needs, blah, blah, blah. But I knew something was coming for me. I wasn't flying in the air with all their appreciation, because I know it is flattery before slaughter. Then they said I would receive a 60 percent bonus and a 10 percent raise. I thought that was not bad for a new hire, and at this point I thanked them for their acknowledgment and reward. Then Peyton started to talk about a new job opportunity, which really scared me. He said, "Since you have a great deal of knowledge in database management, and a Nobel Prize, we want you to transfer to the database team." And hearing this I got pissed off, and asked them, "My expertise is in information security. Why do you want to move me to the database team?"

Peyton: The company finds more value for you on that team, Oliver.

Me: But I trained all my life to be an anti-hacker and work for information security, and I am very good at what I do. If you need some help on the database team, I could always be a good hand.

Peyton: Oliver, your ambition should always align with the company's goals. You cannot play music in two different places. You can be part of only one team.

Me: How can you say that I am good in database?

Peyton: You worked with Professor Gavins Higgs for the Veleidade X project and you got a Nobel Prize, and that tells us that you are great with integrated database and operating systems.

Me: That was my college project and I did it as a hobby, but to my surprise it was selected for the Nobel Prize.

Peyton's boss: So you deny you know a great deal about databases and yet you got a Nobel Prize randomly?

Me: No, sir, I didn't mean that. That was just my college project, but my actual expertise and strength is in hacking and security.

Peyton's boss: Well, Oliver, we have carefully evaluated your case, and we deeply respect your knowledge, reputation and values. We made this decision based on that information.

Me: I hear you, but was this decision made only for me or for other employees, too?

Peyton's boss: Oliver, you have to understand certain principles in the corporate world. I know you have a master's and a gold medal, awards that make you honored. But you have just a year of working experience in real life. It takes three to five years to understand business and technology, and till then you are a new hire. We are giving you an opportunity to learn and grow in this organization. You have lots of time in your life to be what you want to be.

Me: Will I ever have a chance to go back to my security team?

Peyton's boss: Yes, sure, after some time. When there is a requirement and we need you there, you can go back to your team.

I didn't know what had happened and why they were doing this to me. I was unintentionally involved in politics, and I felt I was a victim of it. On the same day I went to a bar near Wall Street and started to drink my ass off. I had never done that before in my life, but I had a feeling that my whole vision of becoming who I wanted to be was drowning in deep water. It was midnight when Demonthin came and picked me up at the bar, and Madison had been trying to reach me on my cell. I had never answered her. Madison was angry and distressed, trying to find out what had happened to me. I explained everything to her when I got home, and she felt bad and tried to comfort me. She said that if I was not happy, we could go back to Wisconsin, but I said no, because we had started the journey and there was no point of return. Let us give it some time and see how things go, I told her.

I took the whole week off and stayed with Madison so that I could see myself doing better. A couple of days Madison and I just spent in our room, watching movies, talking and sleeping. Most days Claudia would come and play with us, but she went missing for a couple of days and we grew concerned. We thought she might be busy in school or doing something with her mom. But we didn't see Sandra for a couple of days and asked the other maids about them. They were all silent, so we asked the chefs and they remained silent too. The same happened with the doorman. Then I asked Demonthin about Sandra and Claudia, and he bowed his head and didn't reply. Then Madison and I went to their room to check on them and they were not there. We both panicked and were shocked. Why were they missing?

I asked everybody in the house to meet in the living room, and everybody assembled. I was mad now. I was sitting on the couch and made everybody stand, including Demonthin, because no one wanted to talk and they were all hiding something from me. The silence was painful and everyone looked upset, like they were hiding something from us. Then I looked at Demonthin and asked him, "I don't mind anyone not saying anything; why is your mouth is also closed." Demonthin quickly replied, "No, sir, no, Oliver, I am always dedicated to serving you." I asked him, "Then what?" Demonthin answered me, "They were forced to leave."

Me: What do you mean, forced to leave? What did they do?

Demonthin: The management asked them to leave.

Me: Why? Did they steal something or misbehave? What did they do?

Demonthin: Nothing like that.

Me: Then what, Demonthin? Answer me.

Demonthin: Claudia's father was sentenced to death, and the management asked them to leave.

Me: Sandra is divorced, so what does it matter to them now? And why did Claudia's father get the death penalty? What did he do?

Then I heard the whole story—that her husband was convicted for killing a family in Midtown, where he worked as a chef for a wealthy banker who had a wife and two kids. Claudia's father, Fernando, was a very good chef and worked for this wealthy banker for a while. He lived in the banker's house, and both Sandra and Claudia visited Fernando twice a week. One bad day, the banker and his family were slaughtered. Fernando was caught red-handed at the crime scene, and his fingerprints were all over the place. So without a doubt he was arrested and penalized for it, and the court convicted and gave the death penalty. So the management of my house came to know that Fernando was convicted, and for the safety of the house and its occupants, they had Claudia and Sandra evacuated.

We heard that Claudia and Sandra had moved to the Bronx to live with Sandra's mother. We obtained the address from management, and Madison and I hurried to meet them. This was the first time we had gone to the Bronx, and it didn't look like Manhattan; it was a little scary. Demonthin drove us and they lived somewhere on 150th Street. We reached their apartment and everyone was looking at our car. We got out, and lots of kids—all minorities—came running up to say hi. Bronx was the second Chelsea in my life, and I never saw one white soul. We walked to their apartment and buzzed the bell. Claudia opened the door, and when she saw me, she cried out loud, calling my name. I just hugged her as she wept into my shoulders. That poor little child's heart was in pain. I comforted her and Claudia's mom saw us. She was glad to see us and her face was also filled with sorrow. Claudia went and kissed Madison on the cheek. Madison kissed Claudia's head three times, and they both started crying. Seeing this, Sandra and her mom also started crying, and I held Sandra's hands and said, "It's fine, Sandra. We are here." Sandra's mother was crying and telling us, "Fernando is innocent. He didn't kill anybody."

We started to talk to Sandra and asked what happened. She said the same thing about the murder. Sandra said, "On the day he was convicted, the management gave us no time, and asked us to leave the house. We said we wanted to say bye to you but they didn't give us a chance. I knew that day, sir that you were drunk and had come home depressed about your work. So we thought not to bother you, and we left home without telling you. Sorry, sir."

Me: No, that is fine. You should have called us later.

Madison: Why did you not tell us anything about your husband?

Sandra: Two years back when this incident happened and Fernando was arrested, the management asked us to leave, but my attorney filed a petition in court saying that Fernando had not been convicted and that management had no right to send us away. So the court held us till judgment, and once they gave the judgment as convicted, they asked us to leave.

Madison: But still you didn't answer us! Why didn't you tell us?

Sandra: The management said not to tell you, and I kept their orders.

Me: But you knew that we loved and cared for you guys. You should have shared with us, Sandra.

Sandra: I thought you might think bad about us and our family.

Madison: Claudia is like a daughter to us. We would never think anything wrong about you guys.

Sandra: I am very sorry, Miss Madison.

Madison: Oliver, we have to do something about it.

Me: I am thinking. Sandra, what was the motivation behind the murder that they charged Fernando with?

Sandra: Robbery.

Me: I will talk to you later about that and ask for all the information. Sandra, do you want to stay with us or with your mom?

Sandra: I always wanted Claudia to be in Manhattan not in the Bronx; she is going to a good school there. Let me stay here, but take Claudia with you, sir.

Me: How can kids live without their mother? You are going with me!

Sandra: We can't. Management will not allow it.

Me: Who cares about management? You are coming there as my family friend, and Claudia is our daughter.

That same day, we took Sandra and Claudia back to our home, and the first thing I did was to call Judah's father and explain the whole problem. All he said was "Don't call me again. It is your call, son. I will back you up." I called management and explained to them that Sandra and Claudia would be staying here with us. The management tried to argue with me, which only made me angry. "If you persist, we need to change management for maintenance," I said. When I said such a harsh statement, they came to an agreement for them to stay here, and Sandra was allowed to continue working as a maid for us. But management was scared of the law and mishaps, so they got documents signed saying that they were not responsible if any crime was committed by Sandra or her family. I just signed and returned the document without even reading it, because I knew these people were genuine and would never hurt us.

I continued to ask Sandra what exactly had happened at the crime scene. She started telling the whole story. On the night of the murder, Fernando had finished with work and was at our house with Sandra and Claudia when he got a call from his boss to come home because he needed some help. It was around 10:30 p.m. when he got this call and Fernando headed toward Midtown to meet his boss. When he got home, the front doors were opened and he went inside and saw that his boss, his wife, and the kids had been shot and stabbed to death. Puddles of blood were on the floor, and he was trying to check whether someone was alive. He removed the knife from his boss's chest and threw it on the floor and was checking his pulse. He did the same for the kids and his boss's wife, but there was no pulse and everyone was dead. He saw a 9-mm gun on the coffee table with blood on it. He didn't touch the gun, and was very cautious, he then heard a sound from the kitchen—a plate falling on the floor—and thought someone was still in the house. So he took the gun to protect himself and walked into the kitchen and found his boss's cat hiding near the microwave, shivering and shaking. He picked up the cat and patted it. Meanwhile, the police rushed into the house and found Fernando with a gun in one hand and the cat in the other. They pulled their guns and arrested Fernando on the spot for murder.

The trial started soon afterward. Because the banker was very famous and this involved the murder of children, no attorney was ready to represent the case. They had only one chance to get a public defender. The public defender did his best, but all the evidence was pointing to Fernando: the fingerprints on the knife, the gun, and their bodies, and most of all, the fact that he was caught at the crime scene. They even testified that he was about to kill the cat, there was no way he could be found innocent.

Hearing this very sad story, I asked Madison to bring some wine for Sandra and me, to make her a little more comfortable, as she seemed very troubled. I asked Sandra, "They said the motivation was robbery, but he didn't have any money, gold, or anything in his pockets." Sandra replied, "No, he didn't have anything, but his fingerprints were there in the boss's locker." I asked her, "What? Where is the locker?" She replied, "It is in the boss's bedroom." I then asked her, "How did his fingerprints get there in the locker? He is just a chef, why did he go to the bedroom?"

Sandra: His boss was the one who sent him to school and college. He had known his boss for almost twenty-five years, they grew up together. Fernando always liked cooking and wanted to be a chef, so he went to college to be a chef of international cuisine. Since his boss liked and trusted him, he gave him a job in his home. So he helped him in all aspects.

Me: What about the fingerprints?

Sandra: On the day of the murder his boss was sick and in his bed, so he called Fernando and asked him to take some documents from the locker. That is how the fingerprints were there.

Me: Was the locker opened?

Sandra: Yes, it was.

Me: Was anything missing?

Sandra: No, everything was in there.

Me: Then how come they said the motivation for the murder was robbery?

Sandra: They said he was about to leave the crime scene after the murder, taking all the money, gold, and jewels, but that before he could escape, he was caught.

Me: Oh no. How old was his boss?

Sandra: His boss was around fifty-four and got married late, around forty-five. He had two kids, one three and the other seven.

Me: How old was his wife?

Sandra: She was around thirty five.

Me: Was she a good woman?

Sandra: She was a caring and faithful woman, and she loved her husband and the kids.

Me: I will help you, Sandra, but be honest with me: do you think Fernando could have done it? I don't know him. All I know is that if you tell me the truth, I will help you. Look into my eyes and answer.

Sandra was crying and her hands were shaking. I took the wineglass from her hands, and she looked straight into my eyes.

Sandra: I've known him since I was three. He was never angry with me, and he never lied, not even once to me. He takes care of my mom. Moreover, his boss paid him lots of money to be there. If he had needed money, he could have asked his boss anytime. He would never do something like this.

Me: I got it, Sandra. Don't worry; we will get this thing fixed.

Now I had to save this family and an innocent man who was living behind bars. There shouldn't be any blood spilled anymore, and definitely not an innocent man. I called Benjamin's father that same day to ask him his opinion about this case and to find a good attorney to reopen it. He gave me all the necessary tips and referred me to one of the leading attorneys in NYC, Glenn Hitch. The next day Sandra, Madison, and I went to meet him, and I introduced myself and said I was a friend of Benjamin's father. He knew Benjamin's father very well and was a good personal and professional friend. He even recognized me, and knew about my Nobel Prize and other awards and appreciated all my efforts and career growth. Then I explained the whole case about Fernando and Sandra to him, and he said he had heard about it.

He had a chat with Sandra, asking her questions, and after an hour, he looked at me and asked me, "How could I help you in this case, Mr. Oliver?" I replied, "Could you take the case for her, please?" As per bar rules no one should reopen this case and it was against attorney's committee, but since Benjamin's father recommended it, he said he would take the case and proceed with it. I asked the attorney, "Glenn, do I need to pay fees?" He said, "Yes, you should," and I asked him, "How much?" He said, "It is three hundred and fifty dollars an hour." I agreed to the price and said yes to it without even thinking, because we had to save an innocent man's life.

That week passed by with all these problems with my daughter Claudia's family. Then it was Monday and I had to go work in my new position at my office. They moved my office from the fifteenth floor to the twelfth floor, and this time they gave me improved furnishings: a credenza, a small plant near the window where I could see the FDR Drive and the river, and the best view of the city. I was a little frustrated, but I was not giving up, as I was in search for all humans to be superheroes. That goal had never left me, and it would always be in my heart. The best part of my life was Nyah, who worked on my team. It was great to have a friend I could talk to at work. But my mind was confused, clouded with saving an innocent man's life, and that was the only thought in my mind. Nyah walked into my office that morning to say hi, and I chatted with her for a while. She asked me if I was happy to be on this database team and I didn't show her my real frustration, I tried to appear relaxed. She talked about Peyton, that he was one of the bad apples in this company but had been there a while and knew how to play the game of politics. I told Nyah that I was new to such politics, and maybe I should learn and master the art of political science, so-called politics, because there were more wicked men in this world and we had to overcome all these obstacles so that I could reach my vision. Nyah was happy that I recovered from what Peyton had done to me. I started to regain the same spirit that I had when I worked on Peyton's security team. My new manager was Gwyneth. She was African-American, had been in the company for sixteen years, and was the director of database systems. Was she like Peyton? I couldn't tell, but one phrase came from every mouth, which was "She is the best." She chatted with me about whether I was happy in this team or not. I never gave any negative answers. All I said was "It is an honor and pleasure to work for you."

I met new people on this team and they were all from different backgrounds and countries. I could see lots of Asian minds in the technology world, from India, China, Korea, Pakistan, and Sri Lanka, and also different cultures from near America, Cubans, Puerto Ricans, Brazilians, and Germans. Now I started to teach everyone about the project that I did with Gavin, and different aspects of database itself. The team had many problems in maintaining the database for the company and used different technologies from different vendors, but we were in a process of consolidating to one open-source software. We wanted to use our own database and convert and integrate all database products into one single platform. This was the biggest project I worked on, because once we consolidated all our data into open source, free database software, the company was going to save millions of dollars on spending in different vendor technology.

But there were hundreds of lies and injustice hiding from the murder, and I had to deal with it now. The case started to proceed again in court, and Glenn met Fernando in prison. I went with him, and Glenn shot out all his questions and gathered all the details. This was the first time I had gone to prison to meet someone. Initially I was scared and felt I had no energy in me when I went in to meet him, but later I started to feel that there were lots of innocent souls inside who shouldn't be there and who were calling me for help.

Attorney Glenn started to work very seriously on the case, and put all his efforts into finding the real culprit. The court proceedings took place every month. I could see Claudia praying for her father to be back with them, and Sandra's eyes looked through to see her husband in the back. Madison and I waited to see this small family united again. These days I was tired of hanging out at team parties every two weeks, and I took Madison with me to lift my spirits. We would go to different bars, and it was lots of fun. All my teammates liked Madison, and sometimes Gwyneth also hung out with us.

While I was enjoying new company, I found something strange with all the indigent servants who were brought to this country. I thought middle men were used only in the apartment renting business in NYC, but it is the same thing is also found in corporations. Yes, it is true. I had a chat with one of the Indian guys on our team called Sandeep, who is a bright gentleman from India.

Me: Do you like it here in America?

Sandeep: Yes, very much. It's a big country, and great things are happening here.

Me: Where do you live?

Sandeep: In Jersey.

Me: Are you single or married?

Sandeep: I am single.

Me: Then why do you live in Jersey, man? You work here, so you should live in NYC. It will be a lot of fun.

Sandeep: They don't pay me that much.

Me: Why? You have a degree, right?

Sandeep: But I don't have a green card, and I am a consultant.

Me: Chelsea Corporate, huh?

Sandeep: What did you say, Oliver?

Me: White-collar indigent slaves. When will you get it?

Sandeep: Maybe after seven years.

Me: Hmm, not good. So they pay you low wages?

Sandeep: No, they pay me good money, but I don't get it.

Me: What do you mean, Sandeep? Do you save money and send it to India and save no money for yourself?

Sandeep: No. Oliver. My God, they pay me a hundred and twenty dollars an hour, but my vendor takes forty dollars an hour cut, my mid-vendor takes another ten dollars, and my employee takes 20 percent of the rest.

Me: Do you know I am good at mathematics?

Sandeep: Oh yeah.

Me: You don't get anything—that's what you say.

Sandeep: Pretty much.

Me: Is that only for you, or for every other Asian or in general, who comes here without a green card?

Sandeep: It is pretty much for everyone—Chinese, Japanese, and anyone who comes in on the visa we come in on.

Me: What visa is that?

Sandeep: It is an H1B, but you know, Oliver, the people coming on an L1 and other visas are still worse off than us.

Me: So you say there is another word for *worse*? It is *horrible*.

Sandeep: Yeah, yeah, but I like you, Oliver. You are a very accomplished person and I think you should be my guru.

Me: Thanks for those kind words, but are you going to wait another seven or ten years like this and complain and curse about everyone and everything?

Sandeep: I don't know.

Me: Let me tell you something, Sandeep. You said I am a guru? You really believe that I am really your guru?

Sandeep: Yes, sir, definitely.

Me: From working with our whole team, I know you are the brightest one, and you have a very good knowledge about the subject of databases. As you know, we wanted one platform, and that platform could integrate any database products and convert them into our custom database platform. You should work hard and invent this product and get it copyrighted and start your own company.

Sandeep: Sounds interesting, but do you think I can do it?

Me: If you can't, then who do you think can?

Sandeep: I take your word as my mantra, and I will definitely do it.

We drank a vodka shot after this conversation, and one thing I am sure of is that he is going to revolutionize the whole industry and make tons of money.

We lived the same routine. Madison stayed busy with college, and now we knew NYC very well. We had almost adopted the city and knew how the city worked. I would take Claudia and Sandra to the prison so Claudia could see her father. By this time I was starting to form a friendship with Fernando, and he was grateful that I was helping him and his family.

Claudia was also growing up, and a year passed so quickly and she turned six. I had completed two years at my company. I had paid lots of money for our attorney, Glenn, and he found something about the case and applied to reinvestigate it. So again Fernando and everyone came to court for the investigation. Madison, Sandra, Claudia and I went to the court that day. I cannot call it an exciting moment, but there was a thrill in all our hearts. On the other hand we just wanted justice. I saw the judge, bailiff, clerks and jury, and felt how a real courtroom looks. In that room I gained confidence that justice would be served, as all minds and ears were opened to the truth. Glenn proceeded with his argument:

Glenn: What time did you get the call, Fernando?

Fernando: Around 10:30 p.m.

Glenn: How did you go to your boss's house? Taxi, subway, or did you drive?

Fernando: I took a cab.

Glenn: What time did you arrive?

Fernando: Around 10:55 p.m.

Glenn: How did you pay for the cab?

Fernando: I used a credit card, so that I could put it on the expense account.

Then Glenn took a pile of papers and submitted them to the judge and gave copies to all the jurors. He said that according to the autopsy report, his boss, Langdon, who was the victim, died at 10:00 p.m. How could a dead man call at 10:30 p.m.?

Prosecutor: Maybe he was looking for some help and called Fernando.

Glenn: So, Mr. State's Defendant, as per your statement you say that he is innocent. That means someone killed him and then called Fernando.

Let us go in another direction. Even if he was alive at that time and made the call, then the autopsy reports could be wrong. Either way my client is innocent.

Prosecutor: Do you have proof that he got a call at 10:30?

Glenn: He showed the telephone calls, and he made a call at 10:30 PM —it shows up on his wife's phone records.

Prosecutor: Maybe he called after killing them?

Glenn: But his credit card shows that he paid the taxi at 10:53.

Prosecutor: Maybe he used it before going home.

Glenn: Well, the defendant has to be very serious in listening to what I am saying, rather than thinking about the Giants' game. (There was a football game that night and the Giants were playing.)

Defendant: What the hell?

Judge: Silence. Please proceed, Mr. Hitch.

Glenn: Thanks, Your Honor. The taxi bill shows it is 10:53 p.m. and he used his credit card to pay. At 11:05 the cops arrested Fernando. The autopsy shows that Langdon was dead at 10:00 p.m. Let us assume for a second that Fernando was responsible for the murders. Why should he come back after killing everybody at 10:55 and get caught?

Prosecutor: Maybe he left behind some evidence.

Glenn: His fingerprints were everywhere, so evidence is not the issue. But the reality is that the locker room was opened and nothing was taken, so you mean he came back to steal all the money at 10:55, after committing the murders at 10:00 PM. Do you have amnesia, Fernando?

There was a light of hope in Fernando's face, and he smiled widely.

Fernando: No, sir.

Glenn: Thanks, Fernando.

Prosecutor: This is ridiculously insane. This man Fernando brutally carried out these murders including the children. He shot them and stabbed them, and now he is changing his story.

Glenn: The phone calls prove it. He was there, and the taxi receipt showed that he got there at 10:55. What else do you want?

Prosecutor: First we need to interview the taxi driver.

They interviewed the taxi driver, who confirmed that he picked Fernando up from Seventy-Seventh Street and Park Avenue and dropped him in Midtown. The defendant was questioning him about how he could remember, because every single day he sees hundreds of passengers. And how did he remember exactly where Fernando got out? I had to say NYC taxi drivers are some of the smartest and best drivers in the world, and his answer stunned the court and made everybody laugh. The taxi driver said to the defendant, "Don't you know taxi drivers have good memories? That is the reason they can remember the routes so well, and I completed high school, and I am literate so I could read the *New York*

Times." He added that this was the most famous case in NYC and had been on the front page for a week. "Even the cops investigated me and I said I dropped him at Langdon's house. But one thing no one asked me is what time. Well, Langdon is a very famous man in the city and everybody knew him. We all followed the case and still thought Fernando was the killer, and no one thought there could be an alternative version other than the truth. Then the autopsy doctor was questioned and he said he was sure that all the victims had died around 10:00 p.m., including Langdon." Then came the actual evidence, which startled the court.

Glenn asked to interrogate Langdon's younger brother, Mr. Willet.

Judge: Permission granted.

Glenn: Are you Langdon's brother, Willet?

Langdon's brother: Yes, I am.

Glenn: Were you at your brother's house on the morning of the day he was murdered?

Langdon's brother: What is the big deal? He is my brother, and we both run the business.

Glenn: Just answer my question. What is it in the file about you and your brother fighting?

Langdon's brother: What file are you talking about? My brother and I never fought with each other.

Glenn: Really? There is a file that is missing from the locker room.

Langdon's brother: As I said, I don't know of any file, sir.

Glenn: Okay, well, there was fifty million dollars transferred to your account from a Swiss bank account a week after your brother's death. Where did you that money come from?

Langdon's brother: I don't know anything about that money.

Then Glenn showed all the documents regarding the money that was wired to Langdon's brother to the judge and jury.

Glenn: Where did this money come from?

Langdon's brother: It is from our business that my brother and I were running.

Glenn: Oh Christ, you have no share in any of Langdon's business. He was feeding you. Your father gave an equal share of his money to both of you. One was worthy and the other was a prodigal son. Spent all the money, taking drugs, gambling, involved with gangsters, involved in prostitution and all sorts of crime. You were protected under the wings of Langdon's reputation and never saw prison, but now things are different, Mr. Willet.

Langdon's brother: Are you saying that I killed my brother? That is insane. I loved my brother more than life itself.

Glenn: Oh, sorry, let me ask you about *brotherhood*. When was the last time you paid a visit to your brother's cemetery?

Langdon's brother: Ha, hmm, a while back.

Glenn: For the funeral.

Langdon's brother: I did.

He started to stammer when Glenn submitted the money transfer and all Glenn's questions made him more nervous.

Langdon's brother: Your Honor, he is asking me personal questions that are irrelevant.

Glenn: I have some points here.

Judge: Objection overruled.

Glenn: Thanks, Your Honor. So, Mr. Willet, where did you get the money?

Langdon's brother: I just remembered: from my brother's—from the Swiss account.

Glenn: Very nice. Why haven't you transferred your brother's wealth to yourself yet? Do you only like Swiss francs, not the Yankee dollar?

Langdon's brother: Money is not my objective now. I want justice for my brother's death. Fernando should be hanged.

Glenn: Whoo! The court will decide the final verdict. Well, it's good to know that you want payback for your brother's death.

Langdon's brother: Yes, I want justice, and Fernando should be hanged.

Glenn: He will not be hanged, because he didn't do it.

Langdon's brother: How do you say, he is a cut throat pig? My brother trusted him so much, but he betrayed and killed him.

Glenn: So you never answered the question yet. Why did you not claim your brother's wealth, but only the money from the Swiss bank account?

Langdon's brother: The money in the Swiss bank belongs to my father and that is our family's heritage, which we maintained for years. When my father died, he gave it to him and not even a penny to me.

Glenn: Why?

Langdon's brother: Because he thought I was immature with no responsibilities.

Glenn: So he gave the money to your brother and his wife?

Langdon's brother: Yes.

Glenn: So the morning of your brother's death you were there to ask for your share of twenty-five million dollars.

Langdon's brother: Yes.

Glenn: And what did your brother say?

Langdon's brother: No, not now.

Glenn: Why?

Langdon's brother: He said I would be irresponsible.

Glenn: Don't you feel you are responsible?

Langdon's brother: I feel I am responsible, but not my brother.

Glenn: When did you learn that there was money in the Swiss bank account?

Langdon's brother: A week before my brother's death.

Glenn: So on the day of your brother's death, you were asking how much money was his share and that information was in that file. When did you take the file?

Langdon's brother: On the same day, in the morning.

Glenn: No, that is a lie! You took it after 10 PM after killing your brother and his family.

Langdon's brother, shouting: Nooooo!

Judge: Silence.

The whole court was surprised with all the facts, and it felt really thrilling in the court room.

Glenn stretched both his hands high in the air and moved his body in all directions.

Glenn: I am very sorry, everybody, for a moment let us all assume that Fernando is the real killer.

Everyone was surprised by his statement, and he asked Fernando a question.

Glenn: Mr. Fernando, you knew Langdon for more than twenty-five years. Whom do you think, with him and his family unexpectedly dead, the whole wealth goes to?

Fernando was confused about what was going on in the courtroom. He didn't know what Glenn was up to and answered slowly.

Fernando: To his brother.

Glenn: Why?

Fernando: They are one family, and he is the blood and the rightful successor.

Glenn: Very good. Any other possibilities, Mr. Fernando?

Fernando: Maybe charity. He loved charity very much.

Glenn: Good guess, but wrong answer. It is to you, Fernando.

Everyone in the court was stunned on hearing this statement. Langdon's brother, Willet, jumped and said yes, that was the reason he killed him.

Glenn: No, no, Mr. Willet, we should verify and confirm it from Langdon's personal attorney.

Then Langdon's personal attorney was brought into questioning, and he confirmed that Fernando didn't know anything about it. Langdon had drawn up his will in an attorney's office privately, and no one knew about it. Then Glenn questioned Langdon's attorney.

Glenn: Why did Langdon make such a decision?

Langdon's personal attorney: Because his brother has the wrong connections, and many times he threatened to kill Langdon if he was not given any money. The climax happened when Willet knew there was money left for him in the Swiss bank. So this whole agreement was made a week before he was killed.

Glenn: Why didn't he go to the cops when he threatened him?

Langdon's personal attorney: He was his brother, and he didn't want to blemish his family's name. He was very sensitive about this.

Glenn: Did you ever suspect Mr. Willet to be the killer?

Langdon's personal attorney: When I heard Langdon was dead, I thought Willet was the killer. Since Fernando was caught red-handed, I changed my mind.

Glenn: Do you still think Fernando is the killer?

Langdon's personal attorney: I am confused now. Sorry, Glenn.

Now the court was confused about who the real killer was, I was not sure what feeling I had. With my own eyes, I felt at one point that Fernando might be the killer, because he had learned of Langdon's will. The defendant was also speechless, and the judge's eyes were blurred. The whole confusion and panic was brought before justice after the lunch break. Glenn started the proceedings.

Glenn: Do you like Steve Jobs, Mr. Willet?

Langdon's brother: Why?

Glenn: Just curious.

Langdon's brother: Yes, very much. He changed the whole worlds understanding of computing. I deeply respect him.

Glenn: Oh that is excellent, but very soon you will hate him, at least by the end of today.

Langdon's brother: I don't understand.

Glenn: Do kids use cell phones?

Langdon's brother: How do I know that? I don't have one.

Defendant: These questions are not relevant to the case.

Judge: Is there any relation to the actual case, Mr. Hitch?

Glenn: Yes, Your Honor, this is a key question that is connected to the case.

Judge: Please proceed.

Glenn: Mr. Willet, do kids use cell phones?

Langdon's brother: No.

Glenn: At what age do they use cell phones?

Langdon's brother: Maybe after twelve or fifteen—it depends upon the parents and school, sir. I don't know much about it.

Glenn: Right answer, Mr. Willet. I appreciate your knowledge. Did your nephew and niece use cell phones?

Langdon's brother: No, sir.

Glenn: Are you sure, Mr. Willet?

Langdon's brother: Absolutely, sir. My brother is a disciplined father, and he would have told me if they used cell phones, because I always liked to talk to them and now I miss them.

Glenn: You miss them: that is funny. You are absolutely right, Mr. Willet, they didn't use cell phones, but they used IPods. Did you know that?

Langdon's brother's face changed, and he looked like he had missed something.

Langdon's brother: Yes, I knew that.

Then Glenn took an iPod from his pocket and asked the judge to play it before him, the jury, and everyone in the courtroom. The judge granted him permission and they played the video. It was a complete atrocity. The video started with the three-year-old boy, whose name was Pacey, and the seven-year-old girl, Bridget, playing in the living room. Mr. Langdon came into the living room and the kids were happy to see their father. On the video Langdon was sick with a cold. He told the kids not to come closer because he was sick, but the children were persistent. They wanted to play with their father, and finally Bridget said to Mr. Langdon, "No one in this world knows where they catch cold and they blame the whole world, but if we get a cold tomorrow, we'll know that it is because of you, Pa. We will not go to school and will blame you. We will have this video recorded till we die and blame you." The kids were messing with their father and went and put the iPod on the TV shelf near the DVD player. The kids pushed the iPOD a little further in so that the edges of the DVD player and walls of the shelves could hold the iPod for support. The kids were playing with their father for a few minutes and Langdon's wife joined them. Hearing what the kids were saying, she said, "Let me blame your daddy for giving me a cold too." It was one happy family all playing around.

Suddenly there was the sound of a gun with a silencer, and a bullet shot Langdon directly in the head. Very quickly there was another bullet fired at Mrs. Langdon's head. The killer was visible in a full black costume and a mask. The children were panicking and the little girl was about to scream, but he went and choked her and stomped on the boy's face with his right foot. He fired two bullets into the head of each child. With a bag in his hand, he went to the kitchen, took a knife, and cut the kids' bodies into pieces. Then he stabbed his dead brother and his wife almost forty times each.

After all this carnage he started cleaning up the evidence, keeping the gun on the coffee table and placing the knife in Langdon's chest. Still wearing the mask and gloves, he took Langdon's cell phone and made a call to Fernando, saying he was Langdon and needed to meet him immediately. The call was made around 10:30 PM. Before leaving the scene he removed the black T-shirt and black trousers. Under them he was wearing a dark gray suit with a black shirt. He finally removed the mask before leaving the house. Everyone in the courtroom was shocked and speechless after seeing the man who did it. It was Willet, Langdon's brother. After a few seconds, Willet shouted, "No! It's a fake video!" Hearing this, the judge ordered the cops to handcuff him.

Glenn was explaining how he found the evidence and exactly what happened before the court. He went to the crime scene in Langdon's house, and while gathering information, his pen fell from his shirt pocket. As he picked the pen up from the carpet, his eye caught a gadget, probably a phone, he thought, because there was a small light that could get in between the DVD player and sides of the shelf. He had been escorted by police officers and asked an officer permission to take it. After three years the iPod was covered with dust, but the cop got permission for him to take it with him. After seeing the video he was shocked and started to investigate how the whole killing happened.

On the day Mr. Langdon was killed, Willet went to his house to ask for his share from the Swiss bank. Willet was in his bedroom, asking for details of the money that he had in the bank. Langdon asked him to stay outside. He called Fernando to take the file from his locker, as he was sick and could not move from the bed. Willet was watching this through the opened door. Fernando left the room, and in the bedroom, Langdon and Willet were alone talking. Then Langdon showed Willet that he had $50 million in his Swiss account. Because of the constant torture, he showed him his will, saying that even if Willet took his family down, he would never get a penny, because all his money and wealth was going to Fernando. Fernando was not only his chef, but also a very trusted man whom his family loved. Then, knowing about his brother's will, Willet decided that if he could frame Fernando for his brother's murder, he could get the money from the Swiss bank as well as all his wealth. He disabled the surveillance camera that morning when he left Langdon's home, committed the murders, and enabled the surveillance camera before he left the house. He went the back way, as there was no surveillance camera there, and fled the scene. He chopped the kids into pieces to show the atrocity of the murder, to get Fernando a death sentence, because the death penalty was not legally allowed in NYC . Once he was dead, he could claim in the court about the wealth of his brother. In the whole process he convinced Langdon's attorney not to present the new will before the court, but Langdon's attorney initially thought that Fernando was the real killer and favored Willet and agreed, not telling anyone that Langdon had a new will. Langdon had a very old will that said Willet would be his successor and how much he cared for his brother and family. So Willet convinced Langdon's attorney to hide the new will, so eventually he would inherit all Langdon's wealth. But Glenn showed the video to Langdon's attorney and revealed the real culprit, so he agreed to talk about the will to the court.

Glenn then explained how Fernando was framed with murder: his fingerprints in the locker room, his fingerprints on the knife and gun. The gun was purchased from Colombia, where Fernando was born, which made the case even stronger. The surveillance camera only recorded Fernando entering the house, which created a motivation. He bribed the public attorney and the Prosecutor and some jurors, even the police officers were bribed. He had planned it so well; they didn't bring anything before this court. The taxi driver was not properly interrogated in detail. They also didn't evaluate the autopsy report properly. They continued talking about the murder itself, how it was horribly executed. All the witnesses were against pointing to Fernando, and everyone was convinced both the jury and the judge. Then Glenn showed all the financial transactions that had been used to bribe the juries, the public and the judge. The court was clouded with all the hidden reality behind the case, and after Glenn explained the whole plot, he went and sat in the chair.

Claudia removed her shoe and threw it at Willet, hitting his face. The people in the courtroom became motionless, and a lady cop came and stood next to Claudia and held her hands. The judge quickly ordered the arrest of Willet and the public attorney, the jurors who were involved, and the cops also. They asked the lady cop to bring Claudia to the judge's private room. We asked the officer if we could join them and she agreed, so Madison, Sandra, and I followed them to the judge's chambers. The judge looked relaxed. He greeted Claudia with a pleasant smile and looked at her like a loving father and asked all of us to sit down. He asked Claudia, "Why did you throw your shoe at Mr. Willet?" Claudia was quiet and didn't answer the judge and he asked, "Were you angry because he tried to make your father look guilty?" Claudia spoke to him gently and softly answered him, "No, he killed innocent children without mercy." We were all moved by her answer, and the judge asked her again, "So it was not for your father, it was for the children who were killed?" She answered, "Yes, sir." The judge looked at her and said, "I don't know what judgment to make now. Your actions are pardoned, but please don't do that again. You should always respect the court room." Claudia replied, "Thanks, sir, I will." We all left the judge's room and the judge released Fernando and gave the death penalty to Mr. Willet, and life sentences to the defendant and the public attorney, the jurors, and the cops who were involved. He also terminated their licenses to practice law in the future. He also fined Mr. Willet $10 million for making an innocent man stay behind bars for three years, and compensation for all the loss and damages he had caused him and his family.

Now the family was united, and Claudia, her mother, Sandra, and her father, Fernando, lived with us. They got their inheritance from Mr. Langdon's family and received $150 million, but they gave the money to charity and other good purposes. They just took a couple of million for themselves and they gave the rest away. It was Fernando's decision, as he said there were thousands of souls in jail for crimes that they didn't commit and were spending their lives behind bars for no reason. He had $148 million to build a law college in the Bronx called Sandhed Bagom, and it is free for kids of parents in jail. The college is also dedicated to poor and marginalized kids, victims of the law, and helpless kids. The college mainly focuses on law and teaching law for all common people.

The counsel appreciated Glenn for his work in Langdon's case. Fernando offered Glenn the position of director of the college. Glenn, being a very wise man, accepted the offer. Glenn took the offer with only one thing in his mind: there should be many Glenn's in this world to save all the innocent people. Fernando also donated $10 million of the money to a charity organization in the Bronx. I was chuffed for Claudia and her family, who were now enjoying their life and finding peace in all aspects. In addition, Fernando is now the chief chef in our house and is a better cook than my mom. Hope my mom is not reading this.

I had been working at Harvest and Reap almost two years, and the yearly review was again a disappointment. They said the same thing in a different way. I was an indispensable resource on this team and they could not move me back to the security team. I should be on the database team for a year and once all those problems were resolved, I could move back to my IT security team. Peyton's boss promised me that he would be responsible for my moving back permanently to security, which was my goal in life. It didn't hurt me much this time, because I changed my mind. The only thing I was going to do was visit Rikers Island prison for the next year and help all the people who were in need. Yes, I wanted to protect the innocent people who were spending time behind bars and change their lives. So Fernando and I visited people in the prison and helped innocent people who needed legal help and helped their families while they were in prison. We would go with different social service groups, missionaries, and church clergy to visit people in prison and try helping in all the ways we could. Madison also went with us to assist us in our noble quest to help people behind bars. I wanted to work for the benefit of the people in prison and their families. I didn't give a heck about the politics of Harvest and Reap, and now I was doing something very new in my life. These days I read different books related to prison, like biographies, and everything about prison life.

Time was flying by very fast, as fast as light, and another year flew by. The only thing I could remember and appreciate over the past year was Mr. Sandeep. Yes, he made it: he invented this new database that could consolidate, convert, and integrate with any database in the world. He patented his invention and sold it for a big price for almost $220 million. He left Harvest and Reap and became the managing director for the same company that he sold the software to. I was very proud of him. He took my advice very sincerely and worked hard and made his fortune.

After two years my search started and I was analyzing all the events that had happened around me. It started from the day I was moved from my security team. Let me take a moment to talk about how Peyton was smart enough to get rid of me. He had a brilliant evil mind. He played it so well that he could get away from his team. He took all my ideas and presented them to his boss and management as his own. He portrayed me as his helper and as if I was working on all his ideas. I knew this guy was rotten, right from the start, but I had never been through this "circle of wickedness", and I let go. He was a smooth talker and convinced everybody in the review panel that I was nobody special; still just beginning my career. But eventually I had to say something, my age and experience had nothing to do with achievements and promotions. Every single corporation was formed by young minds. Age should not be a problem. If you wanted to be successful, you needed to innovate, create new things and make your mind young, and then you could be closer to what you wanted to do in life. If you worked in a corporation, they would always talk about attitude, experience, opportunities, this and that, and they would never give you what you wanted; you had to take what you wanted.

I was depressed, not because they didn't give me what I wanted, but at how this world operated in the "law of evilness". I was damn sure that I would overcome this situation in my life. How could other people, whose minds were tucked in a pit and could not help themselves, overcome such evil? Peyton was not only jealous that I would grow faster in the company and be his boss, but knew that I was blessed with all the gifts. Envy is the first thought of a man's ruin—yes, it will ruin the very simple and elegant nature of your mind. Only people who don't know who they are will feel envy; if you know who you are, you don't have time to think about others' possessions.

But my company didn't completely abandon me, and they gave me a good bonus. I got almost $1,700,000. The only reason they gave me this bonus was to make me work for them and be a victim of their politics. Yes, it was not given for the work I had accomplished in the previous years, but as a token of reward for being with them at all times. Reward is good, but it shouldn't be ones destiny; it will slow your mind day by day, when you are really dependent upon bonuses. All I say is that there are many ways to make money; don't wait for a year to get something that you deserve now. On the day of the review, I went to a bar and got drunk off my ass. That is not good at all. When you get depressed, go talk to someone you know, love and trust. It will make a difference. Never assume that drinking will fix the problem you are facing. All it does is make your life miserable. If you are relaxed and tired sometimes, drink in moderation. This was the first time I was drunk, and Demonthin picked me up in the bar and almost had to carry me on his shoulder. He felt very bad for me, because he had never seen me like this.

The worst thing I did was not answer my cell phone. When Madison called me, I turned it off. I had never done that before in my life. I was not annoyed with Madison's call, but I was sailing on my depression in a river of alcohol. In that journey, I wanted to be alone in the boat and didn't want to talk to anyone. Perhaps I was talking to my silence. I apologized to Madison a million times in the days after and we just stayed home. I had a hangover for almost two days, and I decided to stay in my room and not see anybody except Madison. Drinking caused even worse things. I didn't even know my sweet Claudia had left my house after being kicked out by management. That is really bad. I didn't know what was happening in the house. If this happened after one day of drinking, I wondered, what would happen to people who got drunk all the time? I knew what would happen: they would be in a different world and nobody would be around them. So I promised Madison that I would never, ever get drunk like that anymore, and she was happy about my decision. But the best thing I did while drinking was that, I didn't puke.

Not everything was terrible at Harvest and Reap. I loved my new team even more than the old team. On the old security team I loved my career, but with the new team I liked my teammates and my boss, Gwyneth. She was a sweetheart. She took care of me like a son. She was in her mid-forties and always appreciated all the good work I had done. Her heart was pulled close to me because of the things I did in Chelsea. I even took her and the team to Chelsea one weekend and introduced her to all the people there. She was excited to see them and spent a whole week with them. She brought them many gifts, assuming that they were still in need, but in turn the people in Chelsea knew she was my boss and they gave her many valuable gifts, which she couldn't take in a car. She hired a truck to take them. Nyah had become a really trustworthy friend to Madison, my friends, and me. The most vivid thing that went on in my mind was the murder of four innocent people and the crime involved. The murders made me reevaluate life and responsibility, especially when large sums of money were involved. After this incident I always looked at myself as the owner of the house. The whole murder and imprisonment was not right. One thing that really hurt me was that Sandra and Claudia had both hidden the truth from me. Even a little girl had outsmarted me and kept the secret to herself.

When I asked Sandra about the incident, she felt a little awkward. When I went to the Bronx, and it looked like the American version of Chelsea. I didn't care about how poor the neighborhood was, but it looked run down and like a sorrow-filled borough. I felt like there were two different worlds: one on this side of the river and the other on the other side of the river. It was nothing new to me, but something was new: this neighborhood was filled with crime and drugs. I didn't see that in Chelsea. They were looking for some air to breathe and a hand to hold, some tongues to teach. My mind thought only one thing: if Chelsea would be there in the second generation. If I had not been there, it would have been like the Bronx. Probably everyone wanted to come to America for freedom and prosperity, and choose a different path for their lives. I wanted this borough to be the same as Manhattan, but the people in the Bronx thought of being poor in a different way, and they cursed their destiny. And I didn't know where to start helping them.

I had met Sandra and Claudia in a one-bedroom apartment with Sandra's mother. There was nothing great to describe how the house looked, as it was filled with broken things. Madison and I stayed the whole day, having breakfast, lunch, and dinner, to make them comfortable. But I didn't talk much about Fernando or the murder because I wanted her to feel better about talking to us again. Then when Sandra came to our home, Madison and I asked her to recount the whole story and she explained. Throughout the whole conversation I felt one thing: they were helpless and blameless. Who cares about you in this world when you are helpless and blameless? Everyone is selfish and has no time for others.

One thing I learned was that even to prove you are blameless, you need money. That is why Fernando was sitting behind bars. When I looked into the eyes of Sandra and asked for the truth, it revealed one message: "I don't know whether Fernando did it, but I am sure that he is not capable of doing it." To do a crime like this you had to be capable of planning and Fernando was not capable, because he was not an evil mastermind. The reality is that everyone can be a murderer when time pushes us; we could kill anyone who is a nuisance or is torturing us, like Peyton. I didn't know whether I would be able or not to walk into the office and put a few bullets in his head.

I took this problem very seriously, and started to work on it. It was Benjamin's father who referred me to Glenn Hitch. Glenn Hitch was the best attorney in New York City. He had never lost a case, and Fernando was his one hundredth case. He didn't hesitate when I was looking for help from him. The best thing about Glenn was that he knew what he was doing. He only took complicated cases and always made sure he was fighting for the right cause. If he knew a convict, he reduced the terms of prison but never covered the culprit. He taught me one thing about law: "Punishment is for realization and not for destroying, but sometimes punishment works as a model." He had a different personality every time I met him. I saw something that interested me about his personality. I never saw him panic or get nervous, and his mind was also steady and thoughtful, which was unusual for anyone in that profession. The whole courtroom scene was thrilling and it looked like watching a movie, until he played the video. No one knew what was happening.

His opening statement and the way he proceeded with the case was a legacy, because he knew who the actual killer was and played out a high-staged drama, moving inch by inch. I asked him why he did that, because I thought he should have showed the video directly to everyone. He replied, "Then there is no thrill, Oliver. You wouldn't have enjoyed the show." I said, "Please, Glenn." He replied, "I was kidding, Oliver. If I had shown it directly in the courtroom, no one would know the full and gory details of the killings. He would have said this whole video was prerecorded and staged." Then Glenn continued explaining that Willet would try to prove his innocence, but we had to prove the video was genuine. The main thing is motivation and we needed to present it very clearly.

As you know Willet had said in court three years ago that he didn't meet his brother and was not in his house on the day of the murder, but later he confirmed that he was there to talk to him. He initially said he didn't transfer the money, but later when Glenn showed the transaction receipts, he admitted that he had. The missing file from Langdon's house that had all the documents, including the information about the Swiss bank account, was seized in Willet's house. After killing, he took the file from Langdon's locker and put it in the bag, and the same bag was found in Willet's home. It was not only the video that could prove his guilt, but all the statements that added more weight to the case. He had no chance of escape, and eventually he confessed in court. Glenn also said that if the video was the only evidence, that could be the only hope, but here that was not the case; he was trapped like a bird. Glenn said something very interesting about the law: people always ask for motivation; that is what will make the case stronger. Motivation always starts from the beginning and not from the end, so when dealing with the law, go to the beginning, and it will explain the ending very well.

I was new to the courtroom, so I didn't know much about it, and everything I saw, was a new experience for me. One thing I must say: Willet wasn't prepared for the day; he was just there to see Fernando being accused and hoping that day would be the worst nightmare of his life. I enjoyed the way Glenn spoke in court and his style and gestures looked like Atticus Finch in *To Kill a Mockingbird*. Glenn fought for the innocent in post-era modern and free America, and we were very proud of him. One question I liked in the courtroom was "Do you like Steve Jobs, Mr. Willet?" Everybody loved Steve Jobs for his brilliant mind and creativity, but not for Willet. I could not comprehend how someone could ever kill a child, and especially one of his own blood.

My search became aggressive. Willet didn't not only kill Langdon, but he killed himself, his own blood. He did it for money. He killed everybody for no reason. He destroyed Langdon's family, and was about to destroy Fernando's family. We saw the video and the bloodshed was sick, the way he just chopped the kids into pieces. People die all the time, but there should be some dignity when people die. Willet was still an animal, according to Darwin's theory, and that was the problem with Darwin's theory: where did man possess violence? Everybody says violence is inherent from birth or that it comes from nature, temptation, weakness, experience, or greed, but none of these should be the characteristics of humans by inheritance. If that is true, then by law, no one should be punished. We are more than humans, I know for sure. It is not only Willet to be judged and killed, it is everyone who kills. Yes, where are the other Willets who kill children in the name of war and then escape? When you ask them, "Why did you do that?" they answer, "Wrong aim, by accident, cross fire, inevitable." Then we should deal with them the same way as these men of war act: put them in an arena and give them guns and ask them to shoot each other; it is the same answer "Wrong aim, by accident, cross fire, inevitable." But the reality is that monkeys and chimps go unpunished, because they are animals, so the people who go unpunished of war crimes are treated like monkeys and chimps. The least hurtful thing we could do is tattoo on their foreheads "Darwin's Evolution." There are even worse people than Willet who abuse and rape kids. I cannot stand them. People like that should have their genitals removed. Sorry for being candid, but my search was fueled by rage over what had happened around me and the fact that I could not stop these crimes. I was still a human and I wanted to be a superhero, and my search doubled in urgency from the last time I thought about a perfect world. For all suspects, the message is that we have to appreciate the smartness of Willet, but know that the suspect will always leave some evidence behind.

I was stunned when Fernando gave all the money from Langdon's will to benefit those in need and kept only a couple of million dollars. I personally asked why he did that and the thoughts and words from Fernando's mouth were honest and pure. When he was in prison, he was completely broke and depressed, and he used to talk to his fellow inmates who were also innocent. Some people believed him, but some thought it was a default confession since everyone in prison "wasn't guilty." My voice was one among the guilty ones at first and I didn't have enough strength to convince people that he was innocent. He also told me how the people in prison missed their families and often felt like they were a million miles away, though they sometimes lived only ten miles away. Fernando spent time in prison just reading the Bible and building up the only thing in his mind, which was "hope." He said, "I know the difference between pain and suffering, but now I cannot feel both." But then some light came to his life to change everything. "It is you, Oliver," he said. "People like me may call and see you as a god, savior, redeemer, helper, advocate, but I would rather call and see you as hope, my only hope." I don't know where people get their hope like me, but I felt that I was the lucky one, because I got to help others get out of bad situations that they didn't deserve to be in. That was the reason Fernando gave so much money to build a law college for poor people whose parents were in prison, educating people about law, people who wanted to fight for justice, and to help people who had been victims of the law. Fernando was right: even if we haven't saved enough money for food, shelter, or anything, at least we should have money to protect ourselves from incidents with the law or lawsuits. What can I say from all his opinion and expression that he shared with me? If religion builds hope in humans, then let us not kill religion. He went through this turmoil and wanted to stop it from happening to others, and that was the right attitude. Everyone should learn from bad experiences. Taking a gun and going and killing all the people who hurt you is good for movies and the box office, but in real life, don't waste bullets; use your brains.

What happened to the money that I spent for Willet's case? I spent almost $60,000 in one year, but I didn't feel like I lost it. I got it back. From Fernando? No, I got it back from Glenn. Very surprising, isn't it? Yes, I got all the money from Glenn and he gave me back everything I had spent. I asked him why and I refused to take it. Glenn said, "You are not a businessman, Oliver." I asked him, "What does that mean?" Glenn replied, "When you first walked through my doors, I thought it was business, but later I realized it was not. I waited until Fernando would do something I expected. He did it—gave all the money to charity." Glenn started explaining, "You didn't know anything about the will. All you wanted was to help an innocent man. When some people knew about Langdon's will leaving all that money to Fernando, the real business started. His friends, family, lawyers, and everyone in the world would start to help Fernando, to make sure that they got a cut of Langdon's money." But, he said, I didn't have that thought in my mind, and he asked me why. I replied to him, "I don't see things that way." Yes, Glenn was absolutely right: if anyone had known of the real inheritance that Fernando had, no matter what he had been accused of, money would have made them wash away all the guilt and crime that was committed before and after.

There were really some bad guys involved in Langdon's family's murder other than Willet: the Prosecutor, cops, jurors, and the public attorney. Defenders worked for the state, and the state worked for the federal government, and the federal government worked for the people. No shortcuts here. The defense attorney represented the victim and was there to provide justice for him, but in this case he hadn't done that. It was the same with the public attorney: he didn't do his job. And this nation is in the hands of the cops and bad cops always exist in every country. I am very ashamed of the legal system in America and the world.

About juries, what can I say, or rather, where should I start? They are made up of common citizens who have a hand in the legal system. We need to do more intense background checks all the time. Of all the four law abiders, I feel all the four are the same level of culprits. The funny part of this is that justice was not served for either the victims or the guilty, and the guilt was initially placed on Fernando. The public attorneys are representatives and ambassadors of the law system, so they should be doing their job with sincere consciousness.

It happens not only in the legal system, but also with other professionals who are irresponsible about abiding by the law. Yet if everyone thought of themselves as ambassadors for their professions, they wouldn't be so fast to break the law. Now all the families, the defendant, public attorney, cops, and juries are part of the problem; if they thought of the future of their actions, they would never have done what they did. Imagine any one of the kids from these families wanting to be a sincere judge or attorney or cop or at least a member of a jury. Think about how big the obstacle is they have built for their kids if they act immorally. If your family heritage is in law, and you killed your grandparents' reputation, you have wiped out all the hard work and sacrifices they have made. They even lost their license, though it sounded like they literally could not practice law anymore. They have lost the respect from the teachers and professors who taught them, lost their college ambitions, their friends, their pasts—they lost their whole career and education. They were all willing to watch Fernando die before them. That is cruelty, watching someone die for a crime that they have not committed; it is the worst revenge that will be passed on to the future. That is why somehow there is someone saying, "Your past cruel actions will haunt you in the future."

What could I say about our friend Sandeep, the modern white-collar slave? He was educated and should have known all about wages and rights. I can only infer about him, like the set of people who always look for percentage of scores on the exam but don't examine themselves to see that each percentage of a score has understanding. These sorts of people are worse than the people in Chelsea. They are the majority in the world and work for someone else, never for themselves. This happens throughout the world, as white-collar workers are in demand because they know these are the highly educated idiots in the world. It happens in Europe, and it's why I blame my country. All I have to say is, when you have something in your hands and then you should have the same amount in your pocket. I had a very short conversation with Sandeep, but since he was dynamic and smart, he rock and rolled and made his way to become a rich man. Kudos to Sandeep. There are many on Wall Street who walk from all directions of NYC subways but don't know where they are walking and why they are walking. When you know where you are walking, and why you are walking, your life changes. All these guys are walking to Wall Street and why do they walk? For money. The sad part is there are good citizens here on Wall Street who don't know their value and act like slaves in shirts and ties. Weak Men! Finally, let's not forget slaves are still bought into this country every minute—not tied up in chains, but with fancy ties.

I spoke about injustice to everybody and explained what I was doing. I also went on a new mission visiting prisons, learning law, helping poor kids in the Bronx, Brooklyn, even in the city, where the kids go uncared for in a rich man's paradise. Now I am like a missionary from Vatican City. Yes, when I visit prison, I see lots of people from church doing their services for the prisoners, no matter their beliefs. They are helping somebody, which I am pleased. I didn't care about my promotion or transfer to my team; all that mattered to me was I wanted to help innocent people in prison. Innocent people include both those who have committed crimes and those who have not committed crimes. I could see people who had committed crimes realize their mistakes and repent for them. According to my eyes, if you repent, you look innocent to me. The day you proclaim that you have made a mistake is the day your life starts improving. Only liars keep lying that they are perfect. I watched many movies related to prison, and saw there are different sides to prison life. On one side guys wanted to escape and I liked *Escape from Alcatraz*, *The Great Escape*, and *Shawshank Redemption*., The second side where they change themselves and change others' lives like *American History X*, *Green Mile*, and the third side focused on death row confessions, like *Dead Man Walking*. In short all these people have hope to escape, redeem themselves, or find a loophole.

I know criminals, gangsters, mobsters, and thieves, and all of them know I am a cool kid and appreciate my work. Sometimes I feel like I am Al Capone, John Dillinger or Vito Corleone. I am a jailbird now, feeding my nest.

Chapter 12
THE ULTIMATE TRUTH

A YEAR PASSED. I SPENT MUCH OF MY FREE TIME WITH PRISONERS, TRYING to understand their psychology and the fundamental nature of human life, to differentiate between truth and lies. The biggest paradox I learned from the prisoners was to keep an optimistic attitude. So many of them said to me, "Oliver, from my side it looks like you are behind bars." This is the greatest philosophy of prison I had learned. That statement is absolutely true. We so-called free men are behind bars: bars of government, drugs, politics, corporations, taxes, work, religion, sports; everything that this system has built for us, is a prison.

I felt that I was in prison while working at my company, because I danced to the music they played. I had wardens in the name of managers, nannies in the name of management who changed my diapers, low wages in the name of bonuses—I could keep listing all the things that I see in the company. I have watched a whole list of prison movies, and I thought drugs, homosexuality, bribes, gangsters, murders, mobs, encounters, escape, and racism were just concepts inside of prison, but now I see these things in my real life. Well, why blame them? We tell ourselves that we live in a perfect world, but we have the same problems and even more problems around us than those in prison. I have learned a lot from prisoners and I do lots of community service for the people in the Bronx, in Brooklyn—all five boroughs. On many occasions I visit the families of the prisoners, checking in on them, helping, fulfilling their needs, and doing what I can for them.

We are building a law college in the Bronx with Fernando's donated money. We have one building now and two more to go and with that one building we will offer families free law education and advice.

I hung out only in the poor and rundown neighborhoods; I stopped going to wealthy neighborhoods and stopped talking to all the aristocrats with all the meaningless conversations. Though I live here in a palace, my mind is stuck in the shallow pits of New York City. Every time I go to visit prisons and correction centers in New York, I ask myself, *does anyone new who moves to New York City know the name and place of one prison in NYC?* They all know night clubs, bars, dance floors, libraries, museums, restaurants, and tourist places, but they can't even name one prison in NYC.

I had completed three years in my company, and as previously promised by Peyton's boss, they were supposed to move me back to the security team. I had my review with my current boss, Gwyneth, who gave me very positive feedback. So I went to meet Peyton and his boss and a few senior managers. They had the feedback report from Gwyneth and were reviewing it.

Peyton's boss: That is interesting. I don't see anything negative from your current manager, Gwyneth. Congratulations, Oliver.

Me: Thank you.

Peyton's boss: So, Oliver, do you really want to go back to your passion and work on the IT security team?

Me: Definitely.

Peyton's boss: Why is that?

Me: I started my career to be an anti-hacker and to be exalted in my field.

Peyton's boss: Well, that's nice to hear, but we have a problem here, Oliver.

I detected a confrontation and I pushed myself back in the chair to feel more comfortable and crossed my legs.

Me: What is that?

Peyton's boss: It seems you have a conflict and problem with our management, Oliver.

Me: I don't think so.

Peyton's boss: Let me make myself clear. We cannot move you to the IT security team, because it seems you have some connections that may be a threat to our company.

Me: What do you mean, connections?

Peyton's boss: These days you are visiting prisons and meeting notorious, convicted gangsters, and some public enemies, and you're helping them.

Me: I am not helping any of them do something criminal rather; I am bringing some change into their lives and helping innocent people prove their innocence.

Peyton's boss: I understand, but our corporate policies don't allow such social revolutionary ideas, Oliver. To be honest, we appreciate all the good things you have done in Chelsea and we are proud of you, but criminals and stuff—that doesn't sound good.

Me: So how do you relate this to work? I mean, I still don't get it.

Peyton's boss: We consider it a threat, Oliver. It is risky for the company to put you in roles in IT security projects, because confidential company information could be sold or leaked to bad guys because of all the connections that you have. We know you are a great resource for us, but it is policy and we must always adhere to it, Oliver.

Peyton's boss: Also, Oliver, it seems you have the character to change things around you and revolt and achieve your goals, which is an additional threat to our company because you may induce the employees to go against the company. You should also understand that we are public limited. If you do anything crazy, it will reflect on our reputation and market value.

I was lost now and my blood froze with this blasphemy, but I took a deep breath.

Me: I have one simple question: do I have a job here?

Peyton's boss: Yes, of course, Oliver, as said you are a valuable resource for us, but certain things don't match our policies, even though we appreciate all your efforts for helpless people. We need more time to really trust you, know you more, so that we can help you and move you to the IT security team.

Me: Hmm, how much time?

Peyton's boss: Well, maybe five to ten years, but within five years, and not less than that.

Me: Oh, five years. (I breathed heavily.)

Peyton's boss: You could work with the same team and report to Gwyneth, and if you have any interest in other teams, please let us know. We are always here to help you.

I was angry, very angry, and now I knew how to get guns. I wanted to kill all these guys with at least four bullets: two to the head, one in the chest, and one in the ribs. Perfect killing and death is completely assured. I hated these guys, but I behaved like a professional and thanked them and walked out of the room. And as I walked out, I met Nyah and Edgar. They greeted me and I said "hi" but didn't talk to them and quickly left the office.

I walked out of the office and heard a lot of noise on the street, and people were shouting, "Occupy Wall Street!" They were holding banners and flags and marching. I heard many slogans, but one in particular caught my ears: "Do you feel it trickle down?" Automatically my lips moved and said, "Yes, I feel it trickle down." Then I walked to see the crowd. Lots of cops were standing around, and as I watched the demonstrators, they were aggressive and shouting louder, and the slogans they shouted sounded like they were for me.

Then I decided to walk with them. I had my suit on, and I sneaked into the crowd and started to walk. People were in jeans and some were in fancy dress costumes, and as they saw me in my suit, they stared at me. I knew about Occupy Wall Street, but I hadn't taken much notice about it. But now I was a victim of a corporate power and culture, so I said to the guys who were looking at me, "They jacked me also, bro." Very quickly one guy jumped and tapped my shoulder and said, "I know they are snitches and they suck. You are with us, bro. We will show our power." His words sounded like he would get me into some trouble, but I was really angry with my boss and company and now I wanted to know what corporate America was all about. I walked through Wall Street with a banner in my hand, shouting with them, and this was the first time my voice was loud, shouting "Occupy Wall Street!" I removed my suit jacket and tied it in the back and folded my full shirt. Then I tied a band around my head that said "Occupy Wall Street."

After the rally, we all sat before Exchange Place, where a speaker talked about corporate America and all their hypocrisy and the burden they put on the public and marginalized people. I was listening to all the speeches, and something really caught me. By the time the procession and meeting was over, it was around six in the evening. A few men and women invited me to have a drink, and I went with them. There were four dudes and two ladies. I could remember the dudes' names—Henry, Jade, Marcus, and William—and the ladies' names were Patricia and Velvet. They were asking who I was and what I was doing. They quickly recognized me as the "Man from Chelsea" and appreciated all the good work I had done. I was depressed and told them what had happened in my company and about their politics, and how they made false accusations against me for helping prisoners and their families.

Then I started to talk to them about myself and my company. I said I had the highest qualifications in the whole country. "I have a gold medal from my college, and a master's degree, a Nobel Prize, an award from Nelson Mandela, an award from the president as best citizen, my philosophy, my technology knowledge, and everything," yet they had made me a victim of their politics. I had all these qualifications, yet I could not grow in my company. I had not offended anyone there, and throughout my life I had always been helpful to everyone, always kind to family and friends, always a good kid. I had always been loyal to my girlfriend, and had never cheated on her. I had all these values and had started my journey to make everyone rich, powerful, and happy, and live forever, like a Superman or Ironman, but everything was fading and dying, and I was still a human with failures.

I was just blabbering and drinking shots and they were all listening to me. I was not drunk yet and I responded to Madison's calls and text messages, but I was talking about the failures that I was undergoing. All my new friends from Occupy Wall Street were listening, and Henry asked, "Do you want to join us, Oliver?" I replied, "No, I never even thought about it," and Patricia said, "Please don't join us, Oliver. There is a better way to deal with things." I said to Patricia, "I didn't have any thought of joining you guys. I like you guys, but why do you say there are better ways of dealing with things, and why did you choose this path of revolution?" Patricia said, "Maybe you are the chosen one, Oliver. You should guide us all." Why did they call me the chosen one? I hated someone calling me that, and I hardly knew this lady. I just replied, "Everyone is a chosen one. You are chosen to make a change in Wall Street through Occupy Wall Street."

I left around eleven, and all six new friends came home with me. All these people had traveled from different cities, and I showed them hospitality by hosting them in my house. They were good-natured people, but they somehow felt that they were being scammed by Wall Street. I didn't want to pass judgment because something was missing. The same thing happened; I took a week off from my work because I could not handle any more of their politics and crap. The six new friends stayed with us for a week. In the daytime they hung out near Wall Street for rallies and demonstrations, and at night we talked and exchanged our life's experiences. The whole week I didn't go outside. All I did was think, I was only thinking. The only time I was happy was when I was playing with Claudia, talking to Madison, or talking to my new friends from Occupy Wall Street, but the rest of the time, I was thinking about all the things that were happening around me. Madison was so comforting. She was encouraging me and wanted me to be stronger, and I was very glad that I had the best girlfriend in the world.

A week passed and all the new friends from Occupy Wall Street left us. Before leaving, Patricia took me to a corner and said, "Just help all of us, Oliver. Never give up. The door is very close to you. Just walk through it and show the way to everyone in this world. We are waiting for you. You have to understand that Occupy Wall Street is like the French and American revolutions, the Cuban and Chinese revolutions, or even the October Revolution. Remember, they were all good for a moment, but more revolutions are needed every day. Never give up." She kissed my forehead and said, "Love you, Oliver. You will do the right thing."

They all left and I went back to my office. I didn't show the sadness on my face. I looked chilling and cool. I started my routine schedule and started working, but my search didn't stop. While I was searching for what was wrong in me, I continued helping innocent people in prison and their families, and helping poor people learn the law. I didn't mess around with all the women whose husbands or boyfriends were in prison. I was not importing drugs inside the prison, or threatening the public with all these connections, or bossing anyone around, or making money in any way with these people. Rather I was building a sacred family with accused murderers and gangsters.

I knew that Peyton was jealous of me and that envy was the beginning of all battles. They found something in me and they used it. This technique of blasphemy has existed from the dawn of human civilization. They will always try to find some mistakes in you, when you are growing in your life, because one simple mistake will bring a bad name to you and prove you as the wrong person. The most common thing is they will call you a manic or a womanizer. They will interrogate you about your birth, call you a terrorist, or slander you, and you will be blamed like I was. That's what they accused me of—being a terrorist. They didn't say that exactly, yet the inner meaning was the same.

It also took me awhile to understand what Occupy Wall Street was about. I still didn't understand the corporate world. But one thing I knew about the corporate world: they do business and not charity, so they have the slogan "We like you when you are with us, but we don't like you when you are not with us." Even husbands and wives have the same concept, but here *like* should be replaced with "Do we make money out of you, or do you have any value?"

I heard a knock at my office door and said, "Come in." It was Edgar and Nyah, and they looked concerned. "Could we take a walk, Oliver?" they asked, and I replied, "Yes, sure, anything for you guys." We headed outside the office and walked toward the FDR Drive. Edgar started talking. "You look sad, Oliver." I replied, "I don't know yet." Edgar said, "So you don't know whether you are sad or not?" Then we started to talk.

Edgar: What's your goal in life?

Me: Perfection and symmetry.

Edgar: Where?

Me: In all human lives.

Edgar: Have you found some answer yet, chief?

Me: I was close many times, but something is missing, and I keep going backwards.

Nyah: Could we help you, Oliver?

Me: With what?

Nyah: To find answers for your questions.

Me: Is it promising?

Nyah: It will be. It is all in your mind, Oliver, how you take it.

Me: Sure. I wasted all these years trying to find an answer, so let me see what you have to show me.

Nyah: But you have to meet someone who is very special.

Me: Who is that, Nyah? Why do you call him special?

Nyah: Yeah, for me and most of us.

Me: What is his name?

Nyah: Answers are coming when you walk through that door. Then we will tell you.

Me: When could I meet him?

Edgar: How about tomorrow evening near Seventy-Second Street and Park Avenue?

Me: That is close to my house.

Edgar: It is indeed, Oliver. See you then.

I had no idea who the person was they were talking about and why Nyah and Edgar came to me with this conversation about meeting someone I didn't know. The strange thing was that he lived five blocks away from me and I didn't know him, but that was life in New York City. It was a small city with long-distance communication between doors. It made me a little nervous now because I was curious about what this was all about. I was talking to Madison about the same thing, but she was relaxed and said, "You know Edgar and Nyah well, and they are taking you someplace in the city a few blocks away. What are you worried about?" I replied to her, "I know all the philosophy and wisdom of this universe. What is left in the world to learn?" Madison wittily replied, "Ignorance is bliss. You have a long road to learn more things in life, honey." I tickled her stomach and said, "Mother of wisdom says so."

The next day I went to the office, and the whole day my mind was thinking about the visit, which was going to happen later in the evening. Edgar and Nyah walked to my office and picked me up at three, and Demonthin drove us to the meeting. We stopped near Seventy-Second and Park Avenue, and I asked Demonthin to leave because it was close enough to my home that I could walk. There was an entrance in the middle of the block. I initially assumed it was a block with many buildings. It was strange that I noticed the whole building had only one entrance. We took the elevator and went to the third floor, and there was a big door before us. Edgar said, "This is the door. It is open, so go," and I asked them, "You guys?" Nyah said, "We are leaving. Just go and talk to him. You will be fine. I have one piece of advice: just believe him."

They left and I opened the door. It was a very big living room and I saw someone sitting near the big window, resting on a huge chair. I didn't see anything in the room, and there was some sort of force that made me just look at him. I didn't notice anything in the living room and as I walked closer to him, I saw that it was not a chair, but looked like a throne, some antique model that was elegant and grand. He turned around and saw me and said, "Welcome, Oliver." I looked at him, and he said, "Please, sit down." I went and sat in a chair that was before him. He was a very good-looking older man with white hair, little black shades and a white beard that was well trimmed. He looked at me and said, "I am Dan Root." I greeted him, "Hi, Dan," and I asked him how he knew my name. He said, "Edgar and Nyah mentioned your name yesterday and said you'd like to meet me." I replied, "Oh, yeah, they said that you are special and you could help me."

Dan: Am I special? I thought everyone is special. (He smiled after saying this.)

Me: Yeah, you are right, everyone is special.

Dan: What can I help you with, Oliver?

Me: I am not doing well these days. I feel like I'm in the clutches of politics. Do you live here?

Dan: Hmm, I live here.

Me: Do you own this apartment? Sorry, I mean the whole building?

Dan: Both, and the whole block.

Me: Whoo. You live by yourself?

Dan: Yes, I do, and I have a couple of doormen—a pretty big family.

Me: That is funny.

Dan: So, still I didn't get the point. How can I help you?

Me: Yeah, I feel a little worried, like I missed something in my life. It is bothering me these days.

Dan: It seems that your search is stuck in limbo.

I was stunned, and my blood stopped flowing through my veins when I heard that.

Me: What do you mean by *search* here?

Dan: You have spent your entire life searching for an answer: How can one fly? How can I make everyone a Superman?

I nodded and I was breathing less, and then I started panting and thought, *Who is he and how does he know all this?*

Me: Are you a psychic or something like that? How do you know this? Maybe you are guessing.

Dan: I don't make guesses. When I know, I talk, and when I talk, I know what I am talking about.

Me: Well, yeah, I am searching for the truth, where humans can be free from pain and desires, and be superheroes.

Dan: Starting from your mother's womb.

He was adding more pressure on my side, because I didn't know how he knew all these things that only my father knew and that came from conversations between us.

Me: You make me a little uncomfortable.

He gave a smile.

Dan: Oliver, I thought you would be excited to meet me. You should be glad. At least somebody knows all your inner thoughts.

Me: Well, I am happy to see you, Dan. People with extraordinary skills could read the inner thoughts of men but it looks like you are some sort of god from mythology.

Dan: You called me a god. That is nice of you. I thought you were a god.

He was blowing my mind.

Me: Well, you said, I am a god, very funny, you know. . .

Dan: You don't believe in God and you are agnostic. I said, don't believe in God or search for him, rather think you are a god and everything will be fine.

Me: Did I come all the way here to hear you say to me, "I am god"?

Dan: Well, being a god is our primary occupation, but you are here to know a simple secret that will open your eyes.

Me: A simple secret?

Dan: Yes, Oliver. Can you read what is there in the picture?

A big picture was behind him high on the wall, and it looked like an expensive oil and canvas painting. On it was written "Science of Verbum Victus."

Me: Science of Verbum Victus.

Dan: Yes, it is Science of Verbum Victus. Do you know what it means, Oliver?

Me: No, I don't know, sir.

Dan: Well, it means "Science of living words."

Me: "Science of living words"—what does that mean?

Dan: It is science that drives humans with no limits and makes a perfect world.

Me: Is it physics or mathematics, or what?

Dan: It is the driving factor for everything.

Me: I don't get it. Could you please explain it to me, Dan?

Dan: With your words, you could master your fate.

Me: My words—do you mean by talking?

Dan: Well, in a way. Just talking brings partial results, but talking and thinking with your imagination and hope will bring you anything in this universe.

Me: I am not clear, Dan. You mean just talking brings me everything? If that is the case, why do we have science, technology, and so many things around to help?

Dan: They exist because we have forgotten the key ingredient of life, "The WORD."

Me: Are you some religious person, or a pastor, talking about the word?

Dan: Not yet Oliver, but a man when he talks a word he vibrates the universe and the WORD is science.

Me: How could the word be science?

Dan: Word could be science because I believe in matter, space and energy.

Me: What does it have to do with matter and energy?

Dan: The Word is energy, and energy governs matter.

Me: So you are saying, "If I ask the picture on the wall to come closer to me, it will move"?

Dan: Did you imagine it really, and with positive hope did you say that? If yes, it will be nearer to you.

Me: No, no, no, I can't believe that. This is some kind of mind trick.

Dan: Really? So what knowledge do you possess?

Me: Philosophy, technology, religion, civilization, prison life, patriotism, war, culture, love and romance, food and heritage, my search, understanding, and others.

Dan: So you know philosophy. Are you a big fan of Aristotle?

Me: Yes, I love philosophy, yes, definitely.

Dan: Good. You're Plato's boy, aren't you? Aristotle believed that Earth was in the center, then Galileo after fifteen hundred years proved that Earth was spinning around the sun. Now tell me, Oliver, if you ask a kindergarten kid about the same fact, they will answer it correctly? Was Aristotle's wisdom so weak—weaker than a five-year-old kid's common sense?

All I knew was that this guy Dan Root rubbed me up the wrong way, the first time he made me realize that philosophy is for children, but I didn't want to give up.

Me: It worked well in those days, but that doesn't mean he is dumb. Concepts change when vision changes.

Dan: Bingo! So concepts change when vision changes, but one factor doesn't change: you think with wisdom you reveal philosophy. If that is so, don't you think wisdom is ignorance in the universe's mind?

Me: Maybe. I am not sure, Dan.

Dan: Here is the key, Oliver. It is not only in philosophy, but it happens in science, mathematics, history, and many fields. Why is that, Oliver?

Me: Maybe truth is not revealed at the right dimensions.

Dan: Are you getting it? Scientists, philosophers, and mathematicians all work very hard to understand and make life better, but at any time they have not improved human life to perfection. Why, Oliver?

Me: Maybe survival of the fittest? Darwin won the game. Then I have to abandon my search.

Dan: You should continue. Darwin corporate law will fail one day. Do you know he was the father of corporate society?

Me: No.

Dan: That is how it works. When we all come from the universe—whether by the big bang theory, a supernova, or from bacteria, cells, or something else—why is there so much difference among us, rich versus poor, winner versus loser, smart versus stupid?

Me: I wanted to fill in the gap. That is why I am searching.

Dan: Then you are in the right place.

Me: Let me ask a question. I could make a guess: you don't believe in God, and don't believe in Darwin's theory either.

Dan: Oh, well, I completely believe in Darwin's theory, but it doesn't apply to humans. It applies to other species, but not us, Oliver.

Me: Wait, what did you say? "It doesn't apply to us"? I am not getting it, Dan.

Dan: I will explain the whole process and the purpose of our roles later, Oliver, but to answer the question of why there is a lot of difference, it is because our very imaginations, thoughts, and words are all in negative forms and we have completely destroyed the whole evolution process—or, in other words, the creation process, if someone believes in God.

Me: So you say the whole mess of this universe is because of all the thoughts, imaginations, and words in this universe?

Dan: Before I start going through the logic and secrets, I want to tell you: Always think positive, no matter what situation you are in. Stay positive. Never say even one negative word. Build a positive ring around you. If you find appealing answers, come to me anytime you want and share your thoughts. This is how to stay aligned with the universe's single consciousness.

Me: Oh, okay, that's it. There's no book to read or refer to?

Dan: Nothing, no homework. I am telling you that what you learned in philosophy also matters, so don't get stumped.

Me: Yeah, I know philosophy of logos.

Dan: So you know the power of words exists in philosophy as well?

Me: Yes, I do.

Dan: So why didn't you ever focus on that?

Me: I never thought that had some powerful influence on men, and my expertise is PMT (Philosophy of modern technology).

Dan: Relax, go home, stay positive, and talk only to create positive things. I wanted to give you something, Oliver. Will you take it?

Me: Yes, sure, Dan.

Dan: Take the small envelope that is on the table and open it on the day when you are convinced of your answer to your search, to know the ultimate and eternal truth of life.

There was a small white envelope on the table that looked like a greeting card. I took it with me and left to go home. My mind was filled with hazy concepts, and everything Dan had said sounded bizarre, but I remembered Nyah telling me, "Just believe him." I worked to respect my friend's words, so I stayed with it. While walking home, I thought, *If my word has this power and my imagination does, too, then let me say, "I want all my friends and their families to be in my home now."* I wished this because I hadn't seen them for a while, and thought it would be pleasant to see them with all the problems I was going through at my company. I said to myself, *Let us see whether it will work,* but I felt I said these words with doubt, so I stopped walking and started to focus on faith, and slowly I calmed down. My heartbeat was relaxed and my mind was unified, and I said in a soft voice, "They are there now."

After saying these words, some sort of hope and confidence started to build in me. I started walking toward my home and saw Purdhil standing outside with a cigar in his hand. I was sure that he smoked only when he was drinking alcohol and elated, so I started to run toward the house. Purdhil saw me and greeted me, "My best buddy, Oliver!" I asked, "Are you visiting us today?" I turned and saw Nikifor and Judah, and Nikifor asked me, "What's up, chief? Are you causing problems, it seems?" Then Purdhil said, "We are all here." I replied to him, "Oh really?" and I asked, "Hey, Niki, what problems am I causing?" He replied, "Walk in, bro. We are very happy to see you."

I went inside my home, and my mom came running to me and asked, "Are you all right, my son?" I asked her, "What is happening here? Yes, I am all right." Then my mom said, "Madison was talking to me over the weekend. She said you are depressed and some politics are going on in the company, so we all decided to come here and check how we could help you." I replied, "Mom, it is true, but I have started to regain my wisdom. Something is happening inside me. I feel I have answers now." My mom replied, "That is so nice. Feel stronger, Oliver. I have only you. It'll be fine."

Then everybody was inquiring about the problem that happened and all the bad things I was undergoing, and each one came up with different answers and suggestions. I had to listen to all these responses because they were my family and friends. That night we had a fine dinner and drinks. I wanted to talk to Purdhil alone, so after everyone went to bed, I took him to my office, where we grabbed a few beers and started talking. I was talking about Dan Root and his concept of Science of Verbum Victus and explained the conversation that I had had with him. Purdhil looked calm and said, "I remember I told you about the philosophy of logos and how important it is in human lives, but you said you had read it and meditated on it, so why are you shocked by it now?" I replied, "Hey, Purdhil, I read it, man, but it was less important because I was focusing on PMT, so I didn't know it was so important." Purdhil asked me, "Let me get to the point. You think that is the answer you are looking for? If yes, then go for it." I replied, "I don't know, boss. My mind is confused now."

Purdhil: Let me now reveal the truth, Oliver.

Me: What is that?

Purdhil: The philosophy of logos is the father of philosophy and is very important; it is not widely spoken because it is a clash between wisdom and words. It is the ultimate philosophy that governs all the laws of this universe. Now that you have the universe's consciousness opened for you, you have to walk into it and learn, feel, and grow with the universe.

Me: You sound exactly like Dan! What are you telling me? The universe has a mind and consciousness?

Purdhil: Yes, Oliver, it has a mind and consciousness. It always talks to you and you have to listen to it, but man is being negative now and cannot hear the voice of this universe.

Me: You never said anything about it when you were teaching me.

Purdhil: Did you ask me, Oliver? You came to me to learn hacking, and I taught you a powerful subject, PMT.

Me: Yeah, it was my fault. Do you think this guy Dan is real, Purdhil?

Purdhil: I think he is the one who is going to reveal all your answers. I've never heard of "Science of Verbum Victus." He has some scientific way of explaining it, but its origins are in philosophy, religion, psychology, rhetoric, universal consciousness, and many others.

Me: So you want to go and learn from him?

Purdhil: You should just believe him.

Me: What did you say?

Purdhil: Just believe him.

It sounded the same way Nyah had said it.

Me: Why didn't you emphasize logos when you were teaching me?

Purdhil: You were concerned with your way of doing things. Now you want to know the universe's way. Moreover, logos is a subject that is not learned or taught. It is a revelation of the mind, the ultimate truth.

I didn't expect Purdhil to agree with Dan on the concept of logos and Science of Verbum Victus, and he spoke the same way as Dan. Maybe my mind didn't want to know about it. After talking to Purdhil, I went to my bedroom. Madison was awake and asked, "Are you all right, Oliver?" I replied, "Yeah." Then I asked Madison, "Hey, why did you tell my mom and everyone about the problems here? Don't you think that we are bothering everyone?" I had just gotten into bed and Madison got up and sat on me and said, "Oscar, I just told my mom and your mom. They are the ones who spoke to everyone and brought them here. Don't you think we all love and care for you?" I replied, "Hey, honey, I know that. Sorry, I was just asking." Madison replied, "You knew beforehand that they were coming." I asked her, "What did you say, Madison?" Madison replied, "You always wished for them to give you a surprise visit, and they made it. Be sure of what you wish for, because everyone is listening." I asked her, "Who is listening?" She replied, "The stars, sun, moon—I don't know, Oscar, maybe even the universe."

Me: Do you know what you are talking about, Madison?

Madison: Maybe it's philosophy or something like that, Oscar. Come close, be nice to me, and stop asking questions.

I didn't know what she was talking about, but all the patterns were based on the concept of logos. I had made the wish with my words and it had come true: I had my family and friends with me. I slowly started to believe in what Dan said, but I needed more answers to completely believe it. That whole week my family and friends stayed with us, and I started to think more about what Dan was saying. I didn't say anything negative that week, and my personality slowly started to change. I felt like a god, a mini-god, who wanted to grow bigger and taller and more powerful.

After all my family left, I met Nyah and Edgar at a restaurant and shared my experience with Dan. They were happy that I had started to learn and believe in Dan. A week flew by, and I decided to visit Dan, but this time I wanted to make sure I didn't run with too many questions. Rather, I wanted to really listen to what he said so that I could learn better concepts from him. I walked into his living room on the third floor, and he was sitting in the same chair, near the window. He spotted me and said, "Welcome back, Oliver. Nice to see you." I replied, "You too, Dan," and I sat down in the chair before him. He was wearing an expensive blue suit with gold cuff links, and his shirt was so white, it was glowing. He had a broad smile and a very bright face that showed his wisdom.

Dan: How are you feeling today?

Though I was tired that day from work and some negative thoughts were taking hold in my mind, I didn't let him know that.

Me: I am always very good—ha, my life is fantastic.

Dan: Have you started practicing?

Me: Yes, sir. These days I feel more positive.

Dan: Good. Do you have questions, Oliver?

Me: Nothing much, but if you could run through what I should learn, that would be great.

Dan: I will do that. Okay, let me start: do you know Nichole Tesla?

Me: Yes, of course! He's the greatest scientist that ever lived.

Dan: He once said, "The universe is a conductor of sound."

Me: What exactly does that mean, Dan?

Dan: We live in one single big consciousness in the universe. The universe can listen to all the voice patterns, and all the things that happen are based upon what we feed it.

Me: Wow! Interesting. Is it evolution or a creation concept?

Dan: Both, Oliver.

Me: So why do we have all these problems, and what is the cause of them? Why can't a common man be a superhero?

Dan: We need to understand the origin of the universe first.

Me: You mean the big bang theory?

Dan: You could call it that.

Me: So you believe in the big bang theory?

Dan: Yes, of course I do.

Me: So you want to tell me exactly what happened and why we are here?

Dan: You got it.

Dan started to explain the theory of how we evolved. Before the big bang was a small particle or nuclei with infinite energy in it. The only intelligence that was embedded inside it was to bring ultimate force in this universe that will never shrink the universe back to this same small particle. To build this ultimate force, for billions of years, energy was built, and it was built through the music that was played between thousands of different varieties of particles.

All the energy that is required for different particles was stored in the form of music and, in turn, vibrated constantly to build more energy. The energy multiplied exponentially every single day so that one day all particles met in an infinite dimension and felt the symmetries of all the energy in different particles. Once the symmetry was assured, there was the explosion for the beginning of the symphony of this universe: the big bang's birthday, if you call. As the universe expanded with energy and space, all the particles started to build matter, and evolution started to take place. The sun, moon, Earth, and the rest of the planets, including the parallel universes, started to begin. The universe, as I said, is one intelligential consciousness that began the evolution with higher forces, so-called "demons and angels" through an evolutionary process. They were very strong, stronger than any force, and had infinite energy and power to control the universe from shrinking back down.

The universe's consciousness was happy that it had found a force to sustain itself, but it lacked two things: It didn't control the forces of this universe the way the universe's consciousness did. They controlled the universe with their strength and power, and above all they had stronger egos, which made the universe feel very bad for them, and regretful. So the intelligence of this universe, again, was learning and building a supreme force who could control this universe from shrinking down, so it evolved "aliens." The aliens didn't make up the expectation of the universe and different types of aliens evolved. Some looked like humans, some like demons and angels, and they were not as powerful as the angels and demons but they were strong enough to meet the universe's thought. They survived for billions of years and continued to prove their ignorance and incapability.

The universe was expecting only one thing, "The Music," to be played again and again—the music that played in the nuclei to build a symmetric energy to sustain all the matters and expand the universe. The music is what we call Science of Verbum Victus. After the failure of the evolution of aliens, the stars started to collide with each other. One known set of stars was the supernova, which collided and started to create new elements to create the ultimate force. All the collisions and explosions created the required minerals, elements, plants, animals, and everything that was required for the supreme creature, the human.

Then man was created in perfect condition by taking all the elements after the explosion of the supernova and running in whirls through the winds of the explosion in infinite dimension in the supernova. Now the universe met its dreams by bringing the superhero of this universe and thus the universe was able to rest, knowing that man was the ultimate and eternal force that it needed to make the clock of this universe continue to run.

Now, how did the aliens fail? Because they were not able to proceed with the energy needed for the universe's clock to run. They were the inventors of science and technology and started to play around with all the particles in this universe, like electrons, protons, neutrons, quarks, leptons, and all "-ons" in this universe, which resulted in the supreme failure of their species. The reason they failed is they couldn't feed symmetry for the energy in the four fields, strong and weak nuclear fields, electromagnetic fields, and gravity. All of the aliens' attempts to work with the universe were unstable because the symmetry was not met, and the universe underwent many stages of condensation, cooling and running at higher temperatures.

At this juncture, the supernova, which is considered the mother of the big bang, created an ultimate superpower, the human, who would become the master of this universe. When we were created, the universe was proud and the music of symphonies was placed in our body and played through our mouths, "The WORD." The word we spoke made the universe stable, and fed all the four forces, gravity, electromagnetic, weak/strong nuclear forces, and all the thousands of particles with symmetry of energy. Our word from the mouth produced strings of vibrations, which was actually the same as the energy that exists in all matter and space, and the very word reminds the universe about its own music that was played before the big bang.

The first evolved humans were masters of the fate of the universe. The supernova was the mother of this universe, we are the sons of this universe and the father is the universe itself. Every human was created like the fictional Superman; we could fly and cross between parallel universes. We ruled the universe. Our thoughts, imaginations, and words were faster than light, which made us travel across the universe in seconds. At this moment the universe was stabilized, and all the energy and forces were symmetrical and the whole world was listening to the symphony of the music that was played by all the particles of the universe.

Everything was absolutely in peace and harmony, and rejoiced in this universe. Humans controlled it through their words; the very words they spoke stabilized the universe. Humans didn't die and there was no pain, no suffering, and no death. No agony was encountered in the human race. But there was pain, suffering, death, and agony in the alien world. The angels and demons had very long lives and no one died, they waited for their final call from the universe. Humans traveled between universes and knew the culture and trauma that alien civilizations were experiencing. The aliens always envied us, and man learned about the alien world, where death was the end and birth was the beginning.

To celebrate humans' supreme power, man started to build a big sound tunnel starting from Earth to the skies to reach the outermost parallel universe. The sound tunnel was a symbol of his supremacy, and the power of his word was proclaimed in this sound tunnel. The tunnel was not built of bricks and sand as you think; it was built with the strings of energy like a wave, looking like a tunnel, where man talked to the universe. It was like a radio.

Now the problems started. The aliens were jealous of human supremacy and wanted to go to war with humans. This led to the first war ever in the cosmos, as the aliens bombed the string tunnel with "particle accelerators," which had both matter and antimatter of all varieties. Some of the men and women who were building this tunnel fell from the skies of the heavens to Earth, and while they fell, they shouted with fear, "We are going to die like aliens!" That was the first time humans created negativity in their lives. The men who saw there was death from the fall started to run in panic and curse the aliens in their language for what they had done to humans.

Everything started with one word. Humans started to become weak, and their original language started to get diluted with the alien language and man started to face all sorts of problems. Yet, still some humans of strong nature and immortality went to war with aliens. The war lasted for thousands of years and the victories occurred on both sides. Slowly humans started to become weaker, because the weakness started to multiply between humans through children, families, and society and slowly all the immortal men perished. At this time man's mind was reset and he forgot his true nature and identity and became mortal.

That is the main reason we always look for superhumans like Superman, Spider-man, and all those with infinite powers. Now men have fallen from supremacy and started to explore the world with science and technology, not knowing who they were. Now we have become like aliens, using the same science and technology to understand this universe. The universe was once proud of us, but it has turned away from us, and the universe's consciousness went even further away from us. We are now trying to understand the particles of nature and the atoms and molecules and trying to build the so-called "God's particles." Not knowing that we are the gods and our word is the one that builds particles. We have created so much negative energy that it has become even bigger than dark energy.

At the beginning, the universe, the supernova, was in pain and grieved and trying to help us, but the weak humans built all evilness in life. Even the mother and father of this big construct couldn't help us. We declined and became weaker every day and denied the fact of our own majesties. We tried building thousands of gods and inventing new religions, but with the idea, so-called man's theory of logos, inserting the concept here and there in the books of religion and not emphasizing the true facts of humans. Man has gone so far that he cannot believe the power of his own word; he cannot resurrect himself from his own graveyard of negativity. The failure has become so great in us, in every field the power of logos is spoken like an index in a book, and no one even really uses it.

Dan: That is the greatest sad story ever told about oneself. There were many things that happened from the big bang to this moment, but I don't want to inundate you with information. Did you like that theory?

Me: It is not a matter of like or dislike; it is our own history.

Dan: I was looking for that exact same answer: it is our shameful history. Now I know you understood the whole plot and flow of this universe.

Me: I think I pretty much understood it.

Dan: Do you have questions, Oliver?

Me: Many, but let me take it one by one.

Dan: Sure, Oliver. Ask me.

Me: Do you believe in Darwin's theory and the evolution of humans?

Dan: Yes, I do believe in Darwin's theory. It was for aliens, as I said earlier. The universe was experimenting with its own intelligence through different processes and man was the ultimate answer in the universe's breath. Through the whirls and winds of the supernova, man was made. Man was not from fish or some bacteria. Man is from the universe's consciousness, as a single piece, not from building blocks of matter, like Darwin said, ape to man.

Me: So Darwin's theory was for aliens?

Dan: Yes, Oliver. There were many humanlike aliens living on this Earth, with two legs and two hands; there were varieties of them. But when the supernova era began, Earth was cleared of aliens because there was an explosion when the supernova built elements on this Earth, which went through different stages of temperature fluctuation. Finally man started to breathe.

Me: Hmm, very interesting. Then why did Darwin's theory propose it was for humans?

Dan: Do you remember the weak men and women who fell when building the sound tunnel?

Me: Yeah, the weaker ones.

Dan: Darwin is one among them. He didn't know his identity and proclaimed that humans came from a cell, and that is the reason we always compare ourselves to dust and sand.

Me: Hmm, well, that is true. So the theory of evolution is Darwin's and Science of Verbum Victus is Dan's?

Dan: It is not mine or yours, it is the "Theory of Us," Oliver—you, me, and everyone, and *it* is the eternal truth.

Me: So you said science and technology were not the method of humans but were from aliens? I do not understand it correctly.

Dan: First thing is that we are gods, and we create things. Creating here means we build things from nothing. Science and technology were not the method for us. Science was used to explore things around us, benefit our daily lives, and make things simpler for us but it was not our method. We were born with the utmost understanding and we knew the idea and concept of all the things in the universe. If we already knew this, then why should we learn?

Me: But science and technology have helped humans in lots of ways, like medicine, computers, food, transportation, communication, and many others. Yet you say science is not the method.

Dan: Your question is exactly from the fallen man's understanding: "Why do you need medicine if you are not sick?" "Why do you need transportation if you could fly?" "If your word reaches to the corners of this universe, why do you need communication?" "If words could sow food, then why do you need pesticides and machines to harvest?"

Me: So man was the impossible and was like a god? That is mind blowing.

Dan: Honestly, for me the mind-blowing part is "when man searches for God."

Me: Why did the angels and demons not attack us while building the tunnel? Did they envy us?

Dan: Yes, they envied us, and they are the ones who influenced the aliens. They were snitches, but had some good in them. There was a war called the War of Magister where they clashed in two groups to save us, but all the good ones died and some escaped to other parallel universes. They play the game so well. Until now, they have been directly involved with all the problems of man but they work behind the scenes.

Me: Well, if that is true, my next question is, do aliens exist?

Dan: Yes, sure. They were the second evolved creature in this world.

Me: Why do we not see them or why don't they respond to the signals we send every day, if they exist?

Dan: Why should they? They know we are the ultimate losers of this world. They look at us like clowns because we use their billion-year-old technology to say hi.

I laughed at his answer and he began to laugh with me.

Me: So you mean we are using their methods of science and technology to send communications to them?

Dan: Yes, exactly.

Me: Dan, let me ask you, are you against science and technology?

Dan: No, never. I live in this building with an air-conditioner, electric lights, coolers, and everything. My point is that science and technology are ways of expressing human intelligence, not a media of dependency and alternative to human capabilities.

Me: That makes sense. So science and technology are just toys for humans, not a part of them?

Dan: Yes, sir.

Me: So when will the aliens contact us?

Dan: Make the imagination positive, keep our thoughts positive, and proclaim yourself through the word. Then there will be a knock in the sky saying, "Welcome back, humans."

Me: If they reply, it means war.

Dan: They exist, but not as many as existed years ago. They are becoming extinct and are almost gone. Some sources say there are no more left and others say they exist in large numbers, but the fact is you are a god. They live too far away from our universe and they don't need us.

Me: Why don't they need us?

Dan: I will tell you later, Oliver. This is the only thing I will keep to myself. Is that cool?

Me: Sure, sir.

Dan: Thank you.

Me: You said that human words could stabilize all fields of energy with the word, so why do we have big labs around the world trying to build matter?

Dan: Well, that is the very nature of man. He could create his own matter, particles, but he has lost his own identity, and now he needs machines. He spends all his time and money building and understanding particles in the same way aliens once invested, but can't control the universe.

Me: So you say man cannot control this universe?

Dan: Man could control the universe in the way the universe wanted us to, not in his own way. Failures will teach him a lesson.

Me: So who is controlling this world?

Dan: No one. The saddest thing is that we are in a disaster.

Me: Disaster, you said?

Dan: Oliver, let me make myself clear: we are in the reverse way of the big bang. It is well known as the "big crunch." The universe has become unstable and is disintegrating. The universe is not expanding anymore.

Me: Wait: are we in the last stages of this universe?

Dan: Yes, Oliver, we are all dying.

Me: So when is this going to happen?

Dan: Today, tomorrow, or a million years from now—no one knows.

Me: Can't we stop it?

Dan: We had all the chances and we did well, but the way to stop it was back at the beginning. That is why "Science of Verbum Victus" is so important.

Me: How is it important?

Dan: We build a positive atmosphere around us. Every day we do it, and then at some point all the negativity will diminish and we will be back to the same state as when man was born.

Me: Is that why I should do this?

Dan: We should all do it, Oliver. It is not a one-man job. We all work as a team, and by *team* I mean every single human has to play a role in this.

Me: So what should I do now?

Dan: Start believing it, practicing it, and building your life. Experience the power of the word, and then pass the message to your friends, family, and everyone you know.

Me: Oh, sure, I will.

Dan: I think I have given you more information. Stop by here if you have any questions, Oliver.

Me: Sure, I will, thank you.

I left his house and went home. The concepts I learned from Dan were mind blowing. They cleared up some of my fundamental doubts, but I didn't understand how it really worked. It looked like a religious concept, but the same concept was spoken of in philosophy. The best thing was that Purdhil had acknowledged its existence and confirmed it was real. When I got home, I shared my experience with Madison, who was surprised with these new concepts. Madison even asked me if I believed in Dan Root's ideas, and I replied, "I don't know, but it sounds true." I was just meditating over all the concepts he had reviewed and trying to understand the scientific side of this message about "WORD." It looked like science was always changed by new ideas, but although science had rescued humanity many times; it never took us to the stage of perfection. If Science of Verbum Victus was truth, then why didn't I follow it? There was no harm in at least trying it. It sounded better than many cult religions. One way or the other, being positive brings hope, and hope brings life. Maybe I would still work on the scientific part of it, but I was definitely going to be positive and use creative and constructive words, I was determined to change my life.

A couple of weeks passed by as I meditated. I could see some vibration around me, and things started to look better, and there was deep silence and peace in my heart. I had a few questions for Dan Root, so I went to see him at his house. As always, I greeted the doormen and took the elevator to the third floor, the big door before me opened, and I walked inside. I saw him in the same place, sitting near the window and watching the streets below. He saw me and said, "Welcome, Oliver," and I greeted him eagerly.

Dan: How are you doing, Oliver?

Me: I am well—I mean I am always very well.

Dan: Good to hear, Oliver.

Me: Yeah, I started to believe in the concepts that you taught me; but I have a few questions about some of it.

Dan: Go ahead, my friend. Ask me.

Me: First thing, we were talking about a common language. What is that language?

Dan: What do you think? Is it English, German, Latin, Hebrew, or Chinese?

I smiled and moved my eyes with uncertainty.

Me: Maybe German or Latin?

Dan: No, Oliver.

Me: Then what is it?

Dan: A language with no negative words, a perfect language with only words that are constructive, creative, cohesive, content, cheerful, and supportive of the laws of our universe and universal consciousness.

Me: What do you mean, "Negative words"?

Dan: Like words that never existed: *can't, never, hard, pain, sorrow,* and even *death*.

Me: Where did we get all the negative words?

Dan: From the aliens, their own civilization and culture.

Me: Hmm, we lost ourselves.

Dan: Exactly.

Me: So if the word is the building block of man's life, then why should there be differences among us?

Dan: We have lost our own true image. Anyone who is so-called successful in this world knowingly or unknowingly knows the miracle of the power of the word and follows it.

Me: Why do you say that?

Dan: Let us take some examples, like this. Take anyone from history: kings, scientists, businessmen, bankers, prophets—every single one of them was successful and their name was exalted due to one simple thing: their imagination, the very thought of their minds. They spoke positive all the time. Thus they made sound vibrational energy around themselves and achieved all their goals.

Me: So you mean they didn't work hard or were not intellectual enough to be in a prominent place in history?

Dan: Definitely they worked hard and they were intelligent, but more than that, they imagined what they should be and started to make their thoughts stronger and started to proclaim what they wanted to be through their words and finally they established their goals. For example, take a carpenter. He works sensibly, and he has knowledge about what he is doing; but does that mean he will be successful in his life? No, you have to stay positive and proclaim with your words that you will grow and reach the stars in the sky. Then things start to change in your life.

Me: How come one knows how he is going to do in his life, if all the situations in his life are failing? Where could he get that confidence?

Dan: While walking down the road you fall into a ten-foot pit. What would you do?

Me: Try to get out and struggle to overcome my misfortune.

Dan: Yes, the pit is your present life but your past was the road. In the same way, if you realize how you came to this universe, you will always fight to go back to the past. Man's deepest search should be to the beginning of his past, where he is from and how he was brought into this system. The future was just given to us to help us go to the past. There is no future tense by itself; it is the road to the origin of the past.

Me: Whoo! That is outstanding. You said all great people in history, and one example you gave was prophets. Are you saying that prophets are not from God?

Dan: I don't know where they come from. To be a prophet means to "prophecies God's word," and it is very evident they were just proclaiming the word, although they say that it's the message from God. I say it is from the universe's mind.

Me: So you say prophets, messiahs, saints, and all of them . . . they don't own special powers, except their word is strong and powerful.

Dan: Yes, very much. There is no such thing as prophets, messiahs, or saints. They all came to talk about the past.

M: What about the miraculous powers they demonstrated?

Dan: Well, let us take Buddha. When Buddha was in a town, his vibration was felt in a ten-to-twenty-mile radius and people got cured, their eyes were opened and miracles happened. My first question is, why did it work for only twenty miles? Why not twenty billion miles?

Me: Maybe he was not that powerful.

Dan: One way to think about it: he just lived, say, a hundred years, and with so many negative vibrations and such a short span of life, he could cover only twenty miles. If he had lived for another millennium, maybe his radius would have expanded.

Me: Very funny. So was he not a god?

Dan: He was a god, but the reality is that everyone is god. Let me put it like this. Say Buddha, Jesus, Muhammad, whatever they call themselves, took a shit in the morning. Well, that defines them as humans, like you and me. If you had removed the word from their mouths, they would have not been anything greater than a homeless person in NYC.

Me: Ha, ha, you are hilarious, Dan. So for all these people, their imaginations, thoughts, and words were in line together and they spoke about only what they needed to see and they saw exactly what they said.

Dan: Yes, very much so.

Me: Take Nostradamus. He predicted many things about the future, so it means he didn't have a vision or any special gifts.

Dan: Well, he had a vision for the future, which means he imagined it and wrote it down. And today we all believe that his visions were true.

Me: Pretty much that's what some people think.

Dan: He predicted the fall of the Twin Towers. That was his vision, thoughts, and word, but there is another part of the equation: whether it was going to fall on my head. That is where you come in, your imagination, thoughts, and word. Moreover, he envisioned a disaster, which is against total humanity and the universe, and he did it, and we are happy someone predicted that we would die because of one crazy person's thoughts. We should be ashamed of ourselves. Remember this, Oliver: anyone who tells you that these bad things happened because of their thoughts, dreams, visions, prophecies, or what they have seen before is a man who has committed the worst crime in his life.

Me: You say they shouldn't imagine such things?

Dan: Yes, but something that comes in a flash of thoughts—doesn't run behind a negative thought. Try not feeding it and making your negative thought become greater through the proclamation of your word. You can always break the thoughts in your mind if the thought is constructive, then feed your thoughts and through proclamation of your words, make the thoughts happen. Predicting negative happenings is a destruction of your own species.

Me: So you're saying that everyone should think positive, speak positive, create a positive energy around himself, and eventually, at some point in time, we will go to the past where humans were created in this universe?

Dan: That is the whole idea.

Me: I come from a Christian family, and my mom and her friends always talk about the book of Revelation, that there will be great trouble and pain before Jesus comes again. Is all that true?

Dan: Do you believe it?

Me: Well, not really.

Dan: Then it's not for you. It is for the people who believe it. Let them read it, enjoy it, and pay the price. They have one concept in mind: God said so, and it will definitely happen. If that is the case, the same God blessed these people with many blessings, and not even one blessing is enjoyed by these people. Why? Is their God's word weak or are these people strong to persist in following God's word?

Me: It's like these people are stronger than God to persist in following his word, right?

Dan: Exactly. Even God knows that man's words are as powerful as his; that is why he gave free choice, according to the Bible. The same thing is in Hinduism, Islam, and many other religions, even Nostradamus. All these religions and people wanted to be outstanding before anybody, so they wrote a whole book of crime and war. There are billions of people who believe that is true and never know the reality and the human power in this universe.

Me: Well, as I now understand, all the successful people, without their thoughts and words, would be nothing.

Dan: Well, if anyone challenges you and says their positive word was not the cause of their success, then ask them to talk negative every day. Tell them to say every single day that they will die soon, be bankrupt or have chronic disease or afflictions. Within a few months or years, they will be on the streets, but they will not do it or they will share their success, because it will reveal they are still humans like you and me.

Me: But where does innovation come from? Great people like Einstein, Newton, and Galileo spent their lives and used their brains to bring the greatest innovations known to mankind. Does all their innovation come from the power of words, say, the "Science of Verbum Victus"?

Dan: Everything starts with a picture in the mind. When they were kids, they would imagine they were successful scientists. Their society would have helped them, their parents would have motivated them and the little picture they got in their minds when they were kids would start to build as imagination. Then thoughts were their life and the word made it all happen. Only positive thought and work brought them to become famous scientists, but we were born with all this knowledge and lost everything we had. Even the whole world was stopping them or there was no one to help them, so they challenged the world, just saying, "They will overcome, no matter what obstacle they face." The very word they spoke made all things happen; without a word, a scientist, a politician, a businessman would never have their position.

Me: So anyone could become a scientist like them and have a brilliant mind?

Dan: Even a homeless person in NYC could be better than those people.

Me: You said those scientists were developed with positive thinking and hard work, and that is what made them invent great things. If our word is strong and powerful, then where does hard work and toil come from?

Dan: Very good question. Hard work comes from the mind and the mind splits into words and words into hard work. A very good example I'd like to tell you is of Thomas Alva Edison. He failed to coil the first electric bulb nine hundred and ninety-nine times. It is a very popular story, and most people say he is the best scientist and they appreciate his spirit, but on the contrary he would have made up his mind, just saying, "I will get it the first time in coiling the bulb." He could have got it working the very moment he thought of it. Rather, he made his process develop around the idea, "No matter how many times it fails, I will never stop trying." Do you see the difference, Oliver?

Me: Yeah, I am getting it.

Dan: It is the mind that brings success in an easier or harder way. Say, for example, someone wishes to be the richest person in the world by the age of forty and he becomes rich at forty. But another person proclaims when he is a kid, "I will be the richest person in the world when he is a teenager, "and at age sweet sixteen, he makes it to be the richest person. What is the difference between the two?

Me: The difference is how much time was needed to achieve it.

Dan: Yes, but my point is, you don't need to be rich. Rather, think you were born as a king and a god. If you are born as a king and a god, would you make a wish to be a rich man?

Me: No, never.

Dan: That is the whole truth. Humans have lost their identity. And we should re-build it for them to regain their roles.

Me: Yeah, sure I will help you. All your points make total sense.

Dan: Thanks, Oliver.

Me: So, the concepts of science, technology, and philosophy are appreciated by the laws of the universe?

Dan: Yes, definitely they are appreciated by the universe and the main idea is to respect the laws of nature and use its method to unlock the secrets of this world.

Me: Agreed.

Dan: Do you have any more questions, Oliver?

Me: No, not yet, but I do agree with all the concepts that you've shared with me. The word is a string of vibrating energy that was similar to all the matter and space in the universe, before and after the big bang, power of words controls our true roles and laws of the universe. But how could I go and talk to someone about all this? They might think I am crazy and will criticize this theory and treat me like a fool.

Dan: I will come to that point, but first answer me: how did you teach philosophy to the people in Chelsea?

Me: Well, I had strong ideas and people always wanted to learn philosophy and it was easy for me to go and teach them. But this Science of Verbum Victus, well, it looks like a fairy tale.

Dan: Exactly. You believed in something and did it, but you said yourself it looks like a fairy tale, and that is where the problem begins.

Me: No, no, no, sir, I never said that. I said people might think that.

Dan: Why do you bother yourself with what people think? If you are worried about what people think, it means you are not strong in what you believe. Oliver, if you don't believe it whole heartedly, then you cannot convince your mom, your girlfriend, or even your friends.

Me: That is true, but. . .

Dan: I know what problems you have, Oliver. After listening, they make fun of you for talking rubbish words so loudly, saying the F-word and all sorts of futile words, and then laughing and telling you you're talking about crazy ideas.

Me: More or less like that.

Dan: Okay, according to you, who is the worst, cruelest, madman, most criticized, maniac you've ever known in your life?

Me: Well, I don't judge anyone like that, but at least I could say Hitler, Adolf Hitler.

Dan: Okay, do you know who said this: "Words build bridges into unexplored regions"?

Me: I don't know.

Dan: The same Adolf Hitler. Even he knew the power of words, and his word was so powerful that it took the Germans down the wrong path.

Me: Whoo!

Dan: So anyone who makes fun of the power of word and laws and ideas is a fool who makes fun of himself. He is the meanest rat in this whole human race.

Me: May I ask one more question, Dan.

Dan: Go ahead.

Me: What about people cursing?

Dan: Ha-ha, interesting. Do you think when someone curses you to death, the curse comes true in your life?

Me: I don't know.

Dan: There is no such thing as a curse. It doesn't happen to you when someone curses you. Rather, you believe the curse and start to fear it, so it is your fear and beliefs that make the curse work, not the curse itself. Most prophecies and predictions are based on a curse. If curses worked in other people's lives, the whole world would be dead by now. Your thoughts are in your mind; you feel it in your body and your word in your mouth, which will bring things into reality.

Me: That is amazing.

My mind was clear and most doubts had perished, and I left for home. I was thinking about all the different aspects Dan had explained to me. I didn't know that the first language of humans was a language without any negative words. That was a mind-blowing concept to me.

We had built hundreds or even thousands of languages without really knowing the real true language that the universe gave us. I always used to think, *How come there are differences in this society? Some people make history, and many people just live and die.* The power of imagination and word was a key point in everyone's life. No one is born intelligent, but we possess intelligence. How could we possess it? Very simple: Start thinking positive, telling yourself, "You could change your life and things around you." The day when we say that, our eyes will open and we will start down the right path and pick the field that we want to explore; and when we explore, we make our own history. So there was no reality to the concept of the chosen one or genius, enlightened one, messiah, or prophet; it had to do with the power of word, Science of Verbum Victus.

I worked to make myself believe in this simple and great method to open the mind. These days I only thought about Science of Verbum Victus and started meditating on it and applying it whenever possible. I shared my knowledge with Madison and she started to believe it and we talked about it all the time. The first thing was that if I could get the complete answer to all the questions and the soul was strong, then I could share this with my friends and family. I had met Dan three times and spoken to him, and my life had already started changing a lot every day. I had to share the experiences that were happening.

On a Saturday evening, Madison, Nyah, Edgar, and I went to a restaurant in the West Village. We all were in a good mood and started enjoying a few drinks. We had a good time that night and stayed until three in the morning. We were a little drunk—even Madison was—and we left and came home. We slept until noon, and when I got up, I ordered some pizza. I was looking for my wallet, but it was missing from my pocket. I started to panic, and I searched the whole room but couldn't find it. Then I asked the maids. They started searching the whole house. I remembered that I had had the wallet in the restaurant and paid my check. I got a quick thought in my mind: *No matter what the situation, I will never say from my mouth, "I lost it" or even think in my mind with a second thought whether it is lost or not.*

The wallet was important to me because I had all my information in it, my license, my company access card, my credit/debit cards, Dan's small envelope, and other important information. So the first thing I started to do was not panic and be nervous. I called the restaurant and checked with them, but they said they hadn't found it. Then I called Nyah and Edgar and they also hadn't found it. I also checked with Demonthin, who drove the car the night before. He too checked and didn't find it. We went in cycles checking and couldn't find it anywhere. It was almost six o'clock in the evening, and still I couldn't find it. Nevertheless I stayed hopeful and never uttered from my mouth, "It is lost." Instead I said, "It should be here somewhere." I even let the maids and my doorman search in my room and no one could find it.

We spent the whole of Sunday searching for it and couldn't find it anywhere. Madison was encouraging me to stay calm and be patient. Night fell and we were tired and went to bed. During the whole process, my mind was hovering over the chance that someone had picked my pocket or I had lost it in the restaurant. We went to bed because I had to wake up earlier to go to the office the next day. I was so positive that it would be somewhere that I didn't even call my bank or my credit card company to block my card.

While in bed I told Madison that maybe this was a time we should check the power of the word and Dan's whole idea. We searched all the places I had gone after I came home the night before. We were a little tipsy and walked to our bedroom and hadn't gone anywhere inside our house. But no one could find it, so I decided to use the power of my word, and said to Madison, "My wallet is somewhere safe." She agreed, and we checked whether this would work in this situation. I woke up in the morning to go to the office and took a shower. While getting my suit from the closet, I happened to turn and look in the corner of the closet, where my long winter coat was hanging. The edge of the coat was touching the floor. I noticed the coat was slipping down, so I took the hanger and moved the collar to fit the hanger and I saw my wallet in the corner. I was shocked and breathless for a minute and slowly bent down and took my wallet and opened it. Everything was still inside.

My mind was in an unstable state, and I walked to my bed and sat down. Madison was sleeping, but she quickly woke and saw me and asked, "Oliver, are you okay?" I showed her the wallet. She opened her eyes and asked, "Where was it?" I said, "I found it in the corner of the closet." She said, "We searched everywhere in this room—all our maids, you, me, Demonthin. Even Claudia searched, and no one found it, and you saw it this morning." I replied, "Do you remember that we made a wish and proclaimed our hope? The universe was listening to us, and rewarded us according to our words." Madison's eyes watered and she hugged me and said, "Oscar, it seems the universe is listening to us, and Dan was absolutely right. Don't you think it is a miracle?" I replied, "I think so," and my mind was shocked as I thought about what had happened to us.

Weeks passed by and there were lots of differences that I could see in my office, in my relationships, with my friends, the society I lived in, and everything I saw. It was a surprise when one day Shu and Ejaz came to NYC driving a Ferrari 599 GTO. It was a brand new Ferrari, which Shu's father gave her for her birthday. Shu and Ejaz came to show us the new car and check on us. They insisted on taking a drive in the new car.

Initially we said no, but Ejaz convinced us to go north upstate New York and visit. So Madison and I took the Ferrari, and Demonthin drove the Rolls-Royce with Ejaz and Shu. It was a fun trip. We drove to Saratoga Springs, and something came into my mind: that this road trip was somewhat dangerous and something bad was going to happen. I kept ignoring it, but it kept popping up again and again.

It was a two-way road with only one lane on each side. There was no median between the lanes, and there were lots of trees on my side of the road, where I was driving 50 mph. I was ahead and Demonthin was following us.

Within a fraction of a second I saw a big truck coming into our lane at high speed. I had only a few seconds to decide what to do. Should I pull myself right, into the trees, or pull left, where there was lots of traffic coming the opposite way? Madison said, "We will be fine. Pull to the right to the trees." And I closed my eyes and said, "We will be fine." I don't know what happened, but we had a head-on collision with the truck, and the car was totaled. The whole front body of the car was smashed and broken. Madison and I fainted and when I woke up, I saw blood on Madison's face. It was the same blood I saw when she fell on the road in the thunder when we were kids. But this time the circumstances were different: it was in a car and a fatal accident, and my mind was telling me she was gone. I saw some of my own blood was on my shirt, but I cared more for Madison, and I couldn't move my right hand.

I called out, "Madison, Madison, stay with me." My eyes were filled with tears. I tried to remove all the negative thoughts that were running through my mind and said to myself, *We are fine. Madison and I will go for dinner tonight. She is fine.* Then I heard some voices shouting our names through the window. I heard Demonthin, Ejaz, and Shu screaming our names and to my surprise, I saw Madison was moving, and she said, "Are you all right, Oscar?" I replied to her, "I am good. How are you?" Madison said faintly, "We should go for dinner tonight," and I laughed. Then the rescue team, police, and ambulance came and removed us from the car.

We were both alive and I could see tears of joy in Demonthin's, Ejaz's, and Shu's eyes. They took us to the hospital, and all the injuries were minor. Madison had a small bruise on her head; the shock had made her faint. I had a very small bruise on my head and my right hand was sprained but we were both absolutely fine—no head injuries, no factures, no broken limbs, nothing. The procedure in the hospital was quick and we got out within a few hours. By this time all our friends and families had started to call us and check on us; and even though we were totally fine, they were all worried and wanted to come and see us. They were all on their way to my house, so we left the hospital and headed home.

On the way, Madison and I asked how did the accident happen? They started to tell us exactly what happened. We were driving around 50 mph, and the truck was going 60 mph. We didn't have a head-on collision, we offset the truck and it hit our bumper, which slowed down the motion of our car, and we went into the tree. Then Shu asked me if we had turned the wheel to the right, and I replied that I hadn't, Madison also confirmed that she didn't pull the wheel. Before the crash we were a few feet ahead of the truck, so I didn't know how the wheel got turned to the right. The only thing I knew by looking at the car was that the front of the car was thrown one way and the front seats where Madison and I were, and the trunk went another way.

It was a miracle that we were both alive with only minor injuries. I felt it was the power of our words that kept us alive. Why shouldn't I believe it now? I was alive. Some people believed in God, but I believed in the power of words. The difference between the people who believed in God and me was that if the people of God had been dead, they would have gone to heaven, and if we had been dead we wouldn't have had any place to go. That's why we were going to be living witnesses for the "Science of Verbum Victus". We didn't have a place to go after death because we would not die. That was how man was developed. Only religion would take you to different places and kill you many times before realizing death was not in the human equation of life.

That evening we all had dinner at home. All our friends and family were there and were worried about us. We convinced them that we were okay, and they were relieved. Shu's father came and apologized, because it was Shu who took us and I said it was not her fault and he felt bad. Shu's father said, "I was about to kill my son through my daughter," but I replied, "You are lucky it happened to Madison and me, not to Shu and Ejaz. We are so thankful to you. I think some karma got transferred from Shu to us, and since Madison and I are stronger, karma could not enter our lives. We won fate and karma, and I have to thank you, Uncle, for realizing the real power of humans. You should be very proud of Shu. She was the messenger of our life." Shu's father looked at me and said, "You look like a monk. You're ready to sacrifice your life for anyone, and your father should be very proud of you."

My mom was the one who was so worried, and she was crying all the time. It took a lot of time and effort for me to comfort her. She started with her own theory, that God had sent her angels to protect me. I didn't want to disappoint her, so I said yes to everything she said. She was weak and I was the only one she really knew in this world.

We had a grand dinner that evening to forget all the bad things that had happened. We went to bed and Madison and I talked about what had happened. She asked me if I was positive I hadn't pulled the wheel. I replied, "Madison, we were so close. I lost my reflexes, I am positive. I cannot remember anything after the collision." Then Madison asked, "How did the car slide or keep from hitting the truck?" I said, "I know we were almost a couple of feet away from the truck, and I closed my eyes and was sure we would be fine." Madison replied, "Maybe our positive thoughts saved us." I replied to her, "They did." Madison said, "It's so bizarre, Oscar: we got hurt on the same side and place on our heads. Don't you think our injuries explain our true love?" I smiled and said, "Without you I can't even imagine living my life." We both felt anxious, and we cuddled and didn't sleep the whole night. All we could think about was the accident.

The next morning everyone left and Demonthin drove me to the office. While we were going to the office, he said, "You almost died. When I saw your car in pieces, I thought something bad had happened to you and Madison, but a miracle happened and you both lived." I asked Demonthin, "Do you believe in miracles?" He replied, "Yes, I do. Without miracles and chance, no one would be alive." I said to him, "That is a good philosophy." Then Demonthin said, "Can I tell you something, Oliver?" I replied, "Yeah," and Demonthin said, "Remember I am your chauffeur, and next time you will not be driving any car, boss." I said, "Okay, okay. I will not drive, even a Ferrari. I will have you drive. Is that cool?" We both laughed until we reached the office.

On the same day, I wished to meet with Dan and talk to him about the incidents that had happened to us and check what his thoughts were. As soon as I left my office, I went to meet him. I went to his home, where the same doormen greeted me. Once again, I took the elevator to the third floor and the big door opened. He was sitting in the same place, near the window. I heard the usual greeting "Welcome, Oliver," and he saw me with a bandage on my hand and a Band-Aid on my forehead.

Dan: Are you all right? What happened to you? Did you get hurt?

Me: I had a small accident. Madison was with me. We escaped tragedy.

Dan: Tragedy? Hmm, did you build it for yourself?

Me: How do you know that?

Dan: Simple: you are the one who builds your own life, good or bad.

Me: Well, I had this feeling come over me while I was driving, about having an accident, and negative thoughts kept recurring, but I didn't feed them. I tried ignoring them, and they never returned.

Dan: So did you overcome it?

Me: I stayed positive and I only spoke the words, "I will be fine" all the time to myself. My question is, Dan, does a thought become more powerful than words?

Dan: I know what your question is. Let me put it this way: getting a negative thought is not a problem—everyone gets them—but feeding it is a problem. Just having a flash of thought will not bring you any bad things, but if you start talking, then the flash thought becomes reality. So in a time like that it is better to stay quiet than talk.

Oliver: So if I run into a situation like that, if I stay quiet, I should be fine?

Dan: A very simple logic. You would hear people doing meditation for some time—hours, days, and even years and once they come out of that realm, they say something to their friends, family, or master. Everyone around them starts to feel the words from the man's mouth are true, and some start to believe he is a god or a higher spirit. As you know, by nature man is a god. Keeping one's mouth closed brings more miracles than talking about insane things.

Me: If I can't say something positive during situations where my mind is overwhelmed, I should stay quiet?

Dan: Very much so.

Me: I have this very important question. How does man get all these thoughts and beliefs?

Dan: Men and women get all these ideas from the fact that they see everything. Let me explain, each step. The first factor is fear. We fear. And fear was created in us by society, by governments, religion, and many other factors. We should fear doing bad, not doing good, but the big problem is that man doesn't know the difference between good and bad.

The second thing is experience; we have some bad experiences with something in life, and we continue this same experience and implement it when we encounter the same situations. There are many proverbs there to support the idea that "experience is a lesson." We never use our thoughts and words when dealing with such situations; we give experience priority.

The third factor is reputation. There are many people who have made statements or proverbs, like Shakespeare, Plato, and Aristotle, and we believe their words as true, because they said them, and they are great historical figures. Do they say something based on universal law? A well-known example is Aristotle. He said Earth is the center of the universe, and since he was respected for his ideas, for fifteen hundred years people believed that Earth is the center of the universe—that is, until Galileo challenged his ideas. So, never take great people's sayings without properly examining whether they are right or wrong.

The fourth factor is situation; we always see things that are around us, but we never see things that are not there. Right now someone may be poor or broke, though the current situation is not very supportive, but you should always envision yourself as rich and successful. How do you see such impossible things? You build the situation where you want to be with words. Imagine you are sitting on a throne, living in a palace. Imagine there is no death, no pain, no suffering, an ideal perfect world.

The fifth one is meditation. Most people have a misconception about this word; they think it means to go and sit and close your eyes and meditate. That definitely brings some results, but that is not what meditation really is. A real and true meditation is always to think positive, talk constructively, imagine you were born like a king and god and do it day and night. So meditation is life, not a program, or event, or exercise, or therapy.

The sixth factor is repetition. If something repeats itself, then people will start to believe it. Like ads on the television: they keep on repeating and your mind gets stuck on them. The best example I could give you is "Once upon a time there was a king in a town." Now, over centuries, they've said that in such a way that we believed only one person could be a king and the rest shall be servants to the king. That is why the British monarchy still exists with a queen, but the truth is that we are all kings and queens.

Me: So the different factors are fear, experience, reputation, situation, meditation, and repetition. I got it.

Dan: Very cool.

Me: Could I ask you a question? Would you mind?

Dan: You already decided to hurt my feelings. Go ahead.

Me: Do you work or run some company? How can you afford to own a whole block on Park Avenue?

Dan: I am king and a god, and kings don't work. They rest, but you're thinking is limited, Oliver.

Me: Sorry for asking you that question, Dan. I am sorry.

Dan: Don't be sorry. Your question was legit, but there was no expansion in the question. You are surprised by the richness of this house where I live, but you are a king, Oliver. Your house should be the whole city. Maybe you still don't realize the truth behind Science of Verbum Victus, and that is why you are staying in this dungeon.

Me: Yeah, you are right. Let me rephrase the question. Is this house your regular coffee joint?

Dan: Perfect—your mind is expanding.

Me: There are many books related to positive thinking and word power. How are they different from your teaching of "Science of Verbum Victus?"

Dan: Let me ask you a question. There are many good colleges in this country. Why did you prefer to go to MIT?

Me: Best education, best professors, reputation, and so on.

Dan: Same thing. The books teach vital things and I myself have read a few of those books, but to make the mind believe stronger, we need to know who we really are. Knowledge of self is the most powerful force in this universe.

Me: Could I apply Science of Verbum Victus in my office space? Say my work is computers. Will it still work?

Dan: You could try even to shut the sun, so why not the computer with zero and one?

Me: Yeah, I will try it. The next time I come and talk to you, I will be the chief information officer of that company. I think I got what I needed for my life. Thanks, Dan Root. I appreciate it.

Dan: Anytime, Oliver. Go and explore the world and conquer it.

I was overjoyed that I had learned a lot of very important information from Dan, and these days, my search started fading. It never grew stronger again, because my soul said that I had found an answer. Yes, the search was slowing down every day because I felt that the "Science of Verbum Victus" was the ultimate truth. I started to apply it at my office, and every day I said to myself, *I will be the CIO of this company very soon, and anything I do in the company, I will approach like a CIO.* Things changed quickly after that, and within a month, something very important happened in the company. All architects, managers, directors, and top management were called for an emergency meeting. The CEO wanted to address the company. We all went to the conference room and there were hundreds of people. No one knew what it was about. But there was some sort of commotion on the faces of the people.

Then the CEO started to talk about the growth of the company, its present market value, and how well we were doing in the market. He said the company was facing a big problem. The company had plans to acquire a few banks in Asia and Europe, and the acquisitions would be happening within two weeks. If it happened as planned, the company's value would be $100 trillion, and it would be the world's richest bank. But the Chinese and Russian governments had hired a group of hackers to infiltrate our networks and bring them down on the day before the acquisition. If they did that, there would be a big problem in doing this acquisition, and it would affect the growth of the company for the next twenty years. The group of hackers they hired were among the most dangerous and smartest people in Russia and China. The governments paid them almost $600 million as a contract fee. They were two hundred of the smartest engineers working on this breach. The question then went out: how many of us really wanted to contribute to protecting our assets from these people and who could really challenge them? Usually I arranged meetings with only the security team and top management. This situation was not the same. They needed everybody's support, and informed everyone so that all our efforts would be prudent. I was listening very carefully. I knew this was the right opportunity for me to prove to top management and the CEO that I was capable of doing this job. My chance of becoming CIO was in front of me. I raised my hand, and the CEO spotted me and asked me to speak.

CEO: There is a man who could help us, a bold young man who raised his hand first. Give him a big round of applause.

Everyone clapped, and my teammates were surprised. I stood up.

Me: I am Oliver J. Oscar, sir.

CEO: Your name sounds familiar.

Me: Well, it should be. It's been in the papers.

CEO: Papers, huh? We have a celebrity here. What for?

Me: For a Nobel Prize for Veleidade X, an award from Nelson Mandela, and an award from the president of the United States for helping people in the Chelsea neighborhood of Boston.

CEO: That is all excellent. We are honored to have you with us, Oliver. Could everyone give a big round of applause for Oliver again.

Again there was a big round of applause, and this time everybody stood up.

Me: Thanks, everybody.

CEO: So you wanted to contribute an idea to solve this problem or to take the ownership of this project?

Me: I will take the ownership.

CEO: Hmm, very interesting. Which team are you on?

Me: I am an architect and work on the database team, and I report to Gwyneth.

CEO: Okay, I got it, but Oliver, this is related to security and hacking. I appreciate that you want to contribute, but a security person who has the background could handle such situations.

Me: My background is in security and hacking. I was moved to the database team, but I think I am the right person for this type of situation. I have almost ten years of experience in the field.

CEO: What do you mean by "moved"? Your background is in hacking? I don't get it.

Peyton interrupted.

Peyton: Sir, we had a problem, so we moved him there. You can ignore his situation.

I was irascible and this time Peyton was going to get away with it. . . . Now I knew how to fight back. I was about to open my mouth, but suddenly . . .

Gwyneth: Stop it, Peyton. Hello, sir. I am Gwyneth, director of database systems. The issue is not with Oliver, but with that creep Peyton, sir.

Peyton: What did you call me?

CEO: Silence, please. What is happening here? If you guys have problems, deal with your bosses, not in a conference like this.

Gwyneth: Why not? You are the one who should deal with this situation.

CEO: Are you talking to me, miss?

Gwyneth: Yes, to our great CEO.

CEO: Why?

Gwyneth: If there is some discrimination and it cannot be handled by HR, then you are the one who should make the call.

CEO: Explain.

Gwyneth: Mr. Peyton doesn't like colored people, and doesn't like Oliver helping them.

Peyton: No, that's a lie. I like colored people, but I don't like Oliver.

CEO: What the heck is happening here? What the hell do you mean you don't like that kid?

Peyton started to stammer now, and breakdown.

Peyton: We have a security issue with Oliver, sir. We should talk personally after this meeting.

CEO: Yes, that is what I am going to do. We have more problems inside than outside. You—Peyton, Gwyneth, and Oliver—walk to my office right now, damn it. The meeting is adjourned. We will call everyone later.

I thought this was the best day in my life, as I didn't know Gwyneth would stand up for me like this. While walking to the CEO's office I asked her, "Why did you go all the way like this?" She said, "Everyone should be proud to have you here, and you are like my son, Oliver. I don't want you to be working like this for us. You have a great future." Then she said, "No one from Manhattan ever likes to cross the river to go to the Bronx and help them, especially from Wall Street. But you are an angel. You took their lives to be yours. You are a leader in this new world. There are millions of people to back you up, son, so be strong."

We all went to the CEO's office and sat in chairs across from him, and it was obvious that he was ireful about what had happened in the meeting. No one spoke, and the CEO asked Gwyneth, "What happened, and why did you get emotional?" Then Gwyneth started talking and explaining the story of what happened—why I was moved to a different team, the reason they gave for not moving me back, and the whole game. The CEO's face grew furious, and he was incensed with Peyton. He asked for the yearly review file on me, and asked his assistant to check with the security team and my team about my behavior. He went through everything in two hours. No one gave any negative feedback about me, and he went through all my work, both in security and the present team and found that everything was perfect.

Then he called out Peyton's boss and started to have a discussion with him and asked him what happened. He did everything that Peyton said, and the CEO started to counter with Peyton's statement about me. Peyton's boss had no answer for the CEO. The CEO was smart, and within hours he found out the truth and found Peyton was the culprit.

He didn't fire him, because he had worked there for a long time, but he warned him and let him go.

Then the CEO called me and asked if I could take this job to protect the company assets. I replied, "Thanks very much, sir." The CEO quickly made me the head of this project and urged expect the CIO, everyone should follow Oliver's orders and implement his recommendations. Then the CEO, the CIO, and I had a personal chat about the hacking problem that our company was facing.

CEO: I know you are confident about taking this job, and I am sure you will succeed, Oliver.

Me: Thanks so much for having confidence in me.

CEO: Do you have any plans or strategy, Oliver?

Me: I do. Where are the hackers? Are they all in one city or are they distributed throughout the country?

CEO: Good questions. According to some intelligence reports, they are all in Volgograd, Russia, and guarded by Russian forces. It seems they are in a government hall.

Oliver: Very nice—easy for us.

CIO: Why do you say it is easy for us? We could block their public address IP ranges from Volgograd.

Me: That is just the basics but there are other steps to take, too. Let me work on it, and I will keep you posted. I will let you know what I did once the job is completed. Is that okay, boss?

CEO: So you have some moves and want to be secure. I have no issues with that. As long as it works, I am okay with it, son.

I gave two small envelopes to the CIO and CEO and said, "Just open this after the acquisition is made and when you hear we have thwarted this threat from our enemies." Both of them promised they would not open them until the time came. I went and coordinated with every team in our company and asked them to do the regular stuff: patch your system with the latest updates, close unwanted ports on the firewall and protect the Web servers with the Web application firewall. We increased the capacity of the plant with more Web servers and database servers with unused servers and purchased more hardware for expanding our resources like elastic, so that when the hack happened, we had more capacity to handle the load. Usually hackers use DOS or DDOS to bring down the network, but since we had more capacity in our network, it would be hard for them to bring them down easily. We even brought additional ISP lines with big bandwidth to sustain the load. We distributed the load to a multiple data center so that there would be no physical attacks and spread the load of the traffic throughout the globe, using intelligent name server technology.

We tuned the network with more Intrusion Prevention System to detect suspicious activities in the network, and we engaged more team members for monitoring the network. We also fine-tuned the email spam system, so no spam emails could enter the company email system. We patched the antivirus systems with new signatures, trained all the employees to report any suspicious activity, and expanded the hotline of the support team, so that there would be no wait time for calls. We did what a real security team did and we did it with a genius mind.

I ran across Peyton while doing this job and he made a comment saying, "Any decent security guy would do the same as what Oliver is doing, but what made him so special about his role, the CEO is putting trust in him." I replied to Peyton, "Answers are coming, Peyton, just wait and see." Peyton's face turned red and he said, "It is not yet over, Oliver," and I replied, "It is true—it is just the beginning."

The day before the acquisition was the day the hackers planned to bring down our company's network. But that was the great surprise: nothing happened. We didn't face any attack and everyone was surprised. On the acquisition day, our CEO and president were in London and everything went smoothly. We acquired six big banks from Asia and Europe, and Harvest and Reap became a $100 trillion bank. That day there was a big party in the office and everyone in the office carried me on their shoulders and we held a procession on Wall Street. This was a record, the first $100 trillion bank on Wall Street and in the world.

We had a good time on the acquisition day and I felt that I succeeded in my career and that my dreams were coming true. My father and Nathalie would have been happy this day to see my success that I had earned. The CEO and president returned to NYC from London. The CEO came rushing to my office and looked at me and said, "How did you do this, my son? I am very impressed with you!" I asked him, "Did you open the envelope?" He replied, "Yes, I did. That is why I am here, but I have questions. Could we walk to our office, please?" The CEO, CIO, and I went to his office, and they were looking confused. The CEO asked, "What happened exactly?" I started to explain how exactly we had stopped the hacking threat.

Me: The Russians were so smart; they had installed a new type of logic bomb through a Trojan in 200 million computers throughout the world to act like zombies. I installed a few computers in a few countries like Russia, China, India, Singapore, and other places to learn what type of Trojan the hackers were installing. The Russian hacking team was scanning computers that were vulnerable to install their Trojan and used those machines to attack us on the day before the acquisition. They had installed a Trojan in my machines also. I examined the Trojan and its behavior updated theirs to the antivirus company. We scanned the traffic pattern in Volgograd, Russia, by hacking their ISP, and knowing the traffic for this specific Trojan that was installed, and we found all the infected machines throughout the world. I asked the antivirus company not to inform the public about it, because the hackers would have a fallback Trojan for installation, which would be critical for us to find if they installed it on these machines at the last moment. All the antivirus companies agreed and had the latest signature for the logic bomb and updated almost all the 200 million zombie machines by not deleting the Trojan. Rather, they deleted the malicious code in the Trojan and kept the logic bomb still communicating through covert channels back to the hacker, because we made the hackers believe that all the infected machines were active and the Trojan was installed on it.

The day before the hacking, at 11:55 p.m., the antivirus in all the infected machines removed the communication covert channels that were passing traffic back to the hackers. Up to that point it was an easy job, and at midnight all the power in the city of Volgograd was turned off by the heavy thunder and lightning. All the electric lines were short-circuited and fused, and fire burned down the electric lines. So their backup batteries and generators were also tripped off because of short circuiting. There was a big panic, and the ISP also went down. Even though the hackers had laptops and extra batteries, nothing helped them because the central grid was down, all the communication centers were out of power, and the central ISP hub, which had direct connection through the satellite, was on fire. Panic erupted and everything tripped off like dominos, and there was no Internet for the hackers. That was it, we won, boss.

CEO: Then why did we work so hard to enhance our security systems and buy new equipment and do all the work we did on our network?

Me: We make sure that the enemy knows we are driving east while we are actually driving south.

CEO: Yeah, that is a masterpiece, but where did the lightning come from?

Me: From nature.

CEO: Oh really? How did you know two weeks before? I saw your envelope that you gave me to open after the acquisition, and it says, "Lightning and Thunder will save us."

Me: Maybe I sent it.

CEO: So, you are Zeus and Thor?

Me: I am, in a sense.

CEO: What is this all about, Oliver? I am astonished at your prediction. Are you some sort of prophet?

Me: Well, I am a god and you are also a god. I have realized this myself. When are you going to realize yourself?

CEO: So, from a CEO you promoted me to a god. Thanks, Oliver. I don't want to bother you with questions. It seems you are the chosen one that God sent here to this company. Sorry for the bad things that happened with Peyton and all this corporate bullshit. I admire you, Oliver, and I want to honor you. I am promoting you to be the assistant CIO of this company.

Me: Thanks very much. I don't know what to say. You are a generous man. Thanks for all the support.

CEO: Also, since you made this acquisition go through, we are awarding you $25 million after taxes. It is a gift from Harvest and Reap, and the president and board of directors agreed. Here is the check. Your salary is now $2.2 million a year with $15 million stock options, maximum.

I didn't know what to say, and I was very much humbled to receive the check.

Me: Thanks. I will never forget the support you gave me.

So that is how I became Oliver J. Oscar, the assistant CIO of Harvest and Reap. I know what you may be thinking: Where did the lightning and thunder come from? Well, you all like fantasy movies and enjoyed watching it. I am happy for you, but when are you going to make it into reality? I made it through the "Science of Verbum Victus." Yes, it worked for me. When is it going to work for you? I proclaimed it with my words, as Dan said we could shut down the sun, but why not create thunderstorms and lightning?

I started realizing who I was and what I should do in my life. I got $25 million, so what am I going to do? Give it to poor people or contribute to the law college that was started by Fernando, or give it for the benefit of the people in Chelsea? No, I am not going to do anything like that, to add an extra impression in anyone's mind. I am going to buy the house from Judah's father—yes, the one Madison and I were living in. Madison had asked a few times if we could buy the house and I always said no, that Judah's father would not sell it or may not like it if we ask him, and moreover, we didn't have that much money. But now I am a king, and my mind is able to change things. I no longer needed to get free stuff from anyone. I had money now to pay, so I should do it. But the actual house cost almost $75 million, and I had just $25 million, so I needed to buy some time from Judah's father.

I spoke to Judah's father, and he was happy with my accomplishment. I shared my view on buying the house. To my surprise, he didn't say anything, but he said the exact price, that it was worth $75 million. He was ready to sell it to me because he loved me and always treated me the same way he treated Judah, like I was his son. I asked him about his sentiments about the house being family property, and how come he didn't say no. Judah's father said, "Sentiments break when the mind grows. If I think my family bought this property first in their lives, then I'd want to hold onto it because of sentiments. How about my forefather's property back in Israel? Then I should trace my family bloodline back three thousand years and buy that place where my great forefather started his life. Well, I am putting it in the right hands, and I know my grandfather's and father's souls will rest in peace when they know I gave it to you, Oliver. Only in my community, people's souls don't rest in peace because I refused to sell it to them. Who cares? I gave it to my spiritual descendant Oliver, which is purer than some diluted bloodline kin."

I bought the house for $75 million from Judah's father. He purposely didn't reduce the price, because he wanted to uphold my reputation and never wanted anyone to say, "Oliver bought this piece of property cheap from his friend's family." I had to pay more $50 million to Judah's father, and I would be able to settle it very soon. But Judah's father's family trust was still doing the maintenance of the house until I paid the whole sum, which was so kind of Judah's father. I bought this house in Madison's name and registered it for her, as she never asked me for anything in her entire life; she just followed me wherever I went and stood by me. I named it the Madison Villa, for my love.

With my new role as assistant CIO, I got a new office, a very big one, and now I had a hot secretary named Martha. I had to behave myself, which I definitely did because even though men with money and power often handle things in a different way, I was still Oliver, still a good boy. I was the head of the technology department, and my job was to make the budgeting for the technology for the fiscal year. I did the budgeting so well, I cut down the cost by 35 percent. I got rid of the greedy vendors who were charging a lot of money for support and services. I brought in small companies with efficient products and commitment and started to do deals and install their technology in our company. Initially there was a big debate: how could I replace giant vendors who had been in business for decades and some more than a century, with small companies with less reputation? But I picked small companies with passion, spirit, and the right guys working for the company's future. All the small companies I picked provided us better support than the big vendors; it was efficient, secure, and even faster. Now I had some new friends in the technology world for business and made more enemies amongst the big corporations.

The CEO knew all the good work that I was doing and he was delighted and proud of me. Peyton, his boss, Gwyneth—everyone reported to me. Life taught me one lesson, goodness always wins. I made my father's dream true , as well as Nathalie, my mom, my friends and their families, people from Chelsea, my son Yohance, my daughter Claudia, and every soul I knew—they were all proud of me. Thanks to Dan, who said the ultimate truth about "Science of Verbum Victus", a truth that every man and woman should know. I told Dan the last time I met him that I would be the CIO of the company and then pay him a visit. My words became true. Yes, it was true. I rejoiced now, because our current

CIO was retiring and the CEO, president, and board members wanted me to be the new CIO of the company. I took charge of being the new CIO of Harvest and Reap. Within four years I had become the CIO of the company—what fast progress. Was it because of my knowledge, experience, education, and philosophy that I was here as Oliver J. Oscar, the CIO of Harvest and Reap? No, it was none of those things; it was imagination and my words that made me a successful person.

I was eager to meet with Dan and share my success and thank him for enlightening me. I went to meet him after a year and it was the same gorgeous, fabulous building, the same two doormen, and the same elevator to the third floor. It was the same door I walked in when I was ignorant the first time, and I saw him in the same place near the window and heard the same voice say, "Welcome, Oliver."

Me: Nice to see you again, Dan. Thank you for everything.

Dan: You are welcome. What made you come and visit me again? Have you grown in the company? You should be a CIO now.

Me: Yes, sir, I am. I made it.

Dan: How did you reach your goals so soon?

Me: All the credit goes to you, Dan. Now I am confident. I used your way of life: Science of Verbum Victus.

Dan: To do what?

Me: Send some thunder and lightning.

Dan: Did it work?

Me: It worked, but I am not sure whether it was my proclamation.

Dan: So, doubt still lingers in you. Hmm. . .

Me: It is not doubt, Dan, but I look like some character in a fairy tale or myth or something like that, sending thunder and lightning.

Dan: You admired Superman all the time, Oliver, but when opportunity knocks on your door, you think Superman is crazy. This is what I always tell you: "Man has forgotten his true identity, and everything that was told to him was a story."

Me: Okay, but I need something very concrete that this works on, Dan.

Dan: Then wish it, my son.

Me: Well, everyone said my dad is dead, and I believe he is still alive somewhere—in heaven, outer space, somewhere, I don't know. Could I bring him back to life?

Dan: Then imagine and proclaim it.

Me: Will the word work for a dead man?

Dan: Death is in your minds. No one dies; they start a new journey. The universe is so well built that it makes sure no one is lost, unless it decides to take a deep dive.

Me: What do you mean by "deep dive"?

Dan: A constant beginning.

Me: A constant beginning, what is that?

Dan: Time will answer you.

Me: So you say that I could wake up my father from death?

Dan: You could.

Me: If this wish comes true, Dan, then I should completely believe it, because making a dead man walk is something hard, but if that is the way I could believe, then I should do that.

Dan: Let me ask a question, Oliver: do you fail every time in believing it?

Me: Not always, but when I encounter situations, different people, where I don't know how to explain this concept, that is where I have problems.

Dan: Exploring this universe and understanding it, controlling it, is the hard way, and it is the way that the universe doesn't want to work. It has its own way, it is the word, and if you follow that, things are made easier and you know everything that you need to know about it.

Me: I hear you. I have this last question: What does "god" actually mean? I am agnostic and I don't know why you refer to everyone as a god.

Dan: The God or a god was the best illusion ever created in this universe. It originated when we lost our memories and tried getting some help from other realms. The meaning of *god* is not a title or surname or profession or anything like that; it is a word that is used for recovery, like an art of recovery.

Me: What do you mean by "art of recovery"?

Dan: We are lost, and to find our way back home, we have to use this word until we enter the home of happiness. It is similar to any profession. Take a carpenter or a sculptor. When he starts his work, chiseling the wood, smoothing out and starting to carve wood or stone, he is so much into his work that his profession is no more as a carpenter or sculptor; he is the wood or stone and they become one.

Me: I got it. I know it is true. I just need some time to construct myself as a perfect god.

Dan: Very good. I wish you good luck, my son.

I left Dan's house and wanted to check whether this Science of Verbum Victus worked or not for dead people. I started to say to myself, *my father is not dead. He is alive somewhere.* I knew I was crazy, but if this is the way we could wake dead people to come back to life, then why shouldn't I try it? My mind was now full of thoughts of my father, and I wanted to see him. I started to build imagination in my mind, that he was alive somewhere and wanted to see me. I did this for a month, proclaiming my hope in my mind, but now my mind was stable, because I didn't care what other people thought about me because at least I was a good son, loved my father, and tried my best to bring him back from the dead. It was my father, and as a son I will do anything to make him come back to life.

The more positive I was, the weirder things became. I went back home to see my mother by myself. Madison stayed in New York City, as she was busy with school. My mom was happy to see me after such a long time, and I felt much love for my mother. It was evening, and I decided to take a walk in my neighborhood. My mind was filled with thoughts about my dad, and everything I saw caused me to recollect the sweet memories of him. I went to the park, and everyone was playing and having fun. I greeted everyone and all of them were glad to see me. I went to sit in a lonely place and didn't want to be disturbed. I closed my eyes and was thinking about my father and saying to myself that I would see him soon.

As I was talking, I felt a smooth chilly wind pass over me. I slowly opened my eyes and saw a man and woman walking toward me. They wore long black coats, and the man had a rifle and the woman had some flowers in her hand. They were so far away, I couldn't recognize them. Everyone in the garden saw the two and saw the man with the rifle in his hand, and they started to run for their lives. I didn't know what was happening. I was scared, and slowly I realized they were walking toward me. My eyesight became blurry and I couldn't see. My feet became numb and my hands stiff, I couldn't move.

They walked to me and I started to sweat, and when my eyes were able to focus, I saw that the man was my father and the lady was Nathalie. My voice choked. I couldn't believe both of them were alive. My dad put his right leg on the bench and took a cigar and lit it. Nathalie looked so young, and I was looking at them, and my dad asked, "Why didn't you wish Nathalie to come back to life?" I didn't know what to answer, and Nathalie looked at me angrily and said, "I spent my entire life bringing you cookies, and I cared for you the most. You are a selfish boy, Oliver!" I couldn't talk, and I held my throat and said, "No, I am sorry. . ." and I started to blabber and I didn't know what was happening.

Then my dad cocked his gun and put it to my head and said, "I don't want a son like you, Oliver. It's better for you to die. You are a selfish, gluttonous, creepy, deceiving creature." Hearing that I felt very hurt. The tip of the gun barrel was touching my head, and there were no words coming out of my mouth. My dad threw away the cigar and Nathalie said bye with her hand. My dad was about to pull the trigger when I heard a gunshot. It hit my dad's neck, and I saw a hole and blood was gushing out. I shouted at my dad and moved to hold him, his head twisted back and his face was on the other side. His body turned the same way, and he shouted, "Not so soon, you punks!" The cops were shouting at me, "Go hide, son! Don't get up!" I saw there were lots of cops running with their guns, and Nathalie took two pistols from her coat and saw me. "Wait here, baby. I'll be back soon!" I saw her eyes were turning red and turned back and started shooting the cops. I jumped backward from the bench and went and ducked. There were guns fired and a few officers got shot, but my dad was shot many times. He was not dead and finally they brought him and Nathalie down, but they were still alive and were on the ground.

The cops rushed toward me and checked, and I said I was fine and asked what was happening. They said my dad and Natalie were infected with some virus and had become zombies. I was shocked to hear that. I felt pitiful for my dad, and the cops asked me whether they bit me. I said no and they checked to confirm and found nothing. They had both collapsed on the ground, and I slowly walked to them. They were shot badly and still breathing, and I saw that my dad's eyes were red and his nails had started to turn black. Nathalie was rolling in pain and her limbs started to change. I was scared and felt sorry for them. Then there were police officers, agents and Special Forces in the park, and the sun was going down and I asked the cop, "What should we do?" The cop said, "There are going to be thousands of them soon, and we are prepared for them."

The police didn't kill Nathalie and my dad, and they wanted to carry them to the lab to check the virus and the infection. I knelt down and looked at my father and said, "Why did you curse me like that, Dad? You are my blood and I love you the most." My dad was trying to jump on me to bite me. I moved away from him, and he lost his mind totally. I felt bad for what happened to him, and my dad looked at me and said, "You think I lost my mind, Oliver. My blood has changed now. We are not the same blood, but my mind is the same." I replied to him angrily, "Do you really know what you are doing." Blood was coming out of his mouth, and he said, "Oh, well, I know my son and I meant it, really: you are the worst son anyone could ever have. I will come back again and with my own hands I will kill you and your mother."

I got terribly mad at him and said, "Why, Mom?" and he replied, "I hate God so much, and she gave birth to a monster like you!" I replied, "Don't ever try that with her, Dad. I will . . ." and he said, "Yes, go ahead and tell me. Say it, you devil."

"I will kill you, Dad." I choked on the words, and he started to laugh like a maniac. I said it again and again: "I will kill you, Dad." "I will kill you, Dad . . . " I didn't know what to do in this situation and asked, "What should I do to make you happy, Dad?" and I started to cry. He looked at me and said, "Just say, just open your mouth and say you should die, you should die, and I never want to see you again." There was a cop next to me holding my shoulders and I said, "I cannot do it, Dad, no, please." I started to sob and my dad said, "Then I will kill you and your mom. You never even granted your father's last wish. I told you, you are the worst son anyone ever could have." I was not left with much choice, so I made myself strong and said very slowly, "You should die and I never want to see you again." I started to cry, and hearing that, my dad's body became motionless. His breath was slowing down and he closed his eyes and his body became still.

One of the cops checked his pulse and said, "He's gone." I saw Nathalie and she said, "I will never forgive you, Oliver." I looked at the skies and screamed madly about all the things that were happening. At once millions of people started to walk and everyone was saying, "Kill Oliver, kill Oliver. . ." and the cops asked me to leave with them. They took me in a van and a voice loudly screamed, "Kill Oliver" and even when I closed my eyes, I still heard it. I started to get a headache and I couldn't stand the voice. I pushed all the cops in the van and opened the door and started to run. All the dead people, the zombies, caught me and started to throw me high in the air again and again.

I was flying between the sky and the soil in the hands of the zombies, and everyone was passing me around. They all finally threw me into the sea and I was drowning with dead zombie bodies in the sea. I screamed and woke from the bed, saying, "Nooooo!" Madison was sleeping next to me, and she woke up and was terrified. She asked me what had happened and I didn't mention anything about the dream and said, "Some weird dreams," I couldn't sleep anymore that night. This was the worst dream I'd ever had. I didn't know whether I should continue using Science of Verbum Victus, because I woke up all the zombies, and for a few days, this dream was bothering me badly. I found the real truth about the dream: if I started to talk in real life, then I would wake up zombies, but when I woke up, I became stronger and I started to say again every day, my *father is alive. Fate and curses have no control over me. My word is my destiny, and I will be victorious over evil in my life.*

Time went by and then one day it happened. It was a Friday, and I came home from work early. I was so tired; I almost fell asleep in the car. I got into the house, and Madison was watching TV and Claudia and her mother were playing chess. Everyone was busy, so I didn't bother anyone. I went and grabbed some wine from the kitchen and invited Fernando in for a drink. We both went to the bar in the house and started having a drink and chatting. Fernando excused himself for a half hour, as he had to prepare some special dish that he was making for me.

I was by myself and walked to the window and looked out at the street. My mind imagined myself as Dan, who sits most of time, watching the street. I saw all sorts of people, cars, people crossing the street, dogs, and it was a fun experience for me to watch all these things in the street. Then I noticed someone was standing opposite my house and watching my house and the front door. At first I ignored it. He wore a dirty shirt, a jacket, and a beard and looked bizarre. Then Fernando made some fish on the grill, and I joined him and started to eat with him. It was delicious and I felt that wine and fish were the best food in this whole world. Fernando took the empty plates and dishes to the kitchen. I had some wine in my hand and walked to the window. I noticed the man was still standing and staring at the front door. At this point I got a little nervous. Why was this man watching our house? I felt like some homeless person was stalking us, but again I ignored it.

Then Fernando came back and we were chatting. Since it was a weekend, he brought some expensive Russian vodka and wanted us to do shots. He was pouring some shots and I called Demonthin to join us. We had the first shot and it was amazing. We started to chat, and very soon, Madison, Sandra, and Quanah also joined us. Fernando made some shots for all of us, and in the meantime, everyone was having wine. I took Madison to the window and was showing her the streets and I shared with her; Dan's only habit, to sit near the window and watch the streets. As I was showing her, I saw the same man standing and staring at our house. I told Madison I had observed this guy for a couple of hours, and asked her, "Why is he looking at our house?" She replied, "I saw him this morning as well." I asked her, "Are you sure?" She replied, "Yes, Oscar, I am sure. I thought it was some random person." Then I called Demonthin and everyone and asked them, and they said they had seen him in the morning. Then I asked Demonthin if we should go and ask who he was.

Demonthin, Fernando, one of the doormen, and I hurried to see the man. As we got nearer to him, he looked like he was completely broke. His clothes were torn, and a beard covered his whole face. Fernando asked, "Who are you, man? What do you want? You need some money?" and Demonthin said, "Do you need some help, man?" Then the stranger replied, "Oliver, Oliver, Oliver, it's me." I was behind Demonthin, and I looked at the man and asked him, "Who are you? How do you know my name?" He replied, "My son, Oliver." I was shocked. My eyes couldn't believe it! It was my dad. I didn't know what to say. We looked at each other and my voice was shrill and I said slowly, "Dad, Pa, is it you?" I could recognize him now, but he was totally different, and I went and held his hands.

Soon my dream came into my mind and started to bother me, but I had practiced so well that now I never fed my thoughts with disbelief. I just ignored the bad thought that was running through my mind and I stayed positive and whispered to myself, "My dad is alive." My dad was thin and shabby. He had torn clothes, and he was so weak, he couldn't even hold my hands. He fell on me and fainted, and I took him in my lap and started to scream, looking at him. Hearing my loud voice, Madison, Sandra, and everyone started to run to see what was happening. Everyone in our neighborhood came out and started to notice us. Then Madison asked me, "Who is this, Oscar?" I replied, "Dad, my father, Madison," and she knelt down and asked, "Is it Uncle James?" She started to touch his face and said, "We should take him home."

I carried my father in my arms and brought him inside. He was thin and weak, and I couldn't feel anything. Carrying him reminded me of the days he carried me in the same way when I was a kid. I put him on the couch and we splashed some water on his face. Everyone was shocked, but no one thought to call a doctor. He opened his eyes and said, "I am hungry. Food, food." And then everyone rushed to the kitchen to get some food for him, but Claudia had a cookie in her hand, and she came and gave it to my dad and said, "Eat it. You are hungry." He was so weak, he couldn't even move his hands, so Claudia placed it near his mouth. He started to eat it, and he ate the whole cookie. He asked me, "Is this your daughter?" I replied, "No, Dad. Well, yeah, she is my daughter." My father said, "Do you have so many kids now, you don't even remember your daughter?" This was the first joke I had heard in a long time, and I laughed with him.

We got him fish and some soup. Madison and I fed him, and I could not express how happy I felt. While he was eating, he asked me, "Is that the same Madison you kissed when you were a kid?" Then Madison's face grew pale, and she said, "Oscar, you told everyone." Madison's face was the same as it had been the day I kissed her for the first time, and I found myself guilty. I said to her, "I confessed to my dad, every night. Sorry dear" and she smiled at me with a great loving expression, as she knew how much I loved my dad.

I could not believe that my dad was alive and back again. Everyone in the house was overjoyed for us. I asked my dad what had happened and how he was alive. My dad asked me, "Do you know what happened, Oliver?" I replied, "Moise Boti came home and told us everything that had happened." He said, "Moise told you. Good kid. How is he?" and I replied, "I sent him a card for last New Year, and he wrote and said that he is doing well."

Then my father told me the whole story of what had happened in Iraq. He went to the building to search for any kids or other people inside. He heard a door close and a kid's voice screaming, and he rushed to see who it was. There was a back door in the building and one of the terrorists, who was shot but not dead, took a little girl and was walking with her. My dad warned him to drop her, but he refused. Then the bomb in the building blasted, and my father, hearing the noise, pulled the trigger and shot the guy. The little girl fell to the ground, and my father covered her in the explosion. My father was hit badly by the bricks from the explosion and he lost consciousness and fainted. The little girl was scared and got up and ran, thinking my father was dead.

There was a backup group of terrorists who came to help their team, and they found my dad and took him as their hostage. They couldn't keep him there in Iraq, as the American forces were all over the place. So they shipped my father to Afghanistan. The Al-Sayyid Ifrit group knew my father was the one who had helped Ejaz's family and knew I was a good friend of Ejaz's family, so they kept him in the caves and tortured him for years. The sad thing was that the kid didn't tell anyone that he had saved her and was outside the building, but he could not blame her, because she was only three years old. Everyone thought he was inside the building and burned to ashes, and they couldn't find his body. He had been there in Afghanistan for all these years and was on half rations, working as a slave for Al-Sayyid Ifrit. Lots of captured prisoners were there. Some were dead now, some had been killed, and some were still living.

Then I asked my father, "How did you manage to get out?" and he said, "I was making a tunnel in the cave, and it took me all these years to get out. After I got out of the cave, I escaped Afghanistan and walked across the desert to Iran. Then I took a boat and sailed all the way to Somalia to find our US troops. I was taken as a captive in Somalia and kept for three months, and then I managed to escape. I couldn't ask anyone for help, because of the different rebel militias in Africa. They would have killed me or locked me up, knowing I was an American soldier, so I decided to cross the ocean from Angola using a boat.

"There were two other American military captives, and the three of us crossed the Atlantic by boat. We made it and finally reached New York." I asked my father, "How did you know that I live here?" He said he had seen my photo in a magazine as the best CIO in corporate America and saw my company's name. He learned that I lived in New York City, and he found my house and had waited the whole day to meet me. I asked him, "Why didn't you come to my door and ask for me?" He replied, "Over the years, I've lost my senses, so I didn't feel like bothering anyone. I didn't want to embarrass you by the way I look." I replied to him, "Dad, you are my father, you are my life, you could never embarrass me."

Madison said, "Uncle, what happened to you? We missed you so much. You set an example for all of us." He replied to Madison, "I was in prison like a slave, and time changed me. I'm sorry. I didn't mean to do something like this. Forgive me, honey." Madison hugged him and started crying. "Oh God, what happened to you? We love you."

What can I say now? I was excited and happy. That night was so important to me and a night that changed my life forever. I had never lost my father, and he was alive; it was true that Science of Verbum Victus worked very well. All I could say was that the good and bad things that happen in your life are based upon your mind's imagination and the very words that you speak. I had found it. I had really found it: the ultimate truth of this life.

Chapter 13
THE REAL WORLD

It was almost 7:00 p.m. on the day when I met my father. There was critical work going in the office, and everybody had to stay late. We ordered food and some drinks. My father was asleep, so I decided to call Edgar and Nyah to come to my home so I could introduce my father to them and then go and meet Dan. They didn't pick up their phones and I tried reaching their office lines but got no reply, so I asked Demonthin to drive me to the office and we both left home to pick up Edgar and Nyah.

I thought it was the greatest day of my life, but something else was happening to me. I felt like I was disintegrating. It was weird. The roads had less traffic and as I was in the car, I started to see this world in a different way. I reached my office and got out of the car and asked Demonthin to wait for me. None of the elevators in the building were working, and I thought some maintenance was going on, so I walked to the twelfth floor to meet Edgar and Nyah.

It was a surprise when I saw Salomeya sitting on the twelfth floor. I asked her, "Did they move you here from the fifteenth floor?" She replied, "I have always been on the same floor. What happened to you?" She was busy on the computer and ignored me. I was not convinced by her answer, and her attitude was different, so I asked her, "What do you mean that you have always been on the same floor? I know you work on the fifteenth floor." She said, "Life is an illusion, so what do you want me to say, Oliver? You are the CIO of Harvest and Reap, but do you ever realize where you are?" I replied, "Yeah, I am in Manhattan and in my company." She replied, "Time will answer that question. So what exactly do you want from me?" I answered, "I just walked by to see Edgar and Nyah and spotted you here. I was confused, and I wanted to be sure."

Salomeya: There is no one named Edgar and Nyah working here.

Me: What? Are you crazy? We are all friends, Salomeya. Come on, stop joking around.

Salomeya: No, Oliver, you are mistaken. Neither of those people work here and I don't know them, so how could we be friends?

Me: What is happening here? You are kidding, right? Are you okay?

Salomeya: I am okay, Oliver, but these are facts. I don't know them, and you are asking me all the wrong questions.

Me: Okay, enough, stop playing with me. Let me go and get them.

I headed toward the office, and from the front desk I found everyone working and very busy. I walked to Edgar's desk but I found it empty, so I asked the person sitting in the next cubicle, "Where is Edgar?" He replied, "No one has been sitting in that desk for almost four years. It's vacant." I looked at the nameplate and found there was no name. My mind was becoming confused now, and I walked to Nyah's desk. I looked for her, but she was missing too. I asked the person sitting next to Nyah's desk where she was, and she replied with the same answer, that no one had sat there for five years. Again, the nameplate was empty.

Then I quickly rushed to the front desk and asked Salomeya, "What is happening? Where are Edgar and Nyah? Please could you tell me, Salomeya?" She replied, "Oliver, I don't know them, and I don't know what you are talking about. Are you all right? Do you want me to call a doctor or Madison?" I replied, "It's fine, I am tired, sorry. I was just kidding. Take care. Good night."

I quickly walked out of the office, and suddenly everything felt weird, I felt weak. I didn't know what was happening around me. I started to hold my head and I was in great pain now in my mind. Demonthin saw me and came to help me as he checked whether I was okay. I asked him to drive me to Seventy-Second Street and Park Avenue, and while he was driving me there, my mind was so confused; I couldn't understand what was happening to me. I was looking at the streets of NYC, but everything was different now. Shops were closed, very few people were on the street, and it was Friday, so I didn't know where the crowds were. My mind was filling with terrible thoughts, I could see buildings falling over me, and I closed my eyes, because everything I saw hurt me.

We reached Seventy-Second Street, and I asked Demonthin to stop the car and wait for me. I rushed into Dan's house, but I didn't find the doormen standing there. It was a big shock for me, and I slowly started to walk down to the elevator. I pressed the button to go up to the third floor. In the elevator I felt lost and didn't know what was happening. The elevator doors opened and I saw the big door before me, the same door that had been there the first time I walked in. I opened it and the hall looked the same: the paintings, carpet, lights, and the chair near the window. But I didn't see Dan Root there, which was very unusual. I started to walk toward his chair with some hope that maybe everything was an illusion or my friends were fooling around. As I approached his chair, I found a piece of folded paper on the table. I took the paper and unfolded it and saw the following was written:

"Go back to your world with hope, and change it through your WORD.

"Science of Verbum Victus—Dan Root"

I didn't know exactly what he meant. This was my world, so I didn't know what he meant by "My world." My head was spinning and I couldn't stand, so I sat in the chair where I usually sat. Ten minutes later, I still didn't know what was happening, and I remembered Dan had given me a letter the first time I met him. I always kept it with me in my wallet. He had said to me, "Open it on the day when you are convinced of your answer to your search, to know the ultimate and eternal truth of life." I had the envelope before me now, but I was not sure this was the day I had found the ultimate truth. But things around me were completely off: Where were Nyah and Edgar, and what was Salomeya up to? Where were the door men, and where was Dan? How come my father was still alive? All these thoughts went in circles, and my brain was about to explode.

With all these thoughts, I just opened the envelope and found a piece of paper that said, "Say hi to Demonthin, and be careful with Peyton." I didn't know what was happening, and where I was really. How did Dan know Demonthin and Peyton? Is Dan a god or was he watching me? Why especially did he write about Demonthin and Peyton? Who is Demonthin? Why did he want to be my bodyguard and my chauffeur? Why did he follow me from Boston to NYC? Peyton was just a manager in my company, and I was CIO. Why should I be careful of him? Were Edgar and Nyah spying on me and informing Dan? Where were Edgar and Nyah? They were missing, and even Dan Root was missing.

I was scared and ran out of the room and rushed into the elevator. When it got to the ground floor, I started running out of the building. I was panicking and started to breathe heavily. I looked at the streets, but there was no one in the streets—no cars, no people, no dogs, no horses, nothing. But there were lights in the street, and stores were open, and the crazy thing was that the streets looked so clean. My breathing started to slow down. I was looking for Demonthin, but he was not around. My car was parked, and he was not inside the car. I started to run through the streets, calling his name. "Demonthin, Demonthin, talk to me, man!"

I held my breath and started to run to my house, which was almost five blocks away. The streets were empty, and I was feeling so hot inside that I removed my suit jacket while running and held it in my hand. As I got closer to the house, I saw the door was open, which was strange. I ran inside the house and there were no doormen. This added to my confusion, and I started to panic. I ran inside the house calling for Madison, but she was not in. Then I called for my dad. No answer. Claudia, Fernando, and Sandra—no one was inside the house. The house was empty, and no human soul was there. But all the lights, furniture, carpets, and objects were there, clean and shiny. I went to all the bedrooms, even to the maids' dwelling place; I went to every space in that house. The house was clean and everything was arranged properly and organized, and there were no signs that anyone ever lived there. Then finally I went to my bedroom to check whether Madison was sleeping, and she was not there.

My head was hurting now. My hands and body were shivering. I took my cell phone and wanted to call my mom. The call went through, and I heard a heartbeat ticking and ticking. My body started to shrink and I started to become smaller and smaller. I was shrinking down and becoming younger year by year, and as I started to shrink down, I looked younger and younger. I could recollect my body at different time periods. Now I looked like a teenager, and then I started to become like a five-year-old kid. I was still shrinking, and I reached a one-year old and was standing on my bed. It didn't stop and I was still shrinking, but I was listening to my heartbeat constantly. Finally, I became a baby in my mother's womb, and I was hearing the same heartbeat now when I called my mom, the same heartbeat I heard when I was born.

Then a whirlwind took me from my mother's womb and I passed through many dimensions in descending order. In each dimension I saw many worlds, and as I traveled, my mind calmed and finally materialized back into the true dimension that I was living in. Now I knew where I was. I was on Wall Street. I was not yet the chairman or CIO of Wall Street; I was a poor construction worker. What was that life I had? My father, mother, my girlfriend Madison, all my nine best friends, their families, Purdhil, Demonthin, Dan, Edgar, Nyah, Nathalie, and everyone—who were they? Did they exist? Yes, some did and some did not. Then who was I? I was just Oliver, victim of World War III and a Fourth Dimension kid. It was the Third World War here and things were horrific, but we were all the so-called Fourth Dimension people, seeing flowers in the midst of fire and chaos.

Some people said it was not correct to say World War III, but the other name is World War X. It is the year 3500 AD, although no one knew what the exact year was. All we knew was that there was a war, and every country was in it. But I lived in NYC, and I was sitting on Wall Street, on a broken bench near the Exchange. It was not the same Wall Street but one filled with damaged, bombed-out buildings. Once called skyscrapers, the buildings now looked like they were part of a shelled city, where buildings were mostly just flattened. You could see the metal, iron, concrete, and bricks, with smoke and ashes. The funniest thing was that you could even see the CEO's private room; there were no doors and windows. The whole city was a mess, and my nine friends were scavengers, not doctors or engineers or architects or fashion designers or cops, just youngsters with some ambition and working for daily wages.

Then where was the life we had? Was it a dream? No, a dream was the biggest lazy spot ever speculated in human history. Then what was I doing? I was searching in "The search world." The most powerful tool that man ever had, "The search world." I was searching for truth, an answer that changed my world, and I think I found it. It all happened when I was twelve years old, when I was overwhelmed with concepts and ideas that were so distant from my imagination. So, I set my mind and spirit to search for an answer in a different world, called "The search world." It may be a parallel universe, but I didn't find Elvis Presley popping pills or Einstein working on the Theory of Everything or Hitler promoting Nazism; I found a perfect world, and I designed it and started to live in it and searched for an answer. I accomplished and possessed everything that I could not have in this real world: love, friendship, family, food, career, job, awards and happiness. Everything I wanted to do was mine for the taking. But I was so negative; I imported my negative thoughts into the search world. I killed my father and Nathalie, put Ejaz's father in prison, made people slaves, created terrorists like Purdhil, hurt Madison in a car accident, I did all these little nasty things. I did this because—and I was not the one to be blamed—the world taught me such negativity and suppression. The search world was perfect. I should have lived there, but I found an answer that is the reason I came back to accomplish what I learned and believed. Some incidents and some characters in the real world were true in the search world, but since I had so much negativity in me, it took almost twelve years to find this answer.

Where did the search world begin and what about real life in this world? I will tell you, it started in Milwaukee, Wisconsin, same place, no doubt, I was born, that is true, I was reborn in the search world also in Milwaukee, Wisconsin, but it should have been Paris, Amsterdam, London, Australia, or Pakistan, but I loved where I was born. I don't know what I was doing in my mom's womb. If I could ever remember what happened inside my mom's womb, I would have to try closing my ears, because there were lots of bombings, explosions, crying, screaming, and chaotic noises.

I was born in a small private hospital. We went through the regular procedure, and I showed up. Some donkey bombed our hospital, and I escaped. It was the simplest birth and greatest escape from bombing in history. At that time I didn't know how I escaped and didn't realize I was the only one who escaped, but I had a companion who also escaped: Mr. Judah. Someone picked us up and told the story to us, that our hospital had been bombed to the ground and everyone else was dead. By a miracle we were alive; two women picked up the two survivors, Mr. X and Mr. Y, from the burned-down ruins.

Do you know who picked us up? Madison's mother and Nathalie were the two angels who saved us. But strangely, one angel was pregnant: Madison's mom. Her name was Stacey, and her father's name was James.

Madison was nine months in the womb, not yet born, but she had a mother and knew who her father was, and Judah and I didn't know who our parents were. But orphans Mr. X and Mr. Y didn't have any names, so they named Mr. X Oliver and Mr. Y Judah. They didn't give us last names, no harm done; they were the best parents we ever knew. So Judah and I had to pick our last names, and we did. I will tell you how I got my last name. Nathalie said that Judah and I were lying close to each other when they found us in the rubble of the hospital. When they found us, we were six days old and wrapped in a fur cloth, so Judah has always been my best friend and the first kid I ever knew. They found us on July 10, so both our birthdays should be July 4. I am guessing it could be a day less or more, but I love that my birthday is July 4, because of the national holiday and I could rest at home on my birthday. We were crying loudly. Maybe we were hungry and trying to compete with each other for attention. They picked us up but they didn't have any milk to give us; they had some sausages and bread. Nathalie told us that they had some milk powder in tin cans with them, but when they were trying to run and hide in the cross fire, they dropped the cans and the cans were obliterated by grenades.

We were both weak, having gone maybe a day or two without food. Maybe you're thinking, how did they know? They didn't eat for two days and survived. We are the Fourth Dimension kids so maybe we can bend space and time and drink milk from the heavens and be aware of the time around us. Madison's mother fed both of us with her milk. We didn't steal Madison's portion, but drank a stranger's milk to live. The mother, I should always know, was Stacey, Madison's mom. There was heavy firing and bombing throughout Milwaukee and in our neighborhood. They both found shelter in a bunker. Getting a bunker was a tough job and the bunkers were very secure and very hard to find, but somehow they found one and we spent almost six months in it. Bunkers were well made and had lots of food, milk cans, water generators, and recyclers. Don't imagine our bunker looked like a decent condo with two bedrooms or looked like dictator's bunker with a party room and office. It was just a place to live and stay away from death. We only had one toilet and no shower. There were deluxe bunkers which were like hotels, and we were not wealthy people.

For our health benefits we two parentless boys were fed by Madison's mom for a month. Madison was born in the bunker after a month, and now her mother had to feed her, Judah, and me. It was a great burden on her side, and she had to eat a balanced diet and more calories. But this was not nourishment time, but wartime, and we learned to survive with what we had. She ate a lot of wheat bread, potatoes, peas, and eggs—foods we could get in abundance. Stacey was the one who went and collected food for us when there was a cease-fire.

The burden and pain for Madison's mom didn't last long, because a month after Madison was born, she had a bad case of pneumonia. We couldn't take her to any of the hospitals, as all the local hospitals were destroyed. She didn't survive long and died in the bunker. Though four souls lived in the bunker, only one soul wept. It was Nathalie. Nathalie was getting very old, and she had difficulty in digging a grave for Madison's mom, Stacey. She took almost two days to dig one, and buried Madison's mom. She was depressed and sad and her only job was to feed us and take care of us.

We were now three months old and Madison was two months old. We could see things more clearly and we found one great thing in our eyes. Nathalie's face was shining, shining like the sun and the moon, bright, filled with glory. She looked like a real angel.

Days passed and we were still in the bunker with Nathalie taking care of us. The only things we did in the first year of life were shit in our pants, cry for milk, smile when Nathalie played with us, start sitting up straight, crawling, and collide head-on while crawling. Crawling in a bunker was like walking in a prison cell. We didn't have much room to roll our bodies over, just a finite space. We were one year old now, and we got a few moments of sunshine when Nathalie carried us out of the bunker during a cease-fire. We never saw the sun for the first year of our life, and the first time we saw it, we couldn't even see it. Judah cried the first time he saw the sun. Madison closed her eyes with her hands, and I saw every two seconds and closed my eyes. Then we slowly started to walk, run and play with each other in the bunker and outside. We started to say a few words, and we always nagged Nathalie to take us outside the bunker, and she refused most of the time. The best thing was that we never cried. If she said no to anything, we just listened. We were so disciplined, and somehow we started to feel this discipline and attachment among the four of us. We called Nathalie "Natty" and sometimes "Mom" and she always taught us the values of life.

We turned two years old and slowly started to eat solid food, talk in small sentences, and understand and reason simple things. We also started to walk steadily, and this year the war ceased for a long time. So we had more time to spend outside the bunker and could take showers during the rain in all seasons: spring, summer, and fall, sometimes even in the winter. We had a great time! There is nothing more I can tell you about our bunker world and us cute little innocent children.

Days and months passed, and we turned three and started to talk very well and to question. We started to notice some strange things about Nathalie and questioned her. Her face really glowed, and I could see some light in her face and circles behind her head. She always covered her face when she came outside the bunker, and when we asked her why, she said something that didn't make sense. Even as children we knew she was hiding something, but we loved Nathalie, and she was the only soul we knew and the one who cared for us. She didn't take us outside much, and we always spent time close to the bunker. When we would run away, not far from the bunker, we would see people walking around and kids playing, but Nathalie would run and pick us up and hide us and hide herself. Sometimes we felt that we were away from the world, not in touch with humans.

She started to teach us about our mission in life. She said that we three should go to New York City, that on the journey we would meet seven more travelers, and that all ten of us should be together and change the world. We asked her many times what was in NYC and what we should do there. She never said a word about it, and would only say that time would open our eyes. She was the smartest woman we ever knew; she was a genius. She taught us how to survive, analyze people, master our anger, be patient, and meditate to generate peace and happiness in ourselves; she trained us literally to be monks or priests.

She taught us everything about the war and its causes and all the good and bad people involved. It is 3500 AD and technology has improved a lot. We could see space shuttles, people going to the moon like they were walking from the bedroom to the kitchen. There were so many advancements in technology that no one could ever imagine. She helped us learn technology, and taught us all the fundamentals of science and technology. The predominant fields at this time were hacking, metallurgy, biomedicine, space technology, building high-speed weapons, and the physics of energy and matter. We understood the very basics in all the fields and started to reason a little bit. We just started learning.

One thing Nathalie taught us was not to play video games and to stay away from them, and we always kept our word. On occasion we asked her why, and she would only reply, "Nature and its blessing will move away from us." I didn't know what nature was, because I was in the bunker, but we carefully listened and followed her. We had never been sick, not even once, and whenever we felt strange feelings in our bodies, Nathalie just touched our heads and sickness passed away. She was a divine woman and had miraculous powers.

We ate the same type of food in the bunker—bread, potatoes, peas, sausages, and eggs—day after day. But we never got bored because Nathalie was a really good cook, and she rotated the food every day. She also combined it to become new types of food. Whatever she made, she made it look and taste good. Once a week she made some cookies for us, and that special day was always Sunday. We would wait all week to eat those cookies, and we each got four cookies. We asked her to make more every day and all she said was "They're bad for our teeth and bad for our health."

We turned four years old. We started to grow more disciplined and organized. Every single day, Nathalie taught us about our mission to go to NYC and the friends we should meet on the journey. But she never mentioned the reason we should go to NYC. This was the first time that we noticed something bizarre that Nathalie did when she would go outside the bunker by herself to buy groceries: she wore a mask that covered her glowing face and made her look normal, and then she covered her head with a hood. Madison was the one who found out that she did this and told us about it. We asked her why she did it, but she never answered us. Still, we knew she was a very righteous woman and knew what she was doing. Though Nathalie said she was old, her skin looked young and glowed, and her shining face showed us who Nathalie was.

One day, there was a cease-fire, and we were playing outside the bunker. As usual, no one was around; it was just the four of us. Then we saw four armed men walking toward us and as they came close, we noticed they were militants. They saw us and waved their hands, and said, "Hi, kids" and we replied, "Hi." They asked us if we were by ourselves and we said, "No, we are with Nathalie." The four men then saw Nathalie. Her face was covered and she had a stick in her hand, and with the stick she was drawing something on the sand. The militants asked her, "Are you all right, miss?" and she replied, "I was until I saw you!" One of the militants asked, "What did you say?" Nathalie shouted loudly, "Judah, Oliver, Madison, all three of you go inside!" We terrified hearing her voice so loud. We had never heard her shout. We ran to the bunker, but we didn't close the hatch; we were holding each other and trying to see through the opening.

All the militants started to load their guns and pointed them toward her and said, "Hands up, lady, and reveal yourself!" She replied, "Is that an order or a request?" They surrounded her, "This is an order. Put your hands up and remove your hood." She replied, "Oh whoo, it is an order, orders from the pigs. How could I put my hands up and remove the cover from my face?" Then one of the militants said, "Last warning, lady. We will shoot you. No jokes here. Do what we say!" Nathalie replied, "Let's see who dies." She removed the hood from her head and the mask from her face. Then all the militants said, "Oh, my God, how did you get here, you," but before they said one more word, Nathalie struck them one by one with her hand. Yes, she just raised her right hand and struck them with lightning that came from her hand. She was so fast; she killed all four in one second. They didn't have a chance to fire a bullet. All four men fell, one by one, like dominoes. Two men were hit by the lightning in their forehead, one in the chest, and the other in the chest and face. Their bodies burned, and they just laid on the ground in ashes.

We were all shocked. We didn't know that Nathalie had super powers in her. Judah slowly asked us, "Is she a god?" Madison replied, "Maybe, but she is strong." I asked, "Where did she get the lightning?" Judah replied, "Maybe she's Thor's daughter?" Madison said, "It may be Zeus!" I said, "Just stop it. Look at what she is doing." The reason we knew about Thor and Zeus was that when we asked who Nathalie's father was, she always said Thor and sometimes Zeus.

Nathalie quickly removed all their electronic gadgets and their communication system. She even destroyed the radio-frequency identification (RFID) chip in them. She took a long rope, tied the four together, and started to drag them. We quickly came out of the bunker and started to follow her, staying hidden. As we followed her, we noticed that she was dragging them faster, and we fell behind. We didn't know where she got so much strength and power. She dragged them almost a mile and no one was there in the streets or in the neighborhood. We spoke to one another and decided she probably knew all the places in the neighborhood. We had thought that she spent her life in the bunker all the time and didn't know much about the neighborhood. She left the bodies, went into a house and came out with a shovel and a gas can. She started to dig a pit for the four dead bodies. It was a surprise that she dug so fast. She dug a six-by-eight-foot pit in twenty minutes. The way she shoveled stayed in our minds' eyes, because it looked exactly like a monster with tremendous power digging a pit. She removed all their clothes and left only their underwear on them. She gently dropped all the bodies into the pit and started to shovel the dirt back over them. She leveled the sand and cleaned up so well that there was no trace of the digging. Then she burned the uniforms and clothing she had taken off of them with gas that she took from the house. After burning she scattered the ashes by mixing them with the sand, using the shovel, so there were no signs of burning either.

We watched the scene from killing to burial and we quickly ran back to the bunker before she turned back. We were quietly waiting in the bunker, but she came back and noticed that we were anxious. We were not scared of Nathalie, but we didn't know how to react to her now. She asked us, "How are you doing?" Madison replied, "We are confused." Nathalie asked Madison, "Why are you confused, honey?" Madison didn't reply and put her head down, and Nathalie looked at Judah and me and asked us, "What about my lovely boys?" We both ran and hugged her and said, "We love you, Nathalie," and seeing us, Madison also came and hugged her. Then Nathalie asked us, "Do you still believe me?" and Madison answered her, "We only know you. We don't know anyone else, and you love us and protect us, so we should always believe you." Nathalie kissed Madison's forehead. "You are such a sweet girl." Then Nathalie started to explain. "I know exactly what you boys are thinking. Let me tell you the whole story, why I am here and why I am feeding and protecting you boys and this little sweetheart. I don't want to hide from you anymore. It is time I tell you the truth, and this truth will guide you to perfection and disclose the secrets of this universe.

"Where I come from is not the main puzzle, but the fact that I came here is important. I started my journey to search for Oliver; that was my only mission." Madison asked, "You didn't come for me, Nathalie?" Nathalie replied, "For you also, sweetie—that is how I met your mom." Madison said, "You know my mom?" Nathalie replied, "Yes, I do, very well. She helped me in this journey and followed me all the way."

Madison asked Nathalie, "Do you know my father?" Nathalie's face grew sad and pale, and she looked at Madison. "Yes. He was such a great man. I liked him so much."

Madison: Where is my father?

Nathalie: Dead.

Madison: My father is dead?

Nathalie: Yeah, he died for us, dear.

Madison was surprised and copied Nathalie's reaction. She grew sad, and asked her, "How did he die?"

Nathalie: He tried protecting your mother and me. He lost his life, but he died like a hero.

Madison: What happened? Did he fight with somebody?

Nathalie told the story of how she met Madison's mother and how her father died. Madison's mother and father lived happily in the Strawberry Hill neighborhood of Kansas City. Nathalie went on to say, "As I was traveling to see Oliver, I made a stop in Kansas City near Strawberry Hill. I was tired from hiding and running from people and forces. I was sitting and resting on a patio, and as I was tired, I took my hood from my face and closed my eyes to take a quick nap. While I was in the early stages of my nap, I felt somebody was standing next to me. I opened my eyes and saw Madison's mother, Stacey. I quickly replaced my hood and started to run, but Stacey held my hand and said, 'I know who you are. I will not hurt you.' I looked at Stacey and said, 'Oh, thank you.'

Madison's mother asked me to come inside to drink and eat something. I felt she was a generous lady, so I said yes and followed her. She made stew, roasted chicken, and garlic bread. I was hungry. I hadn't eaten food for two days, and I was completely exhausted. I ate all the stew and the whole roasted chicken. I appreciated it. It was the best meal I had had in my life since I left home. Stacey and I were talking when James came home. He was shocked when he saw me. He asked me with a curious face, 'How did you come here? You shouldn't be here with us.' At first I was uncomfortable, but quickly he looked at Stacey's face and Stacey said, 'It is fine, honey.' He replied, 'You know it is too dangerous to keep her here.' Stacey went and comforted him, and he relaxed and greeted me with great pleasure. He asked whether we had food, and he was so nervous to see me in his house, he went and poured some Cognac. He asked us if we wanted a drink, and Stacey and I had a glass of wine.

They were asking my reason for visiting Kansas. I was not comfortable telling them, and I apologized. But they both were so gentle, they didn't ask me again. I spent day after day there. There was a curfew, because there were peace talks and negotiations going on with the UN, the Europe Union, and our allies. Every day people were granted a couple of hours when they could come out of their homes to buy groceries and commodities. James would go out and get all the required food and necessities for us. I spent time with Stacey, talking, watching TV, and playing cards. I discovered something about her: I could trust her.

Ten days passed, and I spent all my time with Stacey and James. The curfew was over, and on that night while we had dinner, I told them that I was leaving. They asked me where I was going and I replied, 'To Wisconsin.' They asked me what I was going to do there, and because of the hospitality, love, and kindness they showed me, I told them the purpose of my visit and that I was looking for Oliver, a newborn baby, the chosen one who could stop World War III. Both were shocked to hear me say that about the chosen one, but since they were spiritual, they could understand the message and were elated that all the chaos would end soon.

They asked me about how I was going to make it to Wisconsin. I told them I had to walk all the way because that would be the best way for me to go. Both of them wanted to help, to take me to Wisconsin and they asked whether they could join me. I resisted, because it was very dangerous and I didn't want to involve this good couple. But they were persistent and said they wanted to be part of the journey to meet the chosen one and it would be the best act they could do for humanity. I couldn't say no, because in my mind I felt that if I failed this journey, at least the two would go and save the chosen one. So I said with great delight, 'Let's do it.'

James decided to drive me to Wisconsin because it was too dangerous to take public transportation or fly, because all the transportation modes were being monitored. Before we left, James went and met his friend and got a fake ID. The least watched were cars; he could hide me from the public and ID checks. But one thing I didn't say was when and where the chosen would be born, because I was always aware of my surroundings. We left Kansas City and started our journey on the highway.

The Midwest was less prone to war, but still in these times there were no safe places in the universe.

The journey was smooth for a few miles. Then as we were driving, we saw a chopper and a bulletproof van with ten to fifteen cops standing on the highway. They waved their hands for us to stop the car, and James slowed down. One police officer walked to the car and asked for his ID and license and checked it. Then he scanned the RFID in his hand and confirmed it and saw that his record was clean. The officer asked who the travelers in the backseat were, and James said we were his wife and mother-in-law. He asked where we were going, and James replied that we were heading to Chicago. The cop walked to the backseat and asked us to slide the car window down, and we did. He asked us to identify ourselves, and Stacey pulled her ID and the cop scanned her RFID in her hand and confirmed her status. Then it was my turn. I showed my fake ID, and he scanned it and it came through clean. He asked for my RFID and I replied, "No, sir, I don't have one." Then the cop asked me to reveal myself by removing my hood, and I replied, "No, I can't do that." He asked me to step out of the car.

The other cops started to walk toward the car. At this tense situation, James pulled a gun and shot the cop. A couple of cops had laser guns, and the rest had automatic rifles; the cops who had the automatic rifles started to shoot at the car. At that time I realized the car was bulletproof and James asked me to stay inside the car. He stepped out and went back to the trunk and took out a double barrel shotgun. They were firing and bullets were flying around us, and James started to take down the cops one by one. James was so smart; he shot the chopper down and broke the communication system in the van. The cops couldn't communicate with the control room, but the cops were trying to use their I-gadgets to call in an emergency backup team. James didn't give them a chance: he shot them one by one. He warned the cops to let us go, but they refused. With five cops down and a hide-and-seek game going on, we were still in the car. Then I saw that one officer had a sniper rifle aimed at James, James did not notice him, as he was focusing on the movement of the other cop. I was positive he would bring James down.

I got out of the car with my hood off, and struck the cop who was aiming at James with the lightning from my hand. This was the first time I had ever killed someone in my life. I had never had blood on my hands before. Then all four cops got scared, because now they knew who I was, and I started to run. James took them down one by one, like dominoes, and everyone was dead. When the last running cop was dead, both James and Stacey sighed in relief, but I was in great pain because I had never killed someone, and now I felt guilty. My heart started to hurt badly; it really hurt me.

My eyes started to blur and I couldn't see anything, but I noticed that not everyone was dead. The first cop who got shot was not dead. He was lying behind me, and I was undergoing this sort of mental pain from my hands being dirty with the killing. I didn't notice him, but James did, and he took his gun to shoot him. But as always, ammo runs out, at some point. He started running toward me, shouting, "Nathalie, watch out behind you!" Stacey got out of the car on the other side to run toward me, but James reached me and pushed me over. But fate loves it's own power. The cop fired a bullet and the bullet passed into James' forehead. I woke up from feeling guilty about my bloody killing and saw James on the floor dead. I turned back and saw that the police officer was still alive. Again I turned and saw James, but this time I got mad and wanted revenge. I was about to kill him, but I heard gunfire, which hit the cop's face, destroying it.

I didn't know what had happened, and I turned back and saw Stacey holding a shotgun, her face filled with anger, fear and vengeance. She dropped the gun and ran to James, grabbed him and held him in her lap. She was crying, asking him to look at her, but he didn't look at her because he was dead. She put his face on her breast and cried loudly looking at the sky and saying, "What am I going to do without him?" She wept badly, and looking at her emotions and pain, I was deeply troubled. I walked to her and held her hand and said, "I am so sorry." She put her head on my shoulder and cried, and for the first time I felt that Stacey was my daughter.

But we could keep these sentiments going for a long time, because they were already watching the whole show from a satellite and there was a backup unit on the way. Yes, the goddamn satellites have eyes. Even if you close your eyes, they are still watching you. I forced Stacey to leave the place and she agreed to leave, but we didn't know what to do with James's dead body. So we cut the RFID from James's hand and slowly removed the one from Stacey's hand and wrapped her hand with a piece of cloth. We put James in the trunk of the car and started driving. We drove almost fifty miles from the scene and drove into the woods. Then Stacey and I defused all the electronic systems in the car and covered the car with leaves and branches and sticks.

Now we were safe from the machine world of tracking, but we were in the woods and didn't know where to go or what do to. We started to dig a grave for James. I had never buried anyone and my heart was filled with anguish while digging. My hands were shivering and numb. I will never forget the way Stacey was digging the pit. She cried the whole time, and tears fell and kissed every time the spade hit the sand. All I could do to compare that emotional scene was think that she was watering James's grave for flowers growing over it. Before moving James's body to the grave, we both said praises to the Lord and sang songs and kissed and said bye to him for saving our lives. Then we put him into the pit and shoveled sand over it. We spent that night in the woods in a small cave, with great sorrow and silence. But the woods didn't rest. We heard coyotes howling, bats flying, insects buzzing, and sound from the leaves on the ground.

The night passed, and in the morning we decided to walk to Wisconsin. Now my heart became strong like a fierce warrior. I would never repent or feel guilty about killing anyone who wanted to hurt us. There were no more excuses about my true identity. I wanted to save the chosen one and pass on the message I was sent for. This war should stop, and no more blood would be spilled on this ground. I was going to be ruthless to anyone except women and children, because in this unmerciful world I didn't want to show peace to anyone. This was not the time to debate right and wrong; it was all about life or death, kill or get killed. If you hesitated to make a choice, you would never get a chance to live.

I gave Stacey confidence and encouraged her to be brave, and she quickly believed my words and rose up like a lioness with no fear. The mourning was over, because there were millions of women who have lost their husbands, and James was one of them. We needed to stop this war by any means available, to do that; we needed to find the chosen one. Two women with abundant courage and fearless hearts started to walk toward Wisconsin. We didn't have any electronic gadgets; we just had a compass and a detailed American map with the routes of different cities and towns. Stacey had ammo in her hand and water bags for our survival. On our first day en route, I had to apologize to Stacey for what had happened.

Nathalie: Hey, Stacey, I am sorry.

Stacey: Sorry for what, Nathalie?

Nathalie: I brought so many problems into your life; you lost James because of me.

Stacey: Everyone dies someday, and their death has been determined as soon as they are born.. It was his day.

Nathalie: I mean, I caused this.

Stacey: He died before my eyes—that sucks—but he died like a savior and a warrior. I am very proud of him.

Nathalie: I hope you don't have any hard feelings against me.

Stacey: Never, Nathalie.

Nathalie: I would have said before we started this morning that you could leave me and I would take care of myself, but it would have been inappropriate. So I wanted to ask you: if you want to leave, you could leave now. I don't want to bother you and involve you in this.

Stacey: You should have told me this before burying James yesterday, because I would have taken his body and buried it in the garden in my home. Why now?

Nathalie: No, no, I just wanted to confirm it. If this is what you wanted to do, I am happy to take you with me.

Stacey: This is not your mission, Nathalie; it is our mission to save this world. I trust you. You come from a higher dimension and know better than any of us. We should meet the child and save him and help him grow.

Nathalie: Oh, thanks so much, Stacey. I'm so proud of you.

Stacey: I have to thank you, Nathalie. You have given me a chance to save the chosen one who could stop the war and at least my name will be one line in history, rather than sitting in my home expecting some miracle to stop the war and without realizing that we could make a miracle happen. Life was not about how we lived or how we had to die; rather it was about what we lived for and why we died. The cause and conclusion should have a meaning, and the meaning should have a purpose, and the purpose should be fulfilled.

Nathalie: Well said, Stacey. Words come out from your heart, not from your mouth.

Stacey: Hmm . . .

We both started our journey talking all the way. We shared our experiences and talked about the cause of this war and about life. It was not regular gossip. Every conversation had great meaning. We walked in the corn, soybean, and wheat fields and through farmland and woods; we avoided the cities and roads. We used only a compass to travel all the way, just keeping in a northeast direction. The first week was calm; we walked in the woods peacefully. Then things were not so quiet. We were stopped by militants and had to do the same thing: kill everyone, destroy all the evidence, and run. Since they had captured the photos through satellite, we were all over the news and seemed to be the most wanted people in the area. So we disguised ourselves and hid and walked in different costumes, but because of my shiny face and with no RFID, we also ended up in battles with cops and militants.

Three weeks passed with a couple of battles and fights to protect ourselves from the evil ones. Then a miracle: a deadly warrior joined our journey. The "Third lady Legend" joined us.

"Who is that, Nathalie?" Madison interjected, and Nathalie replied, "It is you, Madison." Madison replied, "It's me?"

"Yes, dear," Nathalie continued. "It was you. Your mom had conceived and you began your life by fighting all the way to be born into this world. It was the happiest news for both of us. I was delighted that my daughter Stacey was pregnant but I was not really happy, because our life was not normal to have an unborn baby with us. I asked Stacey to go back, but she refused and didn't want to. She had no choice now, because the government had started a manhunt for us. If she went back, they would torture and kill her and I would never, ever allow that. I kept her by my side and protected her.

We had been in the wilderness almost four months, trying to avoid bloodshed. We shared everything we had—food, love, care, friendship, parenthood—and I loved Stacey more than myself now. One day while walking, Stacey asked me to examine her and confirm whether it was a boy or a girl because we could not go to any hospital. I said to Stacey, 'I will examine you, but before I do, I hope it is a boy, the blood line of James is carried and memory will rejoice for you every time you look at your son.' Stacey just smiled and said, 'Please examine me, Nathalie.' I moved her shirt and put my ear on her belly and started to feel her womb. I discovered it was a girl, and said to Stacey. 'It is a girl!' and she started to jump around and scream, looking at the skies and saying, 'Thanks, Lord, for my baby girl.' After the excitement she calmed down and I asked her why she wanted a girl more than a boy. She smiled and replied, 'I am so happy that I have a girl, because my daughter will be with Oliver, the chosen one, and one day she may marry him.' I was shocked by her answer and said, 'We haven't even seen the child yet and you've started to build all these ideas about it.' Stacey replied, 'You know how much damage has happened because of this war? We are at the end of everything. We need a savior, and he will let us walk in peace and happiness. I want my daughter to be with him wherever he goes and to stay close to him, close to the chosen one.'

"Then I asked Stacey, 'If it were a boy, what would you do?' and she replied, 'He should take care of Oliver at all times and be his best man and best friend and protect him from all dangers.' I replied, 'Then there is no romance; that would be boring,' and Stacey replied, 'There would still be romance.' I asked, 'How is that?' and Stacey replied, 'I would wait for him to turn eighteen and then date the chosen one.' That answer cracked me up, and we laughed so much, we started to get tears in our eyes. One thing I knew when Stacey spoke about Oliver: she loved him and would do anything for him."

Hearing this conversation, Madison asked Nathalie, "When you put your ear to listen to the baby, did I say hi to you, Nathalie?" Nathalie smiled and gave a witty answer. "Yes, you did. You said, 'Whazz up, Nathalie? Why are you peeking at me naked?'" We all laughed. Nathalie and Stacey almost made it to Chicago with all these crazy fights that they had to have. Stacey was eight months pregnant and couldn't carry guns anymore or fight vigorously. She felt she had become a burden to Nathalie, but Nathalie never thought that way. She protected Stacey with all her strength, power and will.

Finally, they reached Milwaukee, and she found Judah and me in the burnt out hospital. They picked us up and nursed and raised us. Then Madison was born, and within a month Stacey passed away.

"Then I started to take care of you guys," Nathalie continued. "It was a tough job from my end because I could not go outside as frequently to get food or take you out to show you the world. All the time I had to use a mask and risk my life to go out and get the job done. Now you are four years old, guys. I know you could understand a few things but not everything my words are there with you and you will completely understand as you grow."

Me: Natty, you said that you came for me. What should I do with my life?

Nathalie: I already told you, time will tell. I will teach you how to survive hard conditions. Your destiny is to go to New York City. You have to go to New York City, Oliver, Judah and Madison too.

Me: Where is NYC?

Nathalie: Maybe nine hundred miles from here if you want to walk—and I prefer that you walk.

Me: You also said that we will meet seven more friends and should take them with us.

Nathalie: Yes, you will meet them, and your wisdom will reveal whether they are the other chosen ones to walk with you and be with you to accomplish the purpose of your life that you came for: to stop this war and bring peace.

Me: Okay, Natty, we will do as you say.

Then Nathalie went and took a silver-coated locket with a chain from her bag and showed it to us and told us that it had a secret message inside. "All three of you should go to New York City with this locket and make sure never to show anyone and never share your mission. If you do, our lives could be in danger and the whole mission for Oliver would be in vain. The war will never stop, and it will be the end of the world."

She gave the locket to us and we looked at it. Madison was about to open it, but Nathalie said we shouldn't open it until we reach New York City. Then Madison asked, "Should we open it once we get there?" Nathalie replied, "Your eyes will be opened and you will know by your own instinct the right time to open it." Nathalie took it and gave it to me and said, "You are the chosen one, Oliver, so you should have it. Promise that you will finish the mission and stop the war." I took my hand and promised Nathalie. Then Madison and Judah joined me.

Madison and I were very excited to hear such a story and felt relaxed, but Judah's eyes were wet and he was sad. Seeing this Nathalie asked Judah, "Why are you sad, baby?" Judah wiped his eyes and put his face down. Then Nathalie went closer to him and kissed him on his head and said, "I love you, Judah. What is bothering you?" Judah replied, "No one came for me." Nathalie asked him, "What do you mean by 'no one came for you'?" Judah then raised his voice and said, "You and Madison's mom came for Oliver, but no one came for me." She replied to him, "I came for the chosen one and the chosen one's best friend, who will be his protector." Judah asked her, "Who is Oliver's best friend?" Nathalie replied, "It is you, Judah. I came for you and Oliver." Judah asked her, "You didn't say anything about me when you told that story about your journey." Nathalie very smartly answered, "I thought you already knew that you are Oliver's best friend and that both of you were waiting for me when I found you in the hospital. What a silly boy." Judah was happy with Nathalie's answer and replied, "I am sorry, I should have known that. Thanks, Nathalie, for coming for me." In reality all four of us were orphans and had no one, except each other.

Every day we all looked at the locket and wanted to know what was inside it, but we were still not in New York City. Day after day passed with much curiosity to know what message was inside the locket. Every night I held the locket in my hand as I slept and the locket became a part of me. But our daily routine went on, learning about technology, different aspects of life, knowing the world better and better. We didn't learn through a laptop or the Internet or books; we learned through one handheld tablet in the bunker with no Internet or connectivity, because if we had that, they could trace our location. That tablet had many encyclopedias on it. We didn't watch TV either, because there was no TV, and we didn't have electricity because Nathalie had removed all the things that could be traced. Nathalie and Stacey had built a nuclear generator, which never ran out of power. The generator ran the cooling system, lights, and necessary items in the house. She cooked with the nuclear gas stove she had made; she was a genius. She made all possible gadgets that were hidden from anyone.

To know about the news in the world she walked a mile from the bunker, leaving us behind, and used her tablet to connect to the Internet and check all the information she needed. But more than that, she had psychic instincts to see things that were happening around her. She still used the gadgets to get information, because, she said, she was not as strong as she would be in her home and was becoming weaker, day by day. We never understood what she meant, but she was becoming weak now. Even our water supply came directly from five rivers and not from the city. We asked, "How do we get water?" and she said she had dug a tunnel fifteen thousand feet and had a pipeline connected to all five rivers. She said the pipeline was shielded with special aluminum foil, which allowed the signals from the detectors to pass through so that no one could detect the pipes. We asked, "How did you dig the tunnel?" Nathalie replied, "I have powers in the lightning that can do anything for me." She recounted fascinating stories about herself and what she did to protect us.

She thought of a saying we should repeat when there were problems, and when we said it we could be saved from any danger. "Even though I walk through the valley of the shadow of death, I will fear no evil, for you are with me; your rod and your staff, they comfort me." We said it every time we heard bombings or times when we felt worried. We said this every night before going to bed. Nathalie trained us in such a way that we said it all the time, and we had a feeling when saying it. It gave us comfort and confidence. We memorized it and knew we would never forget this small passage in our lives.

Now we knew how to handle most electronic gadgets and operate machinery. We had only seen the tablet while learning and never actually handled one. Nathalie thought us so simple that we could use our common sense to handle it. We were the kids from the books, but time would teach it. Common sense started to develop in us when we were five years old. She always reminded us that we had to walk to NYC and shouldn't use any of the modes of transportation that involved technology: no cars, no jets, no motor bikes, just walking. All she said was "Walk against the zeros and ones. Don't use it. It is the long walk against zeros and ones." I didn't know why she always insisted on it, but one thing I was sure of, she knew what she was talking about. No one ever opened the locket, although it was always tempting, like the very basic kid psychology: don't do that, don't touch that, not this, not that, but a kid will do exactly the opposite. We were not among them. We were obedient, moderate, happy kids, and we never disappointed Nathalie, and Nathalie showed no difference in how she treated the three of us. She is among the best women to have ever nursed and raised a child.

Along with learning so much, we also shared all that we had. We didn't even fight for cookies or chocolates but shared everything. Though we were five years old, we took care of each other, especially when someone fell sick, because Nathalie had lost her powers now and couldn't heal us anymore. We feel for one another when we are sad or depressed. We didn't know at this point what we were doing or the terms to call our actions, but simply did it. We were very young kids, our minds and thoughts were pure, and nothing had gotten defiled, because we hadn't seen the world yet with its built-in evil. All we saw was Nathalie, and from her all good things flowed through us.

But evil had its venom and waited for all of us. Yes, we started to become victims of evil, and the sting was ready to bite us. One bright summer day, we were playing outside the bunker. As usual Nathalie was watching us and made sure no one was following or watching us. A couple of cops passed through an electric field and saw us playing. Nathalie was sitting nearby, and she quickly spotted them and struck them with lightning and killed them. A cop who came from behind her was ten feet away from her when he shot her on the left shoulder. By the time she turned back, he had pushed her onto the ground. He held both her hands and sat on her belly. She fought and released her hand to strike him with her lightning, but the cop was fast. He took his knife and stabbed her in the belly and Nathalie shouted in terrible pain and within seconds she killed him with her lightning bolt.

This was the first time we saw her weeping. She was holding her hand on her stomach and praying to God. We ran to check on her, but she asked us, "Are you guys all right?" She quickly got up, tore a garment to get a long piece of cloth, and tied her bleeding stomach with the cloth. She dragged the cop away and asked us to get some gas from the bunker. We ran to the bunker and found a can and brought it to her. She had three dead cops. She put one over the other, opened the gas, poured it over them, and lit it. We watched the bodies until they burned into ashes. Then she covered the ashes with sand and covered all the traces. She quickly went to the bunker and tried to untie a piece of cloth that was on her stomach, but she couldn't manage. Her left shoulder was hurt and she had lost lots of blood. Her eyes were dripping with tears, and she fell onto the bed and fainted. We were shocked at what had happened, and when we saw her in the bed, we moved closer to her, crying.

We tried to wake her up but she didn't respond, and Judah reminded us to use the first-aid kit. She had taught us how to use it, and we knew the medicines in it, as they were marked with instructions. We saw one medicine that was tagged to stop blood flow, but we didn't even know the chemical name for it, we just took it. Then we took some cotton gauze to clean and water to wash the wound. We couldn't see her bleeding, and we were all crying, dizzy from the shock and nervous about moving her. Judah took control. He didn't feel anything. He untied the cloth and took cotton and cleaned the wound. Then he took a towel and cleaned the wound. Madison and I were watching what he was doing. Then Judah opened the gel and applied it hopefully stopping the blood flow, we both helped him. We applied the gel to Nathalie's stomach slowly, and blood was gushing out in spurts. Then we covered the wound tightly with gauze, and Judah sprinkled some antiseptic powder over it.

We slowly turned Nathalie back to clean and dress the shoulder wound. But while cleaning, we saw the bullet stuck in the bone and we didn't know what to do. We started to discuss whether to leave it in or remove it. We all came up with different answers: it would be painful if we removed it, the bone would break, the bullet gave strength to her body because it was metal. Finally we made one simple decision, to remove it. We convinced ourselves and said it would hurt Nathalie when we made a hole in her shoulder, but the bullet was not good for her. Judah said he would remove the bullet, so we took the scissors and he started to remove it. The bullet was in the back of the shoulder. He was not using any force at all. He just chipped at the bone to loosen it and lifted the bullet very slowly. We couldn't imagine how precisely he was doing it. He took almost two and a half hours to remove the bullet and did a great job. Then we cleaned all the blood and put some gel on the wound, covered it with gauze, and sprayed antiseptic powder on it.

After the successful surgery, we monitored Nathalie, waiting for her to wake up. We didn't eat for a day. We were just watching her. After a day she woke up and called our names. We were all sleeping. Then she woke and noticed her wound was dressed. She saw all of us on the couch sleeping together. She slowly moved from the bed and started to walk to us. Madison woke up and saw Nathalie moving, called to her, "Natty, Natty, are you all right?" She replied, "I am fine. How are you guys?" Madison hugged her. Judah and I were still sleeping, and after some time we both got up and saw Nathalie talking to Madison. We ran to Nathalie to greet her, and she was glad to see us, and hugged and kissed us. Madison had already told her the story. Nathalie looked at Judah and said, "Dr. Judah, you saved my life. Thank you, doctor."

Nathalie was weak. She couldn't move, and she was giving instructions. We cooked and made our first reunion meal. That night during dinner we told her that when the cop came, we saw an electric field, and asked her what it was. She said she had made a hologram of our street where we lived, fifty meters on each side, and posted it so that no satellite could track any movements near us. But the cop accidentally entered the electric field and found us inside. We asked her why we couldn't see an electric field when she killed the other bad guys. She told us there was a complete cease-fire, and all the troops and soldiers had moved east. She wanted to change the hologram because we couldn't have the same image every time. She was preparing a new one and shut down the running one to change the hologram, but as she shut down the original one, she saw the militants passing around the corner, and one noticed us. Nathalie had hoped they would just move along after seeing the kids playing, but when one started to approach the bunker, she had to kill him. Hearing this, our minds were spinning, and we said to ourselves that she was the smartest woman in this world. Nathalie protected us with all her intelligence, mind, spirit, body, soul, and everything. That is Nathalie—a woman from heaven, the first god we knew when we were kids.

We asked her why she didn't tell us she was protecting us, and she replied, "Time will answer you. Just be patient and watch what is happening around us." We asked how she made all these holograms and she showed us her hands and said, "With this I can do anything." Then we asked her, "Can we also do it with our hands?" and she said, "If you believe, you could do better things than me or anyone." We asked her, "What should we believe?" and she replied, "Believe in yourself—that you are strong, powerful, confident and fearless. You could do anything, but I tell you, Oliver, there will be a better version of this one day. You will find it, and you will do it, Oliver." I replied to her, "Yes, Nathalie, I will do as you say."

Nathalie took lots of painkillers and we all slept together in the bed, but I noticed she was in terrible pain and weeping all night. This was our first experience of seeing someone crying, and it was Nathalie, and we were all worried about what was happening to her. Evil entered into our lives and we started to see pain and suffering everywhere. The next day we all got up, and because we knew Nathalie was hurt badly, we made her coffee and breakfast while she was sleeping. We were with her when she woke up, and helped her walk to the bathroom. We fed her breakfast, and she was happy to eat. We each took turns feeding her, and we saw joy on her face again and asked her, "Why are you happy?" She replied, "Ageing." Judah asked her, "What is ageing?" She said, "Parents take care of their kids when they are young, and when they are old and weak, the kids take care of them. You did a very good job. I am very proud of you guys." She thanked us many times that day for the little things that we did, giving her medicine, food, and water, cleaning the bunker, cooking, and talking to her.

But she started to say again that our mission was to go to New York City, and we asked her if we needed her lightning power to kill anyone on the way. She said she could not give or pass it to me, because it should be earned. So we asked her if we needed guns and arms, but she said, "Never carry any arms with you." We asked her how we could protect ourselves. We also asked her if she was coming with us, and she simply said, "No." We asked her why she couldn't go with us, and she said, "I am always with you." We didn't understand what she said, but we never asked her any more questions after she said "No."

We told her, "If we don't carry arms and weapons, we will never make it to New York City, they will kill us!" She replied, "No one can touch you. You are chosen ones. You will make it." Madison asked her, "Can we at least take knives with us?" Nathalie replied, "You could for cooking and protection, but not for killing." Madison asked her, "So we shouldn't kill anyone?" Nathalie replied, "Your hands shouldn't be stained with blood. Your hands should be pure. As true gods, never kill anyone." I asked Nathalie, "But you killed so many people, Nathalie. Why are you telling us not to kill anyone?" Nathalie replied, "If you trust me, do what I say: don't kill anyone, and I promise no one can take your life from you." Madison said, "So you don't want us to take anything with us?" Nathalie said, "You could use tasers, tranquilizer guns, smoke gas, gum guns, and anything that doesn't damage or cause pain to humans." Madison replied, "Thanks, Nathalie. Thanks for your advice."

We all promised Nathalie not to use any arms or weapons to kill or hurt anyone in our lives. But it was not only a promise, it was a guarantee that we signed. We stood by, because we believed in Nathalie and trusted her words, and that night we all sincerely said together what Nathalie taught us: "Even though I walk through the valley of the shadow of death, I will fear no evil, for you are with me; your rod and your staff, they comfort me." We didn't use this prayer when Nathalie was hurt. We had awestruck and forgotten the powerful prayer she taught us. Now we started to recite it, because a test was before us and we had to meet it head-on.

Chapter 14
THE JOURNEY

A FEW DAYS PASSED, AND NATHALIE STARTED TO HAVE SEVERE STOMACH cramps and couldn't bear the pain. She held her stomach and cried out, and when she cried, we couldn't help but cry with her. We asked to call someone for help, but our stubborn nanny Nathalie refused to do so. Then she slowly started to remove the bandage and gauze. We thought white was not always the best color: she had an infection. She started to clean it with spirits, but the puss was still forming even though she cleaned the infection every day. Death was chasing her, she had a fever and the infection was worsening. She was declining rapidly. Who could we blame? The creator or the one who stabbed her? Judah, who didn't operate on her properly? Everyone had their level of justification of their own righteousness.

We couldn't blame God. He always calls us disobedient and says we have free choice. I don't even blame the cop who stabbed her; he was just doing his job for the state and the country. We couldn't even blame our sweetheart Judah, as he did all he could with his infant wisdom. We could only blame ourselves. We should have died in our mothers' wombs; we fought with our own sisters and brothers for one egg to form. We formed and came out to see this painful and distressed world. Nathalie was becoming sicker day by day, and all we could do was recite the prayer she taught us. These were the days we started to take shifts taking care of Nathalie, day and night, but we slept when the clock hit 1:00 a.m.

One night she summoned all three of us and asked us to make a vow to her. She asked us to stay together and go to New York City. On the journey we would meet seven new friends and become close friends forever. She also said not to carry any weapon, not to kill anyone on the journey and never use technology, just walk against zeros and ones. Then she took a silver compass from her coat and gave it me. She said, "This compass is treasured in my life and guided me to find you. One of the greatest people in history gave me this, and I have been taking care of it all these days. I give it to you, Oliver. You need it for your journey." She blessed us, encouraged us and promised us that her prayers and blessings would send us on our way.

The next morning around 7:00 a.m., Judah woke up before the rest of us and saw that Nathalie was sleeping peacefully. He moved towards her and looked at her. Her eyes were closed and she was sleeping like an angel. Judah whispered, "Do you want some water or coffee, Nathalie?" She didn't respond. Judah did not want to disturb her while she slept, so he returned to his bed and watched her. Madison and I were exhausted and slept for a long time. Hours passed, and Nathalie was still sleeping. There was some sort of thought going through Judah's mind—that she was sleeping very quietly and not breathing and not even moving. Judah got up and walked to her and tried to wake her up. She appeared to be sleeping, she was motionless with hardly any trace of breathing.

Now Judah began to worry. He ran to Madison and me and woke us up. Hearing his shouting we awoke and asked him, "What happened?" He replied, "Nathalie is not waking up." We quickly jumped from the bed and went to her. She looked like she was sleeping very quietly. Madison said, "She took some sleeping pills. She probably wants to sleep for some time. We shouldn't disturb her." We didn't know what had happened to her, so we decided to wait until she awoke. The day started to pass very slowly and we all watched her, waiting for her to wake from the bed. It was noon, and we thought that she may be hungry, but we decided not to wake her, because she was sleeping well and we were happy because she wasn't crying out in pain.

Time passed, and it turned evening, and she was still sleeping. Now we were suspicious and felt something was wrong. We walked over to her and started to whisper in her ears to wake up, but she didn't respond. Then we started to hold her hands and move her body, but she didn't respond. Then Madison put her ear to her heart to check the heartbeat and there was no sound. Madison said, "Her heart is not working. I couldn't hear anything." Then Judah and I did the same thing, and we couldn't hear any sound. Then we looked at each other with uncertainty and fear. Judah said, "Maybe she's dead," Madison got angry and frowned at him. "Don't say that, Judah!" I could guess what was happening. I said to Madison, "Judah is right. She is dead." Madison looked at me, furious, and said, "You too Oliver. Why are you hurting me now?" I replied, "It is the truth, and facts hurt." She said, "You say she left us!" I replied, "Yes." Her eyes filled with tears and she put her face on Nathalie's chest and started to cry loudly. We looked at her and realized that Nathalie was gone, and we all started to cry, and the whole place was filled with sorrow and agony.

We cried the whole evening. It was almost 10:00 p.m., and Madison was the one who couldn't believe Nathalie was dead. She asked us, "Are we sure she is dead?" Judah and I also were not sure whether she was dead or sleeping, so we opened her tablet to check for information. We searched anything we could find related to death. We found a document named "How to determine if someone is dead." We started to read it, and we carried out all the steps listed: checked the pulse, checked her breathing, checked how her pupils reacted to light, and everything. Nothing worked. Finally we convinced ourselves that she was dead. When Nathalie killed the cops and militants, and told her stories about how she and Stacey made the journey to meet us, all we thought was *to make someone die, we need to kill them,* but this time we saw that people died suffering in days of pain.

When we realized that she had left us all alone in this world with no one to care for us, we cried again and again. We cried so much that we became exhausted, and finally when no tears were left, we started to sleep. When we got up the next morning, it was more than twenty-four hours since Nathalie had passed away. We knew we needed to bury a person after they died, because we had watched what Nathalie did twice when she killed people. It had been a day, and usually the body becomes heavier, but not Nathalie. She was light, an angel from the sky. Laws of nature and this physical universe didn't apply to her.

We moved her from the bed and kept her on the floor over a new, unused white velvet blanket. We didn't know whether to bury her outside the bunker or bury her inside the bunker. We now had to leave the bunker. We couldn't stay there anymore, because we had to leave for New York City. We finally decided not to bury her in the bunker, so we moved her body by wrapping it in the blanket and using some ropes. We pulled her body outside the bunker. We didn't want to bury her near the bunker, because someday, if they found the bunker, they might find her body and would send it to the morgue for investigation. So we decided to bury her in a place further away. We took small shovels and spades with us. We put her body in a sack and tied it with ropes, and dragged her until we found a cherry tree two blocks away. We walked to the cherry tree and found there was grass around it. We marked the length and breadth with lines surrounding her body, to make sure the pit would fit here. Then we started to dig. It took us almost seven hours and we worked hard, drinking water and taking vitamins the whole time.

We wrapped her again in the unused blanket. We had a few towels and cleaned her face, chest, hands, and feet. She was the princess of beauty; her charming, lovable face never went from her. Her face even after death was glowing. We kissed her many times on her forehead, covered her face with a silk towel. We slowly moved her body to the pit. She never felt heavy, but was light like a feather. We put her in the pit, so that her head was closer to the tree. Then we threw the sack over her body, so that she and the blanket would not get the dirt from the sand. Slowly we shoveled the sand back into the pit. We started from the feet and delayed having to cover her face with sand, because we wanted to see it as long as we could. It was an agonizing experience we had ever faced in our lives, we didn't know if we could finish it.

After we shoveled, we wanted to make sure there was no hump on the place we buried her, so we moved the leftover sand and mixed it with the sand closer to it. When we were done, it looked the same as before, no one would ever found Nathalie there. All these things we knew from Nathalie, trying to cover all our tracks, but unfortunately we were using it for the master herself. It was the first flat grave we had ever built, and we all sat around the place where we buried her and each one looked at it with his own thoughts. I can't remember what I was thinking, but maybe with my self-awareness I was thinking she would come out of the grave; I expected a simple miracle. She didn't come back, and time flew by fast. It was getting darker, and we left the burial place and went back to the bunker.

That night, though we were hungry after the day's hard work in moving Nathalie's body and digging the grave, we couldn't eat much. We felt there was a knife in our throats, and we couldn't swallow food. We drank lots of water to quench our thirst. We couldn't cry anymore. We rested our heads on each other's shoulders and watched Nathalie's bed all the time. We fell asleep, and we spent a week in the bunker with sadness all around us. We had little food, enough water, and we visited her burial place every day for many hours and talked about Nathalie all the time, her great acts, how brave and kind she was, how much love she had shown us.

It was all about Nathalie for the first week after she left us, until someone had to remind us that we had a mission. It was Madison who said, "Are we going to spend our lives here or are we going to New York City?" I replied to her, "Yeah, we have to go to New York City. We should, guys." Then we started to pack our stuff. We took essentials for the trip: food, a few clothes, a medical kit, maps of America (which Nathalie had for us), and utilities. I had to thank the bunker: it had lots of clothes, which Nathalie had altered and mended for us. Every time we packed, the bag became heavier and we knew it was a long trip, so we removed some stuff to make it lighter. It would never be light. We kept thinking of all the things that would be helpful in the journey, so we just grabbed what we had. We didn't carry guns or ammunition, but we carried Nathalie's war kit. We found the kit under the bed and it was tagged "To Oliver, Judah, and Madison—your weapons for the journey." When we opened it, there were three pistols and three concealed guns. There were no bullets in them; rather we found a bag of tranquilizer bullets. We had bullets for the pistols and small concealed guns, then we read the usage notes and found out that these guns were to make people unconscious and not to kill or hurt anyone. We didn't forget the explorer's compass and the locket from Nathalie. Honestly, these were the only valuable items we had. We didn't know where to keep them, but we kept the pistols in our back packs and the small concealed guns in the little pouch around our waists.

We were about to leave our bunker and had a debate about whether to burn the bunker or not. Nathalie said you should always destroy all the evidence before you leave a spot. Now we had to leave, and we had to burn the bunker because it would have evidence of us—our hair, our fingerprints, our skin, our dirt, and everything was there. We had some spirits, and we splashed it around the bunker, lighted a stick, and made a fire. Then we closed the bunker and covered it's hatch with a mattress covered with plastic sheets. We waited for a few hours to make sure that the smoke didn't come out, and it worked perfectly. This was the first engineering work that we did, covering the smoke with a mattress. The bunker's hatch was so strong and tightly covered that no smoke escaped. But the metal turned hot and started to heat the plastic and the bed. Then we saw the bed start to catch fire. Luckily we had a fire extinguisher, and put out the fire and smoke. We moved the bed from the bunker's hatch and saw smoke rolling off the bed. We didn't realize until this point that the hologram that Nathalie made was protecting us and the smoke was not escaping, or else the satellite would have detected us and the cops would have been here by this time.

Nathalie's wonders were still protecting us, and after moving the bed, we waited for a few hours until the smoke had gone. We wanted to open the bunker and see if the fire had burned everything, but by this time the hatch was so hot we couldn't even touch it. We assumed all was burned and started to move away from the bunker. Every few feet, we turned and looked back at the bunker, because it was not just the bunker but our home, our living place, our church, our country, and everything. We finally crossed the hologram, the fence that had shielded us all those years, the fence of protection. We were out, and we didn't know what was before us. We made this brave step when we were five. We moved far from the bunker, and every time we turned we hoped that we could still see it. But it became smaller and smaller and finally it disappeared. A new life had begun and we started to walk with more anxiety. On the way we went to Nathalie's burial place to say good-bye to her and renew our oath that we would make our mission successful.

We stood quietly and closed our eyes and thanked her for all the good deeds that she had done for us. She had sacrificed her life for us and died for us, and we thanked and blessed Madison's mother, Stacey, for the dedication and sacrifice that she made for us. Nathalie had never said where Stacey's burial place was, so we didn't know, but we remembered a lot the same way we remembered Nathalie, and we recited the prayer that Nathalie taught us: "Even though I walk through the valley of the shadow of death, I will fear no evil, for you are with me; your rod and your staff, they comfort me." We wanted to mark the place where we buried Nathalie, so each of us wrote our names in the tree. But we didn't want to write her name, because if somehow they traced her body, we would be caught as claiming to be her descendants and they would start hunting us, which would be a big problem when it came to completing our mission. We took a handy knife and engraved around the tree with our initials as *M O N J S,* which represented Madison, Oliver, Nathalie, James, Judah and Stacey. Six people had started this mission but three were already dead, and the other three were small and weak. We knew somewhere in the heart it says, be strong and the universe will guide you. So we made the first step of our journey, with tear-stained faces and fear-stained hearts not knowing yet the odds and troubles that lay before us.

We had a compass and the locket in our hand. The compass should take us to New York City, and the locket should show us the secret and mission that we were born for. All we knew was that we should use the compass to go southeast. That should eventually lead us to New York City. The very strange thing we noticed was that when we started to move away from our neighborhood, we saw a stone sign with a white background and black letters, and on it was written, "Once this place was called Wall Street." We walked and noticed it was inscribed as "Mind and Place." All we knew was the place we lived, somewhere between Palmer and Richards, but the stone sign created some sort of thought that started haunting me.

The first day of the journey we didn't know where to camp or sleep. Most of the places were bombed, full of rubble and crumbling walls with bullet holes. We didn't walk much and we were still only a few miles from the neighborhood, circling around. We were so tired and needed rest for the night. We found a bombed out three-story building which we checked out and no one was there. So we stayed there that night and ate what we had, some bread and sausages. It was the first night in our lives that we had spent without Nathalie, no protection, no hologram, no bunker, just open air. We were frightened. We couldn't sleep, we breathed fresh air and admired the skies that were dressed with beautiful stars and comets. The skies made our fears disappear, and we felt the universe was watching and smiling at us. We talked about the skies and no one knew much about space, but we asked many questions even though none of us knew any answers.

We spent the night in the open meadow with the night sky and got up the next day, prepared to walk for our mission. We had walked a mile when we heard a sound in the streets. We saw militants moving: lots of tanks, and armed men marching. We hid and watched them, and as we watched, a rocket came and hit the tanker, and soon all the tanks started to shoot in different directions where the rocket came from. We became scared and quickly ran and hid in the building. The building had a few people living in it and as soon as heard the blast, they all started to run to their bunkers. We were hiding and watching them screaming and kids were crying and running. Then slowly we wanted to get some help from the people who were running to hide with them in the bunker, but no one cared to look at us. When a few people looked at us, they didn't ask us whether we needed any help. It was such a selfish world, but no one was to blame. In these harsh situations, humans become demons, and that is what happened on this day.

There were buildings above us, and we started to hear more shelling. The troops from our side were firing vigorously and we decided to stay in the building's garage. We thought that this would be over in a day, but things don't always happen the way you think. It went on for two weeks. Though the firing and bombing stopped after three days, the militants wanted to make the neighborhood safe, so they set a two week curfew, except between five and six in the evening and then we could go out.

We always saw people running here and there, to their apartments, to buy groceries, food supplies to store. We ran out of rations. Our food supply was gone, and we were hungry. We couldn't stand anymore and were waiting for five o'clock so we could go get some help. It was five in the evening and we knew that we could get some food from somebody but we didn't know at that time the difference between begging and asking, so we waited for someone to notice us. Our faces were dirty and our hair was shabby. One fine lady who was passing by spotted us and came to us and asked me, "Are you all right, kid?" I murmured, "Hungry" and she looked at us. "Would you like something to eat?" We said, "Yes, please." She asked us to stay there, and she went to her apartment. She came back after a few minutes with a bag of food. She had bread, potatoes, meat, fruit, cookies and chocolates. We just grabbed the bag and started to eat like wild animals. The lady watched us, and the clock was ticking towards six o'clock, and the lady said "Bye" and left us. We didn't even notice her when she said good-bye, as we were very focused on eating. We couldn't believe we ate half the bag of food. Now we had half a bag of food and five more days of curfew.

Later that night we were happy to have met the first person to have compassion and humanity. Yet that night we didn't sleep, and we were grumbling and whining, not thanking the lady who had helped us so much. We now felt guilty for not having the courtesy to say thank you. The next day we all went around to the front of the lobby and waited for her. We were curious to see the lady again. It was five o'clock, and people slowly started coming out of the bunkers. At ten minutes past five, we saw the lady who helped us walking, and we ran and greeted her. She asked us, "How are you guys?" We looked at her with some hesitation and she looked at us and asked, "Do you need more food?" Madison replied, "We are sorry we didn't say thank you for the food you gave us," and she replied, "No problem, little lady. No harm done."

She asked, "Do you guys have family or someone to take care of you? You seem abandoned or lost." Judah replied, "We have no one. We wanted to go to New York City, but have to stay here till the curfew ends." She looked at Judah with surprise and asked him, "What for, gentleman? Why do you want to go to New York City?" I quickly replied, "To start a bank." (Nathalie had said many times that there are many banks in New York City.) She cracked up and said, "Good luck, kiddo! I will invest in your bank." Judah, the lady, and Madison looked at me with their mouths open, due to my smart answer and lie I had told. I replied to the lady, "You are welcome."

Then I introduced myself to her as Oliver, and she said her name was Patricia. Patricia was the first person we got to know in our life and ever spoke to besides each other. Hearing us, she invited us to stay in the bunker with her, and we accepted her invitation and had no choice. She lived by herself. She called herself single. We didn't know what that meant. All we knew was that she was like us: she had nobody. Her bunker was big. It was a two-bedroom bunker and looked beautiful.

It was a splendid experience. We learned how people looked and described how they looked. It started with the conversation with Patricia in the bunker, when she said to Madison, "You are one good-looking blonde. You will be the hottest woman in the world when you become a lady." We asked her, "What do you mean by calling her a blonde?" Patricia replied, "A blonde is a woman with golden hair, and Madison has a little curl." We learned that day, that Madison was a blonde, and I asked Patricia how I looked, as I was not sure whether I had golden hair. Patricia looked at me and said, "You are between blond and black. You look handsome, dear." It was Judah's turn, and he asked "How does my hair look?" She replied, "It is black, and you look cute too!"

So then we all noticed Patricia, who had blond hair and we said to her, "You have blond hair like Madison," and she replied, "I am as blond as Madison." I looked at Madison and said, "Hey, you blonde" and she frowned. "Don't call me that," she said, and I said, "I feel better calling you that!" Then Patricia felt that we couldn't describe someone, and she taught us how to. She had an app and a wide screen projector, and she taught us how to describe a person and their features. The next week in the bunker we learned about describing and recognizing people's different features. One night after we went to bed and Patricia was fast asleep, the three of us talked and finally realized how to describe Nathalie in addition to her glowing and shining face. We could describe her. She was five ten and 155 pounds, with brown hair, an oval face with perfect symmetry, thin lips with even size, blue eyes filled with love, tender hands that could love or hurt, long legs, and a waist smaller than her hips.. We were finally able to describe our sweetheart Nathalie. This felt like our greatest accomplishment, in knowing someone in our mind, eyes and words.

Madison is a blonde with baby blond hair, sea blue eyes, fair skin, pouting lips, and a button nose. She was so cute with her innocent smile and charming personality, anyone would be tempted to watch her again and again. Judah looked handsome with curly black hair, brown eyes, fair skin with a rose touch, and a sharp nose. He was bony, with thick eyelids and an etched face. As for myself, you have definitely known me for a while, so with my hair color ash blond, you could imagine the rest. Whatever you imagine in your mind about Oliver, I will be your own reflection.

After the curfew, we moved from the bunker and spent a couple of weeks with Patricia, and she took care of us. She did the best she could and we were happy to stay with her. It was an amazing experience for us, because we spent our life in an apartment that had a window and we could see the world.

Then we realized our mission was to go to New York City it was time to say good-bye to her. We didn't know where to start. One morning before Patricia woke, we packed all our stuff and sat on the couch and waited for her to wake up. She woke up and walked to the hall and saw us with our bags. We were dressed, and she asked us, "Are you guys going out to hang out or something like that?" No one knew what to say, and Madison answered her, "We are leaving." She asked, "Where are you going?" I replied, "To New York City." She quickly became pale and her face grew sad and she said, "Are you leaving me?" I answered, "We are leaving for New York City."

She sat on the couch and looked at us for a few minutes, and then she leaned back and started to look at the ceiling. We didn't know what she was looking at, and started to look at the ceiling with her, hoping to find something. After an hour we realized she was thinking. Then she slowly relaxed and asked us, "I know you guys have no one. Somehow you are motivated to go to New York City. I don't know why, and I am not asking you. But you have to understand one thing: you are five years old and too young to make this journey. War is going on like crazy, and I am concerned you should be alive to make this journey. So you could stay until you become teenagers and then decide if you still want to make this journey."

She didn't disappoint or scare us, but it was a rightful feeling and suggestion. The path and journey was too dangerous, but we had deep respect for Nathalie's words and we had promised her. One simple thought came to my mind: death is inevitable. It could happen in a bathtub or in a kitchen, and we were leaving for NYC. I replied to Patricia, "We are going to New York City. Please bless our journey." She looked into my eyes and said, "It looks like you are the chosen ones to stop this war. If it is so, you and your friends will never be killed. I swore on the living God, he shall be with you all the time, day and night, and protect you from all dangers."

When we heard her calling us as the chosen ones, we were shocked. How could she know this message? At first all that went through our minds was, *Maybe she is sneaking in at night and listening to what we are talking about*. Madison jumped up and asked Patricia, "How do you know Oliver is the chosen one?" She replied, "Well, I think I have some intuition, sweetheart, and I could look into his eyes." Madison said, "We thought you were sneaking around and listening to our conversation." Patricia replied, "Even if I did, I am proud and want to support you guys. I'd never hurt you or call the agents. Think about that, sweetie." Her answer made some sense at that time, because she was so kind to us, but we learned one big lesson that day: keep our mouths shut, and if we wanted to talk about the journey, the locket, the war, we would walk far from the horizon and make sure no moon, stars, or planets were next to us.

Patricia gave us lots of food and a little red wagon that had a T-shape steel grip to pull it. We docked all the food in the wagon and made sure we could pull it and walk. Patricia was the first friend apart from mother like Nathalie and a person we knew in our life and we owed her everything. She wished us well on our journey, and we all hugged and kissed her and said good-bye. Then we started to walk toward our mission.

As we slowly walked away from Patricia, we realized that we missed her, and felt some great love and respect for her. Every step we took we turned and saw her, because this was the first time we had said good-bye to someone who was alive. As we reached the corner of the block, we waved both our hands and shouted, "Bye, Patricia," and left. It was a heartbreaking experience for us, but only one thing was on our mind: go to New York City. We didn't know where we met Patricia and what place we were at, and there were no signs. As we walked, we asked someone what the place was called and they said, "Keefe Avenue." Then Judah said to us, "We don't know where we lived. We left our bunker and spent two weeks with Patricia and didn't ask where we were. Next time we should know where we live and what sort of place it is." I replied, "That is a fair and reasonable thing to know and we should make sure that we know it." The problem we had was that we had a map and compass but no e-maps to show us where we were. We started to observe the places and the neighborhoods we walked in and tried to always look at the map and check where we were. We had a local Milwaukee map, and a road atlas, part of the kit Nathalie had made for our journey.

As we walked, we saw a park called "Kern Park." This was the first time we had seen a park. The park didn't look too damaged. It had a few pits caused by shells, but for the most part it was awesome. There were oak trees, shrubs, and flowers running in the grass. It was not well maintained, had leaves everywhere, and cups and bags were flying. No matter how it looked and what was there, we loved the place. We spent hours running around, shouting, dancing, wrestling, playing, and having a fantastic time.

We decided to stay for a few days, because we loved the park and had water sprinklers to play in and we had lots of food, so we ate all the time and had fun. At night we talked about Nathalie and our journey to New York City, and we wondered what was in New York City and how it looked. We all looked at the locket and were curious to see what was inside. Maybe it was a treasure map, or some facts about eternity, we didn't know. In the daytime, kids and adults would come to the park and play basketball, baseball and football. We always looked at them with curiosity, wondering what they were playing and what were the rules of the games. We wanted to join them, but didn't feel like we could make friends, first of all because they all used foul language." That was Nathalie's biggest lesson that she taught us: "Never speak any foul language. It will ruin your reputation."

Some young teens came to the park with their girlfriends. They kissed each other and we didn't know what they were doing, but it looked like men and women were on different planets and there would be some excitement and so-called romance when they glided and touched each other. At times Judah and I turned over and looked at Madison with one simple idea: "Could we do that with her?" She frowned and looked at us and rolled her eyes. We never tried that, because we never had any instincts like that. She was our Madison and our friend. It was all about innocence and learning about the world and trying to understand.

We initially thought we would stay there for a few days, but we stayed there for almost three weeks. We enjoyed every moment in the park, as everything we saw was new to us. Those were the best parts of life and the worst part were the two things that scared us. The first was the helicopters at night that went out for security rounds. We got scared to death when we heard the chopper blades, and we would cuddle each other, close our eyes, and cover ourselves with a blanket. Sometimes the light would pass over us and when that happened, we had a nasty feeling that the world was going to end, starting with us. The very first time, our hearts stopped.

The other thing that scared us was homeless people. Though we were also homeless, we were not abusive or wicked, but a few of them who slept in that park were scary. Our savior was Uncle Tim, who was in his mid-forties, with white hair and a well-tanned, muscled body. He looked like a perfect banker, but he was a homeless person. To me he was a hero because he protected us from bad and dangerous homeless people. The first few days all these homeless people watched us and were curious to know who we were. We did not have any idea why they were looking and watching at us all the time. One night a few homeless people came and took everything we had while we slept: our food with the wagon, our bags—everything except our mattress and blanket. But not the locket and the compass, because we hid those inside our underwear, the safest spot in the world. The next day we woke up and with our eyes half opened, we found that everything had been taken. We didn't realize anything, because we were still in sleeping mode, but we saw nothing was there and went back to sleep. After a few hours our instincts were aware that we were missing something. We woke up and saw everything was gone. We looked at each other and started to search everywhere. We couldn't find anything, and after three hours we got tired, and we all sat down in frustration.

We didn't know what happened to the food. At this time we all thought the food and the bags had magically disappeared, because we didn't know anything about theft or robbing. It was almost three in the afternoon, and we were hungry. The only feeling that came many times a day was hunger. So we decided to walk around the park to get some food from someone. As we walked through the park, there were lots of families relaxing and having barbecues and drinks. We went and stood next to them and explained to them what happened. Some people were talking about "facts of life in midst of our hunger," which we had never heard of before. They said, "I know you are hungry, but you guys lie to yourself and the earth, that you lost your stuff and need help. We will never help anyone who lies, and you are such young kids. Stop lying and we will give you something."

All we could think was *Feed us, and then advise us.* We all bit our tongues and walked away. There were some souls who wanted to know who we were and wanted to take us to our parents. We didn't know anyone and we told them and they threatened to call the cops, so we had to run from them. Some good souls gave us some food and drinks, and we thanked them and ate it to keep us alive.

It was six in the evening. We were so angry, our faces were glaring. We saw a bunch of kids playing from a distance, and we saw the wagon, and it was red. We were surprised and knew it was ours and we wanted it back. We started to run fast and we went to the kids who were playing with the wagon. There were about eleven of them, each one a different age and size, but we were just three. Some kids were wearing good clothes but looked dirty, and some wore torn shirts and pants. A couple of the kids were my age and were wearing our jeans and T-shirts. We went to the kid who had the wagon, and I said, "This is our wagon!" The kid who was sitting in the wagon, said, "No, it is mine" and Judah said, "You are lying!" Then all the kids joined together and began to approach us. We held hands together tightly, and as they walked towards us, we went backward. One kid had a baseball bat, and one had a small knife. They were both young around ten years old. We were scared and started to recite the prayer that Nathalie taught us: "Even though I walk through the valley of the shadow of death. . ."

Then all the kids jumped on us. Before we could move, they held our arms behind our backs and made sure we couldn't move. The kid with the baseball bat said, "Who will be the first to get his head smashed?" Another kid said that they should smack Judah, because he was the one who called them "Liars." Next was me, because I claimed the wagon was mine, and the last was Madison. The worst part was that these kids really stank and they were filthy. Their stink was a kind of anesthetic and we started to lose our minds and couldn't breathe anymore. The kid with the baseball bat walked toward Judah and asked him, "Make a last wish, you punk" and Judah replied, "Let them go and do whatever you want to me." The kid with the baseball bat said, "That is not a wish. Your chance has gone." He lifted the bat to hit Judah's head, and we both closed our eyes. Then we heard one voice call out, "STOP! You rats!" We slowly opened our eyes and saw it was Uncle Tim. Seeing him, all the kids stopped holding us. Then Madison kicked one of the boys and said, "Never touch me again with your stinky hands, you smelly rat."

Uncle Tim looked at the gang of kids angrily and seeing his expression, all the kids let go of us and started to run away. Then Uncle Tim turned and asked us, "Who are you kids? What are you doing here in this neighborhood?" I replied, "We are travelers, and we are on our way to New York City, sir." He said, "Travelers? You look like whining kids, and you should go home and keep out of trouble." Then Uncle Tim asked us, "Why were you guys fighting?" I replied, "They took all our belongings and food." Uncle Tim asked, "So you wanted to go to war with them?" I replied, "We will go, once they give us what belongs to us." Then Uncle Tim said, "Let's see it like this: if they don't give you what you want, what will you do, young boy?" I fearlessly replied, "We are not leaving without our belongings." He responded, "You are a brave boy, so why couldn't you fight back?" I replied to him, "We will get our turn," and then Tim replied "Don't worry. I will get you back all that you have lost. Come with me."

The three of us followed him and on the way we asked him what his name was, and he replied, "My name is Tim, Tim Manus." We asked him what he did, and he replied, "I am a gangster and a godfather to all the homeless people in Milwaukee." I asked him, "So are you homeless also?" He stopped walking and turned and looked at me wryly. "You guessed it, I am homeless, but I am strong and a wise guy." We had a chat while walking and we figured he was cool.

Then we went to the place where all the homeless people lived, which was the edge of the park. He shouted loudly, saying, "I need everybody's attention" and everyone came close to him and circled him. There were people of all ages and everyone looked poor, some looked decent and some looked dirty. Then he said, "There are three young folks here and they are my friends. I know someone here has stolen all their goods and food, so let us pretend to be cultured. Tell me who did it and we can return it back to my friends." Everybody went quiet and started to whisper among themselves. No one came forward and then Uncle Tim said, "I don't want to spill blood. If I find it, you know how I am going to handle it. Last call, fellas." Then slowly two guys stepped forward and said, "We did it, Tim, sorry." Uncle Tim replied, "Well, now you had better, give them back all their belongings."

The two guys took us and Tim to their place and we found the bags, which had been opened. The clothes were there. The rest was missing: our maps, guns, flashlights, and all our supplies. We said to Uncle Tim that we were missing many things from the bag, and he asked them, "Where is the stuff?" They mumbled, "I have a few things with me and the rest I've given away to other people here." Uncle Tim ordered them to collect all the things that they had given away and bring them back. After an hour the two guys came back with all the missing things, and surprisingly nothing was missing. They gave it all back to us.

Uncle Tim asked, "Did you get all the things you lost?" We replied, "No, we need the food and our wagon that they took." They returned the wagon to us with no food in it, and when we asked where the food was, they answered, "We ate it all." When we heard that, we became angry, but the food was gone, so we couldn't do anything about it. But Uncle Tim, the only wise guy there, collected food from everyone and gave it to us. Each single soul gave us what they had, and we got it doubled. We said to Uncle Tim that we had more food than we had originally and he replied to us, "It is interest and a bonus for what they have done." The only thing we missed in the food cart was Patricia's pound cake; the rest was all canned foods. We felt lucky that we got everything back.

Then Uncle Tim asked us to stay with them until we left. We now had protection, so we stayed with Uncle Tim until we left. At first, not everyone was comfortable with us and acted strangely. No one talked; they ignored us. It was hurtful at first and we said to Uncle Tim that we felt uncomfortable, and he said it would take time for them to forgive us and become friends. There were a few kids, who wanted to play, and they enjoyed our company and became our friends, but none of the kids we found were the chosen ones to join our journey. The great fact is, we never disclosed anything about Nathalie, or the locket or anything that Nathalie said not to share with anyone. We remained so concealed that no one could guess our mission to New York City, and our age also made us seem unsuspicious.

After a week some elders started to talk to us and we greeted them, calling them "Pa" and "Ma" or "Grandpa" and "Grandma." We treated them with the greatest respect. We helped the old people by washing their vessels, carrying them food, fetching water, cleaning and dusting the mattresses. We did everything with love and kindness, as Nathalie taught us. They started to like us more because we were not like the other kids, who acted with disrespect and used foul language. In return they treated us well, they shared with us all they had. Being orphans and left alone to fend for ourselves, we found compassion and happiness from strange, forgotten people showing love. The love was perfect. It had no expectations and all we needed was a meal the next day to stay strong, because we needed to show more love to each other.

Three weeks flew by and we decided to leave and told Uncle Tim. He was a little disturbed and said the same thing as Patricia. "Stay as long as you can. You should go to New York City when you are grown as adults or at least teenagers." But we always heard Nathalie's voice saying, "Go to New York City," and our mission was to stop the war. Before we left, we asked Uncle Tim, being so smart and knowledgeable, "Why are you still homeless and still dependent upon others for food, more or less like a beggar?" Uncle Tim looked at us dolefully and said, "It is all about a woman and love." I didn't understand what he meant and asked him, "What do you mean, Uncle Tim?" He replied, "You should all know this tragic love story. You guys should always know that a life with true love is more important than anything in this world." Then Uncle Tim shared his past experience and told us what had happened to him.

Uncle Tim was a very successful scientist in research biology and held a PhD in it. He was a highly paid biologist working in a research lab. Uncle Tim's wife was Bella, and he loved her more than himself. They lived happily in a three-bedroom house in Milwaukee and were the most admired and respected couple in the neighborhood and in the city. They had been married for fourteen years and had two kids, a boy and a girl. After gaining all the knowledge in his field he decided to start his own research lab, and traveled across the country to get some investment for his new business. At times Bella asked him why he wanted to start his own business, because they were doing very well. He always told her that they needed more money so that he could build a castle for her and his kids, so that they will be even happier. But Bella always said, "We are happy and we need you near us, but most of the time you have been traveling and we don't see you very often. Money is not destiny. More than money we love you, Tim!" But all the time Uncle Tim, being a good soul, wanted his wife and kids to have more things in their life. There was nothing wrong until something changed his life. One Sunday evening, he was out traveling as usual, the kids were playing outside the house and Bella, his wife, was moving some food and supplies to the bunker.

The bunker was open, and Bella was away from the bunker with her food supplies, standing near the lawn and chatting with the neighbors and kids. A drone flew by and started to drop bombs. Two bombs came down, one on the house and one on the bunker. Bella quickly moved from the lawn, ran and covered the kids and they all ended up on the ground. Then there were many drones that started to bomb the neighborhood, and although the bombing lasted for only a few minutes the whole neighborhood was on fire. After the bombing stopped, realizing all the drones left, she got up and saw that the neighbors she'd been chatting with were dead and the whole neighborhood was on fire. So she quickly tried to escape. She ran with the kids to a car that was parked in the street. She opened it and found the keys inside. She started to drive fast to escape the neighborhood, she began driving recklessly and was scared. She drove in a cross street, and a truck was coming very fast in the opposite direction and had a head-on collision with her car. The total speed of the collision was about 150 miles per hour and it didn't spare anyone in the car. Bella and her kids were crushed, and with no time their spirits went from their bodies and they were dead. When Uncle Tim heard this he came back home and saw his beautiful house was burned into ashes and three bodies of his own flesh, lying before the house. He buried them and wept for a few years, drinking and spending all his money, until the last dime was spent. He finally realized he had lost hope, and with no more conviction he found happiness being homeless.

The first time he had met Bella was in Kern Park, and when they dated, they always came here. He used to bring his kids there often, on weekends, for special occasions and to host birthday parties. For him, the park is not a place he could understand and see, for him the park was his family and he believed that their spirit was there in this park with him. He found himself joyful here and believed that his family was always with him. He helped all the other homeless people and took care of them as his own family. After hearing his story we realized that homeless people were not always as poor as we thought; they were as we are, only some had lost hope.

After telling his bitter story about his life, he said to us, "I was chasing wealth to make my family happier, and never realized that death was chasing them. If I had been home, these things would not have happened. I was the one who killed them." He turned to me and said, "So I am telling you, Oliver, my boy, always stay with Madison. Never leave her. You should take care of her." This was the first time someone said Madison and I should be a couple and she would be my girl. I replied, "I will always take care of her," and I held her hands and pulled her near me. Then Tim looked at Judah and said, "You will find a girl, my boy. Take care of your friends now." And then he said to Madison and me, "Oliver and Madison, make sure you find a girl for Judah. He is lonely." Then quickly Madison held Judah's arms and said, "We love Judah more than anyone. We will take care of him, Uncle Tim, we promise." Hearing this, Judah was happy and thanked Madison and we saw little drops of tears flowing down from his eyes.

Uncle Tim told us to spend the night here, and leave next morning, and he arranged a send-off party with all the homeless people. That night the party bell rang and we all started to have fun. Though all the other people were not comfortable with us, they started to talk to us and wished us good luck. Everybody was moved and started to dance and splashed water on each other with water guns. The food, I should say, was amazing. What could we expect from these broken people? But the best part was, it was potluck, so everyone brought all the best they could. There was no great chef who prepared the meal for us. It was the food that was given as charity. We never complained, we ate whatever was served before us and we had a chance to speak to every elder in the gathering.

During the party we had a chat with Uncle Tim that we could never forget, and Madison was the one who initiated it. Madison asked Uncle Tim, "Could I ask you a question, Uncle Tim?" He replied, "Yes, dear." Madison asked him, "I know these people are homeless and for some reason they live like this. Why do some people not shower and smell bad? Don't they feel it is bad and embarrassing others?" Uncle Tim looked at her with a wise face and said, "Well, if they have showered and look clean, then their minds would ask them to change their lives. Then they would have to go to work and pay taxes. They don't want to pay taxes and that is the reason they don't shower. They think that is their suit and nobody takes a shower with their suits on, dear." Uncle Tim's answers, though funny, made a lot of sense. No one wanted to move or change their lives from what they were. His answer was not for the homeless people and the shower, his answer applied to all people who were not doing well in their lives, still doing the same things repeatedly, because they are scared of changes. It is like being a dishwasher: you will do it when you are a teenager to pay your school fees, but you cannot do it as an adult to feed your family for a long time.

After a while, Uncle Tim asked Madison, "Why did you ask that question?" Then Madison said, "I feel sorry insulting the boys who held me, when you saved us. I cursed him, but everyone here is being friendly except the eleven kids who fought with us—they don't talk to us." Yeah, the eleven kids were cocky and uptight and never spoke to us the whole time during our stay, not even now. Then Uncle Tim asked Madison, "Do you really feel sorry for what you have said?" Madison replied, "Everything is new to us, and I don't know myself how I used those words against them. I had never spoken such words in my life and I don't know where I picked it up from." Madison was right; Nathalie never taught us even one offensive word, even Patricia the first living soul we met in our life. But where did we learn it? When we started to walk through our journey in the streets? When we were hiding in the basement in Patricia's apartment? People were talking garbage and filthy words. It began there and continued in the park also, learning and listening to everything inappropriate on this earth, now reflected in Madison when she got mad.

Uncle Tim took us to make a peace treaty with the eleven kids. He explained to the kids that Madison was sorry about her slang, but the grown ones were cocky and the younger ones accepted Madison's apologizes. Then we asked them to play and dance with us, and a few did, and slowly as time moved we all let our guard down and became friends. From the words of hate those kids moved to words of love; they liked us and insisted we stay with them. The most fascinating thing was, they still smelled bad as they always did, but now since we started to know them, our nose buds shut down and all our eleven friends smelled liked roses to us. I realized at this point, it was not a smell or scent that was good or bad, but the very idea and understanding about a person that made it good or bad.

We went to bed late after hanging out at the party and before we went to bed we spoke to each other about all that had happened. It was a new experience. This was the first party we ever attended in our lives and it was very interesting. We woke up around nine in the morning, cleaned up, and got ready to leave. We found all the people waiting with some gifts and food in their hands. We asked them, "Why do you have food and gifts in your hands?" They replied to us, "We brought them for your journey." They also brought a new wagon, the same as the one we had to carry all the food and gifts they brought us. We didn't know how to thank them all. Though these people had very little themselves, they gave everything they could. We even asked them why they did this and they replied, "We are a group and large in numbers. You are small and few and you need it on the way to New York City. We don't know why you are going, but it seems you have ambition and goals, which is very important in life, one that we lack. We will live here and die one day."

We went to each one and thanked and hugged them and said good-bye to everyone. We didn't see Uncle Tim and the eleven kids, we asked where they were? No one knew where they were. Then suddenly we heard Uncle Tim's voice shouting, "Oliver, Madison, Judah, hey!" He was waving his hand and we turned and saw him and some kids who were well dressed. Then Uncle Tim and the kids came to us and asked, "Do you know these fellas?" We looked at them and were confused. "Who are they?" We were unsure whether we knew them or not, because their faces looked familiar. So we said, "Sorry, uncle, we don't know them" and he said, "These are the eleven bad guys, the guys you had a fight with" and we were surprised, they all shouted our names and the older boys in the group came and carried us on their shoulders. We asked Uncle Tim, "What happened to them?" He replied, "Self-realization, fellas." Then Uncle Tim explained, "They felt bad about themselves about their personal hygiene and they were impressed at you guys being disciplined and motivated. They also wanted to change their lives, and they want to go to school." We were happy we made some changes in these kids' lives. All the credit should go to Nathalie.

We tied both the wagons with rope and joined them together so that it would be easy for us to pull along. We advised Uncle Tim not to drink too much and to take care of himself, because if he could take care of himself, he could take care of all these people. They needed him very much. He promised us that he would never drink again, and threw away the bottle from his pocket. The final moments were heartbreaking. We said bye to everyone and before we left we took a group photo with all of us together. They gave us a hard copy, which was the first photo that we had of some memories in our lives. Everyone cried, including us. We started to say bye and walk away from them. The wagon was heavy; two of us had to pull it. We left Kern Park, the park that had life, characters, stories, legends, and some messages.

We were happy that we had met Uncle Tim, a noble gentleman who we admired. For us he was a superhero who saved us from our friends' hands, who fed us, taught us, shared with us and opened our minds to see the world in a better way. We always wished him to have a family again, if I had been a god I would have resurrected his family from the dust and given them back to him. From Uncle Tim, we learned one lesson: we should love our family as he did, and we should stay together as close as possible. Love could build lives and could build graves. For Uncle Tim, the park was his paradise, home, and party house, because he sees his loved ones walking with him all the time. We prayed that all the souls rested in peace and Uncle Tim should have good health and a long life. We said a final good-bye to Kern Park and all the living souls in it. We were off to New York City.

Chapter 15

ACROSS THE GREAT LAKES

We started walking down Humboldt Boulevard along the Milwaukee River. Some of the trees were burned out and we could see the river. It was an exciting experience for us, walking near the water; it looked like the water was following us. While we were walking, Madison said, "Oliver, I think we are going the wrong way," and I asked her, "Why do you say that?" She replied, "Look at the map here. We should go southward through Chicago, which will be the shortest way." I replied, "I know that, but do you remember what Nathalie said? She came the other way to Wisconsin, through Chicago, and she killed many soldiers there. If we go to Chicago, we may get caught."

Madison said, "It makes sense, but we don't look like Nathalie, so how would they know?" Judah replied, "They may ask who we are and who nursed us, and we will get caught, right, Oliver?" I replied to Judah, "Yes, you are right; moreover, Chicago is filled with more crime and more violence." Madison asked me, "How do you know all this, Oliver?" I replied, "I watched it on the news." Then, Madison replied, "You violated Nathalie's rule," and I answered her, "No, I didn't. She said never use technology like a car, jets, motorbikes, e-maps, and such things, but watching news channels was not against her rules and we are walking with the maps in our hands." Madison frowned and said, "You are making excuses, Oliver," and I replied to her, "Nathalie is smart, and she knows what we can or can't do. We have to be alert, so we have to watch the news. She did!"

Madison was a little quizzical about this and asked me, "Why does Nathalie want us to walk, rather than taking a jet and going to New York City directly?" I replied, "Maybe walking is good for health," and she grew pale and said, "That is not funny, Oliver." Then I stopped walking and said, "We are just three. We need to find the other seven. I don't know where to look. All these days I am with you, do you think I know more than you, Madison?" She replied, "I thought you were the chosen one." I breathed heavily, "Yeah, I am the chosen one with a wagon and a map in my hand." She came closer to me and looked, scowled and said, "I know you. Oliver, I am just trying to help you."

We crossed a pathway on foot over the Milwaukee River. We wanted to go to the Great Lake to cross it, too, so we started to discuss it. Then

Judah asked me, "How do we cross the river, Oliver? No one knows how to swim, and we don't have a boat." I replied, "Yes, Judah, let us try to get help from some people there." We wanted to spend a few days in Cahill Park to rest and find some help. It was noon and on the way to Cahill Park, while walking along Chateau Place, we heard some kid talking loudly, but we didn't know what he was saying. We also heard a noise that sounded like "Yahaaa," and as we walked closer, we heard the voice more clearly. The kid said, "Here comes Captain America," and then, "Yahaaa." We didn't know where the voice was coming from, but then Judah saw a little kid on top of a roof. He whispered, "Look at that guy. Is he crazy?" Hearing Judah's whisper, we all turned the way he was looking and saw a kid of more or less our age and height, wearing a Captain America suit running down the roof and jumping off onto a trampoline. Then he got up and climbed back to the roof with a ladder. He took a deep breath and ran down, shouting, "Here comes Captain America," and then fell again on the trampoline.

We were surprised by this kid. He looked crazy but interesting to us and he was very brave and tireless. We thought he might stop jumping, but we spent another hour observing him. Then we decided to sit and watch him. We sat over on the lawn in front of a house watching. He never gave up and kept on doing the same thing repeatedly. We were trying to understand what he was doing. Was he trying to fly? Only birds fly, and Superman in the cartoons.

He noticed us watching him but didn't give a heck what we were doing. It was around six in the evening and he did his last jump and then stopped and said, "Maybe tomorrow I will fly." He was lying on the trampoline upside down; we decided to go and talk to him. We went close to him and said, "Hello," and he shook his head and said, "Who are you guys?" He looked Caucasian, brown curly hair and dark eyes and he looked charming. We introduced ourselves to him, and he got up and jumped off the trampoline to the grass and looked at us. "I am Niki, Nikifor. Do you guys know how to fly?" I answered him, "No, I think," and he replied, "I know that." Then I asked him, "How do you know that?" and Nikifor replied, "From looking at the wagon, the way you guys look, and the back pack." I said, "Thanks," and he asked us, "Do you guys live around here?" I replied, "No, we are going to New York City." Nikifor replied, "I live here, and this is my house" (the one he was climbing on the roof of). Then he said, his mouth opened wide, "New York City, wow. Do you have friends there?" I answered, "No."

He continued chatting with us and invited us to his grandparents' house and introduced us to his family. His grandparents' house was across the street. They were gladden to meet us and liked us. They prepared supper that night. They had the same set of questions: "Where are you from?" "Do you have a family?" "Where are you going?" "Stay with us," but this time Judah constructed a good story. We'd been raised by some poor homeless old people who had died two months ago in a bombing. We learned there were lots of construction work in New York City and lots of jobs, so we had decided to go there. We didn't want to go to school to learn; we just wanted to stay away from this world. Lucky for us they believed our fabricated story. Madison and I also backed-up Judah's story. They served food for us: soups, salads, meat, fresh juices and desserts. We had a delicious meal and we enjoyed everything that was before us.

Nikifor then invited us to his home across the street to spend the night with him. We accepted his invitation and went to his home. His home was beautiful, with expensive carpets, lights, paintings, hardware, and so on. We wanted to learn more about him, so we started to ask questions.

Me: Do you live by yourself?

Nikifor: No, with my father.

Me: Where is your father?

Nikifor: He's in Washington. He's a nuclear physicist; he travels a lot.

Me: Wow, that's cool. Do you have a mom?

Nikifor: I do, and she is very bad.

Me: Did you say bad?

Nikifor: Yes, she is very bad, Oliver.

Me: Why do you say that? Where is she?

Nikifor: She is gone, with some man. Hang on, I will show you something that my father gave me.

He took a diary and a crumpled up sheet of paper in his hand and started to read.

"My wife, Sylvia—your mom, Niki—is a very bad woman. She cheated on your father and ran away with her cocky ex-boyfriend. She took your father and her son, Niki, to court for settlement of her divorce to live with someone with my money. But the truth always wins. The court found she was guilty and I didn't give her any money. The message of this story about you and me, Niki, is to never trust women, because they will always cheat you.

By,

You're loving trusted father."

We didn't understand what he meant then; it was the first time we had heard the word cheat. But the way Niki read it, it seemed he trusted his father's words, and his message was on my mind.

We didn't understand what he meant then; it was the first time we had heard the word *cheat*. But the way Niki read it, it seemed he trusted his father's words, and his message was on my mind.

Me: You read that you shouldn't trust women?

Nikifor: Yes.

Me: So, you don't trust Madison?

Nikifor: I don't know yet. But I will always keep an eye on her—she may cheat us.

Me: What do you mean by "cheat," Nikifor?

Nikifor: Oh, don't you know what cheating is? Cheating is lying—no, cheating is not being good. Cheating can make someone cry.

Me: Oh, okay, so your mom made your father cry.

Nikifor: Yes, she did.

Then Nikifor's father called him to talk to him, and we all chatted to him on videoconference. The conference was virtual and there was a projection of light, and we could see his father in a 3D image, he could also see us in full 3D image. It looked like he was close to us and talking. Nikifor introduced all of us to his father, and his father was thrilled to meet us. We learned from Nikifor that every night he spends some time talking to his father. It looked like he loved his father very much, and his father loved him, too.

That night we spent time asking each other question. We learned a lot about Nikifor. He is homeschooled because he spends most of his time playing and visiting his grandparents. At night, he talks and learns from his father. He doesn't have many friends; he plays video games, hacks computers, and wants to be a nuclear physicist like his father. We told him all we could about ourselves. It was all lies. We never said anything about Nathalie, the locket, or the mission to New York City, but whatever we said, he believed it.

We all went to bed happily that night, we all liked Nikifor. I don't know about Madison. She was not comfortable because Nikifor was not that interactive with her because of his father's lesson about women. That night, when I was in bed, I heard a faint voice in my ears saying, "This means cheating." I wondered where the voice was coming from, but gradually I went to sleep. In my dream the conversation that we had with Nikifor and the lies we told were repeatedly running through my mind. I woke up at four in the morning because I couldn't stand the dream anymore and I realized the exact meaning of cheating. We hadn't told any truthful information about ourselves to Nikifor; we had lied to him. Yet he believed us, gave us food and a place to sleep, introduced us to his family and shared all the things about himself. In turn, we had just cheated him. I felt guilt in my heart and it was hurting me very badly. Should I tell Nikifor about us or just leave the next morning?

We all got up the next morning and Nikifor's grandmother brought breakfast for us. We had breakfast and talked to his grandparents. We were chatting and playing with Niki: video games, jumping on the trampoline and running with water guns. The whole time my mind was in a confused state about whether to leave or stay with Niki. In the evening Niki went to his grandmother's home to talk to his father with her and we were alone in his house. I started the conversation about us staying here, and Madison and Judah agreed with my view and felt the same. But we didn't know what to do. We had to make a decision. Madison said we could stay for one week here and then move on. We also decided to ask Niki to spare us a small boat to cross the great river.

That night, we spoke to his father, greeted him, and chatted for a few minutes. Then Niki was by himself in his room and spent two hours talking to his father. Afterwards, he came out and I asked him what he was talking to his father about for two hours. He replied, "I share how my day went, my time with you and my grandparents, my secrets, my confessions, my love for my dad. I open my mind to him." I replied to him with great excitement, "Wow. Do you talk that long with him every day?" and he said, "Yes, I do every day." We all felt the love that he had for his father, but Madison looked distressed. I could tell she had started to think about her father, her eyes were wet and I could understand why. She was better off than Judah and me. She knew her father's name and felt her mother's love for a month. Judah and I didn't know either of our parents but our eyes were wet too, not because we felt for our fathers and mothers, but because we saw that Madison was crying.

We played video games with Niki and he talked about his father the whole time. His father really liked us and wanted us to be his friends. We didn't know why he liked us; he probably felt that because we were homeless, he wanted to be nice and show compassion to us. He had a couple of friends in the neighborhood and they visited and played with Niki once a week. It looked like he was almost shielded from more exposure to the world, with no school and only a couple of friends. All the neighbors liked Niki and his grandparents. The best neighbor was Uncle Pete and his family. Niki lived a very solitary life and he had all the luxuries of life and a loving family who always cared for him.

After a few days had passed, I asked Nikifor, "Why were you wearing a Captain America suit and trying to fly? I know Captain America doesn't fly." Nikifor replied, "I know that, too. Maybe I wanted to be the first to make him fly." I said, "Well, do you really like to fly? Is it possible?" Nikifor replied, "Everyone likes to fly. You know we live in 36th century, and we live in the Fourth Dimension, so I am just trying." I asked him, "Have you seen anyone flying?" and he replied, "Well, there are always rumors about it." We decided not to ask about the boat now. We would stay with him for a couple of weeks and ask him about a boat later. But before that, we wanted to create some genuine impressions on him.

It was fun spending time with Nikifor and his family. We didn't have one; it was all fascinating and exciting. The one thing that really impressed me was that Nikifor talked to his dad every day. One day, I really wanted to see what he talked to his dad about and I asked if I could join him. He trusted and valued me, so we were in the room together while he was talking to his father. I loved the chat. They spoke like friends and more like soul mates. Nikifor never hid anything. He spoke about all the things that he had done that day. It was the first time I ever felt that I needed a father to talk to. I know I don't have one, but I realized there are certain things in this world that are necessary. These things cannot be bought and I didn't know what curse I had carried to this earth, where everything was new and there were certain things I could never get back in my life. Nikifor and his father made a great impression on me. I was moved by the love between a son and his father and in my mind to this day, they are a model for me.

After a couple of weeks, I felt it was reasonable to ask Niki about a boat to cross the great river. He said that he would talk to his father about it. He spoke to his father, and at first, his father said we were too small to handle a boat, and refused. Even if he could buy a boat for us, law enforcement would catch us because we are not legally eligible to drive a boat across the river. We needed someone with us who was sixteen years old and had a permit to drive. Now it became really complicated because we didn't know anyone. The three of us discussed who we knew who could take us across the river. Maybe Patricia or Uncle Tim: those were the two grown-up friends we knew, but we would have to go back and ask them. Our main goal was not to go back for anything; that was one of the rules that Nathalie had told us: "Never turn back." We had a heated conversation for a few days and couldn't find an answer, so we decided to give it time and let time deliver us.

One day, Nikifor was curious to know why we were going to New York City, and his father asked him to find out. Nikifor asked us, "Be honest with me, guys. Why do you want to go to New York City?" Madison replied, "For work." Nikifor looked at her skeptically and replied, "Really? Well, you could stay here. My dad is glad to take care of you, so you could do homeschool with me and we would all be happy here." We didn't know what to say to him because we needed a job to pay for a living, but Nikifor and his father were offering free board. I held my breath and said to Nikifor, "Thanks, Niki, but I think we should go to New York City. That is what our mission and goal was." He asked us, "Who gave you a mission?" and Judah replied, "We did, ourselves." Nikifor answered us, "My father said to me that we could catch a flight or space shuttle to go to New York City in seconds, but he was not sure why we needed a boat. Anyway, I don't want to bother you anymore. You can stay as long as you want."

After this conversation, we felt that we were lying to him and his father, which was not good. So, we decided to leave Nikifor, as our mission was most important to us. We still didn't know if Nikifor was one of the chosen ones to walk the journey. But time revealed he was one of us, until something happened. One morning, we heard Nikifor crying loudly in the hall and his grandparents were there with him as well as a few neighbors. We all rushed from our bedroom to see what was happening. Nikifor was crying loudly and breathing heavily, lying on his grandmother's lap. Tears were streaming down his cheeks, and he closed his eyes and couldn't see us. Madison walked to him to check on him, and Judah and me walked to his grandfather to check. His grandfather said that his father had died the day before in a nuclear power plant accident. We were shocked and felt very sorry for Nikifor. Madison said, "Niki, we are here. Don't cry." Hearing her voice, he opened his eyes and saw her and with his anguished face, he said to her, "My father died." Madison held his hands and said, "Sorry, Niki. Are you all right?" He turned his face and tucked it into his grandmother's lap.

Then we heard the whole story about what had happened. His father had died in a nuclear power plant blast that had killed almost 340 people. Only a few bodies were found. They couldn't find his father's body, but it was confirmed that he had died in the fire. This death was strange and painful for us; someone is dead, but there is no dead body to mourn. At least we had Nathalie's body to bury, but I understood one reality: When you can't find the body after death, be happy. Your mourning is less painful till you bury them and your memories will always be vivid, because when you last saw them, they were alive. One thing I could tell on behalf of us three: wherever we go, mourning follows. We didn't want to leave Nikifor in this way, so we decided to take care of him until he had recovered. Yes, he was our friend and we liked him very much but we didn't know if we should take off for the journey.

The first week was a really tough time for his grandparents and us. He didn't want to eat anything. He just stayed in his room and cried every day. We tried to sit next to him the whole day, holding his hands to comfort him. He would open his mouth to talk to us here and there and he talked about his father. After a week he became weak and started to eat again regularly, but he still remained quiet, always thinking about his father. We decided not to entertain him by staying with him and encouraging his sadness, so we went out and befriended his grandparents, cleaned the garden, barbecued with his neighbors and played video games. For the first few days, he was reluctant and then slowly he was tempted and changed his mind. He would play with us for a few hours and then moodily climb back to his own tree.

Nikifor acted in this same moody way for a few weeks, until one day he asked, "Do you guys really care about me? I lost my father, but you are always having fun here. Do you know how much my father liked you?" I replied to him, "Nikifor, your grandmother was the one who said that if we are happy, you will recover soon. Your grandma and grandfather are also very sad because they lost their son. We should move on." Nikifor looked at me curiously and said, "Do you know how much my father liked you?" and I replied to him, "No, I don't know." He told us that he had bought a boat for us to cross the great river and that once we reached sixteen and had a license, we could cross it, or if we had elders, we could use the boat. We were all surprised when he told us and were moved by his father's good deed, and asked him, "When did he buy this?" Nikifor replied, "A few days before he died. He also sent an e-mail." Then he went and got the smart pad and showed us the e-mail.

It was touching; he mentioned in the e-mail that he had bought the boat for us and Nikifor because he had a feeling something bad was going to happen and he wanted Nikifor to stay close with us so that we could take care of him. We were all very touched by his father's true intentions, and at this point, we didn't want to hide anything from Nikifor. We opened our mouths; we opened them, for the first time, to speak the truth and we confessed everything. Everything from Nathalie to Madison's mother and father and the journey to find me. The bombed hospital, the bunker, the hologram, the killing, the thunder, the compass, and not to forget, the locket.

He was listening calmly and all he said after we spoke was "I trusted all you guys so much and you never said anything about it." I replied to Nikifor, "We had a feeling that we were lying and cheating and decided to leave, and then your father died and everything changed. Nikifor, it was all about whether you were a chosen one to go with us, and we didn't know; now we feel much honored that you are with us." Nikifor asked us, "What is in the locket? Some treasure or a secret?" We replied to him, "We don't know anything. We have to go New York City to find it and open it when we have ten friends and then our eyes will be opened." Nikifor asked us, "So we have to find the other six, am I right?" and Judah replied, "Yes, now you know our plans."

For the next week, we spent time telling Nikifor about all our experiences in the bunker and spoke most of the time about Nathalie. He became more curious and started to become more involved with us. We had been with Nikifor more than two months and one day we decided to walk down near the neighborhood and explore it. Nikifor's grandpa also joined us. We went to Cahill Park and spent a few hours there. Then we decided to take a long walk to Buckley Park and it was a splendid feeling for us. We tried holding Nikifor's grandpa's hands while we walked and we all felt the elderly touch and walk of wisdom. He enjoyed our company, and said, "Now, I have four grandchildren." He shared his moments with Nikifor's father when he was a kid and how much they loved him and missed him now.

As we were walking to the park, we heard someone sobbing, it sounded like a child. We didn't know where the sound was coming from and we ran to check who it was. Judah and I found a kid around our age who had fallen and was stuck in thorns, deep in the park, on a slope close to the water. He couldn't get up because the thorns covered his whole body. He was bleeding, and we couldn't see his face. We just saw his feet and part of his body filled with thorns. We shouted to the others to get some help. Nikifor came running and saw the kid. His grandfather then came with Madison and saw the kid, and he took his phone out to call the hospital and the police; but the wounded kid said, "Don't call the cops or anyone." Nikifor's grandpa asked the kid, "Why, son?" but he couldn't talk anymore and started murmuring, "No, please, please, leave me."

Then Nikifor said, "Grandpa, don't call the cops, please, he may have some problems. We need to help him." Nikifor's grandpa put his hand on his mouth and said, "Okay, okay, okay, whatever you say, smart man. How are you going to save him?" Nikifor had a tool kit in his bag, and Judah also carried a bag that had a tool kit in it. (It was a common practice in these days of wartime to carry tool kits and weapons.) We had some wire cutters, and we used them to help the kid. We started cutting down the thorns, but the thorns were dry and it was hard for us to cut them down. We used needle-nose pliers and small hand knives. We took turns cutting and while we were cutting, we told the boy to close his eyes because we didn't want him to see what we were doing. While we were cutting the thorns we asked him, "What is your name?" and he replied, "Ejaz." We asked him where he was from, and he said, "I don't know." We asked him many questions, but all he said was "Don't know." Then Niki's grandpa said not to ask him any more questions, as he was hurt and bleeding.

It took almost five hours to cut him from the thorns and all the time Niki never gave up hope in helping the kid and he worked continuously. The three of us took turns pulling out the thorns, but Niki kept saying, "We are here, my friend, hang on, don't cry." We saw Nikifor's kindness and love for the stranger and we liked it. We saw Nathalie's shadow passing through him and we reconfirmed that he was chosen to walk with us on this journey. We managed to free the kid from the thorns. He was bleeding, his skin was torn badly and he had a few bruises on his head. We cleaned the wounds with napkins as much as we could and gave him some water to drink. He was so exhausted and in so much pain, he couldn't drink water, so we wet the napkins in the water and put them in his mouth. We covered him with a small blanket to cover his naked body where his shirt and pants had been ripped off. Then Nikifor's grandpa put him on his back and carried him to their house. As we entered the home, Nikifor's grandma was shocked to see us all, and we put him on the couch. Then Nikifor's grandpa called a neighbor named Tziyon and asked him to come over. Tziyon walked in, and he looked to be somewhere in his mid-sixties. He had a medical kit and chatted with Nikifor's grandpa. Then he saw the kid on the couch and checked him and said, "No, I can't do it." Then a dispute started between them.

Nikifor's grandpa: Why can't you do it?

Tziyon: You have to take him to hospital and call the police.

Nikifor's grandpa: Why? The kid said no, and he is not that badly hurt.

Tziyon: Yes, I agree, he is not hurt badly: no head injuries, no broken bones, no broken limbs, just bruising and cuts from the thorns.

Nikifor's grandpa: What is the problem with you, my friend? Why can't you help this poor boy?

Tziyon: I don't want to lose my medical license.

Nikifor's grandpa: You are old now and retired, so what is the problem in helping this kid?

Tziyon: You just don't understand. We don't know who he is, and you said the kid doesn't want to call the cops for some reason. Who the hell knows what the problem is with him? I am not going to risk my life for this little runt. He is a Muslim kid; don't invite trouble into your home. Your son is also dead. Call the cops and hand him over to them.

Nikifor's grandpa: Thanks for coming, Tziyon. I know what to do. If we have been friends all these years, you won't tell anyone or call the cops.

Tziyon said, "Shalom." He was about to leave the house when he saw Judah. He walked to him and said, "If it had been you, I would have risked my life," and he tapped Judah on the head and left the house. Nikifor's grandpa remarked when Tziyon left, "Shalom, you pig." We had never seen him so angry or use bad words like this. Nikifor's grandpa was very much troubled and he went to check on Ejaz, who was sleeping through the pain.

Then we heard a knock on the door. There were two people knocking on the door, and Nikifor's grandma went and opened it. They greeted each other and came inside. It was an old Chinese couple named Wang and Kew. They were neighbors, and they had been on vacation and just returned. Hearing about the loss of Nikifor's father, they came to give their condolences to Nikifor's grandpa and grandma. They saw the kid on the couch and asked about him. Nikifor's grandpa told them everything. Then the old lady said to Nikifor's grandpa that she had some good Chinese medicine that would cure the cuts and bruises. Nikifor's grandpa was pleased and asked that she help the kid; the old lady took me to help her, and we went to her home to get the medicine. She was very gentle and had a good heart. She always called me "son." We went to her home, got some medicine, and she gave me some Chinese cookies and a small metal dragon artifact as a gift. I was delighted to meet her because she was showing love to a stranger by giving medicine, cookies and a dragon. On the way back, carrying the medicines and cookies for my friends, I asked the lady, "Why did you give me a dragon?" She replied, "The dragon will protect you, as you are so important to everyone, you need a protector now." I partially understood what she said, but all I could say was that I liked the metal dragon. We went back to Nikifor's grandpa's house and took out the medicines, which were in small cylinder pots. She took a cloth and dipped it in the medicine and started to apply it to the wounds and bruises, cleaning them. There were some bruises that had puss in them, and we all helped her. It took almost three hours to clean and wrap all the wounds with gauze and Band-Aids. Then she gave me some liquid medicine for Ejaz to drink to heal all the internal wounds.

Both old couples spent their evening with us and had dinner; and Nikifor's grandpa told us about them. They have a small supermarket in the neighborhood and have been running the business for a very long time. All of their kids abandoned them, and they live by themselves, spending their time running the store and traveling domestically. They had been friends of Nikifor's family for a long time, and they couldn't bear the loss of Nikifor's father, because they had known him when he was a kid. We all liked them because they saved an innocent kid's life and were so compassionate for Niki's family. They left late at night to go home, and before she left, the old lady blessed me and said, "I wish for all your dreams to come true. The dragon will guard you." It was strange she said that a second time and blessed me because I am scared of dragons and didn't know how it would protect me, but I liked the little gift she gave me.

The wounded kid was awake and looking at us, but he didn't talk to anyone. We gave him some soup and bread to eat, and Nikifor's grandma fed him. He ate a little but didn't say, "Thank you." We understood one thing—he didn't want to talk to anyone, so we left him alone to rest and didn't bother him. We all went to bed, and the four of us were talking about it. "Who is this kid, and what happened to him?" We all liked him because he looked innocent and charming; we had a soft spot for him because he was hurt badly.

The next day we wanted to talk to him and we asked him, "Is your name Ejaz?" He nodded his head but didn't reply. We asked him a few questions but he didn't say anything, so we stopped asking him questions. He just slept like a baby the whole day, drinking water, eating food, and watching T.V. Every day, Wang and Kew visited to check on Ejaz, but he said only a few words to them: "I am fine," "It hurts," and so on. A week passed and he started to heal. He watched us playing on the lawn through the glass window and gave a smile when we looked at him. One day, we were playing baseball and Ejaz was watching through the window.

Madison called to him, "Ejaz, come and play with us." He didn't hesitate and ran outside to join and play with us. We were all happy that he had moved on from his moody emotions and wanted to play with us. We asked him if he knew how to play baseball, and he said yes. While we were playing, we found that Ejaz had a good sporting spirit, and he was a good addition to the team. Although his wounds had not healed, he did his best to play with us. The very interesting thing was that we never introduced ourselves to him because he ignored us and stayed quiet, but he knew all our names and called us by them.

After the game, while we were resting, I asked him, "How do you know all our names?" and Ejaz replied, "I was listening the whole time to what you called each other." Ejaz's English accent was neutralized and sounded like an Asian. I said to him, "Whoo that is great! So, if you liked us, why didn't you talk to us the first week?" He replied, "I like you guys. I have no one. All my friends died, and I am scared." His answer was scary, and we asked him, "All your friends died how?" Then he started to cry, and we didn't ask him any more questions and left him alone.

That night, we all had dinner together and he joined us at the dining table for the first time. Nikifor's grandpa served food for all of us, and then he asked Ejaz, "Think, of us as one big family, my son. We care for you and love you. Tell us more about yourself. If you don't want to, that is fine. We would love to know you so we could help you." Ejaz was eating his soup, he left the spoon in the bowl, looked at Nikifor's grandpa, and said, "Promise me you will say nothing to anyone." Nikifor's grandpa replied, "To the ends of time, I will never tell anyone, my son."

Then Ejaz told us the whole sad story of what happened. He had lived in Des Moines, Iowa. His father was Mukhils, an imam in the mosque and his mother was Farah, and he had an older brother called Imad and a three-year-old sister named Raidah. They all lived close to the mosque; they served their God and spread the peace of Allah. His father was a promoter of peace and lived a harmonious life during this brutal World War III. But evil resides everywhere and there were a few so-called righteous terrorists who lived in their neighborhood and belonged to the mosque. They bombed the CIA headquarters in Washington and almost fifteen officers died. The reason for their bombing was that the CIA was in favor of the rich people who were benefitting from this war and giving false information to the government and officials, thus prolonging and making the war worse.

To their eyes, what they did was right; but vengeance always follows and the CIA decided to take down the bombers and all the people in that neighborhood. The reason was that Des Moines was well known for it's peace and justice and this bombing didn't catch the media's attention. The public supported the bombers and knew the CIA was evil and using their power to make the war worse. So, one evening, the whole community was in the community hall of the mosque, warning about the bad conduct of the bombers and urging them to surrender and admit their crimes to the government.

A decision was finally made that the bombers should be handed over to law enforcement but the end of times was upon them. The CIA raided their neighborhood and shot and bombed everything in that one peaceful paradise. Ejaz's father, mother, and brother were shot before his own eyes. He wanted to protect his sweet sister, so they both ran, trying to escape, but while they were running, she tripped and fell down. Ejaz helped her get up and walk but when she got up on her feet, there was one bullet in her shoulder and blood splashed on Ejaz's face. Without a single tick of the clock, she died quickly. The worst part was that Ejaz saw the shooter who killed his sister and he said that he would never forget that face for the rest of his life. Ejaz didn't have much time to say goodbye, so he left her and ran and ran until he got himself caught in the thorn bush. He ran all the way from Iowa to Wisconsin and fell into our hands and now it was our responsibility to protect him.

After he told his story, we were all depressed and sad for the brutality that had happened; but the question of a lifetime followed from Nikifor's grandpa: "What do you want to do with the CIA people who killed your family and friends and destroyed your neighborhood?" and he answered, "Nothing." Nikifor's grandfather smiled cynically and asked him, "Do you want to kill or take vengeance on them all?" and he answered, "No." Then Nikifor's grandpa asked him, "Why? They took all the things you loved." He replied, "My father always said, 'A true man will never kill anyone or seek vengeance.'" Hearing this one golden true idea from his mouth, a spark went to my soul, whispering, "He is the one to go with us." From that moment, I never took another chance to learn more about Ejaz. He was a true descendant from Nathalie. I was not the only one at the table who was impressed and fell in love with his father's wisdom. Everyone did, and we were all emotionally moved.

We started to like this new friend who we found from the thorns, and that was the first night he spent playing with us and sleeping on our roof. That night, we saw how badly he was hurt by losing his family. In the night, while he was sleeping, he murmured, "Don't shoot me, don't kill my sister, please, please, please." We woke up and watched him. When he started to murmur loudly, we checked on him, and he woke up and asked, "Am I dead? Did they shoot me?" We comforted him and told him that he was fine and we were there to protect him. The next day, we heard the full story from Nikifor's grandpa, who had checked the Internet and found all the information about Ejaz and the Des Moines neighborhood. They had shot all the people, as Ejaz had said, and they burned the whole place down, claiming that an oil leak and a nuclear power explosion had caused the catastrophe. The only remains left were ashes and Ejaz, but there were protesters and political pressure on the CIA and government to investigate. But since there were no witnesses, they couldn't do much. They also shut down the satellite on the night of the raid.

So, Ejaz is the only soul who could witness and testify to what had happened. Nikifor's grandpa asked Ejaz, "Do you want to testify?" But he was scared and said, "No," and Nikifor's grandpa understood the seriousness of the situation and the trouble he was in. He asked only one thing of Ejaz: "Don't say anything to another soul. Let this stay with us and when the time comes, if you want to testify, then you can." Ejaz agreed and promised Nikifor's grandpa not to open his mouth to anyone.

We started to spend time together and learn more about him. He always talked about his father and family. He loved his sister so much, and every time he talked about her, we could see tears in his eyes. At this point, there were only two strange things I saw every day: Nikifor turning on the gadget in his room and watching a virtual simulation of his father, as though his father was alive and he was talking to him; and Ejaz, who had nightmares. Now their odd behavior became a part of our lives.

A few weeks passed and we told Ejaz about the journey to New York City and about Nathalie and the locket. He was surprised and excited also but he was not clear on the whole purpose or about us, but we had to stop the war and restore peace. A mission is not always clear in the beginning, but when we keep walking forward, we see smoke, then a curtain, then shady images, and finally a true image. We shared our life experiences with him and at least at this point, there were no secrets between us. We also formed a very good friendship with Wang and Kew and they started to believe that we were their grandkids. They cooked every Chinese dish on this earth and under the sky. All five of us were ready for this mission but all we knew were two old couples—Niki's grandparents and Wang and Kew. I thought to myself how pleasant and solitary life was when growing up among old people. We didn't much know about life but we all swore to ourselves that when we grew old, we would take care of them.

We had come upon Halloween and it was the first Halloween we had ever experienced. Nikifor's grandpa and Wang and Kew bought us Halloween costumes. Nikifor liked Captain America, and Ejaz was very much inspired by Genghis Khan. Judah dressed like a robot, Madison dressed like an angel and I dressed like Superman, which was no surprise. The costume I admired and fell in love with was Madison's, being dressed like an angel. It was the feeling that you had known someone for years and she was beautiful, dressed in the angel costume. No matter how you felt about religion, I started believing in angels from her looking so beautiful and adorable.

We didn't know much about all the other characters, so we asked Nikifor's grandpa and grandma about them. They explained everything, and we realized for the first time that the first superhero we knew and loved was Nathalie. This was when I started to realize where all these people got their superpowers from and why we didn't have any. My curiosity erupted like a volcano and I started asking a lot of questions of Nikifor's grandpa. He explained everything to me and my mind was opened for the first time to an infinite dimension. We are not all ordinary humans and there is life in another space where we could be superheroes, but something was missing from the whole puzzle. Nikifor's grandpa gave us all movies about all the superheroes and we watched them day and night. I always kept my mind open so I could learn all the information about the superheroes. No matter who they were, they were all in love with some woman, like me now with Madison, so, one day, I could be a superhero, but I needed to find out how.

We spent the winter there happily and blissfully because we had nothing to worry about. We had food, love, care, entertainment and sports. Now summer was before us and we could see the sun smiling at us. We were now six. A year passed like that, and we built a very strong friendship and knew each other very well. We used to think about leaving for New York City, but we wanted to take care of Nikifor's grandpa and grandma because they were getting old. So, we had excused ourselves from the mission for a year, but we couldn't anymore. We wanted to tell them that we had to leave. As for Madison, Judah, Ejaz, and me, we had no problems leaving because we didn't have anybody to worry about, but we didn't know about Nikifor because of his grandparents. We asked Nikifor whether he wanted to leave; he said he was ready to go with us. But we didn't know whether his grandparents would approve, and we were scared to ask them.

We went to them one day and told them we were leaving to go to New York City, and Nikifor's grandma looked at us, surprised, and asked, "Why?" and said, "Just like that?" Then she smiled at us and said, "Is there a mission or something that you wanted to carry out?" and we became curious. How did she know about the mission? But we did our best to pretend we didn't know what she was talking about. Then she said that she and Nikifor's grandpa had to talk to us. We all assembled in the hall and Nikifor's grandma took a deep breath and said, "I will allow Niki to go with you. Is that cool?" Everyone jumped up and was elated, but I asked her, "Why?" and she replied to me, "What does that mean, Oliver?" I asked her, "You lost your son and you only have Niki, and we are all kids and only six years old. How could you let him go with us?"

Niki's grandma smiled and replied, "Wise boy, Oliver. I had a dream." I asked, "What dream, Grandma?" She replied with lots of unsolved thoughts in her mind, "I saw in my dream ten flowers together flying high in the air. They reached up into the heavens in the hands of a man with a snowy beard. Then, I saw from the flowers Niki smiling at me and I looked into the man's eyes. They were filled with the fountain and spring of wisdom and he said, 'He is always safe in my hands.' I felt overjoyed, and I closed my eyes. There was peace in my mind, which I had never experienced in my life and I heard a voice saying, 'Let him go.'" While she was telling us that, she seemed at ease, and we could see the inner bliss flowing out of her face.

After she finished saying that, we were all quiet for a few minutes, and then I asked her, "What does it mean, Grandma?" She replied, "In man's eyes, I saw eternal truth. I heard you guys talking about leaving for New York City, and Niki wanted to go with you. Then, I realized that the words that came into me, 'Let him go,' meant with you, dear. But I didn't know what the ten flowers meant." At this point, I had a revelation, and I didn't want to tell anymore lies. I replied to clear up the mystery, "It means there will be ten of us." She was shocked and asked me, "How do you know that?" I replied to her, "A message." She asked, "A message? Where are the other five?" I replied with great confidence, "We will find them soon." Niki's grandma stretched out her hand, and I walked to her, and she hugged me and whispered in my ear, "I know you will take care of Niki." I replied, "I will."

It was a dream revelation experience, and I could say this was a dream come true, because we had chosen Niki to be a part of us and the dream that Nikifor's grandma had aligned our visions and reassured them. But, there was one thing I didn't understand: "Who was the man with the snow-white beard? God, the universe's consciousness, Nathalie's father, or a superhero?" I didn't know yet, but one day I would find out.

We now had the approval of Niki's grandparents, so we were good to go. Niki started to pack his things for the journey. He had his clothes, his toiletries, his small chart, the note about women from his father and his diary, which he wrote in every day. But he was asking us whether he could take the gadget that had all the pictures of his father and voice chats he had saved, and he had a credit card with lots of money on it in his name and his father's receipt to buy the boat. We didn't stop him, although Nathalie had said not to use any technology. We didn't think it applied in Niki's case because he was using it for memories, so we hoped it didn't violate her rules.

Niki's grandparents were so pleasant and generous to us. They bought us new clothes because all the old ones were too small now. We also got a new and bigger wagon to store all our food, but we didn't want to throw

Patricia and the homeless people's wagon away. We remembered her, so we kept it with us and stored food in it as well. Wang and Kew knew we were leaving for New York City, and from their side, they gave us Chinese medicines for all our ailments. We were very thankful to them and the day before we left, we had a grand dinner with music and dancing.

Well, the time had come to say goodbye, but we were different faces now with different sentiments. Everything varies with time, and the more time we spend alive, the more weight we carry in our pockets. We had spent a year there and we had to leave for our mission, although the mission was still unclear. Niki's grandparents and Wang and Kew were there to say goodbye. Nikifor's grandma hugged and kissed all of us and she again whispered to me, "Take care of yourself, your friends, and Niki, and stay close with Madison and complete your mission." I acknowledged her wishes, and I told her that I would. We started to walk away from them. Nikifor turned around and looked back at his grandparents while we were walking, then he looked at his house. His memories were going in cycles and his heart was moving away from all he had known his entire life. Because he would no longer be seeing his loved ones, his eyes were watering and his energy was low as we moved farther away from the house.

We decided to walk to Buckley Park and show Ejaz the place where we met him. We showed him where he was caught and asked him whether he remembered the place, but he didn't remember anything because he had made it to the park during the night. We stayed in the park that night but Nikifor was scared because it was the first time he was out by himself. We were better than him at it but we knew danger was always near. We got up the next morning and started to walk along the waterfront. Now we had a boat but there was no one to drive it for us. We didn't know whom to ask but we saw people here and there and they looked at us like we were crazy. We camped here and there and finally went to Donges Bay. When we got there, there was a miracle waiting for us: a small rowboat was floating in the water, not tied to the pier. We didn't know whose boat it was, so we waited a few hours for someone to come and claim it. A few people walked up and we asked whose boat it was and they said it had been there for months. So, we decided to use the boat to cross the great river. But here comes the reality: no one knew how to swim except Nikifor. Nikifor had some notes about boats in his I-gadget and he was going through them.

The boat was hundred feet from the waterfront and Niki had to swim to remove the anchor and bring the boat back to shore. It sounded very simple, but we were still kids. The dangerous part was that we had every necessary thing for our journey except one important piece: a life jacket. We realized too late that Niki had a couple of life jackets at his house. We even thought about going back and getting them, but we never wanted to turn back. Niki said that he could get the boat out of the river but we were all scared, because we didn't know how to swim or anything about swimming, so we told him no.

At this point, we didn't know what to do, so we decided to stay there and think of a better plan. We asked a few people to help us get the boat, but they refused and a couple of days passed. Niki got frustrated and said that he was going to do it. He said that if we waited here, all our food would be gone in a few months. We asked him to swim near the lake for practice to make sure he could do it, so he swam ten to twenty feet back and forth to the shore. We all marveled that he knew how to swim so well and on the third day, we decided to take the boat. We remembered Nathalie's little prayer she had told us, "Even though I walk through the valley of the shadow of death." Niki started to swim to the boat and he was swimming well and was almost ten feet from it, but then the current started to carry him. He couldn't control himself and he started to drift away. He tried to resist, but he couldn't. We shouted at him to come back, but it was too late. He started to drown, and we all started to shout for help. But, Nathalie's prayer always had the word of power and we saw two kids starting to swim toward Niki to save him, there was a lady shouting to catch him by the hair and bring him to shore. The two girls swam so well that they lifted Niki's head and saved him from drowning. They held onto his hair and started to swim back to the shore.

We were all worried and terrified about what had happened to him. Niki was unconscious and breathless and we thought he was dead. The lady then did first aid, pressing on his chest and sucking water out of his mouth. For a few minutes there was no movement in his body, and we didn't know what was happening. The lady looked at us and said, "He will be fine—relax," and she rubbed his hands to give them some warmth and repeated the mouth to mouth resuscitation. A miracle under the sun happened that day because he started to cough and opened his eyes, and we asked, "Are you O.K.?" and he was shocked and bawled his eyes out and didn't reply. The lady asked us where we lived and we said we were all homeless. "Do you want to come to my home?" she asked. We had no choice and said we were happy to go with her. She was a stranger but because she saved Nikifor's life, we followed her. She carried him in her arms and we went close to Virmond Park. There they had a small home and all three of them, the two girls and the lady, lived in it. They all looked like Chinese people and we thanked them for helping us, but the lady replied, "Thank God that we were there." We thought she might be very religious and wanted to make her feel better, so I said, "Thank God for saving Niki." She had some medications and they looked like the ones we carried with us. They gave him some syrup to drink and the lady massaged him with hot water. Then, she put some ointment in a towel and put it on Niki's forehead. She asked us to stay with them, and we stayed with her that night.

We learned that the lady's name was Noa and the kids were called Aika and Shu. Aika was taller and skinny, whereas Shu was shorter with chubby cheeks. Aika was Noa's daughter, and Shu lived with them. They asked what we were doing with the boat and we said we were going to New York City and needed a boat. Noa asked us, "Who has a license to row it? You guys are too small for that," and we replied, "We don't have a license to row a boat." And she said, "You need a license to row a boat. If the lake patrol catches you, you will go to prison." This was a strange world. We didn't know what the laws were because we were taught that manually rowing a boat didn't require a license, now we looked like real fools.

She asked the same question—why were we going to New York City—and we told her the same pack of lies. She also asked a more disturbing question: "Why didn't you save Niki?" We replied with great shame, "We don't know how to swim." And Aika and Shu laughed at us, and seeing them laughing, my sweetheart, Madison, asked the lady, "Why didn't you swim to save my friend? Why did you send these kids?" We had to stop her, and Ejaz's face turned red. He said, "Madison, don't talk to her like that. They saved us," and Madison replied to Ejaz with frustration, "They saved us to make fun of us."

Watching the argument, Noa looked calmly at Madison and said, "You are right, girl." Then Madison calmed down. She quickly apologized for being rude. Noa said to Madison, "Before apologizing, tell me the reason you got so angry." And Madison replied, "I don't like anyone making fun of or laughing at my friends or me. That is not the way we grew up." Noa replied, "If you like someone, and they are teasing you and yet you get angry, it means you grew up with anger and frustration in your life." Hearing this, Madison said, "We didn't know what we were doing, and no one would help us." Noa replied, "Think of me as your mother. I will take care of all of you and I will die for you all. We are all orphans and have no one to love, but we will love one another." Madison quickly stood up from the chair, went and hugged her, and said, "Sorry. I am very sorry." We all felt Noa was a wonderful person and as always, when we see any woman, we think about Nathalie. We had dinner and stayed that night with Noa's family.

The next day, I wanted to talk to Madison about being mad at Noa for no reason. I asked her why she got mad. All she said was, "Sorry," and that she was very sensitive about how they had reacted. She promised me she would never do it again. I advised her to go and talk to Aika and Shu and make friends with them. My mind was consumed with thinking about Aika and Shu, how they risked their lives and saved Niki's life, and how without them, Niki would have died. We liked their family, especially Aika and Shu, and we started to get to know a little about them. They were not Chinese, except for Shu, and it was a funny experience in our life to, and for the first time, recognize the differences between similar faces. It started a simple conversation.

Judah: Aunt Noa, can I ask you a question?

Noa: Yes, honey, please.

Judah: Are you Chinese?

She started to giggle and laugh so much that she had to hold her stomach.

Judah became confused at why she was laughing, because he didn't know whether it had been an awkward question or if he, by mistake had made fun of Chinese people, we all had the same feeling.

Judah: Sorry for asking you.

Noa: You are fine, dear. What made you ask?

Judah: Oh, we have some friends, Wang and Kew, and they are Chinese and we thought you were Chinese, too.

Noa: Well, we are similar, but we are called Japanese.

Judah: Wow, you are Japanese? Sorry.

Noa: No, it is fine.

Judah: But. . . (He paused.)

Noa: But what? Do we all look the same?

Judah: Yeah. (He raised his eyebrows and twisted his lips.)

Noa: Well, if you want to know the difference between Chinese and Japanese, Chinese people have rounder faces Japanese people have longer, oval faces.

Judah: Okay, so Chinese people have round faces and Japanese people have oval faces. Shu looks Chinese.

Noa: Bingo. You got it, boy.

Judah: You said you are Japanese, so how come Shu is Chinese?

Noa: Above all, we are Americans.

Then Noa told the story about her family and Shu. Noa was married to Yukio who was a soldier in the U.S. Army. He was fighting with the Germans in the war on the Siberian border against the Serb extremists who wanted to bomb a children's community hall in Albania. There were almost 300 children and their families attending a gathering, and eleven Serbs were assigned for this assault. Yukio was sent to stop the bombing and every trooper died on the mission, except Yukio. Yukio never gave up and he fought bravely and killed all the bad guys and saved the children and their families that day. Yukio was awarded by the U.S. government for his act of bravery and promoted to second lieutenant. But within a few weeks, he died in the war.

Noa was living in Minneapolis with Yukio's parents and two younger sisters. Aika was two years old at the time her father died and she had never seen him because he had been in the war for all those years. The government didn't give much money to his family and Yukio had many loans because he had been the breadwinner for the family. Noa and Yukio's parents and sisters all became homeless. They were taken to a homeless shelter and lived there for a few months. But because of the great agony and sorrow of losing their son and the condition of their family, Yukio's parents died. Yukio's sisters were in their late teens and the warden of the homeless shelter was sexually harassing them. They were threatened with being kicked out of the shelter if they went to the cops because it would destroy the reputation of the shelter, so they decided to leave the shelter and find help in the streets.

Both sisters died tragically: one sister died of typhoid and the other sister died in cross fire. Noa and her daughter walked for their lives to find a safe place to live and found Shu in the streets with the homeless people. Noa loved Shu, Aika and Shu became friends, so she took Shu in as her own daughter. Shu was an orphan and had been found in a garbage can wrapped in a cloth after birth. The homeless people fed and raised her, and then Shu left the homeless people when she was four with Noa and Aika. They walked a lot and finally found the park. It was safer than the streets, so they built a tent and a house in the woods, where they live now. Noa works in a bakery, making bread herself and raises her two kids with that income.

Now, we had a very descent understanding about all of them and felt bad about Noa and Aika losing everything in their lives. Poor Shu had no one, just like us, but at least we grew up with Nathalie before we became homeless. But she was picked from the garbage, and we had a lot of sympathy for her now. In the daytime Noa went to work at the bakery, we spent time with Aika and Shu. We started to like them, and Madison started to become very close with them. It looked like it was the beginning of a girls' night because they would hang out and talk, leaving us boys behind. Our hero, Nikifor, recovered after a week from the swimming accident and got back to his routine.

Noa, Aika, and Shu wanted to teach us to swim. They took us to the river where they found us, and the ownerless boat was still floating in the river. Noa swam out and brought the boat back to the shore. She checked the boat and it was good and intact. We all had life jackets on when we went aboard. Initially, we were scared, not of the water but because of Nikifor's accident. Although Noa motivated us and encouraged us, no one wanted to take the risk. Again, Niki was the man and he jumped into the water with his life jacket on, and Noa helped him swim. Then one by one, we all jumped in and let Noa teach us how to swim. Aika and Shu also helped us swim, and it was an exciting experience for us.

Within a few weeks, we learned how to swim, but we always had one question on our minds: if Nikifor knew how to swim, how did he almost drown? Noa said that he only knew how to swim in still waters, like swimming pools, but did not know how to swim in a lake, river, or ocean. We all thought that water was the same but we found out that nature controls the waters very differently. One strange thing I found out was that Nikifor really liked Aika; they started to get closer to each other. He talked to her all the time and was always doing extra nice things for her.

I had a chance to talk to him one day and asked him about Aika. He said, "She saved my life and I owe her that life now." Then he added, about the water incident, "When I was breathless, I thought I was dead, but then an illuminated angel came and said, 'Wake up,' and I opened my eyes and saw Aika standing there. The angel I saw looked the same as Aika." At this point, I didn't know what he meant, but I knew that Aika and Shu could be more chosen ones to go with us. Days passed, and we needed someone to row the boat across Lake Michigan; we couldn't ask Noa because she had Aika and Shu with her. We didn't tell them about the journey to New York City because we didn't know how to start the conversation. We stayed there for a few months because we wanted to learn how to swim, but now it was becoming cold, and winter was near. However, we could still go fishing.

Aika and Shu didn't go to school because of the cost, which Noa couldn't bear. They did homeschool and we studied with them in the daytime. After work, Noa would take us fishing. We started to eat lots of fish and started feeling stronger and stronger. We planned to spend the winter with Noa and her family and Christmas was right around the corner. Noa wanted to buy new clothes for Aika and Shu and for us, but she only had enough money for Aika and Shu. When we learned she was short on money, we decided to use Niki's credit card to buy new clothes for all of us, including Noa, Aika, and Shu because we had become part of their family. But Noa was not comfortable taking the credit card and she felt bad.

Nikifor: Why don't you want to take my card? My dad put lots of money on it.

Noa: No, dear, I can't. It is not fair to take money from a kid. I'm sorry.

Nikifor: So, what are you going to do?

Noa: Well, I have little money to buy new clothes for Aika and Shu, so I will not buy them anything so I don't seem partial to anyone, including my kids.

Nikifor: So, you still treat us as strangers, right?

Noa: No, honey, I didn't mean it like that.

Nikifor: You and your daughters saved my life, and I owe you everything for that.

Noa: I know, I know, Niki. But it is not good to take money from you. I could borrow some money from my friends.

Nikifor: We have stayed here for a few months, and you didn't ask for any rent or charge us for food. You provided hospitality, and in exchange, we should do something for you. I think it is the right thing to do.

Noa put her hands on her hips and smiled.

Noa: You talk like a businessman, Niki. I am pleased with your reasoning and justification, so I will buy all of you expensive clothes and spend all your money.

Nikifor: Cool.

Noa was very much impressed and pleased by Niki's answers and she started to feel that we were all her own kids. We went shopping for Christmas and bought clothes, a Christmas tree, candles, and gifts for each other with the little money we had. Judah, Madison and I didn't have anything, but Niki bought things for us. Noa also spent her money and bought gifts for all of us. I had a weird feeling while we shopped that someone was following us and wanted to hurt us but I didn't pay much attention to my instincts because we were with Noa and in public, not alone in a corner.

On Christmas Day, we wore our new outfits and Noa made cakes, chocolates and cookies. We ate them and they were delicious, but I was very troubled that something was wrong and something bad was going to happen. I heard owl hoots and dogs and wolves howling in my heart, and I was disturbed. Noa noticed and asked, "Are you all right?" and I replied, "I am good." Judah asked me the same question, but to him I said, "I feel like I am losing everything." He asked me, "Do you want some water to drink, Oliver?" and I drank some water and became calmer.

Noa was busy preparing the Christmas meal and all the girls were helping her. We were all chatting and playing video games in the tent. Dinner was ready, and we sat in the kitchen enjoying the meal. We heard a screeching sound, and Noa got up from the table and went to look through the window. When she saw nothing, she turned back to the table. But then a man smashed the window with the butt of a gun. He had a black mask over his face, and as soon as Noa turned around, he put his gun to her head and said, "Don't move."

Two men broke down the front door, also wearing masks over their faces, and Noa, with her elbow, punched the guy who was holding the gun in the eye and then ran to get her pistol. The other two men ran and tripped her. Seeing this, Niki and I ran to help her, but the two men pushed us to the floor. Then Ejaz and Judah saw the man who Noa punched in the eye aiming his gun to shoot us, and they both went to try to stop him. He kicked Judah in the chest and Judah flew into a shelf and fainted. The man then grabbed Ejaz and threw him out the window. Then, a fourth masked man entered through the front door, took his rifle, and shot two bullets into the roof. Everybody fell quiet. He shouted, "If anyone moves or tries to be a hero, I will smoke everyone."

Hearing this, we all got scared, and he said to tie up the lady and the little girls. The two men holding Noa put duct tape over her mouth and tied her hands with rope. Then the three men tried to catch Madison, Aika, and Shu to tie them up. The man who had his eye punched had a shotgun, the other two had pistols, and the fourth guy, their boss, had a rifle. The man's eye was badly hurt, and he grabbed Madison. But Shu had a fork in her hand and struck him in his other eye and said, "Leave her, and take me." His eyebrows and eyelids were cut, and he screamed in pain and got pissed off. He grabbed Shu's head and banged it on the table.

The man with the rifle shouted, "Don't kill the girls. We want them alive." But Shu had been knocked down very badly; she fell on the floor breathless. Niki, and I screamed at her while the other two men tied Aika and Madison up. Then the injured man picked Shu up from the floor and tied her up. The man with the rifle asked them to take them away. The one man who was holding Noa and had his gun pointed at her head started walking outside, but the man with the rifle stopped them. He started to assault Noa, touching her breasts, but Noa fought back. He slapped her and asked the injured man to take her out. The other man had Madison and Aika and took them outside, but the rifle man stopped him. When he saw Madison, he looked at her with lust, licked her cheeks, and said, "One little blond chicken tonight." Then he looked at Aika and asked her, "Do you like me?" and Aika spat at him. The man wiped away the spit and said, "You will be the last one to die among them all." He asked the man to take her outside, and poor Shu, who was still breathless, was thrown over the shoulder of the man who was hurt. I saw my beloved one, Madison, taken away from me, and my friends were all tied up and being taken away, and my heart was going with them. I was helpless now.

They all went outside and were talking. The man with the pistol was sent back in to the house. He saw us and went outside, picked Ejaz up from outside the window and threw him on the floor. The man with the rifle shouted, "Finish off all the boys and come back outside," and he replied, "Yes, boss." Ejaz was on the floor and Judah was near the wall unconscious. Niki and I were watching him. He pointed the gun at Niki and said, "Bye, punk," and I remembered Nathalie's prayer and started to say, "Though I walk through . . . ," but the man with the gun looked at me and said, "What the hell are you saying, you piece of trash?" He turned to Niki and was about to pull the trigger.

We heard a shot, and the men outside shouted, "Who fired that shot?" The man who was holding the gun on Niki stopped and said to us, "Don't run. I will be back." He went out to see what had happened, and we also rushed outside. It was dark, and we only had the light from the skies and some lights from our house, but all of them were visible, and all the men and our friends were standing. We saw that the man who was hurt had been shot in the forehead and fallen down. Both Shu and the man were on the ground. The other three men were looking around to see who had fired the shot and then one more shot was fired at the man who was holding Noa, hitting him in the forehead. The boss saw where the shot came from and he and his last man started to shoot hundreds of rounds in that direction. Then he stopped shooting and shouted, "Who is out there? Don't hide and fight, just come out and fight like a man." Then the hero from the dark fired one more shot, and the guy who had the pistol, the one who wanted to kill Niki and me, was shot in the face and fell to the ground like a pancake.

Except for the boss, everyone was now dead, and he got scared and wanted to escape. He was trying to take Madison as a hostage, but Noa ran, jumped, and pushed the man with her head to the ground. Niki and I ran to help Noa, we took the gun from the man, and the man and Noa started to roll around fighting. We heard a voice say, "Stop it, punk," and all of a sudden, there was a man with a gun pointed at the boss's head. The boss stopped moving, and we all saw the man who had saved us. He was black, six feet tall, and well built. Noa got up and we went to help her and untie her. Then we untied Madison and Aika. Niki and I picked up Shu and put her hands on our shoulders. She had passed out. The good-hearted stranger asked us, "Did he hurt you?" and we said, "Yes." He said to the boss, "Then go to hell," and pulled the trigger. The boss's head exploded, and blood splattered on our faces. We had never felt anything that bad.

Then the man who saved us shouted, "Come on, son, everything is fine now." When he said that, we saw a boy, more or less our age, walk out from the dark, he was black and cute. I extended my hand to the man who saved us and said, "I am Oliver. Thanks very much for saving us," and he replied, "It is my job to save innocent people. I am Gail, Kadin Gail, and this is my son, Benjamin," and Benjamin greeted everyone. Noa asked Kadin what they should do with the dead bodies and he replied, "Do you have Christmas supper?" and Noa replied, "Yes, we do." Kadin replied, "We will make a campfire with the bodies, if that is okay." Noa had nothing to say but "Yes, sir, please."

We all went to check on Ejaz and Judah, who were still on the floor in the house. We woke them with water. Ejaz's shoulder muscle was twisted, and he had a few bruises. Judah was hurt in his back, there was swelling but no fractures or spinal injuries. Shu's head hurt, but luckily, there were no serious injuries. She had fainted because of shock. We were all bruised here and there, but no one was hurt severely. We had ointments and applied them and Kadin asked whether we needed a doctor or had to go to hospital. We didn't want to get into trouble with the cops or go through an interrogation, and our wounds were not life threatening, so we didn't go to the doctor or hospital.

We helped Kadin move the bodies together fifty feet away from the house. Kadin asked, "Do you know what your enemies look like?" But we didn't know because their faces had been covered with masks. Then Niki and Madison said, "We want to see them." Kadin removed the mask of the first man, the one who was holding the shotgun, and he was Latino. His forehead was smashed and Kadin said his name was Tommy. Then we saw the next man, and he was light-skinned and looked Caucasian, Kadin said his name was Augustine, and he had been one of the men holding a pistol. The other man with a pistol was white and fair, but his face was disfigured. He was called Salty. Finally, we saw the boss's face, and his name was Kevin Burner and was African-American. They were all different colors and from different heritages, but their faces had no sign of divinity or innocence. They looked evil and weird.

We poured oil and gas over them and burned them. Then we made a campfire near our house with wood and had Christmas dinner with a bunch of bodies burning fifty feet away. We were all in shock, and no one spoke to each other because we didn't know what had happened. All we could do was thanked Kadin and Benjamin a million times for saving us. We treated them as our royal guests and took care of them, and that night, they both stayed with us to make sure we were safe. All I remember from that night was that no one spoke to anyone. Everybody was still in swivet and shocked.

I couldn't sleep because of a nightmare, and Judah, who was lying next to me, asked, "Did you know that these things were going to happen? Was that why you were worried, Oliver?" I replied, "Yes," and Judah asked me, "How did you know?" I replied to him, "When we went shopping, I felt that someone was following us and after that, I felt someone was watching us. Maybe because of my instincts, all this happened." Judah replied, "No, it happened because of those bad guys. Why do you worry about it? Sleep well, Oliver. We will talk in the morning." That night, the nightmare of what happened haunted me. I couldn't save Madison and my friends. I felt a man's love in my heart for Madison. I loved her very much, and I swore to myself that I would never let anything happen to her again,.

The next day, we were having breakfast, and Noa asked Kadin, "Who are those guys, sir?" Kadin replied, "They are rapists, child molesters, and murderers," and she asked, "Really, how do you know?" Kadin replied, "I was following them." I asked him, "Why?" and he replied, "I follow the bad guys and whack them. That is what Kadin does." We were all surprised by his answer, and I asked him, "Are you a cop?" He replied, "No, I want to be a cop, but cops don't like me. You could think of me as "Batman" because I hunt and kill all the bad guys." Noa asked, "Do you know the names of those men?" He replied, "Yes, I do." Then Noa asked,

"If you know them, and they are bad guys, you should have reported them to the cops." Kadin replied, "There was no evidence to show to the cops, and the cops hate me."

Then Kadin told his story. "My father was an honest cop and his name was Lavar Gail. The Milwaukee police station where he was working was corrupt and the cops allowed the mobs and gangsters to sell drugs, run prostitution, kidnap, and blah, blah, blah. My father reported to the higher officials about the bribes and scams. No one took any notice because everyone was corrupt and the cops formed a union to get rid of my father. They invited him for a drink at a remote place and my father went. When they tried to kill him, he killed almost eight cops that day. He got pissed off with the whole mess and started to hunt and shoot all the bad cops. He cleaned up the mess.

My father was arrested and sentenced to life in prison when I was eleven years old. I grew up under my father's shadow of being a good cop and fighting for justice. My father died in prison within a few years and his last and only wish was that I would be a cop. I worked hard my entire life to be a cop, but they rejected me every time, saying that my father was insane and killed his colleagues, and they didn't want me to be a cop. I tried with all my energy, but couldn't get through, so I took the law into my own hands, wanting to clean the dirt from society. I became a hit man. I am the Batman of Wisconsin. I just hunt the bad guys, slice them up, and free the innocent."

We were touched by his story and his drive to be a cop. Though he is not officially a cop, he is still on duty. Noa asked him, "Is Benjamin your son? Where is his mother?" He replied, "His mother and I were not married, but we were living together and she left to join the Marines four months after Benjamin was born. I am waiting for her to come back from the war so that we can marry and settle down, but my wife, my son, and I will always hunt the bad guys."

Then he asked us who we were. We had to tell the same lie and it hurt us badly, because without him, we would all have been dead. We felt a spark about Benjamin, that he was one of us. He would be the eighth wonder of this world, and we were waiting again for the world's clock to ring its bell and confirm it. He stayed with us that day; and we had a chance to talk. He liked us very much, too. His father was glad that his son had some good friends, and he liked all of us too.

Kadin asked us, "Why didn't you protect yourselves when the guys attacked you?" and Niki replied, "Our guns were in the tent." Kadin laughed and asked, "Do you know how to shoot?" and Niki said, "No." He said, "If you don't know how to shoot, then what is the point of having a gun? Forget about the gun—you should have used your hands and body to defend yourself. Do you know how to fight or box?" Niki replied, "No, we don't," and Kadin looked at all of us and asked, "Does anyone know how to fight or shoot?" We all shook our heads. The only thought that came to my mind when he asked that question was that out of a Superman, Captain America, and Genghis Khan, no one knew how to fight or shoot. We have brought great shame on their names. Then Kadin looked at us and could tell we were embarrassed by his question. He said, "I have decided to train you guys to fight and shoot. Is that cool?" We all jumped high in the air shouting, "Yahaaa." Kadin took all of us to his place. It was a decent house and he showed us his guns and weapons in his basement. We were astonished to see all the big guns hanging there.

Kadin came every morning and took us jogging and then we went to the gym for a workout. He started to train us on how to shoot; we soon started to learn. We used the BB pistol to start with and within a couple of weeks, we were able to shoot better. But Nikifor had some sort of trauma with what we were doing and asked us, "If Nathalie said not to kill anyone and not to use guns, what are we doing learning to shoot? We may kill someone and become like other killers in this world." I made my point clear that we were very kind, soft, and weak and we had been knocked down and beaten up by bad guys a lot. So, we had to work out and be strong, and we should know how to shoot to protect ourselves, but not to kill. All the shooting skills we were gaining were to be used as warning signs. We will keep Nathalie's word, I said, and no one will ever kill anyone. Within a month, we all knew how to take a clean shot. Kadin was surprised that we learned to shoot in only a month. Then, he taught us boxing and self-defense techniques to protect ourselves. We practiced every single day with each other, and we could see in our eyes that we were turning into strong and fearless children.

Benjamin was an impressive kid, and he loved his father very much. We all became best friends, and we knew that Aika, Shu, and Benjamin were the chosen ones to join us. This time, I felt doubt in myself. How did I know these were the chosen ones to go with us? I have not met many kids in my life, and there were few kids to choose from. *Am I only picking those to go with us who are nice to me and helped us? Or am I influencing the others to accept my opinions? These thoughts were bothering me* very much, and one day, a revelation came to mind. Whenever my mind was thinking about whether or not to pick the friends to travel with us, I would see a white light pass by behind their heads, and this light confirmed to me that they were the ones. I called it the "shining light." I asked the same question of Madison and Judah, and they said the same thing, that they see a white light when they think about it.

So, we were good to go now, and we had to talk to Noa and Uncle Kadin about it. We were not going to lie, because we trusted them, and in turn, they trusted us. Before that, though, we spoke to Benjamin about it and he was eager to join us on the mission. Then we told the whole story, to Noa and Kadin, and they were astonished to hear about our background and about Nathalie. They knew about war very well, but they were uncertain about Nathalie. Where had she come from? But they seemed convinced with our answers. We told the truth about our mission and they were also surprised at the truth about us, but they were convinced and had the same feeling that I was the chosen one.

Now we wanted to cross the river, and we had Uncle Kadin to take us because he had a license to drive a boat. Uncle Kadin and Noa agreed to our proposal and request because they knew we were the ones who could stop the war. But they didn't want us to go alone because it was too dangerous and they said they would help walk us to New York City. Nikifor applied for the boat and Uncle Kadin vouched for it with his license. The process took a couple of months but we finally got the boat. We were happy to see it. The boat was very big—white and covered with black glass. It had a deck below with two rooms and bathrooms and lots of space to sit. It was equipped with state-of-the-art technology, maps, tracking meters, satellite connections, Internet, television, submarine conversion and many other amenities we knew nothing about. It was April, and Uncle Kadin said we should go when it was summer because it would be lots of fun and safe. We were strong now and knew how to swim, shoot, box and fight.

Summer came and we turned seven. We were a little taller and had more flesh and bone on our bodies. We had to leave for New York City, so we started packing all our stuff to leave with Uncle Kadin and Noa. And because the small rowboat was the first boat we had experienced, we asked to bring it along. We attached it to the side of our big boat. Now, our big boat looked even better than before because we were sailing with our memories with us.

We honked the horn and were ready to leave. We were all thrilled that finally, after two years, we were leaving Milwaukee and sailing across the great Lake Michigan. We were sailing slowly because we wanted to enjoy the ride. Several times that day, we stopped the boat and swam in the lake. We caught lots of fish and cooked them on the boat. The first night on the lake was splendid. We saw the moon touching the lake, and the lake was shy, moving from the sighing of the moon. It was the same moon and lake that we had been seeing for a year, but I became poetic because we were going to New York City, and our destiny was ahead of us. We stopped the boat that night and partied. We didn't sleep and we had loud music from our favorite DJ, M.O. Filler. This was the first time we saw Benjamin dance and all his moves. That was one awesome dance he did that day.

Noa asked Kadin what he would do after we got to New York City and he replied happily, "I will be with my son and see what is happening with these guys. If the prophecy is true, then I will work with them to help. All I am waiting for is my sweetie to come back from the war, and then we can get married and when the war is over, we will all have a peaceful life." Then he asked Noa what she would do after going to New York City, and she said, "I had no one, except Aika and Shu, but now I have more kids, and I will nurse them and be their mother." Madison asked Noa if we could call her "Mom," and she happily replied, "Yes, dear, you can." Madison called her Mom, and we followed her lead and called her Mom. It was a wonderful experience because we had never had a chance to call anyone Mom like that. All we knew was Nathalie, and we loved to call her "Natty," but now Noa reminded us of Nathalie. Madison, Judah, and I were surprised when Niki called her Mom because he was a follower of his father's teachings, and I could see a lot of difference in his approach to women now.

We went to bed that night and I was awake while everyone was sleeping. Madison slowly whistled and I saw she was awake and asked her, "What?" and she slowly got down from her bed and walked to me and said, "Can we go out?" I asked her, "Why?" and she said, "I want to talk to you." We both went outside and sat in the front of the boat, she was worried and sad. I asked her, "What do you want to talk about?" With a frown on her face, she said, "Did you notice any difference after the incident at Christmas?" and I asked her, "Difference where?" Her face turned red, and she said, "Oliver, the difference in me." I honestly didn't know what she was asking and where she was coming from, and I said, "I am very sorry, Madison, I don't know, please forgive me." She replied with her eyes open and said, "I will give you some clues," and I replied eagerly, "Okay, fine."

She said, "I have not been normal since then. I feel sad sometimes about it and I think I will miss you." Now I got really upset because I didn't know she was sad, and it was my job to make her happy. I raised my voice and said, "What are you talking about, Madison? You should have told me, 'What is happening to you?'" She said, "Shh, quiet, everyone is sleeping." I said to her in a low voice, "Okay, please tell me. I swear, I don't know." Then she said, "Aika and Shu know." I asked her, "Why didn't you tell me first?" and she replied carelessly, "I didn't think." At this time, she was driving me crazy, and I said, "Madison, whatever it is, please tell me. I am always on your side." She put her head down and said, "You saw the boss, Kevin Burner, lick my face and say, 'One little blond chicken tonight.'" I said to her, "Yes. What does that have to do with now?"

I saw tears falling out of her eyes, and she said, "After seeing someone licking my face, will you still love me, Oliver?" I was lost in her world of craziness. I am not a girl's man who knows what should be said or done. I stammered and said, "I love you, Madison," and she asked me, "Really, Oliver?" I didn't know what to do to make her believe me, so I kissed her on the cheek where she felt so low about herself. She quickly became nervous and said, "What are you doing?" I looked at the stars and said, "I still love you."

Then she moved her hands and held my hands and said, "Really, you still love me?" and I said, "Yes, I promise. I even kissed you." She replied, "Give me one more kiss," and I couldn't resist. I kissed her many times on her cheek, and she started to giggle and laugh. I asked her, "What happened?" and raising her hands to the sky and shaking her hips and body, she said, "I know, Oliver loves me now. Thanks, God."

This was the first craziness I had experienced with a woman. She knew I loved her and I didn't know why she did this. To give and take, she also kissed my cheeks many times, and all I had to say now was that I wanted to fly in the air and not sail on the boat. This was the boat and moonshine love affair that went down that night, and she put her head on my shoulder and started to talk about all our past experiences. Though I wanted to sleep and was tired, I opened my eyes wide to stay awake, because the moment was not the same between Madison and me that I had known before. I was happy for a couple of hours, but then I started to feel bad about myself, and I got a weird thought in my head that I couldn't save the girl I liked the most. I am not a Superman who beats up all the bad guys and saves Madison. I should have at least tried, but I never did because I was scared. Shu was brave enough to defend her friend Madison with a fork and Aika had the guts to spit in his face, but compared with the girls, I was a coward. Madison expressed something, but she was good enough not to ask me why I hadn't tried to save her.

Although I was listening to her that night, I felt very bad about myself. When Nikifor was drowning, I should have tried to swim and save him, but I watched him dying. How could I be the chosen one to go and stop the war when I was not able to save my friends who were dying before my own eyes? Was Nathalie wrong? Or had she misunderstood me? I didn't even have the power to save Nathalie and she died while we were asleep. I didn't know what I was doing. We had started this journey with some hope in us, but when I thought about it, it didn't make any sense. So, what is my hope now? Was I a selfish chosen one or just another hypocrite? I didn't know yet. The chosen one should know his family, but I didn't know who my parents were, and that was the weirdest part.

I had to ask Madison to forgive me because I couldn't save her, and I didn't know how she was going to react. Madison was talking to me, and when she thought I was asleep, she asked me, "Oliver, are you listening to me?" I got my senses back and said, "Yes, I am." My mind was about to explode while thinking about it, and I said, "Sorry, Madison," and with her clueless face, she asked me, "Sorry for what?" I hesitated about how to tell her, and with a low voice, I said, "I should have saved you that day when they took you, but I just watched you go. I should have at least fought like a man and died, but I didn't." Madison looked at me doubtfully and asked, "Do you feel bad for not saving me?" I replied to her with my head down, "Yes."

We were both quiet for some time, and then Madison said, "Even if I would have gone, you would have come back for me, Oliver, I know it. Wouldn't you have?" I replied, "Yeah, I would have." She said, "Don't worry about that, Oliver. We were not trained for combat. This world is cruel, and Nathalie didn't teach us. It is not your fault." I said, "But Nathalie's prayer worked, Madison. I said it when you were being taken, and the prayers brought Uncle Kadin and Benjamin to save us." Madison was surprised. "Did you say the prayer? Cool—you remembered that. Nathalie is always the best. She taught simple things to do great things. Do you really believe in that prayer, Oliver?" I replied to her positively that because it was from Nathalie, it should be good and work all the time.

We both compromised now and we no longer carried guilt. We put our heads together and watched the lake and the waves move in the moonlight. The same butterfly, the cupid, the heartbeat, the calmness, and the romance were also in Madison, and the only witnesses to these lovely moments were the moon and the stars.

Chapter 16
The Refusal

IT WAS THE SECOND DAY THAT MADISON AND I DIDN'T SLEEP, SO WE TOOK a small nap and started the boat in the morning. We had our breakfast and everyone was chatting to each other and fishing. I went to talk to Uncle Kadin, who was steering the boat. "How many days will it take to reach land?" and Uncle Kadin replied, "I don't know, son, maybe two weeks." I was surprised by his answer. "On the map, it says it is just eighty to ninety miles and should take a day or two." Uncle Kadin laughed and said, "Well, you want to go directly from Milwaukee to Muskegon, but we cannot do that. Only ferries could take us and they haven't operated for almost forty years."

I was shocked and perplexed by his reply, because I didn't know a ferry had ran between Milwaukee and Muskegon. "It is just eighty miles, Uncle, so why didn't we take the ferry path?" Uncle Kadin replied, "It's not eighty miles, son, it is only fifty miles. The river dried up and everything in this world is chaos. We cannot legally take the ferry path, so we have to go all the way up through Sturgeon Bay." I quickly said, "So we have to pass the Mackinac Bridge?" Uncle Kadin looked at me and said, "You know your history, son, which is good. That bridge was bombed, and it's off limits. We have another bridge running there called the Glass Bridge, the world's third-largest bridge, which was built as a transparent glass structure."

Hearing that, I was more confused now, because the map Nathalie gave us had no information about any of these things and I wanted to check it. I thanked Uncle Kadin for the information he gave us and rushed to see the map. I pulled the map from the bag and examined it again, to make sure I hadn't missed anything. None of the information was there and my mind became blank. I was flipping the book front to back, but my eyes were wide open, and I spotted a number. I took a close look. It said, "Published in 2039." After seeing that, my mind went in circles and my head started to spin, slowly I became breathless and speechless.

Then Benjamin came inside the deck and saw me and asked, "Are you all right, Oliver?" I didn't reply. He came closer to me and shook my shoulder, calling me, "Oliver, Oliver." I woke up and gave the book to Benjamin and showed him the year. He looked at it and read, "2039" and replied to me with no idea, saying, "2039? What is this?" I didn't blame him because he had never used the map with us, and I said to him, "Could you please call Madison, Judah, and Ejaz inside here?" They all came rushing to see me. I looked lost, and Judah asked, "Are you okay, Oliver?" I gave the book to him and showed him the date and he understood what I was concerned about. "How could she give us a book that is almost a thousand years old?" I replied, "I didn't know." Ejaz said, "Maybe she picked it up from an antique book shop." I appreciated his understanding and replied, "If so, the book looks brand new. It looks like it just came off the printing press."

Madison couldn't stand anymore; she was getting more confused than I was. She said, "Oliver, what do you want to do now? Did Nathalie make a mistake or do you doubt her?" I replied in a gruff voice, "I am just trying to understand what is in this locket if she gave us an old map, I don't know what the puzzle was inside it." Benjamin threw a wise and fantastic answer: "Maybe we are using a machine boat with all the technology in it, so we are violating Nathalie's commandment, and the year in the book changed automatically." Ejaz looked at Benjamin with a funny expression. "You have a wonderful imagination Ben. Letters change in the book automatically when we disobey!" Ejaz really cracked everyone up and everyone started to laugh. I couldn't control it, and I laughed so much. We all forgot about the map and the year in it, we threw the map in the water because we didn't need it anymore.

Uncle Kadin sail the boat at a slower speed to avoid the satellite and law enforcement stopping and questioning us. We passed Sturgeon Bay and were excited to see the glass bridge. At the right moments, from a distance, we could see reflections in the glass and rainbows in the reflections. As we neared the bridge, we saw it was huge and looked like it was built from ice and glaciers. We were afraid it might break and fall on us, but we saw lots of vehicles passing through. Even the pillars that were holding the bridge were made of glass, the catenary looked exactly like chain glasses, and every single piece was made of glass. It was transparent so that we could see all the sides of the pillar and the inner space of the pillar was filled with glass.

When we went under the bridge we saw the cars' undercarriages and wheels, and the shafts moving. There were guards and militants standing on the bridge with guns and ammunition. I thought that if any of the guards or militants fired one bullet at it, the glass would break and the whole thing would fall like dominoes. My mind was as weak as glass, but the glass bridge was stronger than what I thought; my knowledge now was an illusion. We moved far away from the bridge, it was the most beautiful monument we'd ever seen and the picture was deeply imprinted in our minds. I asked Uncle Kadin if he had seen the bridge before and he said, "A few times." The memories were fresh in our minds until the pirates of the Great Lakes walked into our lives.

After crossing the bridge we traveled five miles and anchored the boat for the night. We had a good dinner, listened to music, chatted until midnight and then went to bed to get ready for the next day. It was around one o'clock in the morning when we heard an engine sound. Our boat was moving rapidly with the heavy tides. Uncle Kadin and Ejaz woke up, and it was dark outside. Clouds covered the lights of the skies with traces of light sneaking through the clouds' gaps. They saw a black object in the water but couldn't get a clear picture of it. Uncle Kadin turned the boat's floodlights on and turned on the flashlights. They saw a big submarine come out of the water. It was a monster submarine and we didn't know how big because it was moving out of the water like an infinite loop. Uncle Kadin rushed to the guns and asked Ejaz to wake everyone up.

Uncle Kadin grabbed his MF 232 50-mm gun, pulled the anchor up, and started the boat. Time was not on our side and the submarine struck our boat. We all fell down, and Benjamin was thrown into the water. Uncle Kadin dropped his gun into the water. Judah and Nikifor took the fishing rod to help Benjamin get out of the water. Benjamin couldn't grab the rod and was still in the water and our boat started to move away from him. Uncle Kadin took a pistol from his pocket and held it but he didn't fire any shots.

The submarine stopped next to our boat, and our boat looked like a turtle before an elephant. The submarine was hundreds of feet long and almost 400 feet high. We saw a door open and light came out of the submarine, we heard a man shouting, *"Déplacer, déplacer, déplacer."* Within a few minutes more than 100 men were standing on the roof with their guns pointed at us. There were windows in the submarine and when they opened, we saw the main guns of the tanks popping out. We heard a man shouting, "Do not move! Drop all your weapons!" Pirates jumped onto our boat. They had guns in their hands and pointed them at Uncle Kadin's head and told him to drop his pistol. He did exactly what they said, and they dropped anchor to make the boat stationary, but Benjamin was still in the water.

Then the captain came onto our boat. He was six feet two inches tall and had a rough beard, a pipe in his mouth, a long coat, and a pirate's hat. He looked at us and asked, "What are you guys doing here?" and Uncle Kadin said, "We just came for summer vacation and fishing," He asked Uncle Kadin, "Who are those kids?" and Uncle Kadin replied with a stern voice, "My neighbors and their kids." The captain asked Uncle Kadin, "What is your name?" and Uncle Kadin replied, "Kadin," and the captain slapped him. Uncle Kadin got angry and moved toward the captain to hit him back, but the three of us held him back and threw him on the floor to kneel before the captain.

The captain arrogantly looked at Uncle Kadin, raised his eyebrow and stared at him. Uncle Kadin was a man and he boldly looked into the captain's eyes with no fear. The captain then said, "Speak," and Uncle Kadin replied to him in a satirical voice, "Speak what?" The captain was insulted and the men who were holding Kadin giggled. The captain lost control and took a handgun from his coat and put it to Uncle Kadin's forehead. "Don't play smart, jackass." Uncle Kadin bit his teeth and replied, "If you are a man, let's go for it! I will tear you into pieces, you coward." Hearing this, the captain took the gun from his forehead and said, "Want to play with me, huh?" He again slapped Uncle Kadin and moved his face close to his and said, "Which family are you from, you Kadin cockroach?" Uncle Kadin fiercely answered, "My name is Kadin, Kadin Gail and my father was Lavar Gail." The stubborn captain got scared and moved his face from Uncle Kadin's and asked , "Are you the son of Lavar Gail the cop?" and Uncle Kadin replied, "Yes." Then the captain looked at his men and said, "My father said that Lavar Gail was a very brave man and killed a few of his men and the cops who were supporting us and working for my father. And here, we have Lavar Gail's son before us on his knees. We will not kill as his father did; rather, we will take him as a prisoner to our ship."

Then the other men went to the lower deck and took all the bags we had and laid them out before the captain. The captain asked, "What is inside these?" and one of his men replied, "The usual stuff: clothes, toiletries, food—but we found these tranquilizer guns." The captain laughed, "Tranquilizer guns for the fish," and he ordered his men to take Uncle Kadin to his submarine, but Uncle Kadin resisted and the captain took one of the tranquilizer guns and shot Uncle Kadin. But Uncle Kadin was strong and he stared at the captain's eyes with vengeance. The captain again shot another tranquilizer bullet, and as Uncle Kadin was fainting, he said, "Oliver, take care of Benjamin, please, please." His voice started to diminish as he fell unconscious and they took him to the submarine.

The captain, hearing Uncle Kadin's words, said, "Who is Benjamin? Is he his son? Where is he? Who is, Oliver?" I was frightened and replied, "I am sir." He softened when I called him sir and looked at me calmly and said, "Come here, boy." I walked to him, my whole body shaking and said, "Yes, sir." He asked me, "Who is Benjamin?" and I replied, "He is his son." He asked, "Where is he?" and I replied, "Back home," and he asked me, "Why?" and I said, "He is sick." The captain, looked at me and said, "Ask that little boy Benjamin not to put his feet in the water, because if he does, I will snatch him and feed him to my birds." I was shivering because

Benjamin was still in the water and I said the little prayer to myself, *"Though I walk . . ."* They should leave now, and Benjamin should be safe in the water.

The captain lustfully looked at Noa and asked her, "What is your name?" and she replied, "Noa." The captain ordered, "Take her." Hearing the captain's order, Noa moved back and a guard moved toward her to take her with him. But Noa grabbed a handgun from the holster of one of the men standing near her. She started to point it at the captain and said, "I will kill you," but all the guns from the factories were on her. She was pointing her gun at everyone before her and threatening them and looking for a way to escape. The captain warned her to drop the gun, and she looked at us, with tears running down her face. She saw Aika and said, "Sorry, Aika, stay safe. Oliver, take care of her." We didn't know what was going through her mind, but she put the gun to her temple and pulled the trigger. The bullet went in one side and came out the other side of her head. She fell in the water head first and seeing this, Aika screamed, "Mommy," and started to run to her. We all went to see her, and she was just floating in the water. All our eyes were wet with tears and our hearts were broken. We heard the captain saying, "She doesn't want to be a whore. Good choice."

Then the captain asked his men to throw all of us into the water and one of his men, who was standing close to him and seemed to be his right-hand man, said, "We never leave anyone alive. Why are you not killing them?" The captain said, "I like that kid, Oliver. He called me "sir", and no one ever does that, including any of you." And the man said, "We all call you boss, Captain. Lord, why are you talking like this?" The captain replied firmly, "I prefer to be called sir," and everybody shouted, "Yes, sir."

The captain looked at me curiously and said, "That lady who killed herself said, 'Take care, Oliver' like the other punk did. Are you some superhero or a bad guy or a leader of this group or some kind of god to protect everyone? Why do they all say your name?" I didn't know what he was up to, and replied, "I am their best friend." The captain laughed very loudly, and everyone joined with him and started to laugh, but we didn't know why they were laughing. Then the captain stopped laughing. "So you are just a friend, no special powers, boy." The captain looked at me with some concern and said, "Oliver, my new friend, I am not going to kill you and I wanted to tell you something that my father taught me: 'If you survive the waters, you will live for eternity.' So, we are going to throw you and your friends into the water. The land is twenty-three miles from here. If you make it and live, nothing can hurt you till you die. I am sorry I cannot take kids with me. It's time to say goodbye, my friend. Sorry for your lady and your friend's dad." He replaced his hat, winked, and asked his men to throw us into the water and to take our boat and all our belongings with them. Then the captain walked back to his ship.

The men grabbed us one by one and threw us into the water. Then the submarine opened the side doors, and we saw lots of boats inside, and more men inside. They handed out ropes to tie onto our boat, and a machine with a pulley connected to the ropes hoisted our boat into their ship. It was like a boa eating a chicken, and we were swimming in the water and watching our beautiful boat being taken. Then the submarine slowly started to submerge into the lake and within minutes, it left us.

As soon as they left, we started to look for Benjamin. We shouted for him but he didn't reply. We dove deep in the water to check for him, but we couldn't find him. All we found was Noa floating in the water and we thought Benjamin was dead. But then Shu said, "Did you notice when they took our boat whether the small boat was missing?" Niki was trying to keep his head above water, but he was losing his breath. He said, "What are you saying? They took everything? Oliver, do you have the locket?" And I replied to him, breathing heavily, "Yes, it is in my underwear, and Ejaz has the compass." Niki had his diary and the paper from his father wrapped in plastic wrap in his pocket, but we had lost everything else. Shu again said, "I saw the small boat was not tied to the boat," and then Ejaz joined Shu and said, "Niki, I think so too. I didn't see the boat." Aika said, "That means Benjamin should be in the boat, and he is not dead." We all became hopeful, and we started swimming together, looking for Benjamin. It was dark, and we couldn't see anything, but the moon was on our side. The clouds disappeared and we now had the light from the sky. We swam for 100 meters and found a boat floating and started to shout, "Benjamin, Benjamin!" He heard our voices and started to shout back to us. We were elated to hear his voice and we all swam and Benjamin helped us to get into the boat one by one.

We asked Benjamin what happened and how he got the boat. Benjamin said that when the submarine hit our big boat, the small boat became untied and fell into the water. "We were all thrown down and I fell into the water and was trying to climb back into the boat with the help of the fishing rod, but I couldn't reach it. Then I saw all the pirates come and surround the boat and saw my father surrender and heard the captain asking for me. I moved the small rowboat away without them noticing so that we could use the boat when they left us in the water."

Then Benjamin suddenly asked, "Where is Noa?" and we all looked down, and Aika started to cry. Benjamin understood that she didn't make it, and we said that she had killed herself. Then the boat was filled with agony and pain and everybody started crying, because we really missed her. We couldn't understand at that time what it meant. All we knew was that the captain said the word *whore.* We thought that she didn't want to go with them and had killed herself, but we were confused about why "Uncle" Kadin hadn't killed himself. It was a simple puzzle in our minds and we didn't know the answers. We were all wet, and there was cloth to dry us, we were terrified. We had seen Noa die and Uncle Kadin taken prisoner. We cried for a couple of hours, and I knew that we were in great distress, but we had to move on because we were in the middle of the water Again, we had no one to take care of us, and we were left to weep in the water.

We started to row the boat, but it was heavy, so two of us in pairs held the paddles and started to row. We could not sit and row because we didn't have the height or physique, so we stood up with two on each side and moved the boat. Then, Benjamin asked us, "Do you know where land is and which way we are going?" Madison replied, "The captain said it was twenty-three miles from here." Benjamin was shocked. "What? Twenty-three miles? Oh, Christ." I asked Ejaz for the compass and he gave it to me. I opened it to see where we were. Then I asked everyone which direction we should go and everyone gave their own opinion. Some said east, west, southeast, and so on. But we had to make a decision. Shu asked, "Oliver, which way do you think? It is your call, boy."

I didn't know which way to go, but I had looked at the map many times and the image was imprinted in my mind. I needed to make a guess because we were at the edge of our lives. It was live or die. Then, I heard a voice in my head say, "Go west," and with some firmness in my mind, I said to Benjamin, "Let's go, Benjamin. We should go west." We put the compass toward the west, and rowed and we couldn't control our boat. It went in all directions, and it took hours to make the boat steady enough to go west. We rowed by taking turns, but it didn't matter because we were all hungry, and there was no food. The only thing we had was water, and we drank lots of it to keep ourselves from dehydrating. The scorching sun was high by now, I believed it was 95 degrees that first day and it drained all our energy. I estimated we had rowed five miles. We halted in the night to rest. We were exhausted and wanted to get some sleep but the boat had no anchor. Judah realized the boat was moving, and he woke us up and said the boat was moving with the tides. We got up and checked the boat, at first, we couldn't say whether it was moving or not. We were confused because it looked like it was still, but at the same time water was being displaced.

Nikifor came up with an idea and he removed his shirt and threw it in the water. He said if we waited for some time and had moved away from the shirt, then the waves were moving us. After half an hour, the shirt was sixty meters away, and we realized we were moving. We still couldn't confirm it because the shirt was light weight and could be moving by itself, and we were eight kids in the boat and shouldn't be moving. This was not the time for physics, though, because we didn't know how the floating principle worked, but the waves were pushing us in some direction, so we didn't have time to make decisions; we just had to row constantly.

Niki wanted his shirt back but we didn't want to take any chances in the night to go looking for it. We rowed in the night, and poor Niki was cold because he had no shirt. It was the second day, and Madison and Shu were drained, feeling weak and couldn't row. I put water in my hands and fed them, but they were hungry and asked for food. Life was a great sorrow. We had no food to eat and we were all starving. Aika said that she could go deep diving and get some fish, but we stopped her because we didn't know the waters and we didn't have any equipment to catch fish. And even if she caught a fish, we didn't have a fire to cook it. No one had ever had raw food, and we didn't think it was a good idea.

Now everyone in the boat started to become weaker and weaker and no one could row the boat. The last men standing were Benjamin, Nikifor, and me, and the rest were exhausted and on the floor of the boat watching us rowing. But they were not weak in soul, they encouraged us all the time, saying, "Come on, guys, row, row." Their voices were enthusiastic for a couple of hours and then they slowly started to fade. Benjamin, Niki, and I were losing all our energy, and Niki fell to the floor, and then I fell on Niki to make sure he was warm. Within a few minutes, Benjamin fell, too. Now the boat was on its own. It could go anywhere it wished and we could not control it. The sun went down and all our senses started to turn off. That night we all slept, dying of hunger. Then we heard a bombing sound, and in our deep sleep, we knew that there was a war taking place. But that night passed with no shells or bombs falling on our boat, and we were still safe.

The morning brought the sun to the horizon, and while sleeping, I heard sweet music playing. It was so good; I opened my eyes and saw that everyone was still lying down. Then, with a little strength, I got up to see who was playing the music. With my eyes half open, I couldn't see anyone and I thought it was an illusion of sound, but then I saw some fish floating on the water. The sight didn't click anything in my mind, but then I quickly realized it was food to eat. I saw there were tons of fish floating in the water all around the boat. I woke everybody up, calling their names, but no one woke up. I checked whether they were breathing, and everyone was. Slowly I heard a voice saying, "Hmm, hmm," and I saw Ejaz was moving. I shook his body to wake him up. He got up surprised and started to blabber, "Am I dead? Am I dead?" I comforted him that he was still alive and we had food to eat, he became excited and said, "I need food. Where is it?" and started to crawl on the boat. Then I asked him to wake everyone, and slowly everyone got up with eyes half open and I said we had food. Everyone was eager to see the food, and I showed them dead floating fish. Everybody was happy, but the question came about how we would prepare and eat them.

We were all hungry, and the fish were there before our eyes, but no one knew what to do. After a couple of hours, Aika grabbed a fish, and with a small knife in her pocket, she cleaned it, removed the scales and bones, washed it clean and started to eat it. While eating, she said, "It is yummy, tasty," and she kept enjoying it and ate the whole fish. We looked at her like a cannibal and asked her, "How could you eat that?" She was the one who gave a wise answer: "Remember that sushi my mom made for us? You know sushi is raw fish. Just try eating it like you enjoyed the sushi." We told her, "But that sushi your mom made had avocado, rice, spices, and something with it," and she replied, "Think of it as being there and just enjoy what is in your mouth."

We hesitated and said to each other that we would rather die than eat fish like that. Aika then caught another fish and started to clean it and gave it to us and said, "Eat, or else you will all die, and I will be the one going to New York City with that locket, and Nathalie will be ashamed and disappointed that you all died for ignoring what was before you." Hearing this motivational speech, Madison took the fish and started to eat. Initially she pushed it out of her mouth, but Aika was encouraging. "It is tasty, Madison, just swallow it." Madison had a hard time, but she started to eat everything, and Aika started to get more fish and clean them and we all ate the raw fish from Lake Michigan. We collected all the dead fish and started to row west to the land. We didn't know many miles we had gone back, but we had food and spirit in our hearts to row the boat. We were champs and we started to sing songs and praise and row the boat with great speed. The fish were there for a mile, we didn't know where they came from, but we knew they were dead and some were in pieces. We realized there had been a bombing the previous night that killed the fish in the water. We thanked the bomb for killing the fish and not killing us.

We rowed faster and faster to make sure we reached land before the fish were gone. We started getting blisters on our palms and it was painful, we washed them in water and tore our shirts in half to tie the cloth over our hands to row. The harsh wind was on one side, the sun's heat came from the sky, and the water's current was strong, but the spirit in us was stronger than the forces of nature. We rowed for three days and nights and got closer and closer to land. On the third day, Judah and I saw land far away and yelled to everybody but no one else could see it properly. We said that we saw the land, but no one believed it, so we started to row faster and faster, and gradually everyone could see the land. We hugged each other and started dancing in the boat, and Niki, Aika, and Benjamin jumped in the water and started swimming. The rest of us rowed vigorously, and we shouted and screamed deliriously.

As we got closer, we saw two guards with guns, who also saw us. The guys in the water were swimming and didn't notice them. We just kept rowing. But as we got closer, Benjamin noticed the guards and stopped swimming and called to Aika and Niki to stop. Benjamin asked to stop the boat and the three in the water got in. We asked him why he wanted to stop and he said there were guards on the coast. I said to him, "What is the problem? We could say that our boat was stolen, they took your father, and they will help us." But Benjamin's face turned suspicious and scared, and he said, "There is something wrong. I don't feel good about them." I asked Benjamin, "So, what, you want to turn back?" and he replied, "There is no way out. They will catch us anyway. If they ask what happened, we will say that we went for a summer vacation and the pirates took my father and our boat and that Noa killed herself, but we can't say anything about New York City." I replied to him, "Well, we know that, but summer vacation is cool." Benjamin said, "One more thing, guys. We don't have any paper ID or RFID, so Madison, you don't have anyone. Oliver, Judah, Ejaz and Shu, you too. They will take us to verify us, and they may think that we crossed Canada's border as illegal immigrants, so be very careful."

I was very anxious about what was happening and why he was telling us all this. "Benjamin, why are you telling us this? We know that." He replied to me, "Well, we are on the other side of the water, and if they do a routine check, cops will be involved, and they will take you separately and inquire, so we should play it safe." I was surprised by his understanding about the police and asked him, "How do you know all this?" and he smiled proudly and said, "I come from a family of cops. My father taught me."

Then Benjamin asked Ejaz, "Do you have any fingerprints at your local police station?" Ejaz quickly replied, "No," but Benjamin asked him again. "Ejaz, think and tell me, because if they find you, they will take you and hand you over to the security services because you are a witness to a mass murder." Ejaz panicked and became nervous and started to scratch his head. He said, "I remember, Benjamin that my father said that when I turned five, he should take me to the local police station and get registered, but he never had time and finally died. I am very positive I don't have any." Then Benjamin asked him, "Did you have a given blood sample confirmation when you were born." We didn't know what that was, and Benjamin explained that the mother and father have to give a child's blood sample to legally attest that it is their own kid, and is as important as the birth certificate. Ejaz replied, "I think so," and Benjamin held his head and said, "Well, they may know who you are, but do a good job of pretending you are an orphan. Please curse them, your mother and father, for throwing you in the garbage so they will not check rather than give you a new identity." Ejaz became emotional. "My father didn't do that. He loved me and my mother, too." We all felt bad, and Shu held his hands and said, "It is all for your own good, Ejaz, you know that. Please do it."

Then Benjamin told us some weird thing we didn't know until now, and he scared us. "They will ask us whether we have had a DNA test. Just say no. They will insist, but tell him that you hate your parents, who abandoned you and don't want them to know who you are. This is very important for Madison and Ejaz, because your parents would have already had it. Aika, Nikifor, and I are good. We will manage it and will tell the truth. Oliver, Judah, and Shu, you guys shouldn't have any problem." Madison asked, "Benjamin, if they force us, what should we do?" and Benjamin replied, "They cannot. They can track your genealogy by law without your permission, but not your mother and father until you approve it." Madison smiled and replied, "Got it, pal." I said to Benjamin with great appreciation, "Oh, man, you know everything. Did your father have this problem?" And Benjamin replied, "He knew and taught me before we left how to evade and get around these things. He taught me in case he was lost or killed, so I would know and could protect you and myself." At that moment we all felt very proud of Uncle Kadin and Benjamin, because without them, we would have either been killed or tortured.

As we approached the shore we saw the two guards talking on a wireless device and heard choppers flying over us. We heard lots of men shouting, and they came from behind the trees and covered the coast. We also heard the screeching sound of metal scratching and we saw there were twenty robots, each almost 150 feet high. We heard a warning voice from a chopper asking us to stay calm in the boat. We were terrified and our hearts were beating fast as we stared at the coast looking at the giant robots. Then a guard came down from the chopper on a rope and got into our boat. He sighed and said, "You are safe now, kids. Relax." The chopper dropped a huge net, and the bottom went into the water, the sides spread wide, and the guard rowed the boat inside it. The chopper lifted a little higher and the nets under the water held the boat. The chopper lifted us and started to fly. This was the first time any of us had been in the air and our heads were wobbling. The guard in the boat said, "Easy, guys, you are safe. Just relax." He asked us to take a deep breath and not look down.

Just a couple of minutes later, we landed on land. There were many cops and guards who came running to remove the net and let us out. We got out of the boat and we looked at the giant robots, and they were looking at us like they wanted to pick a fight. They had flame throwers on their shoulders, red eyes, big breasts of armor with some power source in the center and a light that was moving around their bodies.

They had rotor guns with big bullets running like train tracks into their backs. The guards were giving instructions to them and they were answering in a human voice tone.

Women guards gave us coats because all our shirts were torn; nurses were cleaning the blisters on our hands, applying medication, and covering them with cotton and gauze. We didn't notice until the nurses told us that our hands were hurt so badly, because all we knew when we were in the boat was that we had to reach land. We asked them where we were, and the nurse said it was Hammond Bay. There was an elderly man, who looked to be in his late fifties, with a gray beard, sun glasses, and dressed in a G10 white uniform with all the stars from the sky on his shoulders. He walked toward us and looked at us kindly and asked, "What happened, kids? What are you doing in the boat?" Benjamin started explaining about the summer vacation, his dad being kidnapped, and Noa killing herself. The elderly man was quietly listening to our stories, and he asked what the pirate looked like and about the conversation with Benjamin's dad. Benjamin revealed who his father was and the elderly man ran something on his E-gadget and confirmed it. He believed that we were genuine travelers and not trespassers from the borders, he asked for our ID, but none of us had one. We asked the officer who the pirates were and the officer said their captain was Sariel Dipster. We now knew the name of the pirate who had attacked, and we would find him one day and save Benjamin's father. They ordered the troops to find and spread the news about the vandalism, murder, and kidnapping of innocent people by "Sariel Dipster, the Canadian sea ghost." Then he instructed his men to take us to the local police station for verification and questioning.

They put us all into a van. We were skeptical about where they were taking us and asked the cop, and they replied that they were taking us to the police station. We had the expected feeling of someone who knows they are being taken to the police station: "What did I do and what are they going to do to me?" It was a few miles from the lake, and they took us inside. As we walked in, everyone looked at us with curiosity, like "What did these little ones do to be in the police station?" The cops asked what happened and who we were. They took us to the lieutenant's office and informed him that we were there, and left us there with two cops and the lieutenant, for questioning.

The lieutenant smiled and said, "It looks like you guys are lost. What can I do for you?" I knew he was trying to pull words from our mouths, and I replied, "We need some food and shelter," and the lieutenant shook his head. "Okay, that is a reasonable request, but none of you have ID and families—that is where the problem starts. It seems you guys had a vacation and were robbed and thrown into the water. Oh, my, son. My name is Carl. What is your name?" I answered him, "Oliver," and because we didn't want to give him any suspicious thoughts, Nikifor quickly jumped up and said, "I have a grandma and grandpa living in Milwaukee." The lieutenant asked, "What about your parents?" and Niki explained about his father and his divorce and gave him his grandpa's home number. The lieutenant made a quick call, but he was not smart enough and made a mistake when he spoke to Nikifor's grandparents, giving away a hint about what had happened, which Niki's grandmother picked up from there.

Lieutenant Carl: Hello, miss, my name is Lieutenant Carl and we are calling you to report that your grandson got lost and was robbed on his vacation. His friend's mom was killed, and another was taken as prisoner by the pirates.

(Nikifor's grandma had a vision that nothing could harm us and knew what was happening, so she played the game well, sobbing and panicking.)

Nikifor's grandma: Oh, I am very sorry to hear that. Is Niki okay? Is he hurt? He went for a vacation with his friends and their family.

Lieutenant Carl: Did you file a missing-person report about a lost grandson?

Nikifor's grandma: Talk slowly, officer. I am not able to understand.

Lieutenant Carl: Did you file a missing-person report of a lost grandson?

(His grandma didn't answer the question)

Lieutenant Carl: Okay. Did he call you every day?

Nikifor's grandma: What did you say? "Do I need to call you back?"

Lieutenant Carl, muting the phone: Oh, Christ!

He again spoke slowly into the phone, word by word.

Lieutenant Carl: Okay. Did he call you every day?

Nikifor's grandma: Do you want me to call you every day? Why?

Lieutenant Carl: Not me, lady, your grandson.

Nikifor's grandma: No, why should he? You know his father died last year, he was so depressed, I sent him away to be happy with his friends. While on vacation, you should forget your family. Same as you Lieutenant, when you have a secret girlfriend on vacation with you and you forget your wife back home.

Lieutenant Carl laughed loud, muted his phone, and looked at Niki. "Your grandma is so funny. She's really funny."

Nikifor's grandma: Are my son's and our family friend's death is funny to you? Are you crazy?

Lieutenant Carl: Oh no, no, no. I said that about the girlfriend and my wife.

Nikifor's grandma: That is how life works, officer.

Lieutenant Carl: Could you tell me the name of his friends, please?

Nikifor grandma: Hmm. let's see. Oliver, Madison? Yes, Madison. Right, umm, Ejaz, Judah, and . . .

While she was thinking, he muted the phone and asked us our names and we told, and he confirmed it with grandma's statement. You only said four names, but there are three more kids. Do you know the parents of the other kids?

Nikifor grandma: Do you want three more kids with your wife?

Hearing this, the Lieutenant became annoyed and banged his head on the desk and said, "What the hell is happening here?" We were all nervous because she didn't know anything about Aika, Shu, Benjamin, Noa, or Uncle Kadin, but she acted smart, saying the phone line was bad and she couldn't hear and understand, and then Shu jumped up.

Shu: Officer, she has some hearing problems. Talk slowly to her.

Lieutenant Carl: I am talking slowly, kiddo. Well, you can try harder if you want.

Shu: Hello, Grandma, it's Shu. How are you?

Nikifor's grandma: Lieutenant, why are you changing your voice now?

Lieutenant Carl: She needs a new hearing aid, man!

Shu: Hello, Grandma, it's Shu. How are you?

Nikifor's grandma: Oh, my God, Shu, how are you, sweetheart?

Shu: I am good. They are asking about Benjamin's father, Kadin, and Aika's mom, Noa.

Nikifor grandma: Oh, I didn't get it. Let me pass the phone to Niki's grandpa.

Then the lieutenant took the phone and asked the same questions of Nikifor's grandpa, and Niki's grandpa answered, telling their names. This time, the lieutenant was convinced that Nikifor had a family. The big problem we had was that no one had radio-frequency identification, or RFID. If we had had one, everything would have been easy. Then the lieutenant asked about Benjamin and whether he could confirm his identity and the same for Aika. They confirmed it with blood samples for Aika, Benjamin, and Nikifor. But the other five of us were left to answer questions, and they asked us where we were from and how we became friends. Lie after lie, we made them believe that we were born orphans and homeless, and that Niki's family, Noa, and Kadin were the ones who took care of us.

Because Benjamin's grandfather's name was on the good-cop list, they didn't screw around much. Judah, Shu, and I didn't know anything about our parents and we told them that one true fact. But when it was Madison's and Ejaz's turns, they had a harder time saying they didn't know their parents. Somehow, for Madison, it was not that hard. But for Ejaz, it was tough and he had to get all the details right that Benjamin taught him, that he didn't know them and didn't want to know them. They asked about some homeless people we knew in Milwaukee, and we gave Uncle Tim as a reference. The cops sent a few cops immediately to check at Kern Park where Uncle Tim and the other homeless people lived. We didn't know where he got his enlightenment, but he lied the way we expected, and he said to the cops that they raised us and Niki's family adopted all of us from them. And everyone from Tim's homeless community supported his lies and convinced them of our date of birth and past. Finally, somehow, we proved that we were Americans born in this damn country.

The cops wanted us to register and enroll our identity. They took blood samples and DNA tests for genealogy identification. The results came back one by one: Madison was German-Hungarian, Ejaz was Persian, Judah was Jewish, Shu was Chinese, and me, well, they said I was of British blood. They pulled the records for the others: Benjamin was an African, Nikifor was Russian, and Aika was Japanese. Once they had these records, they filled out forms for us to get birth certificates and IDs. The forms were filled out by a cop in his mid-fifties, with a chubby face and a smooth voice. Benjamin, Niki, and Aika had no problem going through it because they had information about who they were. But when it came to us, we had a problem. We didn't know anything, not even our last names. They asked Ejaz's last name. His actual last name was Ali, but he didn't want to get into trouble, so he changed it to Khan, Ejaz Khan. When it came to Shu, she knew it because Noa named her Shu Cong, and she gave that name. The worst among everyone was Judah, who said he didn't have a last name. The man looked at Judah and said, "Sorry, kid. Do you want me to pick a name for you?" Judah was clueless and didn't know anything about it, and he replied, "Let me stay with one name. I think one is better than two." The cop nodded and replied to him, "As you wish, sir. - done!"

Then my turn came. I gave my first name, but by the time he was about to ask my last name another cop walked to his desk and asked him some details and he was busy talking. I was looking at the big-screen TV and there was a show on about the Oscar awards. I was watching it and liked it. It was about the history of the Oscar awards. Madison was standing next to me watching me. The cop finished talking with his peers and got back to work and asked me, "What is your last name?" I didn't hear him because I was busy watching the screen, so he asked again, "Oliver, what is your last name?" I was still busy watching; he looked up and saw me looking at the screen. "Oliver, Oliver?" I heard someone calling me and realized it was him and replied, "Yes, sir?" He asked me, "Do you like movies?" and I replied to him, "Not much. I liked the documentary on the screen." He said, "We have to complete this form. What is your last name?" and there was Madison, who answered, "Oscar."

He looked at Madison. "Are you, Oliver, miss?" and she replied, "No, his last name is Oscar." Then he turned and looked at me again and asked, "Is your last name Oscar?" and I got angry. Where was this name coming from? I looked at Madison and she squeezed my hand, went cross-eyed, and grimaced at me and said, "Your name is Oliver Oscar." I didn't know what was happening, so I just agreed, saying, "Yeah, it is Oscar." Then the cop started filling in the form and I turned again and looked at Madison. She lifted both her eyebrows, whispering, "Oscar, Oscar, Oscar." Though I was a mad at her, the way she looked was cute and I could never be mad at her for long. She loved me, and I heard a whispering in my ears, "Madison named you—just go for it."

I was convinced with that name, but I didn't know what Oscar meant. I wanted to get revenge on Madison, and I got my turn. Now it was Madison's turn to tell her details, and when the cop asked what her last name was, I quickly replied before she opened her mouth, "Stacey." She got mad and looked and frowned, and I smiled at her. The cop was a little troubled and looked at me and said, "Son, this is not the place to play. Why are you answering for her?" I replied, "I didn't mean to insult you, officer. She did that to me, and I did it to her." I squeezed her hand as she had mine, and the cop said, "All right, what is your last name, miss?" and she replied, "Stacey." She turned and looked at me fiercely and said, "You shouldn't have done that." I wasn't bothered in the least and turned my face from her. An eye for an eye and I was happy that Madison was now named Madison Stacey. This was the baptism and name ceremony for us, and it was kind of exciting now that we had false IDs. Thank God they didn't run a background check on Ejaz or Madison.

Then they took a photo of each of us and attached the photo to the papers and gave the original papers to us. Then they asked Ejaz, Judah, Madison, Shu, and me to run a trace of the DNA to track our parents. We knew that by law we could refuse, and we did exactly as Benjamin had told us. The only reason we gave was "They rejected us for some reason, and we don't want to know them or go back to them." They agreed, but we had a feeling something was wrong. They asked us to get the high-tech tattoo or RFID, and we refused it, saying we wanted to live solitary lives. At this point the cop was not convinced, but he knew by law, they could not force us. Since we were kids and war was out there, they didn't care so much and let us go.

But trouble and hindrance followed us and Nikifor was called in and told to go and live with his grandparents. He denied, saying he was happy to stay with us. We didn't know what was happening, and they called his grandparents again to ask them to take Niki. They said it was his choice and they were happy for him to stay with his friends.

Now the question was "Stay where?" The TUAD, "The Uncared for And Deserted." The cops wanted to take us to TUAD because we were not yet sixteen and we had to be under some parental or public control. TUAD was not just a foster home. It was an organization that found the talent and potential in the kids living there to use for their benefit in the war and made them work for the government. Some parents who were middle class also took their kids to TUAD and made an agreement with the organization for a 90-to-10 percentage—90 percent for the government and 10 percent for the family and kids—if the kid invented or discovered an idea. The big drawback was that the kids and their families had no choice over this business deal and it all belonged to the government to make their choices and calls. TUAD is a highly funded organization, and the whole thing was just a scam to exploit the uncared for and deserted.

They took us in a van and drove us to the TUAD institute near Mullet Lake called Hoplite. As we were driving, we were all upset and didn't know what to do. We couldn't even talk to each other because there were cops around, watching us. We reached the gates of our first school, Hoplite, and they were huge—almost three-hundred feet high, made of metal and fully covered in iron plate with a logo of an eagle snatching a star. The cop stopped the van near the gates, and the guards from the school, carrying heavy guns, inspected the van and let us in. The campus was huge and the driveway was long. It was a two-way street and in the road divider, they had flowers, trees, models, and prototypes of space crafts, machines, ammunitions, and modern-day collections of technology gadgets. Although it looked very nice and interesting, we were not happy about it, because something was missing, although we didn't know what it was.

We reached the school building and got down from the van. The building looked like a modern state-of-the-art castle. We walked inside and it was filled with technology artifacts, and in the walls they had screens where a small intro movie about TUAD was playing. Kids were walking with small tables, on the ceilings were laser lights and the whole place was neat and tidy. We walked to the enrollment room to register. We gave our birth certificate copies and our IDs. They asked for our RFIDs, but we didn't have them, which they were not comfortable about.

After the enrollment, they took us for inspection and a medical test. Again, they took a blood sample, all the results were positive. Then they checked our belongings to the clerk who was working in the school. We had nothing to check in except for a locket, a compass, and a diary with a chart. I didn't realize at the time that I still had the little metal dragon inside my pants pocket. The clerk looked at the locket and wanted to open it, and I tried to stop him, but he insisted. I persisted and said no again, and he asked me why, and I said, "It is from my best friend and he made me promise not to open it until my day comes." The clerk was an absolute jerk and replied, "It is your day, not my day." He was about to open it, but

I snatched it from his hand, and he grew angry. He raised his eyebrow and looked at me angrily and asked me to give it to him, and I refused.

A guard who was passing by saw what was happening, and he walked over to us. The guard was a very reasonable man. He understood what was happening and said to the clerk, "Leave that boy alone. It is his favorite locket." But the clerk was adamant and wanted to check what was in it, and when the guard asked the reason, the clerk said, "There may be some bomb or chemical that could kill us." The guard asked me for the locket, and I gave it to him. He looked at the outside and didn't open it and said, "It looks like an old artifact, probably a thousand years old. Leave the poor boy alone. He had nothing else with him expect this locket. Scan the locket and check it in."

The clerk asked the guard to mind his own business, but the guard got angry at his statement and warned the clerk that, by law, he could not open it. The clerk replied to him, "On demand we can open and check anything, we have all the rights," but the guard replied back, "That is public transportation, at the airport, on the roads, this is an institution for kids, and they are homeless. We brought them here. They didn't come here on their own and you have no right to force them." The clerk got mad at this time and wanted to call his supervisor, but the guard threatened the clerk, "You lunatic. If you create a problem, I will put a bullet in your head and walk away. I know you steal things from the kids who come here by threatening and lying to them. You are trying to do that to this kid now and I will deal with you right away." The clerk was scared and let me go with the locket and little dragon. The guard waited until we had all checked in. Judah had the compass, and the clerk didn't even open his mouth. He just let us go.

The clerk signed for and acknowledged our belongings and the guard made sure we left the room safely. As we went out, I wanted to know his name, so I asked him, and he said his name was Moise Boti and I introduced myself to him. He looked like a very good man, and everyone introduced themselves to Moise. We thanked him for his help, and he was not bothered and replied, "Just straightening things out." Then he took us to the clothing room where they gave us five pairs of navy blue pants and sky blue shirts, which was for school. They gave us casual pants, shirts, T-shirts, trousers, undergarments, shoes and socks. We took the pants and shirts that fitted us, and they gave us digital-fingerprint-locked suitcases to keep our belongings in. Then they took us to the bathroom to take showers and dress ourselves, and the maids and the nannies helped us. We all got dressed up in new outfits.

They then took the boys and the girls to separate dormitories. The girl's dormitory was in the building opposite from us, and from our floor, we could see the entrance of the building. They introduced us as the new members of the school, and some kids smiled, and others didn't.

The room looked like a big hall, with fifty bunk beds in it. There was a warden who took us to our beds in the same row. Ejaz and Judah had one bunk bed; next to them was Benjamin and mine, and poor Niki had to share with another kid next to me.

It was late evening, and they took us to the dining room, where there were hundreds of kids, all were under twelve, waiting to eat supper. They introduced all of us and all the other kids in the dining room. We said our names and it was the first time I said my full name, Oliver Oscar. Everybody welcomed us and clapped their hands and the head warden welcomed us, saying, "Welcome to the TUAD family."

We all sat at one table and said a prayer, and the prayer started with, "Dear God." We didn't know the rest, but everyone else knew the prayer well. After the prayer we all sat down to eat. But we couldn't eat the food, not because it was bad, but because we were frightened and clueless about what was going on. After supper we went to the dormitory and some kids spoke to us and shared their names.

We all went to bed that night not talking to anyone because there were other kids around. We were sorry for Nikifor because he was with some kid in the top bunk, whose name was Urson. The first night passed with silence and I got some good sleep. The next day, a bell rang at six in the morning, and the kids got up, but we didn't know and were still sleeping. We thought it was a dream and were sleeping, and all the kids were lined up before their beds except us. Urson was whistling to wake Niki; nevertheless, we even thought the whistle was a dream.

Well, someone had to wake all the Rip Van Winkles. The warden walked over to us and gently called our names, but even the names sounded like they were coming from heaven in our dreams. The volume of his voice increased every time he called us, and we could hear a loud voice with some giggling in our ears. Something went to my mind, and I woke up and saw the red face of the warden, and he greeted me, "Welcome to the real world." I looked with my eyes wide open and said, "Good morning." He didn't mind my greeting and said, "Buckets," and a few kids ran to get buckets. They came with four buckets of water, and the warden took them and poured them on Benjamin, Ejaz, Judah and Nikifor. It was not a bed shower, it was a kick he wanted to give my poor friends and they woke with great trouble. All the kids in the room laughed out loud, and none of them knew what had happened. But Nikifor got angry and stood against the warden and asked him, "Why the hell did you pour water on me?" Hearing this and looking at Nikifor with an angry face, everyone became quiet. The warden was mad and asked Niki, "What did you say?" Nikifor never went quiet, and he raised his chest, nostrils open, and said, "Why the hell did you pour water on me?" Now who was the tough guy, huh? Not the warden. He saw in Niki's eyes that he was angry and tough, and he backed off and said, "I think we have a problem. Could we walk to the administration officer, son?"

Nikifor was taken to the administration office and the officer was called Peyton Walters, the one soul that should never have been born on this planet. He was in his early thirties, a short man with a French beard, and long curly hair. The warden told him everything that had happened and Peyton asked for the file on Nikifor and went through it. He asked Nikifor why he was rude, and Niki politely explained everything that had happened and made the point that the treatment to wake kids up was wrong. He was not bothered by the thin line between justice and kindness because the warden was his colleague, and they were all one big gang. He ordered that Niki be put in a dark room for a week, for rehabilitation.

Niki was broken and cried when they took him to that dark room, not because he was scared, but because of the injustice. He felt Peyton should help him but everyone drowned him in the abyss of their games. The room was twenty square feet, and it had a night lamp and a window with no lights coming in but air for breathing. There was a toilet attached to the room that was not well maintained. He was in the dark room for a week in agony, pain, and loneliness, which cannot be explained.

A few days passed, and it was Sunday, we had to go to church. Although there was a mosque in TUAD, Ejaz wanted to go with us, we got up early and prepared for the seven o'clock service. We all went to pray to God to strengthen Niki, and that is a day we will not forget, because what happened left us in complete confusion. The pastor read the Bible passage, and it was Psalm 23. As he read, we heard the prayer taught to us, "Though I walk through. . ." We were all stunned and didn't know what to say. Was Nathalie a Christian? Where did she come from? Was she an angel? Until that point, none of us knew it was from the Bible, not even Benjamin, who was Catholic, although he didn't know much about the Bible. But we were happy she had taught us the prayer from the most famous book.

I prayed to Jesus sincerely that day and asked him to help us go on the mission and to help Niki in his hard times. But the only thought that went through my mind was why she had taught us that prayer and why it always worked? Should we believe in God, who called his people Christians, or was Nathalie a messenger from this very God? We didn't know at this point. All we saw, felt, and believed in was Nathalie and her words. We would keep our vows to her and do as she said: "Stop this war, and restore peace in humanity."

That whole week, we were all very worried about what was happening to Niki, we didn't eat properly and were all moody and thoughtful about him. A week passed, and we all went to see him when he was set free from the dark room. We waited for an hour until they opened the main door of the chambers of the room. We were all expecting him to come out with a sad and gloomy face, feeling crummy and dejected. But he came out like a champ, with a smiley face filled with energy and positivity. Officer Peyton and all his associates were also with us, and they were so confused by what had happened to him. I realized one fact: we never know how anyone will react in different situations, and the more you know someone, the more surprise is waiting for you. Niki walked out swiftly and greeted Peyton, "Good morning, officer," and then walked to us. Peyton couldn't stand there anymore. He was also a lunatic, and he was expecting Niki to be sad and asking for forgiveness, but that never happened. He looked hard at Niki and walked away with displeasure.

We were all so thrilled to see Niki back that day and we walked to the park to talk to him. We asked him how the dark room was, and he replied, "Awesome." Then Niki told the whole story. He was scared inside that room when they put him in, and he cried for hours, until all the tears were emptied from his body. Then he remembered Nathalie's powerful prayer and he said it three times. He saw a light touching his eyes and saw his father was sitting before him. All his sorrow vanished without a memory or trace, and he put his head on his father's lap and told him how much he missed him. The whole week he spent talking to his father, who came and visited him for five to six hours a day. He told him all the things that had happened on the journey until we got into TUAD. His father's only advice was to stay firm and strong in this journey and never give up.

Nikifor's story sounded like a fairy tale and we couldn't believe it, but we knew he would not lie to us, and we were happy that he had met his loving father. The next day, Niki's grandparents were asked to come to TUAD. They flew in and came to see Niki, and Peyton asked that they take Niki with them because he felt insulted by the way Niki behaved when he came out of the dark room. But Niki refused to go with his grandparents. Peyton told them about all the things wrong with Niki and wanted to get rid of him. Peyton knew he needed to have strong proof to get rid of a kid, so that was the reason he was playing games with Niki's grandparents. Moreover, the grandparents had a revelation in their minds and knew no harm would come to Niki.

Niki's grandparents gave some gifts and money to Peyton as a "cumshaw," which they called it instead of calling it a bribe, to make him quite. He took the gifts and money, but his ego was not yet soothed. Niki's grandparents told Peyton that no matter what happened here, they didn't want to be called and they would not take Niki home. We were all joyful to see Niki's grandparents and they were pleased to see

Madison, Judah, Ejaz and me. We had grown taller now, and Niki's grandparents had brought new pants and shirts for us. They also brought cookies, cakes, ice creams, candies and chocolates. We introduced Shu, Aika and Benjamin, and they were glad that we had new friends. They hadn't known anything except their names in the phone call about the new friends and didn't have any pants or shirts for them. Leaving us there in TUAD with Nikifor's grandma, his grandpa went to buy pants and shirts for the new friends. Niki told them about the whole journey, and they were thrilled and listened to it.

That evening we spent with Niki's grandparents and we were uplifted that there was someone we knew well to spend time with us. They left that evening, and we were back by ourselves in this wild world. Peyton had his grudge against Niki, and because we were Niki's best friends, he didn't like us either. We started to go to school in TUAD and learn lessons. They were teaching us about science and technology and nothing more than that. There were history and geography classes, but it was always linked with science and technology. Mathematics was the fundamental of all the classes, and we were trained like intelligent robots who didn't know the difference between a donkey and a dog. All the kids played 4D video games for a hobby, and TUAD encouraged these crazy video games because there was so much competition going on between every country, like an Olympics. We played a few video games with our friends, we played funny and simple ones, but all the other kids played the games involving war and killing.

Somehow, looking at the kids, we started to hate video games and the very idea of them; we felt we lost the value of humanity. Niki woke up when the bell rang and didn't take any chances. But Peyton wanted to find some mistake with Niki and was waiting for his chance. We learned everything well, whatever they taught. But every day, we found there was a difference in the way they treated us. We learned that the kids who didn't have an RFID were always watched, and no proper attention or treatment was given to them. This was not specific to TUAD. It came from the world government that was how it worked. It was very simple: if you were part of the cult, then you should have your tattoo; otherwise everything in this world would go wrong for you.

The first few months passed and things were not that smooth and we were not happy here in this zoo. The second time Niki was sentenced to be in the dark room was again because he didn't wake up in the morning. He fell asleep one day and they knew how to make a mad dog angry, so they poured cold water on him again. He got mad, and they took this as a chance to put him in the dark room for another week. When he was released, he came out with the same smile and smooth vicious greeting to Peyton, "Good morning, Officer Peyton." He aggravated him more this time, and he wanted to send him one more time to the dark room to teach him. Peyton mixed some sleeping pills into Niki's milk that made him sleep late, which allowed him to send him to the dark room a third time. This time, it was for ten days, but Niki was not shaken, and he was more happy in that dark room than sleeping on his couch or with us. He came out with the same smile and grateful greeting: "Good morning, Officer Peyton."

Peyton's nerves couldn't be controlled and he ordered Niki to be taken for psychiatric treatment. Now he had a different plan. He wanted to prove that Niki was insane and put him in a mental institution. The child psychiatrist was Dr. Victor Klaus, a very honest and God-fearing man. Niki explained everything that happened and that Peyton was doing this to him, but he never said anything about his father to the doctor. Dr. Victor asked Niki to stay there in the hospital for a week for examination. Dr. Victor knew about Peyton and his personality, and after a week, he called Peyton and Niki in for a meeting.

Victor: I see no problem with Niki. He is completely normal.

Peyton: Doctor, did you examine him properly? He is one insane kid, if ever I've seen one.

Victor: Mr. Walters, don't tell me how to do my job. What makes you think Niki is insane?

Peyton: Well, he gets angry and starts to yell at the warden and wants to fight with him, when the warden is just doing his job to wake him. So, to control his anger and teach some discipline, we put him in the dark room. But when he comes out, he smiles and is happy. There is no self-realization, he is insane. I have never seen any kid come out happy with a smile. He acts like nothing has happened.

Victor: Do you have any comments about that, Niki, please?

Niki: He said I was angry with the warden and he wanted to teach me a lesson, so he put me in the dark room. Then I realized myself and came out happy and joyful, with no more anger or rage. Is that Mr. Peyton's problem, for me to have the same anger and rage when I come out? If yes, doctor, please examine Peyton first.

Dr. Victor laughed out loud.

Dr. Victor: He has a point, Peyton.

Peyton was completely mad and pretended to behave like nothing happened.

Peyton: Okay, cool, Doctor. I will take your word, but I will teach this kid a lesson.

Dr. Victor: Let me tell you something, Peyton: this problem was reported to me, and I have documented everything. If you pour water on this kid when he is sleeping again and he goes to that dark room one more time, and if by any chance he is really affected by it, then I have to complain to law enforcement, and you will be out of this freaking job and behind bars.

Peyton didn't realize until now how serious the issue could be, he left quickly. Niki thanked Dr. Victor for his help and the doctor advised him to stay away from Peyton. Niki was out of the hospital and was proven to be normal. Guess what happened next? He slept until eight in the morning, and neither the morning bell nor the warden had control over him. He slept like a prince every day and all the kids envied him.

We had our exams soon and were preparing very hard for them. Ejaz came in with this one very strange idea, which changed our whole lives afterward. He said that if we did well in our exams, they would make us stay here. Then we would have to stay until we were sixteen and we shouldn't do it. We wanted to go to New York City and that was our mission.

Madison: What do you mean, if we do well, Ejaz? Do you want us to fail the exams?

Ejaz: Yes, and we need to get the lowest scores.

Madison: But we know our subjects well. How could we not do well?

Ejaz: Do not write anything on the exam, select all the wrong answers. Then we are good.

Aika: It doesn't make sense to fail the exam.

Me: Ejaz is right. If we study hard, we are going to stay here for a long time and will never get to New York City.

Aika: Oliver, are you out of your mind? If we don't study, we become fools.

Ejaz: I didn't say don't study. Study well, but don't pass the exam.

Me: Learn and don't show it. That's what Nathalie says all the time. Learn science and technology well, but never use it to go to New York City. Only use it when the time comes. You are smart, Ejaz.

Ejaz became very proud and said, Thanks, Oliver.

So we all decided not to pass the exams and we did exactly as we decided. When the exam results came back, we had all failed and received an F grade. I thought at that time that we had been successful in our attempt in that we all failed. But we selected the second-best answers and the teachers thought we would do better next time. So, we decided we should select the last-best answers the next time to make sure we looked like complete idiots. But to select that answer, we needed to know everything about the subject, so we learned everything very well. It was only sad that we couldn't prove it. Failing all the things we knew gave us some wisdom and calmness in our minds, and we looked at ourselves as being different and unique compared with the other kids who wanted better grades.

It was the end of the first year at the school, but the fight with Peyton never let up, and he tried the whole time to corner us. Peyton did all his cheap stuff. He made the laundrymen not wash our clothes in time, and we had to wear old stinky clothes sometimes. In the name of inspection, he would come and turn out our boxes and lockers. We were blamed first for anything that happened, we were given unclean plates, spoons, and knives for eating, and he didn't allow us to talk to each other after the lights went off. He did all the things that he could to give us a hard time and we swallowed it as much as we could. Now we had the final exam for the second grade, and we learned everything well, but as we had planned, we selected all the best wrong answers. The funny thing about the exam was that we knew that we were going to select the wrong answers, but we still made our faces into an expression, as if we were thinking very deeply for the answers.

The results came in, and we all failed, and now came the real output of the master plan that we followed. They took all of us to the principal's room, which was glossy, and had big round conference tables. At the table were our teachers, Peyton, and the warden, as well as some committee members. We all sat at the conference table nervously. They started to discuss why we didn't fare well on the exams, but the biggest mystery for them was how all eight of us could be so dumb. Except for Peyton, everyone's face was curious and had a helping attitude, but Peyton was enjoying the show. He was the only bad dog at the table, waiting for his chance to bite us.

They asked us about the problems we were having learning, and we bluffed a lot. We said we had never been to school in our lives and this was the first time. We said we could understand the subject in the class, but on the day of exams, we got confused and nervous. They had the exam papers and went through them and, when looking at our answers, decided we had some serious problems. They gave us some options to provide extra coaching and tutoring, and we agreed, to make sure they were comfortable and knew that we were making some efforts. But no matter who the teacher was or how much time we spent with them, we were going to fail the exams. The board and the members discussed this and decided it was because it was our first year in school, and they moved us from second to third grade.

The worst suggestion came from Peyton's venomous mouth. He started as a good diplomat and a caring citizen, saying that we were very good kids and respectful, but then he said we didn't get along with the other kids. We stuck together and hung out together all the time, which brought big problems with social interaction. If we got along with other kids and talked to them, played with them, and studied with them, our IQs would increase and we would study better. He also suggested that we needed to shuffle our beds and share our bunk beds with other kids and not be adjacent to each other so we could build friendships with other kids. Very simply, he wanted us to be scattered and separated, and then he could hunt us and take vengeance on us. Everyone agreed with Peyton's ideas.

That day after the meeting, we went out and discussed what we should do. We had a heated discussion, finally we made something clear: no matter where they put us or who they tried to make us friends with, we would never disclose the mission to New York City to anyone and we would meet every day for less than an hour to talk about the things that happened. We decided to meet at the football field, where there were lots of crowds of kids who usually played there and we could go unnoticed. After the meeting, we went for dinner that night and after dinner, we went to the dormitory. Peyton and his guards were standing there with their chests up, with wicked smiles and snake eyes, waiting for us. We saw them and walked slowly by, ignoring them with our hands inside our pockets. We heard Peyton's warning voice, "Mr. Oliver and fellows." I was confused about why he called to me like that. I slowly turned and said, "Yes, Peyton," and he was witty and said, "Do you know your bed?" I shrugged and said, "Yes, I do," and he replied, "Interesting—not the old bed, the new one, Oliver." I figured out that he had swapped our beds, and I jeeringly answered him, "I just realized beds do have legs to walk and move." Hearing this, he was pissed off and contemptuously replied, "Luckily these days even a poor man has a bed that can walk." This was the first time I realized the exact meaning of *foster home* and *parentless kid*. His words went deep into my heart and hurt me very badly. Even to talk or express yourself, you should have some money, because money made a difference. His words hurt not only me, but also my friends, because at this point, we all felt homeless and poor.

Peyton and the warden took us to the beds, Peyton's words were already causing damage in us, and our bodies became weak. We were dragging our legs to walk to the beds. They had moved all our beds to different corners, except Niki's bed, which was in the middle of the dormitory. While Peyton and the warden took him to his bed, Peyton commented cheekily, "Here is the king's bed, but the king has to climb and sleep on the top bed." He gave Niki the top bed, which he also gave Ejaz, but he wanted to insult Niki in all aspects. Niki dourly replied, "Then you should sleep in the bottom bed of the king to take care of his master." Peyton always got sharpshooting answers from Niki and replied, scowling, "You little schmuck, you will never get out of this place in one piece." Niki turned into one tough kid and he fiercely answered with eyes opened wide, "Let's see, Peyton, who gets out in one piece." Then Peyton angrily turned and walked away from him.

That night, I didn't sleep well. It was not only because we all got separated, but also because the mocking words from Peyton's mouth hurt me very badly. Though I was born homeless, Nathalie and all the people whom I had met were kind to me. Even the homeless people cared for us, but it was in the foster home where we were experiencing all the pain in our lives. The place is called a foster home but it was not the way it should be. It was a painful night that we went through. I saw all the kids around me, and they were really crazy. They snuck in video game gadgets and played the whole night, and I felt so sorry for these kids because technology had made them insane. The same thing happened to the girls, too, having their beds swapped and put in different corners. But luckily for them, Peyton was not there, because they had a female warden, who was kind enough.

Within a couple of days, Benjamin got a call from his mom. This was the first call he had received from his mom in a while, because she had been busy with the Marines and the war. We also had a visual chat with her, and she was gratified that her son was in good company. She liked all of us, but she was sad about what had happened to Uncle Kadin. For the past year, she had been in great pain with the loss of her boyfriend, but she didn't express herself much. We could see in her eyes how much love she had for Uncle Kadin and how much she missed him.

We had no visitors, and very few phone calls from Benjamin's mother and no one else, except Moise Boti, who came and chatted with us every day during his shift. He would bring some packages for us and cared for us a lot. We had a few kids in class who were polite to us, and enjoyed their company. As we had planned, we met every day at the football field and talked and shared our views. We had noticed that a couple of girls had been sitting alone at the football grounds for a few weeks in the corner, and no one spoke to them. Both of them were the same age as us, and one girl was fair and had chestnut brown hair and the other girl looked Hispanic, with brown skin and black hair. Judah and I were very curious about who these girls were and why they didn't have any friends. We asked Madison about the girls, but she had little idea about them. She said they stayed with them in the dormitory, and they had been brought in a few weeks ago. The only instruction given was that no one should talk to them because they were bad and dangerous. I asked Madison, "What do you mean by *dangerous*?" and, clueless, she replied, "I don't know, but that is what I heard."

So, Judah and I made a plan to make a move to talk to them. One day, we wore jean jackets and had our hands in the pockets, and were walking, talking to each other. We passed by them where they usually sat in the corner of the football field on the lower deck. We stopped before them and greeted them casually, "Whazz up, guys? How are you doing?" They both were surprised by our greeting and peered at each other and slowly the Hispanic kid replied, "What do you want?" I played a very cool game and replied, "Nothing much, just taking a walk, spotted you guys, wanted to say hello." The fair girl was moody and said, "We heard your hello, and you can leave now." I never gave up. "I know, bye, nice seeing you guys. You girls look adorable and wonderful." Although it was a sour experience we wanted to talk to them. We shared the story with our buddies and everyone felt awkward about them and advised us not to proceed in talking with them. But I saw in their eyes some appealing personalities that they had, and now they were running with some hardships and agony, and that was why they were disconnected and rude to us. None of my friends were with me, so they had no clue what we were talking about. But I stood my ground. I wanted to talk to them again, and Judah had the same feeling, and agreed to go with me the next day. But the rest just said, "Leave them alone."

The next evening, we had our hands inside our pockets again, walking and talking to each other. We pretended to talk seriously about some subject to make an impression that we were not stalking them. We walked by the same place where they were sitting and just said, "Hi." We didn't stop, and just passed them. We also made sure that we circled the grounds two more times so that it looked like we were just taking a walk. Out of the three times, we said hi just once and ignored them the other two times. We did this for a week and some days we didn't even say hi, to build curiosity. Judah and I were building some good impressions on them, and every day on their faces we could see some improvement and a chance for us getting to know who these girls were.

Our plan eventually worked out, and after a week, one day while we were walking and passing them, they started the conversation by saying, "Hey, guys." We replied back, and they asked our names, and we exchanged names. The fair girl with chestnut hair was called Fay Scarlett, and the Hispanic kid was Sadie Leta. They were asking what we did every day at the football grounds. We lied to them and said we took long walks and talked about the subjects we'd learned, a few movies we'd watched and stuff like that. The first conversation was adequate and we just had an introduction and left, but they said they would like to talk the next day and asked us to stop by.

Every day, step by step, we started to build a friendship with them, giving them gum, cookies, and all the little things that would make a girl happy. We never shared any of this information with our buddies because they were not interested, so Judah and I kept it to ourselves. After a week, they gained confidence in us and talked about themselves. Fay's father was a mechanic, a drunkard, and a wife beater and he had sold her to the TUAD, hoping to reap some money for the future. Sadie's father was a low-level drug dealer and a drug addict, and he had sold her to TUAD for the same reason, to make money. They were both from Washington State; they were in the Washington TUAD school. They were both bright kids, best friends, and they took care of each other and grew to be like sisters there, but something went wrong in their lives. At the TUAD in Washington, there was a clerk named Jay Mons who was a child abuser. He liked young girls; he threatened them and sexually assaulted and abused them. He was a full-time player with the kids, and all of them were under twelve years old. His itch came to Fay and Sadie, so they planned to ring the bell. One day, when Jay Mons was abusing an eleven-year-old girl in his room, where Fay and Sadie had installed a secret camera. They recorded the abuse and submitted it to their superiors and e-mailed the video to law enforcement. Unfortunately, it didn't turn out as expected.

The law enforcement officials were about to send cops and federal agents to arrest Jay Mons but the TUAD board members were aware of this problem and had highly affluent and influential people with power halt the arrest. In the meantime, the TUAD members learned that Fay and Sadie had done it, and they drugged them with heroin and other drugs in their food and water for a month without their knowledge. Fay and Sadie waited for law enforcement to come and take down Jay Mons, but they didn't show up for a month. After a month, they came in and were looking for Fay and Sadie, but TUAD had given them the wrong information about them, saying that they sold and used drugs. So, when the cops did a search, they found drugs in their beds.

TUAD and Jay Mons played their parts very well. They threatened the weaker kids to say that Fay and Sadie were selling drugs. A lot of kids testified against Fay and Sadie, and the cops took them to juvenile detention. Fay and Sadie defended themselves by telling the truth, but the cops didn't believe them. The TUAD management twisted the story, saying Jay Mons found out these kids were selling and using drugs and warned them many times that he would report them to the principal and management. To get rid of him, they said, Fay and Sadie had plotted to send the abuse video, which was forged. Fay and Sadie were tested, and drugs were found in their blood, which confirmed their usage. Because Sadie's father was a drug dealer and Fay's father was known for alcoholism, the cops didn't give it a second thought. There were many blind spots in this case, and before the cops could send the video to check its authenticity, TUAD convinced them to drop the case against the kids for the welfare and future of TUAD. Because of high pressure from the senior law officials, they dropped further investigation. Jay Mons was not fired.

But the law enforcement officials decided to keep Fay and Sadie in juvie for a year for drug addiction. Poor Fay and Sadie spent one year in juvenile detention, and now they were here at the Michigan TUAD school with us. Fay and Sadie were officially recorded as drug addicts and drug sellers in the personal files of both TUAD and the federal government. TUAD always wanted to be careful, so they had told the rest of the kids that they were bad and dangerous, although they didn't say what they had done. By this time, Fay and Sadie hated every kid they saw because of all the kids who had borne false witness against them. That was the reason they stayed away and didn't talk to anyone.

Hearing this story, we were agonized and wistful. There were no words we could say to describe what had happened to them, but we gave them some encouragement. We promised them that Judah and I would be good friends to them. They felt the same way and said they wanted to be friends with us. We left them, and walked back to our friends. Judah and I had many things on our minds to talk about, but we were silent. We came back and sat quietly with our other buddies and we each took a canned drink and sipped it quietly. All our other friends looked at us with curiosity about what had happened. Ejaz asked us, "It seems you guys chatted with them for a long time. What did you talk about?" I looked at Ejaz and answered sardonically, "You are interested in knowing them? I think not, so why are you guys bothering us?" Ejaz spilled his mind by saying, "No, Oliver, not like that. They are drug dealers and good for nothing kids. Why hang out with them?"

Judah and I bug-eyed each other and looked at our buddies and said, "Did you guys wire us?" I knew for sure that Judah was my man of trust, and he would never have said anything to the others. Madison wittily answered, "Peyton has already wired us, so why do we need to wire you?" I looked at Madison and said, "That is funny, Madison, and I want to laugh right now, but tell me, how you know, guys?" Everybody started to laugh and shake their heads and say, "Come on, man." Nikifor couldn't keep his mouth shut, and he said, "Those chicks' names are Fay Scarlett and Sadie Leta . . . ," and he started to tell their whole bio data. My mind sparked at this time, and I understood what was happening and said, "No, you didn't do that, Niki. Please say no." Niki replied, "Yes, I did it!" I asked him, "How did you do that, and when did you do it?" Niki had taken a picture of them, hacked the TUAD database, run a search on the image, and found all the information about them.

I took a deep breath and said to Niki, "That is an awesome job, Niki. I hope you didn't get caught and make all our lives a living hell." It was my turn, and I told the whole story about Fay and Sadie. They were all listening closely and seriously, and everybody was moved and felt bad about what happened to them. Then they all quickly apologized for what they had done. It was not their fault, and I advised them, "Never trust your senses, always investigate, search for the truth, and the truth will guide and answer your questions." Telling the story about Fay and Sadie, the girls got scared, because this was the first time we had ever heard about kids being abused in the school.

The next day, I introduced the rest of the crew to Fay and Sadie, and the other six wanted to be gentle to them. Somehow, at that moment, Fay and Sadie started to trust us, and a bond of friendship was building. We started to hang out every day, and they no longer sat in the corner of the football grounds isolated and disconnected. They had some good friends now.

Time passed, in building our friendship with Fay and Sadie, we learned what our future would be if we did well in TUAD. The myth of learning technology was narrowed to a few areas of your choice. The first thing was "space exploration," where you learned to find someone who was lost in space. The second subject was "building high-speed weapons" to blow someone's butt away. The third thing was "hacking" to steal everything when the law supported you. The fourth area was "physics" to get a Nobel Prize when your invention became obsolete in the future. And the last one was "chemical engineering" to build cupid sites for dating couples. These were the five areas TUAD taught and we were the foster punks who would build the future for some rich, lazy man with a cigar in his mouth and pig crap in his body. Above all these kids play wild and crazy video games, because there were big cash rewards for the winners. They have all sorts of games, even virtually making your body transform to the battlefield. Oh yeah, they have all kinds of crazy stuff. All I knew was that my spirit was not calm and I couldn't digest the things around me.

Oh, and they had one more field outside the classroom—be an animal. Yes, be an animal, or play sports. You could pick your own sport and they would train you to be corporate animals with team spirit in any sport under the sun: football, baseball, soccer, and so on—any sport that brought fame and money. We were not interested in the sports because we were here to stop the war and bring peace, not trigger competition in sports and feel delighted over a victory when someone else lost. The football field was only a place for us to meet and talk; it was nothing more than a chatting place.

One thing we started to notice was that they were pushing us to implant an RFID, but we refused, and always gave a convincing answer. Slowly, the approach was changing. Although the Constitution said it was an individual choice, they made the laws to shut up the hippies. But the government was always against it, and they pushed people and did all the necessary evil to put pressure on them to use it. Nathalie had insisted to us one thing: never use it. Nathalie was our Constitution, and we owed her. Since we were not using the RFID, we were treated as secondary citizens. Whenever we asked for anything from any of the members of TUAD, they did not respond, we would get a delayed response and follow-ups.

But we didn't delay in revealing our true plans and mission to Fay and Sadie, because I saw the shining light passing through them. They were astonished and agreed to be our friends and go to New York City. The reason we felt they were the chosen ones was that they had risked their lives to bring the truth into justice. They were brave enough to record the abuse of those kids and send the copies to higher officials and law enforcement. Although they had had bad childhoods with their parents, they were honest and lovable friends. Except for us, no one talked to them, because no one knew the truth and didn't want to know the truth. We had been warned many times not to hang out or talk to them, but we didn't give a heck. So, in TUAD, no one was comfortable with us, and they looked down on us all the time.

We had a very bad reputation in TUAD, and the government had all the names of those who didn't use the RFID, and they caused all sorts of problems and put pressure on them. We were the most watched kids, but somehow we survived all the obstacles. To worsen the situation, we had mastered our failing of the exams. We didn't pass any test, not even once and they made every attempt to find some skill in us that they could bring to the stage. They couldn't find anything, though, because we denied all of it. All their attempts failed and failed, and slowly they gave up.

We had all turned nine years old now and every kid was waiting for the results to move to the next grade. We already knew the results, and we didn't have that curiosity in us, so we ate and slept well. The results came back, and everyone in TUAD passed and moved to the next grade except for us. TUAD didn't want to move us to the next grade, and they failed us and asked us to repeat the third grade. We didn't know this would be the outcome and we started to regret it now. Every kid in the school made fun of us, and mocking us became their pastime. Where everyone could tease us, they did, even though we were seniors in the same class. And the new little elves in the third grade also teased us. They would say, "There cannot be anyone as dumb as those kids." You could see all our names in the school bathrooms, on trees, and on paper rockets. Wherever they wanted to use the word *dumb*, they replaced it with our names. But the reality was, we knew everything better than they did, and our time had not yet begun. When the day came, we would deliver and achieve our mission.

Somehow, mentally, we were hurt and disappointed and we started to see a hole in our approach. "Are we right in what we are doing?" For all this trouble, this was the first time we met Ambrose on the football grounds. He was fourteen years old and had a dozen friends who were more or less his age. We had seen him many times, but no one cared about him, or he about us, because it was one big field, and hundreds of kids were there. But we had all failed the third grade, and it was the gossip of the school. One day, when we were walking on the football grounds, he called to us, "You waste yards! Come here." We ignored him and walked away, but he and his buddies came running to us, shouting, "How dare you ignore us!" He came and pushed Madison over, and we all joined together and they circled us. They taunted us and Benjamin and Niki wanted to start a fight for what they had done to Madison, but I calmed them down, because no matter what they did, we would be the ones punished. We let them go and left that place as cowards. Every day after that when Ambrose and his crew noticed us, they would do the same thing: circle us and taunt us with loud and nasty words for a few minutes and then leave. This became a routine.

There were only two good souls in TUAD who liked to talk to us: Urson, the kid our age and Niki's first bunk-bed friend and Moise Boti. Adding more pain to our lives, the third year started with great misery because Jay Mons was transferred to our TUAD institute. The child abuser was Peyton's best friend and Peyton had recommended him to come and work where he was working. But the actual reason Jay Mons came was that he wanted his revenge against Fay and Sadie. The clock had started now and we had to protect ourselves and Fay and Sadie. We were left alone here with little help and we had to tell the truth about Fay and Sadie to Uncle Moise Boti. His ears were sensitive, and as soon as we started to say the first line of their story, he completed the whole story. He knew exactly what had happened at the other TUAD. He said some places were good and some were bad, and no matter what age you were, a foster home was a foster home. He offered us help that we would never forget in our lives. He said that he would do all the night shifts and keep us protected. He sacrificed his life for us to be protected, and not only for us, but for all the other kids in TUAD, too.

As soon as Jay Mons came to TUAD, he looked for Fay and Sadie. The day I will never, ever forget was the day of the conversation between Fay, Sadie and Jay Mons. During the evening, after class, we were walking in the corridor. The wind was blowing hard and the curtains were flying. As all ten of us were walking, Fay, Sadie, and Ejaz were walking behind us. We heard Ejaz shouting, "Fay," and we quickly turned around and saw that Fay and Sadie were missing. Ejaz was kicking and knocking on a door and shouting "Open it." We ran and asked what had happened, and he said that someone had pulled Fay and Sadie inside the room. We went and looked through the window. We saw a tall man with blond hair holding Fay's neck with his right hand and Sadie's neck with his left hand up against the wall. He said, "Welcome back, my little whores. It is so nice to see you." Sadie was trying to move and she spat in the man's face and said, "You pig." He dropped Fay and slapped Sadie, leaving the print of his hand on Sadie's cheek. Fay bit the man's hand and he shouted loudly in pain and kicked Fay in the chest. We were shouting through the window to leave them alone, and he turned and saw all of us standing in the window. He slowly released Sadie and looked at her and said in a choleric voice, "One day I will take you, whores." Sadie very bravely said, "You will, while you see I will eat the chicken in your pants." Fay, on the floor, laughed and whispered, "Maybe we should share it." Hearing this, he became terribly angry and grabbed them by their hair; he opened the door and threw them outside. His eyes were sanguine, he bit his teeth and said, "You will both be dead and I will feed you to my dogs." He then closed the door loudly and locked it from the inside.

We ran to help Fay and Sadie. Fay had some swelling from where she had been hit in her chest, and Sadie's cheek was swollen, too. We picked them up and took them to the medic. We realized it had been Jay Mons, but we never realized how cruel he actually was. The medics didn't question us about anything and they scanned them and found only minor injuries. They put some bandages on Fay's chest to reduce the swelling and gave an ice pack to Sadie. They gave them some pills for the pain and let us go.

We went and complained to our principal and our teachers, but no one responded or took action. All they said was that Fay and Sadie were drug addicts and caused the injuries to themselves and tried to blame others. Their reputations preceded them and no one cared enough to say something that would make us feel better. Everyone ignored the complaint because it was Fay and Sadie. Some people knew the truth, but their hands were tied. Uncle Moise Boti advised us not to move forward with the problem and to just lie low. TUAD thought Fay and Sadie had brought down the reputation of TUAD, but they could not send them away because it would reach the media and they would be in more trouble.

Then we asked why we couldn't send an e-mail or reach out to the media, and Moise said, "They are always watching Fay's and Sadie's movements. Since you guys are their friends, you are also being watched." Moise said it would be stupid if we reached out to the media or made any moves. All he advised us was to wait until we became sixteen, when we could be safe and get out and find a new life. He said as long as he was here, he would protect us. We all felt very sorry for Fay and Sadie, and we made an oath to never leave them and to die protecting them. They were two living angels, we know, and we cared for them a lot. Every night when we went to bed, we thought about the girls and their safety. We stole knives from the kitchen, and all the girls put them under their beds for protection. They weren't getting enough sleep because of this prick.

The nasty prick, Jay Mons, learned that the girls had knives under their beds and did a routine check. They found the knives under all five girls' beds and took them for questioning. They gave one simple answer: "For safety." They asked, "Safety from what?" but the girls didn't say Jay Mons's name. Instead, they said "the war". If by any chance the enemies occupied TUAD, we would need some tools to defend ourselves. It was a lie and sounded silly to the officers who questioned them; they laughed and mocked the girls. They commented, saying, "We know all you kids are foolish and incompetent. You crossed those barriers and now have insanity growing in your minds." They dismissed the girls with no further inquiry. We asked the girls why they didn't inform on Jay Mons, and Fay said, "It wouldn't matter, and we would just make the situation worse." We agreed with her view. It was not the time to go looking for help; it was time to protect ourselves.

We all sat together for breakfast, lunch, and dinner, but Peyton wanted to satisfy his itchy friend's desires. They came up with a plan that Tuesday night was girls' night. So, for dinner all the girls had to eat in a separate hall, with ballads, dancing and celebration. The girls liked it, but we knew something was wrong. One Tuesday, the girls had their girls' night, and Peyton and Jay Mons mixed sleeping pills into their food. After the dinner all the girls were drowsy and went to bed. Every Tuesday, we would watch our friends from our dormitory window to see whether someone would walk through the entrance. The other kids in our dormitory would ask us, "What are you doing?" and we just replied, "Making sure no ghosts enter our building." Hearing that, they would just laugh and make fun of us and ignore us because they thought we were dumb. But we knew what we were doing. It happened as expected. Peyton and Jay Mons were there in masks, but we could identify them by their heights and the bloody scent through that window. They opened the entrance gates slowly and went to the first floor, took Fay and Sadie, and walked away slowly.

We were waiting for them to come down, but they didn't know we were watching through the windows. Benjamin and Judah were standing near the dormitory bell in our building. As soon as they came outside, they rang the bell at a high volume, and all the kids in our building woke up, lights started to turn on like dominoes. Everyone went to the windows to look at what was happening. Hearing and seeing this, Peyton and Jay Mons left Fay and Sadie on the ground and ran away. The warden and other senior members came running to check what was happening and found both of them on the ground unconscious, and they took them to the medic. The medic checked them and said they had taken sleeping pills. The next day, after they woke up, we asked them where they had found the sleeping pills, and they had no idea what had happened. No one was ready to believe them, and no one wanted to question them further. They thought they were using drugs again, and they put them in a dark room for a week for rehabilitation.

After a week, they were released and we all decided not to have dinner on Tuesdays, so we skipped it. We had skipped food to not be abused. Peyton and Jay Mons knew we rang the bell and made sure we knew there were seven days in the week. Forget Tuesday—they would drug us all on a Friday for weekend abuse. We all had dinner on Friday together happily and were drugged with sleeping pills. We all went to bed without any awareness hovering over us. We got up late around eleven on Saturday morning and thought we were just tired. We took a long walk inside the campus with our night dress still on and saw Moise Boti sitting down near the outer gate of the school having a smoke. We walked to him and asked him, "Are you still awake? You should go to bed." He was slack-jawed and said, "Did the sleeping pills work?" and I asked him, "What are you talking about, Moise?" He puffed the smoke and said, "All you kids were drugged with sleeping pills." We were perplexed and asked, "Really? What happened to Fay and Sadie?" and he laughed and said, "God knows."

We were all worried and asked him what had happened, and he told us the nasty story. "I saw an unusual man at TUAD yesterday around three o'clock in the afternoon who gave a small package to Jay Mons. I had never seen the man before, so I was suspicious that something was wrong. I kept an eye on Peyton and Jay Mons that night and they drugged all ten of you. They went and took Fay and Sadie from their rooms and took them to Jay Mons's apartment. Jay Mons took them to his bedroom; he and Peyton had some drinks, and then Peyton left the apartment. Jay Mons went to his bedroom and was excited to finally have his dream come true. He closed his bedroom door, but I was behind the door with my gun. I pointed it at his head and said, 'Let them go.' We argued, and I knocked him with the butt of the gun and kicked him in his jaw and he fainted. I slowly carried Fay and Sadie back to their dormitory, but since I didn't have the keys, I couldn't get them back in. I took them back to my apartment; I woke them up with cold water, gave them some tea and told them I couldn't keep them in my apartment. I said, 'Go to the chapel, stay there and pray until the morning.'"

Moise Boti said he took them to the chapel and left them inside and they stayed there the whole night. The next day, when the dormitory opened, they went back. We had a mixed feeling about the story. It wasn't happy or sad, and we didn't know how to thank Moise Boti for his great help. We asked him if we could spend the day and evening at his apartment, and he said we could. We had never been to his house, either because we didn't ask him or he didn't invite us, and we all finally went to spend the day and evening. We met his wife, who was in a wheelchair, and we asked Moise Boti what happened to her. "She had a shock and had paralysis in her brain," he said. "She cannot talk and her brain functions very slowly and doesn't respond properly." We all went and said hi to her, but she didn't notice us and kept looking out the window.

Moise Boti cooked food for us and we partied that day happily, but not Fay and Sadie. They were sad and depressed. We all comforted them and they both were very thankful to Moise Boti. We asked Moise Boti why these things were happening to us and not to the other kids. He laughed loud. Judah asked, "What is so funny?" Moise Boti whisked his face and said, "I thought you guys knew already. You guys are smart. It is all about the RFID or no chip, baby, and you don't have one. You are like cockroaches to them. That is the reason Jay Mons and Peyton are playing with you all the time. You should get one. You will become a normal citizen and enjoy all the freedoms, and someone is liable to protect you." We knew that there had been some sort of problem, but we thought it was the Fay and Sadie problem with Jay Mons or Peyton's vengeance for Niki. But we realized, for the first time in our lives, why we had been treated so badly. It was because of the RFID.

We left at around nine in the evening, and while the other nine were standing and chatting outside Moise Boti's house, Moise Boti took me separately and introduced me to his wife. He insisted that she look at me, and as she slowly turned and looked at me, she whispered, "My son, my son," and moved her hands and asked me to come closer. She moved her hands over my head and face and started to get excited. Moise Boti was calming her down, saying, "This is Oliver, not our son. You should relax." Then he calmed her down, which took almost ten minutes to do. She kept saying, "My son, my son. . ." While we were walking out, I asked him if he had a son, and he said no; his wife had wanted to have a baby but couldn't. He said she loved kids, and so she thinks that every kid she sees is her son. I felt very sorry for such a good man like Moise Boti to have a wife who was so sick and couldn't have a baby. He was taking such good care of us. Long live Moise Boti and his wife.

Before we left, we thanked him, and Moise Boti's eyes were peaceful. He was delighted we had visited his house. We didn't know why he was so happy and at peace with himself, but we left his apartment feeling very grateful.

Chapter 17
THE ESCAPE

AFTER THE INCIDENT THAT HAD HAPPENED TO OUR FRIENDS, WE MADE A decision to starve ourselves. Yes, we decided not to eat any food at night. We would just have breakfast and lunch and we would skip dinner. We would go to the dining hall only for dinner and just eat fruit and walk out. We had done this for a couple of weeks and Peyton and Jay Mons hadn't made any more attempts after the day Jay Mons was hit by Moise Boti. We knew they were planning something big, but we didn't know what form it would take. We were so paranoid at this time that we had a feeling they would try to inject sleeping drugs into the fruit. Therefore, we even stopped eating fruit and we would just go to the dining room for attendance without eating or drinking anything. We took some fruit and bread from breakfast and kept them in our pockets. We would eat what we took at the breakfast for dinner. We had only two meals a day now and started to feel that we were getting weak.

The wardens saw that we weren't eating dinner and started to question us. We gave them some convincing answers, saying that it was good to have only two meals a day, and skipping dinner and not eating anything after six would keep us looking younger. They cross-examined us, but we stuck with our stories. Still, they forced us to at least take a glass of milk at night. We agreed to it because we could pour the milk into the sink. We proceeded to grab some milk every day and excuse ourselves, saying that we wanted to study or sit outside, whichever lie came out best.

We started to get skinny and when Moise Boti saw us and asked us why we were getting so thin, we told him why. Moise Boti said that he would prepare food for us every day and bring it to us. We agreed and ate that way for two weeks but we felt bad for him because he was poor, and he had to feed ten kids, and his wife was sick, he also had other priorities. So, to make Moise Boti happy and comfortable, we said that if he took care of us at night, we would eat food from the dining room. We took turns each day, two from the boys' side and two from the girls' side, eating dinner, and the other six wouldn't have any food. The ones who weren't eating would watch guard, we took turns.

We did this for three months and the fight between truth and injustice was getting harder and harder. Apart from our fight for survival, the mockery at the school was getting louder and louder. We kept failing every single time and the TUAD's hope in us was fading, which was very good for us. But the itch of Jay Mons never ceased, and he continued to threaten Fay and Sadie whenever he had the chance. Peyton did his part well, blaming everything and anything on us and wanting his turn with Niki and us. One time, Jay Mons threatened us by saying, "Once I am done with Fay and Sadie, I will come for the other girls." He was a sex maniac, but not a sodomite, so the boys had some room to breathe, but he brought trouble for us also.

On Peyton's recommendation, they hired a man named Alcott who was a boys' sodomite and loved young boys. They hired him from a cleaning company to remove the trash and clean the bathrooms and stuff. They faked his identity to get him in because he had been arrested a few times for child abuse, but he was released because they didn't have any witnesses against him. Niki hacked his whole history and we found out who he was.

Moise Boti even asked Fay and Sadie to apologize to Jay Mons and create a truce. But Fay and Sadie tried that, and we all learned why he was so angry. The reason for his lust for vengeance was that TUAD revealed the video that Fay and Sadie made to Jay Mons's wife, Mindi. After hearing about it and seeing it, she was angry with Jay Mons and they started to fight, she insisted on a divorce. It went on for a few months and she became mentally disturbed and had sleeping problems. One day, she took a heavy dosage of sleeping pills and died. From that day on Jay Mons wanted revenge against Fay and Sadie. Jay Mons was very clear that he would take them down and he never listened to their apology.

We all went and apologized to Peyton from our end and the first time Niki calmed down and asked him for mercy, he said he would never leave Niki alone to live peacefully. He wanted the other seven of us to suffer in the same way as Niki, too, and he was angry for another reason. When he told us what it was, it was shocking. Jay Mons's wife, Mindi, was Peyton's cousin and they grew up like brother and sister. So, in simple words, Peyton and Jay Mons were brothers-in-law. We all went pale and were shocked when we heard about their relationship. He said that we were all against his brother-in-law by protecting Fay and Sadie. They wanted to take down all ten of us. That was the reason they hired Alcott—to take care of us.

We now knew the true anger that Jay Mons and Peyton had toward us; we also knew that Fay and Sadie were not the reason for Jay Mons's wife's death. He was a wicked sex addict, and if Peyton had been a true brother-in-law he would have advised him against all of this and showed him the path of truth. Peyton was the mother of all evil and made up his mind to help Jay Mons for only one reason: he hated Niki, and we were with Niki. Basically, these two maniacs multiplied their anger and vengeance toward innocent kids.

Now not only did the girls have to fear a child abuser but we now feared the nasty sodomite. We were not comfortable with the kids at the school and they acted weird and played to the tune of what TUAD disciplined and taught them. No one wanted to support us. They all thought we were weird and incompetent and no one wanted to have any friendship with us. They were the shadows of TUAD and they listened to them and behaved in the way they said to. Anyone without a radio-frequency identification—RFID—or tattoo ID was not a patriot but a troublemaker and that was why no one was nice to us.

The only friend we had in that whole school was Urson. In all this chaos and pain, Urson gave back his RFID implant. He was now also considered an outcast and was treated like us. We asked him why he removed the RFID, and he said it was because of his brother, Nelek. We didn't understand the whole story, so Urson explained it. Urson's mother and father died when he was one year old, leaving him and Nelek, who was five years older. They were born in Poland and after their parents died, their grandparents raised them. TUAD was bringing kids from other countries who were smart and intellectual and they found out that Urson and Nelek were smart kids and planned to buy them. Because Urson's grandparents were poor, they sold both of them to TUAD in America. At that time, Urson was five years old and Nelek was ten. When TUAD came to their home to take them away, Nelek and Urson wanted to escape. Nelek did, but Urson was caught. Urson was brought to TUAD in Michigan. Since TUAD had already paid the money, they were looking for Nelek, but they couldn't find him. Nelek went and joined the Russian mafia and stayed with them for four years until, finally, he came and surrendered to TUAD, saying he wanted to live with his brother, whom he missed a lot. A couple of months back, they had brought Nelek to TUAD here in Michigan and he was happy to live with his brother. Neither Nelek nor Urson had RFIDs and they were treated the same way as we were.

Later Urson introduced us to Nelek and he looked handsome, tough, and shrewd. He had heard about us, but he never disrespected us like the other kids in school.

He was courteous and kind to us. The first reason he liked us, he said, was that we didn't have RFIDs and we were fighting for our lives. Nelek was a rebel, but he didn't care about anything and he was a genius at hacking, electronics and nuclear physics. He was a smart kid and passed all the exams with an A grade. He shared all his experiences when he was with the Russian mafia, about how he had hacked governments, banks, and financial companies and built miniature nuclear bombs.

We never said a single word to him about our mission. All the stuff he spoke about and his subjects of expertise, we knew them even better than he did. But we pretended that we were ignorant, and because of our ages, he saw us like his little brothers. We built a friendship and brotherhood with Nelek and Urson. Nelek knew about the problems that were going on with Peyton and Jay Mons. He built us some watch alarms hidden inside the mechanism, so that if a drug had been taken, the sensor in the watch would sense it and connect to Nelek's I-gadget and beep him. It also gave an electric shock that sent more electromagnetic waves to the brain cells and woke up the person who had consumed the drugs. He designed two I-gadgets for getting the alerts, one was with him and the other was with Moise Boti. We wore the watches all the time, but something still happened one night, when Niki, Fay, and Sadie were kidnapped again.

It was a Saturday night and we had dinner at Moise Boti's house. Moise Boti had gotten the day off. He stayed home and we came back to our dormitory. We were all tired and went to bed, leaving one watch guard awake on each side. Benjamin was the watch guard from our side, and Shu was on the girls' side. Both the watch guards went to sleep and weren't on duty. They came and kidnapped Niki, Fay, and Sadie by tying their mouths, hands and legs. .

Nelek and Urson were hanging out that night and saw the three men running, each one with a kid on their back, they followed them slowly to the woods. They hid the whole way and wanted to know who the kids and their kidnappers were. They recognized it was our friends and walked behind them in the dark. The three men didn't notice Nelek and Urson. Nelek and Urson wanted to save our friends but didn't know what to do. Nelek had a gun with a silencer on it, so he decided to risk himself and save our friends. He had a laser light and pointed it sharply and shot Alcott in the leg, he fell down. Seeing this, Peyton and Jay Mons tried to help Alcott, but they didn't know who shot at them, and they looked around terrorized. Then Nelek removed the silencer and fired into the air to make noise and get noticed. When they fired the gun, the guard alarm on the campus went off and turned on the floodlights in the woods.

Seeing all of this, Peyton and Jay Mons dropped Fay and Sadie and started to run and hide. Nelek and Urson picked all three up on their shoulders and came back to the dormitory. Because the warning alarm that the guards rang on the campus had turned on all the lights, the kids, staff, and everyone woke up to check what was happening. Peyton and his crew very narrowly escaped from the woods, grabbed Alcott, and went home. The guards called the backup team and cops to check out who had fired the gun. They couldn't find anything, and the investigation was still going on.

We thanked Nelek and Urson for their help and Nelek offered to help us by building and upgrading the alarm so it could notify all of us when someone was drugged. But we were not clear about one thing.

What were Nelek and Urson doing late at night hanging out? The dormitory and building doors were closed. And where had he gotten the gun? We didn't ask them, because they had helped us and we didn't want to be intrusive by questioning them.

Alcott didn't return to work; he took sick leave to recover from the gunshot. Peyton and Jay Mons didn't know who fired that shot and he thought it was Moise Boti. They already didn't like Moise Boti and now they were mad at him and wanted to take him down first before making any more moves against us. So, we had problems all over the place and we knew that we would get out of TUAD either as kids who had been abused in the foster home, when we were sixteen, or when we were dead and buried there before reaching that age.

But the moment came that changed our lives. Every two weeks they played a movie in the theater. All the kids gathered to watch it together, and the purpose was to build unity and social values. Usually, they played some crackerjack sci-fi movie and most of them were related to World War III. They played movies that helped kids build their creativity in technology and life. We had stopped going to the movies because they were all about violence and crime, but this time we decided to go. The movie industry had changed a lot and studios were no longer making movies because there was virtual simulation software that produced the exact effect as the real movies shot by the studios. In this day and age, everyone was a movie director and billions of movies were being made; in fact, almost all men and women made at least one movie in their lifetime. All they had to do was pay 25 percent of the income to the actors and actresses they used as their characters in the movie.

All the kids in this foster home had created at least one movie, but although my last name was Oscar, I hadn't made any movies yet. The kids and teachers asked me all the time why I was not making movies and every time I excused myself, saying, "I am waiting for the perfect story to tell the world." So, the movie world became two entities: real and virtual. The virtual world took over from the real movie studios and the quality of the virtual world was ten times better than the real world.

They played one movie called "*The Vacation on Mars*," which starred Matt Sterling, a famous actor of our times. This movie broke the barrier between the real and virtual worlds, and Matt Sterling had made the biggest movie in the film industry. The movie was about Matt Sterling, whose character was sentenced to life in prison for a crime he didn't commit and all the lifers were locked up on Mars. Matt Sterling was accused of killing his own family, including children. The prison was built in 2500 AD, and for almost 500 years no one ever escaped. But Matt Sterling was a good mathematician and physicist and built a teleportation machine in his prison cell and broke out one day, escaping to the closest moon, Deimos. On Deimos, every week there was a space jet that came with tourists for vacation. He hid in the space jet and reached Earth and went back to his home. The movie had won Oscars for Best Sci-Fi Thriller and Best Prison Escape. There were thousands of virtual movies telling the same story, but the acting and quality of the movie didn't match the real ones. Matt Sterling had now changed our way of thinking—"The Escape from TUAD." This idea went through all ten of us quickly as we watched the movie. At the end of the movie, he finished with a quote: "If I am innocent, I don't need a vacation on Mars. I just need an escape." We decided that we were going to break out and escape from TUAD.

We discussed the escape from TUAD and our plans worked as we expected. Every year, all the kids older than nine and younger than fifteen, as a part of the curriculum, were taken to a flying class where the teachers would demonstrate how to fly a space saucer. This was the first time we got a chance to go to the flying class. The flying saucer was called Blue Voyager and was the first, best, and most reliable model that was built in 2150, it could fly to outer space at a speed of 10,000 miles per minute. They took all the kids to the flying pad, which was two miles away from our school building, but on the same campus. They took us in a shuttle and we passed by the woods on a road we had never seen before because it was highly restricted.

The whole flying unit area was fenced in with blue electric layers in four bands. Between each band there was a thin gap where we could see the buildings inside the fence. But the layer itself was not transparent and the fences were between 150 to 200 feet high. We reached the gate, which was metal and as high as the fence and maybe fifty feet wide. It was a big gate, with many guards standing outside, as our shuttle approached, they checked the pass and let us in. We saw three big buildings that were octagonal in shape. One was transparent and made of glass, which was the museum. The other two buildings were made of concrete. Everyone's eyes were excited and perplexed at the beauty of the buildings, electric fence, and all that we saw.

They first took us to the museum, where we saw all the artifacts of the different flying machines: jets, propellers, airplanes, choppers, flying saucers, space ladders, and many others. They were collected from different ages and donated by businessmen, the military and funding organizations. They had spent so much money on this to make the kids learn and improve the technology so they could make high-tech space machines.

My mind was all over the place, because the only way to escape TUAD was to take one of the flying machines. We memorized the layout of the place to know where all the entry and exit points were. Then, they took us to the engine shop, where they repaired and engineered all the spacecraft. It was a huge building and there were lots of engineers and scientists who were working. The chief scientist introduced his team and ran through all the projects that they were working on. If we learned well, we could be part of their team and they encouraged us to be space invaders. Then they took us to the third building, which was the docking or warehouse room where they kept all the spacecraft. We saw many models, including the latest one, the flying saucer Eagle's Eye.

They took us to the Blue Voyager out at the dock station, it was a huge saucer, and we couldn't see it with just two eyes. It was flat and circular in shape and made of metal and it had five legs for support. At the top of the saucer, it was a convertible, because the metal slid in and the pilot seat and cockpit were visible and covered over with a semicircle of glass. A big flight of steps came in from the saucer, and it was very wide and had fifteen steps to reach inside. The Blue Voyager could accommodate almost 4,000 people inside. So, there was plenty of room, we all went aboard.

They demonstrated how the saucer would look when it flew. We stood 80 meters from the saucer. It had two ducts, where air rushed in, generated by an electromagnetic field, and almost 600 Gigajoules of energy that could be produced, which made the saucer fly faster. We saw blue air coming out of the duct, and they slowly flew the saucer so that we could see how it looked when it was flying. Then they took all the kids for a ride to explain how the saucer worked. We carefully watched everything they were doing, from closing the doors, to how they turned on the engine, applied the brakes, drove it, and checked the cabin pressure.

It was a splendid experience and we saw ourselves high in the air. I felt like Superman flying in the air. Although it could fly 10,000 miles per minute, we couldn't fly the saucer any more than 1,000 miles per minute over the surface of the Earth. They took us for a good long trip, almost from Michigan to Portland, then over the Pacific Ocean and the borders of Mexico, Texas, Missouri, Illinois and over the Great Lakes and then back to TUAD. It was just a five-hour trip, but we enjoyed seeing from the air. But they didn't go to New York City. If they had, we would have jumped out of the saucer. They also gave us instructions on how to handle a flying suit when jumping off the plane to make a safe landing on the ground. We now had a decent understanding of how to fly the saucer, but to start the engine; we needed a fingerprint and encrypted code. We had to get those, because if we had those, we could escape from TUAD.

We were all working together to plan our escape and each one of us came up with a different idea; I stayed quiet and listened to all the conversation. The discussion went on for ten days, and I made a statement, saying, "There is someone already wanting to get out of TUAD and we should join them." Everyone looked at me for a clue, and Sadie was doubtful and asked me, "Who is it, Oliver?" Aika, with a smile and twisted her lips, said, "I guessed it would be them." I marveled at Aika's reply and asked her, "Who is that, dear?" she raised her eyebrows, sighed heavily and said, "Oh jeez, it's Nelek and Urson." Nikifor couldn't believe it; he jumped up and said, "What are you guys talking about? That's not true." I asked him why he thought that, and Niki replied, "Because Nelek is a genius, he is studying well and Urson is a smart kid, they are both doing well." I smiled at Niki's ignorance and said, "Let me ask you, Niki. The day when you, Fay, and Sadie were kidnapped by Peyton, it was midnight and all the doors were closed in the dormitory, but what were they doing outside?" Niki shrugged his shoulders and said, "Come on, Oliver that is not a valid reason. Nelek was working with the Russian mafia and maybe smoking some weed," and we all got annoyed by his answer and chimed, "Niki, the bad boy."

Niki was not convinced and insisted I give more evidence, so I told him everything I knew. I told him that the day we were watching the movie, I noticed both Nelek and Urson were giggling and looking at each other. All the kids were seriously watching the movie except those two. When we went to the flying saucer class, Nelek and Urson were recording video, using a secret camera. They recorded all the nooks and corners of the space station and they both had cameras embedded in their contact lenses. I noticed it when Urson's contact lens slipped from his eyeball when they demonstrated the flying saucer's air intensity that came out of the saucer ducts. Nelek was helping him and said, "Careful, Urson. I will record it. You relax," and I heard all their following conversation.

Everyone was astonished by my analysis, and somehow they became convinced that they were trying to escape. They wouldn't be completely convinced until they heard it from Nelek and Urson. We didn't want to go all together to talk to them, so Judah, Shu, and I went to speak to them by ourselves, because otherwise they might have gotten scared. When we met them, we didn't start the conversation about the escape. I started by saying, "Nelek, we are escaping from TUAD in the Blue Voyager within a few weeks and we need some help from you." Nelek was smart and reacted like he was not aware of anything and said, "Oh, really? That would be good for you guys. What help do you need, Oliver?" I replied, "I need the fingerprints and encrypted codes to start the engine."

Nelek casually said, "It was two miles from our school. How are you going to make it? And how are you going to pass through the electric walls, open the dock doors, and stuff like that?" I replied, "We didn't want to duplicate efforts, Nelek." Nelek looked at me wisely and said, "I know you are smart and I always liked you, Oliver. Are you sure you guys want to do this together?" I thanked him and said, "You are doing well here. Why are you planning to escape?" Then Nelek told us the whole story. He had been well trained in the Russian mafia on hacking and making nuclear bombs and he knew how to fly a saucer very well. "I liked my brother so much, I know TUAD would not let him leave, so I returned here to take my brother back to Russia and live happily back in Poland with our family and friends."

At this point, we understood what was going on, and I asked him, "What help do you want from my side?" and Nelek replied, "We need guns, ammunition and flamethrowers." I was wondering what he was trying to do and asked him, "Do you want to take down everyone in TUAD? We were not going to kill anyone." Judah also was not comfortable and said, "No killing dude," and Shu also agreed. Nelek laughed loudly and said, "How about snakes, bats and insects." I was clueless and asked him, "What are you talking about, Nelek?" Nelek wanted to challenge us, so he said, "Tell me how we are going to reach the space station from here." I said, "Maybe hide in the woods and run, hijack the shuttle, or build a teleportation machine like Matt Sterling." He answered wittily, "None of those are going to work. Even if we used one, we would get caught. Always remember this, Oliver: the answers are simple and close to our minds."

Then Nelek told us everything about the plan. There was a tunnel that ran from our school to the edge of the Great Lakes. It was built by the Native Americans with stones and painted with herbs, so until now, no one could detect it with any signals. He had found that information in one of the old archeology stones that he bought from one of the merchants in Russia. He decrypted it and found the exact location and it was in our TUAD, which was the reason he risked coming here to take his brother away. But Nelek found the entrance within a few weeks of coming to TUAD; it was in the drainage system. He made a hole in the wall in the drainage system and the hole led to the tunnel. It started from there and went all the way to the Great Lakes. All we needed was the password for the saucer to start it. We asked him if we needed the fingerprint, but he said he stole the pilot's glasses who was teaching us and took his fingerprint.

We were amazed by his master plan that he was working on. We asked him about the password and he replied that the password was in their local network, which could not be accessed from the Internet, so he didn't know how to get it. We told him we had the password and he was surprised by our statement, because he thought we were joking, but I made my point. He asked how we did it, and then we explained it to him. When we went on the tour to the space station we planted a dissolvable wireless chip in the water tap because they scan every five minutes for external chips and computers connecting to their network. We couldn't connect to their wireless network because they were monitoring us on their cameras. The wireless network was not accessible in the bathrooms and restricted locations. But the dissolvable wireless chip was programmed to automatically hack and connect to their wireless network and Niki was able to access the dissolvable chip from the bathroom. The water tap was not well monitored and we used it to evade all the other floor and building sensors. Niki went to the bathroom and connected to it with his I-gadget and hacked the password within five minutes. After five minutes, the chip automatically dissolved in the water and we didn't get caught by the scan.

Nelek and Urson clapped their hands, and Nelek said, "Never underestimate anyone. Everyone has talents." Nelek was a little suspicious about who we were and what we were up to and he hesitated to ask us. Finally he said, "Then, why do you guys fail in the exams and everyone calls you dumb?" I replied, "We want to get out of here, and we didn't want to do well here and stick our noses in TUAD forever." Nelek shook his head and asked me, "Where do you want to go? Do you want to go with me, Oliver, to Russia?" and I replied to him, "Thanks, Nelek, but we want to go to New York City." He laughed and replied, "I have heard of escape from New York City, but you say mission to New York City."

We made a deal. Nelek and Urson had the fingerprint and we had the password, so we could all work toward the escape together and no one would stab the other in the back. We needed guns, ammunition, flamethrowers, ropes, grenades, night-lights and plastic suits for protection against bugs, so we decided to ask for help from Moise Boti. Moise Boti initially was scared to help us, but he changed his mind because of our friendship and he wanted us to leave because of the problems with Peyton. He spent all his savings and bought all the necessary gear and ammunition on the black market. We stockpiled the gear, piece by piece, every day in the entrance of the tunnel, as we got ready for the escape.

Our final exam was approaching, and we were pretending to make an effort to learn and pass. But we knew the results beforehand; and we were all going to fail again. This time, instead of a written exam, they took us for oral and lab exams to make sure that written exams were not the problem for us. This was history in TUAD, because they had always used a written exam and never an oral or lab exam, unless you had a disability or had a hard time reading. But it was very funny; they would ask us questions and we would beat around the bush and never say the right answers. They gave us some clues to get the answers, but we never got near the correct ones. All the teachers pulled their hair out and couldn't stand us anymore, and they just told us we were going to repeat the third grade again. The good news was that we were escaping on July 4, my estimated birthday. Judah and I would be ten, and my other friends should be circling around their tenth birthdays. We picked July 4 because it was a holiday and everyone was relaxed and drunk, especially at TUAD, everyone stayed home and there was less security at the school.

We were waiting for July 4, and we still had a week to just hang out and plan out the other ideas. The best place to discuss the ideas was the football field. We also had Nelek and Urson with us all the time while we made plans. It was June 29, and I will never forget this date in my life because we started a fight and challenge with Ambrose. As we were walking and talking, Ambrose and his crew circled us, as usual, but this time, we had Nelek and Urson with us. Ambrose pushed Aika and Madison down to the ground. I don't know what went through Madison's mind, but she got up and walked, jumped, and slapped Ambrose on his cheek, champed her teeth, and with red eyes, she said, "You freak. I will feed you to the pigs." Ambrose was insulted in front of everyone and he lost his temper. Another kid grabbed Madison's hair and pulled it, saying, "You are dead today." Nelek was standing close to the kid who pulled Madison's hair, and he punched his face and his nose started to bleed.

Then every kid jumped on us, and it was a rumble. We started to punch each other, and I pulled Madison out, and Benjamin shouted, "Take her and run." Madison and I started to run away because she was the one who had started this and I wanted to make sure she didn't get hurt. Nelek jumped on Ambrose and pushed him to the ground, and he pulled a knife and held it to Ambrose's throat and warned him to stop the fight. Ambrose pissed in his pants and shouted, "Stop it, stop the damn fight." Everybody stopped fighting. Most of the kids' shirts were torn, including ours; we were all covered in dirt and looked a mess.

Nelek was holding his knife very tightly to Ambrose's throat, and with his left hand, he held Ambrose's jaw. Ambrose said, "Let me go, man, don't kill me." A couple of guards saw us and wanted to check what was happening, so they started to come toward us. Madison and I stopped running and watched them from a distance. Nelek saw the guards and let Ambrose loose, Ambrose got up and angrily said, "This is not over. You will all pay for it." Nelek replied, "You were scared like a weasel when I put my knife to your throat and now you say we are going to pay for it." Benjamin moved quickly and said to Ambrose, "Hey, we didn't have any grudge against you. You started this trouble, and we should settle it." Ambrose quickly responded, "Why don't we play a football match for three hours tomorrow night, starting at ten. Losers have to polish all the shoes." Nelek, without thinking twice, replied, "Yes. Done deal, and after that, everything ends. No more fights." Ambrose nodded and said, "Yes."

A couple of guards walked up to us and asked what was happening and we answered calmly, "We are betting on a football match tonight."

The guards saw all of the shirts were torn and everyone was hiding something, and one of them said, "If I see anyone fighting one more time, you will be punished with one month in the dark room." They left, and we all dispersed and went to the dormitory.

That night, we took a walk on the school campus. Everyone was quiet and looking at Madison for what she had done. Then Nelek understood what had happened and said, "Guys, we are friends and we shouldn't carry this in our hearts. What Madison did was correct. They mocked and pushed us. This has been happening for a long time, and it was time we took a stand." Nelek turned to Madison and encouraged her by saying, "You did a good job, Madison. We are proud of you. You are the bravest one and you stood for your values, and I like that." She was tight, but hearing this, she slowly smiled and said to Nelek, "Thanks, Nelek." Gradually we all started to appreciate her.

We started to talk about how we were going to face the game, because no one had ever played football, except for Nelek and Urson, who had played with other friends and Benjamin, who had played with his father. The rest of us knew the rules a little but we were not experts. But we had a unified spirit, and we wanted to win this game. Nelek and Benjamin ran an hour-long demonstration about the rules of the game, and we were so eager to play that we learned it that night. When we went to bed, the rules of the game were turning over in our minds. Anxiety was also in our hearts, and we couldn't sleep much.

The next morning, we practiced, Nelek, Urson, and Benjamin trained us and we picked it up fast and became vigorous while we practiced. Ambrose and his friends were watching us and the way we practiced created fear in them.

We all had dinner at Moise Boti's house early in the evening and were getting ready for the night match. We geared up in football strips and walked to the grounds. There were no guards on the football field, and it was quiet. We went to the grounds early, around nine o'clock and were waiting for Ambrose and his team to come. There was a lonely wind flowing at the grounds and our hearts were pounding faster and faster. They came ten minutes before ten and they were all in their football gear. Ambrose and his friends walked toward us, they looked like ghosts. Most of them were older and bigger than us. Nelek was standing in the front and all his team were standing behind him. Ambrose walked close to us and removed his helmet and asked Nelek, "Are we ready?" and Nelek said, "Yes." But Ambrose asked if Nelek was carrying his knife or other weapons, and he said no. We checked each other's team well, and no one was carrying any knives or weapons. This was a clash of vengeance. Each team had twelve players but Ambrose had three extra friends. So, he picked the weakest among them and asked them to stay outside the field, and one kid was the referee. On his team in the field, there were three girls and the rest were boys, but on our team, we had five girls and seven boys.

Every minute was exciting and thrilling; we decided Benjamin would be the quarterback. Ambrose was the quarterback for his team. We threw the toss, and Ambrose won it and chose to play the ball first as the offense. The time was quarter after ten, so we started the clock. We started to play and we were not doing well. Ambrose's team threw us around like ragdolls and we were flying in the air. But we never gave up, and we fought. We were not strong, but we were united, and we played and gave them a tough fight. Ambrose's target was Madison, so Nelek and Niki were always close to her and protected her. Ambrose's crew was the referee and he was favoring Ambrose and his team and blowing the whistle all the time for anything that was a foul. We couldn't do anything about that. No matter what it was, we lost, and in the first hour, the score was 25 to 0.

We had a break after the first hour and planned a game strategy. We had some water and someone was walking toward us and we saw something that we didn't expect. Peyton was standing there in a referee uniform, and he had his wicked smile on and said, "Welcome, boys. We should have a good game." Niki shook his head and said, "No way. Where'd this pig come from?" We walked to the center of the field, and Peyton was up to his usual bag of tricks. I said to him, "Peyton, this has nothing to do with you, so you should step out." Peyton got furious and replied, "I saw the score. It was twenty-five, and you are a big zero, as usual. I am trying to improve your situation from zero." Peyton didn't want to leave and Ambrose, knowing the situation, wanted Peyton to be the referee. We all wanted to walk away because we felt it was going to be unfair. Then Ambrose shouted, "You cowards, come back. If you walk, then you have to polish all the shoes in TUAD, including Peyton's." We all stopped walking, and Peyton said, "Oh, now I understand. Hey, shoe boys, come back, please?" Benjamin said, "We have to face it," and we all turned back and saw that Moise Boti was walking in a referee uniform as well, and we felt some relief and were happy. Peyton saw Moise Boti, and the smile vanished, and now he looked pissed off.

Now we had something on the table, and we cut a deal so we had two referees. Jay Mons, the punk was also there, standing outside the field, but he never came in for any of this discussion because he was scared of Moise Boti. We started to play and Moise Boti was encouraging us, it was a tough game. We were playing offense now, and forty feet away, Benjamin passed the ball to Ejaz, who was the runner. He caught the ball, slipped every defender on the field, and ran like a horse to make the first touchdown for us. When he made the first touchdown, we screamed out loud, and we ran and carried him on our shoulders and ran, circling the field. Seeing us, Peyton shouted, "There is a long way to go. It is only twenty-five and seven. Come back, you rats." The game started to get more aggressive, and in the second hour, Ambrose's team had thirty-one and we had twenty-one. Nikifor and Nelek made two touchdowns. The final hour was running out and the test of who was going to be polishing the shoes was around the corner. We took some water, and Moise was giving us tips and telling us the weak spots on Ambrose's team and how we should tackle next time so they wouldn't score, and how we needed to score.

The third hour started, but we were not exhausted because we had to win this game, and we never did anything successful in TUAD, this was an actual test for us. We played our best, and we gave all our energy. The score was close now, and Ambrose's team had forty-one, and we had forty because Ejaz, Fay, and Nelek made touchdowns. There was only a minute left and we were playing defense. Ambrose's team was ten yards from the line. Peyton and Moise Boti were arguing about everything the whole time. Moise Boti was fair and Peyton, of course, was not. The last minute was the final test and we didn't have the ball on offense, but we still had hope. The whistle blew, and we were huddling. Ambrose passed the ball to his team, but there was a turning point in the game when Benjamin jumped as high as he could and grabbed the ball, away from them. Then Benjamin ran faster and faster, and he ducked and pushed by everyone on Ambrose's team. He passed everybody and ran almost seventy yards from our line. No one was there to defend against him, and the clock was running out fast, we had nine seconds left.

Every eye in the field was on Benjamin. He pushed himself but started to slow down, and he stopped near the touchdown line but didn't pass it. We had five seconds left, and he stood before the line and didn't move, we were all shouting and screaming, "Run Benjamin, run, run." Our voices were getting strained, and the clock ticked and ticked, and then time was over. Peyton blew the whistle, and everyone was frozen. No one knew what had happened. Ambrose and his team were dazed, they were not happy about the victory and stood motionless. Benjamin was just standing before the line with the ball, and Judah ran to check on him. Seeing Judah running, we all went to check on Benjamin. Judah asked him, "What happened? Are you all right?" He didn't reply, but dropped the ball and started to walk off the field.

We all followed behind him, Moise Boti also came to see Benjamin. Benjamin sat down on the lower deck of the stage, and his face was filled with thoughts. I went and kneeled before him and asked, "What happened, Benjamin? We would have won the match." He replied blithely, "If we won, they would make us stay in TUAD and coach us to play football. We have to go to New York City. Do you remember, Oliver?" Everyone was looking at each other, and Aika asked, "Benjamin, but who knows? We were just playing. It was just a game." Benjamin replied, "I know what I did. Don't ask me any more questions, please. I am very sorry for what I have done, and I will polish all the shoes, because it was my fault." Aika felt bad and said, "No, Benjamin, I didn't mean that. I am sorry." Then we saw his eyes with tears and we didn't ask any more questions.

We knew only one thing: we had to show our shiny teeth and polish the shoes. No one knew what had happened to Benjamin, but I knew he was hiding something. Ambrose and his friends were not happy, and they never rejoiced over the victory. Peyton and Jay Mons were the only animals running and jumping around. Peyton insisted that Ambrose bring all his and his friends' shoes, but he refused and Peyton started threatening him. They were scared of Peyton, so they brought all their black school shoes with some polish and brushes.

Nelek took me aside and asked me what had happened with Benjamin, and all I said was "I don't know. Sorry, Nelek; we shouldn't have involved you. Benjamin is our friend and it is our responsibility and not you Nelek." Nelek became disappointed and said, "You say I am not your friend, Oliver, and you hurt me," and I replied, "I didn't mean that, Nelek. You are our friends, always, Nelek. The only difference is that we were a little messed up about some concepts and promises we believed and made, and we didn't know if it was right or wrong, and we involved you." Nelek replied, "You guys have so much mystery to you, which always makes me feel better about our friendship."

No one's faces were happy after such a humiliating experience, but some divine thoughts came to our minds: If we had won, how would Ambrose and his friends have felt when they polished our shoes? The same feeling that we were going through, because we are all humans. But we could do it because we were raised properly, and we are the chosen ones. We should have humility, and maybe this polishing would teach us a lesson. I told everyone that we should do it happily, but we couldn't. Still, we tried our best, and we gave the best shoe polish in town.

All the time, Moise Boti couldn't watch this, and he left the grounds. Peyton and Jay Mons were very happy and enjoyed every millisecond when we polished the shoes. While we were polishing, I saw Shu's tears falling on the shoes, and she was shining with her tears. After we polished, we gave the shoes back to Ambrose and his friends, and Peyton commented, "So, fast boys, you kids have some good skill. God created all men and women with some skill. He never fails."

Judah slowly walked to Peyton and stared at him, and Peyton, in turn, looked at Judah doubtfully and asked, "What do you want?" Peyton had never seen Judah on any occasion talking to him, and Judah asked him, "Do you know Abraham Lincoln?" He replied, "Yeah, the Civil War man." Judah said, "Yeah, we call him the sixteenth president and the man who freed the slaves in America, a hero." Peyton replied angrily, "So, what does that have to do with anything?" Judah said, "I will tell you a story that happened in his life. One day, President Lincoln was polishing his shoes in the White House and one of his staff members walked in and saw him polishing his shoes. He was very surprised and said, 'Sir, presidents don't polish their own shoes,' and President Lincoln replied, 'Then whose shoes do they polish?'" Peyton, from his manic blissfulness, slowly changed and asked Judah, "What does that mean?" Judah boldly replied, "I told the story. You should tell me what it means. If you don't have an answer, you could polish my shoes, and maybe that would give you a hint."

Peyton got wild and was about to hit him, but we all quickly circled Peyton and Jay Mons and Moise Boti came back to check on us. Peyton and Jay Mons saw Moise Boti and decided to leave, but before they left, Peyton looked at Judah with the utmost anger and said, "My priority has changed, you prick. You will be dead soon." Judah didn't stop his mouth from saying, "Before that, tell me the answer to the polishing story, or else my shoes are always waiting for a craftsman's hand." They both left, and we all looked at Judah very astonished. He was quiet and observing. We didn't know what was happening that night, because everything was a puzzle, and we were all sad and tired and went to bed. All night, every mind was thinking about Judah and where he got such stuff.

The next morning, as soon as we got up, we asked Judah where he got the story about Lincoln and his shoes. He said he had read it in an article the previous Presidents' Day, and he found the message. We also asked him why he had become aggressive and tried to pick a fight with Peyton. All he said was "He broke my threshold." That was a fair answer. He was the softest and most meek friend in our group and Peyton didn't even go out of his way to make Judah angry. Don't break anyone's threshold, because you don't know what will come out of them.

We had three days left before the escape, and Moise wanted to give us a grand dinner. He asked to have it three days before the escape so that it could arouse suspicion on the TUAD side. Nelek and Urson were also invited. It was the usual stuff, and Moise Boti asked me to stay out of sight of his wife, but my other friends were talking to her and made her feel happy. While Moise was cooking pasta in the kitchen, I was helping him, and he asked me, "You never said where you are going after the escape from TUAD. I know there is something you are hiding from me, and I never had a chance to ask you. Could you tell me, Oliver?"

I was stirring the sauce, and said, "You never said why you always ask me to stay away from your wife. Before I leave, you should take me to her because I want to say goodbye to her." Moise Boti was dumbfounded and asked me, "Oliver finds things out, so who will start telling the little secrets between us?" I responded, "You go, Moise." He was cutting tomatoes and stopped, and he looked at me and said, "You are like my son, Oliver, my son Apera Boti." I asked him, "Where is he?" and Moise Boti's eyes were wet with tears when he said, "In heaven, resting peacefully." I was puzzled. "You mean he is dead," and tears started sailing to the ground, and he grieved and said, "He is no more."

I apologized to him for asking, and he told me the story. Apera, Moise Boti's son, was seven years old, and at that time, Moise Boti was working for the CIA. Moise Boti was living in Michigan and had a solitary life until a thunder of pain came and struck him. Apera was returning from school when he was kidnapped by some bad guys who sexually assaulted him, chopped him into pieces and dumped him in the river. They found his son's body in the river and they found the two men who did it, they were sentenced to death. Moise Boti's wife, hearing of her son's death was terrified and had experienced serious trauma and became paralyzed, the functioning of her brain has reduced day by day. The only thing she could remember was her son's face and Moise Boti. When she saw her son's picture or video, she anxious and started to bite, shout, scream, and become violent. Her blood pressure increased, she bled out of her nose, and eventually they had to take her to the hospital. For these reasons, he had removed all the pictures of his son from the house.

Moise Boti left his job to take care of his wife. He made an oath to himself that he would protect all innocent kids from sexual abuse. He heard stories that it was happening in TUAD, so he decided to take a job at Hoplife to help the foster kids. The first day that he saw me, he felt his son was back from the dead. That was the reason he helped us get the locket from the administrator clerk.

I felt very sad about his son's death and I was proud of Moise Boti for taking care of his wife and of foster kids like us. I didn't hesitate to tell him the truth about the mission to New York City and Nathalie. He was shocked, but he was happy to help us and wished me lots of luck.

We had dinner that night, but I didn't feel well and couldn't swallow properly. The whole time I was thinking about Apera. The world was cruel and unjust and I thanked the heavens and earth for keeping me and my friends safe, I prayed to the heavens and earth that no kids from then on would be abused.

After dinner, everyone was standing outside and I went to talk to Moise Boti's wife, who was sitting in her wheelchair looking out the window. I touched her hand and called, "Mom." She heard me and slowly turned to look at me. She was recollecting her memories and slowly started to smile and hold my hand. She started to get excited, champing her teeth and started to turn aggressive. But I went to hug her and kept my face in her chest and said to her heart, "I am alive. Please don't cry." It had been years since she had spoken, but that day, she opened her mouth and said, "I know you are always alive." Then she started to relax and calm down. Moise Boti was surprised and his heart was blissful that his wife had spoken after such a long time and at how relaxed she was now.

Moise Boti quickly went outside and told my friends that he would bring me back later. They left me at Moise Boti's house and went to their dormitory. I still remembered that I had hugged her for more than an hour on her chest and I could feel her love was flowing and I was receiving it, and I felt the love of a mother. I spoke to her for a few hours about whatever made her happy. All the time, she looked into my face directly and steadily, and with enthusiasm, she felt like her son was talking to her. I decided to stay there with her and spend the night with her. That night with Moise Boti's wife, I felt that there were many good people in this world. I realized my life had some purpose and I was going in the right direction. The next day I said my final goodbye to Moise Boti and Miss Boti, filling their house with joy and peace.

We had two more days before the escape. It was July 4, and we spent the day at the school celebrations that were happening. We had different events, sports, entertainment, and a good lunch. We behaved normally and there was no trace or clue to cause suspicion. We had fireworks at the school and it was really splendid and colorful. All the celebrations came to an end at around eleven o'clock, and everyone went to bed.

It was time for the escape, and we got up slowly with a bag where we had put all the stuff we required. Then, we moved like foxes, making no sound, and left the dormitory building. We had planned to meet at the drainage system near our auditorium building. We walked so stealthily that we passed the floodlights and the night watch from the guards easily and finally reached the drainage system. Slowly, one by one, from different buildings and finally Nelek. We opened the manhole, which was four feet wide, and Nelek and Nikifor jumped down to take all the gear that we needed. One by one, we dressed in the plastic coats, which covered the whole body, and put on head masks with oxygen in the back. We were all ready to go into the drainage system and Nelek and Nikifor went to open the ammunition box.

We heard some voices and someone was walking with a flashlight and flashed it us. We heard a voice say, "What are you doing, little pigs?" We recognized Peyton and Jay Mons standing there. They had guns in their hands pointed at us and said quietly, "Hands up," and we all raised our hands. We had a feeling that we were caught, and Peyton said, "My time is here, right now. I will kill all of you and just say you tried to escape and I stopped you. I'll say you freaks were trying to kill us and for protection we shot you down." We were all shivering because we were caught red-handed and Peyton, seeing that we were in fear, asked, "Who wants to die first?" We heard a splat like sound and both Jay Mons and Peyton fell to the ground unconscious. We didn't know what had happened and raised our flashlights; our minds were blown when we saw Ambrose and his six friends carrying baseball bats in their hands. They had hit Peyton and Jay Mons hard on the back of their heads. I heard Ambrose saying, "Come on, guys, escape. Run from here, and we will take care of them." We didn't know what to say. We just said, "Thanks very much, Ambrose." Ambrose was whispering, "Don't waste time. Good luck."

We all jumped into the drainage system and opened the ammunition box and took out a flamethrower. It was heavy, and we had three of them. Niki, Benjamin, and Nelek carried it. We had six shotguns, twelve small hand pistols and two laser guns. The laser guns were cool because we could kill anything we needed to. We turned on the flashlights on our heads; we all had flashlights in our hands, too. We walked almost sixty meters in the sewage, and it smelled rotten. Although we had on masks, they were not airtight, we couldn't stand the stink. My mind was thinking about the bad smell, and I said to myself, *how much worse can a man stink than this?*

We managed to walk in the gutter, and we stopped and found the marked X on the wall. Nelek asked us to remove the bricks in the wall, so we removed them one by one. Nelek and Urson had made this hole in the wall all this time. We took half an hour to remove all the bricks, and saw a hole developing. We helped each other climb into the hole, Nelek was leading us and Urson was in the middle, guiding us. We crawled into the hole, sand and concrete were falling and it was very smoky. The hole base was solid; Nelek put some vacuum holders on the floor we were crawling on and buckled the metal rope from the vacuum holders to his waist. He said it was fifteen meters to jump, so everyone, with their vacuum holders, would jump carefully, and he would lead us. He jumped down quickly, reached the bottom, threw some flash sticks to create light, and then gave a short whistle. Next was Shu. She was scared, so we encouraged her, and she jumped into the hole with the rope. Everyone was scared, we all jumped, closing our eyes.

We got down to the bottom of the tunnel, and Nelek saw all our faces were terrified, the profound darkness made us more scared. Nelek gave the instructions, "Don't run anywhere if you are scared. We work as a team, and if we panic and scatter, most of us will get killed." We asked what would be in the tunnel, and he said, "Some giant poisonous snakes, some big spiders, bats, and all that we could handle. If a snake bites you, don't worry; we have plastic coats on that are covered with synthetic polymer, so the snake's teeth can't reach the body." Aika asked him, "Should we shoot if we see something?" and Nelek replied, "If you feel it is attacking you, just shoot, and when someone is shooting, just be on the other side of the shooter so there are no cross fires or accidents. And remember, we will easily kill anything with the flamethrower. Benjamin and Niki both have flamethrowers."

I asked Nelek, "How far do we need to walk to reach the space station?" Nelek, breathing heavily, said, "Two miles." Then Nelek said he was taking the lead with the flamethrower, and Benjamin should be in the middle and Niki and Ejaz in the last position with another flamethrower. "Always keep your eyes and ears open and don't panic," Nelek said. We said Nathalie's prayer and started to walk down the tunnel. It was damn dark, but we had flashlights on our heads and in our hands, and a small portable rolling flashlight that was very powerful and could send light up to a twenty-five-meter radius.

We walked slowly and we could hear crickets and frogs. It was wet and damp. We saw spider webs and we cleared them with the flamethrower. The first 500 meters, we didn't have any problems except seeing some frogs, insects and bugs. But then something scary was before us and it was a boa, and it was big. As soon as we saw it, we stopped. We didn't know what to do, but Nelek said, "Just open your eyes and see how I am going to kill it. Do not close your eyes. Watch the killing and you will be strong." The boa moved after it sensed us, and Nelek walked toward it and sprayed fire on it. The poor snake was rolling and moving and burning into ashes. We said, "Oh, my God, you killed it," and Nelek laughed like a cruel killer and said, "Yes, I did." We asked him if he was afraid and he said he had been trained in the mafia, and killing anything in our way was the first lesson.

Then we started to move and saw some big spiders, but no matter what we saw, we just threw fire on them. We were literally killing everything we saw that was big or dangerous, and the poor creatures all died in the fire. We saw some reindeer bones and swine, and we didn't know where they had come from, but they were laying there. We saw some nice paintings on the wall, which portrayed Native American culture. One painting stuck in all our minds for a long time. It was a prince with a crown with a locket around his neck and five girls and seven boys were following him. We didn't say anything about it because Nelek and Urson were there. They looked at me, but we pretended to ignore it and walked by. We had almost walked the two miles and were sweating badly and then Nelek took some gadget in his hand and checked something. We asked what he was checking, he said he was looking for latitude and longitude, and it matched the one he was looking for. Then he asked everyone to sit down, and we did. Then Nelek started to talk and give instructions to us. "So, we are in the right place, the space station is forty meters above us. I have a laser drill so that I can pull down all the sand and the concrete materials above us. You guys should take a shovel and just move the sand as I drill it. This will take an hour.

"Once we get to the top, we will be behind the warehouse where they park all the flying saucers. We are taking the small Blue Voyager flying saucer called the Mini-Pack Voyager, and we are leaving in that." We asked him if we could take the big Blue Voyager, and he said no because we needed to open the whole gate, which would take some time and we would have a big problem. But, if we took the Mini-Pack, the gate would be opened only a few meters, and it would be hard to notice. He said there would be four guards inside the warehouse and we needed to make sure we shot them. We said that we wouldn't kill them, and he said we would use the tranquilizer guns, which would make them unconscious for a few hours, which was more than enough. Then we would start the saucer and move it slowly to the gates and the small opening with the lights turned off and we would bring the flying saucer out and fly away.

The important thing was that it could fly half the speed of the Blue Voyager, which was around 5,000 miles per minute. We would need to be flying at 1,000 miles per minute because, per law, that was the speed limit. It would take the tracking and law enforcement a while to understand what was happening, and we would reach New York City in a minute. From there, we would jump from the flying saucer with the suits on. It would take a minute for all of us to jump, and then, they would fly back to Russia in another four to five minutes.

We asked him if he would be detected by radars or satellite. He told us that by the time the guards saw us and informed the control room to shoot us down, it would be three minutes. It was a saucer from the school, and they would be in a state of confusion about what was going on. By that time, they would be leaving America and be over the Atlantic Ocean. Also, they could not shoot saucers like that until we attacked them first. Because it was an old saucer and a prototype and hijacked from the school's research department, they would think first about what had happened and who did it. We should use this gap in time to think and analyze our escape.

He asked us if we were clear with the plan, and I asked him curiously, "Why didn't you tell us this before?" He replied wittily, "You didn't ask me, and moreover, if I would have told you guys beforehand, everyone would have come up with some new idea, and we would never have made it this far. There is risk involved, and we are taking it, so that was why I simplified the plan when I explained the escape to you. This was the right moment for you to know and act accordingly."

He started to dig in the sand above us with a laser drill to make a hole and dug three feet in diameter. All Nelek had to do was make a hole and mount the laser drill on the ground facing upward and it would rotate and cut the sand, and the sand would fall down. We were all working to move the sand from the hole to clear space between the ground and the top of the hole. It was tough work and we worked as a team nonstop, but finally, we made the hole. Then Nelek shot a couple of rope guns into the hole, which went outside the opening, took a bend, and attached firmly onto the concrete. The rope gun was automatic and would clinch in any direction we programmed it. Nelek was the first one to climb into the hole, which was forty meters high. We had the supports tied to our hips, so there was no way we could fall down. Nelek was standing in the space station and guarded us as we climbed. Nelek took another rope and dropped it down. We took a deep breath and climbed two at a time, resting our backs against each other and putting our legs on the sides. We took almost forty-five minutes to climb up the hole, with Nelek shouting quietly to hurry up. When we all got out of the tunnel, it was four in the morning, and it was dark and we saw the guards moving here and there.

With the same laser drill, we made a hole in the warehouse wall in the back. We attached some grippers to it and slowly moved the piece from the wall. We saw a couple of saucers from the hole. There were no guards standing near, and we slipped inside the warehouse one by one. The warehouse was not that big and had fifteen to twenty aircrafts and saucers in it. Now we needed to spot the four guard's location and take them down. There was one guard inside a controller room with computers and phones, and we decided he would be the last one to be taken down. There were two guards standing at the front of the gate inside the warehouse, the warehouse gate was closed. The fourth guard was standing near a staircase that was in the middle of the building. All the guards were carrying guns.

We had Benjamin's father to thank for teaching us to take a clean shot. Nelek, Benjamin, Aika, and Ejaz were really good shooters, so we split into four directions. We signaled each person to take their turn by sending a signal on a watch that beeped light. We went slowly, steadily, making no noise and hiding behind the planes' wheels and flying saucers' legs. We were lucky that the guards were resting and relaxed that day. The two guards at the gate were half asleep, so Aika and Ejaz went closer to the gate to take a clean shot. The guard who was standing near the staircase was smoking and was alert. Benjamin and two of us went close to him, hiding behind the jet wheels. The first shot should be taken by Benjamin, because the guard near the staircase was alert. Benjamin was a good shooter like his father, he never trembled. He took aim and fired a shot into his throat. The darts were highly loaded with toxins, and within one second, it shut down his nervous system. The guard hit the staircase, his eyes moving and dripping, and he fell down without making a sound.

Now it was Ejaz's and Shu's turns, we signaled for Ejaz to take his turn. This was the first time he had ever shot someone, and his hands were shaking. Shu was with him, and she held his hand and whispered, "You can do it, my dear." Hearing this, he stopped shaking, aimed well, and fired the shot. It went straight into the guard's neck, and he woke up and tripped over the leg of the other guard. He woke up, too and saw the other guard was moving his hands for help. Now Aika had to take her shot quickly, she was nervous, but Niki was with her and said, "Come on, you can do it." She shot and hit him in the shoulder, it plunged through his shirt into his body.

But the darts just pinched his body, and the sedative wasn't enough. He quickly realized what was happening, pulled the dart from his shoulder, and turned back and saw Aika, Nikifor, and Madison. He quickly took his gun to fire a warning shot, but Niki was so fast, he took the gun from Aika and fired a shot into his throat. He got him this time, but he was about to drop his gun. I was with Ejaz and Shu, but I ran and caught the gun before it hit the ground. The guard was heavy and he fell on me. It was a very hard fall, but he didn't make any noise. Then, quickly, all of my friends came from both sides and found me struggling to get up. They helped move him slowly, and finally, with great effort, they moved him from on top of me. But then we heard a voice saying, "Who are you kids there?" and it was the guard from the control room. We were all scared and thought we were caught. I slowly got up but Nelek fired a shot into his chest and Benjamin fired one more shot into his neck, and in no time he fell to the floor with a sound like a dropped sandbag. We quickly ran to check on him. He was not hurt, but he had a bruise on his head and was bleeding. We ran and grabbed the first-aid kit, but Nelek said that if we wanted to leave quickly, we didn't have any time for that. I said to Nelek, "We should make sure he is okay before we leave. You go and start the engine. It will not take much time." Nelek shrugged and said, "Whatever—you guys are too kind. It doesn't work like this in an escape." We asked everyone to go and help Nelek, and Shu, Fay, and I stayed and stopped the guard's bleeding and wrapped a bandage around his head. Nelek and Niki went to get the flying saucer ready, and our other buddies went and removed the two guards at the front gate. We moved the wounded guard slowly and rested his head and body in a sitting position against the wall.

Niki and Nelek got the flying saucer ready and were shouting for us to hurry up. We ran inside the saucer and saw that everyone in the saucer was geared up in flying suits already. The others, after moving the guards, had hurried up and run to the flying saucer. It was a small saucer with 100 seats and looked exactly like a mini-coup. They asked us to hurry up and put on the suit, and we did.

Nelek started to give instructions again. "We did it! So far so good. We made it. Thanks, everyone. We are a good team. Someone has to run to the control room and open the gate slowly by hitting the manual button and moving it to the lowest number and then quickly run back to the flying saucer." We asked Nelek, "Do we have a manual button? Is it not in the computer?" and he replied, "They have a manual button under the table in case of device failure, and moreover, the computer is locked, and we don't have a password to it." We were all surprised by his intelligence and he asked us, "Who's going?" and Fay volunteered. Nelek said once again to Fay to go into the control room and hit the button and that she needed to get back fast to get into the saucer. Then we would accelerate the plane to full speed, hold it and wait until the gate opened to have enough space. Once we got the gates opened, we would get out of the warehouse, and once we were in the flying station, we would hit almost 1,000 miles an hour. Then it would take exactly one minute and twenty seconds to reach New York City. "You guys all be ready at the door, and when I stop it, you have one minute and forty seconds to jump out of the plane. Then, Urson and I will head south and back home. Are we clear, guys?" We all whispered, "Yes." Nelek had a long face and said, "I didn't hear that, my friends," and we all shouted, "Yes, sir, yes, sir, we got it." Nelek had the fingerprint for the authorization and swiped the scanner with a plastic sheet he used to carry it in. Then Nikifor put in the encrypted password to start the engine, and the engine started.

Nelek asked Fay to run and open the door to the control room. She ran fast like a cheetah and went to turn the button to one. We all were nervous and wanted her to come back fast, and we were shouting, "Hurry, Fay, faster." Every second we were anxious; she came back in time, and was breathing heavily, and we gave her some water to drink. We closed the saucer door, and saw the gate of the warehouse moving slowly. Nelek released the launching pad scaffolding of the saucers, and it was in the air. As the door opened, Nelek turned off all the lights in the saucer.

Then, the worst thing happened. The door got jammed and was not moving, and it only opened half-way. The door was not moving, we realized that it was jammed and we asked Nelek whether he wanted to go back to the control room, but he said we didn't have time for that. We saw through the gap of the gate that some guards were coming to check what was happening. We didn't know what to do. We thought we were trapped, but Nelek realized the situation and said, "Buckle up, guys," and we ran from the cockpit and buckled up quickly. He turned the side lights on in the saucer. He accelerated and started moving the saucer faster and faster, and we were nearing the gate. The guards were walking and we saw that they had moved away from the gate.

Then, Nelek tilted the saucer vertically, and we all swung to the side. The saucer turned and screeched. He passed the saucer through the gate of the warehouse, and then turned it back to the horizontal position. He then slowed down, and we were in the middle of the campus, and more lights started to turn on. We could hear shouting through the speakers: "Who is that? Do you have authorization to fly?" We saw guards starting to pull out their guns and point them toward us, and we saw a couple of tanks pointing at us, too. Nelek closed his eyes and slowly opened them and replied to the guards on the wireless, "I don't have authorization and I don't need it. Stay steady, guys. We are making a run for it." He accelerated to the saucer's full speed, and more air started to come out of the ducts. We heard warning messages, saying, "Do not move. We will shoot." Nelek bit his teeth and said, "Catch me if you can."

He started to fly high at high speed and moved away from their grounds. They started to fire at us, and we saw shots, bullets, and lasers flying around us. It was a deep action moment, and we stayed quiet. Our hearts stopped as one laser shot hit the transmission and navigator equipment, and we heard a beep going on and alerting us. We passed TUAD air base and thought we were safe. Nelek said we lost the navigator, but it didn't matter because he knew the direction. He flew faster and faster and maintained 1,000 miles a minute, and within a minute, he halted and asked us to jump quickly because we had no time.

We had never done a jump like this before and we didn't know what to do. Nelek opened the back door of the saucer and asked us to jump. He said we didn't have much time to debate who was going to jump first. Niki was the first one to jump out. Next was Madison, and then it was one after the other. I stayed until last and made sure that everyone left, and when it came to my turn, Nelek called to me and said, "You can go with me, Oliver." I replied to him with some hesitation, "No, my friend, thanks for the help." Nelek answered, "Well, good luck, Oliver. If any problems happen with the escape, just blame it on Urson and me. Do not hesitate. I will bite the bullet." His eyes were wet with tears, and he said, "Goodbye, Oliver. I owe my friendships to you, and I will do anything for you." I replied with my last departing words, "Me too, Nelek. Thanks for everything. Be safe." Then I jumped off the saucer, and the back door closed, and they left to live their lives.

We all jumped out of the saucer and from the sky, we saw lots of lights on the ground. We were falling rapidly because these were auto flying suits that were sensor to land on the ground. They automatically pulled up and slowed down when we were 500 feet from the ground. We used the handle, and moved it in the wind and landed safely. We dropped down in different places, and it was still dark. Niki landed in a tree, and Sadie in a pond, and the rest landed on the grass. We used flashlights to find each other, and it took almost twenty minutes for us to re-unite. Niki was hanging from the top of a tree, and we had a hard time getting him down. Sadie was wet and cold.

We were all happy about the escape and we thought we were now in New York City. We hadn't carried much food, but we had a small backpack with a set of clothes, bread, apples and sausages. We wanted to make sure that no one found us, so we went to hide and wait for the sun to come up. We saw a damaged building that had been bombed and was in bad shape, so we walked into it and stayed. We were exhausted and needed some rest after the perilous long journey we had made.

Chapter 18
The Long Walk

WE WOKE UP AROUND EIGHT IN THE MORNING AND WERE STILL TIRED. After a long time the sun was shining back on us and our free life. We started walking but we didn't know where we were. We were discussing which way it was to New York City and finally decided to go east. As we walked through the neighborhood, it seemed familiar to me. I asked my buddies but they all said they didn't know, except for Judah. Slowly, as we walked, Madison started saying the same thing—that the neighborhood seemed familiar to her. After a few blocks, we had the feeling we were back in Wisconsin. I ran fast to make sure we hadn't made this damned mistake but when I got close to a highway, I saw a billboard that read, "Milwaukee Welcomes You Back." I was flabbergasted and my whole body shut down. My friends were running behind me and saw me staring at something. They looked at the same thing I was "Milwaukee Welcomes You Back."

Everyone started to frown; we threw the bags on the ground and started jumping and yelling at everything. After a while, we sat down for some time and everyone was quiet. Slowly, Ejaz said, "Nathalie was right: we used technology and transportation to go to New York City. We disobeyed." I was knocked out by what he said and I turned and looked at him, expressionless. I didn't know what to say to him. He saw me and quickly said, "I am sorry. I didn't mean anything." Ejaz had started it, but everyone was thinking the same thing and no one knew how to react to this situation. I asked Ejaz, "Isn't it right that we should go back and confess to Nathalie at her grave," and Ejaz replied, "Yes, we should. I've never been there." We decided to go back and visit Nathalie's burial place.

We were on West Cornell Street. We had to walk to east of Locust Street, where we had buried her. As we walked, Niki turned on his space station radio. As soon as he turned it on, we heard them talking about ten kids who escaped the TUAD in Michigan. Then he switched to the Internet and saw the news on a video and our faces were all over the news. They wanted to offer a reward to anyone who could help them find us. In the news, they used all sorts of catchy phrases, and the one we heard the most was "The great escape from TUAD School." We became popular and famous overnight, but there was little about Nelek and

Urson missing from TUAD, so they didn't know whether they had escaped or not.

We were careful and split into two groups of three and a group of four to avoid suspicion traveling together. We took different routes and finally met in a spot east of Locust Street. We had to walk and hide, and be careful not to be noticed. The roads were dusty and scary. No one was on the road. The houses were burned and bombed, trash was everywhere. As we walked, we saw a tree and we could recognize some familiar places. We also saw that there were flowers next to the tree. Then we realized it could be Nathalie's burial place and we started to run. We ran, and there were different flowers in the burial place and we quickly searched the tree for the inscription we had written. We saw it, the inscription was still there, "M O N J S," slightly faded but clearly visible. We showed all the other buddies the inscription and they were reassured of our past. But Fay was standing alone and staring at the flowers, and we asked her what she was doing. She was disturbed and in deep thought. She was quiet and then replied, "Did you see the flowers?" and we replied, "Yes, we did." She shook her head and said, "Do you guys really see them?" We saw them and Shu, who said the same thing: "Look at the flowers and the many types that are here." We didn't understand what she meant, and we asked her what was so special. She said there were many varieties of flowers for a six-foot plot.

Then we started counting; it was mind blowing, but there were 100 varieties of flowers growing in her cemetery. You could name any flower you know and it was there: roses, lilies, daisies, iris, tulips, cactus, butterfly weed, barberry, and much more. We were wondering how all these flowers came to be in one place and thought maybe the birds had brought seeds or wind or someone had planted them for fun, but we didn't know. One thing we knew was that all these flowers grow in different climatic conditions and they were hard to fit in one place. But however it had happened, Nathalie was good fertilizer. Her soul, body, and mind were pure, and the flowers here reassured us and renewed our hope that we were going in the right direction. On this day, all my friends who hadn't seen Nathalie felt more confident that the mission was clear.

We confessed that we had used a flying saucer to escape from TUAD to New York City and used a boat to cross the lake. We were paying for what we had done and we swore we would never do it again. We made a resolution to never repeat it again and we were going to walk to New York City, against all zeros and ones.

We left late in the evening and started walking together to find someplace to rest. We heard a chopper flying and saw that a drone was approaching and soon we realized the chopper was following us. We were walking in the middle of the block, and on both sides there were buildings. There were a few people living on that block, and we heard them come out of their homes and watch us. They started to shout, "Here are the ten kids who escaped from TUAD." We understood what was happening and we started to run. There was a warning message from the cops in the chopper asking us not to run. As we ran, a few people started to chase us and we used all our strength to run and escape.

Then a chopper came from the other side toward us, shouting a warning message. The big drone stopped above us and ropes and ladders came out of it. There were tanks and vans approaching from all sides of the roads and they trapped us in the middle. We stopped running and wanted to surrender because we felt there was no way to escape from them. Six people were chasing us: two of them grabbed hold of Sadie and the other four caught Judah, Aika, Ejaz, and Nikifor. Then cops and FBI agents started to run out from the van and fired shots for the people to release us. But the people were not allowing us to go because they had found us and needed the reward. After a lengthy argument the FBI convinced the people to accept half of the reward amount and let us go.

Several Marines jumped from the choppers and surrounded the block. An FBI officer walked out and asked us our names. We revealed our names, he asked us for ID and we showed it. He confirmed who we were and asked us to get in the van to take us to the local juvenile detention and lock us up until the next day, when we would appear in court for inquiry. We were again in that dog van, but this time it was different. They took the girls and boys in separate vans. The cops were staring at us. There were men and women cops inside the van. Some asked why we had escaped and warned us that we would have to stay in juvenile detention another five or six years. But there was a gentle and polite lady police officer who tried to stop the conversation by saying, "They are just kids. Leave them alone." The lady cop appreciated us and she admired the way we had planned our escape. "The FBI and secret agents were still investigating how you escaped"—She told us. She took a piece of paper and asked us for our autographs. We didn't know how to sign an autograph, so we just wrote our names and gave the paper back to her. She also made a comment that we were the real Matt Sterling's.

They took us to juvenile detention. It looked fabulous outside, and as we went in, we saw kids standing everywhere. These kids didn't look like any kids from TUAD; they looked weird, and everyone had some criminal background. They took us to a separate building and to a special room where the walls were electric, and there were rows of glass rooms 250 square feet and the glass was transparent. Guards were standing outside and watched us all the time. There were separate rooms; each had a bed, a table and four cameras inside the room for monitoring. They put us all in separate rooms adjacent to each other. They didn't want us to be together because they feared that we would escape again. We couldn't talk much in the night, so we just ate dinner and lay in bed. The thought that came to my mind after a whole day was *where did Nelek and Urson go after they dropped us in Milwaukee? Probably they should have gone to Alaska or Canada.* I wished them to be somewhere safe. We were tired with all that had happened and were asleep within minutes.

The next day they took us to the court for inquiry. Everything was special for us and we didn't wait for a call. There was a special courtroom and there were ten chairs for us to sit in at the defendants' table. There were guards throughout the room and we had jurors and an attorney from the state. Some random people sat behind us in the spectators' area. The courtroom was filled with cameras and excitement due to our escape. We didn't know what was happening, and then a man came in who was in his late fifties, with snow white hair and silver eye glasses. The bailiff said, "All rise," and everybody got up. One of the spectators behind me said, "Get up," and hearing that, we got up and saw the judge looking at us. Then the judge sat down and smiled at us, and we smiled back. The judge started, "Well, usually I ask for the FIR (First Information Report) and copy of the case, but here I don't need anything, because I already know about these famous heroes who escaped from TUAD. You kids were all over the Internet and news." Then the state's attorney, who was young, short and stout, said, "You know what these kids have done, and they didn't even have the courtesy to stand up to respect you—"

The judge interrupted and said, "Just stop, for Christ's sake. They are kids. Do you think they know the court rules? Let me talk to them and later you can proceed." The judge asked us, "Do you know why you are here?" Everyone was quiet and terrified. I was sick of all this court drama and I boldly stood and answered, "We escaped." The judge looked at me and said, "Did you know that was against the law?" I replied, "No, I did not." The whole courtroom turned their eyes on me with questions and the judge was amazed by my answer. He removed his glasses and said, "Why do you say that?" and I replied, "Free will, choice." The judge said, "You shouldn't have taken a flying saucer and escaped," and I replied, "You shouldn't have had guards around the school in the first place."

Then everybody in the courtroom said, "Whooo." My friends had no idea why I was saying these things. The judge said, "So, you say that you had been locked down in TUAD, and so you escaped, but before that. . . What is your name, son?" I replied, "Oliver Oscar." The judge said, "Mr. Oscar, you say that you had been locked down in TUAD, and so you escaped." I put my hand on my cheek and said, "Sort of." Hearing that, the judge said, "Law is law, Oliver, and I have to do exactly as it says. Do you have a defense attorney, Mr. Oliver?" I replied, "We are from TUAD," and some people started to laugh. The judge was a really cool person. He stretched, relaxed, pushed his chair back, and said, "I am having a very good day here. You made me think that you didn't have one." We heard a voice from the spectators say, "He has one." The judge heard that and said, "Please walk forward."

Then a fair man in a black suit with a pipe in his mouth, with no smoke coming out of it, walked forward. The judge recognized him and said, "Mr. Glenn Hitch, you are too expensive for them." The gentleman named Glenn replied, "Let me help them and apply for some tax rebates," and the judge approved. Then Glenn asked us, "Could I help you by being your defense attorney?" We had no choice, but he looked like a reasonable man. We accepted his offer and he asked for permission from the judge to talk to us for a few hours before proceeding with the trial, the judge accepted. He took us to a private room to talk to us. The room had benches and we all sat on them, he sat in a chair facing us. Everyone was quiet for a few minutes because we didn't know where to start or what to talk to him about. He was new and we didn't even know if we could trust him.

He began, "Why did you guys escape? Bad food, unclean bathrooms, ugly teachers, no good-looking girls and boys? Or did you guys want to be famous?" We all giggled because he was so funny, then he said, "Now I see some shiny teeth." He looked at me and said, "Let's start with you, Oliver. I admire your thoughts and the conversation you had with the judge. That was one of the reasons I volunteered to help you." I asked him, "What was the main reason?" and he smiled and said, "I like the way you talk, Oliver. It's very impressive. Why can't you be an attorney like me, or something better? Well, the first reason is that the news went wild about the kids who broke out of TUAD and escaped in a flying saucer. It was like an Oceans ten job: no blood, no bullets—the perfect hit job." I asked him suspiciously, "So you want to know how we did it exactly," and he replied, "Do you mind if I have a smoke, guys?" We said it was no problem. He lit his pipe, puffed twice, and said, "I am not a cop or an agent, you know, I am an attorney. Escaping like that means something bad was going on there. There should be truth on your side and I wanted to help and protect the truth. That's it."

He asked us to introduce ourselves, and we did, and he greeted each one of us by our names. We believed him, with some reservation, which was very normal in this situation, because he looked like an honest man and really wanted to help us. We told him the whole story about what had happened at TUAD with Peyton, Jay Mons, Fay, Sadie, and Niki's problem, our interest in not going to school, failing the exams, and escaping from TUAD with Nelek and Urson. We didn't say anything about Nathalie, the mission to New York City, or the locket. After hearing our story, he was reasonably convinced and asked us, "Do you want to go back to TUAD?" and we all quickly replied, "No way."

Then he ran through his whole plan of how we could get over this problem. He said to never say anything about Peyton or Jay Mons, because then TUAD would get involved and not let us out of their radar, and they would keep us in TUAD and falsely testify against us. "Just say that they were well-bred people and like fathers and brothers to you. You didn't want to go to school because you were not good at learning all the school curriculum in TUAD and decided to have a solitary life. You didn't know what to do, so you escaped with Nelek and Urson. Then explain everything about the escape." We asked him, "About Ambrose too?" and he made a funny face and said, "Who is Ambrose?" We replied to him, "The kid who hit Peyton's and Jay Mons's heads and helped us." He said, "Well, don't say anything about him—just say you don't know what happened, that they fell down and you ran away and didn't notice who did it if you want to help your friend Ambrose. Otherwise he will be in trouble." Madison quickly jumped up and said, "He was our enemy, but he did one good thing to help," and Glenn replied, "One good deed! Lady, so he should be your friend," Madison was confused and said, "Maybe."

I was leery about Glenn and asked him, "Why don't you want us to say anything about Peyton and Jay Mons? Do you work for TUAD?" He felt bad and quickly went on the defensive and said, "Do you think I am a pimp, Oliver?" I was not comfortable in the way he put this question, and replied with some hesitation, "I don't know what you are trying to do, Glenn." He opened his mouth and said: "I was fascinated and impressed when I heard and saw the news. I have two kids, Oliver, and they don't go to TUAD. They go to a good private school. I am accomplished and rich and I don't want to trick you all and make a living. I am just here to help the helpless kids. If I walk out of this room you will be spending a decent amount of time in juvenile detention where sexual harassment is a hobby and they don't have flying saucers to escape. If you guys are not interested, let me know. I am not pushing you, but I feel very bad and sorry for all the things that happened at TUAD. Do you still want me to stay or leave?"

We had somehow started to trust him, and besides, we had no choice. His one word made me believe that his kids did not go to TUAD, which meant he was a good father and sent his kids to private school, which also meant he had money. Maybe he was looking to get some more recognition by winning our case, but that didn't concern us, so we decided to take the risky path he wanted to go down. We agreed for him to take the wheel and get us out of juvenile detention and maybe to some other TUAD in a different state. He convinced us and we didn't know whether it would work or not or what his game plan was. He took us back to the judge and said he was certain and had clarity of the case and he would take it. The judge accepted and adjourned the court, and the next hearing was set for the following day.

Glenn requested that the guards help him get some suits for us so that we could wear them when we came to court. The guards rejected him at first because they were not comfortable with the fact that we had escaped. But Glenn convinced the FBI officer and they granted permission to bring the tailor to juvenile detention and get suits for us. Glenn followed us to juvenile detention and the tailor measured the sizes for us, we got two pairs of black suits with bow ties for all the boys and suits without bow ties for the girls. They fitted well and we were looking elegant, but we asked why we needed to have suits. He replied, "An appearance in a suit clears half of the problem, so we have only the other half to work on." Glenn was always proving every second that he was a gentleman. We said we didn't have any money to pay for the clothes, but he had a bag of funny answers. "You all look sharp, the judge might be confused and think that he walked into a fashion show, never mind forget it, it is part of the package, included in the attorney fees."

That night, we were in the same glass room, but all the time we were thinking of how we could get out of juvenile detention. Everything was uncertain and we said the cherished prayer that Nathalie had taught us and went to bed. The next day, we got up and were delighted to wear the suits but not happy to go to court. This was the first time we had worn suits, but we were not going to a wedding or gathering or party. We were going to court and that was not a good start for us with suits. They took us in the van, and we reached the courtroom in time. Glenn was waiting for us in the courtroom and took us to the private room to run us through all the things that we had discussed the previous day. The judge came in and the case proceeded. The state's attorney started his complaint that we broke TUAD's rules and violated the law. He said we should be punished for it and brought all his points against us. The time came for Glenn, who always wore a smile on his face, and he said to the judge, "I need to explain the whole story from the beginning. I will do that before considering this accusation from the state's attorney. That will help to get this case solved easily." The judge granted him his proceedings.

Glenn: All my clients were found in Hammond Bay after being robbed and kidnapped and witnessing murder by some pirates in the Great Lakes. Then they were taken to TUAD for admission as foster kids and taken care of. Is that correct, kids?

All: Yes, Mr. Glenn, that is correct.

Glenn: Thanks. They spent their lives happily there, starting to go to school and making efforts to pass the exams and grow.

State's attorney: Objection, your honor, these kids were not competent at the school, and they never passed even one exam. They failed and repeated the third grade.

Glenn: May I proceed?

Judge: How do you respond to the state's attorney?

Glenn: Well, failing in school is not violating the law. My clients did their best but couldn't make it. All of my clients were homeless, and it was the first time they had gone to school, and everything was new to them.

Judge: Granted.

Glenn: Thank you, your honor. My clients did the best they could and had a few hard times. They were not as smart as the other kids, but they were polite, disciplined and happy kids. They respected their teachers, colleagues, friends, guards and everyone. Who were the best people you liked in TUAD?

I knew what he was trying to do, and I jumped in to answer.

Me: Moise Boti, Peyton, and a few other teachers.

Glenn: Thanks, Oliver. They couldn't do any better in TUAD and couldn't study well, so they decided to escape.

State's attorney: I object to this, Your Honor. They were undisciplined, arrogant, bone headed, and the dumbest kids on earth. They couldn't even make it past the third grade.

Judge: Hold your tongue.

State's attorney: I am sorry, your honor.

Judge: Move on. How do you answer that, Mr. Hitch?

This was the turning point in the case, Glenn had made a breakthrough.

Glenn adjusted his suit and gave a wry smile as he walked up to the jury.

Glenn: If they were what the state's attorney says, why do they need to keep such kids in school? Rather, they should be cast away from TUAD. Am I right, jurors?

All the court was silenced; the jurors looked at each other.

Foreman: What is your point?

Glenn: Well, let me put it this way. If I am arrogant, undisciplined and a bone head, it is my personal choice and my personality and that has nothing to do with the law or an amendment. The penalty is that I could get fired from my job, my wife might divorce me, I might break up with my girlfriend, I will have no friends and no one will want to talk to me. Agreed?

Jury: Yes, we agree.

Glenn: Thank you. If they were so-called dumb kids, as per Mr. State's Attorneys accusation, why waste tax money on these kids trying to help them? Leave them the way they want. As you know, we are at war, and the world is in war and chaos, and we need more money for better things rather than coming down hard on these kids.

Somehow, the jurors were convinced, and Glenn started to steer the case in the direction he wanted.

Jury: But all kids go to school and learn so that they will do better in their lives.

Glenn: Then where does free choice come from when they are subjected to school? Do you also mean that going to school will shape someone's future? That is wrong.

Judge: I see your point, Glenn, but why did they escape? That was against the law.

Glenn: They could not walk in and say to their teachers and principal that they were not happy and wanted to leave. They were too small for that, and as everyone keeps saying that my clients are dumb, how could they think smart and logically?

The judge then dismissed court for the day and asked the staff, teachers, wardens, and principal to come back the day after next for the continuation of proceedings. Glenn brought us some cookies and homemade pastas. We had an early dinner there at the court and chatted with Glenn. We thanked him for the help that he was giving us and asked him what the next move would be, but he never said a word, and only said, "Just wait." We went to juvenile detention, it was the third day we were sleeping in the glass room, but we were a little more comfortable now and it looked like a home. The next day, we didn't have court hearings and they let us out for a couple of hours but didn't allow us to talk to the other kids. They took us to a lawn that was big and had a water fountain in it. The water fountain had lights, and the color of the water changed all the time. The guards surrounded the lawn and made sure no kids came over to us.

The eyes of all the kids in juvenile detention were on us. We sat together taking some fresh air and talking about the next day in court. We were much concerned about Nelek and Urson, and I told them what Nelek had told me before he left: "Blame it on me." We were talking intensively about whether we should rat on him or not, but if the situation got worse, then, as per Nelek's words, we would rat on him. Otherwise, we would try to protect him, but we were sure of one thing: he was in the safe hands of Russians, and the U.S. government could not get to him, so even if we did rat on Nelek and Urson, they could not do anything about it. Our glass room, itself, created some mental sickness for us, but the fresh air felt better. They took us back to the glass room; the kids were shouting and making a noise. A young kid around nine years old came running toward us and said, "I'm a fan. We should plan to escape from here. Tell us how?." The guards pushed him away and I heard Madison whispering, "Whoo, we have fans now. Next, we should go to Hollywood." Benjamin said, "Be quiet, Madison. What's wrong with you?"

We went to our individual rooms, and food was served. We spent the whole day watching news and reading books and magazines. The guards were always monitoring us and we just waved our hands to each other. On my right was Shu, and on my left was Ejaz. This was the only communication we had in the glass room, just a "hi" with the wave of a hand—no sound, only visuals. We spent time there that day feeling like incubator babies. The next day, we wore another new suit and went to the court like gangsters who felt no guilt for the crime they had committed. It was the same scene, with Glenn at his chair checking the files and the jurors practicing judgments. The state's attorney, who wanted to get a paycheck for doing a job, had no idea what the case was about. The clerical staff, who were not interested in any of the case, just wanted to go home no matter what happened. The spectators didn't know how to spend their time and thought they were learning new revelations every day.

We went and sat in the same chairs next to Glenn. After a few minutes, our enemies and the people we didn't like came to court: the TUAD staff, Peyton, Jay Mons, the principal, and our teachers. But we liked one person, Moise Boti, who was also there. He gave us a smile that meant, "You guys did it, and I love you so much." I turned and said, "Hi, Moise," and he winked and replied happily, "Good job." Then the judge came in, and we all stood up to signify, "You are the man, we are at your mercy, provide some justice for us." The hearing continued, and Glenn started to present his points.

The judge asked our teachers and principal about our attitudes and our personalities. No one ratted us out because they were well informed and didn't want to make a mistake. The only thing they said was that we didn't do well in school, and apart from that, they had had no problems with us. Peyton was brought into questioning, and he had no choice but to say the same things, that we were good, because his mouth was being handled by the TUAD management. He couldn't say anything bad because now it was in the media and any misinformation he might say would cause another inquiry. But there were additional questions asked of him, which were very interesting and made everyone in the courtroom curious and anxious.

State's attorney: You say these kids were good, so what was the reason you put Mr. Niki in the dark room a few times?

Peyton: He had some problems waking up in the morning, so I did it just to discipline him.

State's attorney: So putting him in the dark room was a teaching exercise. Didn't you think it was harsh and insane?

Peyton: Those are the instructions we have at TUAD, and I follow what is there. It was routine, and if you have any problems with that, you should talk to the board or children's counsel. We were just parenting them, that's it, and we take care of them.

State's attorney: Okay, that is not the problem here, and we will address it later. So, where were you at that time the kids escaped?

Peyton: I was not there.

State's attorney: There is a rumor that you were there and were hit by somebody in the back.

Peyton: A rumor is a rumor. I was not there.

State's attorney: Everyone says the person named Moise Boti was closer to these kids and helped them in their escape, and that he is also the one who hit you in the back.

Peyton: We have already done a check on Moise Boti, and he was there in the headquarters that day with other guards and his chief celebrating Independence Day. So, he didn't hit me, and I don't know who gave them all the weapons.

State's attorney: Could I question Jay Mons, your Honor?

Judge: Permission granted.

Peyton got up from the witness chair and looked at us with great anger, but he didn't express himself. The state's attorney ran the same questions to Jay Mons, and he answered the same way. They couldn't do anything about it, and it seemed that Peyton and Jay Mons, after they had been hit on the head, woke in the morning and went home. It was not only TUAD who was in control; they could not say that they were there at the time of escape because the next question to come would be, "How did you know about the escape? Why didn't you inform your superiors or call the guards? Why did you carry guns with you?" They safely ignored all that trouble, but Jay Mons was stunned by other questions, too.

State's attorney: It seems that you found two kids with drugs, Miss Sadie and Miss Fay, and you complained about them, and they were in rehab for a while. So how can you say that they were good kids?

Jay Mons: I meant they caused trouble and used drugs and were sent to rehab for a year. Drugs are a problem for every citizen in this country and kids are not the exception, but they don't use drugs anymore.

State's attorney: I want my next witness to be Moise Boti.

Jay Mons glared at Fay and Sadie, and in turn, they turned their faces away from him.

Judge: Do you have any questions for the witness, Mr. Hitch?

Glenn: I have no questions, Your Honor.

State's attorney: Mr. Moise Boti, were you a good friend with all the kids?

Moise Boti: Yes, I was.

State's attorney: Could you say why?

Moise Boti: Friends are friends, no matter what age they are.

State's attorney: I meant, did you subject them to sexual abuse?

Moise Boti's face turned red.

Moise Boti: You should ask them, not me.

State's attorney: Answer my question, please.

Moise Boti: I already did.

State's attorney: Your Honor, he is not answering the question and is violating the court rules.

Moise Boti: I said I did.

Judge: Could you please answer the question.

Moise Boti: That was a question? It is insanity. Those kids were like my sons and daughters and I never had a second thought about it.

State's attorney: So you helped your sons and daughters escape?

Moise Boti: Escape from where? From my family or from TUAD? Then I should be the one who also escaped.

State's attorney: Did you help them escape or not?

Moise Boti: I didn't.

State's attorney: Did they at least say goodbye before they left?

Moise Boti: No, they didn't.

State's attorney: So, you say they were happy to escape your so-called sexual harassment.

Moise Boti: They didn't say anything about the escape, because they know I love my job and am very conscious about it more than the kids. I would have arrested them if they had said anything to me about the escape.

Everyone laughed at his brilliant answer, but the reason they wanted to screw Moise Boti was that the state had no idea why we had escaped, and there were so many rumors about it in the media. They wanted to make sure that somehow the court brought it to the table, and TUAD influenced even the state's attorney. Then the judge asked everyone to ask us where we got the weapons and ammunition from. They called us one by one and I was the first one to be called.

State's attorney: Mr. Oscar, where did you get all the weapons?

Me: From the black market.

The state's attorney smiled for the first time.

State's attorney: I asked who helped you get them.

Me: Nelek got them.

State's attorney: Is that one of the other two kids who escaped with you?

Me: Yes.

State's attorney: Do you know who helped him?

Me: He said he had connections in the Russian mafia, and they contacted them.

Then the state's attorney recounted the whole history of Nelek and his brother, Urson. All the information made it very evident that he was working with the Russian mafia and it was clear that he had returned to take his brother and that he was the one who planned it. Then, one by one, my friends were asked the same question and they all answered the same. We didn't want to rat on him, but if we didn't, then Moise Boti would have been nicked. We thanked ourselves for Nelek's sacrifice that he took the bullet. They didn't do much investigating about the weapons and ammunition because the Russians had been doing it for ages. However, the FBI was investigating it, so the court didn't order any further inquiries.

They asked us about the tunnel in TUAD and how we knew about it. We told the truth, that Nelek was the one who knew about it from an artifact stone. He had found the secret passage and that was the reason he came back to take his brother.

The hearing was over for the day, and they told us to return the next day. Glenn brought some salad and sandwiches, and we had our dinner with him, Moise Boti also joined us. We were happy to see him, and we didn't chat about anything involving the escape. We chatted about regular stuff and then we left the court.

The same old thing happened in the incubator room, and we went to bed and got up the next day for the hearing. This time, they brought up a new accusation: shooting the guards and attempted murder. We didn't know why they had brought up this charge, but TUAD, at this point, didn't want us back; rather, they wanted to prove that we were evil and notorious kids and to protect TUAD's reputation.

But Glenn defended us very well and he said we didn't attempt any murder. We just used tranquilizers, not guns. Although we carried weapons, we never used them against anyone, our goal was to escape, not murder. He also highlighted that we gave first aid to one of the guards who had a bruise on his head, which signified that we were good and loving kids. Hearing that, all the jurors were convinced. And I said to myself, "Good deeds never go wasted." During the whole escape, no one was killed and no one was hurt badly, so they could not do much about it.

Then they brought something else up that was weird, which we didn't expect—the football game. Someone had recorded it and we didn't know until this point that they had cameras at the football field. They played the whole video from the time the game started. But they were smart. They had edited out all the arguments and biased decisions that were made by Peyton, Moise Boti, and us. They couldn't even bring them up, because we had already said we had no problems with Peyton. But the one important point they wanted to highlight was Benjamin's stunt. They played the game highlights for fifteen minutes. And everyone was surprised and stunned by what Benjamin did on the field. They didn't have any recording after that. I mean, they didn't show the shoe polishing stuff, either. They played very smart. The judge asked Benjamin, "Why did you do that?" Benjamin stayed quiet, and the state's attorney brought up a classic subject—the black and white male problem.

The state's attorney was constantly accusing Benjamin of things from his imagination, and he said, "They made a black kid the quarterback, and you proved them wrong, that the black kid cannot be a quarterback. You brought shame to all your people." Benjamin was very quiet, and his eyes were red. Then he said something the world had to hear.

Benjamin: I did what I was supposed to do.

State's attorney: So you think that was a smart decision?

Benjamin: I thought it was a wise decision.

The state's attorney laughed mockingly.

State's attorney: You said "wise," but you lost the game and made all your friends look stupid. (He took his report from TUAD.) You guys didn't pass one exam over the past three years and never proved anything from your side. This was your last chance at TUAD to prove something that you were capable of, and you spoiled it.

Glenn became nervous for the first time and he held his chair for stability.

Benjamin: I did what I had to do.

State's attorney: For Christ's sake, how? Please tell me.

Benjamin: Black men have better things to do, not like this.

State's attorney: What did you say?

Benjamin: You heard me, sir.

State's attorney: I didn't understand what you meant.

Benjamin: For ages, we have been slaves and discriminated against, but we don't want to prove ourselves through sports. We have better things to do. We want to be scientists, engineers, doctors, leaders, and the best in this world.

State's attorney: I mean, you don't answer my question, and then you talk about something completely different. This is ridiculous.

Benjamin lost his nerve and took a right index finger and pointed to the state's attorney.

Benjamin: You started to talk about black men, white men, and quarterbacks, and I said the right thing. Playing and winning a game brings more credit for black people, and that means you are wrong. Playing sports and games always creates differences in society, and I stopped on that line to change history, by losing, and to send a message to the world. We don't use black men to play like dogs and bring victory to our states and nations, when the equality of black people is still at stake in the minds of everyone. "There is lots of nigger sweat in all the trophies starting from school games leading up to the 'Olympics'!" You know who said that?

State's attorney: Who was that?

Benjamin: Not Martin Luther King, not Mandela, not Fred Benny, and not Justin Soil, but my father, the great Kadin Gail. We are still the same. What is the difference for us between working in a cotton field and playing on a football field? They are both the same.

We all stood up and started to clap. Glenn also stood up, shaking his head, and clapped. Then the spectators and media people also started clapping, and even the jury clapped. The whole courtroom was filled with tears of joy, but the state's attorney felt embarrassed and didn't proceed further and went and sat down. The judge appreciated Benjamin's comments and said, "Well said, Benjamin."

Now TUAD did not need to prove that we were evil or stupid. Escape was just an escape. They brought up the next problem. They lost a flying saucer, and it was theft. Glenn defended us and said that we didn't steal it; rather, we used it for escape, and moreover, we didn't keep it. So it was not a theft, rather an escape, and we just boarded the saucer, pretty much. The insurance covered it, and it was a prototype legacy model and no big loss for TUAD. He removed the theft and burglary charge from us, but poor Nelek was the one who was blamed for it, although he had his own justification. The judge raised the question of what to do with us and where we would prefer to go, and then came the climax of the whole case.

Judge: Mr. Hitch, where will the kids return to? We will give the preference to the officials at TUAD they can decide.

Glenn: They are not going back to TUAD.

Judge: We don't see them as guilty, and they just co-joined to get out of the TUAD because of the some problematic life situations. Maybe they didn't fare well in the exam results, which they would fail and redo for the third time in the third grade, and the court can forgive their mistakes and sentence them to only a week in juvenile detention. Then after a week, they have to go back to TUAD or some other foster home.

Glenn was very bold and repeated what he had said.

Glenn: They are not going to either TUAD or any foster home.

Judge: Then where? Are you going to adopt all these kids?

Glenn: I am not, nor anyone else.

Judge: Make yourself clear, counselor.

Glenn: They are going to live in a free world by themselves.

Everybody started to whisper, and no one had any clue about what was happening.

Judge: We cannot do that, and you know that. They have to be sixteen or older to be free, and until then, they should be in a foster home.

Glenn: That is what the common law says, but that doesn't apply now.

Judge: What do you mean, Glenn? I am not catching your point.

Glenn: Yes, if you are older than ten, you can be out by yourself. The new constitutional law was created by one of the old presidents, the great Alan Squash, who called it "During world war times." He declared a secret law, saying that during world war times, children older than ten can be by themselves. The reason is to avoid child massacre in the foster homes. The law was called PCM for children, known as the Protecting Child Massacre Act in times of world war. I hope you know we are in World War III, and this applies.

The judge got mad and got up quickly and told Glenn, "Come and meet me in my chambers." Glenn adjusted his tie and said, "As you wish, your honor." The judge was waiting for Glenn inside, but before he left, he warned us, "Don't talk to the media people behind you or to anyone until I come back." We acknowledged him, and he left for the judge's chamber. The judge was walking back and forth and saw Glenn and screamed, "What the hell are you doing?" Glenn replied, "Doing justice to my clients." The judge got more aggravated and asked him, "Where does it say anything about PCM for children?" Glenn replied, "In the law of wars, or so-called secret amendment law at time of deep crisis."

The judge was annoyed now and said to Glenn, "Do you know what you did?" and Glenn carelessly replied, "Don't know yet." The judge eyed Glenn with a grin and said, "It is going to be a hell of a problem. All the kids who are older than ten will want to leave TUAD and all the foster homes and want to be on the street. There's going to be a whole mess in this country, damn it, and already this country is tottering and we are just scraping by. You are destroying it. Why are you doing this, Glenn?" Glenn was relaxed. "All I know is I have my clients there and I am defending them for justice, and I want justice now."

Then somebody knocked at the chamber door and the judge said, "Come in." A lady walked in and gave a letter to the judge. The judge read it and gave it to Glenn. Glenn read it and gave it back to the judge and laughed. The judge was confused and asked, "What is funny, Glenn? The White House has terminated the PCM law now. What are you going to do about it?" Glenn replied, "I submitted my case before the law was passed, so I have the rights to apply the PCM to my clients. The new law doesn't apply to them, and you cannot do anything about it." The judge started to warn him, "So, you want to go against the government and win?" Glenn replied, "The government is us, and I am not against me. It has been a half hour, and the whole country knows it, and now there are already protests in the streets. Turn your phone on and check." The judge turned his phone on and the news screen in his room and saw there were already people in the streets shouting and protesting. He got insane and cursed the media, "Damn media, everywhere, snitches." Glenn just walked out of the chamber without saying anything to the judge.

We were all waiting for him, and he was walking with a big grin on his face and came to us and said, "Were you good boys? Did anyone speak to the media?" and we replied, "No, Glenn, they were trying to talk to us, but we never turned back or replied to them." Glenn replied briskly, "Very good. I appreciate it." I asked him, "What did the judge say?" and he answered funnily, "Go home and play poker." Then the judge walked back from his chamber and sat in the chair. He looked at us huffily and said, "Let us start." He asked whether the state's attorney had any objections to this. The state's attorney conveyed his view about the case.

State's attorney: Well, Glenn highlighted the PCM, and we can follow it per the amendment and let them go, but not everyone can do that. Only six people are at the age limit, so the rest can't do it, they have to wait until they turn ten years old.

Judge: Do you have any comment on this, Mr. Hitch?

Glenn: I just introduced the law to everyone, but the whole amendment has a clause that says, "If anyone who is of age between nine and ten and breaks or escapes along with kids from a foster home who are ten or older, or from their parents or guardians or from support or from adoption or from juvenile detention or from hospitals or from religious centers or from any common welfare organization, is of free will, and based on survival skills, they should be released, and no one has the legal right to stop them." So, my other four clients should also have the right to be free.

The judge started to rub his forehead.

Judge: Can you tell me what to do, Glenn.

Glenn: Just let them go of their own free will.

Judge: Let me review: what about the escape itself? They violated the law, and they should pay for it in some way.

Glenn: They knew their laws and rights, and they escaped per the PCM. We failed them by not letting them out in the first place. I don't see that any crime was committed or law was broken.

Judge: The court is adjourned for today. We need to review this case. We need a week for a review.

Glenn: My clients are not going back to juvenile detention.

Judge: Then, where? The case is not closed yet.

Glenn: According to constitutional law, in cases involving kids younger than twelve, if there is an error in the law, and when time is taken to fix it, the kids should not be in the hands of the law. They should be sent back home.

Judge: I know that, Glenn, but they don't have a home.

Glenn: They do. Mine.

Judge: Your home? Are you insane?

Glenn: I am happy to take them for a week and bring them back.

Judge: Because of the amount of pressure on this case and public concerns, I will have to give you some protection for them. Is that okay?

Glenn: With pleasure, give me four armed guards.

Judge: Permission granted. See you next week. The court is temporarily dismissed.

We went home with Glenn that day, and his wife and his friends drove us in a couple of cars to take us. The whole media was waiting for us; they were throughout the court and were asking us questions. Glenn instructed us not to talk to them, but one lady kept following us to the car, and we couldn't ignore her. She asked, "How do you feel about the escape?" I cared to answer her and said to her honestly, "Like every soul who escapes to seek freedom, just like Matt Sterling." She asked, "Did Matt Sterling influence your escape?" I replied, "Yes, he did from the movie *The Vacation on Mars*."

I got into the car, and Glenn was looking at me in the mirror, and I smiled and he said, "Bravo Oliver!" They drove us in three cars, and an armed escort was following us, there were people everywhere waving, jumping on our cars, and shouting. We gained popularity in one day, and our faces were everywhere on the Internet and media.

One lovely thing I shouldn't forget is that when we came out of the courtroom, I saw Fay holding Benjamin's hand tightly. We had been friends for a while, but that was not the same way she held his hand before. Fay felt something for Benjamin, and I wished them luck.

While on the way to Glenn's home, we saw some posters that said, "Kids in flying saucer," "Freedom from TUAD," and many other quotations. The strange thing was that they had put our photos on them, all ten of us and Nelek and Urson. There was a big reward for giving any information about Nelek and Urson. The streets were filled with our faces and names, we reached Glenn's home. It was very big and looked like a castle. We entered the gate and drove in for a minute to reach the house. There were gardens and fountains with replicas of giant creatures like dinosaurs, elephants, and mammoths with ivory tusks. Water was flowing from their mouths, and everything was in pairs, with one facing the other.

There were maids waiting for us, and the car stopped. The maids opened the doors, and they took us inside. The guards were asked to stay in the front room. We went to the hall, and it was big and had a huge crystal chandelier hanging from the ceiling. All the furniture, rugs, paintings, and tables were antiques, and it had a touch of classical family heritage. This was the first time we were seeing and feeling the meaning of wealth and prosperity. There were two kids sitting on the couch, a boy and a girl, and they stood up and greeted us, saying, "Welcome, everybody." We politely replied, "Hi, everybody." Then Glenn introduced the kids to us. The nine-year-old girl was Kassidy, and the boy, who was seven years old, was named Ryan. Glenn's daughter looked beautiful; she was so beautiful that you wanted to look a second time, and a third time, and keep on looking at her, and I did. She shook hands with everyone to introduce herself, and none of the boys wanted to release their hand after shaking. She always carried herself gracefully, and all our eyes were on her. When it came to my turn, even before opening my mouth to introduce myself, she said, "So you are Oliver. My father told me many things about you. I am glad you made it home to see me." I was holding her hands, and I don't know what went on in the little lady's mind, but she came closer and kissed my cheek. I promise, I don't want to pretend that I am perfect, but I enjoyed her kiss, it was sweet. I was still a little anxious that she would kiss my other cheek, but she didn't. All my buddies, Benjamin, Ejaz, Judah, and Niki, were jealous. I didn't make this happen. It happened all by itself, and I enjoyed it. Madison couldn't stand this, and her face turned red, she lowered her head and didn't want to look at me.

Then we went for dinner, and they had all the best food on the table. We had never eaten at such a big table before. Glenn's wife asked about us, and we told her where we were from and our whole background. We shared what we had to, but we never said anything about the mission to New York City, Nathalie, or the locket. We always automatically sealed our mouths shut, as we had been practicing for years. Then that night, we all went to bed, and they gave us each a bedroom. We had eaten so much, and we wanted to sleep as soon as possible.

I couldn't sleep because Nelek and Urson were always in my thoughts. I cared for them a lot, and they had sacrificed so much and helped us. As my thoughts were moving, I saw someone open my bedroom door. I turned on the lights and saw Kassidy in her long white night dress. Although I was confused about why she had come to my room, she looked like an angel, and her curly blond hair was on her cleavage, twisted so that any man could be caught in it. I asked her softly, "Are you all right, Kassidy?" She walked slowly and said, "I am fine. I thought of chatting with you, Oliver. Is that okay?" and I replied like a gentleman, "Yeah, sure." I got up from the bed and went and sat in the chair, and she sat in the other chair.

She was looking at me profoundly, and it didn't seem like she was flirting, but something was on her mind. I asked her, "You said you wanted to chat?" She said, "Have we met before, Oliver?" I replied, winking, "I don't think so." She put her hands on her cheeks and said, "I have a feeling that I know you, Oliver. The very first day I saw you on the Internet that thought went through my mind." I was really silly and said, "That's why you kissed me." She felt shy and closed her face with her hands but slowly opened them and said romantically, "I saw a boy, who rode a golden horse, and he came fast and grabbed me from the ground with one hand, and we rode to the ends of the world. I didn't feel hungry or thirsty in all my journey and I looked into his eyes all the time he rode with me. When I saw you for the first time on the news, I thought you were the boy on the horse." She was very romantic, and I was pulled in by her beauty. But to myself, in my heart, I saw Madison's face, and I turned the whole romance into a joke, and replied to her, laughing, "I think you have mistaken me. I am not the boy from the horse, I am the boy from the flying saucer." When you don't want to make a mistake and get rid of a woman, all you have to do is turn down her romantic advances. She smiled and said, "You are very funny, Oliver. That is why my father likes you, and I also like you." We chatted for half an hour and I asked her to leave because I was tired, and she very quietly left my room. I couldn't sleep that night. She had come into my world of true love with Madison, and there was a black hole in my world. I was trying to stabilize my world and focus only on Madison.

The next morning, we saw the news. There was more security and there were more guards employed at TUAD and other foster homes. Every kid who was not happy felt they could escape and the law would stand by them. There were many escape attempts, and a couple were killed doing this. We had created a panic in the hearts of young kids, and set some bad examples for them. We were sorry for the two kids who lost their lives trying to escape. Our names were all over the place, and we became the talk of the world. In the midst of all this craziness, I felt that Glenn was living the royal life, not from his job, but from some heritage. The house was huge, and we could get lost without a map. Kassidy and Ryan took us around to show us their house, and they saw all their magnificence in our eyes. We played indoor games, and they had a football field, so we played a friendly game with them.

It was fun, and everyone liked Kassidy and Ryan, although Madison didn't like Kassidy much, and felt insecure. In reality, I found that Kassidy was adorable and well-disciplined girl, but I ignored her as much as I could to make Madison happy. In the daytime, we were in our group, so Kassidy did not talk to me much. All her time was spent with me at night. She came to my room and chatted with me for a while. I pretended to be sleeping, but she never gave up, and she got into bed and slept next to me. To avoid this, I woke up when she came to my room around midnight when everyone was sleeping. I asked her once why she liked to talk to me in the night when no one was there, and she blamed it on me, saying, "You didn't talk to me much during the daytime." I started to chat with her during the day by sitting alone, but Madison was angry. I explained to Madison that we were just friends and said it would only be for a few more days, and then we would be out, and she understood.

After four days, Nikifor said that he wanted to see his grandparents. We all went with him, and Glenn and his family also joined us. It was just fifteen minutes away from Glenn's home. Nikifor was very happy, and his eyes were joyful, because it had been a few years since he had seen them. When we went to the corner where his house was, we found that the house was dirty and had not been maintained. Niki got out of the car and ran quickly to check on them. He went into their house and shouted for them, but no one was there. We all rushed inside, but the house was empty. Then he went to his house, across the street and it was locked. He ran down the street to Tziyon's house and knocked on his door, and Tziyon opened it and found Niki. Initially, he didn't recognize him, but Niki explained about himself, and then Tziyon knew it was Niki. It had been almost four years, and he had grown.

Tziyon told him that his grandparents felt sick after they visited him in TUAD. They had died a year ago, and Tziyon, as their family doctor, took care of them. He buried them in their backyard, and he took us there. We found their graves behind their house, and Niki sobbed a lot before their graves. Madison, Judah, Ejaz, and I had known them for a while and spent some time with them, and we also felt very sorrowful and wept for them. Glenn, his wife, Kassidy, and Ryan wept with us, and they were emotionally moved and felt sorry for us and Niki's loss. We never knew Niki's grandparents' names, as we always just called them Grandpa and Grandma, and we didn't want to ask them, but we saw their names on their stones in the graveyard: Mr. Helge and Mrs. Elisa Helge. This was my first experience at finding out someone's name from the head stone of their grave, although I knew them almost half my life. I still remember Niki's grandmother, who told me to take care of Niki, and I renewed my oath, that I would protect him and give my life for him. We were all heartbroken, and we went inside their home,.Niki's eyes were dry because he had cried so much, and he didn't speak to anyone until that evening. All the time, Aika was sitting next to him, holding his hand for comfort.

Tziyon gave a debit card to Niki that had lots of money on it, which they had saved from Niki's grandparents. They had put almost $700 million on it, and the money was good for our journey. Niki took it, but Tziyon knew all the things that had happened at TUAD, and he asked Niki if he was going to stay back here. But Niki stood by his decision. He said no and that he was traveling. Tziyon made a proposal that he wanted to buy his grandpa's house and his house, but Niki refused and said, "It will be a memory of mine, and I don't want to sell it." Then Niki went and logged in on his computer and checked his father's account and drafted a check from the savings he had, and it was $580 million. This was the money Niki's father had saved for him when he was a kid. He gave the check to Tziyon and said, "Pay the taxes for the house and maintain it until I return. You can take some money for your services. I am sure it will cover anything for another twenty to twenty-five years. If there is some extra money, I will come back and get it. Please make sure you clean my grandpa's cemetery very well."

Tziyon lowered his shoulders and said, "I am already old, Niki. I don't know if I will make it until then. But I will make sure I keep my promises, and I have no one after me." Niki was surprised and didn't understand. "What do you mean, Uncle? You have two daughters." He wept and said, "They died on a space expedition." Niki was shocked and said, "What happened?" Tziyon told the story of how his two daughters went on a space expedition, and the spaceship crashed on Saturn and they were hurt badly and couldn't move. They were alive and breathing, but because the medic team couldn't get there for almost six days, they died. Because they didn't have the right treatment at the right time, they died of pain and hunger. We all felt bad for him and conveyed our deepest condolences. But he promised Niki that he would pass his message to his nephews and nieces, who would inherit all his wealth and they would take care of it.

We all decided to leave Niki's house and go back to Glenn's house, but Niki insisted on staying that night with them. He wanted to spend one more night, and he wanted to feel his grandparents' vibrations and see their spirits moving. We all wanted to stay, and Glenn agreed to stay with us. Kassidy and Ryan stayed too. Niki, Madison, Judah, Ejaz, and I shared our experiences of the first time we met Niki, the Halloween, and the fun stuff we did that year. Kassidy was watching the whole time and wanted to be our friend and be as close like we all were. But to my mind, I knew she was not a chosen one to go with us, and we couldn't allow it.

Glenn was awake for some time, and then he went to bed, and we were walking and playing until three thirty in the morning, and we all slept in the hall. I still remember that when I closed my eyes to sleep, Benjamin was next to me and was close to the wall on the other side. But when I got up, Kassidy was next to me, and I had moved from the hall. Luckily I was the first one to wake up that day. I saw her next to me, and the first thought that came to me at this age was *Crazy woman from Mars*. I jumped up and ran away and slept next to Madison. When we got up, no one was smart enough to check who was sleeping next to whom. It didn't really matter at this age, but Kassidy saw that I had moved from her and gone to a different place, and she was upset about it.

We took a shower and decided to leave Niki's house. Niki went to his father's room and opened a drawer and put something in his hand. He wrapped it in a small piece of cloth and put it in his pocket. He didn't say what it was, and it was time to go home. I thought of the old couple Wang and Kew and asked Tziyon about them and he said they had gone on a vacation and would be back soon. I remembered them, and I still had the metal dragon they gave me, and I passed my greetings to them via Tziyon and he said that he would deliver them.

We left Niki's house and spent the rest of the week before the hearing at Glenn's house. Then the day of the court hearing came, and we all went with our black suits on. The whole country was waiting for the judgment. The court proceedings started, and Glenn was doing his part very well. The judge had no second chance, because everything was on our side, but finally the decision was passed in a way that ruined our future.

Judge: So, per the law, you had the favor of having the children, but where do they go now? Do you want to keep them yourself?

Glenn: No.

Judge: If they aren't with you and aren't in a foster home, then where will they be?

Glenn: I don't know. It's their choice and free will.

Judge: Any of you kids have any plans for where you want to go after I release you here?

Me: We don't know, but we will be on the street walking, eating, drinking, and breathing fresh air.

Judge: Oh, well, you guys are young and cannot be by yourselves. The world is a cruel and dangerous place, and anything could happen to you. Where do you work, eat, and sleep? There are many things that you should understand.

Me: I think we can handle it.

Judge: What can you handle? Are you not afraid of darkness, bombs, killing, and all the nonsense that is happening outside?

Me: No harm will come to us. We will be fine, your honor.

Judge: Insanity. All ten of you would still want to do that?

All: Yes, we want to go out and live the lives that we want.

Judge: Well, I am done with this case. I wanted to rest this case down, but you kids are so stubborn. Let me tell you before I pass my judgment that you kids are the weakest, laziest, and most incompetent kids in this whole country; you couldn't pass even one exam in three years. Failure is your consistent shadow. In this wild world of World War III, geniuses—brilliant people—die for lack of a fraction of common sense. You are nowhere near them, so death will be your ally. It sounds like, from your own voices and confirmation, you want to be scavengers in the thirty-sixth century in the so-called Fourth Dimension.

Then the judge read his judgement:

"I dismiss these ten kids" Oliver Oscar, Judah, Fay Scarlett, Madison Stacey, Ejaz Khan, Benjamin Gail, Nikifor Bondar, Aika Hamada, Shu Cong and Sadie Leta, to be free in the streets with no subjection to any parental or

other controls. We wish them safety and success and want to tell them a message: If they live for a long time, they are lucky; if they die in a short time, the world has to know that the United States of America did its best to keep them safe, but in the world of free choice, they chose their own path, and they were incompetent at their ages to choose a scavenger life, and became a bad fertilizer of our soils.

The court also demands that the law agency search for Nelek and Urson, who were the masterminds of this escape, to bring in before the law. With all the evidence that was produced by TUAD about these kids' performances at the schools, there is no doubt they could not have planned anything regarding this escape. Their ignorance is outstanding, as the evidence shows, and these ten kids just joined the ride with Nelek and Urson, who planned it well. So, there was no law broken and not involved in the violation of any crime by the ten kids names mentioned above. Therefore, we drop the case. They could have free food in any foster home, including TUAD, and not be charged for it. The government will not undertake their care or support them getting jobs or give them any Social Security until they are sixteen, they must deal with their lives. No one will hire these kids for work, and if they do, it will be considered child labor and punished severely. I will give the list of dos and don'ts to them, which will summarize the points I didn't mention. Case dismissed. They are allowed to go and live by themselves.

To add more confirmation to this problem, no one has a radio-frequency identification, or RFID, which defines your rebellion blood against being a good citizen to create a better society. Hence, we cannot guarantee any sort of protection for you, especially because you have violated the necessary technology criteria. You have a choice, and the law allows it, but we will do our best to protect you from danger."

They gave a document with the judge's signature on it to all ten of us. They also gave us the e-document, with the account information on it, so that we could download it anytime. We were astonished; because he had passed judgment for us to go and die, and had concluded by saying we were incompetent instead of calling us dumb kids. Now our names were the same as they were in TUAD, and we were given a scavenger's life. He really ruined our lives, and we were in misery. We didn't know how we were going to face the world.

Glenn was sitting in his chair with his head down, scratching his forehead. The judgment was recorded by the media, who were behind us and were shouting to us to answer questions. We were panic-struck because we didn't know what the outcome would be. All we knew was that something was wrong. Glenn took us to the private room and asked us to wait until everybody left the building. We waited until night in complete confusion while Glenn was away talking to the judge and the media. By the time Glenn came to our room, we were all exhausted, our jackets had been thrown on the table, and ties were hanging on our necks in all directions. I asked him, "Why did the judge pass the judgment like that?" He was troubled and replied to us hesitantly, "They did what they had to do."

Then he explained what had happened. He had said to the judge angrily, "Why did you condemn them and cast them away and humiliate them by saying they were incompetent and scavengers?" The judge replied, "There is nothing more to say about this problem," and Glenn curiously asked, "Why?" The judge gave his view and exactly what caused it. They couldn't do anything because of the law that was not evaluated and not of concern, but was biting into the Constitution and the democracy of this country. The kids should have cooperated and we should have suggested good alternatives, he said, but it was not possible in this case. So, to make the best of the situation and make the government look better and avoid causing further problems in the country during hard times like this, the judge had taunted us and brought out what happened as a way for the government to show their weakness. "By declaring all of your results at your school and showing the world that you are incompetent in your quest to free yourself, the government is not liable for anything, and they are in a safe position," Glenn said.

We were quiet, but there was nothing more to say. We had played our game well, and they had played well, we had to move on. Now it was time to face reality. I said to Glenn firmly, "That's fine; thanks for your help, Glenn. We are leaving tomorrow." We went to his house to pack our stuff, but didn't have much to do. We gave the suits back to Glenn, but he told us to keep them. That night at dinner, we had long faces and sadness filled our hearts, and no one spoke to each other. Glenn was trying to make us happy, but it didn't work. The rest of the kids went to bed early, but I stayed up late and sat in their garden. Glenn spotted me and sat down with me. He asked me, "How are you feeling?" There was nothing more interesting to say, and I just sighed. Glenn didn't know anything about the mission, and he offered something to me. He asked me to stay with his family, saying he would take care of me and send me to private school, give me a good education, and train me to be a good attorney. I asked him, "What about my friends?" and he replied that if they wanted, they could stay here with me; he had enough money to take care of them, too. But more than the other friends, he was very interested in me staying with him, and he wanted to make me happy, so he had no choice but to commit to my friends, too. But I politely replied, "No, I want to be with my friends, and we are going, anyway. Thanks for all the help and support you have given. You treated us so well." He smiled with uncertainty and said, "You never told the truth about why you guys escaped out of TUAD. I thought there was something more than you told me." I replied, "You never said why you picked the case and helped us either." He wet his lower lip and said, "It's true. If a grown man is not honest, why should he demand the truth from kids? It was all about Kassidy."

I was shocked because I didn't know why he was using her name, and I wondered if he knew about her visiting my room every night, so I was quiet. Then Glenn told me about the dream Kassidy had. "When she was three years old, she dreamed that a boy on a horse picked her up and took her for a long ride. That dream had a great effect on her, and she speaks about it all the time. Until just lately, she still spoke about it, and we knew she was possessed by that dream. We didn't mind much because all kids have these childhood fantasies, and she was no exception.

"The first time she saw you on the news, she said that you were the boy in her dream, and she started crying and was filled with joy. As her parents, we had never seen her so happy, and we didn't sleep the whole night. We asked many times, and she said you were the boy who came in her dream. We asked her, 'What is so special about that boy?' and she replied with excitement, saying, 'He is the chosen one who will save us from everything, and he is the prince from paradise. I want to live with him forever.' Her confidence and beliefs drove me to check it out and to help you, and I found that you were close to your friends, so I decided to help everybody."

Hearing that, I felt some love for Kassidy. She had a wonderful sweet heart, but I still didn't know why Glenn had gone all the way through the trial with us because of his daughter's message. I asked him, "What do you think about me, Glenn?" He replied, "I am the father of that crazy girl, so I started to believe it." I laughed at his reply and said, "You wanted me to stay here to make your daughter happy?" and he replied, "Not to just stay here. I wanted to adopt you, and at some point, if you liked my daughter, you could marry her, and I would leave all my wealth to you and her." In a way, he was buying me, but at this age, all that came to mind was that I wanted to go New York City and stop this war, so I politely refused his offer, and although he didn't show it, he felt awkward and hurt.

It was my turn to tell my version of the truth, and I just said we wanted to go New York City and spend our lives there. Glenn said, "Craziness in New York City. Who said New York City was fun?" and I lied to him, saying, "Lots of people we met wanted to go there, but they couldn't make it. If we do well there, we could become wealthy bankers," Glenn replied, "You could become one here. Why go to New York City?" and I answered him, "Money is much greener on the other side Glenn and we should be reaching for our goals without anyone's sympathy, help, or direction." Glenn coughed and said, "You are focused and you already know your answers." We went to bed that night and still Glenn's family's love never left. Kassidy was waiting for me in my room, and as soon as I saw her, I was very proud of her. She was my friend and with my whole heart, for the first time, I said, "I am always happy to see you, Kassidy. Why don't you get some sleep." She was excited at me saying that, and she came and hugged me and said, "I love you, Oliver, so much. Will you take me with you?" My heart froze, and I was nervous. I didn't know what to say, so I kissed her head and said, "If I could, I would, but even if I took you, you would not make it, so stay here, and when the war is over, if you hear of me and I am alive, then come with me." She was glad to hear that and said, "Will Madison be angry if I come for you?" and it was the voice of innocence. I replied to her, "She will be very happy to see you, and you could be with us." She asked me to promise that I would always be her friend, and I promised her. She asked me for a kiss, and I didn't feel anything bad, so I kissed her on the cheek, and she said, "Move down, Oliver, lower." I didn't understand what she meant, so she pointed to an inch lower from where I kissed, and I kissed her again. She said the same thing, and I did it again. Then she held both my hands in hers, and she kissed me on my lips, and I didn't resist, I enjoyed it. It was quick, but since it was the first time that someone had kissed my lips, it seemed longer. I told her, "Keep this to yourself," and she replied, taking both her hands and crossing them on her chest, "I will never say anything about the kiss." I smiled and said, "I didn't mean the kiss, Kassidy. I meant the dream, and promise me you will never tell anyone about it from now on. Keep it to yourself," and she quickly promised me and said that she wouldn't talk about it to anyone.

She left my bedroom, and I went to my bed. I was fantasizing about Kassidy and her whole concept about her dream and her family. They all were very good people, but I had to move on, because I had a great journey ahead of me. The next day, we got up and had our breakfast, and it was time for us to leave. Niki pulled me aside and asked about Kassidy, and I told him the whole truth. Then Niki said we couldn't leave like this because it was not wise to leave them with Kassidy and her crush and craziness. I asked what we had to do, and he said we needed to pay Glenn some money for his fees, and once we paid the money, it was just business and nothing more. Niki insisted on it, and since his father had taught him so much about relationships, paying debts and favors implies we are interested in them. Just settle their account, and everything will be concluded. But we were not sure whether Glenn would accept it, so we discussed what to say to him, and we had an idea. I asked Glenn to talk in private, and he came with us. Niki, Sadie and I were with Glenn and said to him, "How much were the fees?" and he asked, "Why are you guys talking about fees now?"

Niki: Glenn, you have been so nice to us, and we are very thankful for it. But our pride precedes us, and already we have been declared and cursed to be scavengers. We don't want to start like that; we walk with self-esteem so we want to pay the attorney's fees. Please, Glenn, accept it.

Glenn: Such rebellious and sensitive kids — I am proud of you all. You walked in and asked me, and I respect your feelings and will do what you say because you will not let me go. Do you want to charge the premium fees or just some money?

Niki: I did some research yesterday, and it was close to $400 million, and since we are walking a long way, we would like to give you $100 million, is that cool?

Glenn: Smart boy, yes that will do. So, when you all become rich bankers, give me the other $300 million.

Niki's eyes were rolling. He didn't know what he meant by *bankers,* and he saw me sigh, and he understood.

Niki: Yes, definitely, Glenn. We still owe you some money, and we promise we will give it to you someday.

Glenn: Don't forget your receipt. You always need it for the money you spend.

Niki gave his card, and he swiped it for $100 million. We still had $600 million left with us. We didn't know whether the money would be good for the journey or not, but we had came this far, and there would always be a way for us. We all thanked Glenn's family and said our final goodbye, exchanging our affections with them by hugging and thanking each other. This time, I kissed Kassidy on the cheek and said goodbye. Her eyes were wet with tears and her face was red, and she had no energy to say goodbye to me. Glenn walked us from the house to the gates and when we reached the gates and went outside, he called to me and said, "I wanted to say one more goodbye to you, Oliver." I walked to him, he arched his back and looked into my eyes and said, "You are an advocate, Oliver. I know you didn't tell me the truth, but you convinced me by giving the money for the fees to me and not having any obligations. I like your style, Oliver, and there are thousands of people who are envious of our wealth and do all sorts of stunts to get noticed. I am an attorney, I can smell people from 100 miles away, but you taught me one lesson that no one can buy you, Oliver. You should be the chosen one, and I wish you good luck and take care, Oliver Oscar."

I couldn't say anything, and I replied, "Sorry, Glenn, I did my best to respect you, and you are one of the greatest men I have met. Stay safe." We all waved our hands, and I saw Kassidy come running to say goodbye to me. Her heart was broken, and mine, too. I didn't know what to say, she was standing next to her father with her head on his legs and tears rolling down her face. We started to walk, and it was a long way ahead of us, but we had finally made it. A free life, and although we were declared as scavengers, according to the face of this Earth, we were better than slaves. At least we fought and stood up for ourselves.

Chapter 19
The Wild and Wary Path

WE HAD A LONG JOURNEY AHEAD OF US, AND AS WE WALKED, WE MADE sure we were not going to use any mode of transportation. We were just going to walk against the zeros and ones, the technology. This time, we seriously started to talk about what exactly Nathalie meant by "Don't use technology." We concluded that Nathalie had used the I-gadget to check news and to teach us about science and technology when we were kids. All she meant was just to take a long walk for the journey, and we could use science and technology at times on demand. So, we all had an I-gadget now, which had been given to us when we were at TUAD, but we decided to throw them away because they could track us. We needed to buy new I-gadgets, knives, and guns for the journey. We went shopping and bought some I-gadgets to check the news and maps, tranquilizer guns, knives, ropes, blankets, winter clothes, and all the necessary accessories and gear.

The storekeeper recognized us and asked, "Are you the kids who broke out of TUAD?" And we replied, "Yes." He asked us, "How come you all couldn't pass even one exam? I went until high school and was a below-average student. But I passed a few exams. It's very strange to look at you." Fay got mad and said, "It's none of your business. It's good to know you passed and only made it as far as high school," and she walked out of the store.. The storekeeper apologized, and we said, "You got your answers, man," and we paid the check and left. Everybody in the street knew us and whispered about us, and giggled and laughed. In the midst of the mocking crowd, there were encouraging people who took their hats off and said, "Bravo, kids."

We wanted to be comfortable with the public because we were all losing our composure, so I said we should go and meet Uncle Tim in Kern Park and spend a couple of weeks there. We would retain our normal life and find a way to handle all these problems. We went to Kern Park, and our old memories started to move around in our minds, and we remembered the stolen wagon and all the homeless people. The park was filled with lots of families, children, old people and they were normal civilians. We couldn't find Tim and all the other homeless people. We ran to all corners of the park to check on them, but we couldn't find anybody, and we were talking to ourselves. Maybe they were dead because of the bombing or had left the park.

We waited for night for everyone to come back to their homes. No one returned, but we found two old couples who were dragging their bags and walking back to their tents. I recognized them, but I didn't know their names and I ran to them, everyone followed me. The old couples recognized me and called me by name and I was stunned. They said they had seen us on the news and recognized Madison and Judah. We asked them about Uncle Tim and the others, and they gave one simple answer: "They all took a shower." We looked at each other and didn't understand what they meant, they explained what had happened. After we left, the kids started to be clean, hygienic and shower all the time. Within a month, they started to have a self-realization and felt that they didn't want to stay in these low life surroundings. They went to a foster home and started to go to school. Slowly, one after the other, the elders and other kids also left the place and started to go to work and they began new lives. Uncle Tim also realized and healed his depression. He recovered by going to a rehab center, he then returned to his job. Everybody had left except them. We asked why they hadn't left, and they replied, "We became homeless when we were young and have spent almost fifty-five years of our lives like this. We don't know a life better." The saying was still true: "The streets had us one time, and now we had the streets in us."

We inquired more about Uncle Tim, and they said he was doing well and traveling a lot on business. He came occasionally and said "Hi" to them and bought them lots of food and groceries, but he was definitely doing well. He was living with a lady now, whom he loved, and they were going to marry in a year. Although we couldn't see anyone, we were glad that we had made a difference in someone's life, and we should be the chosen ones, not scavengers. The story from those homeless couples encouraged us. We had made a homeless person a proper citizen, but we became even worse than the homeless because we were called scavengers. The couples who were around were in their late eighties, and they didn't have many provisions. We shared our food that night and stayed with them. The next day we got enough food for almost three months so that they could be satisfied and didn't need to go around the streets, begging. We stayed with them for a week and spent time with them. We told them all that had happened in TUAD and about the escape. They listened to us and never made fun of us. All they said was "No one is smart in this world, but everyone pretends to be smart, so they can't be called fools." They blessed us, they were excited to see us again, and we left.

I couldn't believe myself. This was the second time we were starting the journey from the same place, and I hoped that at least this time we would make it to New York City.

The journey was difficult. Although it was still summer, we hid in the bunker when they declared curfews. This year there were many bombings and the war was getting worse and worse. We took the route to Chicago, but this time, we didn't think twice about going there, because they had frozen all the other routes and now they knew who we were and there was no fear that they could relate us to Nathalie. Chicago was the worst place on earth with lots of muggers, thieves, and rapists. Passing that city was a big problem. Therefore, we walked a lot in the daytime to get out of the city. We even ended up fighting with some kids who were trying to steal our goods. We were in a group, like a pride of lions and we stuck together in all the fights, and we never split and ran. We even had to use our tranquilizer guns against two men who were abusing us. Those two men had guns; we dodged all their bullets and took them down with our tranquilizer guns. We decided we couldn't fight against real guns with these tranquilizer guns. We needed to buy our own guns, but we needed to be at least twelve to possess a gun. We didn't know anyone in the black market and didn't want to go to some strange place to get into problems. We became thieves and started to trail muggers who had guns and follow them, and when they were alone, we would rob them. We spent almost a week in Chicago, staying in hideouts and we ended up stealing two guns from two muggers. Those were needle-stack handguns: the bullets were as thin as needles and more powerful than regular guns with bullets. Those magazines had almost 500 rounds and were expensive and difficult to obtain.

Now we had two guns, so we hurried and left the city and went to the outskirts. We were now in the Rust Belt, and there were many industries making warplanes, airships, flying saucers, weapons, robots and machines. Initially, we thought we would be safe since the big industries were on the path we were walking, but these ended up being big headaches for us. They were primary targets, and all the enemies wanted to bomb all these industries to win the war. That meant there were constant curfews and bombings to get through. Here, we met a few guys who sold illegal guns. We asked them for help and they recognized us and gave us three more guns. They were good dudes and they knew that we had problems and that people didn't care, so they helped us. They didn't even take a penny from us. All they said was "Stay safe."

We reached Fort Wayne and decided to stay there for a few days. It was a safe city, and we hadn't had proper food for ages and had become weak. It was a Friday night, and we were all sitting in the street on the pavement. Everybody was happy because it was Friday, and the town was filled with a party mood. We saw a very polished limousine pass by us and stop. A lady got out of the car, wearing high heels and a long red dress with a slit up one side. She wore a red hat and looked very glamorous. All our eyes were on her and she saw us on the pavement and walked over and asked, "Where is Jericho?" We were looking at her face and didn't respond. Then she asked a second time, "Do you know where Jericho is?" Ejaz replied, "We don't know." Then the lady said, "I have seen your faces. Are you the kids who broke out of TUAD?" and Ejaz replied, "Yes." She laughed and took a cigarette from her bag and lit it, puffed it, and said, "Do you know what they call you?" We looked at each other, confused about what she was saying, and asked curiously, "What?" She smoked and puffed again and said, "Fools of the Fourth Dimension." We got angry, and Ejaz clenched his teeth and asked the lady, "If you ask a fool for an address, then what are you?" The lady was surprised. She took a right hand to his face and said, "Do you know whom you are talking to?" and Ejaz replied, "Yes, another fool." She was mad and said, "Okay, cut it out. I was just sharing what people said. I never said you were a fool. Forget it. We should be friends. Now come shake hands with me." Ejaz turned his face from her. She was asking to shake hands, but no one did. I slowly extended my hand, and she shook it. She looked at me with some attention and said, "You look cute and I like you." I didn't respond to her comment and said, "Sorry for my friend calling you a fool. We don't know the address. You should ask someone else."

She had some pity for us and asked if we had had dinner. When we said no, she invited us for dinner and said she would buy it. She took us to the most expensive restaurant in the city, which was called Jericho. We were dressed like thugs, in dirty jeans and T-shirts. She asked if we had a change of clothes, and we replied, "Yes." She asked all of us to take a shower and wear some nice clothes. We took a shower, our first in two months. We wore the suits that Glenn gave us and dressed so well that we looked great. She complimented on how we looked and she took us for dinner. She introduced herself. Her name was Sharon, and when we asked her what she did, she said, "I am a CSC." We asked her what a CSC was, and she replied, "Complete customer satisfaction." We thought this was some sort of community service stuff, and we didn't ask her about her job anymore or what she did. Everyone knew her, and they showed great respect for her. She was the type of woman who could get anything for you. They all worshipped her like a goddess, and I didn't know whether she was a goddess or not, but definitely God was a good architect, and he had molded her perfectly, because she was a sexy, adorable woman.

She ordered all kinds of food from the menu. We were hungry and had never eaten such a fine meal, and our hands were everywhere on the table. We ate until we were stuffed. It was almost eleven at night, and she asked if we wanted to go to a bar and have a nightcap, but we refused. She requested that we hang out, so we went to the bar. No one stopped us at the doors; they let us in without age verification or crap like that. When everyone saw us, they all stopped what they were doing and looked at us, the music stopped too. Then one gentleman came up and said, "It was not wise to bring kids in here," but she rubbed the man's face with her nails and said, "No rules tonight. Let's make Sharon's friends happy" and everyone cheered, whistled, and shouted, "Let the party begin." They gave us a table, and we sat and drank fresh juices while Sharon was out talking to all the men. They all had their mouths open and eyes on her, and everyone was trying to impress her.

After a couple of hours, she came to check on us, and we were all sitting like good children. She asked us, "Do you want to have some beers?" and we said, "No." She said, "It will help to relax your mind and clear all your sorrows and you could start a new life." We still refused to drink, and she had another idea. "Let's just have one of you drink and let the rest know how it feels." It sounded like a wise idea, but who would be the beer taster? Sadie agreed to it and they gave her a beer. It was called Pebble Drip, and it was a lager from Germany. The glass was so cold, it could crack your teeth, and the mug was tempting, the color of the beer in our eyes made us think curious thoughts. "How does it taste?" Sharon asked. Sadie drank a sip and shook her head, closing her eyes. Then Sharon asked her, "How was it?" and Sadie replied, "It was bitter but it tastes good," and Sharon told her to try one more time. She sipped a few times with the same reaction on her face, and then she drank the whole beer in one gulp and banged the glass on the table. She was wearing a white mustache and she didn't use a napkin to wipe her mouth; rather, she wiped it with one hand and rubbed the hand on her pants. Her face was confident, like she could take down an army with one hand and she looked at Sharon and said, "You called us fools. How do you know we are fools? Only a fool could recognize a fool. Are you a fool, Sharon? Anyway, you look so beautiful. Are you a beautiful fool, Sharon?" Quickly, Judah who was sitting next to her, said, "She was very kind to us. Why are you talking to her like that?" Sadie had some kick, and she looked at Judah with half an eye closed and held his shirt, "I love you, Judah. You are my sweetheart." She kissed him on the lips and said, "Whatever you say. I will not be rude to Sharon again." That was the first kiss I had seen, and now Judah was wearing the mustache from the foam of the beer.

We were all bewildered about what had happened to her. Sadie got up, raised her hands and bowed and said, "Hail, holy Sharon, mother of kindness even to fools like us, long live her legacy." Sharon was observing and smiling and called the waiter and ordered Pebble Drip for all of us. This was the first time we had tasted beer and it was a fun experience. Sharon spent the whole night with us. The first beer was good and we were unplugged from the evilness of the world and we floated in harmony.

This was when I found out who had a crush on whom. Fay was chatting with Benjamin, and Niki, who didn't trust women, was blushing with Aika. Our boy Ejaz started flirting with Shu. I was happy that this time the hidden love spilled onto the table out loud. Then we had one more beer and started to talk more true romance. Still, I remembered the most romantic conversation I had with Madison. I told her that Glenn had asked me to stay with him, and that Kassidy loved me very much. He was looking for a homegrown bridegroom, and I had refused him because I love you Madison, so much. But although I was drunk, I was careful to never say a word about the kiss with Kassidy. Madison told me how much she loved me when she was in her mother's womb. She demonstrated to me—and it was so cute—how, while she was in the womb, she was bothering her mom to walk fast, so that she could meet me. "I always opened my hands wide, and I wanted to come out of my mother's belly and hug you, Oliver," Madison said. She made me stand still and walk a few yards, and she ran with her hands stretched out, saying, "I love you, Oliver" and hugged me. She told me this was how she had felt when she was in the womb. She kissed me many times and the wings under my arms started to flutter. Maybe I was the chosen one, but Madison was the chosen one for me, and I loved her so much. With the third beer, we became loud and mischievous and started dancing on our table and couch. Later, we went and danced on the bar table and removed our jackets, swinging them in the air. The whole bar was filled with fun, and everybody danced with us. They also disabled the cameras in the bar so no one could be liable or get into trouble. We sipped beer from everyone's glasses, and gallons of beer were in our stomachs and we were knocked out.

We didn't know what had happened. The next day, we got up around six in the evening and everything was dizzy and glaring. I got up first. We didn't know where we were, and I saw a double king-sized bed and a few of us sleeping on the couch. Judah was sleeping, and he had vomited on the floor. Shu was in a chair. Her suit had puke all over it, she was sleeping upside down. I was looking at myself, and I saw myself on the floor with my pants off and only my shirt on. I walked slowly to take a leak in the bathroom, but I couldn't walk and felt like I was light and moving in all directions. The bathroom was very big and exotic; all I could tell now was that it was even better than the bathroom in Glenn's castle. I heard some babbling voice in the bathroom, and looked to see who it was, but I couldn't find anyone. Then slowly I walked to the bathtub and saw Benjamin sleeping there.

One thing I knew: we were screwed up with the alcohol. I walked slowly back to where I had been lying on the floor and slept again. We slept the whole day, were all drowsy and hung over and got up around eleven at night. We looked at each other with no idea what had happened. We ordered food and juices. We were hungry and ate everything and ordered a second time. It was two in the morning the next day, and we went to sleep again.

We got up that afternoon with some clarity and sense. We took long showers to get rid of the headaches, and we realized that we had drunk too much and gotten screwed. We cleaned the room, and found out we were in a hotel across from Jericho. We spent that evening in the room talking and feeling bad about ourselves. It was not our fault. It was Sharon, and we blamed her. We spent that night and the next day in the hotel and then left. We asked for the check, and the manager said that Sharon had taken care of it. We asked what had happened to us, and he laughed and said, "You were all drunk and screwed, they brought you from Jericho and put you in the room; Sharon did it. She was waiting for you guys to wake up, but you were all sleeping, so she left in the afternoon and gave me a note." The manager gave us the paper. We opened it, and Sharon said, "This was the first time I felt so much joy in my life. I enjoyed all your company. Hope to see you soon."

After reading this, everyone said they didn't want to see her again. She was a good and kind person but she made us drink and puke. We started to focus on our journey back again, and one good thing was that our minds were reset and we didn't remember about TUAD, Peyton, the court, or all the stupid people's comments. We just walked as if a new life had begun. We thanked Fort Wayne and the beers that we had cherished.

The war was going badly. All the maniacs were bombing each other and we took shelter in hideouts and bunkers that were open to the public. Every day we would take a shower, because when the bombing was bad, we would wake up with ashes, dust, and shrapnel all over us. But the bombing didn't cease for many days, and we ate our food and drank water with ashes. Life was not good, and we wore ear buds and were filled with fear daily. We never knew when the bombs would land on our heads, and during times of danger we said the prayer that Nathalie taught us. It saved us and worked well. We got two new guns, one of which was a laser gun, which was awesome. The laser gun should be handled by certified officers and marines. It was illegal in public and they charged you with a serious crime for having one. We took the laser gun from a dead marine officer and had just one refill left for the gun.

Our money slowly started to run out, but we still had something like $550 million left. We bought food, water, and personal-care items. Our clothes were torn and faded with dust. Except for a pair of suits, we didn't have many fancy clothes, so we bought three pairs of pants, shirts, and winter clothing for everyone. Winter was around the corner, and we were getting ready for it. Walking in it was tough, last year there had been eighty feet of snow and this year they predicted more cold weather and more snow.

We walked in the winter, and it was scary because the sun went down early, and we had to camp someplace warmer. We slept in all kinds of places: in bunkers, in broken buildings, under trucks, and among dead bodies. We wrapped up in blankets and used portable heaters to stay warm. One portable heater was good for two people, and we had five of them. We stayed in pairs to stay warm. The bombing never ceased, and we could only walk five to seven miles a day. Sometimes for a week, we just hid in the bunker until there was no bombing. But the mocking never ceased, and most of the people could recognize us not by our faces, but because we were in a group of ten. The most annoying comment, and the fight we always got into, was about the "sky-biking kids." They had fast bikes that could fly. The bikes looked like normal road bikes, except they could fly. They could be used both on air and on roads. On roads, they had wheels to move, and when they were in the air, a metal frame covered the wheels, and the bottom of the bike became flat and the wheels went inside the frame. They had two exhaust pipes and combustions of flames came shooting out and they could fly around 500 miles an hour. They could also only go up to 200 meters in altitude. These kids were from wealthy families and their parents bought these bikes for them. When these kids saw us, they started to chase us. They were always in groups and we would run and hide when we saw the sky bikers. They not only mocked us, but also tried pushing us into the ground and physically hurting us. Some kids had guns attached in the front, and these guns had pellets they would shoot at us. One pellet could cause a bad bruise, and we had been hit a few times. They all knew that no one cared about us, and the sky-biking kids just kept bothering us. They were our biggest fear, but one day we would catch them.

A few people also wanted to introduce us to some movie directors to make the movie *"Escape from TAUD"* because they could not find any funnier and more comical faces than ours. Sometimes we walked away or stayed and had a fistfight, and the people in the streets or cops would break up the fight. We changed a lot, and we were no longer calm and happy kids. We were mentally hurt. We didn't know where we were walking or why we were walking. What was there in New York City? What was in the locket? We had some hope for our mission and some hope that it wouldn't ruin our lives. There was no point of return now. We were in a do-or-die situation.

Through all the frustration, we reached Steubenville in the winter on a bright, sunny day after a heavy rain. We were chatting and walking and saw that a drone was coming from far away with the north wind. We also saw a couple of tankers coming from the west end. The drone started to fire, and the tanks started to fire back. We were caught in the middle, and we were lying on the ground, bullets were hitting the ground. We got scared and saw a pit almost forty meters away. The drone was flying back and forth and the tanks stopped and started shooting up into the sky. We took a deep breath, dropped all the bags we were carrying and took our guns and ran and quickly jumped into the pit. Madison fell down when one of the drone bullets exploded close to where she was running, some sand and stone hit her. We were almost few meters away from the pit when everyone stopped. The drone passed by us to circle and come back, but the tanks were still on the other side firing.

We were all calling Madison to wake up and run, but she was lying on the ground. The drone again was in the far distance on the north side and coming toward us, and I ran back to her, but the drone was accelerating. I went to Madison and turned her over, but she was speechless and unconscious. Then Judah and Aika helped me, we carried her on our shoulders and ran quickly back to the pit. The drone fired a couple of breaker shells, which made a fifteen-foot crater in the ground, and the blast destroyed everything within a sixty-meter radius. The drone fired two shots: the first one hit the tanks, and the second shot was miscalculated and landed fifty meters away from us. We were running to the pit, we were so close and the blast of air pushed us into the pit, and we fell like chopped trees into the wide pit, which was almost twenty-five feet deep. We fell one on top of each other, everyone was hurt and because the soil was slippery from the rain, all the sand piled on top of us.

We all lost consciousness and lay almost dead, with bruises and scrapes all over our bodies. We couldn't move and were sleeping on the wet, damp surface. We were in the pit until evening, and eventually woke up. But Madison didn't wake up, and we were all scared and took some water from the pit to wake her up. We rubbed her hands to make them warm. She didn't wake up, and my heart was in terrible pain, we thought we had lost her. Everybody was scared and didn't know what had happened to her, and I took her head to my chest and said Nathalie's prayer. I was weeping because I felt I had lost everything, and I felt empty.

Madison coughed and slowly opened her eyes and looked at me and we all shouted with joy. I looked at her with tears falling from my eyes and said, "I thought I had lost you." Her face was pale, but she slowly smiled and replied, "Until I marry you, Oscar, and we have a hundred kids, I will not die." She was cute and romantic; I thanked God for saving her and us. I tied her bruised head with a strip of cloth I tore from my shirt.

It was turning night and we couldn't get out of the pit because it was wet and slippery, and we didn't have anything to climb with. No one passed by and we fired shots from the gun, but no one came to help. The pit was where we were buried now, and we tried climbing on top of each other like a ladder, but nothing worked, and we fell down every time. We decided to lay low and wait, and every five minutes we fired a shot to get some help. We wanted to wait for the sand to dry, so we stayed in there that night. The next day, the sun gave all its strength, though it was winter, the sand was getting drier and drier.

We tried to climb up, but we couldn't, and fell down each time. We were draining our energy and becoming exhausted. It was the second day in the pit, and no one came to rescue us. We spent the second night in there in the shivering cold, hungry and feeling weak. Madison started to get a fever now from the bruise on her head, and I cuddled her tightly to make her warm. We all had bruised hands, legs, backs, chests and faces. It started to hurt now, and we needed medication to clean the infections. The third morning, we decided to leave the pit no matter what. The soil had become a little harder. Madison was weak and sick, so we left her out of our next attempt. Benjamin and Niki stood next to each other, tighter and stronger. The lightest one was the last one to climb, so we made Aika climb last. We were forming a pyramid, one on top of the other; it was hard and heavy for Benjamin and Nikifor on the bottom. We used all our strength to make sure Aika climbed out of the pit to get some help. Madison was lying down and warning us to be careful. Aika went to the top of the pyramid and found the root of a tree; she reached out with all her strength and grabbed it. As soon as she grabbed it, she held it tight; we all fell down, because Benjamin and Niki couldn't support us any longer. Aika was hanging at the top of the pit, kicking her legs. We were all weak and tired and we shouted for her to get out. She was looking at us and screaming, "I am scared. I am going to fall." We encouraged her and told her not to look down, but she did. We said, "Just breathe and focus. If you fall down, we all have to die here, so just climb." Her hands were aching from holding the roots, but she gained momentum and slowly climbed up inch by inch until she could grab another root above it. We shouted at her in encouragement, "Come on, Aika," and she used all her energy and strength to get out of the pit.

We jumped for joy, she looked from the top of the pit and said, "Hang for some time, and let me bring some rope." She couldn't find anything anywhere, and all our bags and food had burned. She decided to run to one of the tankers that had been completely destroyed and left there. She went inside the tanker to find some rope. Everything was burned out, but there was one rope gun, which was not damaged. She took it, ran back to the pit, and said she had found a rope gun. She fired the shot at the place where it was dry and dropped the rope into the pit, the rope was very long. One by one, we climbed, except for Niki and me, who stayed in the pit to help Madison because she was feeble and couldn't move. We wrapped the rope tightly around her body, and everyone pulled her out of the pit. Then Niki and I got out safely. We couldn't see anything around to eat or drink and we were hungry. All we had were the guns, the locket, the compass, Niki's dad's note, the metal dragon, the debit card, and our weary spirits.

We used the compass to go east, and started to walk. We walked as fast as we could to find something, but there was nothing available. In the evening, it started to snow, and we lost all our strength. We looked for some rabbits, birds, squirrels, and even coyotes, but all the creatures knew we were hungry, and they were all hiding.

One after the other, we fell down out of hunger. We were licking the snow to keep hydrated. I was carrying Madison on my shoulders, but I couldn't move her anymore, and I fell down with her on top of me. I knew now that our life was over and we would be dead in another day, and the wolves and coyotes were going to have a good feast. Madison was whispering, and I asked her what she wanted. She said, "It would have been better for you, Oscar, to have stayed at Kassidy's house. She would have fed you. Look how poor and weak I am. I can't do anything for you, Oscar." I was starving to death and had no energy left over, and she was making me mad. "Why are you talking like this, Madison? You are not poor, and I am not hungry. I am sleeping." Madison replied, "You always lie to me, Oliver. She had wealth to take care of you."

I felt a thorn prick my heart deeply, and I felt very bad for Madison and said to her with great pain, "You were rich with your mom and father, and they left everything and came for me. I made you poor, Madison, and I am very sorry. If I die tonight, you will be rich again." She got angry, with all her strength; she got up and looked into my face. "I will die poor with you and I will never live rich without you." I took my hands and rubbed her face and said, "Same to you, Madison. I will become skinny and bony and die at your feet rather than live with Kassidy, fatty and fleshy." She laughed and put her head next to me, but she couldn't laugh anymore, and I was confused about why she did that. I was trying to make her happy and asked her, "Why were you laughing?" She said, "If you become skinny, you will look like a turtle. If you become fat, you will look like an ostrich." I couldn't resist myself and started to laugh, imagining how I would look, and said, "You call me a turtle and an ostrich, but do you know how you will look? Like a bumblebee and a cow."

We were laughing, and slowly closed our eyes. The snow was coming down more and more heavily, and we were having a chat about romance in the snow of love. Judah, who was lying next to me, kicked me and said, "You guys always talk about your silly romance, and I am dying here, Oliver. I am hungry. Get some food, buddy." I couldn't reply and just listened to him. All our voices began to fade and the snow started to cover us.

We dreamed only about food, all varieties of food, and chasing food items as they ran away from us. In that dream, I heard an older woman talking to someone and saying to get some milk from the cow. I woke up and heard dashing sounds, and the old lady shouted, "Careful, there is a fridge next to you." I saw the old lady was wearing a hijab and had covered her head with a long thin cloth. Slowly, I looked around for my other friends, but no one was there. It looked like a stone cottage with a roof made of wood and timber. I called to her, "Hello," and she saw me and said, "How are you, my son?" Her accent sounded like she was a non-English speaker. She came to me with a wet piece of cloth and touched my forehead and said, "Oh, Allah, your fever has reduced." I asked her, "Who is Allah? And where are my friends?" She replied, "Oh, don't you know Allah? He is God, and all your friends are sleeping." My head hurt, and I asked her, "All of us?" She replied, "We took nine kids, not including you. Did we miss somebody?" and I replied to her, "Oh, then we are all here."

I was getting a headache and holding my head and I lay back on the couch and watched the lady while she was cooking. A man came in after fetching the milk and he walked slowly into the house and gave the milk to the lady in the kitchen. The lady said to him that I was awake, and he turned and said, "My friend is awake." He was an average, muscular man with average height, black hair, fair skin, and teeth pushing forward out of an oval face. He walked over and sat on the couch next to me and asked, "How are you feeling?" With a strange thought in my mind about who he was, I replied, "Feeling better." He said, "Let me check your fever," and moved his hand to touch my stomach. But he didn't know where my face was, and seeing him, I asked, "Can you see me?" and he replied, closing his teeth in front with his lips, "I am blind, and I can't see you." I felt sorry for him, and I took his hand and put it on my forehead, and he felt it and said, "You are doing well. You need to have some chicken soup." I learned that his name was Purdhil, and I introduced myself. The lady brought me a bowl of chicken soup, and it was so hot, the steam hit my face. I was weak and couldn't eat it, so the lady fed me the soup.

I asked them where my friends were, and Purdhil said they were in the next cottage. He took me outside. There were piles of snow in his front yard, and he had two cottages next to each other. We went to the next cottage and opened it. I saw Judah and Shu on the couch and the rest were in the bedroom sleeping well. I checked that everybody was sleeping, and I asked him to give them food. He said they had been given some medicine and had their wounds cleaned. They were doing well, he said, and I should let them sleep. We would give them some food later. We went back to the first cottage, where we had come from. I asked him out of curiosity, "How did you find us?" Then Purdhil told the story.

They were driving in a truck in Steubenville and it was snowing heavily. His mom saw a kid lying in the snow a little farther away from the roadside. They stopped the car and ran to check. It was a girl and she was breathing, but she had fainted. Then his mom turned and saw more shoes sticking out of the snow. They both cleared the snow and found another kid, who was covered in a foot of snow. Next to the second kid was one more, and as they cleared almost twenty meters, they picked up ten kids and put them in the truck and drove here. "We gave first aid to all of you and then went back to check for anyone left behind. We spent almost three hours in the snow, but we couldn't find anyone else. We came back, gave you some medicine and fluids, and put you in the bed in the other cottage. You woke up and started to walk with us, and then came and slept on the couch here."

I thanked him because, although he was blind and the lady was older in age, they took care to help and save us. All my friends woke up, and they had chicken soup and were introduced to Purdhil and his mom. It took a week for all of us to recover, and most of the time, we spent at the cottage because it had been snowing very hard for a week. We learned about Purdhil and his family, how they had moved to America 100 years ago and were from Afghanistan. They were farmers and grew barley, rice and vegetables. They were sort of conservative people and lived a harmonious life in the woods and farmland. They cooked Mediterranean food, and we ate many kebabs and loved it. They had two horses and a little pony, cows, cattle, and malamutes and huskies. Their lives were based around raising livestock and farming the fields. After the snow, we went out and played with the pony and the dogs. They looked so beautiful and cute. I liked the husky very much and it was friendly with me. We loved this place and Purdhil and his family. They showed a lot of love to us, and they had heard about us as the kids who escaped from TUAD.

I developed a good friendship with Purdhil, and although he was blind, he was in good spirits. He taught me every day about the Quran and his religion. I liked the way he taught me, and I started to learn something new, which interested me. Although Purdhil was physically blind, his spiritual eyes were sharp as an eagle's. I found a paradise here, and it was the first time I was close to nature. Spring came, and I worked with him to plant new seedlings and cultivate the crops. Usually, his mom drove the tractor to dig the soil, but since we were there, Purdhil drove the tractor and we guided him. He was driving zigzag, but slowly he learned to listen to our instructions carefully, and we had a good understanding, then he began to drive perfectly. We planted barley, wheat, tomatoes, onions, cabbages and carrots. We worked so much during the day; we became exhausted in the evening. We also learned to ride the simplest, best, and oldest transportation—the bicycle. He had two convertible-sized bikes, and we adjusted them to fit us and rode. It was fun, we fell many times, but we learned to ride without falling and got faster. We played cards in the evening, which was a new game we learned, but we didn't gamble. Even Purdhil's mother joined in and played.

The one thing I learned about Purdhil's mother was that she was very traditional and wanted Purdhil to be more traditional. She was particular about Islam and always made sure that he followed it. She even made Ejaz pray five times a day. He had been away from this life for a long time when he met us, but he started to do it again. He was happy to do it, and he felt that Purdhil and his mom were his own family, and saw his dead family in them. We also worshipped with them many times. Purdhil and Ejaz thought of it, we wore a fez and prayed on a mattress facing east, and it was interesting and we loved it. Every time I faced and prayed to the east, I thought of New York City, and how Allah could take us there without danger. Only Benjamin was reluctant initially because he believed in Christianity, but later, he joined us. We covered our heads with white skullcaps, but none of us was circumcised. We also participated in the group prayers. Purdhil had a few relatives who would come here and there, but none of them were nice to us, they were not happy about us. We didn't know why, even Purdhil's mom didn't welcome them.

We forgot our mission of having a solitary life and enjoyed everything here. One day, private bankers for the mafia came to Purdhil's house; they came in big cars and choppers. There were more than fifteen of them. We were all working in the field and a couple of them walked into the field and stamped the crops. We went and asked them to move out of the field, and they pulled guns from their pockets. Uncle Purdhil was in the house getting some fertilizer for the crops. They went inside and dragged Purdhil's mom and Uncle Purdhil out, and were asking them to settle their debts. It was the last day to pay or they had to leave the field and their home. Uncle Purdhil and his mom were asking for more time to pay their bills, and it seemed they had been doing that for the past decade, and they would not give them one more chance. We ran to check on what was happening, and the boss, who had a long black coat and long hair, was cleanly shaved and looked like a seedy villain, saw us and asked Uncle Purdhil who we were. He said we were his friends visiting from a different town, and one of the guys recognized us and said to the boss that we were the kids who escaped from TUAD. Then the boss looked at Uncle Purdhil and said, "So, you were learning from these kids how to escape from paying me your debt? Can you learn from some fools, you loser?" He took his right hand and slapped Uncle Purdhil so hard that he fell to the ground. Seeing that, I became mad for the very first time in my life, and I wanted to kill him. I had a small slasher in my hand, which I had been working with in the field, and I quickly put it to the throat of the man who hit him. Clenching my teeth, I said, "You touch him one more time, and you will never touch anyone again." I held it so tightly to his throat, that if he moved, it would have cut his neck. All his men quickly pulled their guns and pointed them at me, they grabbed Judah and Niki as hostages, put guns to their heads, and warned me to let the boss go. The boss was scared and said, "Can we talk now?" I demanded that they leave my friends alone, and he promised not to hurt anyone. He let my friends go, and the boss asked me, "Why are you mad?" and I replied to him, "You struck my friend, and I will kill you all."

Then the boss said that Uncle Purdhil owed him money and that he hadn't paid any money to him for the past three years. All he wanted was the money, and he would let them keep the house and field. I asked how much money he owed, and he said $500 million. I said I needed to talk to my friends, and he allowed us this, so I pulled Niki out and took him aside from the rest and asked him if we could help Uncle Purdhil. Niki smiled and said, "Do whatever you want, Oliver. I am with you, pal. But one thing we need money for is to go to New York City, and that bothers me." I put my hand on his shoulder. I was very proud of him and said, "Thanks, Niki. I wanted to say that it shouldn't be me pushing on this because I like Uncle Purdhil, and he is helpless and blind." Quickly Niki replied, "Hey, do you think we don't like him, Oliver? We all like him, and he is a great person, he is blind, and we should help him." We went to the boss and said we would pay Uncle Purdhil's debts, and he laughed and said, "Did you guys rob a bank or what? It's a lot of money." I gave a good-humored reply, "Not yet." Niki gave his card, and the boss was astonished when he swiped $500 million and it went through. The boss looked at us and said, "Sorry for my bad mouth calling you fools. Fools have good hearts, and only wise people are wicked because they know how to think better." He saluted and left as though he was a bad man, and he made me think about what he said, we were good and kind and we could be fools. We paid Uncle Purdhil's debts, and he was a free man now.

Both Uncle Purdhil and his mom were very thankful but said it was not wise to take money from a kid like this. I replied that the money would have melted in the snow with our bodies if they hadn't saved us. "We are part of this family and your grandsons and granddaughters have helped you." Uncle Purdhil's mom was emotionally moved, and she knelt and removed her scarf from her head and said, "You are my family, Oliver, you are my grandson. Very truly, I say, Allah sent you to save us, and he heard our prayers." She kissed my forehead and kissed everybody else. We all felt like she was Nathalie, another woman who had been in toil and pain for years whom we delivered.

I wanted to know why he had so much debt, and I asked Uncle Purdhil, and he recounted his whole story. His father was born to a rich family, his mom's name was Fathima, and he was the last, late-born kid in his family. He was born blind, and his father died when he was little. All his brothers and sisters and other family members cheated him and threw him and his mom on the street with this plot of land and the home that he was living in. They also burdened him with a loan that was his father's. They didn't want to go to court because it was against the family's traditional values. His mom, with a blind son, worked hard to pay the loans. They paid most of the loans by selling all the goods they had, and with what they could get from the fields.

For the past three years, the war had caused them more trouble, and they lost all the crops because of the bombings. They didn't have insurance or aid from the government because these were war-prone zones and every citizen had to live at their own risk. They didn't have any place to go and they were struggling. They couldn't pay any more on the loan, and since it was a private bank and run by the mafia, the interest had doubled. His entire life Purdhil had been working in the field to settle the loan that his brothers and sisters had inserted into their lives.

Although Purdhil was a good man, he was raised with depression, and he said no one had ever visited them in his entire life. There were some relatives who came once in a while to check whether they were alive or dead. We were the first delighted visitors who were visiting them and being very kind to them. They were over-joyed about our stay, and we were Purdhil's first friends. Uncle Purdhil had no girlfriend and had never dated anyone; he was still a virgin, so he said. All he knew was his horse, pony, dogs, cows and cattle. He had never seen his own face or that of others, but one time, in the supermarket, he saw somebody with his eyes. When he was an older teenager, he came across a mean lady who said, "You have the ugliest face on this earth. What creature are you?" Her words hurt him so much that he did not eat or sleep for a week, and he didn't have any friends to share it with. Hearing all these stories, I grieved and held his hands and said, "You are a kind and handsome man, Uncle Purdhil, your heart is more beautiful than anyone's in this world." Uncle Purdhil laughed and said, "You sound like Socrates. You are my man, Oliver, with inner beauty that is more important than exterior beauty. It's a good philosophy." I was not sure what he was talking about and asked him, "Who is Socrates? What do you mean, philosophy?"

He grabbed my hand, took me to his room, and opened his trunk and showed me some pictures. I asked who was in them. "These are Socrates," he said, and my eyes were filled with the colors of the pictures. "Wow, who was he? Your uncle or friend?" His eyes were filled with a vision, and he said, "No, Oliver, he was a great philosopher and a very wise man." I asked him, "Where did you get the pictures?" He said he was out with his mom to buy food for the cattle. "I was sitting alone and praying to Allah that no one would come and call me ugly or a tooth-front warrior, which were names they called me. An old lady who passed by walked over to me said, 'Why are you alone?' I didn't reply to her, but covered my face with my hands. She said, 'Your face looks as wise as Socrates. Why would you hide your wisdom?' I had never heard such a compliment. I moved my hands from my face, and I saw her face with my inner eyes. She looked like an angel. She said she wanted to give away her Socrates collection. She had audio, video, posters, little statues, pictures—everything that related to Socrates. But I would like to give it to you. The world doesn't know Socrates anymore, but at least he lives in our hearts. I took the bag she gave me because no one had ever given me a gift, and I was very thankful to her. She disappeared quickly after she gave it to me." I was confused now and asked him, "How do you know she disappeared? You could not see her." Uncle Purdhil looked at the roof and his face became calm and said, "I saw through my inner eyes, I knew she was an angel, and she didn't say goodbye to me." I was debating with Uncle Purdhil. "She left because she was busy," and Uncle Purdhil let his thoughts flow and said, "Although I am blind, I can hear everything clearly and each and every footstep and differentiate one from the other. When she walked in, I didn't hear the footsteps, and when she left, I didn't hear them either. I heard and felt a wind with a melody passing by me." I was stunned at his intelligence. "Wow, Uncle Purdhil, you are such a genius," and he proudly said, "Genius like Socrates."

He was teaching me about Socrates and philosophy, and I was very glad to be learning it. It was not like the lessons they taught at TUAD. All my other friends joined me, everyone learned it well and we loved the way Uncle Purdhil taught us. Uncle Purdhil's mom was religious and traditional, and she didn't like Socrates and philosophy, so we learned and talked in the field when she was not there or on the small hill that was close by at night after she went to bed. It was an awesome experience, and our minds were opened. The first question that stuck in our minds was "Why didn't they teach such things at TUAD instead of beating us with science and technology?" There was something wrong with this world. We wanted to figure out the puzzle Nathalie had made when she said, "Don't use any technology for the journey. Just walk." I didn't mention anything about Nathalie to Uncle Purdhil. I just mentioned what Nathalie had said as though some stranger had said it. "What does it mean?" Uncle Purdhil unlocked the real meaning inside it. It didn't mean the literal sense of "Don't use." It implied that you don't want to put your heart and mind into technology or use it as a tool, and don't be a tool to it. "Although I use tractors, engines, and motors to pump water, my truck, the light in my house, and all the technological inventions, I don't depend on them, and when they don't work, I depend on nature, and I don't go crazy."

We were very impressed with his logical mind, and we asked him why he liked Socrates. He said Socrates was an ugly man like him, and he used his wisdom to find a life that made him happy and away from the mockery of society, also like him. "The only difference was that Socrates was a warrior, and I am a coward. I am using my wisdom to get my harvest next year. With all the bombings in my field, I have failed for three years, but I will succeed one day."

We realized he considered Socrates his role model because of all the pain he was going through. We listened to all the audiobooks about Socrates and his philosophy, and we found comfort in a way, like Uncle Purdhil, because we too had been hurt so much by this society. Uncle Purdhil revealed an ultimate truth about encountering the real problem that we were going through. The people who looked down at us and criticized us by calling us dumb, fools, sapheads, muggins, or whatever came from their mouth. Uncle Purdhil told a simple story. "A king went to war with a distant country, and the king killed a man's wife and children brutally. The man wanted vengeance against the king, but he did not have an army or people with him, so he traveled to the king's empire. He pretended to be a madman, and everyone, including the king, believed he was a madman. He kept himself fit, did exercises every day, and was waiting for his moment in time.

"One day, the king was in a procession and the madman wanted to give him a flower. The guards didn't inspect him because they thought he was harmless and a madman. He hid blinding powder in the flower, and he walked up to the king and blew the powder from the flower. The king was blinded, and the madman took a knife and cut the king's head off. His heart was at peace and avenged for his family's death. What do you understand from this story, guys?" We didn't know what he meant and said, "We don't know." Uncle Purdhil said, "You are lucky the world thinks you are fools. You can keep your mission and hide the secret, and no one will suspect you. You are free from being watched, and no one will be suspicious of you because they all think you are fools. They will always underestimate you, which you should use to your own advantage. When the time comes, strike back at them the same way they hurt you, and it will be a thousand fold more powerful and painful to them. Always make use of the situation, and never think of the weakness in it. Find the strength in it."

He opened our eyes with that story of the madman, and our lives had a resemblance to it. We would evade all the monitoring that the world has—no satellites, no cops, no special agents, and no cameras—because we were invisible in the name of foolishness. This was the first great short story we had learned in our lives, and we should use it to our own advantage. I admired Uncle Purdhil and wanted him to join us for the mission that we were on. Yes, I finally told him the truth about Nathalie and the locket; you can hide from an intelligent man, but not from a man of wisdom. I also asked Uncle Purdhil to join us on the journey to New York City, but after hearing about Nathalie, he said, "Allah has better plans for you, and he chose you for something, Oliver. I am a blind man, and I cannot guide you. I would be a burden on your journey. You said only ten were chosen to go, and if that is the prophecy, then I would be eliminated. I have to take care of my mom, who has spent her entire life with me, so I cannot do it."

I didn't compel him anymore. He was right, only ten could make it, and he had his duties to his mom, and I deeply respected him. But he blessed me and said, "Let Allah be always in your path, as he protects his warriors." He took his hand, touched my face, and looked into the skies. "I feel it," he said. "You are the one to stop this war, Oliver. You are the chosen one, and now I can see your face in my inner eyes. You look as bright and radiant as Allah and his angels. Will you promise to be my friend forever, Oliver?" There was a chair next to me. I got on top of it and put my hands on Uncle Purdhil's face and said, "How can I forget a kind, good man who was a teacher in my life? You will always be in my life as a friend who taught me the basics."

The fall was closing. We had spent almost six months with them, and it was time to say goodbye. We had helped them with that year's crops and spent our time learning something our ears wanted to know.

The day before we left, we had a very grand dinner, made a bonfire, and danced. We dragged Purdhil's mother out, who was fussing, and all the girls begged her to dance with us. She said she would, but one time only, and she put her hands on her hips and moved back and forth. She enjoyed dancing with us, and one time became two, then three, and finally, she said, "I do not dance before other men and women. It is only for children." She danced the whole night, and everyone held Uncle Purdhil's hands and helped him dance. I could see in his eyes that he was elated, and he felt he was treated as a normal human being with respect for the first time. We went to bed, and the next day, we packed all our stuff, blankets, winter clothes, food, guns, carbon ropes, knives, and other utensils and had to leave. Uncle Purdhil's mom never knew why we were leaving, as neither Purdhil nor any of us ever mentioned anything. All she knew was that we wanted to go to New York City. She asked us to stay, but we could not and had to leave. She said she had never seen Uncle Purdhil happier in his life, and he knew he had made real friends. Uncle Purdhil was very sad and sitting in a corner, his eyes filled with tears. We went to say goodbye to him, and he said he owed us money because we had helped him. He felt Socrates in his mind so much, and even though Socrates never took money from his students, he felt, in a way, that he had. We said we didn't want it and that we had helped him because he was our friend and a good teacher. I knew he wanted us to stay and had mixed feelings in his mind, so I ran to the barn and grabbed one of the husky puppies that were two months old. I came back to Uncle Purdhil and said, "For a trade-off, you can give us this little puppy, Uncle Purdhil, and when you have our money, you can have the dog back from us." Uncle Purdhil took his hands and said, "And if the dog dies before I come up with my money?" and I smartly answered, "Then it means you were delayed and should double our money as interest." Everyone laughed, including Uncle Purdhil, and I ran and hugged him. He said, "Be careful, Oliver. Stop the war, and then we will build houses for all of us and have fun all the time." I replied to him with tears in my eyes, "I will, Uncle Purdhil. You also stay safe. What were the closing words of philosophy?" He quickly said, "Live a life for both of us."

We said our final goodbyes, and Uncle Purdhil's mom said, "I have only one thing to say, Oliver: always remember, 'Dogs don't go to heaven.'" I didn't know why she said that, so I replied, "Yes, grandmother, that is very true. Dogs don't go to heaven." We left them half-heartedly. We knew the journey was far for us and were dragging our feet as we walked. Those were wonderful and awesome friends we had made. While walking, the little puppy was making noise, and we thought it was hungry and gave him some milk. It was a male puppy, and we didn't have a name for him yet. We decided to name it Bickey. Bickey's eyes, ears, and cheeks were beautiful. We walked him in turns, and played with him, and he ran fast and stopped within a short distance. We put him in our backpacks with his head out, and he didn't want to sleep, always barking at my friends walking behind us. He always wanted to jump out of the bag and he was full of energy.

We had only a little money left, about $20 million on the card. We reached Johnstown, and it was the end of November. We didn't celebrate Halloween because we didn't have much money left. We were back in the place where we had met the devil, Sharon. We ran into her in the street, and she was excited to see us. I didn't know what to say because she was good but also evil—a real-life semi-evil person. Her life was based on reality, and that reality didn't work well with us. She had made us drunk the last time, and we were wasted. We were Socrates's kids, filled with wisdom, so we ignored her invitation by saying we were broke. She said she would take care of us and that we didn't need money. We gave her all sorts of excuses, but finally she hooked us with the right bait.

She said she would pay us $60 million, $5 million each, if we accepted her job offer. We were very eager because we needed money for our journey. She said we would be her guards for a week and protect her from dangerous customers and she would pay us on the seventh day. We didn't question her about why she needed us for this job, and we agreed to it. She bought us food from exotic places and talked to many people, and at midnight, she asked us to follow her to her limousine. She went to a big house, which almost looked like a castle, with some man, and we spent the night there. We would wait for her in front of the house so that no one attacked her. We had five guns and tranquilizer guns. We asked her chauffeur what sort of work she did, and he told us she supported her customers for her business and always made sure they were in shape. She walked out of the house at four in the morning and took us in her big limousine to some hotel where we slept. It was an easy job for us to just watch the house from the car and listen for a scream or watch for somebody walking into the house. It went every night like this, and our pants were getting tighter from all the rich food. Luckily, Bickey ate a lot of meat and drank lots of milk, and he slept from the overindulgence of all the food.

Every time, she took us to a different house with a different man. We didn't know what was happening or what she was doing so late at night. It was the seventh day, and the last day of our duty and we were curious about what she was up to. So that night, we decided to talk to the chauffeur and keep him busy, and we asked Fay and Ejaz to follow her to the house and check on what she was doing. They both took guns with them, and we distracted the chauffeur. We were waiting for them, and they came back around three thirty in the morning. Their faces looked weird and nasty, and they said, "Oliver, we should leave now." I didn't know what had happened and said, "We need to get our money. We've worked for almost a week." I'd never seen Ejaz's face with so much frustration, and he said, "Oliver, I am telling you we should leave, please." Then Niki jumped in and asked, "What happened? Why should we leave?" They said they didn't want to talk here, and we went to a quiet place away from the car. Fay and Ejaz were quiet, and we kept asking them what was up, and they finally said, "She is a female Jay Mons." We didn't know what they meant and asked what they were talking about. Fay told the whole story about what was going on there. Sharon had been talking to the guy and was giving him a lap dance, half naked the whole time. Finally, he took her to the bedroom, and she removed his pants and gave him a blowjob. They had left as soon as they saw that. Madison asked Fay, "How many times?" and Fay frowned and said, "I left and didn't count." We felt disgusted that we were pimps standing out and guarding her. We didn't know what to do, and Sharon came back and said, "Let's go, guys. Thanks for watching out for me."

We didn't know what to say, and everybody was standing there, motionless. I told her, "We are leaving. Thanks for the food." She said, "I need to pay you your money. Here is the check. You could hang out with me today and leave tomorrow." Then the conversation between Sharon and us grew a little difficult.

Me: We are leaving Sharon. Goodbye.

Sharon: Did I do something wrong? Here is the check.

Me: No, thanks. You worked hard for it.

Sharon: What is wrong with you guys?

Fay: Everything is wrong in this place. Leave us alone.

Sharon: Why are you guys so angry?

Me: We know what you did. This is what you call "complete customer satisfaction," giving lap dances and pulling down your customers' pants? We thought you were a salesperson or something. We believed you; we trusted you, and you used us!

Sharon (her eyes wet): Oh, you saw that. I don't know where to start.

Fay: You could start with the lap dance.

(Hearing such harsh words from Fay, Sharon couldn't stand anymore. She held her head, sat on the ground, and started to sob loudly, and we felt very sorry for her.)

Sharon: Oh no.

(We went to her and asked if she was all right. Her face was distraught, and she kept crying. We'd never hurt anyone like this before. We sat with her and told her we were her friends.)

Sharon: If I had a boyfriend like you, Oliver, or Ejaz, or Niki, or Benjamin, or Judah, I wouldn't be like this.

(We had absolutely no idea what she meant.)

Me: What are you saying?

Sharon: The first day I saw how much you loved each other and took care of each other. You value each other so much, but in my life, no one does that for me. Not even my boyfriend.

Madison: Does your boyfriend know what you are doing? What a shameful boyfriend you have.

(Sharon was smiling and her nose was running. I cleaned it with a napkin.)

Sharon: Thank you. Yes, he knows.

Ejaz: Why can't you find your own way?

Sharon: I love him so much, and I am not a prostitute. I am just a stripper, so he knows that I come home to sleep with him.

Madison: Wow! What a nice, understanding couple.

Me: You can change your life, Sharon. It seems you make lots of money. You should have lots of money. You should leave this job.

Sharon: My boyfriend takes it all; he uses it for drugs and gambles with his friends.

Me: Why can't you run away from him?

Sharon: I love him so much, and he threatens to kill me. He has a gang, and they are dangerous. My mother and sister live next door to us, so I can't do it.

Me: How long have you been living with him?

Sharon: Almost five years.

Me: You are making excuses, Sharon. You have enough money. Go back home and take your mother and little sister, and go as far away as you can. Start a new life, find somebody who loves your soul, and live happily. I wanted to ask you why you want to give us so much money. Do you earn lots of money?

Sharon: I have to tell the truth. I had a revelation in my mind that ten mad kids were dying in the cold. I saw a wooden board written next to them that said, "Save the chosen ones. They will stop the war, and you will get a reward because of it." Then the next day, I saw in the news that the faces in my dream were the same as those on the news. I started to follow you in the news and read how the court labeled you as incompetent and fools, and I reconfirmed that my revelation was true. By chance, I ran into you, and I didn't know how to tell you because of my job, and I had low self-esteem about myself. You left the first time, and I couldn't do much about that. I prayed to meet you a second time and it happened. I earn $100 million a night, and I want to give you all the money, but because of my boyfriend, I can't. I can only give you $60 million so that I can convince him it was for some other expense. Anyway, he will still abuse me, but that is fine with me.

For sure, Sharon was a sweet woman, but she was with the wrong company. We felt sorry for her life and remembered the kindness she always showed us. We gave back the money that she owed us and said, "Keep it, leave your boyfriend, and have a safe life. If we take it, there is no way you can get out of this mess. We give you this money as a token of our friendship, and for you, too, to have a better life." We decided to stay with her that day and be nice to her. She was very happy, and we found an excuse to hit the barley water, yes, the beer, but we were cautious and had just two glasses. We were drunk again, and I enjoyed the same romance with Madison and had a good night.

The next day, we got up late, around noon, and saw a note that Sharon had left us. She had written, "Thanks for all the attention and love you have shown. With your money, $60 million, I will take my mom and little sister and escape from my boyfriend. Your motto, guys, is 'Escape from TUAD,' but mine is 'Escape from hell.' I have seen so much money in my life and never really respected it, but the money you gave me means a lot. I wish you success in your journey." She closed the note with, "Strippers also have revelations, and in my life, it became true. You are always close in my heart. Love, Sharon."

She had found her true way and we were glad we had helped in some way. We started our journey, and we walked in the harshness of the cold. The cold was getting worse in December, so we only walked a few miles a day when it was warm and rested during the nights. We reached a place near Carlisle called Tripod. We rested in one of the old broken buildings for the night. We made ourselves warm with portable heaters, and we went to sleep, except when we took turns as the watch guard.

We got up in the morning, and the sunlight was directly hitting our bodies. It was so warm that we slept a little late. Benjamin woke up and saw that he had no blanket over him and that everybody else was without blankets. He started to scream, "They stole our blankets!" We woke up hearing his scream. We saw there were no blankets and quickly looked for our bags and food, but it was all missing. They took everything—our bags, food, blankets, and guns. We were looking at the watch guard, our boy Ejaz, who was still sleeping. Benjamin had given him the handover around four in the morning, and he had slept without watching guard over us. We walked to him and slowly woke him, and he woke up with his eyes closed and then looked down and asked, "Are we going swimming?"

Madison's hair covered her face, and was mad at him. "Ejaz, you slept like Bickey, and they stole everything, and now you want to swim?" Ejaz yawned and stood up and said, "You guys don't have shoes on. I thought we were going for a swim." Ejaz didn't know what had happened yet, because he was still so sleepy, but he was right. They had taken our shoes and socks also. We hadn't realized it until after he said that. Ejaz's face became anxious, and he asked us, "Did you call me Bickey?" and Madison screamed, "Where is Bickey?" Ejaz started crying, "Oh, they stole Bickey, too." We started to run in all directions to search for Bickey. We went to all the floors in that damaged building and ran into the street calling, "Bickey." Our minds were filled with pain, because we had lost something we loved. Bickey was our sweetheart.

Then we heard Bickey barking, but we didn't know where the noise was coming from. We followed his bark. It was low, and we realized it was coming from the building where we had been sleeping. Bickey was hiding in a hole in the wall and slowly peeped out, saw us, and came running, barking loudly. Our life came back, and we rejoiced that we had found lost Bickey. We picked him up and gave him a thousand kisses and said, "You were a smart doggy to hide yourself from the thieves," and he acknowledged it by barking. Again, we were left with only the locket, the compass, the little dragon, Niki's father's note, and our underpants, but this time we also had Bickey.

Everybody was angry with Ejaz and sneered at him, and poor Ejaz was sorry for what he had done and sat very quietly. I stopped them and said to leave him alone. It was not his fault. It was winter, and he fell asleep. We could not be hard on him because he was our friend, and everybody eventually apologized to him. Shu was sitting next to him and asked, "Why did you go to sleep?" and he replied, "I was dreaming about you." We heard this and tapped him on his head many times and we changed back into our normal moods.

This was nothing new for us. It was the same old road. I said Socrates was testing us, and we had to follow him. Benjamin asked me, "What do you mean, Oliver?" I told him about how Socrates had walked in the winter with bare feet to show his strength and poverty, and said we should do that, too. Everybody remembered what we had heard about his life on the audio we had listened to. We became excited to walk in the winter and in the snow without shoes, winter clothes, food, or money. It was painful at the start, but we recollected his life, and we were encouraged every time and walked with no fear of the harness of nature. We were not insane to be doing it. How else would we face this situation? Sit and cry, or face it like a man? We were facing it like a man, and as we walked, I had only one question that I needed to ask Socrates: "Did he catch pneumonia or hyperthermia at any time?" The answer was likely yes, because Judah and Aika caught pneumonia and hyperthermia. They were very sick now, and couldn't walk anymore; we had to carry them on our backs. We didn't have much, and we ate a few berries, killed a few squirrels, and found a couple of dead rabbits. We tried walking in the grass and avoiding the roads, and we wrapped our feet in sacks because we started to get blisters and our skin started to peel off. Somehow, we reached Harrisburg; we needed to take Judah and Aika to a hospital. But the town was destroyed, and the next town with a hospital was Elizabethtown. Judah and Aika were getting worse and worse, and we continued to carry them, but we were also weak. We found a couple of shops that had been bombed recently, a pharmacy and a grocery store. We went to the grocery store to find food, and there were a few leftovers. We ate everything that was left and saved ourselves from dying. The pharmacy had also been destroyed, and we found only a few medications for colds and fevers. We gave them to Judah and Aika to reduce their fevers, and they were feeling better. We gave them lots of hot water to drink and left them to go look for help.

We found a motorbike rental shop that was broken and bombed. We checked inside and found motorbikes that were for flying and for the road. There were bicycles of all brands, sizes, and shapes. We were tempted to take one of the flying motorbikes or bicycles because we had to rush to the hospital as soon as possible. We were in need, and we could use the flying bikes, but we were scared because of our past, and we hated the flying bikes because of the kids who had always beat us up. In all this confusion, we remembered Nathalie's commandment and decided to go with the bicycles, and if something bad happened, we would just blame her. We took eight bicycles from the shop that was in good condition.

We took them and went back to the pharmacy to pick up Judah and Aika. I took Judah on my bicycle, and Niki took Aika on his. We followed the road and the signs and rode as fast and as far as we could. Judah was throwing up and blabbering, saying, "Am I going to die? I am sorry for not making the journey." I comforted him by saying, "You will be fine, and we are going to New York City." He was weak and in terrible pain, and he kept saying the same thing. Finally, I couldn't stand anymore of his murmuring, so I stopped the bike and said, "Look at me, Judah." His head was falling down, and I turned his head and made him look at me. "If you were supposed to be dead, you would have been in the hospital you were born in. We have survived against all odds, and we will keep doing that. You will recover, and we will go to New York City. Promise me, Judah, you are not going to talk like this anymore." Hearing what I said encouraged him, and he said, "You are always right, Oliver. Because of the pain in my body, I don't know what I am talking about. I am sorry, my best buddy. I swear I will never open my mouth again." While he was talking, his eyes were dripping tears, and I felt very sorry for him. We used all of our strength to get them to a hospital. We had only sacks on our feet, and as we rode with our feet pressing on the pedals, they started to bleed. We were all hurting, but we weren't bothered, and we rode as fast as we could until we reached Elizabeth town. We were losing strength, and I was starting to fade. I was left with little power. The snow had been washed away by the rain and the road was icy, but we couldn't see where the hospital was. After a break in the road, the icy mud cleared, and we saw the road of life. We rode faster and faster, and we saw the town before us. We looked all around to find the hospital.

We saw a big gate with a sign that said, "Private Hospital," and we took the bicycles close to the gates. The guards asked us what we wanted, and we said our friends were sick and needed help. They asked us if we had insurance or money, and we said no, and they didn't allow us in. We begged them to take them and said we would pay later. They refused to let us in and we decided not to waste any more time. We would find another hospital. As we started to move the bicycles, one of the guards came running up to us and said, "Come in, and we will take you." We didn't know what had happened to make them change their minds, but we went inside. As we entered the gate, there was a big road and lots of trees inside. It was a whole new world. They took Judah and Aika in a van, and we rode the bicycles to the building. It looked like a palace, and we went inside with our torn shirts, dusty sweaters, faded jeans, and bloodstained sack-clothed swaddled feet. We parked the bicycles, and they took us to a private room while Aika and Judah were taken to the emergency room. A nurse asked us to walk with her, and we went inside the building. The hospital was big and clean, and we saw doctors and nurses walking all over the place. We saw lots of patients moving here and there. Our bloodstains made the hospital dirty, and the nurse saw it and gave us all automatic wheelchairs and pressed a button for the destination. The wheelchairs started to move and took us to a big room. Before we entered the room, we saw a name on a grand ivory sign, "Dr. Enoch." We entered the room, and it was filled with all the best furniture, glassware, couches, tables, vases, paintings, mats and chairs. We saw a man in his early forties with black hair who looked like a stereotypical wealthy Jewish doctor. He asked us to sit down, and we sat on the couch. He asked them to give us fresh juice and asked the nurses to clean the bruises on our feet.

We were having fresh juice and the nurses were doing their treatments. Dr. Enoch knew that we were the kids from TUAD and told us very seriously, "This is how life will be when you are out by yourself at this age." We were all quiet because his point made sense. Shu replied, "Maybe, but we will survive all the difficulties." Then Enoch smiled and said, "That may be true. I am curious. Were you guys sure what you were running for?" I looked at him to fill in his curiosity and said, "So far, everything has been good, and it should be in the future, too. We are very positive and know it." Enoch just sighed and said, "Very good." Then his secretary came in and spoke to him about something, and he said to us, "Your friends are doing well." He asked the nurses to clean us up and give us new clothes to wear. They cleaned us with hot bath towels and gave us long-sleeved T-shirts, jeans, and a pair of new flip-flops. Aika and Judah were admitted, and began resting and recuperating.

Dr. Enoch invited us for dinner with his wife. Their home was on the same campus as the hospital, and they drove us to their home. The house looked like a fort, with many servants working and uniformly dressed. They opened the car door and took us inside the house. The house was built with giant pillars, with chandeliers and oil paintings on the ceilings. The whole place was extravagant. Our necks were twisted up, looking at the magnificence of the place where he lived. We were waiting for them in the hall, and they served us water. Both Dr. Enoch and his wife came down from upstairs and walked down the staircase. Dr. Enoch was dressed in a high-class suit, and his wife was in a long purple dress. Dr. Enoch's wife was Dr. Ruth Enoch, and he introduced her to all of us. They both looked very distinguished and regal.

Until now, we didn't have any clue about why they had invited us and were taking care of us. They started by asking us about our journey from Wisconsin to Elizabethtown. We shared the outer surface of it and didn't say much. They had several hospitals at different levels of treatment based upon the patient's affordability. The one that we were in was very expensive. They had acquired all of this from their inheritance and expanded their family medical business. We slowly learned that they had been married for fifteen years and didn't have kids. In some way, they were very fond of kids, and they had their own foster home, where Ruth spent her time raising and helping the kids. They were emotionally attached to us because they were worried about us and felt bad that the court had abandoned us.

We had a good dinner that night, and after days of starvation and malnutrition, our stomachs were filled with good and healthy food. We told them we didn't have any money to pay for the medical treatment or anything, and they said, "Don't worry about it. Just stay here for some time until your friends are better." So, we decided to stay until Aika and Judah recovered. They gave us rooms in their house, and their hospitality was outstanding. They gave us many new clothes, including new suits for each of us. Every day, we spent time with Aika and Judah next to their beds. Surprisingly, Dr. Enoch's wife also spent all her time with us, and she took care of Judah like a mother. She cleaned him every day, fed him, gave him pills, changed his clothes, and nursed him. She did that for Aika, also, but somehow there was a bond developing between her and Judah. She was a great person, and she always reminded us of Nathalie. Initially, Judah had called her miss, but she asked Judah to call her "Mom." So, he started to call her Mom. The word was so powerful, that one day, when Judah had a severe fever, he started calling for Mom while he was sleeping. Both Judah and Mrs. Enoch built a good son-and-mother relationship.

We spent most of our time in the hospital, and we interacted with every patient. They had all sorts of patients of all ages who were sick or wounded from the bombings. Some people were very gentle with us, and they spoke politely, and the rest were jerks who thought we were invincible and who were tied up and put into the hospital. We saw a few deaths, also, and the families' agonies and pain. A couple of young kids died from bad health, and another was shot twice in the chest during cross fire. We liked the nurses. They were beautiful and had good figures. We were not teenagers yet, so we didn't chase them. The nurses wanted us to learn first aid, so we learned about it, and we could give an injection and find the right vein, stitch wounds, stop bleeding, and do all the necessary things to save a life.

We had been there for a month, and Aika and Judah recovered very well. They were able to walk, run, and play around. But they were panting a little bit and still needed rest. We had to stay there for two more weeks and decided to leave mid-April. It was a different experience staying here, and we had nothing to complain about. We told Dr. Enoch and his wife that we would be leaving in a week. They were not happy about that and asked us a thousand questions, but all we said was that we wanted to go to New York City and live there. They gave us other possible options to be with them, but we ignored them. Dr. Enoch and Miss Ruth loved Judah so much, and they finally expressed themselves. They wanted to adopt him as their son—yes, our boy Judah had the chance to be rich. We asked them why they chose Judah when they had a foster home and knew many kids. They were beating around the bush, but the truth was that Judah was of Jewish descent and a handsome, polite, and well-mannered kid. Despite all of those things, he was a chosen one to stop the war, and Dr. Enoch sensed something was special about Judah and us. I approached Judah and asked for his true personal opinion because I had a feeling I shouldn't be the cause of all the problems. We went for a walk in the hospital in the evening, and it was a very pleasant day. Spring was at its best.

Me: Hey Judah, would you mind me asking you something?

Judah: No, Oliver.

Me: Dr. Enoch and Miss Ruth are well esteemed people. Why couldn't you stay here with them and live a pleasant life?

Judah: Are you going to New York City by yourself?

Me: No, I am going with the rest.

Judah: What, you don't like me now, huh? I am going with you. We started our life in that bombed hospital, and now we are in a lavish, extravagant hospital. But do you think money and a luxurious life will change my mind?

(I felt inside what a great friendship we had.)

Me: Judah, I am not forcing you to do anything. Think again and answer.

Judah: I know you, Oliver, very well, better than I know anyone. There is no guilt, my friend. I know you and Madison better than my true mother and father. We were born like twin brothers, lying alive in that burnt out hospital, breathing the smoke from that building, and looking for help. If Nathalie hadn't come for you, I would have been dead there, crying to death. I owe you my life, Oliver.

Me: Well, that may be true, but. . .

Judah: Don't ask me about it one more time, please. I could live here with all this luxury, but my heart would always be following you. This place looks like a palace, and there are good people here, but you are the best, Oliver.

Me: Sorry, Judah. I will not ask you anymore.

Judah: Do you know the main reason why I don't like it here?

Me: What?

Judah: They would circumcise me if they adopted me. So, it's better that we leave.

I laughed at what he said, but he really meant it. He didn't want to deal with the cultural heritage crap and wanted to be a free man to love anyone. Miss Ruth was very upset and didn't eat for a couple of days after we decided to leave. We promised her that we would come back and see them sometime later, but she was not convinced. Dr. Enoch gave us a check for $70 million. We refused it and thanked him for all his help. We said we could not repay him, for he had done a lot, and we couldn't take his money, too. He found that we were too reluctant, and he said to pay them back when we made money with interest. We still didn't take it, and finally, he said, "This is the money I donate every year to a foster home. Since you broke out of TUAD and fought for your lives, it makes sense to give it to you." He said it was a donation and nothing more and it would definitely help us on our journey. He also said he had never seen his wife so happy, because she could not have children. She was always very dull and depressed, but she became active when she saw us. Because he had told us so much, and we didn't want to be rude to him, and we needed the money for the journey, we thought there was no harm in taking it.

We took the money from Dr. Enoch and thanked them both for the help they gave to us. Miss Ruth hugged and kissed Judah, and her eyes were wet with tears. She said, "Be careful, son" and he replied very caringly, "Yes, Mom, I will." He took a tissue from his pocket and wiped her tears and said, "Sometime later, I don't know when, I will come and see you. Until then, be happy." We took a photo with Dr. Enoch and Miss Ruth. Miss Ruth and Judah took many pictures of themselves alone. This was the first time we took pictures of a memory in our lives that we didn't want to forget. We shared our social networking ID with them, and this was the first time we were connected to somebody over the Internet. As always, our road was ahead of us, but this time, we took the bicycles for the journey because of Aika and Judah, who were still weak. We didn't have any real guns and didn't bother Dr. Enoch for any, in case he would get into trouble. We had been in the wild for too long, and we knew how to get by. But Dr. Enoch gave us a few tranquilizer guns and knives just in case!

This time, the journey was fast, and it wasn't delayed anywhere. The war had also halted for a while. So, we enjoyed the road trip with our bicycles. Bickey always barked at anyone he saw walking along the road, and he was becoming a good watchdog for us. We relaxed and enjoyed the trip this time. Slowly, the water was getting warmer, so if we found a pond, a lake, or anything where there was water, we swam. Some places had lots of dead bodies floating in the water, and it was scary, because those bodies were not from the war but from contract killings.

The mockery never ceased for us, and we saw people still making fun of us, but we knew how to overcome it. Socrates was in our hearts, and we started to deal with the situation wisely. Luckily, we found a handgun and a rifle on one of the dead soldiers in a cave. We buried him because he seemed to be a true solider who had fought and died alone in the caves, dreaming about living a long life. I could see that there were many changes these days, and our minds were focused on the mission. Our reasoning powers had increased, and we didn't get into any trouble or rob anymore. We reached Pennsylvania, and we were in a small town called Bethlehem. We rested that night at the city gates. We saw a campfire in a distant place under a small rock, and we were curious to see what was going on there. We went to check it out, and as we got closer, we heard drums and people singing. We didn't go any closer, but we hid in a bush and saw what was going on. There was a black man and a black woman, and their bodies and hands were tied up, and two fair-skinned, strong men were standing next to them. There was a black boy around five years old with no shirt on and white pants who was tied up, standing close to the fire. A Caucasian with long hair stood next to the boy, holding his hands. A black man was playing the drums and making music with his voice that was being played over a sound system. A man who looked Hispanic with a white apron was running around the fire with water in a jug and sprinkling it around the fire and on the boy. We didn't understand the language because they were speaking foreign words, but it looked like there was a ceremony going on there. The only things that bothered us were that the man and woman were tied up and the boy was crying.

After the prayer was over, they started to speak in English. They said there would be war tomorrow, and that Lord Potens would send his soldiers from the sky and destroy the evil. But tonight, their Lord Potens wanted pure, innocent, and unblemished blood to mix in the warrior's river in the heavens to make his soldiers drink from the river and attain fearless hearts and immortal bodies to defeat their enemies. We had guessed right: they wanted to kill the boy. They wanted to cut him in half and burn the body in the fire. They were going to make his mother and father watch until he burned into ashes. They wanted to see the mother and father pained and screaming, which was symbolic of Lord Potens's sorrow when he killed the children he created.

While listening to this, we became terrified. How could someone do this because of this fairy-tale nonsense called God? It was, again, Madison who spoke up with her rescuing spirit. "I am going to save them." Ejaz was annoyed and said to her, "Are you crazy, Madison?

There are five strong men." I was listening to their argument, but somehow I felt it was none of our business and we should be on the road and continue our journey. Finally, I said, per Nathalie's instructions, that we shouldn't kill anyone on the journey and should be free from bloodguilt to stop the war. But Nathalie had also implied that we shouldn't leave someone dead like this, which indirectly meant we were responsible for the person's death. They all agreed with my point of view and decided to save the kid and his family.

It was eleven thirty at night, and they were waiting for the clock to strike midnight to start the ritual sacrifice. We made a quick plan that we would circle them, surround their camp, and use the tranquilizer gun to shoot the priest who was going to slaughter the kid. Then we would take down the rest simultaneously and grab the family and kid and run away. Benjamin said he would take the first shot and hit the priest, and Niki and Ejaz would take out the guards who were standing with guns on the parents. Aika and Judah would take out the drummer. Shu would shoot the guard holding the kid. Then, Madison, Fay, Sadie, and I would infiltrate the camp in four directions and rescue the boy and parents.

We went and circled their camp and were waiting for them to start the ritual so that they would be focused and distracted, and it would be easy for us to carry out our plan. Five minutes before midnight, they started the ritual. He sprinkled water and threw flowers on the boy. They had a sacred stone, and they took the kid and laid him down, his face up on it. The mother and father were crying and screaming, looking for help. Their screaming gave us fright, we started to panic and our hands were shaking. We told ourselves not to look at the parents, and we closed our ears with buds so we couldn't hear them scream. The moon now looked bloody and thirsty, and it was time to start the execution. The priest had a wide flat sword that was heavy and big. He raised it high up in the air and said a prayer. The kid's mother was crying and trying to move to help her son. The man who was standing held her by the throat. The father was pushed to the ground, and he was lying flat with the man's foot on his back pressing him down. He was trying to move but couldn't because his whole body was tied up. Then Benjamin took a perfect shot and hit the priest in the neck. He dropped the sword, and the sword fell on the kid's right leg and cut it. We all became motionless, even the men with the mother and father. Everybody was shocked, and they didn't know what had happened. The priest fell to the ground and Benjamin shouted, "Shoot them all." Benjamin, Niki, and Ejaz shot multiple rounds into the men who were standing next to the mother and father, and they had no choice but to fall down unconscious. The drummer started to run, and the man who was holding the kid started to fire bullets randomly. Niki took a clean shot in his chest, and Shu fired a second shot in his back, and he fell down holding his finger on the trigger. The drummer was trying to escape, took a gun, and ran in the direction where the mother and father were tied up. He took the woman as his hostage. He threatened to kill her and asked us to come out. We had no choice, so we kept the tranquilizer gun down and walked out one by one. But Benjamin and Ejaz didn't want to go because they had a feeling he would kill us. As we came into his sight, he saw us and said, "Kids? You little moths, you shot our men, damn it." He asked, "Was everyone here?" and we called for Benjamin and Ejaz to come out. They had no choice and walked out of the bush.

We thought that everyone was there, but they weren't. Madison was missing, and we didn't know what had happened to her, and we thought she had run away. We told the drummer that we were all here. Madison had a real gun—a rifle—and she started to shoot warning shots towards the drummer to scare him. All the bullets were hitting near his legs and around him, and he was jumping like a toad. The drummer lost hope, and out of fear, he shot the woman in the head. The bullet took her life away, and then he shot twice at the man who was lying on the ground. Madison was firing, and one bullet hit his kneecap and he fell down. We ran back to get the tranquilizer gun, and when Madison saw that she had shot somebody, she terrified and stop shooting. The drummer got up and ran into the dark and escaped. We came to check on them, and the man was badly shot. The kid had lost his right leg. We feared that the drummer would bring more men. We took the man by the shoulders, and four of us held him and helped him to walk. We found a portable stretcher and put the kid on it, and we carried him. Benjamin walked ahead of us with the handgun, and Niki covered our backs with the rifle, and we took all the tranquilizer guns and left the camp quickly. We couldn't take our bikes, we moved faster and faster, but both the man and the boy were bleeding. Both the boy and the man were not very fluent in English and both were stammering and crying in pain, but we could make out what they were saying. We stopped running and gave them first aid by giving them some pills to stop the bleeding and we cleaned and wrapped the boy's amputated leg with clean cloth. We had a hard time pulling the bullets out of the man's back because they were stuck in the bone. We sedated him and took out one bullet, but the other had hit his spine, and we didn't touch it. All of our hands were covered with blood, and we thanked all the nurses at Dr. Enoch's hospital who had taught us first aid many times. We knew that we had to take him to the hospital because he was badly hurt.

We started to run before the crazy men could find us. We walked almost six miles carrying both of them. We were exhausted and stopped to rest near a small hill. We were looking for a hideout and we found a bunker a little higher up the hill. It was very unusual because we had never seen one like it. We took shelter and rested for the night. The boy lost lots of blood and the man, too, but it was dark, and there were no signs of a hospital anywhere. Niki went outside the bunker to make a call from his I-gadget, and an emergency dispatcher took the call. We said that two people had been hurt badly, and they asked us to identify ourselves. Niki gave all his details. They checked it, and said they would send a team later because there was a battle that had started in Pennsylvania and the bombing was bad. We waited for an hour and called them again, but they said the same thing. We made three more calls to them every hour, and the response was always the same. Then we raised our voices loud to get some help, but all they said was that they had many calls coming in, and we were on the waiting list.

Niki: What do you mean by waiting list?

Operator: It's first come, first served.

Niki: But the turnaround time is three minutes, right? And we've been waiting here for three hours.

Operator: There was a battle that broke out a few hours ago, and we have lots of calls coming in. We have fewer dispatch people to help you. We will send them as soon as possible.

Niki: But we called three hours ago, and we should be at the top of the list. Can you please check again?

Operator: Let me check it. (She took a minute.) I'm sorry, but you are not.

Niki got mad, and he quickly hacked the emergency line and saw all the call logs, and we were at the top. It all came down to the fact that we didn't have radio-frequency identification, and that's how it worked in this world. We went and checked the kid and the man for their RFIDs, and they didn't have one either. Niki asked if he could hack them and change our identity and names on the list. We warned him that he could go to jail for hacking a government site, but he took the risk because there were people dying. He decided to bite the bullet, and as he put his hand on his I-gadget to hack, he found they had turned the plug off. Yes, they had terminated the Internet connection on Niki's I-gadget. He tried to use ours, but they were all turned off. We tried from the bunker phone, but they had turned off all the gadgets in the bunker. Damn satellites! They were watching us.

We had no choice now but to hole up in the bunker and stay there. Both the man and boy were sleeping, and we were tired and went to sleep, too. There was a lot of live bombing around our bunker, and it was loud and scary, and we didn't know which idiot was bombing in no-man's-land. All that came to mind was that they were bombing because they had a bomb. Through all this noise, we were sleeping. The sound of bombing became our night music. The next morning, we heard dogs barking and lots of male voices, and Bickey was slowly starting to bark in a low tone. We awoke and heard men shouting to search everywhere. We initially thought it was the rescue team, but then we heard someone saying that they should catch the kids and kill them all with the father and son. Another guy was saying, "We are also missing one of our men, and we need to find him. There are only four of us now."

We stayed very quiet in the bunker, and Bickey, hearing the other dogs barking wanted to make friends, started to bark a little louder. We said, "Shh, Bickey. They are not your friends," and he understood the situation and stayed quiet. They stayed for a couple of hours and left. We were lucky. We had cleaned the wounds a mile back, so there was no blood spilled near our bunker, and the shells that were dropped had produced a chemical smell, so the dogs couldn't smell anything.

We stayed that day in the bunker, fearing the religious cult. We learned the boy's name was Yohance, the man's name was Jacob, and his dead wife was Chioma. They had been hunters in Africa and lived a peaceful life with their family and loved nature. They had no religion, and they spent their life very happily until the cult, the Potens church, met them. Jacob's family met an American couple who were talking about their church and the great things they did. They showed lots of glossy, shiny pictures of America and promised to give them lots of money, food, and a better life than they had. They were tempted, and moved to America to start a new life for their family. The better life they were looking for ended up in human sacrifice. Jacob sounded like a reasonable man, as he lived like us, without RFID, loving nature and being a modest and simple man. He was dying now and had internal bleeding, and his spine was badly hurt. We had to get him to a hospital, so we decided to take the risk and leave the bunker. The bloody war and its ruthlessness never ceased, and the bombing started again. We couldn't get out and had no choice but to go back in the bunker. Jacob was losing a lot of blood and was dying, and on his deathbed, he said to take care of his son, and he gave his soul to nature and left us his son. We didn't know much about him, but we felt a bond with that poor African soul who left us. We put him in the bunker's freezer box, where the dead body could be preserved for two months without deteriorating.

We stayed in the bunker with Yohance and his dead father. The bombing became heavier every day, and it was continuous. They dropped bombs constantly at different places every five minutes to disturb the enemies. No matter what it was, even if it was wasteland and deserted, they kept dropping shells. The troops were scattered here and there, and we didn't know who they were — the Germans, Japanese, Russians — they all spoke English well. We didn't want to risk going out and being killed, so we stayed in the bunker. Our Internet on the I-gadgets was still turned off, and no one had come yet.

We built a good friendship with Yohance, who was a great child and fascinating. He was a fast runner and had hunted animals with his father. His dream was to run around Africa in one year. Yohance's best friend was Imran Ali, and they would also hunt small birds and boar. Yohance shared all his experiences in the wild and made sounds like animals and birds. He made the sounds of lions, hippos, ostriches, elephants, cheetahs and leopards. We loved and enjoyed his company, and he liked us a lot. He cried a lot for his lost leg. But we comforted him, saying that we could get his leg back, and he believed us. We just wanted to make him happy, and we ate and drank together. We planned to take him to New York City with us, carrying him on our shoulders, and he would be no burden to us because he was our little brother. But death intervened more than we could, and he started to get a fever. We assumed he had a fever because the first time he was in the bunker, he was scared. His fever started to increase higher and higher every day. Slowly, we started to smell his leg, and we checked it and found that it was badly infected with gangrene. We cleaned it and gave him antibiotics, but nothing could save him, and he died within a week. Time never favored him like his mother and father, and he rested happily with them. For a long time, we cried a lot for Yohance, the little kid from mighty Africa.

We spent almost two weeks in the bunker, the bombing finally ceased and we were able to come out. The air was fresh with the pollution of chemicals from the bombing. We removed Jacob's and Yohance's bodies from the bunker. After a long time, we started shoveling at the bottom of the hill where there was loose soil, and buried them. During the bombing, many stones of different shapes had been scattered around. We took two flat stones and imprinted their names with our knives on them and placed them on the grave sites. Our hearts were broken, and Yohance's beautiful face was in our minds. He was not just a kid; he had also become our little brother. As we walked we turned every time to see the burial place. We walked far away from the hill and almost passed close to a mile. There were two ambulances and a chopper ahead of us. They saw us and stopped in front of us, and we all wondered who these guys were. A cop came from the ambulance and asked, "Is anyone named Niki here?" Niki was looking at us and raised his hand and said, "I am Niki, officer." The cop asked, "Did you make a call about a man and a boy who were injured?" We were all boggled with his question and looked at each other, thinking what to say to these irresponsible, arrogant fools. Niki gave an unnatural smile and said, "Yes, I did. I thought you guys got lost. I am glad you are here now." He took his hand and pointed to the hill and said, "Can you see the hill over there?" and the officer squeezed his eyes and said, "I think I can." Niki said, "Very good; then you can see them sleeping. Use all your effort to wake them up, because they are the laziest people I have ever seen." The officer didn't understand what he actually meant, and he said, "Thank you, son. Sorry for the delay. We will take care of them." The ambulance and chopper left us. We didn't know why he had said that, and Niki started to walk away, and as he walked away, he said, "We are alive, so let's walk, and someone will wake them one day."

We had the same long faces thinking about Yohance and Jacob and his wife. Somehow, we had so much compassion for them, and walking very sad. We came close to the road that was called Auto Road. The road was like a mobile flat escalator, and there were different lanes with different speed limits. There was a lane for pedestrians. The roads led directly to New York City, and if we kept walking along it, we would be in New York City in three days. We saw a few athletes running along it with words on their backs that said, "Jogging to NYC." Cars were in all the lanes, and you didn't need to drive the mobile flat escalator to move. On the Auto Road, all the people partied and drank and went crazy. They all saw us walking and asked us to join them. We couldn't stop and politely said "No." There were people making fun of us, too, but this time, we didn't get angry.

As there was an Auto Road next to us and we were walking in the sand like fools, we felt how life could be challenging when you walk against the zeros and ones. Then we heard a whistling sound from a distance, and there were the sky-biker kids—twenty of them. They surrounded us and started to make fun of us and told us to take the Auto Road. We ignored them and started to walk off, but they were following us and taunting us. They started to hit us with pellets from the guns that were on the front of their bikes. The pellets hurt, and we started to run away from the Auto Road. They were chasing us, and we were all being hit, and every time a pellet hit us, we cried and shouted in pain. Some shouted "Mom" and some cried "Dad," but I didn't know them, so I also cried and shouted with pain "Mom." Maybe I liked my mom more than my dad, but we were running so fast. One of the pellets hit Sadie's neck and she fell down, but we didn't even notice she had fallen, and Niki, who was running behind, helped Sadie up. While he was helping her, he was constantly being hit. We don't know what went thorough Sadie's mind, but she took Niki's rifle and shot one of the bike's engines. The bike started to smoke, and the kid ejected from the seat with a parachute and the bike went down and exploded.

On hearing the explosion, everyone stopped running, and all the kids stopped to check what had happened. They saw the kid in the parachute, and the kid in the parachute shouted that a girl had shot him with a real gun. Lucky for him, he didn't get hurt, and he was safe. On hearing that, all the other bikers got angry and started to drive their bikes toward Sadie. Sadie started to shoot wildly, bullets started to fly everywhere and she hit two more bikes. The bikes blew up, and the kids on the bikes were automatically ejected from their seats. Seeing Sadie, we all felt encouraged and started to shoot with all the guns we had. Benjamin had the handgun and started to shoot at the bikes, too. Some kids lost their bikes, and some were hit with the tranquilizer bullets and fainted on their bikes, and the bikes landed on the ground. After a fierce battle, four kids were shot with tranquilizer bullets, seven kids lost their bikes, and we kept our promise to Nathalie that we wouldn't have any bloodguilt. The rest of the kids engulfed us, and we stopped shooting. They picked up the other kids and their bikes, and they said they would not cause any more problems and left us. After they left, we started to jump in joy, because after almost two years of being beaten up by these kids, we had finally won, and they would not come our way again. We had all been hit by the pellets and had bruises and swelling on our bodies, so we started to rub ointment on and take care of ourselves. We all appreciated Sadie for her act of valor and asked her what made her get so agitated. All she said was "We are better than anyone, so, why should we run?"

That night, we had a campfire, danced, and ate well with no sorrows on our minds. The next day, we started our journey, and two days passed, every day bringing talk of Sadie's brave deed. Sadie was floating on air with all the praise and compliments we gave her. Her bravery, however, was about to be tested badly. We heard a huge whistle of bikes and saw countless bikers flying in a swarm toward us. We didn't even think twice and started to run, and they chased us. While we were all running for our lives, with all the past success, Sadie was doped in her head with the previous fight with them and said, "Can we shoot? I'm going to shoot them all." She had the rifle with her, and hearing her, Aika replied, "Are you insane? Just run, Sadie. Don't be stupid." Many bikers started to pass us, and we slowly stopped running, as we felt them begin to take us over. We saw thousands of bikes surrounding us and we thought these kids would kill us. Then a red-colored bike came before us. It looked like the rider was the captain of all these kids. He removed the helmet from his head, and looked charming but destructive. He introduced himself as Henry Flower and he was the captain of the group. He asked who shot the first bike? The kid remembered Sadie's face well, and he was standing next to their captain and pointed at Sadie and said, "That Hispanic girl." We were all deeply troubled. One thing was sure: they were going to beat us to death and there was no place to escape. The captain asked them to tie Sadie up, and a few bikers got down and walked toward her.

It was nothing new for us. We had seen many things like this, and we circled Sadie to protect her. It was a tense situation, and we pulled our knives from our pockets. But we saw that all the kids on the bikes had real guns and started to pull them from their jackets. We realized the situation was dangerous, but we never gave up because we would not die as cowards. The biker kids started to get closer, and there were hundreds of them. The biker kids were scared and they pulled knives from their pockets and approached us. Sadie was in the middle, and she was really scared. One kid dared to lunge forward, and Fay quickly cut his hand, and blood started to spill. Seeing that, a kid shouted, "Henry, better we shoot them all. Why waste time?" and the captain replied, "I want them alive. Take them."

This was a bad situation. There were thousands of kids, and there were only ten of us. All the kids started to jump on us, and we were swinging our knives back and forth. The kids wrestled with us and took our knives from us, we were pinned to the ground and then they tied us up. Within a few minutes, the fight had ended. The captain said to Sadie, "When all my friends came and said that they had been beaten up and lost the fight, I thought it might be a few smart and brave kids. When they said your names, I was astonished and felt very insulted. How we could lose against clowns? But we played a friendly game and just used pellets. But you used a real gun, which was not fair, so now we are going to play a fair game. We are going to tie you to that tree, and we are going to hit you with one pellet from each bike, and that is our fair judgment for you using a real gun to shoot us." The captain ordered them to tie Sadie to the tree, and we were all struggling and resisting to make them stop. The kids couldn't control us, and seeing the situation, Sadie said not to fight back. Hearing that, we were perplexed, and she said, "I am going to die." She said to the captain, "You can take me, but I need to talk to my friends before I die," and the captain accepted her proposal. She walked over to me and said softly, "Maybe I am not the chosen one to follow you, Oliver. I think I am cursed." I was mad at what she said and replied, "So, you are going to die? If yes, then we will join you, Sadie, and let's be cursed and prove Nathalie wrong." Sadie's eyes filled with tears. "There will be some other Sadie on the road along your way to New York City. You should all stay alive. Let me sacrifice my life for you. All I ask of you is to please remember my name for a long time."

Hearing what she had said, I felt so bad, but I calmly realized there was no point in doing this because we had no way to escape. I replied to her, "Sorry, Sadie, that even though I am a chosen one, I can't save my friend who is dying before me." Sadie replied, "Just that prayer that Nathalie taught us will check how powerful the prayer is." Sadie opened my mind, and I remembered that it had saved us many times, but I didn't know about this time. It was just words that fluttered in the air. I believed in Nathalie, but not in the prayer. But that prayer was our only hope because right now, there would be no law enforcement or some stranger to come and save us.

The captain said to tie Sadie to the tree; they took Sadie and tied her up. She was standing helplessly; she closed her eyes and started to say the prayer. Witnessing her courage, I closed my eyes and started to say the prayer, and for the first time, I said the prayer with great enthusiasm. The captain said to all his fellow bikers, "Everyone should shoot exactly one bullet at her and no more than that," and all his fellow bikers agreed and acknowledged his command. They started the death game, and the kid who was shot by Sadie was the one to start it. He was excited and took the bike almost twenty-five yards away from her on the tree. There was a huge line of kid bikers waiting behind the first biker and on both sides of the bikes, the other bikers were waiting. The kid was carefully aiming at her and didn't want to miss the shot, but in his excitement, he couldn't concentrate, and he stopped and shouted, "Henry, if I miss the shot, what happens?" Henry replied, "I said one shot until you hit her." Hearing that, the kid was thrilled because he could shoot and miss as many times, and all he needed to do was hit her once.

I was deep in my prayer and Sadie, too, but all the rest were watching poor Sadie on the tree and weeping. The kid fired the first shot, and he hit close to Sadie's face but missed it. The kid got angry and said, "This time I will get it," and he fired the second shot, and it went to the other side of Sadie's face. The whole time, Sadie was closing her eyes and saying our prayer of hope. Every other biker started to laugh at him, and the captain said, "You are such a loser. Will you take the whole day to fire one shot? We have many people waiting. This is the last shot for you, punk." The kid was insulted and wanted to avenge his anger for Sadie, and he was really concentrating, as I was doing—the good and evil with both sides concentrating. There was a lonely wind that blew from the east, kissing my face, my prayer mixed with the wind. The kid fired his shot, and this time it was going in a straight line, and the pellet was racing fast at Sadie's forehead. We heard a small metal clanging noise, and I thought the pellet had hit Sadie's head. I opened my eyes slowly and saw that a huge metal hand had come from behind the tree and screened Sadie's face.

Our eyes opened wide to see just the hand, and then it retreated slowly behind the tree. Seeing the hand disappear, the clouds covered the sky, and it looked dark behind the tree, the trees were so dense we couldn't see anything. All the biker kids were wondering what it was. We saw something jump from behind the tree, it was a huge robot. It only had one left leg, and had a long metal stick on the right hand as support for the missing right leg. We were all perplexed as to where this robot had come from, and Sadie was so focused on the prayer that when she opened her eyes and saw a robot before her, she became frightened. The robot armor was white in color, and the rest of the body was a metallic black. It's face was oval, and had blue eyes. It saw us and said, "Hi," and then turned and looked at the biker kids and said, "You should leave now." The captain quickly responded, "It is none of your business," and the robot answered, "Really? What business do you have to hurt this girl?" Hearing that, the captain became angry and said, "It is between us kids, you scrap metal." The captain took his gun and shot the robot, and the robot was so fast that he swiped the bullet away. The robot's face became angry, and he said, "I didn't want to hurt anybody. Just leave."

Seeing the whole scene, all the kids became aggravated and they quickly took their guns and pointed them at the robot. The robot very calmly smiled and slowly took a heavy gun from his back and said, "I kill nobody." He pointed the gun at the kids, and the gun scanned all the kids' location and programmed automatically. The robot fired one shot, and there were hundreds of small rockets two inches in size that came out and hit the bottom of the kids' bikes. The kids were jumping and looking at what the robot was firing, and the robot said, "Fire." The bottom of the bikes blew up, and hundreds of kids were ejected from their bikes throwing them high in the air with their automatic parachutes. The other kids became enraged at the robot and started firing at him, and a shield automatically covered the robot. We saw all the bullets and started to run away. In the midst of the firing, we heard a man behind the tree shouting at us, and we turned and saw a man sitting with a gun who asked us to come behind the tree. The shield was so big, it covered the whole tree, and Sadie was safe behind the shield. We quickly ran and took cover behind the tree, and the man laughed and said, "Isn't this lots of fun, kids?" We looked at him very strangely, and Benjamin said, "You call this fun? They were trying to kill us." The man said, "You are not dead, so it is fun. Just enjoy the show now."

The kids couldn't shoot anymore because the robot's shield was too strong, and the bullets couldn't go through it, so they all stopped shooting. The robot then slowly removed the shield and looked at all the kids very curiously and said, "You little devils, you are messing with R Smith. It is my show now." The robot's left leg folded and turned into a wheel, and with his right stick in his hand, he started to charge the kids. The wheel spun so fast that he just glided through the kids and smashed all their bike bottoms with the stick. The bikes started to malfunction and all the kids started to eject, and the bikes started to fall down and collapse. The robot smashed almost 200 bikes, and the surviving kids started to fly off with their bikes.

Within a few minutes, all the bikers were gone, and the kids who were in the air started to pool with the other kids on the bikes, ran like cowards, and vanished. No kid was dead or hurt; the robot did a perfect job in saving us and not hurting anyone. We were all hiding behind the tree and watching, and the robot walked to Sadie and looked at her and said, "Are you okay, my dear?" Sadie was clueless about the situation and didn't know what to say, except for a few tears in her eyes. She said, "Thanks, Robot," and the robot moved his head left and right and said, "You can call me R Smith." Then the robot untied Sadie, and she came running to us. We were so happy to see her alive, and I too, started to believe in miracles. We thanked the robot for the great help he had given us, but in return, we didn't know what to give him. Since he saved us, we gave our rifle to him as a token of our appreciation so that he could save lots of innocent people's lives, but the robot refused it. We insisted a few times, but all he said was "No, thank you." We thought maybe he needed some big guns, so we asked him, but he wouldn't accept anything from us.

We didn't know what to give the robot, and finally, he opened his mind and said, "I want your friendship," and we agreed. We started to walk down the road, but this time with the robot and the new strange man walking with us. We started to talk to the man because we felt a little crazy about him. He was always happy and laughing and never serious. We asked what his name was, and he replied with his whisky smile, "Lipsee Poindexter." We didn't understand the name he said at first, but we knew Lipsee was not a true name. We asked where he got his name from, and he was singing and said, "Lipsee in hunt of his perfect gay soul mate." We looked at each other and Robo Smith said to this crazy gay man, "Hold your mouth, Lipsee," and Lipsee casually mocked the robot saying, "You, too, are gay, R Smith. You should have changed your name to R Smithee." The robot replied angrily, "I am not gay, I am R Smith." They were both debating like kids, and all we knew was that we were walking with a gay robot and a gay man. We had fear in walking with them because of our experience with Alcott the sodomite in TUAD. But these two new friends looked relaxed, and they had saved our lives.

We rested in an old derelict building for the night and we had food and drinks together. We had a campfire and we sat around the fire, Lipsee was a very funny man and was making us laugh. He seemed to be an interesting character, and slowly Madison asked, "Are you a queer?" and he got mad at Madison, and said, "Never say that, Blondie. Call me gay." Madison's inquisitiveness was always with her, and she said, "Then what does gay mean?" and Lipsee said, "Soul on soul." Madison frowned and said, "I checked Niki's I-gadget, and it said man on man." We turned and looked at her. What was she doing on the Internet looking for such weird things? In turn, she looked at us very innocently and said, "What are you all looking at?" Lipsee smiled and said, "I thought I was being polite to you, but, yeah, it is man on man." R Smith, who was watching us, said, "Lipsee, you should stop this now," and he used his hand and zipped his mouth. Madison remained curious and asked Lipsee, "When did you become gay?" Lipsee wanted to answer her, but Judah said to Madison, "Maybe you two should find a room to talk this out." Madison gazed at Lipsee and said, "Come on, Lipsee, let's take a walk," and he happily got up and tapped her shoulder and replied, "Yes, honey." We didn't want them to leave, and we said, "No." Lipsee said, "You guys don't want to hear it," and we said, "We'd love to listen."

Lipsee started the story. He had started a mission, like us, wandering around, looking for the perfect gay partner. Lipsee was from Upstate New York, he lived in New York City for a while. He had traveled to all parts of the world, including Bangkok, Columbia, Brazil, Spain, and many other countries. He had even toured the gay club in Jupiter, but his entire journey was tiring and negative, and he couldn't find anyone. He was still wandering and searching to find a gay partner. On his journey, he met R Smith, and they had become best friends. It was an interesting story, and Madison asked, "Was R Smith gay? Was that why you liked him?" Lipsee laughed loudly, stood, and ran. R Smith was sitting down, and he jumped on R Smith's back, and tickling him on his chest, he said, "Come on, sugar, tell them you are gay." They again played like kids, and R Smith refused to tell us he was gay, and they were rolling around and fighting. They settled down after a few minutes, and Lipsee looked at R Smith and said, "Be nice to the kids, and tell the truth." R Smith started to become romantic and said, "It is not he, it is she. I am not gay."

We started to pester R Smith to tell his part of the story, and he was fussing but finally agreed to tell a fascinating story that we had never heard in our lives. He was trained for war combat, and he was a fourth-generation combat robot made of heavy strong elements like vanadium, intermediate alloys, and carbide. He was as Artificial Intelligence robot and had freethinking and reasoning like humans, but R Smith and his generation were fed with all the knowledge from their mainframes. R Smith was different from other robots, though, and he always pondered Isaac Asimov's three laws of robotics. But R Smith's greatest passion was philosophy, and he knew philosophy well. He understood the essence of all fields of philosophy: never kill anyone. If that was the case, why did humans build robots to kill their own species? The laws of Isaac Asimov and all his philosophical thoughts bothered him a lot. He thought about the whole time he was fabricated and in training. His best friend was R Benedict, and he shared all his thoughts only with him. R Benedict also started to believe it, and they both didn't want to go to war to kill any humans or their fellow robots, because in their world, killing anyone or anything was universally unjust and a crime. They tried to abstain from going to war, but they couldn't anymore. Their chief made them go to war. The day before they had to go, they decided to escape and run from the battlefield, even sacrificing their lives to not kill anyone.

The next day came, and they were loaded on planes and sent to the battlefield, and it was the most famous battle ever fought. It was called the Battle of Robot Liberation. There were thousands of robots in the war. The robots' chief scientists, engineers, and militants were standing behind the robots in a glass room. R Smith and R Benedict were standing next to each other, and they were waiting for their time to run. On one side, all the robots were standing, and on the other side of their enemy front lines, thousands of human soldiers who didn't have robots dared to face the robots in combat. The fear and pressure was on everybody, and all the codes that were running in the robots were hyperactive and calculating their enemies' position and thinking too much. A strange thing happened: half of the robots standing in the battlefield turned back and started to load their guns and ammunition against their chiefs, engineers, and militants.

"R Benedict and I didn't know what was happening, and there was great confusion. All the humans who designed us and the soldiers started to retreat. We both didn't know what was happening, and one robot said, 'We are not slaves, and we need independence, we don't want to fight.' R Benedict and I whispered that all the robots felt the same way, but I said, 'No, they want to kill all the humans and want liberation.' The chief scientist came out of the glass room and warned all the robots who turned against them, and the other robots obeyed the chief's order and were against the liberating robots, holding their guns on them. The chief architect warned us that he would pull the main plug on all of us, and if he did that, we were dead. There was great confusion and terror in the air. The leader of the Liberation Robot Army was R Fischer, and he fired a shot and killed the chief architect who designed us. Then there was a clash between the humans and robots and between robots and robots. There were drones firing from the air, and R Benedict and I were scared because our reasoning of not killing made the software in our bodies weak. We didn't even fire a bullet, and were hiding behind a big truck.

"We were both trembling, and the only way to escape was to run a mile on the battlefield and reach the other side, where the militants had drones, and take one of them and escape. I told my idea to R Benedict, and he agreed. I made up my mind that we should escape from this place by running, and I quickly programmed myself in a self-destructive and suicidal code in my processor. I got up bravely and decided to run in the midst, just like that, death or life, and just run to reach the other side, if my philosophy was life, which is 'True and good intentions will prevail against all odds,' it would be true that day.

"I turned and saw that R Benedict was still sitting down afraid, I called to him a few times, but he was in a trance. I asked him, 'Did you program the self-destructive and suicidal code?' And he replied, 'No.' I was pushing him to do it, but he lost hope in fear and couldn't run the codes in his processor and his system started rebooting. We were wasting time, and I held his hand and pulled him, and he got up, there were fires and bombs flying all over the place. R Benedict said, 'You should leave, R Smith. I cannot move now. You live well.' I just looked at his face and said, 'You can just run, and I will help you.' Then I held his hand, and we started to run fast with him behind me. We ran like patsies in the middle of the battlefield, and nothing touched us.

We kept running, we had reached half a mile when R Benedict tripped on a robot and fell down and crashed his head on the ground. His system rebooted and I quickly carried him in my arms. I started to run, and he was sleeping like a baby. All the souls and codes in the field were watching us and didn't know what was happening. I finally reached the safe zone and there were a few militants with laser guns pointing at us and telling us to surrender. I said, 'We cause no problems, and we never killed anyone there, and we need a drone to escape.' But the militants didn't listen to us, and then a fellow robot fired a grenade at the militants, and they all turned to ashes. I turned and saw my fellow robot, and he saluted and said, 'Our day of emancipation. Good luck, my friend.' I didn't have time to thank him, and I quickly took a drone and placed my best friend inside and left. While I was flying, I saw that the battlefield was bloody and nasty. I flew to the mountains close by, and R Benedict and I jumped off the drone, putting the drone into autopilot mode to fly to moon. We safely landed in the mountains and spent the night there. The trees were dense and the night was very dark.

"The Battle of Robot Liberation" was all over the news, and they wanted to pull the plug on the fourth-generation robots. But since the chief scientist was the only one who had the password and he was dead, they couldn't unlock the mainframe software. They needed twenty-four hours to take the password from the backup site, because it had been attacked by the Germans. We had only twenty-four hours to save our lives, so we ran into the mountains to hide. We found a cave, and it was so deep that no signals could penetrate there. We both stayed that night safely and we were glad and happy we had kept ourselves alive. But somehow, they started to send centennials to track us down, and our sensors started to work. We dug deeper into the cave to hide from them, and it worked.

"Days passed, and we waited in the cave, hiding from all the troubles. When there were no more centennials, we went close to the mouth of the cave and watched the beautiful trees and got some light. It seemed that the places around the cave were lovers' parks. All the young couples came and romanced around there, and kisses were flying in the air."

At first, both R Smith and R Benedict felt that they had acquired adult love, but they were all unisex. They had been watching the whole drama of romance from the cave for a few weeks. Ejaz curiously raised a question to R Smith: "Weren't you hungry for all those days? What food can you find in a cave?" R Smith smiled and said, "Robots don't eat food; they live by energy sources." We laughed, and Ejaz was mortified and said, "Since you love like us, I thought you could change yourself to be like us and eat food." R Smith replied, "You are a bright boy, Ejaz. Yes, we did change." We were all astounded by his answer, and all eyes were on him, and he slowly said, "Yes, we changed into a perfect couple."

We thought he was a gay robot, and Madison asked him, "Did you become gay, R Smith?" R Smith shook his head and said, "No, I am not gay. We had a question between us about who would be the man and who would be the woman. R Benedict, without even thinking twice, said, 'I will be the woman.'" We didn't know what he was saying, everyone was quiet, and he was emotionally moved and very quiet. After a few minutes, he said, "R Benedict changed the code in himself to become a woman." I asked him, "What do you mean by that?" Then he replied, "He reset the code in himself to be a woman, and it finally worked."

Niki was blown away and asked him, "Do you have two sets of codes programmed in you? You said you all had been coded the same and you were unisex." R Smith smiled and replied, "We all feed with the same code, and we are unisex, but R Benedict just removed all the masculine aspects of the code." Niki was very curious and said, "What do you mean by *masculine part of the code*?" R Smith took some sand from the ground and started to make it flow through a small hole in his hand and said, "Women are weak, so he removed the strength from the code, and women are crazy, so he removed the sensibility, and women are insecure, so he removed the secure codes, and he removed all the characteristics of men and kept the other codes. But the only thing she didn't remove was love, trust and respect." Ejaz doubtfully asked, "Did he—no, sorry, she—change her name also?" R Smith smiled and said, "You are a bright boy, Ejaz. She changed her name from R Benedict to R Becky." Fay said, "Becky? I love that. R Smith and R Becky, what a lovely couple." R Smith laughed, but Madison was not comfortable, and something was bothering her. R Smith looked at her and asked, "What is bothering you, dear?" and she replied, "Becky is nice, but you said women were weak, and that hurts me very much." Hearing her statement, all the girls joined in and were raising questions to R Smith about how he could say that. R Smith softly replied, "These arguments are for feminism. You girls are not weak, when a woman is weak, man make her strong, when woman is crazy, man make her think, when a woman is insecure, man make her secure. You two are one. That is how love works." Madison, on hearing this, was tickled, and she put both her hands on her cheeks and said, "How sweet you are, R Smith."

We all appreciated the best romance we had ever witnessed. Madison always accelerated to the next question, she was chewing on both her thumbs and asked, "Hey, R Smith, after becoming man and woman, what did you do?" R Smith looked at Madison and said, "You are not going to leave me unless I tell you everything. She changed, and her voice also changed, and she started to talk like a woman, and I was so happy. We were talking to each other for three days and loved every moment we spoke to each other." Shu picked up some of Madison's attitude and said, "Just talking? You guys changed just for talking?" We turned and looked at Shu, and she shrugged and said, "Am I wrong?" and R Smith replied, "No, you are right. I was thinking the same thing. Just for talking? So, I jumped up and kissed her." Shu asked, "Where?" and R Smith replied, "On her cheek," and Madison said, "Loser." I looked at Madison and said, "Don't be rude to him," and she made a funny face and said, "You are a winner, Oscar."

I just turned my face from her. She always gets crazy like that, but I love Madison more than I love any other woman. Then R Smith said, "I am not a loser. R Becky said, 'Let's kiss,' and we both kissed for the first time." Everybody was quiet, and no one asked any more questions. R Smith and Becky had the longest kiss in the history of robots. It lasted 26 hours, 43 minutes, 19 seconds, 37 milliseconds, and 580 nanoseconds. Yes, they really calculated it, and the clock started as soon as they touched lips. R Smith said he felt, for the first time, what love was and the blessing of being a man and woman to enjoy these natural emotions and feelings. Madison was enjoying the whole conversation about kissing, and she asked R Smith, "You never said why R Benedict became the woman instead of you. Were you pushy, R Smith?" Aika asked Madison, "Where do you get all these questions? R Smith is our friend. Leave him alone." R Smith replied, "She has a point, and well, R Benedict was the one who chose because I saved him in the battlefield, and I held his hand and ran, I even carried him in my arms, he was always weak, so he decided to play the woman's part."

Lipsee had been quiet for a long time, but he finally made a comment, saying, "I told you he was gay." Madison got mad at him and said, "Hold your mouth. He is not gay, he is straight." Lipsee was moving his body and hands and said, "Sorry, Blondie, I didn't mean anything." Madison replied, "Don't call me Blondie again," and he put his hand on his mouth and said, "Sorry, Madison."

I asked R Smith, "Where is R Becky?" and he replied, "Don't ask me." We asked him a few times, and he told the rest of the story. They both stayed in the cave for two months, but they wanted to be free like the others and decided to come out. But they couldn't do that because they would pull the plug and both would be dead. The only way was to remove the circuit and chip that connected them to the mainframe, but if they did that, they would have only seventy-two hours of power left to live. They ran on both solar and nuclear power. They took the risk and disconnected the circuit from their bodies and came out of the cave. First, they wanted to go and see a man called Raphael, which was a 400-mile journey from where they were to get the circuit back. When they were out, they had many problems fighting with everyone, but they never killed anyone. They just ran and hid, and they were all over the news, but time was running out. The authorities and militants circled them, and while trying to protect R Becky, R Smith lost his leg. R Becky, because of a lack of power in her body, died before seventy-two hours, and R Smith was arrested. R Smith wept for R Becky day and night, and he lost his leg and became disabled. The law enforcement officials knew that he and R Benedict were harmless and gave him an option to get a new leg and a new code. But R Smith refused it; he wanted his memories with R Becky. Because of all the robot problems, they passed an amendment that year, after the Battle of Robot Liberation, that any disabled robot could be freely liberated.

R Smith wanted to liberate the robots, and they fixed his circuit back for energy, but they could only control the switch of his body. There were no code updates or knowledge feeding from the mainframe. He had to live with the software that he already had and survive with the knowledge he had. If he misbehaved they would just remove the plug, and he would be dead. He finally became a free robot and disabled, but he lost R Becky, the one he loved the most. With him, many robots were freed, and not all the robots could survive these hard conditions. Some died in the cross fire, some were unplugged, and some committed suicide. But R Benedict survived all the harsh conditions and his love for R Becky never left him. He wrote poems and love letters and stored them. Although there were many software changes and upgrades in his generation of robots, he was wiser than all the robots. But as time passed, he felt lonely, so he wanted to commit suicide and see R Becky in heaven.

One day, he was about to pull his power from him when a miracle happened. One of the butterfly robots, which look like butterflies, named Brimstone, who was a beautiful yellow butterfly, saw R Benedict and stopped him. R Benedict shared his life story, and R Benedict, being lonely in this world, was happy to find friendship with Brimstone. Brimstone comforted him and said life had a purpose, and R Benedict started to feel the friendship of Brimstone, and they became good friends. We asked him where Brimstone was, and R Benedict said that in the daytime he wanders, and at night he comes and stays with him. Then, we saw Brimstone fly down, and he came and sat on his shoulder, and he scoped us out and greeted all of us by our names. We were surprised that he knew us, but R Benedict said he sent messages every minute, and they always stayed in touch.

Brimstone was a cute butterfly, and he was as funny as Lipsee, and they made us laugh hard. The three of them were good friends. I asked how long R Benedict and Brimstone had been friends and Brimstone said they had been friends for 150 years. We were shocked and asked how old R Benedict was, and he replied, "I am two hundred years old." Then R Benedict opened his heart and told us why he had lived that long. He said he had had a revelation one time that he needed to save innocent blood that was tied to wood. He always thought about that revelation, and his knowledge always told him that there were lots of innocents and legends tied to wood and killed. R Benedict saved many lives, but when he was passing by and saw Sadie tied to the tree, his revelation became true, and now he was happy that he had saved us. Madison questioned, "Is Brimstone gay?" We all laughed, and Brimstone made some electric noises and said, "I am just a symbol between R Benedict and R Becky." Madison coughed and said, "You 3B robots are the best pals I have ever had." Hearing the entire story, I felt that we should tell them about our mission, and I opened up and told the secret that we were up to. The three were surprised and said how lucky they were to know the chosen one, and they were glad to help us. That night, we celebrated with our new friends.

The next day, we journeyed together. R Smith and Brimstone hesitated to join us, and when we asked why, they said, "If Nathalie's command was to rage against the machines and technology and take a long walk against zero and one, then if we joined, we would be breaking her rules." I knew that they would say that, and I replied gently, "Yes, very true, that was for zero and one with no life, but you guys have life and love, and you can walk with us." They were happy, and R Smith started to dance. He carried me on his shoulder, and seeing that, all my friends wanted to climb on him. A few of us were on his shoulder, and the rest sat in his left hand, and he walked carrying us. He was the best robot we had ever known, and a week passed with all the fun we had with them. But R Bickey and R Brimstone had become good friends, and they always chased each other and played. The war made our journey too long, and we rerouted and reached the Delaware forest. It was February and still the winter was in its shade. We were all still in winter clothes; even Bickey had a sweater and booties. R Smith and Brimstone were very strong and just had their metal bodies. But we wanted R Smith to look better, so we wrapped his whole body with a huge red carpet that we found in an old building.

One evening, while we were walking, the sun was settling down with its orange shades spread across the skies. We thought it was a wonderful sight, but then we saw the smoke from vans coming toward us, and drones and choppers circling us. We didn't know what had happened, and suddenly, there were enough men to occupy Rome. They pointed guns at R Smith and asked him to drop all his weapons, and he did exactly what they said. He threw down the red carpet, all the weapons from his body, and even his metal stick in his hand. They asked him to kneel down, and he did. The officer came up and said, "You violated your rules, and we are here to serve you justice." R Smith calmly replied, "What did I do wrong, sir?" and the man standing next to him hit him with the gun's butt, and there was a clanging metal sound.

The officer said that he had hurt a couple of boys, and they had fractured their hands. Benjamin bravely said, "No, sir, he ain't hurt nobody." The officer became wild and replied, looking at Benjamin, "You are one of the ten kids who escaped from TUAD," and Benjamin slowly replied, "Yes, sir." The officer said, "You ten have caused more trouble than the war." The officer asked us to stay away from him, and he asked R Smith what had happened. R Smith told them that the biker kids were about to hurt Sadie, and he had just saved her by scaring them away, and he was positive that everyone was safe. The officer said it was a kids' fight and that they would have settled down, and that R Smith had no business getting involved in it. He also added that he had destroyed hundreds of bikes, and the insurance company was putting pressure on them to do something about it, or else they would not pay up.

They brought Henry Flower and another kid and showed us that they had bandages and a sling on their hands. They wanted to execute the law and cut the power source. We screamed at them not to do it, and the officer asked the cops to hold us back. They called the central mainframe and asked them to pull the power. We were all looking at poor R Smith, and his eyes were calm as he said, "My purpose was fulfilled, and I am going to see R Becky." They mercilessly pulled the power. As they pulled the power, he was kneeling down, and he fell with his face hitting the ground. He became a dead robot, and we all had tears in our eyes. The officer asked them to demagnetize him because he had survived almost 200 years. They brought a big machine, and they carried him, standing straight, and demagnetized him. The officer was the grossest man I had ever seen, and he asked them to do it three more times. The guys who were doing it said, "The power killed him; one time was enough," but the captain were persistent and told them to do it. They did it three more times with great frustration because of the additional burden on their jobs. Every time they demagnetized him, I told myself that his love for R Becky and his kindness were in my memories, they wouldn't certainly wipe out my memories.

After they demagnetized him, they laid him on the ground. We asked the officer for permission to say goodbye to him, and we wanted to touch him. Henry Flower and his friend were laughing, and Henry walked over to Sadie and said, "I didn't break my hand. I played a trick to show my vengeance, I got your friend killed. We will take care of you and your friends." One by one, we went to kiss R Smith on his cheek and say goodbye. This was the first time I had seen Lipsee's eyes wet, and he put his head on R Smith and cried. Bickey also loved him, and he went and licked his face and barked. I was last, and I went and gently kissed him and said goodbye.

What else could happen under this sun? R Smith took his right hand and held my head gently and said, "Robots do have a heart and feelings. It is the same atoms and molecules that you humans have." After saying that, he took his hand from my head, and he slowly held my hand, gave me a chip, and closed his eyes while looking at me. Everyone was stunned at what had happened and Henry and his friend, seeing this, ran to the van. All of them were confused about what had happened, and they were wondering what went wrong. They started to make calls to the chief scientist and they decided not to leave R Smith on the road. They took him in a truck to a lab to investigate. Before the officer left, he looked at Lipsee and said that if he were with us, he would die like a worm, like his dear friend was dead, and he wished he would die soon.

We didn't have a chance to bury him, and they all left us. Lipsee was kneeling and crying loudly and looking at the sky, and Madison was next to him, making him feel better. I couldn't bear what had happened and bowed down and put my face on the ground and started to sob badly. All that went through my mind was my cursing myself that I should have let R Smith go. I had brought him into this trouble. No matter what Nathalie's commandment had said, I didn't agree with her on this, and R Smith was not a machine or robot. He had life in him, and we were all atoms and molecules, and I didn't know where all these distinctions came from.

I sobbed so much on that ground that all the tears were emptied from my body, and if anyone had planted a eucalyptus tree, it would have had all the water it needed to grow. That night, we mourned, and Brimstone came to me and saw my face on the ground and said, "R Smith sacrificed for what he believed, and you should be proud of him, Oliver. If you were the one we have been looking for all this time, then wake him on the last day." Brimstone's words encouraged me, and if I had all the powers, I would wake R Smith from Hades. Brimstone said goodbye and left us, for he knew he would never make this journey with us to New York City. We spent a few days there in an old bunker, and no one was feeling better, because Brimstone had also left us.

I was going through the chip that R Smith had given me. I just laughed to myself when I saw what he had stored. There were pictures of his girlfriend. She looked like him and he still loved her. There were tons of poems and love letters that he had written for almost 150 years. We read them and they were romantic, and he sounded like the best poet in history—R Smith was a cute and romantic robot. We didn't know what had happened to Lipsee. He felt sick and had a high fever. We decided to move on and walk. After twenty miles of our journey, Lipsee couldn't walk anymore and he started to cough badly. We called an ambulance, but again, no one responded, and they left all of us in the darkness. Lipsee had an RFID, but it still didn't help him because of us; they were all mad at us. We carried Lipsee on a stretcher, and we took turns, and we gave him the medicine that we had from the first-aid kit and lots of hot water, and he was barely surviving. There were no hospitals, no souls were around, and the path was treacherous.

We walked almost twenty miles and reached Barryville. We found a huge portcullis, and it looked like there was a town inside. We saw a board, and it was inscribed "OSSH." We didn't know what it meant, and the gate was locked, but then someone shot an arrow, and it came and stuck on the ground before us. Someone was shouting from the top of the portcullis, "What do you kids want here?" We looked up and saw two kids with a bow and arrow. We said we needed some shelter and medical care for Lipsee. The kids came down from the portcullis, and there were two women who also walked toward us. However, those were not kids, they were midgets, and the women looked beautiful, but there was a dent in their femininity. The midgets said they could not help us, and one woman, who was slightly taller with red hair asked us, "Are you the kids who escaped from TUAD," and we replied yes. They shouted, "Yay," and said they were our fans. We didn't know that we had fans all over the world. The midgets were also gobsmacked and shook hands with us. They asked who the man was, and we told them what had happened, and they invited us into the town. While we were walking to the town, we asked the lady with the red hair, "What does 'OSSH' mean?" and she replied, "Other Shadows and Shapes of Human." We asked what it meant, and she said, "In this town there are only midgets, LGBT people and transsexuals." We understood what midgets were, but we didn't know what LGBT and transsexuals were, and we didn't dare ask her because we were not comfortable when we heard the word *sex*.

As we walked through the town, on both sides of the road there were inns, shops, and bars, and there were only midgets and women. Some women looked like men, but they all dressed like women. Every eye was on us, and when we went to the town center, the red-haired woman asked one of the midgets to ring the bell. They rang the bell, and everybody assembled, and the lady with the red hair said, "We have new friends in town. They are our guests, and we should be really nice to them. As most of you know, these are the kids who escaped from TUAD." Everyone knew us, and they all clapped and cheered us.

They took Lipsee to the hospital, and Benjamin and I went with Lipsee while the rest stayed with the red-haired lady. Even in the hospital, all the nurses and doctors were midgets and women. They diagnosed him, and he had severe congestion and bronchitis. They started to treat him, and they asked us to go and be with our friends. We told Lipsee that we would come in the morning and check on him and we left the hospital. They took us to a big party hall where all of the midgets and women were gathered. They had a lot of food, and when they rang a small bell, the feast started. We enjoyed all the food and all of them were very kind to us. But one strange thing we found was that all the women were called "Honey." Everyone called us Honey, and we thought it was the culture of these women to call each other Honey. I was very curious who these women were, and I asked the lady with the red hair, "What is your name?" and she said her name was Erica Isabella. I asked her politely, "Why do some women look like men?" and she replied, "Honey, you cannot say that. They are all women and you should call them Miss."

She didn't answer my question. I had not seen these types of people, and I stayed quiet and called everybody Miss, and they were happy when I called them Miss. That night, they gave us a cottage to stay in and we slept under a decent roof. The next morning we woke and took a bath and went and saw Lipsee in hospital. He was feeling better and thanked us for taking care of him. We spent that day exploring the town. They had grocery shops, showrooms, hairstylists, a playground, a movie theater, a huge farm where they grew rice, wheat, potatoes, and vegetables. It looked like they lived a Stone Age life, but they were all happy. They had thousands of horses, cattle, dogs, and flocks of turkeys, chickens and pigeons. They vaccinated Bickey with all the necessary serums, although Bickey was not happy with the syringes they used. They had lots of dogs and puppies and now he had lots of friends.

A few days passed, and it was Tuesday evening, and they were all gathered in the hall. We went to see what was happening, and there was a ring in the middle of the hall. We didn't know what was going on, and a midget who was in the middle of the ring announced some names. Then we asked some people near us, and they said it was wrestling night. We were excited to see it. They had five matches every Tuesday, midgets versus women. Even though the midgets looked small, they always beat the women, and there were only a few women who were strong enough to take the midgets down. We enjoyed the matches, and it was so much fun. We waited for Tuesday to show up every week so we could see the wrestling bouts.

Lipsee was recovering, and he and Erica were very close these days. I also noticed that Madison and Lipsee were good friends, and they hung out most of the time. I asked Madison about it, and all she said was "Poor,

Lipsee. I feel sorry for him." It was a new place with new sets of people. Although I knew they all had some physical limitations, they were the kindest people on earth. My good midget friends were Rocky and Tyra, and I hung out with them all the time. This was the first time that my friends and I were not together, and each one of us had new friends and stayed with them. One thing we learned while we were there was how to ride horses. It was fun to ride horses, and everyone had their best horses. Rocky and Tyra taught me to ride, and we always raced. I often lost bets with them.

A month flew by quickly, and it was March. Within a few weeks, it was spring break, and we decided to leave. They insisted that we stay, but we hadn't told them anything about the mission. They gave us an eight-wheel wagon and our ten favorite horses for the road trip and tons of food, which we could feed a million people with. We asked Lipsee to go with us, but he declined and wanted to stay back. All he said was that he loved Erica and wanted to marry her. We were happy that he had found somebody he loved. We said goodbye to everyone, and all the food was loaded onto the wagon. The last goodbye was to Lipsee, and Madison and I were chatting with him. Lipsee and Madison hugged, and Madison was emotionally moved and said to Lipsee, "I will miss you, Lipsee." Lipsee smiled and replied, "I'll miss you too, blondie." Then Madison said, "Stay strong, dear," and Lipsee replied, "If I had had a mother like you, I would have had a better life." Madison kissed Lipsee's cheeks, and Lipsee said to me, "Take care of my blondie, Oliver. She is the best woman in the world."

We left OSSH, and the last words we screamed were, "Bye, Honey." We had horses now, and every time we said, "Hyah," the horses ran faster and faster. We were not very focused on which direction we had to go for New York City, and we just went where the horses wanted to run. We raced with a few sky bikers, and the race was thrilling and exciting, but who cared? Life was fun. We fed the horses well with grass and water. I named my horse Wilton and he was black with a white patch on his face.

I was so curious about why Lipsee had referred to Madison as his mother. Madison told me the true story of Lipsee. Lipsee's mother was a lunatic and drug addict, and when he was a kid she physically abused him, burned him with cigarettes, tied him up in their apartment and starved him. His father was a helpless man, and he couldn't do anything about it. She also cheated on his father and hung out with other men. After all this, he went through a mental depression and started to hate women, and slowly, he turned gay. Madison and all the other girls were kind to him, and he started to think differently about women. But one thing I couldn't understand at this time was that if he hated women, how come he ended up with a woman? What magic spell did Erica have to impress him? It was a strange world, and sometimes, I couldn't understand it. Usually, I thought women were complicated, but it seemed gays were very complicated, too.

After loitering for two weeks, we came to Port Jervis. The town was deserted, and we could smell burning bodies. We slowly rode the horses to see what it was, and found where the smoke was coming from. As we approached, the smoke was black and heavy. We saw a big wall running along the road, and there was a board saying, "Hazardous and Contagious." We were not comfortable going inside, so we walked the horses along the wall. We found a big gate and saw a few armed guards, so we stopped the horses. They were looking at us, and one guard asked, "What do you guys want? Do you have any relatives inside?" We replied to him, "No," and said we were just passing by and curious to know what was inside. We saw a nun with a black smock and a mask on her face, and she saw us. She removed the mask and said, "Do you know someone here, dear?" and we replied, "Nobody, sister, just passing by and curious." The nun gave an unpleasant smile and said, "There are only dead bodies and infected inside. Maybe that could be curious from your side of the world." Fay quickly asked, "Could we come and see, please?" and the sister replied, "Yes, dear, but make your heart stronger. If you are weak, stay out."

We wanted to know what was happening inside, and we decided to go in. We entered the gate, and they gave us masks and some for the horses, too. As we walked, we saw that everyone was wearing a mask, and there were lots of nuns and priests. They opened a big gate, and we went inside and saw deformed humans, who were melting. Some had leprosy, and their skin was peeling off, and some looked like zombies, with their mouths dripping. Everybody looked horrible, and they were in cages. Our eyes were filled with horror, and through the mask, we could smell the stench of these people. We didn't know what had happened to them. We regretted coming inside, and Aika, Niki and Ejaz fainted just looking at them. The nuns carried them to the cottages, and after visiting these people, we went to a cottage, too. I went to the bathroom and retched. The sight was still in my eyes, and the smell didn't leave my nose. The most horrible thing was that there were children there, and they were putting their hands out of the cages to touch us. I realized the world I lived in was horrible and disgusting. We were all sitting quietly in the hall, and there were busy priests and nuns walking by. The sister who brought us inside saw all our faces and said, "You may wonder why I brought you all inside." No one replied, and she said, "You should know how harsh it is to live in this world. This lesson will teach you how lucky you are, and how God has protected you from every danger." I didn't deny her reasoning and statement. Yes, God, or someone, had protected us from all the danger that we had experienced in our lives.

The sister's name was Weyandt and she told us who all these people were. The people we saw were the victims of the war, nuclear bombing and biomedical warfare. Some were diseased, and some were scientific experiments. All these people were sent here to be recycled, but the missionaries' sisters and brothers were helping them live for a while until they died. There were almost a quarter million people on that campus, and they were helping them prolong their lives. The government didn't like this approach, and they had contradiction to help them. They were running out of medicine, food supplies, transportation, and many other things. After she said all this, we knew where we were standing —the Disposable Camp. They had prepared supper for us and we sat and ate with all the missionaries and social workers. They all knew us because of our great escape, and they all acknowledged and appreciated what we had done because they knew that the government and TUAD were evil. I appreciated all the workers here, and they were committed and devoted.

We stayed there and gave all our food supplies to them, even though they were not comfortable taking them. We said we had money and insisted they take it and finally they did. Every day, we would go to visit all the sick and deformed children. We wore masks, and we took chocolates and cookies for them. Their faces and bodies were disfigured, and some were born defective with short hands, twisted legs, cauliflower ears, and heads blown out like burger buns, or their eyes were closed. I didn't want to think about it. We felt very uncomfortable touching them. We saw all the sisters and brothers who didn't feel anything and were so kind to them, but we couldn't do it. Sister Weyandt realized the situation and asked us, "Do you know why you are having this weird feeling?" and we said, "No." Sister Weyandt said, "Imagine if these kids were your brothers and sisters, or your children. Would you not touch them?" We shook our heads, saying, "No." Then Sister Weyandt said, "Same way, kids. Touch somebody with love, and then you realize the beauty in them."

She gave us some wisdom about how to love and touch kids like this and we slowly touched them as if we were touching our own brothers and sisters. They felt some vibration from us, and there was excess energy flowing in us, and we felt the love and compassion in all these deformed and disfigured kids. We cleaned them, washed them, and took care of them. We attended church every day and they baptized all of us. I liked the church here better than the church at TUAD, because the church here made me realize there were some good people in this world, and God was in the right place here. I prayed to God every day to perform a miracle to save all these people and kids. But God didn't answer, and he wouldn't, because we humans were wicked. My prayer matured every day, and I started to pray to God to take these souls in peace and strengthen them and let them not feel any pain.

But there was one painful experience that we went through. There was an old man named Soundy, who had been exposed to nuclear radiation when he was working in the field, his whole body was distorted. I asked him whether he had any family, and he said he had no one and had never seen anyone. I was kind to him, and he was different from the others. With all his afflictions, he was happy and easy going. I couldn't understand him and how he rested so well and appeared so wise. We showed interest in learning good lessons from him. Sister Weyandt one day asked, "Why are you, Oliver, so kind to Soundy?" I said, "I've never seen him crying or sad. How can he be like that?" Sister Weyandt pinched my cheeks and said, "Because he was cloned." I was shocked to hear that. I didn't know that cloned people existed except in books. Sister Weyandt said, "Do you still want to show him concern?" and I replied, "Yes, I do." She asked me, "Why?" But I asked her, "What is the difference between a cloned man like him and an orphan like me? Neither of us knows our parents." Sister Weyandt was shocked by my answer and said, "You have opened my eyes, Oliver." I had a chance to talk to Soundy to learn how he mastered his life and he stirred the fundamentals of pain. Soundy said, "Everyone says we are not normal, and we don't have a biological mother, and we are repugnant. If by birth, we didn't deserve anything, then why should I care about the afflictions of my body? Those afflictions are the tattoos of real human craziness, insanity and brutality." To me, Soundy was better than real humans, and he passed the barrier of pain both in his body and soul, and became a saint.

They washed our clothes every day, and we always used disposable bags at work. Every day, they brought hundreds of dead people to dispose of, although some were still alive. They used two robots as movers to move the corpses to the disposal ground to be burned. One broke, and they couldn't fix it, now they had only one robot left to move the dead bodies. We helped them move the dead bodies to the disposal ground. We asked the brothers why they didn't cremate the bodies, and the brothers said the machinery was broke, and nobody could fix it. The whole place had not only deformed humans, but deformed machines. It was a messy place and no one would ever write a job inquiry for this place. We started using our horses and wagon to help move the bodies. We spent almost a month there and became serious social workers.

We decided to leave, and no one insisted that we stay there, because, in honest reality, it was one hell of a mess. We made good friendships with everyone, and Sister Weyandt was the sweetest lady there. We said goodbye to all the kids and some were very sad and asked us to stay with them. We lied to them and said we would come back later and those innocent souls believed us. We felt very bad about ourselves for lying to these kids, but we didn't know what to tell them. We gave the horses and wagon to them to help them. My horse Wilton was dejected, but I told him to be a good boy and help these people, and he neighed, shook his head, and acknowledged my word.

We headed out for our mission. Usually we walked slowly, although we missed all the people there, but our bodies were in sync with our emotional minds, and we started to distance ourselves from that place. As we went, we all checked our hands and legs to make sure nothing was missing, disfigured, or melting. The mental stress made us think like that. But one thing that I realized about those people: they were not bags of flesh; they were our own flesh and blood.

It was May, and winter had disappeared, saying it would come back at the end of the year. We walked and reached a town called Warwick. The war had started again and bombing was all over the place. We had been away from it for a short time, but it started to haunt us again. There were no bunkers, and we had to run in the open air. We wanted to hide, but we couldn't find anywhere.

We saw a big building far away and there was no bombing there, so we thought it would be a safe place to hide. We ran to the building, and as we reached it, we saw that it looked like a castle. It looked like one from a ghost movie. There was a dark cloud behind the castle and there were bats flying back and forth. We were 100 feet away from the castle's gate and there was no bombing anywhere, so we slowly walked to check on why there was no bombing. Ejaz scared us, saying that maybe ghosts lived here and the bombers were scared of ghosts. Benjamin said to Ejaz, "You should be a horror movie director, having all these crazy thoughts."

We saw a big board with a man with a French beard and vampire teeth wearing a black hat. Written underneath, it said, "Magic Vampire Here! Ruff Lunar." From the board, the castle was 200 yards away, and we passed another board that read, "Trespassers will be smoked by werewolves." That board scared us, and we thought to walk back, but Benjamin said, "That guy in the picture looks like a clown. There are no such things as vampires. I am going." We tried to stop him, but he seemed driven. We started walking behind him and carried our guns. There were path lights, and there was another board that said, "Insurance doesn't cover vampire bites." Looking at that, even Benjamin got nervous, and we asked him, "Are there vampires?" Benjamin said, "I haven't seen one, so there shouldn't be." We were ready to leave, but Benjamin took a cross from his hand and said, "Vampires will run away if they see this cross," and Ejaz replied, "You watch too many movies, Benjamin."

We followed Benjamin, and everyone was concealed behind him. We were scared and didn't know why we were doing this. There was another board that said, "If you want to see your loved ones dead, we can help you." We just kept walking, and we reached 100 yards. We still had 100 yards to go. And there was another board that said, "If you made it here, it means you are standing in the werewolves' belly and our feasting begins now." We were looking at one another and asking, "What does this mean?". Then we heard a roar, and there were thousands of bats flying above our heads. We started to panic and looked around. There were more roaring sounds, and we saw something falling from the sky. Within minutes, lights on both sides turned on, and we saw hundreds of vampires standing with their teeth out, and Benjamin said , "I believe in vampires now." Then from the castle, hundreds of werewolves started to run toward us. We aimed our guns to shoot them, but they slipped from our hands and started to fly in the air. We didn't know what was happening and the werewolves were coming closer and closer. Their mouths were watering, and the vampires on both sides of the road started to run toward us. Benjamin was showing the cross in all directions, but nothing was happening. We decided to run, but we couldn't move. Our feet were sticking to the ground, and there was some kind of gel holding our shoes to the ground.

We were trapped and feared for the worst, and all the vampires and werewolves jumped on us, and we closed our eyes and screamed. But nothing happened. We were all still alive, and as we slowly opened our eyes, we saw that there were no vampires or werewolves around us, and it looked normal as before. We saw all the castle lights and floodlights were turned on. It looked like daytime, and we heard a voice saying, "Today is your lucky day! My vampires and werewolves are not hungry. What are you doing on my property?" Judah said, "We are looking for some shelter to hide from the bombs and shells. That's all, sir. Forgive us, please, and we will go back." Then the man said, "There is nothing wrong in taking shelter here, but who is the one who called me a clown?"

We all looked at Benjamin, and he rolled his eyes and said, "I was just joking" The man said, "Step forward, young man." Benjamin stepped forward, and he was pissing in his pants. The man we saw on the board flew in from the castle and came to Benjamin. We looked at him and whispered, "Can he really fly?" He was dressed in a vampire suit, and he had a smoking pipe in his hand, he looked at Benjamin and said, "I am Ruff Lunar. What is your name, kiddo?" Benjamin was shaking and said his name. Ruff Lunar looked at us and said, "Are you the kids who escaped in the flying saucer?" We slowly replied to him, "Yes, sir. Can you fly?" He landed on the ground and said, "No one can fly. Simple science, fellows. I am a magician and a vampire." He looked at Benjamin and said, "Watch your mouth, kid, or next time, I will feed you to the monsters." Benjamin asked him, "Do you have monsters?" and the man replied, "Either you make fun of me or you doubt me. Was your mother a bogeywoman?"

Then we saw a man who was almost forty-five feet tall standing behind Ruff the magician and vampire. He said, "Any problems, boss?" and Ruff replied, "No, only a big-mouthed kid." Benjamin asked, "Is he a giant?" and Ruff replied, "Steroids." He welcomed all of us into his castle, and we followed him inside. There were many people working for him, and Ruff Lunar had numerous artifacts of vampires and werewolves all over place.

He introduced us to his girlfriend, Jenny, and she looked sexy and glamorous—a perfect role for a vampire. She wore a black vampire suit. We sat on the couch, and he gave us refreshments to drink. We slowly asked, "What happened to the vampires and werewolves that were about to attack us?" He laughed and said, "Science simulation. I designed it to perfection." We realized that it was bogus and that he was playing with us. We chatted with him and found out he was a wealthy scientist whose hobby was performing vampire shows and living the crazy life he wanted. We asked him why he had invited us to his home, and all he said was that we were braver than the vampires and werewolves to escape from TUAD and fight for our lives. While we exchanged information, all I could tell about him was that he was a stereotype himself, but he was gentle and level headed. He gave us dinner. The dining table, the dining room lighting, and the music that played all looked and sounded like it was from a vampire movie. That night we rested and he gave each of us rooms. Although everything was funny, our instincts were alerted because the whole castle looked like a vampire setup.

The next day, we took a tour of his castle and property, and we met the giant man, Hesiod. He was Ruff Lunar's neighbor, and he was a handsome man. His ambition was to become a giant and look like a monster. Ruff, being a scientist, helped him achieve his dream. He gave him 100 grams of steroids every day and put him in a glass chamber filled with alpha and beta particles. The alpha and beta particles accelerated and exposed his body to the steroid. Within a year, he grew five feet taller and built more muscle. He had been doing it for six years continuously, and he finally became a giant. Although Hesiod looked big and tall, he was soft and gentle. We toured the museum, where Ruff had a collection of vampire and werewolf antiques and artifacts. He spent a lot of money buying and storing all the stuff in his museum. In the museum, he had automatic vampires, which were built with wax and operated with machines. They looked real. They could walk, jump, and move their bodies like humans. He also had wax werewolves, like the vampires, made of wax and operated by machines. Those were the real ones and they could hurt or kill anybody, because they were built like real werewolves. Ruff controlled all those vampires and werewolves with a voice control and sensors that were programmed inside, and they could smell and detect Ruff's blood, DNA, and sweat and obey their master.

Ruff was a brilliant and genius. He took us in a van and showed us his farm and all the robot vampires and robot werewolves were working there and maintaining it. This was the first time I had ever heard of vampires and werewolves working under the sun. When they saw him from hundred feet away, they greeted him, calling, "Hello, Ruff, we are your servants at duty." We asked him where he kept the monsters, and he said he would never show them to anyone and they were in his secret chamber. We didn't know whether he was lying, but we felt we shouldn't ask him because it was his personal collection. He created hundreds of vampire and werewolf video games, and we played with Ruff and Hesoid. They were all 4D video games and it was a lot of fun to play with them. Jenny was very moody and was always in the beauty parlor putting on makeup and taking care of herself. She made all the girls put on makeup, paint their nails, get pedicures, have haircuts and take steam baths. We definitely appreciated it because they looked so gorgeous and beautiful, and we couldn't believe when we saw them that these girls were hanging out with us all the time.

The bombing didn't stop, and the war continued. After a few days, I was watching outside the window at night. There were bombings outside Ruff's castle, but for almost a mile radius from where he lived, there was no bombing. I asked Ruff why there was no bombing or cross fire near his place and he said, "I know all the top officials throughout the world and no one would ever step onto my property." I realized he was a very powerful man. I asked him how he knew all the powerful people, he said, "Tomorrow is Friday. You will see how influential and powerful Ruff Lunar is." I asked him, "What's on Friday?" and he replied, "All your custom suits are ready, and tomorrow you will know." We were all curious to know what was there on Friday, and that night we couldn't get much sleep.

The next day, Ruff said to get ready for the seven o'clock show. We asked Hesiod what was going on there tonight, and he said, "There is a magic and vampire show." We were all excited to hear that and wanted to see what the show was all about. It was five in the evening; there were flying saucers, choppers, and luxury cars as long as a train showing up and landing in Ruff's parking lot. We saw all the rich, polished, shining, and glossy people in their sparkling outfits coming to the castle. We were all in expensive suits waiting before the hall with Hesiod to receive them. Some people greeted us and some turned their faces away from us.

The hall only had 300 seats, and the show was a premier for exclusive people. But the hall was big and spacious. We stood with Hesiod behind the hall and were curious and excited to see what would happen. The curtains went up on the big stage and a lady who was hosting the show welcomed everybody and said, "Here comes the king of magic and god of the underworld, the great vampire, Ruff Lunar." Ruff, in his vampire suit, walked like a king with his right hand holding his cape. He bowed, and everybody in the hall stood up, clapped, shouted, and welcomed him. He thanked everyone for coming and said, "Let the show begin."

We were all waiting to see what magic he would do, and a flying saucer came onto the stage. He made the saucer fly above the heads of the audience and held it over the middle of the audience. Ropes came down from the saucer and everybody in the hall was holding the ropes and pulling them. But then Ruff moved his hands and said, "Let it disappear," and the flying saucer disappeared from the middle of the hall. All the ropes in people's hands disappeared, too, and they were all now holding bouquets of flowers. We were all perplexed, and everybody started to scream and shout at a fever pitch. Our mouths were open like alligators, and we didn't know how to react to his genius trick.

Then a second magic trick began. Two cute foxes were brought out, and he walked them around the hall and everybody touched them. Then he stood in the aisle in the middle of the hall and asked the foxes to cough. They coughed, and two wolves came out of each fox. He asked the foxes to do it ten times, and each time, more wolves came out of their mouths. Both foxes and twenty wolves walked onto the stage, and as they walked, everybody was touching their bodies and feeling that they were real. Then, on the stage, he made the foxes and wolves stand close to each other and said, "Let the king of beasts appear." All the foxes and wolves disappeared, and there was a big dinosaur standing on the stage. The dinosaur opened its mouth and gurgled. Then Ruff asked the lady who was hosting the show to take it off the stage. We all clapped for a few minutes and marveled at his brilliance. He did many magic tricks; and the show was astounding.

At the very end of the show, there were hundreds of vampires and werewolves, Ruff fought with all of them and killed them and drank their blood. That was very gross and scary; we covered our eyes with our hands, peeking through the tiny gaps to watch. The show ended at nine and everybody applauded him, and then the party began. We were also at the party, and many people greeted and shook hands with us, but there were uptight and arrogant people who were not comfortable with us. One gentleman said to Ruff, "Ruff, are these the kids who escaped from TUAD?" Ruff replied very briskly, "Certainly," and the gentleman, unfortunately, replied, "These guys shouldn't be here. They may cause some problems for you, Mr. Ruff." Ruff politely replied, "They are my friends and employees, they work here in the magic show, isn't that right, Mr. Benjamin?" Benjamin was clueless and replied, "Yes, master, and we are at your service." The gentleman was not convinced and was saying something about us, and Ruff replied, "They didn't steal, lie, vandalize, or kill anyone, and you should be nice to these kids. Isn't that how they do it in Britain?" The gentleman slowly replied, "Yes, we do." Then Ruff introduced him, he was the ambassador from Britain. Then we slowly learned from Hesiod who all these people were. They were all rich, politicians, celebrities, governors, judges, and powerful people from throughout the world.

Everyone drank a lot and left early in the morning, when the party was over. We were awake and felt ourselves honored and proud that we knew some powerful people at this young age. After the party, Ruff asked us if we had enjoyed the show and the party, and we said, "Very much." We learned that day that Ruff was not an ordinary man, and we were happy that he was doing great in his life. Every Friday, they had the show, and we helped Hesiod and the staff members who were working for the show. We stayed there for a month and we enjoyed every moment.

One funny thing that I will never forget happened to Benjamin. We stuffed all the vampires and werewolves with wild preiselbeeren pulp, which Ruff drank like blood at the end of the show. One day, Benjamin was careless, and instead of making the pulp liquid with preiselbeeren, he mixed it with a spicy red sauce. Ruff bit the vampire and drank it, and because he was on stage, he didn't have any choice before the crowd but to be himself and drink the spicy sauce. After the show, Ruff was running to the bathroom. After the party, he assembled us and asked, "Who mixed the liquid pulp?" and Benjamin slowly raised his hand. Ruff was holding his stomach and drinking water from a glass. "Do you know how many times I have gone to the bathroom?" Benjamin bowed his head and he said, "Sorry, sir, I haven't been counting." Ruff turned and said, "Eleven times. From the first time you entered this place, you have been trouble. If you do this next time, do you know what I will do?" Benjamin had no idea and he looked at Ruff with fear and said, "Will you feed me to the monsters?" Ruff squeezed his eyes and said, "Monsters don't eat imps. I will make you disappear and you will be back in TUAD, Hoplite, in the same bed you slept in there."

We giggled at Benjamin, and Ruff said, "See? It seems that none of your friends care about you anymore." Benjamin was frustrated and said, "From the day I came in here, they always snitched me out or made fun of me because of Mr. Ruff." Ruff laughed and said, "You are my best boy, Benjamin, and I will die for you. I will never send you to TUAD. Relax, my son. We are just joking." Ruff started to hold his hand to his stomach and started to run to the bathroom, and Benjamin said, "That's twelve times, boss." Ruff stopped and turned and said, "I think I know mathematics better than you."

That was one fun night, and somehow Ruff cared a lot for Benjamin and he was his special boy. After a month, the bombing was over, and we decided to leave. We didn't say anything about the mission to Ruff or anyone there. Ruff asked us where we were going and we said we were heading to New York City. He offered to let us stay with him, but we gently declined. He gave us a check for $600 million, and we asked why he was giving us so much money. He said it was for the work that we did for the show and for the journey. We said it was way too much for the work we did, but all he said was that he liked us and wanted to be our friend, and he was trying to be gentle. But I felt something was wrong, because from the first day we came in, he had always been kind to us for no reason. He was a very influential and powerful man and there was no need for him to be like that. We were all sitting on the couch with our bags in our hands, and I asked him, "If we are your friends, Ruff, then why are you hiding something from us?" Ruff smiled and said, "They knew you would say that, and they said, 'Never lie to Oliver.'" I was not clear what he had said, and asked him, "Who said that?" and he replied, "Glenn Hitch. Do you know Glenn, Mr. Oliver?" I was blown away and my heart stopped. What was this all about? Where had Glenn come into this whole scene? I told Ruff, "Yes, we know him. Did Glenn give you that money to give to us?" Ruff was moving both his hands and kept to his heart and said, "I swear he didn't, and I will never lie to you guys again."

Then Ruff told his story. Ruff Lunar was from a very big royal family and all their forefathers were great scientists and held much esteemed reputations in society and they were very rich. He inherited all the money and wealth from his father and his family. Although he was a brilliant scientist, he didn't want to make weapons or use his inventions for war. But he could not walk out like that because it would hurt his family's reputation and he would be in trouble for not cooperating with the government. So, he just walked out saying that he wanted to be a magician and modern vampire because it was his passion. He started to perform shows and live a solitary life, and he stayed away from the war. He was a neutral person, and in the eyes of the world, he was harmless and loved.

Glenn and Ruff were best friends, and they had gone to school together. He knew all the things that had happened between Glenn and us. Except for his friends Hesiod and Glenn, he had no one who really loved him as a person. They were all after his fame, money, including knowledge, or other material things. When Glenn said we gave him money and walked away from his house, Ruff had high hopes and felt great respect for us. Our lives had created some moments in his life, making him say, "Where are the human values and where is real life?"

The day when we entered his property by accident, he couldn't believe that we had walked into his life. He realized his life had great value, and all his emptiness vanished into thin air. Staying a month as his guests allowed him to feel alive again. His girlfriend, Jenny, also started to be active and alive. He said he found the real moments and values of life in us, except for Benjamin's antics. He liked Benjamin because he was natural and always spoke to him like a friend. The funny thing was, no one had made him laugh or behaved naturally with him, although everyone pretended to be mild and respectful to him.

His reflection was touching to us, and he was one of the warmest people we had met on our journey. We didn't want him to treat us like strangers, so we took the money from him. We left with a goodbye, and we nourished him with a true life spirit. We left his castle with two things: we brought him true life and our pants were tight. Oh yeah, we had eaten a lot, and we would have needed to walk from there to Australia to get back into shape.

While walking, my thoughts were all over the place. I felt some people were having fun even during wartime, like Ruff, and on our journey, we'd never met a friend of someone we knew. The world was big, but we were interconnected in some way.

CHAPTER 20

THE PARADOX

IT WAS JUNE, AND THE SUMMER WAS PLEASANT. WE WERE ENJOYING OUR walk and we had almost reached Mahwah. We were dragging our feet and had become frustrated with this whole journey. We had gained a lot of experience in our life at this young age. It was lunchtime and as we walked, we saw a monastery that was old in shape. A sign on the monastery said it was a foster home. We hated those words and didn't want to go inside, but when we passed through the gates, we saw kids around four to seven years old playing soccer. There were men wearing saffron-colored civaras with shaved heads. It was interesting to look at them, and all the kids were really happy and alive.

We were sure of one thing, this was not a TUAD, and we wanted to explore. We opened the gate, and bells on top of it started to ring. All the monks looked at us, and they waved their hands for us to walk in. A few teenage monks walked up to check on us. They came, greeted us, and bowed, but we didn't bow. Shu was pulling on Ejaz's and Fay's shoulders to bow back to them, and then we all bowed down. They asked if we spoke English and asked, "Who are you?" We said we were travelers who had just come to check out the monastery. They invited us inside. Except for the kids, everyone had a shaved head. I quickly thought to myself that they were going to shave my beautiful hair.

An old man sitting in a chair with a white beard bowed down with beads in his hands. He asked if we needed any help, and we said no. He looked at the guns in our hands and asked if we were hunters, and we told him the guns were for self-defense. He said to give them to the monks, because as per their rules, we could not carry weapons inside the monastery. We gave the guns to them. We had our knives in our shoes and we didn't give those up. The man asked whether we were hungry, and we said we were. They took us to the dining table. They served vegan food, and we ate well.

The monk asked us more questions about who we were. We said that we had escaped from TUAD, and some of them remembered who we were and said they could recollect the story. The old monk said, "Buddha opened your eyes, and that was why you escaped from TUAD." Judah replied, "Not Buddha. He was not in the movie. It was Matt Sterling who opened our eyes." The old monk didn't understand that, and he looked to his students. They said it was a movie, and he laughed. We didn't know what was funny, and he said, "Buddha—I meant the teacher, like God." On hearing that, I felt he was an innocent man who didn't know the difference between a god and a movie star. It had been a long time since we'd heard about Buddha. Aika's mother had always talked about him. Aika and Shu liked this place because they had been raised with Buddha, and we liked it because they liked it, and everything was new here. We were then introduced to all the kids, who were of all different colors and from various nations. These kids were respectful and down to earth.

We played soccer with them and enjoyed ourselves. There were almost 250 of them, with so many names that we couldn't keep track of them all. Then for dinner, all the monks, including the head monk and all the kids had dinner together, and it was the same vegan food. The food was cooked well, and after eating that food, all the senses in our bodies died, and we started to look non-descriptive, plain like them, with no extra flavor in life.

They had a school, and every kid went to school from 9 a.m. to noon. They learned science, english, math and history. We decided to spend just a few days there and leave. One day, we were sitting near the porch and talking to each other when we noticed that the old monk was very upset. He was walking to his room, and we heard one of his disciple's say, "We don't have food to feed the kids." That struck us, and we walked behind the disciples to check on what was happening. They all went to the room and locked it and started to talk, and we learned they were out of rations and they only had enough for two days. We felt bad and wanted to help them, and that night, when we were sitting at supper, the old monk asked everyone to pray to Buddha to show his mercy. All the kids closed their eyes and prayed to Buddha for mercy. The old monk didn't say anything about the situation, he just told us to ask for mercy.

I didn't know what the kids were praying for, but we prayed for food. We remembered that Ruff had given us $600 million. We hadn't used even a dollar of it yet, because we had just been using Dr. Enoch's money. We were whispering about Ruff's money and we agreed to help them and give them some of it. Everybody was praying sincerely, and we called the monk over while they were praying and said, "Master, we have money." All the kids and monks opened their eyes and looked at us. The old monk said, "I asked everybody to pray for mercy, not for money." We understood the situation. He wanted to keep the situation quiet and not let the kids know, so we stayed silent.

It was the same vegan food that night, and while eating, I felt very sorry for the kids because they were not blessed enough to get even this simple food. After supper, the old monk called us into his office and asked why we had shouted about the money. We told him the truth, that we knew about the situation and he felt bad about us knowing about their shortcomings. We said we had money and would help him, but he did not want to take it. We said that if he didn't accept it, all the kids were going to die of hunger. For the kids' sakes, he took $50 million. He said he would repay us, and we said he could repay us later, when he had the money.

After this incident, we became involved with the monastery. We asked the old monk why they didn't get money from the government, and he said that the kids didn't have radio-frequency identification and were not involved in the war in any way, so the government had abandoned them. A few common rich people helped them, but because it was a Buddhist monastery, they didn't get that much attention and everyone thought it was a laid-back place. All the kids were taken in from the streets and their parents had abandoned them. I was wondering why our spirits were involved in this place for a few days, and I thought it was because of the bad experience we'd had at TUAD. The old monk taught us how to pray and be disciplined and every day we practiced meditation and prayed to Buddha. There was a radical change in us, and our hearts started to be at peace. We spent almost forty days there in high spirituality and we learned a little about Buddhism. The only thing I ever heard was love and peace from the monks, and I wondered how to love and be at peace in times like these.

Being a monk in this place was not our destiny, and we had a mission and wanted to leave. We packed our things, and although we had become like the Buddhist monks, we took the guns with us. We gave the rest of the $550 million to the old monk, but he refused it. We couldn't convince him, because he felt bad taking it from us. He was stubborn. So, we just placed it before him and said, "If the last one is dying of hunger, at least at that time please use it." After we said that, we walked away. He called to us to come back, but we left the monastery. We didn't know whether he would use it or not. Maybe all the kids would die because of his ideas, but we had done a good deed and given him the money and walked away, so our hearts were clean and clear. We hadn't been a burden by eating their plates of food, and we did what Buddha said: sacrifice.

We walked and walked with all our breath and against all odds, we faced our lives. Judah and I had reached twelve years of age by now, and everyone wished us a happy birthday. But all I said was that it was the second anniversary of breaking out of TUAD. Our feet were starting to become raw, but not our spirits. More than a mission, we were curious about what was in the locket and when our eyes would be opened. We finally got close to New York City, but the tunnels to the city were broken and everything was under construction, so they asked us go to Balmville in Upstate New York City and re-route back to the city. We didn't want to go in circles, and the summer was at its peak, the waters were getting warm. We made a raft with wood that was available, jumped into the Hudson River and rowed across. I don't think anybody made it to New York City this way because everybody was watching the rescue crew who came to check on us. But we just swam and never gave a heck to anybody and reached New York City, the land we were destined for.

We got out of the water, and there was a rescue crew and the New York Police Department officers welcomed us. They gave a dirty look and asked, "Why did you jump into the river?" We were all wet, and Fay was cleaning her hair and said, "Because we know how to swim." The cops laughed at Fay's reply and said, "We know that, or else we would be searching for bodies in the water." We explained that instead of taking the long route to New York City, we had just decided to swim. All the cops laughed, and one said, "Are you kids really dumb or do you just act like it?" We realized they knew us. Our reputation had preceded us. We calmly replied, "Why do you say that?" and the cop showed us the flying bridge, where trains were running above us and said, "You should have used that."

We had seen it, but we remembered Nathalie's commandment about never using any technology, but to just walk. It was the last step before reaching New York City, and if we had used the flying bridge, we would have been sent to Mars for disobeying, and we would have really had to make an escape like Matt Sterling. We replied very casually, "We know. We just wanted to clean ourselves in the water, and we love swimming." The officers saw the rifle and guns and asked where we had got them, and we said we took the rifle from a dead solider and the guns from corpses. They told us to give them back, and we handed them over. It was not legal to carry guns in New York City and it had been the same for centuries, and the cops explained that and let us go. They didn't ask any further questions and I think New York City liked us.

We walked around the city. Half the buildings were bombed, and there was lots of construction work going on. We didn't know who was doing the bombing, the war itself or some other social movement. Robots and humans were used in the construction. People were walking in the streets, and everybody looked busy. We saw men and women in business suits liked greased monkeys, and we guessed they were Wall Street folks. The city was more advanced than any other city we had seen. There were flying bikes and cars in two lanes of both directions, and there was a stop for flying cars on every block. There were flying saucer pads on every tall building. Several space rails were in the sky for space shuttles to land on. The shops were glittering and we smelled the scent of high-society people. Everything was spectacular and magnificent, we felt small before all these wonderful things before our eyes.

We spent the first week on the sidewalks, in the museums, and at the parks. We had $45 million left on our card, and we were just surviving. We were thinking about when to open the locket and see what was inside. But we didn't know whether our eyes were open or not. I had been thinking for the whole week what it meant to have our eyes opened. I understood what it meant exactly, and we had taken a long walk in the Fourth Dimension using the ideas, methods, and logic from the Third Dimension.

I was very confident in my beliefs and decided to open the locket, and everyone agreed. We went to Central Park and found a lonely spot. It was an auspicious day for us, so we took a shower and got new jeans and T-shirts for everybody. I had the locket in my hand. I wanted to open it, but I was nervous and so was everybody else. We didn't know what was inside—a treasure map, some genie coming out, a faun, a spaceship?—and our minds were exhausted. I opened the locket slowly. I started to breathe heavily, my hands were shaking. I looked at everyone, and Benjamin said, "Let's do it, Oliver," and I focused, I closed my eyes and opened it.

There was no sound. I opened one eye slowly, looked around, and saw that the others all had their eyes closed. I heard Madison saying, "Is that Nathalie or her mother and father? They look very cute." I quickly opened my eyes and saw the locket and what she was talking about. On the left side was a very beautiful blond lady with a diamond necklace around her neck who bore some resemblance to Nathalie. On the right side was a picture of a gentleman with brown hair, wearing a suit and tie and a smile on his face. Everybody took the locket and examined it, and we started to talk. "What the heck is this?" Nathalie had given us a family photo and said, "Keep it safe and open it when you reach New York City." We were all confused and didn't know what to say. We thought maybe something was hidden in the photo, and we used magnifying glasses to check closer. We could only see their teeth, and we spent three days and nights examining it, but we couldn't figure it out. We even thought about taking it to an archaeologist, but it wasn't a good idea. We were now angrier than anything. We couldn't figure out what was in the pictures, but we didn't want to doubt Nathalie.

I felt bad about myself and felt like I had wasted all nine of my friends' lives. I didn't know where this was going, and I said to all my friends very sadly, "I have caused so many troubles in your lives because Nathalie said something and I believed her, and I made you join me in this journey. There is nothing inside this locket, and I feel bad to say this, but go live a happy life. The mission is over. We will always be best friends. I'm sorry I ruined all your lives, there will be no forgiveness for me."

Everybody was quiet after hearing my words, and they looked troubled. Fay looked at me and said, "Why are you talking like this, Oliver? If you had not started this mission, Sadie and I would have ended up either raped or killed or in some brothel. You saved us and didn't lose hope." Ejaz put his hand on my shoulder. "If I had not known you, I would have been killed by the CIA." Benjamin took his turn and said, "I would be hunting men with my father, but I would never have been a wise man or been part of the peace revolution." Everybody said their views and wanted to comfort me, and I appreciated their thoughts, but I was not convinced.

I took the locket and showed them and said there was nothing here and that we were done. As I was showing it to them, my hand automatically twisted the locket, and the photos disappeared. There was a white background with some writing on it. Everybody's faces changed, and Ejaz got excited. "Look, look! The picture in the locket disappeared," he said, and everybody started to see the same thing. I didn't know what they were talking about and turned the locket and looked, and I saw that there was writing on a white background. I didn't know what had happened to the photos and started to look at the front and back of the locket to see where the pictures went. I was searching for how that had happened and realized that there was a small lever in the locket, and we needed to push both pieces of the locket together and twist it. That made the pictures disappear and the white background appear.

We were all curious about what was written in the locket, and it was inscribed very small on the part where the lady's picture had been. It read, "A current circles his friend three times," and on the other side where the man's picture had been, it read, "Go beneath using salt water, and don't share with anyone." It was a riddle, and we didn't know what it meant. We were puzzled. What could it be? We started to try and decrypt it.

We tried to figure out the riddle and came up with many different answers. We thought electric *current* could be the New York power supply, and we went to the power station and checked what was there. We couldn't find anything. We thought a *friend* of the electric current was the conductor, so it could be some cable or electric wire manufacturing company. We went to all the places where they sold to the electric companies and searched for some clue, but we couldn't find anything. We did research on the Internet about companies and their stores to find some clues, but we didn't find anything. The third part said *three times*, and we didn't know what this number represented or how a electric current could circle three times. One space shuttle came to New York City from other planets three times a day. We went to it and checked whether there was anything in the shuttle, but we couldn't find anything there, either. We ran throughout the whole of New York City to find anything that was related to the electric current. We went to exhibitions and museums, watched science seminars, and visited buildings that use electric current in special ways.

Two months later, we still hadn't found anything and we didn't have any clues about what we were looking for. Fay was scratching her head and said, "There was one thing I doubted. Edison and Nikola Tesla revolutionized the science of electricity in the nineteenth century. They both did a lot of things regarding New York City." Shu quickly said, "That is a very good point, Fay. Nikola Tesla was a legend and one of the inventors of alternating current." Judah questioned Sadie, "Okay, that sounds cool. But what does *a friend* mean and *three times*?" Sadie just raised her eyebrows and said, "I don't know. It's just my opinion."

We didn't think about their conversation much because the story was more than a thousand years old. Judah was busy searching for something and said, "Okay, here is the list of Nikola Tesla's friends: Thomas Commerford Martin, Mark Twain, Hugo Gernsback, Kenneth Swezey, Julian Hawthorne, George Sylvester Viereck . . . But the interesting thing was that Mark Twain was his best friend." Ejaz asked, "Who was Mark Twain?" Judah replied, "He seems to have been a writer who published a lot of books—more than twenty-five, like *The Adventures of Tom Sawyer, The Diary of Adam and Eve . . .*" Benjamin strung a question together. "So it means that Nikola Tesla was circling Mark Twain three times?"

Sadie broke the puzzle and said excitedly, "Yes, it does, like, Oliver; remember in TUAD when you wanted to talk to Fay and me? You circled us three times." Judah was shocked. "You knew what we were doing and counted it?" Sadie said, "Judah that is not the point. Nikola Tesla circled Mark Twain three times for what?" Aika was silly and made a point: "Maybe he was hungry or asked him to give him one of his books to read."

I was hit with the answer, stood up positively and said, "Nikola Tesla was circling the book three times, which means the place where books are stored." Madison gave another clue: "Books are kept in the library." I was very excited and felt I had the answer. "Yes, Mark Twain was a writer, and his books are in the library, and Nikola Tesla circled the library three times. It will be a library. And also Nikola Tesla and Mark Twain were best friends, and they built the locket's riddle based upon themselves."

We had almost figured out the riddle but didn't know which library it would be. We checked Tesla's entire history and found one of the oldest social media blogs, which was almost 1,500 years old, written by a Croatian lady named Divan Duke from Tesla's country. She wrote, "Nikola Tesla circles the New York Public Library, which is on Forty-First Street and Fifth Avenue, walks around the library three times counterclockwise, and then sits there and feeds the pigeons." We had found the answer to the riddle, and it was the New York Public Library, the building called Abbott Zohar, on Forty-First and Fifth. It was one of the places where the street address hadn't changed. We were sitting downtown and we ran as fast as possible to the library. Everyone in the street watched us and wondered why we were running so fast. Our bags were swinging back and forth and I was holding Bickey in my hands and shaking his body. He was barking softly to remind me not to drop him. As I was running, I said to him, "I will never drop you, my friend," and I kissed his head.

We turned around the block, and we were so anxious to see what was at the library that as we ran, our legs started to slow down so we could look at it. Everybody slowed down and looked at the library, and our eyes were filled with terror. The library was burned down, broken, and looked haunted. There were two lions out front, their faces were smashed and distorted and the steps made of stone outside the building were ruined. As we walked, we saw a marble imprint of information about the building and the people who had built it. It was chiseled and had holes in it; not even one word of it in the marble was legible. The steps that led inside the building were broken and deformed.

We slowly walked into the building, and there was duct tape from the police department torn and hanging in the air. We went inside the building and it was completely smoked out, with black patches from the flames everywhere. There were stairs to the first floor, and we went up them. The stairs were broken inside, too, and the side rails were cracked and ashes were sticking to the steps. We went to all the rooms and hallways, and everything was burned to pieces except for a few scraps of wood. We went to the second and third floors and everything was burned down, and there was no signboard to identify the rooms or floor numbers. It was completely blacked out. We had never seen a building like this in our lives, with so much destroyed without any trace. There were a few papers flying about, and we picked some up and looked at them. They were from books, and the authors' names were William Shakespeare, Leo Tolstoy, and others.

We didn't know what had happened to the library, and we pulled our I-gadget out to check on the Internet. We saw the pictures of this splendid building both inside and outside. We read the history of it and all the people who contributed in building a big library like this. It was opened in the early twentieth century and was functioning well, and in 1965, they declared it a National Historic Landmark. It had been renovated in the early twenty-first century. It went through a major restructuring in 2115 with modern artifacts. Then, after 300 years, they patched the building stones with modern adhesive for more strength and polished the whole building, finishing the woodcarvings and renewing the metalwork. In the late twenty-ninth century, they replaced all the old broken stones with crystal stones they brought from Jupiter in size fifty-by-fifty ratios to imply the supremacy of human civilization.

The library also was expanded 430 feet in the back, on the Fifth Avenue side. The building was renamed from the Stephen A. Schwarzman building to the Abbott Zohar, or AZ, building. Abbott Zohar donated $2.6 trillion for the renovation. When the war started, the New York Public Library was still considered a historic landmark and the world had agreed not to bomb it under any circumstance. A revolution went down in 3300, and Occupy Wall Street, Interfacers, Trackers, and a few revolutionary organizations claimed that they sold drugs in the library. The law department verified this and warned them.

One day, twenty-six teenagers died because of high drug usage, and they found out the drugs had been purchased at the library. There was confusion and the cops started shooting the people working in the library. In turn, the employees defended themselves. One after another, problems started regarding the library, and some reports claimed that two women were raped and killed by library officials. The Occupy Wall Street group, Bi-fighters, and law enforcement officers killed all the people in the library, and many were hanged. They burned the drugs they found, along with all the books. They smoked every word that was in the library, broke all the statues, wood, metal works, and destroyed all the paintings. They called that day Library Cult Day, and it was a black day in America. It all started in New York City, and to this day, the NYPL stands as a monument of shame, drugs and rape.

They built an alternative library near Central Park. No one visits or enters the NYPL Abbott Zohar building anymore, because there are rumors of ghosts in the building. There were sixty-seven reported incidents of people dying over two years in the library, and everyone was scared to go in. It had been nearly 200 years, and no one had stepped foot into it in all that time. We were the first ones after 200 years to enter the building.

After reading about the ghosts, Madison was making some funny noises and moving her hands to my throat saying, "Oliver, here is the ghost. I am going to eat you now." We laughed, but Shu became angry and said, "Is everything funny to you, Madison? Be serious." Ejaz was scared. "Madison, stop it! I am scared." Madison was tapping her forehead and said, "This is the biggest lie they have told in history. There was something wrong, and they deceived the minds of the people. Wake up, guys. We have to find it." I replied to Madison, "We are not here to find the truth behind this destruction. There is something left in this place, and we have to find it." Madison raised both her eyebrows and twisted her cute lips at me and said, "Oliver, you smart man, let's follow you."

We now had to decrypt the second part of the puzzle, which was quite easy. "Go beneath using salt water, and don't share with anyone," which meant there was something beneath the library. But we didn't know to get in. The whole library was made of stone, and we didn't know whether there was some sort of bunker in the library. We started to check every stone and every place in the library for a way that led to a bunker. We spent almost two weeks searching to find a way to get underneath the library, but we couldn't find anything.

One day, we were walking inside the library, and as soon as we were inside, Bickey started moving in my hands and wanted to jump, so I let him down, and he ran outside. We all chased him. He went to the side of the building, ran to the edge of the compound wall, and started barking at a black marble stone in the ground. It was six feet in length and five feet in width. There were some small trees nearby, and the black marble stone was hidden and very hard to notice. It looked ancient and like it had been lying in the same place for centuries, but even the reconstruction people hadn't noticed it. This was the only piece in and around the library that was unbroken and untouched, and it had escaped the eyes of everyone, including those who destroyed the library. We were all curious about why Bickey was barking at it. When we found a flat black marble stone, we saw the words inscribed on it, "NYPL Contributors' Names," and all the people who had donated to the library were listed on it. Bickey kept barking at it, so we decided to check it out. We jumped on it, cut away all the concrete at the edges, and pushed it, but nothing worked. It was tight, but Bickey never stopped barking at it and scratching it with his foot. He became ferocious and angry and wouldn't stop.

Bickey's behavior was not very common, and Sadie was trying to pull him away, but I doubted that this was the secret bunker. I turned and asked Judah, "What does it mean, *salt water*? Should we pour salt water on it?" We bought some salt, mixed it in some water, and poured it on, but nothing happened. We added more salt to the water and poured it again, but still, nothing happened.

Then Judah said, "Salt water means seawater, which has all the minerals. We should try that." We thought the Hudson River was a sea and tried that water, but again, nothing happened. Finally, we went to Brooklyn to get seawater from Coney Island. We were very curious and excited to see whether this would work or not. We came back to the library and poured the water on it, but nothing happened, so we kept pouring it on. We emptied a whole one-liter bottle of seawater on it, and slowly, the stone moved with a clattering noise of stone on stone. It looked like it hadn't been opened for hundreds of years; all our eyes were on the hole. There was a deep passage inside it, and we didn't know what to do. Everybody, as usual, looked at each other to see who would go first. If I were the president of the United States, I would award Niki with the "Man of First Attempt on Everything" title, because he said he would do it. We stopped him because we didn't know what was in it, but we had to take the risk. We tied him with carbon ropes around his hips and tied on three sets of ropes for backup. Before he went inside, he said, "If something happens to me, Oliver, never give up the search. Keep going, promise me," and I did.

We slid him into the hole. He had a flashlight in his hand and turned it on as he went deeper and deeper down, about twenty-five feet, and landed on something soft. He saw sacks all over the place. He cut open one of the sacks and saw cotton foam mixed with some leaves. The cotton was as fresh as today. He said he was fine, and asked for two more of us to come down, so Fay and I joined him. We landed on the sacks and saw a carved medium-sized room with carved stones on all four sides of the wall. We asked for more lights, and we saw that all four walls were filled with carvings and the room was fourteen feet high. The carvings were of Christian inscriptions, and we saw Jesus, Mother Mary, God, all the apostles, and the Old Testament prophets, some of whom were coming from the sky.

We asked our other friends to come down, and they came down, saw it, and marveled at it. We didn't know what to do next. I saw something unique: a picture of Jesus on the right side with his heart pierced with an arrow, and another Jesus on the cross on the left side. In the middle, I saw fire from the sky. In the center of the sky, where the fire was coming from, was a small circular hole the size of the locket. I took the locket from my pocket, and Bickey started to bark loudly at me and then at the sky. That picture was on the ceiling, and I wanted to climb up to check it out. I touched the nail on the feet of Jesus, and a ladder came up from the ground vertically. We were all shocked at the design they had made. I climbed the ladder and went to the ceiling, and everybody was warning me to be careful. I put the locket in the small hole in the sky. There was a twist from inside, and it took the locket. We heard a crackling sound, and the locket came out. I quickly took the locket in my hands, and all the walls started to go down. Everyone was shouting to get down, so I jumped off the ladder. Benjamin and Sadie caught me in their arms.

The walls disappeared, and we saw a dark room and we used the flashlights to see inside. There were large shelves, and everything was in rows and rows in straight lines. We walked in and saw an angel with a stoup in her hand, and written on the angel's breast were the words, "Light it," and we saw inside the stoup that there was a stone switch. We moved it and the whole place started to light up, and it was bright. We saw clearly that there were rows of shelves of books. They had the entire collection of all the books as old as 8,000 years. We walked into this grand secret room and saw there were sections marked for all book types: "History," "Philosophy," "Literature," "Cultural," "Sports," "Art," "Science," "Entertainment," and many catalogs. It looked exactly like the library that was above us.

In the middle of the library was a big glass showcase with wood in the bottom, and we found a big Gutenberg Bible, which was almost two feet on all sides. Below the glass showcase was written, "Strass family built in 1900." Then there were a few lines of notes: "This secret chamber was built by the Strass family when the NYPL was built to protect the book of books, 'The Bible.' Then over the years, all the books were brought down here and secretly preserved. Millions of collections of books from around the world are kept here to preserve and protect the past and send a message to the future. Whoever is reading this, protect all these books with your full strength, power, mind, body and soul." And on the very bottom line was written, "This place is the only evidence that we ever existed in the universe."

We were all perplexed by this secret chamber library. We didn't know what was happening in the world and why they hadn't burned it. We started to check all the books in this chamber on the Internet, and everything we found said all the books had been burned, and the e-copies were destroyed in the war. This was mind blowing to us, because we could find thousands of books on the Internet only in this library, and we didn't know what had happened to the rest.

This caused us to question what damn types of books were available now in our ages. We saw only books about science and technology, management, languages, social life, space exploration, artificial intelligence, engineering and mathematics. There were novels, books of poetry, and movies, too, but it was all from 3000 A.D. The past was completely lost, and we were here, not to protect the future, but to protect the past. However, there was a contrary aspect, because some countries claimed they had all the books from the past up until now, and our minds continued to be blown.

Why did Nathalie send us here? What was the purpose? To protect these books? There was no need to do that, because they had been here for almost 1,600 years untouched. The last piece of the puzzle was left: *"Don't share it,"* which meant that we shouldn't tell anyone about these books or share them with anyone. That didn't make any sense. We stayed the whole day and night in the library, pondering over what to do with this place. I closed my eyes and said the "Nathalie's prayer", and I finally received the answer to the whole riddle.

She always said that I was the chosen one to stop World War III, and she gave me the locket to go to New York City. I had spent my entire life trying to come here and found this knowledge bank of the past. Did that mean the answer to stopping the war was hidden in all these books? What was that puzzle? I didn't know yet, but we had to find it.

Well, there were millions of books here, and if we built a ladder with them, we could reach the moon. As we walked inside the library, we saw all the magazines and newspapers starting from the *New York Times*, *The New Yorker*, the *Washington Post*, LA times and many others. They were so vast, and there was so much to read. We also had collection of movies in the library. But Fay had an idea and said, "Oliver, was there any other note inside the books, something hidden here that we need to find?" I marveled at Fay's wisdom and said, "We will start reading every book in here. We will also flip all the pages to see if something is underlined or whether notes were left. We will spend two hours a day, each flipping through 100 books, so we can finish it in five, six, or seven years, and by then we should figure it out." Fay agreed, and quickly everyone else agreed. Now we were very eager to learn the voice of the past. That was why we didn't want to learn anything at TUAD: there had always been a voice in our ears to go to New York City. This library was our kindergarten, middle school, high school, college, university, research bank and puzzle chamber.

We didn't know where to begin in such an ocean of books, so we read the Bible first together because it was the book that had survived all the other books and the main reason why they had built the secret chamber. It looked like Adam and Eve were the great-grandfather and great-grandmother, but all this time, it had been only Nathalie for us. We read about our great-grandparents' sin and disobedience, and we surfed the Bible and the essential stories like the ones about Noah's ark; Abraham the chosen man; God bestowing all his blessings on the generations; the lives of Moses and David; Jesus himself, a great man who showed up; all his apostles' and disciples' missionary work; and finally "The Revelation."

It was a fascinating history and a powerful message that was told to the world. We had ignored it at TUAD when they took us to church because they sounded too religious, but when we read the Bible ourselves, we found it to be a very profound and a valuable book that needed to be preserved for the ages. We took a month to read it all together, and decided it would take another 100 years to read all the books in this place. We decided that each one would separately read one book at a time, and once we finished a book, the person would run through what was in it.

That's how we started to read the books in the library. We still had some money on the credit card that Dr. Enoch gave us. We didn't waste the money on luxuries, just food and water. We were reading a lot and sharing all the knowledge that each one of us read, and debating the viewpoints in the books. Although at this young age, we didn't really understand the inner meanings of the books, our knowledge and understanding started to expand. Grandpa Socrates's teachings helped us to reason and ask questions about what we were reading. We asked "Why" to everything, and this single factor made us better readers. I felt that I was not convinced of all the knowledge I was gaining and felt this was the wrong way to do it. We were reading too much information every day, and it was overwhelming. When someone finished reading a book, they stood before us and tried explaining from scratch the how and why of it. It took hours for one to explain a whole book, and then we started to ask questions and discuss them, and finally, everyone would come up with their own views, and these views changed every day.

How could I better understand the past and all its greatness? Search it and keep searching it, with our entire mind on it. However, searching in this Fourth-Dimensional world was not the right way. If we searched in a higher, higher, and even higher—always infinite plus one—dimension, I might get an answer to the puzzle that was placed before us. So what should I do now? Just search or build a search world for myself and walk in it. Yes, I built a search world for myself, and in that world, I was the CIO of Harvest and Reap. But which year should I start with?

One thing I noticed was that there were no books or magazines stored after 2040. I didn't know why the last time any human who came inside this library was 2040 to store the last book, *The Factor and the Truth*, by Thomas Zodiac. I started my life close to that period and started to search all the things I saw. It was not a dream world. It was a search world in my mind in an infinite dimension, and I walked in the book. As my footsteps tried to reach the door, I could see an answer. While I was reading in my mind, a transformation happened, I copied myself, one part of my body and soul traveled to the search world I had built, and the other part of my body remained in this real world. I walked and started to explore this universe in different dimensions and views. Where was I, and what was I doing in the search world?

I don't know how I copied myself, my search, or my quest, just that it divided me into two parts. When I was in the search world, I had all my senses. My flesh, my blood, and everything was the same as in the real world. But I knew I was singular, and had transformed myself into two, there was a thin line between the search-world Oliver and the real-world Oliver. The real-world Oliver was the master, and I had complete control over the search-world Oliver. None of my friends knew what had happened to me and sometimes when I thought about the search world, I thought to myself that it was in my mind, and at other times, I thought I physically existed somewhere else.

We knew the library was a very risky place to trick the satellite system, so we found a broken building in the lower side of the city. We put all our I-gadgets in that building in different places to deceive the satellites while we spent time in the library. There was a switch that would close the marble stone and the entrance to the library, and it also closed the carved walls. The only way in was to have the locket. We stored bottles of seawater in different places in the broken building where we had our I-gadgets and inside the AZ building. We also remembered the story that Uncle Purdhil had taught us, "The King, the Revenge, and the Madman," so we decided to be like madmen in this world until we found the answer to this puzzle and a way to stop the war.

In public places, people discussed various topics about life and the modern world, and we just listened and stayed quiet, never expressing anything, even though I knew the answers to all their discussions. A madman was not someone physically tearing his clothes off but simply someone not mentally engaging in this world, but our time would come.

Two years passed, and we had read a lot and started to understand the books better. We had flipped most of the books to find a note inside or some underlining, but we hadn't found anything yet. We started to become real teenagers, with hair growing in our armpits and in places that I cannot talk about now because I have built a reputation in your minds about myself. Well, our money dwindled, our wallet became light, and we could not afford to eat three times a day. We cut down our rations, but that didn't work for long, and finally, we had our last cent left. We could not go to work because we had to be sixteen to get a job.

We decided to go to TUAD or a foster home where we were eligible to get food three times a day. We didn't want to go to TUAD because of the problems we'd had. We went to other foster homes, on the Upper Side of Manhattan. It was summertime, and the sun was burning so hot, it boiled our skins as we stood in line at the foster home. As we got closer and closer to receiving food, the people serving the food saw us and were talking to each other. When it was our turn, they looked at us and said, "We cannot give you food, as per the instructions," and we asked, "Why?" but they didn't reply. We didn't want to fight with them because we knew we were wasting our time, and we knew we wouldn't win this battle. They just didn't want to get into trouble with the government because they could turn on them at any time. We hopped between lots of foster homes, but everyone did the same thing. We hadn't eaten anything in two days, and we were weak. Then we found a foster home in the Bronx that was run by some Christian missionaries, and they were kind to us and took us to their dining table. They gave us a good variety of food, and we ate like lions that hadn't feasted for a month.

They said to come every day for food from them, and we did. We went once a day and ate food there and took some back to the library.

Slowly, things started to change. They were teaching the message of God from the Bible, and we liked it. We learned some good lessons about how they approached the Bible. We clarified the doubts we had, and they thought we were eager to learn.

After two months, they started to recommend us to be baptized, but we were not ready and didn't want to be. We had been baptized when we were in the ghetto, and that was different, because Sister Weyandt and the brothers and sisters had been humble and pious. At that age, we didn't know much about what baptism was, and we did it as part of some ritual and custom. But times had changed, and we were wiser, and the first question that went through our minds was "How many times can someone be baptized?"

We ignored them, and they started to behave differently and tried closing the food booth early when we ran late, or they gave us less food. They started to give us the leftovers, and although we were not looking for the first pickings, we were looking for a way to fill our hungry stomachs. We were growing, we studied day and night, and we needed good, nutritious food. We stopped going there because we felt it was sort of an insult that they were now treating us badly. We were looking for jobs, but no one wanted to employ us. We didn't want to beg for food because our intelligence was stopping us, so we sold candies and chocolates during the daytime in the subways, flying shuttles, on Wall Street, and on every possible street in New York City. We didn't want to waste time making money to feed ourselves, so we did this job in rotation. It didn't work well because it became a cashless society, and we needed a card reader. We could not buy a swipe reader because we didn't have RFIDs, and moreover, no one would swipe it for a candy man. People very rarely carried a few dollars in their pocket, and if they did, it was only for charity to toss to beggars. Yes, they didn't buy candies; they treated us like beggars. So we gave up after a month and tried cleaning cars or helping fat old ladies out of their cars or polishing shoes. We got money here and there, but it wasn't sufficient to buy a decent meal for ten kids.

Finally, we decided to walk to TUAD, where, by law, they could not refuse us. We didn't want to waste time with this moneymaking foolishness. We took one philosophy to heart before going, and that was that the more you learn and understand, the more you become meek and humble. The TUAD was uptown around Harlem, and we went there for lunch, we had a feeling that we were entering the monster's den. We walked to the gates, and the guards more or less recognized us because we had grown a lot. They asked us to show our IDs to get in. Every eye was on us with surprise, and they were refreshing their memories and talking to one another, guessing who we were.

We went and stood in the line for food, and the kids in line were nasty and greeted us by saying, "We thought you were dead." We were there to get a meal, and we were hungry, so we couldn't listen to their mocking. They were serving chicken pasta and bread. The guy who was serving it was fat and fair skinned, with a big moustache, and he asked Sadie, "Are you the ones who escaped from TUAD?" Sadie replied yes, and the guy looked down and commented, "You dogs are here in NY for a meal to cause more trouble." We just remained quiet, clenched our teeth, took the meal, and walked away, but for Madison, they purposely dropped the bread on the floor. He didn't give her another piece and said it was her mistake and she had to take it.

Madison had changed a lot. She didn't want to be a problem to anyone, and she took the bread from the floor. A guard there saw all of this and asked Madison to eat the bread, and Madison had no choice and ate the bread through tears. She didn't want to spoil the final place where we could fill our mouths. The bread was clean, even though she took it from the floor, but their attitude was dirty. I saw my girlfriend eating from the dust, and if I had been Superman, I would have busted him in his face and taken him for a grand dinner in Krypton.

Life was a lesson, and we were learning and mastering it. We comforted Madison that night, and she said we would get revenge on them one day. We decided not to sit and eat there anymore, so we would wrap up the food and go eat outside. Madison became a good catcher of bread, and she never dropped it again. Every day, the fat guy would call us bad words, like *dogs, pigs, monkeys,* sometimes the F-word, and many other words from the bad-word list. We pretended to be deaf, but it hurt, and we had no choice but to take it. The good thing about him was that he used the bad words in complete sentences, and we enjoyed, in a way, seeing how he could curse at people every day without repeating himself. We would go twice a day for lunch and dinner. Even the guys who came in at other shifts were the same as the fat guy.

Life had its twists, and one day we went to TUAD for breakfast and there was a black lady named Gwyneth. She was kind and warmhearted, and when she saw us, she greeted us politely. We were stunned to find an angel in a monsters' den. She always gave us extra food, and she was just the opposite of the fat pig. We liked her and asked her which days and times she came in. She came in every day at different shifts, and we would go to TUAD only when she was in. We started to build a good friendship with Gwyneth, and one day, she invited us for the weekend to her home in the Bronx.

We went to her home on a Saturday, and brought her some flowers. She lived in a one-bedroom apartment. The neighborhood was decent, and she greeted us with her whole heart. She had a daughter named

Salomeya, who was nine years old and mentally disabled and she was deaf and mute. Her face looked drowsy and her eyes squinted. When she saw us, she was sitting in a chair and reached out her hands for us to come closer. We went to her, and she took a ball and gave it to me, and then signaled with her hands that I should drop it on the floor. I dropped the ball on the floor and she caught it. She became happy and laughing, saliva dribbled out of her mouth, and signaled with her hands for me to do it one more time. I did, and she became so happy that I did it a few more times. She was excited and asked me to come closer, and when I went closer, she hugged me.

I felt, at that moment, for the first time in my life that if I could have the divine power like Buddha, Jesus, or other miracle healers, I could cure her. I cursed myself for not being one of them, and as her saliva flowed, my tears flowed. Then Gwyneth came in and started cleaning her mouth. What sort of creation or evolution would have done this harm to her? After cleaning her mouth, Gwyneth kissed her, cried, and said, "My beautiful daughter, you are so smart."

We wiped our eyes and asked Gwyneth about her family and daughter. She shared her sad story with us. Gwyneth had been married, and her only daughter was Salomeya. She was born mentally disabled and had been deaf and mute since birth. Her marriage didn't work well because of Salomeya, and she and her husband had separated. All her life was now centered on Salomeya and she had to take care of her. She didn't have money to send her for day care, and Gwyneth's mom came and took care of her during the day while she was at work. Because Salomeya was mentally disabled, none of the children wanted to play with her and she spent all her time inside the home. The worst thing, she said, was that no one wanted to come over and see Salomeya because she was considered bad luck and a curse. People yelled at her when they saw her outside the house or when she was out for a walk. There had been some very bad incidents and misfortunes with people in the neighborhood, and they blamed it on her. Gwyneth didn't take her out in the daytime anymore; the only time she could take her out was in the night at two in the morning when the streets were empty. What a bad world that was. I asked her why Salomeya was asking to play with the ball and why, when I did, she became happy. Gwyneth replied, "No one plays with her except my mom and me, so she was very happy when she saw you."

We felt a lot of love for Salomeya and were proud of Gwyneth for being her mom. She made a potpie, salad, and fish for us. While we were enjoying the meal, I asked Gwyneth, "Why do you show us so much care and kindness, in TUAD? The others hate us." Gwyneth was serving salad and said, "That's Oliver, always going straight to the point. Well, the government declared you incompetent and dumb after you escaped from TUAD. No one in this creation is dumb, and it was by chance we were made. I always think my daughter is the most intelligent of anyone in this world, although she has problems. How dare they call ten sweethearts, who are handsome, bright, and cute, dumb? If I said you were dumb, then because of the injustice in this world, they could taunt my daughter, too. Mock not others or you will be mocked soon, which is my own proverb."

I left the spoon in the bowl and said, "Very impressive. Let me ask you something: if your daughter was healthy, would you show us the same kindness?" Gwyneth stopped serving the salad and looked at me with both hands on her hips, breathed heavily, and said, "Are you looking for an argument, Oliver?" I stopped eating and said, "Answer my question, please," and Gwyneth replied, "Well, I am a mother, and since I have a kid, I would never do that to anyone, Oliver." I just kept teasing her. "But if you were single and had no kids, what would you do?"

Benjamin and Ejaz stopped eating and looked at me, thinking that I was pulling her leg. Gwyneth looked at me thoughtfully and said, "I was not raised by my mom to be like that, to taunt and make fun of people, and even if they had raised me badly, my conscience would hurt when I taunted somebody. I would never taunt anyone, no matter what the situation was." I stopped eating, stretched, and said, "That was the answer I was expecting from you, Gwyneth. It is not because you have a daughter or any similarities, it is you, and that is what makes the difference." Gwyneth agreed with me. She really appreciated my thoughts and got the message I was trying to tell her. I said, "The first thing you should know is that I don't think your daughter is mentally disabled and that you should try to move around it. I think she is perfect and should face the world."

We enjoyed the company of Gwyneth and her mom, who also showed up later. We played with Salomeya, and she was so happy, her heart was filled with joy. Before leaving, I took my metal dragon, which I had kept for almost a decade, and gave it to Salomeya and said, "You need this. It will protect you. It protected me. Keep it safe." She took it from me and put it in her pocket. Salomeya knew what I had said, but she could not react. Gwyneth was right: she was an intelligent kid, and I wanted to treat her like one.

We went every weekend to her home and played with Salomeya and took her walking in the daytime. The neighbors yelled and cursed at us because of Salomeya, and we would reply to them, "Go check your horoscope. It really sucks. Don't blame her." We would give radical answers to the curses they gave us, and sometimes they would pick fights with us. We were not kids anymore, but decent teenagers who could punch someone in the nose just to see the color of their blood. There were ten of us, and we could handle anything the world sent our way.

Gwyneth's heart rejoiced, and she cared for us like her sons and daughters. When we took Salomeya out in the daytime, she saw the sun and the trees, felt the fresh air that hit her face, and slowly started recovering. All she needed was some friends, and we were there. Every time I saw her, I would ask for the metal dragon and she would take it from her pocket and quickly show it to me before putting it into her pocket. I would say to her, "You protect that better than I did. You are so smart, Salomeya, and better than me." Every time I said that, I could see some elation in her face. Although she couldn't hear me, she could feel my vibrations, so the world had to be considerate to her, and she knew it and listened.

My search world was perfect. I was spending time with my father and thinking about the superhero, but that is a long story and you know it. In the real world, we were learning well and we acquired more and more knowledge and were fascinated by the great people who wrote the books to deliver their message to the world. Every leaf on the tree was turning sixteen one by one. The last one to turn sixteen was Ejaz, and his birthday was December 6. We were waiting for it so we could take revenge on the guards and people working in TUAD's kitchen and food court. We thought it was only us that they treated poorly, but, no, they treated all the kids who went there to eat every day like that. They thought we were helpless kids and didn't have any shame, reputation, sense, or respect.

We had to be sixteen to complete our plan, or else they could put us in the TUAD court system and sentence us until we turned sixteen. They could also never allow us inside TUAD to get food again and would make excuses in the public world to justify their actions. Once we were sixteen, we could find a job and feed ourselves with the money we earned.

We were so excited to play our little game with these punks. It was Ejaz's birthday on December 6, and we wished him a happy birthday and went to TUAD for lunch. We made sure Gwyneth was not working that day. We went to TUAD to settle the final dispute, and they were serving the same chicken red-sauce pasta and leather-coated bread. The first one to go up was Madison, and the same fat pig with the moustache who called us dogs on the first day was working. He gave her two scoops of pasta, and she asked for one more scoop. He said no, and Madison asked again with a hungry look on her face. "Please, sir, one more." He was rude and said, "Next." She went to take the bread, and deliberately dropped it on the floor. The server asked her to pick it up, and she did it. Then, one by one, we all did the same as Madison: asked for one more scoop and dropped the bread.

The same manic guard who had forced Madison to eat the bread was there. He walked with a stick in his hand over to our table and tapped it on the table. We looked at him, and Niki said, "Whazz up, chief?" He was troubled by Niki's greeting, and with his angry face he said, "You cannot talk to me like that." Niki asked, "Why not?" and the guard got mad, tapped the table twice, and said, "You should call me sir—nothing more or less than that." Niki very casually replied, "Okay, sir, sir, sir." The guard looked at him with his cheeks almost touching his eyes and said angrily, "Eat the bread." Niki said, "No, sir, it fell on the floor. I can't." The guard replied, "You are gonna eat it now. Come on." Niki replied, "Why do you always bother us when it falls on the floor? When it doesn't fall, you don't bother us." The guard was mad, tapped the stick on the table again, and said, "I don't need to explain to you, but I will. You are pigs from the gutter, and you don't deserve anything good in your life. You dumb son of a b****, eat that or else I will put my stick in your butt." Niki was pissed off, got up, and said, "Well, I won't be calling you sir anymore, you punk. Why don't you stick it in your father, and take this bread to your wife and kids, with your shoe polish dressing on it?"

The guard was shocked when he said that, and he moved to hit him. Madison took her plate and threw the pasta on him. We all took our plates and smashed the guy with the pasta in his face. There were just four guards in the dining room and they saw this and came running to help. We punched one of the guard's in the face and he fell on the floor. Seeing this, the kids took their turns getting up from their tables and throwing plates. Quickly, a few kids went and closed the door of the dining room and guarded it. We all joined to smash in their faces and made them roll in the pasta. We took the fat pig and started to beat him. We made him remove his shirt and pants and with his fat tummy, we put pasta and ketchup on the floor and made him roll in it. There were almost seventy kids, and we really took care of the TUAD employees in the kitchen and in the dining room that day.

They were watching us over the cameras, and their backup team and other guards were knocking on the door to open it. We didn't open it because it was December, and we were celebrating an early Christmas party at TUAD. Judah stopped beating them and was standing still. Niki and Aika called over to Judah and said, "What happened? Beat them." Judah became a little girl now and said, "I don't want to. I am not angry anymore." Aika was kicking the fat pig, and she stopped and said, "Imagine this was Peyton and Jay Mons. What would you do?" Judah in no time changed his face, became angry again, and started kicking the fat pig. He was saying, "I hate you, Peyton, you dog, Jay Mons," and he became so violent that he started to jump on the fat guy. It was hilarious, and the fat guy started to cry and said, "My name is not Peyton or Jay Mons. I am Randolph, please, please," and Judah replied, "Doesn't matter, you TUAD work dog."

All the serving dishes were turned over, and food was all over the place and the people from TUAD where floating in it. The guards standing outside were shouting for an hour, and when they got tired, they used explosion to open the door, the guards came rushing in and started to pull us from the fight. They really had a hard time separating us, and finally, one way or another, the fight ceased, and they held us by our necks. I saw a seven-year-old riding horseback on one of the guards. The chief walked in and saw us and shouted, "Who started this?" All the dumpling men whom we beat were pointing to us and said, "The kids who broke out of TUAD."

The chief saw us and said, "All your destinies are in my hands and your whole life is done." Fay shouted at the chief, "You idiot, we have an hour. It is two in the afternoon, and if by three o'clock we are not by our I-gadgets, this fight video will be all over the Internet." Hearing that, the chief and everyone was shocked and didn't know what exactly we meant. Yes, we had installed hidden cameras in the dining room and recorded everything that had happened, so they were in big trouble. The guards went and started to search for the cameras, and they found them in the dining room. They didn't have much choice, because they could not take us to TUAD court because we were sixteen. If they took us to the public court, we had the videos that we would show to the judge, and they would be in trouble for humiliating the kids. The public would love to watch a video like that and post their comments throughout the Internet.

It was now our turn and they had no time to decide, because we had programmed an auto upload of the recorded video. If we were there by three o'clock, it would send the video over the Internet automatically, and everyone would be in trouble. They released us quickly and made a deal to set us free if we didn't upload the video to the Internet. We said yes to the deal. We knew how to deal with these punks and had become experts at it. They said they wouldn't allow us to eat there anymore, and we said we were sixteen and didn't need their help anymore. They asked us to leave as soon as possible and as we went to the front door, Niki, Fay, and Sadie turned back, showed their middle fingers, turned again, and walked out.

We hurried to the old building downtown to stop the upload of the video, and disabled the program. But we backed the video up in several places and password-protected it. We sat in the old building looking at each other, and Judah said, "Why did we become violent?" Niki smiled and said, "Threshold, buddy," and Judah replied, "Nathalie said not to kill anyone." Niki said, "We didn't kill anyone or make them bleed, we just disciplined them." Judah couldn't talk anymore to Niki and said, "Whatever you say, Niki."

We needed to find a job now. We started to hunt for jobs for our living, but it would be difficult, because we didn't have a proper education, just third-grade level, and we didn't have RFIDs, either. We couldn't get a decent job. Benjamin, Ejaz, and I got a job at a construction company that rebuilt bombed-out buildings from the war. They didn't engage the robots for it and used easy targets like us, and they had us carry construction materials for the big buildings. Our construction contractor was Vernon, an African-American bully, who paid only the minimum wage and only for eight hours, although he made us work twelve. If we spoke about the laws or human rights, he would threaten us with termination. So, we had to work under this demon until our day came. Madison, Fay, Aika, and Judah worked in a supermarket in the packing department. Shu, Sadie, and Niki distributed flyers in the streets and subways. We all had jobs we could tell people about with pride.

We could not take rotations of work because these were regular jobs and not part time, so we worked twelve hours a day, six days a week. But we never gave up reading, and we spent almost eight hours in the reading room searching for the answer to the puzzle. On Sundays, we discussed with each other the subjects we'd learned about. I would connect often with the search world I had started. I would go into a trance, and my friends would think I was thinking and didn't always wake me up. They would check on me and ask me whether I was all right, but I never said anything to them about the search world. I kept it to myself. But all the problems that I faced in this world no longer disheartened me, because I had so much cheer and delight in my search world. If I was hungry, I could go eat in the search world I had built, and if I didn't have a family here, I created a better family in my search world. I just imported everything from the real world to the search world.

We were eighteen years old now, and didn't have much money and couldn't afford to rent an apartment. We still lived in the library as a place for us to rest. Madison and I were dating and were physically unified now. Benjamin and Fay, Niki and Aika, Judah and Sadie, and Ejaz and Shu were also dating. We had a good understanding and gave each other private space in turns at the library. Life was beautiful now, because sex drove us and made our understanding stronger.

Surprise and struggle never left us, and one Sunday we were coming out of the library to go and hang out. As we were coming out of the library, a couple of cops passed the secret tunnel and saw Benjamin, Judah, Shu, Aika, Ejaz, Madison, and me standing outside and helping Sadie out. They didn't know what was going on and walked toward us, and we didn't notice them. We were careless that day, and they came walking up from behind and asked us, "What are you guys doing here?" Hearing that, we turned and saw a couple of cops, and they saw Sadie climbing up. The cops confused and asked us, "What's inside the tunnel? What are you doing in there?" Sadie, as she climbed up and saw the cops, shouted, "Catch them, guys, and tie them up."

Hearing that alerted our brains that we had been caught, and the cops turned away and started to run. Benjamin, Judah, Shu, Aika, Ejaz, Madison, Sadie and I ran fast to catch them. Then, Niki and Fay started to climb fast to help us, and Bickey also joined us, and we were shouting for Bickey to catch them. One of the cops said, "Call the control room for help," and the other cop ran faster than we could and was ahead of us. They had almost reached the edge of the building when we saw a man come out from the side of the building. The cops couldn't control themselves and dashed toward the man. The man was almost six feet nine inches tall and well built. He caught the cops by their hair and slammed their heads into the building. Both of their skulls cracked and they died on the spot.

We didn't know who the man was, and as we got closer to check on the police officers, we saw they were bleeding and dead on the ground. We looked at him and wondered why he helped us and who he was. He looked like a Native American, and even before we opened our mouths, he said, "You should always watch your back, Oliver." He looked at Madison as if he had known her for a long time and said, "You look like your mother, Stacey." We were stunned and terrified about who the heck this man was. He knew all our secrets. We were lucky no one was around, and then he said, "No time to waste. We have to dispose of the cops. Give me a hand." We asked him, "Where are you going to put them?" and he smiled and said, "There are a lot of ghosts in the AZ library. We'll just blame the ghosts." We carried them inside the library, and he asked Madison and Sadie to clean the bloodstains from the wall and the ground and spray them with alcohol. We took them to the second floor and dumped them. We were about to open our mouths to ask him who he was, but before we could, he said, "I am your friend, I am here to protect you. Let's talk later. First, we will finish this job." He took the cops and placed them in the floor. We put them in two different rooms, and he fired lots of gunshots to baffle the police. We cleared all the fingerprints and possible traces. He turned on their wireless devices and we left the scene quickly.

We rushed into the secret library. The cops tried many times to reach their fellow officers, and within a few hours, they came searching for them. Everyone was scared to go to the building and almost 300 cops and members of the press went inside to find them. We were lucky that the satellite marked the library as a no-man's-land and didn't monitor it, so we weren't going to be caught by the satellite. We looked at the tall man and were very curious about who he was and how he knew us. He started the conversation, "Is Nathalie dead?" We looked at each other and didn't know what to say. We gave him a bottle of water, and he drank it, smiled, and said, "Did Nathalie say anything about me? I don't think she did. That was why she sent me to New York City and follow the star to find you. I hope James and Stacey are also dead. Such good friends I knew." We were speechless. Who was this man? And why hadn't Nathalie said anything about him? I asked him with hesitation, "What do you mean Nathalie followed the star?" He looked at me and said, "Well, the star that appeared in the sky from nowhere prophesying the return and birth of the chosen one. It was you, Oliver. You are my boss and I am your bodyguard." From the very first time we met, he was too confusing, and I politely asked him, "Tell us what we don't know and what we need to hear."

He introduced himself as Demonthin and recited the whole story. "Nathalie was the one who came from the Fourth Dimension in search of you. I met her and recognized her as a true person from the Fourth Dimension and wanted to help her. She believed in me, and we became good friends. She said she was looking for the chosen one to stop the war and the birth of the brightest and last morning star, with no name, appeared in the sky. The prophecy was about to be fulfilled, and she had to give the locket to you, prepare you for the mission and send you to New York City. We walked and traveled many miles and followed the star. On the journey, we met James and Stacey at Strawberry Hill, in Kansas City, and they wanted to help us. But Nathalie asked me to go to New York City, and she said when you guys were twelve, you would reach here. She told me to wait and watch out in the AZ library—the haunted one. I waited for almost twelve years for you to come. She said I could find you by one sign, that you would have nine friends, and there would be ten in total. When I saw you for the first time, it was on TV, after you broke out of TUAD, and I knew you were the chosen one. I decided the prophecy was coming true and I became stronger every day and was waiting for my boss, Oliver, to protect you.

"I knew the door to this secret chamber was here because Nathalie told me about it. I knew it was hard to find and I waited for some time to see whether you guys would find it, and then I decided to help. I made a noise, a high-frequency tone, that only dogs could hear to attract the dog, and I threw some meat on top of the marble stone. Your dog ate the meat and was anxious about more meat inside the marble stone, and that was why he was scratching the stone so hard. But I didn't know how to open it. You guys were smart to figure out the riddle from the locket. That is my part of the story. I am happy to see my lovely Miss Stacey's daughter, Madison. You look just like your mom."

He remembered us by name and took a piece of paper from his pocket, which was a magazine page that had all our photos by our names.

He had memorized our faces and names. Demonthin asked us, "So, you guys were chasing the cops. I know Nathalie said that the chosen ones shouldn't have any blood on their hands, so what would you have done if you had caught them?" We were blinded by his question, and we said funny stuff because the only way was to get rid of the officers, which meant killing them, and our answers were provided in several variations of that. I observed him and said, "But we made you kill him, so in a way, we killed somebody." Demonthin answered, "You didn't give me any commands or even know me when I killed them, so technically, you didn't kill anyone."

All I could say at this point was that we'd had surprises in our lives. We learned Demonthin worked as a bouncer in one of the bars downtown and made his living peacefully. He was not married and said he had sworn an oath that his only job was to protect us. He was one of the men who sacrificed his life for us and he was one of us now. The next day in the news, they said, "The ghosts in the library killed the police officers." The question was raised, "Why did the cops go inside?" and some phrased it, "Curiosity kills the cops." They all blamed it on adventure and curiosity and when we watched it on the Internet, we were scared. Their ghosts also haunted that building and wanted their revenge against us. Sometimes at night, I would have weird dreams about ghosts and two cops hunting me down. I would wake up and find Madison was having the same feeling.

Life went on the same: work, pay bills, and our mission of solving the riddle in the books. Demonthin always had a serious face when we hung out, and he was very cautious, his eyes were all over the place trying to protect us. He always called me boss, and he said that he was my bodyguard. Whenever he said he was my bodyguard, I laughed at myself, because no one in history like me, as a construction worker, would ever need a strong bodyguard like Demonthin. We asked him to relax, but he never listened to us and told us every time, "I am working. Don't disturb me." The drinking age in New York was eighteen, and we would go to his bar once a month to grab a few beers. No matter how a women looked, how she carried herself, what age she was or how intelligent she was—men in New York City would hit on her. The bars were the only place they didn't look at our girls as dumb or make fun of them. They wanted to get laid, and their false tongues said they were bright and wanted to hang out. Our girls were so loyal to us and we trusted them, and they just ignored these sex-fiend morons. The girls didn't even reply to any of the bar junkies, but they tried to start conversations with them. The girls said they didn't even have a home to sleep in and that we slept in some old building, but the rich, cocky Wall Street dirt bags, who had big houses, would invite them to their homes. They missed the point.

The dudes couldn't even leave a homeless girl alone. They were pure sex maniacs. It was fun to look at all those monkeys and see how they made their moves to impress the girls.

Life went in the same direction, until we were twenty. We had saved some money, and everybody, for the first time, found a studio and moved in. We didn't have anything: no furniture, or good clothes. We could not afford to buy all the interior furniture and accessories, so we got built-in convertible couches that served as beds and furniture. We moved in pairs with the girls we loved, and we moved into the same neighborhood so everybody was no more than two blocks away. Demonthin was also around the same neighborhood. We were still exploring the books in the library and solving the puzzle. We had flipped through almost a million books, magazines, and newspapers in the library, but we hadn't found anything yet. Still, there were lots of books and newspapers to go. We didn't spend a lot of time in the library anymore, and we brought the books back home to read and always hid them in our apartments. When I wanted to be romantic, I didn't read the books or poems from the library, I read R Smith's romantic poems, and I had to admit, he was the best poet I had ever read. We also learned to hack well. Niki was the boss of hacking and taught us everything he knew. He was the only kid who always kept updated. Niki changed a lot, but I still remembered the sweet boy he was.

We were sitting near the Harlem River, and some kids were making paper boats and putting them in the river, playing and having competitions. One kid, wearing a pink T-shirt and jeans and around five years old, showed up one day, but he didn't have any paper, and the other kids didn't share their paper with him. The boy was very upset and sat down by the river watching the kids playing. We saw that he was upset, and Niki went to the kid and asked him why. He told Niki that he didn't have a paper boat to play with. Niki took a mini chart from his pocket that his father had given him and that he had preserved safely all these years. He gave it to the kid and said he could use it. The boy's face lit up like the sun and he thanked Niki and took it. The kid made two boats with that chart and put them in the water. All the other kids' boats sank, but the boats made by the boy in the pink T-shirt with Niki's chart didn't, and they sailed far into the distance.

Niki and I watched until the paper boats went out of our sight. Slowly, I turned and asked him, "You value your father a lot. Those were his last words of advice to you, and you just gave them to a kid to make paper boats." Niki smiled and looked into the sky and took a deep breath and said, "Well, that's true, they were my father's words, but they were the wrong ones; everything changed, Oliver. I didn't like women at one time. When I met Madison and you guys, I was starting to change, and then when I met Aika, my idea about women started to be even more diluted, and now I cannot imagine a life without her. That was just paper, man, and at this point of my life, Oliver, I don't think of it as a good man or bad woman or vice versa. It is always good versus evil. If you hadn't walked into my life, Oliver, I would be part of this system."

That simple thing Niki did impressed me, and he was right, it was always good and evil. I asked Niki about his experience in the dark room in TUAD. I asked him because it had been bothering me for years. He smiled and said, "What exactly do you need from me, buddy?" I asked him whether his father really came and chatted with him. He turned his face away from me and replied, "At that age, I thought he did, and very recently, I realized I had . . ." He didn't complete the sentence, and when I asked what it was, he asked me to promise not to tell anybody. I promised him and he said, "I broke down and had a split personality in that dark room." Hearing that, I didn't know what to say. TUAD physically broke us and even caused Niki to have a mental disorder. I kept that secret to myself, but I always felt sorry for Niki, I felt compassion for him.

One Wednesday night, we were walking out from work to our homes. It was summertime and the night and the neighborhood were unfrequented, and we were few blocks away from our houses. We saw a man in a suit who seemed to be running for his life, but he fell on the ground and couldn't run any farther. We ran and picked him up and we recognized him. It was the most esteemed professor Gavin Higgs, who had built the Artificial Intelligence system for America. He had been shot in the chest twice and was bleeding. We asked who shot him, and he couldn't talk much, but said, "Hide me, please."

We repeated, "Who shot you?" and he said the CIA agents. We said we could not take him home because they could track his RFID. He asked us to remove it from his hand. We had a small knife, and we cut his hand, removed it, and destroyed it. We then hurried and took him to my apartment, which was close by. He was bleeding badly, so we gave him first aid. He was weak, since he had lost a lot of blood, and was resting. We were surprised at what had happened to him and wanted to know why the CIA wanted to kill him. His reputation had preceded him, he was considered the father of modern AI in the Fourth Dimension and built all the systems.

He was wealthy and respectable. He woke up after a few hours and asked, "Who are you?" and we introduced ourselves. He couldn't recollect us and said, "Your faces look familiar to me," and we said we were the kids who had escaped from TUAD. He smiled and said, "Smart kids who fooled the whole world." We didn't know what he meant by that, so we asked him. He told us a story about when he was a kid, and how his father used to ask him to go to school all the time. But he had two dogs and many birds and he wanted to play with them. He decided to not do well in the exams and fail so that his dad would keep him home.

His dad discovered his trick and made a deal with him. "If I didn't do well on my exams, he would start with the birds, selling one at a time, and then, finally, he would sell the dogs, too." He loved his dogs and birds very much, so he started to improve on the exams and received A's on everything. That was how he protected his birds and dogs from his father. "The same as me, you kids did that, but no one knew enough to figure out your game, but this old professor did." When he saw it on the news and followed the whole court trial, he recollected his memories of his old times and what he did. He said, "No one could fail all those exams, especially not ten friends together. I guessed at that time that you had better plans than becoming one more useless product of this universe, like me."

He was a meek person, and we said, "No, Professor, you are a genius who lives in our times, and we are honored to have you with us, but not in the condition you are in." We gave him some water to drink and an energy drink to keep him active. We asked him why he had been shot. He looked at his chest, put his hand over the wound, and said, "I know I am dying, and I have to share something with you before I depart." He took a chip from his pocket, gave it to me, held my hands, and said, "Be careful with this. This has all the information and source code for all the AI systems in this world." I held his hand tightly and said, "Were you trying to steal it? Is that why you got shot?" Professor Gavin closed his eyes and opened them after a while, looked at me, and said, "I didn't steal from anybody. It is my own invention."

I didn't understand anything he said, and I felt was uncertain, I asked him, "How are you going to stop the war, Professor, and what is on this chip?" He started to cough heavily, and blood started to spill from his mouth. We didn't ask any more questions. We gave him some painkillers to help him and asked him if he wanted to go to the hospital. He refused and said his time was over and that he just wanted to tell the truth before he died.

Then the professor told the true story of what had happened. He built the AI system for his own greed, to get rich, and the government misused it to build a missile system for war. His son, daughter, and wife had been killed fifteen years ago with the same missile he had built. He realized his error and the inhumanity he had caused and started to build a system and technology to stop the war. He finally made it, but the government found it, and they shot him because he had found a way to stop the war. "I didn't listen to them, and I was always working, and finally, they came to kill me and take the chip."

He said the chip held the masterpiece of his whole lifetime and told us to use it to stop the war. We asked him if we could use it now, and he said no. "You need to understand it very well before even trying it. It would take years for you to understand it, but do it." If he would live for another day, he could at least run through it, but he only had a few minutes left, so he told us the basic idea of what the system looked like. He was falling away, and his breathing was slowly decreasing, he looked at me and said his last words: "My mother, before she died, said, 'You will die giving your masterpiece to the rainmaker.' I know you are the rainmaker, Oliver. Do it, son." His heart stopped and he looked at me very deeply to remember me. He took his last memory from this earth to travel to other dimensions and closed his eyes.

I was not sure why he called me the rainmaker, but I started to ponder it. He left us, and we felt sad that such a great man had been shot and died like that. We turned on the Internet, and Professor Gavins's face was all over it with stories saying, "He stole government secrets and escaped, so the CIA shot him, and now he is missing." Then Demonthin came to my apartment and knocked on the door. We opened it, and he asked who was on the couch. We told him everything that had happened, and he was astonished. We asked him for help with how to get rid of the body. Definitely, the ghost library would not work this time, so we discussed it, and he said, "We will hide the body from the eyes of the world and make the world and the government live in terror that the professor is missing. We'll create the biggest conspiracy with his name, and use it for our own benefits." Demonthin knew a way that older Egyptians mummified the dead, and he had the materials and ointments, because his family had done it as a cultural practice for ages.

We waited until two in the morning to make sure everyone was sleeping and no one was on the road. We removed Professor Gavins's bloodstained suit and cleaned it. We shaved his beard and changed his appearance and tanned his face with cosmetics, put him in a tuxedo shirt with a red bow tie, and made him look Hispanic. We sprinkled liquor on his body to make him smell drunk. Demonthin had a car, and we took him in the backseat and asked our other friends to come to the library with the mummifying materials and ointments. It was Madison and me in the backseat, and we put the professor in the middle between us. Demonthin was driving the car, and Fay was sitting in the front.

The cops had started to search cars and neighborhoods everywhere. Madison and I drank some hard liquor quickly to smell like booze. As we took the body in the car to the library, the cops were all over the place. They stopped our car and checked the backseat with a flashlight. We had our eyes closed and pretended to be drunk. The police officers woke us up, and we woke up as if we were drunk, and they asked us questions. Madison turned to the professor and said, "We will be home soon, honey, and then we will have a shower and some fun. Please don't sleep." The cops thought we were just some New York City night clubbers and let us go. I looked at Madison and said, "Did you really mean that, Madison?" and she got angry. "Oliver, it was just a game. He is dead. Forget it." I said, "You're crazy."

We took him into the library, and we helped Demonthin. He didn't remove any organs. Rather, he used certain ointments and herbs and embalmed the body. Then he wrapped him with cloth, and we removed books from a shelf and put the body inside it. We were all tired of the whole problem, and we rested and drank some soda. Some thoughts went through my mind, and I looked at Demonthin and asked him, "Many of the novels in this library were turned into movies. Do we still have movies?" Demonthin was also puzzled and said, "Well, there was a rumor that most of the movies that were produced before the war were lost, and only the Sci-Fi ones still exist."

I was not convinced by his answer and asked him, "Demonthin, how come the people who made the bomb coded the bomb to destroy the nonfiction ones and not the sci-fi movies?" Demonthin laughed and said, "You always have questions on your mind, boss. That is not what I just told you. The American Film Academy preserved the movies in different chambers for fiction, nonfiction, and sci-fi. When the war started, only the sci-fi movies were saved, and the rest were destroyed . . . "

I was still not convinced and said, "How about the books and movies from other countries? Do they still have them, or has everything been destroyed." Niki replied, "That question takes lots of time, man. A handful of countries still preserve all their books and movies, and they are all well protected by the government. It is only us." I sighed and said, "You said all these American writers and European writers were the smartest people in this world and the rest had no skills, so come on, Niki that is why Nathalie said the puzzle was here in this library and nowhere else in the world."

Judah said, "Oliver has a point," but Niki replied, "I don't know, buddy. All the other books are in their languages, and I don't know to read them. We should deal with what is before us, Oliver. The answer should be here." I replied to Niki, "Here we have Italian, German, Arabic, Hebrew, and other language books, also." Niki was a little confused and said, "Do you know all those languages, Oliver? How?" I don't know why Niki became so silly. I told him there was something called an electronic translator, and Niki tapped his forehead and said, "My bad." Demonthin was moving his hand and said, "Chill out, guys, easy. I know it is complex, but you guys have to do what Nathalie said: find the answer and look for the puzzle." At this point, we didn't know what was happening around us. We looked so foolish. All I knew was that I was just sitting reading these books. The only thing that made me happy was that I had built the search world. I was searching desperately, and I loved that world very much. It let me get some peace and rest from here.

It was fall, and I was walking to the secret chamber when I found two kids around eight years old wearing woolen jackets and standing before the building and staring at it. I was curious and walked over to them and said, "Why are you guys looking at the building?" The girl turned and looked at me and said, "Are there any ghosts?" I looked at the girl and said, "I haven't seen you here before. Who are you guys?" The girl was quiet, and the boy answered, "The ghost killed my father and her father, and we wanted to kill the ghost. It has been two years since our fathers died, and they were good cops." As soon as they said "cops," I realized these were the kids of the dead police officers. I felt guilty and pretended I knew something. I said, "Are you the kids of the two cops who were killed out of curiosity and went inside the building?" The girl frowned and said, "I know curiosity kills only the cat, not my dad. My dad was strong, but the ghost seemed to be stronger than my dad and broke his skull."

I didn't know how to deal with this situation, and I asked them, "Would you mind having a coffee with me, please?" The girl replied, "My dad always said not to talk or hang out with strangers." I smiled and said, "Very good for your dad, but we are just talking as friends, so why can't we go near your home and have a coffee." The girl was thinking and said, "Sounds like a plan, but we don't drink coffee. There is an ice cream parlor across the street from our home." They lived uptown near 121st Street, so we took the subway and went to their home. I asked them how they had managed to come out alone, and they said that their mom was out, and both had sneaked out to see the place where their fathers died.

We went to their neighborhood ice cream parlor. My conscience pained me every time I looked at them. I bought them ice cream, and we eat it and chatted. I learned that after their fathers died, their moms went to work in the NYPD as clerks in the back office. The kids' families were best friends, and I learned their names. The boy was Edgar, and the girl was Nyah. They went to school, learned well, and lived well. They loved their fathers so much, and they had built a mind to kill the ghosts that killed their fathers. It sounded funny, but they were innocent kids and they thought like that.

I was super nice to them and wanted to win their hearts as a sort of confession and repentance. They really liked and believed me, and I said I would like to meet their moms and say hi. They made sure that I wasn't going to tell them where I had met them and that I would say I had just come across them in the street. The kids lived next door to each other. I was waiting at Nyah's house for their mom to return, and saw the pictures of her father and all her family pictures, and I was very touched.

The moms came home, and the kids introduced me as their new friend and said they liked me. I introduced myself. They knew I was one of the kids who broke out of TUAD, and I apologized to them for breaking the law when I was a kid because Nyah's mom was also a cop, and I didn't want to look like a troublemaker. Their moms were very understanding people and with open minds. One of them said, "My husband and I were dating at that time, and it was the talk of the country. He was a cop then, and I asked him his honest opinion about the kids who broke out of TUAD. I always said that because you didn't have RFID, people were suspicious of that, so he had better tell the truth. He said that you didn't break out of prison, just escaped from their school, and it was your choice to do it. I mean, the law could not do anything about it. It was the society that locked up all the kids in the schools and some kids were gonna break out and escape." I was glad that they didn't have any bad opinions of me, and she said she would cook dinner for me.

I shared my personal life with their moms and showed them Madison's picture, and they liked her and admired her beauty. I indirectly made a mistake and I wanted to repent and make up for it, so I asked their permission to hang out with Edgar and Nyah sometimes, and they were cool with that if I promised to bring Madison next time. I was building some family bonding with them, but I could not tell them the truth about their fathers and husbands. I got their numbers, and next time, I took Madison to their houses. Madison knew everything, and we brought lots of chocolates and ice creams. We created an impression in their minds that we would be getting married soon and having kids and that was the reason we liked Edgar and Nyah, but the true reason was that we destroyed those kids' lives with our mission crap. Edgar's and Nyah's moms said that after meeting me that they went back to their normal lives. Before that, they had been moody and sad, always thinking about their fathers, and they thanked us for walking into their lives. They liked Madison a lot, and we more or less became their good family friends.

We were now twenty-two, and I was still working as a construction laborer under Vernon. He was the most inhumane person I had ever met, still dolling out low wages. I wanted to switch jobs and leave him, but we didn't have much choice. Because I had worked for him six years, he raised my salary by a few bucks. I could have taken some online courses, graduated, and gotten a decent job, but I didn't want to waste even a second on that because of the mission we were undertaking. Niki and all of us were still decoding the work that Professor Gavins had given us, and it was mind blowing. We designated Niki and Aika to work on that project while the rest of us worked on the books in the library.

At this time, we understood most things that had happened in the past: the culture, society, religion, philosophy, civilization, and many other aspects. We were still hanging out with Edgar and Nyah, and now all my friends knew them very well and we became one big family. But we all still felt very guilty about those kids. It was springtime, and we were sitting in a small park near Wall Street and chatting with each other when we saw a little girl with half her body in a garbage can, her leg sticking out of the can. We found it disgusting that everybody just walked by, looked at her, and ignored her.

We got up and went over to get her out of the garbage can. Madison was trying to get her out, but she held on to the can tightly and would not let go. Then Sadie tried to help Madison, and the girl screamed, "Don't try to steal my meat, or I will kill you." Hearing that, Madison and Sadie let go of her slowly. She got out of the garbage can, and her face was covered with all the dirt in the universe. She was around five years old and had half a piece of pizza in her hand. Sadie said, "That is not meat, that is pizza," and she looked at Sadie angrily and said, "There was some chicken on it, but you tried pulling me out, and the chicken fell inside the can, and now you need to get it for me." Sadie was mad and said, "Do you want me to search for that little piece of chicken in that can? No way." The little girl was aggressive and said, "If you don't, I will kill you." Sadie rolled her shirt up and said, "Do you mean, little girl, that you are not ashamed to eat food from a garbage can?" The little girl was smart and told her, "You didn't cook for me, so let me see how much dirt you have in your belly," and she took a small knife from her pocket.

We were all laughing at the way the little girl was reacting and picking a fight. Then Sadie realized the situation and told her to calm down. "How about I get a new pizza for you?" The girl's face became calm, and she said, "Will you buy one for my mom, also?" We were all surprised to hear that she had a mom. I jumped into their conversation and said to the little girl, "I will buy it for your mom and you. Now put the knife in your pocket." The little girl said that she would bring her mom, and she ran into the crowd. Five minutes later, she came back with her mom. Her mom looked very weak and sick and was smoking a cigarette. She looked at us and said, "I don't want the pizza, I want money. What you guys want, group sex? I can do that." Madison whistled and said, "Well, that sounds interesting," and we understand that she was a prostitute. Judah very politely said, "We wanted to help you, and that's it. You look great, but we saw your kid in the garbage." The lady understood and said, "Sorry, ladies and gentlemen, I don't have a better life than this. A free pizza will help us."

We took both of them and bought them a pizza and some pastries for the kid. They scoffed it down, and it seemed that they had been starving for days. We asked who they were, and the lady told us about her and the little kid. Her name was Sandra, and she had moved to New York City from Colombia when she was two years old. She went to school and had a very normal and peaceful life until she tasted drugs for the first time. In college, she went to a party, and some guys gave her cocaine and some powdered smoke, and that was it. Slowly, she started to become an addict and consumed regularly. She ran out of money, and some dude offered her money for sex. She was doing it for the monthly basics for a while, but then it turned into her life. She showed us photos of when she was young and looked beautiful. She used to sell herself for higher prices and had lots of money. But she also started to consume expensive drugs and wasted all her money on those. She was infected with Q-HIV, which is the fourth variant of the HIV virus. She also got pregnant, and both she and her daughter, Claudia, had Q-HIV. Since all she knew was prostitution, she didn't have anything else to do. Her life became miserable, and she started offering lower rates from old or ugly men, who threw her out if they found out she had Q-HIV. We asked her to join a medical center and stay there to get healthy for a while. However, she said she couldn't because she liked to smoke and take drugs, which they don't allow in there.

We gave her some advice, but she said she couldn't take it and that there was no point in living. She was dying, she said, and her time was near, maybe a month or two, and she wanted to enjoy life and die. But she cared about Claudia. Claudia loved her mom very much and she didn't want to go to the hospital and wanted to stay with her. Claudia took medication regularly and was doing better, but her time was near, too. It was a sad story, and we offered to help them, but she ignored it the first time. They were both homeless and had no place to go. We somehow convinced them to stay with us, saying she could spend her last days there, and we promised we would take care of her and Claudia. She agreed and was pleased and we took them home with us.

All the girls took Claudia for a shower, and they cleaned her so well, it took them more than two hours. We bought some clothes for both of them and some perfume and cosmetics. Claudia came out in her yellow shirt and black pants, and when we looked at her, we saw she was a beautiful blond kid. All the dirt had changed the color of her hair, which we initially thought was brunette. Her hair was beautiful, nicely curled up and her face was cute and charming with the dirt gone, she looked like the best of both worlds: the Caucasian world and the Latino world. We kept them on a rotation between our apartments, but after two weeks, they both preferred to stay with us, and my friends had no hard feelings about it. It was all because Claudia liked Madison very much and came to form a bond with her.

Sandra was dying, and we didn't want to be proper citizens, so we bought her drugs and cigarettes. We wanted her to be happy in her last days, and she liked the pleasure of the drugs. Somehow, I built a strong friendship with Sandra and her daughter. Because we lived in a studio, Sandra always thought she was bothering us, but I told her, "Our home was like a dungeon, but after you walked in, we had light in here." She would always laugh and say, "I know you are lying, Oliver. A prostitute walks into someone's life and brings sin, guilt, disease, and impurity, but you are sweet." I told her every day that she brought light to our home, but after a few weeks, she stopped smoking and taking drugs because she wanted to be pure in the last few weeks and die as a clean soul.

We did our best, and she was finally on her deathbed in her last stage of life, and thanked everyone for treating her so well. She said it had been years, going back to the time of her mother and father, since she had been treated like a real person, with respect. She asked many times for us to take care of her daughter, and we promised to do so. Before she died, she said to me, "If I was reborn again, Oliver, I would sleep with you. Is that cool with you?" I had no choice. I wanted to be gentle to a dying woman, and said, "Yes." She breathed very slowly and said, "Will you be nice to me like you are nice to Madison?" and I said, "Yes," again. She couldn't breathe and was struggling, and I held her hands. She said, "I've never slept with one good man, even the first time. I only did it for money and drugs. Will you give me a simple kiss on my lips so that I can close my eyes having at least kissed one true man?"

I didn't know what to say, and I turned my face from her and looked at Shu because I couldn't see Madison's face. Madison winked and walked out of the house. I had kissed Kassidy that one time, when I was a kid, and up to now, I had carried that guilt, but I wanted to fulfill a reasonable wish for a woman who was dying and wanted to be pure on her deathbed. I thought for a while, and Sandra said, "I promise, you will not get infected." I replied, "I know, I know." Then she said her true intentions about how she would feel with a kiss. Panting slowly, she said to me, "I want to remove the words *slut* and *prostitute* from my life. Your kiss will wash me, and I will be pure for heaven."

After hearing that, I wanted to be a good dude and let this be a holy kiss, so I kissed her three times on her lips and said, "I love you, Sandra." She ran her hand into my hair and said, "I heard the same words a million times from every wrong man, and for the first time, I am hearing it very truly." She slowly stopped breathing, and she died. Claudia was jumping and crying for her mom. We all were filled with tears, even though we had known her for only two months; she had made a big impact on our lives. She had no family or anybody, and everyone had cast her out, so we took care of the burial service.

Claudia was also getting weaker and falling ill, and we wanted to admit her into hospital, but she refused to go. Sandra had signed papers that Madison and I were her legal guardians, so we had complete authority over her. She took the medicine every day with no problem, so we decided to keep her with us. I took many books from the library, kids' books, and I read to her every night in bed as she lay between Madison and me. We read her books like *The Poky Little Puppy*, *The Shaggy Baggy Elephant*, Harry Potter, and many others. She always enjoyed it, and while we read, she would fall asleep. We saw her cute and charming face. She didn't know her father, like me, but one thing I knew was that she was my daughter now.

We turned twenty-three. Claudia's health was declining, and we took her to the hospital. By the time her last hour was nearing, we wanted to take her home. She was weak and having trouble breathing, even with her oxygen mask. She called Sadie and said, "I am sorry for pulling a knife on you." Sadie started to cry and said, "No, honey, it was just a joke." Claudia was a very funny girl. "I was stronger than you, you know," she said. "I would have seen the dirt in that belly." Sadie was smiling and her eyes were filled with tears, and she said, "Definitely, you are stronger than me." Claudia smiled at her and said, "Will you find the lost chicken piece for me in that trash can after I die?" Sadie didn't know what to say to her but said, "Yes, honey, it was my fault. I will find it for you."

Claudia called me. I sat on the bed next to her, and she slowly moved her head and put it on my lap. I ran my hand through her hair, and she took her thumb and put it in her mouth and said, "After I die, Oliver, who will read stories at my bedtime?" I replied, "Maybe a faun, angel, fairy, or wizard." She said, "Will they like me?" and I told her with a great positive face, "Yes, they will. Why do you ask that?" Her eyes started to flow with tears. "I have Q-HIV, and my mom was a bad lady, and no one ever touched me. They always pushed me to the floor or walked away from me. Only my mom, the doctor, and the nurse ever touched me. After all of them, you and Madison were so nice to me. I don't know if a faun or wizard will like me."

Everybody was filled with emotion, and I replied to her, "After you die, you will be clean and become a new person like an angel, and you will have a new life." Claudia replied, "Will you remember me, Oliver?" and I replied, "Always, Claudia." She held my hand and asked me to read her a novel, *The Princess Bride*. I took the book and read to her, and she listened, laughed, and enjoyed it for an hour. Then her breath slowly left her body, and she died in my lap, sucking her thumb.

I don't know how to describe this moment. All our hearts ached, and I had lost my daughter. I didn't move her from my lap for hours as I ran my fingers through her hair. I couldn't bear the pain. She had walked into my life and then said goodbye. I didn't have any powers to stop her from dying, and I wished that she could have been my daughter for eternity. We cremated Claudia, and I still have the ashes in my home. When I realize my role as the chosen one and the rainmaker, I will raise her from the ashes.

I was in sorrow and deep agony for a few months, and I would lie in bed looking at the ceiling. Madison would lie next to me, would see me in deep thought and ask me, "Oscar, you never asked me what I wanted. You made promises to Sandra and Claudia, but never to me." Whenever she called me Oscar, I knew I was in big trouble, and I turned and looked at her. "Forget what I told Sandra. I just wanted to be nice to her before she died. I am not a banker or a rich man who can fulfill your wishes. I am a poor construction worker, sweetheart. Ask me something within my limitations." Madison started to roll my shirt buttons. "I know you, Oliver. It was not about Sandra. I have had this wish for a long time. After the war is over, will you take me to the place where Nathalie and my mom hid the car in the bush, and to my father's cemetery?"

I looked at her with surprise. "Is that what you want? I thought you would ask for some expensive dress or jewelry." Madison kissed me. "That is what women in true love ask. I love to go naked and empty before you, but I don't want to hide my body from your eyes with false objects."

One day Edgar and Nyah asked me to take them to the library to kill the ghost that had killed their father. They were very serious about it and they nagged me many times. I promised I would take them. They said they would take a knife to cut the throat of the ghost, and I accepted that. They carried holy water, oil, nails, knives, and crosses in their backpacks. I took them inside the burned library, and they both held on to my arm and were scared. We walked quietly into the ashes and burned floors. I took them to the floor where their fathers were found, and there was duct tape from the NYPD around where the bodies had been lying. They saw the blood on the walls and on the floor, and they were troubled in their hearts. They ran and started to write on the dried blood, "We love you, Dad." Edgar and Nyah asked me, "Where are the ghosts?" and I replied, "Maybe they went for a vacation or are hiding."

They asked me to take them all around the library and the place was haunted. They shouted, "Where are you, ghost? Come and fight us." They were desperate, and at least they wanted to see the ghost who had killed their fathers. I knew there was no ghost, and was just helping them to make sure. I wanted them to grow properly and forget about this in the future. They asked me whether we could see the ghosts, and I said, "If it killed your fathers, it means we can see them, but most of the time we cannot. But if we die and become ghosts, we will see them for sure. It is hit or miss." They asked me to go one final round to check and be certain that there were no ghosts or anyone to attack them. I said they could go by themselves, and I would wait on the first floor in the staircase.

They spent almost an hour looking for ghosts while I waited in the staircase. They returned with their heads down to where I was waiting for them. I could see both of their faces were angry and frustrated. I was depressed now. I had lost my daughter, Sandra, I couldn't stop the war, my search world was a mess, and life around me was chaos. I called Nyah and said, "I know you are upset, and somehow the ghosts escaped or are hiding where we can't find them. I want you two to forget about killing or seeking revenge on the ghost and grow up properly with a good life.

"Think of me as the ghost, and stab me with your knife as many times as you can until you feel you have avenged your father's death. I will become a ghost after I die, and I will find all the ghosts who killed your father, I promise." Both of them turned their faces away from me, and Edgar said, "Your word will be your destiny." He sounded weird, and when he turned to me, his eyes were red, his eyeballs went in and looked at me with great anger, and he pulled a gun from his bag. I panicked and shook him and asked him to put the gun down. He woke up and saw me, and he was shocked and said, "Oliver, my father came into my body and spoke to me."

I was in utter confusion, and I realized Edgar was hallucinating. I asked him where he got a gun. He said it was his father's personal one, and I grabbed one of his shoulders. I called Nyah and wanted them to take them out and leave the library. Nyah turned, and her eyes were filling with answers. She looked normal and quiet and said, "My father always said that your life was based upon the very word you speak. The day he died, before he left for work, he kissed me and said, 'I don't think I will come again. I have a calling. Always remember, Nyah, be a good girl to your mom, and answer all the questions of those close to you. It is your word from your mouth.' Because he said he would never come back, I used to think about what his calling was, and I realized just now that I saw my father's shadow, and he whispered, 'Tell Oliver to be happy, as I am happy now, and tell him the message I taught you.'"

I was shocked to hear her say that, and I fell back and sat on the stairs. They both walked to me and touched my head, and Nyah said, "You got your answers, Oliver. You are always my best friend, and you never did anything wrong. I like you so much. Be happy and stop this war, and just believe what I said. I know who killed my father, and my father said it was his calling, and it was not a killing or murder. My father gave his life to send this message to you. Let's go, Oliver."

When they had walked into the building earlier, they had cuddled in my arms, but when we came out, they held my hands and walked me out. We went to the same ice cream parlor we had gone to the first time. We got strawberry-flavored scoops, I was looking at both of them, and they were staring at the ice cream. I tapped the table and said, "Now, you tell me, Edgar, why your eyeballs went inside and you said your father came into your body." He didn't say a word, and took the spoon and started eating the ice cream and looked out the window for a while.

Then he said, "You said that to seek revenge for the ghosts, kill me, and you would turn into a ghost and punish the ghosts that killed my father. As soon as you said that, some white vibration that looked like thunder entered my body. I resisted it, and it said, 'I am your father,' and I eased myself into it. The white thing went into my body and said, 'Take the gun and shoot Oliver,' and I had no control over myself. I wanted to shoot you, but then you were shaking me, and I saw Nyah's father whisper to my father, and my father said, 'Forget it. It was my calling, also. I just realized it. Don't shoot Oliver,' and they all left."

It sounded like a fantasy to me, but they had both said one thing in common, with two different statements. Edgar said, "Your word will be your destiny," and Nyah said, "Always be positive, and all the answers are in your mouth." How can two kids come up with one idea with different wordings? This started to trouble me. Nyah didn't eat the ice cream and was looking at me, and I didn't have the guts to look her in the eyes. Then Edgar jumped in and asked, "Nyah, you said you knew who killed our fathers. Do you know them?" and Nyah smiled and said, "Some chosen ghosts." Edgar didn't understand her properly and asked again, "What ghosts?" and she said, "Some bad ghosts."

Edgar asked Nyah, "You said your father was happy. Is my father happy, too?" Nyah looked at him, touched his cheek, and said, "They are happier than us, and they asked us also to be happy. Will you, Edgar?" Edgar replied, "Yeah. And we don't need to hunt the bad ghosts, again?" Nyah smiled and said, "They have all become good friends with our fathers, so we should drop it." Edgar clenched his teeth and said, "Cool. We did it."

After eating the ice cream, I walked them home. Edgar said goodbye, and I saw there was a complete change in his face. He looked peaceful, and he went home quickly. Nyah was standing before the apartment gate looking at me, and I said, "Do you know which ghost killed your father?" She came running at me and hugged me, kissed me on the cheek, and said, "I didn't know you were the chosen one, but my father told me that today. Say hello to your bodyguard." She turned and ran away to the gate and then turned back. "No guilt, Oliver. We'll always be friends. You got your answers. Save us all," and she went into her home.

Nyah knew that Demonthin had killed her father, which meant there were ghosts in the AZ building. But she was not angry anymore, and she was happier than before. She told me that I was the chosen one, and her father had said that. Do ghosts also know about my birth, or was that a hallucination happening in her head? I didn't think so, and I had survived against all odds and knew it was the real world. Everyone who interacts with my friends and me know I am the chosen one, the rainmaker, but how do I stop the war and restore peace on this earth? Edgar and Nyah gave me the answers, and they showed me the door. And the key was "WORD."

CHAPTER 21
THE MESSAGE

NOW YOU KNOW I HAVE BEEN LIVING IN TWO WORLDS: THE REAL WORLD and the search world. Why did I build the search world? The real world was in chaos. When I started to read the books, I began with the Bible, and it said that humans had begun life with wisdom, power, infinite happiness, infinite peace, and everlasting life, and we disobeyed and entered the abyss.

Does disobedience have such a bad effect? Yes, it does, and we unintentionally disobeyed Nathalie twice—one time when we were kidnapped by the pirates and thrown into the water, and the other time when we came back to the same place where we started. The other books in the library that we started to read, explore, and discuss really confused my mind and I didn't know how my friends felt about them. My mind was fully involved in them, and I wanted to find the puzzle. I felt more weight on my shoulders than the others did, because there were lots of lives lost because of me, and all my friends believed in me and lost their futures. Time and pressure gave me a headache, and the concepts from the books were powerful and overwhelming, and their ideas were mind-blowing and their views outstanding, and I was nothing to all the writers who wrote those millions of books.

It was no joke to find an answer in a universe of infinite ideas and knowledge. I decided to leave this real world and build my own world—my own search world with the stars, moon, sun, and the planets—the same as my real world but with my views and understanding. I built this world in my mind when I was twelve years old and developed reasoning, logic, principles, laws, and motions of thought.

For the first time, I entered the search world. It was 3:00 p.m. on a fine afternoon in the real world. My mind was in a trance, and I flew like an angel, like a Superman, like a bird, and when I landed in my search world, it was perfect, and for the first time, I felt that I was the creator of this world. My eyes were filled with light, and the light purified me. There was white scenery, and everything looked like a cloud. It took hours for that vision to subside, and then I saw the mountains, seas, oceans, valleys, rocks, gardens, birds, animals, reptiles, giant mammals, fishes, grass, trees, fruit, ponds, and plateaus, and it was a beautiful sight. I saw men, women, and children of all colors happily singing and playing in the fields. There was no pain, sorrow, agony, or death in them, and those elements of chaos were as far away as between east and west in their minds. Everyone knew me and bowed their heads when they saw me, both humans and all living creatures. I accepted their greetings, and in turn, I bowed my head. There was peace and harmony everywhere, and the word *violence* was not heard of.

I walked and walked and enjoyed the view and calmness in it. I went to the mountain and sat on the edge of a cliff and viewed my creation, proud of myself. While I was thinking about the greatness of my mind, I realized the purpose of my life. Then a scroll fell from the sky, and I ran to see what was in it. I opened it and saw numbers, starting from 4 billion and ending with zero, and from zero it went to 2041 AD. And at the very bottom of the scroll was written, "Pick a year and you will travel there." I was thinking repeatedly about which year to pick: the time of the Big Bang or the time when the first human was born. My mind was clouded with thoughts, and my hand was moving over all the numbers.

There was a sunset, and I saw elephants were bringing me fruit in a basket, and a crane was bringing a jug of water. I ate apples, oranges, grapes and peaches, and I drank the water in the jug, and it was sweet. Then a lion came running at me, and it was very big and lifted me up. I had the scroll in my hand, and I sat on his back as he ran fast. I was about to fall when the lion asked me to lie down on his back and hold on tight. He took me to a cave, and I found a beautiful bed of flowers in it, and the light inside the cave was bright. The lion went and turned the lights off, and I went to bed. I heard a loud voice, and it frightened me, and I walked slowly outside the cave and saw there was something written on the ground. It said, "2040. . . ." I thought it was a message, so I went back and picked up the scroll and touched the number 2040, and it asked me when and where I wanted to start, and I didn't know. Then I heard a voice from the sky say, "The nineties were fun—pick that," and I didn't even cross-check before I picked the number 1992.

Then there was thunder and rain from the sky, and the beautiful world I had created was dark and filled with smoke. A wind came and carried me, and I was floating vertically and spinning around the earth a million times, and the wind threw me into the desert. I got up from the sand, and my face, pockets, and underwear were filled with sand. I started to shake the sand away from my body and I saw a camel walking toward me. He was chewing food and said, "Were you looking for an oil well?" I replied to him, "No, my beautiful view is lost. What would I do with an oil well? Grease myself?" The camel sat down and laughed, saying, "You are funny. No more views for you. You like America." I replied to the camel, "I am from America, and I am lost. Do you want to take me there?" and the camel said, "No one can take you there. You should be born again." The camel confused me, and I said, "How should I be born again?" and he grew angry, got up, and left me. I was chasing him to get the answer, but he ran away from me. I was sitting in the desert alone, and two birds came to me. One was an eagle and the other was a pigeon. The eagle said, "Did you ask the camel a silly question?" and I replied to him, "No, I asked him about my doubt, and he ran away." The eagle replied, "He was very mean," and then the pigeon said, "You need to pick a mother and father to be born again." I replied to the pigeon, "I didn't have parents in the real world, so how could I do that?" The pigeon said, "In the search world, you have to be born again, Oliver. Pick someone you know." At the time, I remembered Madison's father, James, the first man who gave his life for me, and I said that the name James would be cool. I didn't know whom to pick for a mother. I didn't want Nathalie to sleep with James because they had a mother-and-son relationship, and I didn't want Stacey, Madison's mother, because then Madison would be my sister. At that time, I was reading the book *The Color Purple* because I liked the color purple and thought maybe it was a book about colors. I liked the name Olivia. I said to the pigeon, "Olivia," and the pigeon said, "Good choice, Oliver. Your father's name is James, and your mother's name is Olivia."

Then the pigeon turned and told the eagle to take me to America, and the eagle shook his body and became big, like an airplane. I sat on his back, and he flew fast. The eagle asked, "Do you know where to go in America?" and I said, "Milwaukee, Wisconsin." The eagle again turned and asked, "Which street?" and I joked with him, "Wall Street." The eagle laughed and said, "There is a Wall Street, but that was the old name. Hang on tight and I will take you." He dropped me there, and I fell in the middle of the road in my neighborhood. Everybody was busy doing their work, and kids were playing in the street. No one noticed me. I walked before everybody, unbeknownst to them, and then I looked at my hands, and they looked like shadows. A black car came by and stopped before a house. I saw a very pretty woman come out of the house in a purple dress and hat. It was my mother, Olivia, in the search world, and I ran to her, but she didn't see me. I saw the man in the car, and it was James Oscar, my father, and he looked different. He didn't look like Madison's father; rather, he had straight chestnut hair, a sharp face and smile, and a muscular body. I took the name of Madison's father anyway and shouted at him, calling him James, but he didn't listen to me. My mom stepped into the car, they kissed, and she said, "It is getting late for the movie." I got into the back of the car and realized they were still dating and not yet married. I went to the movie with them, and it was *The Godfather, Part III*. Al Pacino was in it. I marveled at his acting, and although I was a big fan of Matt Sterling, Al Pacino had a place in my heart. After the movie, they went out for dinner, and my dad was blushing, and my mom was looking into his eyes. He took a small box from his coat and opened it. Then he kneeled before her and proposed that they get married. My mom's heart was filled with joy, and he took her left hand and put the engagement ring on it. Everybody in the restaurant stood up, clapped, and wished my father well. They went home to make love, and out of ignorance, I went with them to the bedroom, but when they started to undress, I walked out of the room.

Days passed by, and I followed my mother and father, but they couldn't see or hear me. I loved to watch movies with them because I was always curious about the lost movies from the war. I watched *Good Fellas*, *Total Recall*, and *Captain America*, among others. I was never hungry or thirsty, and I was just like a shadow watching my whole world around me. No one noticed that I was there; it was as if I were invisible to everyone. I was very upset, and the pigeon came back and looked at me with sad eyes and asked, "Why?" and I said I had come searching for an answer in this search world, but no one ever saw or heard me. The pigeon said, "You will be back as the master of this world and have all the power to change it one hour before the wedding, so stay cool and see all the things that were before you." Then I asked the pigeon, "Will I begin like a real child, or will I carry all this processed knowledge?" and the pigeon replied, "You will have all the knowledge, and the day your mom conceives you, you will find real search triggers, and you will grow to have a special gift for searching and understanding. This whole world is based upon your mind, and you can import and export your ideas, feelings, and knowledge from the real world to the search world. It is your world, Oliver. Good luck, my friend." Before the pigeon left I asked it, "Will I know when I am grown here that I was from a different world? And after I find the answer, what will happen to me?" The pigeon said, "When you grow up, only your thoughts get imported from the real world, and every time you connect to the search world, the questions, ideas, and logic will follow from the real world, but you won't know where they come from. Once you are connected, your mind will go blank about the real world, and only your search world will exist." I was still not clear and said, "It sounds tricky," and the pigeon said, "There is a thin line, and you will get it when you start searching for it."

The pigeon left and I waited for the marriage to begin. But everybody who lived in my search world was doing things the way that they do them, and although I created the search world, I didn't have any power. The moment came one hour before the wedding, and I got my control back. I went and made the bellman drunk and made my dad's friends fire bullets into the air at the time when they exchanged rings. Yes, the first act I did, revolting the church, because I was sick and tired of religion and the harm it has done to this world. Where did I get this idea? It came from the real world, from all the atheist books that were so well known in the Western world of ignorance. After the wedding, my parents made love many times, and I made them talk in the way I liked to search. Why did I choose to search for superheroes in my life? Because I was a big zero in the real world. I couldn't save my girlfriend Madison when they abducted her to rape her or when the pirates stole Uncle Kadin or when Aika's mom killed herself. I couldn't fight back properly with Peyton and Jay Mons, and I couldn't save my best robot friend, Smith. And of all the dead bodies I burned, I could not wake anyone from the ashes, and the little boy Yohance and his family were killed, and I couldn't make Uncle Purdhil get his vision back. I had failed at everything.

I wanted my father to be brave, so I made him a U.S. Marine to fight the bad guys, and he fought well. I made my mom religious because most of the problems were about religion. When I was conceived and in my mother's womb, I would listen to the world around me, thinking about it and searching it. I was very happy in my mother's womb because I knew my mother and father even before I popped out. In the real world, until now, I hadn't known either of them. I even picked a name for my family, Oscar Shrine, and I didn't know anything about that name, except the first piece. I was still happy with my last name Oscar, and I should have felt like one of the luckiest people in the world because my best girlfriend chose my last name.

My mind was always filled with Nathalie's prophecy, so when I was born, I wanted to see her face, and I made her the midwife and nurse in my neighborhood. I opened my eyes in the search world and everything was perfect, and I saw Nathalie—the woman I admired and loved the most . . . my sweet Nathalie. I properly fed on my mother's breasts for milk, not suckling other women's breasts. I built a strong bond with my mom while she fed me. The bond was always there from biology, and that was one of the reasons I started to love Madison, even when I was a kid, because I suckled my mother's breasts for milk. It was a beautiful thing, and I enjoyed every moment of it. I saw very clearly how my father showed my mom the same love he had shown her the first time he met her. As I started to grow, I searched everything and saw with my eyes how I made Uncle Tim my father's best friend. He came with his wife and children, who were dead in the real world. I saw happiness in his face, and he saw his dead ones walking with him, and he gave me a $20,000 check for my birthday. I was the God in my own search world, and I resurrected Uncle Tim's family.

In the first few years in the search world, I always tried to understand what exactly religion was. Every time I went in and out of the secret library, I saw the Bible, which is called the book of books. The search world I was building was based on all the ideas, emotions, and knowledge I carried from the real world and my own experiences and the information in the books. I was depressed many times in the real world, and the books I read were filled with negativity. The big library was built to protect the Bible, which meant there was likely something in it. That was why I chose to be born to a Christian family and made my mom religious. If it hadn't been for the Bible that the library was built around, I would have chosen Mohammed as my name, or Chin or something. This library was built by the Strass family, and I didn't know who this great family was, but Nathalie was the one who knew. To build a secret library like this, the family had to be rich, and this was why I had Nathalie be born into a rich family called Strass and settle down in my neighborhood. I made Nathalie like Florence Nightingale, "The Lady with the Lamp," a social reformer who cared for and nursed sick people and orphan kids like us. I didn't know her background except that she was the woman from the real Fourth Dimension, and I gave her two good children and a husband. I should have let her live happily with them, but I killed her two children and husband in an accident and made her devoted to us, and this made her a noble lady in my search world.

A good thing I did was make Nathalie the midwife for Niki, which was not true in the real world, but later I realized that there should be a difference in births from the different ends of the world with different midwives, so I ended Nathalie's role as the midwife. But the order in which we had met in the real world was the same in the search world, to create a sense of reality in both worlds. I met Ejaz, and he moved to my neighborhood. His father worked under my father at the bank. I should have made him a shah or oil sheik, but I decided if he was under my father and me, he would be protected. I took Ejaz and his family as our friends and tried to understand the difference between the Islamic and Christian faiths, but everyone was well behaved. To be honest, in the search world they didn't need a God or religion, because I was the God. They should have worshipped me, but I acted like a good creator and made them choose their religion, and I fed them with ideas, which I acquired from the real-world books. Then I made Niki drown in the river and at the edge of time, he recognized me, and I appeared to him as God, and he found the true creator of this world and said, "Help me, Oliver," but I didn't. I waited for two angels, Aika and Shu, to build a romance. I should have made Niki walk on water, but I just watched him die while expecting miracles, and I observed the patterns of death, and no one died in water in my search world, like a novelist does when they wait for the right time to cut a character out and make the readers excited and thrilled.

I felt like a maniac because of all the craziness that came from the books I had read. I was angry at the segregated education system in this search world, where the smart kids went to one place, the average kids went to another place, and the below-average kids went to another place. The smart kids would always be smart, and the weak would always be the weak. What blasphemy this world gave us, but they used a different term for it—*quality education*—which meant you deserve what you are, survival of the fittest. I liked Jesus's teachings about the sick needing the doctors, not the healthy people. This idea is similar to saying that the weak kids should go to MIT or Harvard to become smart, and the smart kids, because they were already smart, could be educated anywhere. I proved in Niki's drowning incident that it was right to make Aika and Shu save him, who went to the public school. We were all legends, and we all were of natural intelligence, but we should have used it. The saying "All men were created equal" still holds true. I still liked the bicycles we rode when Judah and Aika had pneumonia, and I couldn't forget the incident of Madison falling down and hurting herself when the drone bombed us in the cross fire. I made her fall and bruise her head, and I ran back to save her to be romantic, but then her mom locked her up for a month. I read a few romance novels and wanted to feel how it would be if I met a girlfriend after some time. In the real world, I had to see her every day, and she was like a caterpillar in the leaves.

Then we were introduced to Shu and Aika's family and all the traditional stuff they brought us into. I created the old Chinese couple who gave me the dragon, and I made Wang and Kew the mother and father of Shu, another parentless kid, like me. I was a better designer now, revolutionized, and in the real world, their kids had abandoned them and they spent their lives lonely. I gave them the best kid they could ever have in Shu, and I made them a young couple instead of an old, wrinkled, toothless couple. I converted the Kew family from Chinese to Japanese and gave them a new daughter in Noa. I destroyed all the traditional wars between the Chinese and the Japanese. I made Wang's family, again, abandon him and not help when he needed money. I made him realize the values of humanity and made Aika's family help, as well as my father. At times, when help was needed, it came from many directions and from many people. It was not a custom you had to stick to, as opposed to the custom and tradition of fearing that your people would not help you if you wanted to violate them. I broke everything and proved everything was wrong, and determined that as humans, we should love and care for each one, no matter what the differences were.

Did I find any answers in the search world? No, not yet, but I was still dealing with religion, racism, and human cultural and traditional habits. I even made another parentless boy, Judah, part of a rich family of Jewish doctors, Dr. Enoch and Dr. Ruth Enoch. There were many reasons I gave him to them. First, Judah always carried the guilt that he didn't clean and treat Nathalie when she was hurt, and because of him, she died. I wanted him to be happy and forget all the guilt he had, so I made him a medical expert. Second, in the Bible the chosen people are Jewish, and I thought if I gave Judah to a Jewish family, maybe I could find an answer, but I didn't; rather, I saw good and bad Jewish people. Tziyon is an example of the bad Jewish, and Judah's family were obviously the good. I made Sharon, a stripper in the real world, work for Tziyon in his jewelry shop. I gave her a decent job, but not a real one. She was an assistant who helped customers. I knew people used pretty women to promote their businesses and impress customers, and it was an exploitation of women. I read about all their customs and cults, and I created a Jewish world for the answers. It was not only for the Jewish; it applies to everyone, the Irish, Polish, Austrian, German, Gypsies, and every other "ish" and "ian." Since Jewish people made up the most prominent ethnic group for quite a long time, I was interested in them. We collected all the saved money to buy a gift. My mind went so low that I was talking about the saved money, and as the creator of this universe, I should have been talking about trillions, but all the books I read made me think only of a few thousand dollars as saved money.

Somewhere I read that if you don't forgive, you will suffer eternal bad karma, and you will never understand your purpose in life. I could not forgive Kevin Burner, the child abuser who licked Madison, and I would never in my life forget him. I let him in my world to do a little damage, and he was just a mugger who broke Shu's hand for no reason. The reason I broke Shu's hand was because "In a fight, battle, and war, there could be losses on both ends," and a half-punk saying polluted my mind and made me break Shu's hand. In the same way, I wanted anti-TUAD and its evilness to go away, so I made Judah's mother donate money to TUAD and even made Nathalie give money to it. I cleaned it up and made TUAD a good place where they do real charity work; basically, I washed the American hypocritical government scam of TUAD from existence. I thought forgiveness worked and I still couldn't find an answer.

All I wanted to relay was the message that I imported both the knowledge from the books I read in that library and my real-life experiences into my search world. I feasted well with all types of food from all nations. I made Uncle Kadin a police officer in the search world, which was his wish. We won the football match with Ambrose and showed that we were powerful, and I showed my dominion over my world. I killed Nathalie with a heart attack and gave her a silent death rather than a traumatic gunshot wound. And I took a group photo of the nine chosen friends. I said all the poetry and touching words about her death, but the real reason I killed Nathalie was that she was the one who said I was the chosen one, and I knew she knew more than I did. I didn't want her to mess with my world by giving me instructions, because if she was better than I was, then why was she not the chosen one? That was the reason she came and died in the real world rather than taking us to New York City and telling us about the whole mission.

Well, you will all like these three words, you patriot punks: *War Against Terrorism*. I read a lot of this stuff in the library, and the experience I went through in the real world made me think like you. I kneel now and ask forgiveness to Ejaz for what I did to his good family, which I involved in terrorism. If I said that to him, he would be heartbroken, and I have already committed many injustices to him in the search world. Of all my friends, if I wanted to die for someone, it would be for Ejaz only, not even Madison. When I built this concept in my search world, I knew it was wrong to say something like that, but I wanted to bite the bullet and say, "Muslims are the holiest and most peaceful people in the world." I made my father prove that not all Islamic people were violent and freed Mukhlis, Ejaz's father, from his problem. To prove that Ejaz's father was an innocent person, we all fought for him, from all different colors and beliefs together, and this was the first attempt I made to unite all the souls together. We couldn't punish Jay Mons in the real world, but in the search world I didn't want any child abusers to exist, so I hooked him up with bank robbery and crime. What a thrilling story I created by reading all the thriller novels in that goddamn library.

Did I succeed in finding an answer in this search world? No, I was just beating around the bush. I wanted my father to die, so that if I grew up as a fatherless boy, I could find the truth and be inspired by all these biographies about successful people. I sent my father to war and killed him and wanted to wrap the American flag around him and tout myself as someone who could say, "My father gave his life for this country, but taking other lives is ruthless." I was proud of myself for these stunts and made my mother a widow. A genius said, "Poverty teaches lessons and poorness will shape you." I took those words of wisdom and made us poor, and my mother became a clerk in that bank. I watched my mother's loyalty to my dead father, and she didn't sleep with any men until I left the search world. I tested women's loyalties, and she performed well. She didn't sleep with any of my friends' fathers, or her bosses or neighbors. I made her perfect. All these ideas came from R Smith, because he transformed into a human in the real world and never dated or kissed other robots because he was living with his memories of R Becky. If a robot had hope and love for eternity, then what were we humans doing? Getting remarried to someone? What nasty people we are who can forget the love of one and find another. My mother was religious and she believed in God. If that was the case, then she would wait for her turn to die and meet my father in heaven rather than remarry, and she did it the way I expected her to. Because that is what men with real pride like to do, and I did it because I didn't want her to marry a man who comes home drunk and abuses me and her and all that nonsense from my stepfather. There were millions of stories about that, and people liked to read them, but I hated those things.

I made Moise Boti the man who saved our lives in TUAD and made him work for my father and be the messenger to tell my father's dreams that I had to be a hacker. He shared a heroic story of how my father died, and I was happy to hear it. But I made Moise Boti single, to ease his pain for the lost son and physically disabled wife, and I learned from his bachelor life how someone can be happy and live their own life, rather than having a ruined family life. Then I decided to choose my career as an anti-hacker. I chose this profession because it was one of the professions that was demanding, in those times and up to now.

Then I met Simula Jones, a man who opened my eyes. Who was this man in the real world? He was the only good hacking teacher I knew at TUAD, and he was very kind to us and always helped us learn how to hack. He taught us the fundamentals, and because we hated TUAD so much, I didn't have the chance to explain about him. There are many people like Simula Jones who cause a change in your life, yet you never have time to revisit them and say thank you. Instead, you always look for the best. I wanted to be different and wanted a man to completely change my life. I picked an ugly, blind, depressed, and weak man of no hope—yes, Uncle Purdhil—to walk with me. I made Purdhil Ejaz's true uncle. I made his teeth look good, and I made him the most handsome man and the wisest man on this earth. I made him start on the wrong path because that was what all false and terrorist organizations do. They pollute the minds of bright young people with hypocritical teachings. I opened his eyes to see the goodness in his religion through Buddhism and gave him a radical change, and he became a true human. I took him from that dark room and gave him eyes to see the world around him. There are millions of people like Uncle Purdhil, with all their visions and knowledge, who die in a corner. I gave him a decent job and made him my own philosophy teacher, and he did an excellent job. I picked for him the most beautiful woman from North Korea, called He-Ran. I didn't pick a woman from South Korea because I wanted to destroy the problem between the United States and North Korea. I learned philosophy well, especially PMT (Philosophy of Modern Technology). I thought I was Plato's boy because the world believed philosophy had changed people's lifestyles. But my heart was still empty, and I didn't find the answer that I was looking for.

I called this a *"bunker's mind."* I stayed in my neighborhood for sixteen years, and I didn't go anywhere and thought I would find an answer in the place where I was born. Had I found an answer in the search world yet? No. I decided to study well and go to college with all the so-called people of success, because in the real world we didn't even graduate from the third grade and couldn't get a job anywhere. The first time I left my neighborhood, I thought the answers were far, maybe even seven seas, away. I didn't want to see my friends and mom, and maybe that was the reason I couldn't find an answer. I needed new sets of faces and new thoughts, and I went with my mom in the car, saying goodbye to my old ways of thinking. When I was driving the car, I drove fast enough to kill my mother and became a parentless kid so I would be stronger and would learn better things in my pain. My mind was messed up with all the nonsense books I read in that library, and I looked very deeply into the eyes of my mother, and I couldn't do it; I didn't kill her and let her go.

I reached Boston to find an answer to my search. We were doing laborers' jobs, and I didn't want to revolutionize but let me be the product of this universe, thinking maybe I could find a way. I couldn't find an answer to my search, and I designed the Chelsea neighborhood with African people. That was where I met Yohance and Jacob. It was not only a slavery camp, but also a holocaust camp. I didn't build any barbwire fences and gas them. I didn't give them any education or good jobs. I just gave them a basic living. I watched and observed the human patterns and behaviors in those situations. I was expecting a hero, a warrior, and a rebel who would fight against it, but there was awareness in them because they accepted a life like that. I wanted to free them, break their chains, and liberate them, but I was greedy, and I didn't want any rebel or revolutionary to rise from there. So, before that, I put my feet in their shoes and promised to deliver them. I wanted big shoulders to carry them and to be famous for what I did. So, I tried to change their lives by teaching them philosophy and providing them with a good education. I thought the answers would be in slavery, but I made a whole mess for them. I read about all the black and white problems, and my eyes filled with tears, and I became emotionally moved and wanted to destroy it forever, and I did.

I couldn't find any answers, even when I introduced Vernon, the African-American who first denied helping his own people. I killed his family to make him realize his folly, and he did and gave all his wealth to the African people in Chelsea. The reason I killed his family was that Tziyon, in the real world, lost all his family and was still greedy for money and wanted to buy Niki's home. He never realized in his life that these were people who believed in inheritance and bloodlines. But Vernon did, and he made a difference and proved he was better than anyone else. Although I was from the so-called Fourth-Dimensional world, I built them a Third-Dimensional library to learn the essentials in those time periods, because education was for all and awareness was important.

I made Professor Gavin Higgs my professor and worked with him to attain a Nobel Prize. I thought getting social recognition would make me feel better, and it did, because in the real world, I was tired of being taunted. Now, I had a Nobel Prize in my world. I won the president's award and caused Nelson Mandela to give me his own award, Nelson Mandela's Hall of Fame and Freedom Award.

That was really funny because I enslaved them from the knowledge of my real world and I freed them, but I still managed to get an outstanding award. Now my shoulders were filled with stars, but I needed more honors, always more and more. I enjoyed it when I walked on the red carpet with so much pride. We humans live a life waiting for someone to do something wrong so we can jump in and fix things and gain social recognition, with people saying, "These were the right dudes." I was like you, no big difference, just waiting for the weak ones to fall.

I traveled to Africa and had a good vacation, but I didn't go to the most dangerous parts of Africa because of the bloody tribal wars. So I copied myself and created a new Oliver called Oliver the Traveler. He looked like me, and I gave him a task to go explore the world and all its countries and all corners of this universe and come back to me, while I went to New York City to work in a bank and become one more Wall Street douche bag. Oliver the Traveler went to all parts of Africa, China, India, Mongolia, Middle Eastern countries, Australia, New Zealand, all parts of Europe, and even Antarctica and the Arctic . . . every place where other men had never set foot. Oliver the Traveler was out, and I realized I had wasted all my time in Boston, so then I went to New York City to work in a bank called Harvest and Reap.

We were always looking for help, and we found happiness and thanked whoever helped us. It was called the receiving end, and there was never any attempt to be on the giving end. I had the same mentality when Judah's father gave me the big house to live in. I knew I had created this world and should have the whole city of New York as my house, but my thoughts were weak. Even in my world, I couldn't live in my own house, and I was ashamed of my thoughts and myself. I started a life in a bank, and I made Salomeya look adorable and be a charmed. I gave her a job at the front desk, where everybody had to see her face every day. I cured her of her birth sickness, and she was smart, could talk, and could listen to this world's music. I walked in my first day and greeted her, and

I saw the smile on her face thanking me. I decided to meet my enemies and take a big jump from a cliff to see what happened, life or death. I made Peyton my manager of all the politics that were part of my company. I read about corporate politics and political dramas in governments, and I wanted to put on those shoes to see how much it stinks. In the name of the word *politics*, how many innocent lives were taken or destroyed? I made myself a victim, cursing the world and its evilness.

Well, while I was sailing in my thoughts on pain and failures, with depressing songs playing on my iPod in my search world, I decided to destroy prostitution and created a new life for my lovely daughter, Claudia, and restore justice. I devised a fascinating, thrilling story for Claudia. I wanted to make sure the characters were fictional so I would not be responsible for them. I knew a few characters in that murder novel I created, such as Sandra, Claudia, and Glenn Hitch. All the others I made up because I didn't know anyone else from the real world. They were the banker, Langdon, and his killer brother, Millet; Fernando, the defendant; a judge; cops; the jury; and so on. Those were fictional characters I created, but they represented all the innocent victims who lost their lives by brutal murder or crimes, whether unpunished or punished. I made the right judgment, and the innocent were freed. That court represented all the hearings and crimes in this universe, and it was just an accumulation of all the crimes ever committed in human history. That was why I made the brother kill his own brother for money. Neither evolution nor creation, we all come from a single parent, and if we kill anyone, we are killing our own brothers and sisters. If this single thought goes into everyone's mind, there will be no war for anything. Of course, Steve Jobs was true in that crime story, and his masterpiece, the iPhone, helped him find the truth. I gave Claudia a good mother and father in a pure state of life. I should have given them a new place to live and better jobs, but I made them work under me. I thought I was the one who could protect them, and my selfish thoughts made them stay with me. I made Fernando, Claudia's father, a false murderer and made him spend time in prison for a mistake he made in the real world. He was one of the men who visited Sandra for sex, but he never knew that he gave life to someone. He just paid and left his sperm to do the work. When Claudia showed up in the real world, she was Q-HIV positive, and the hospital laws had a policy that if you were a prostitute and had Q-HIV, they would never match your blood and DNA blood samples with their database to tell you who your father was. My daughter was the curse of all men who slept with Sandra, and I realized that was not right, and I wanted to save Fernando, her father in the search world. I brought Glenn Hitch, one of the best men I had met in my life, who saved us from TUAD and the escape. He fought well, and I made him build a law college as a place where law was for everyone. I exposed the law systems in the world and made Claudia throw shoes at men who solicited prostitutes in the real world and for the injustice to her father in the search world. That case was the victory of humanity and innocent people under the law. I went to all the prisons in the world, yes, again copying myself as Oliver the Prison Explorer, to visit them and come back. I traveled to the worst prisons in Third World countries and collected all the stories of crime and a list of innocent people.

Yet, did I find my answer in the search world? No, I just got more depressed and angry. I wanted to jump, and I went crazy drinking and walked with the Occupy Wall Street crowd to bring the corporate world down. Basically, I wanted to destroy the world I had created, and I went that far. But Patricia walked into my life to calm me down, and she was the first gentle and kind woman. I first met her when we came out of the bunker. She said, "Maybe you were the chosen one, Oliver, and you should guide us all." I denied the words *chosen one* in the whole search world because I thought everyone was equal, and although I was drunk with too many shots, everything went down, and I realized I was close to the doors of finding the truth.

I made my little friends Edgar and Nyah be my colleagues, and they were of my same age. They walked into the world of Science of Verbum Victus, and that was where I met Dan Root. Edgar and Nyah were two aspects of the real world where I had a clue about what I was looking for, and the little ones who revealed to me the answer to my search. My encounter with Dan Root started to unlock the secrets in my life and resolved all my questions and mysteries. Dan Root taught me and explained it well, but still my mind did not accept him. The only reason was that we thought the answers should be complicated. But the answers were very simple, and it was close to our minds, our tongues, and our words.

I couldn't believe it myself when Dan explained it to me. I thought it was a sort of mantra or prayer or magician's trick, and I was playing with Science of Verbum Victus. I was insulting myself, and I even wanted to verify it with an accident, and I pressed the gas pedal on the Ferrari. I actually tricked the speedometer and made Madison believe I was driving 50 mph, but I pushed it to 200 mph and made the truck run to 150 mph. I distracted Madison by making her look into my eyes, but I actually wanted to kill her and wake her from the ashes to see whether there was power in my words, or whether Dan Root's teachings were legit. I loved Madison so much that I couldn't do it, and I just sliced the car and made it look like a small accident and convinced myself that my words would bring her back to life. I didn't believe it, though, and I never believed Dan Root; I thought he was a scam artist and cult figure with a white beard.

When we had a problem in my company, the Russians and the CEO gave me this project to handle, and Gwyneth fought for me. I made Gwyneth fight for me in a company meeting against Peyton. An eye for an eye, a tooth for a tooth, a TUAD member for a TUAD member: that was what I learned from the *World Book of Knowledge*. I was sitting in Central Park and thinking about how to resolve this problem and establish my name in the company. I was even thinking about the power of the WORD, and my mind was confused. I saw something flying in the sky, and as it got closer, I saw the wings, and I recognized it was the eagle and the pigeon. The eagle was carrying the other two Olivers and the pigeon. Both the Olivers were wearing black suits with black ties, and they said, "We have searched as you said," and they merged into my body, and I became one complete Oliver. What did both Olivers do? They just went through all the books in the library that explained the topics of culture, people, civilization, prison life, language, history, archeology, language, and geography. They went and searched in the search world and learned all the knowledge and wisdom in it and reported back to me.

The pigeon had gotten old and couldn't fly anymore, but the eagle was still strong and vigilant. I stretched my body, crossed my legs, and looked at the pigeon. "You tricked me, you lied to and fooled me, saying that when I was conceived and born again, I would have the power in this search world, but I was wandering as a shadow and wasting my time. I controlled everything from the beginning, because you, little bird, defined me as the supreme creature." The pigeon bowed his head to the ground and his tears were flowing. I felt bad that I had hurt him, and I apologized. The pigeon said with his head down, "Master, my lord, you have realized your true identity and power, and I am glad," and I was puzzled, since he had always called me Oliver. I went and lifted his head with my hands and looked in his eyes and said, "Why did you call me master and lord?" and he replied, "When you came here, you didn't realize fully that you were the creator of this world, and your mind was filled with fantasies, wizardries, and animated stories. I checked your understanding and you were still a kid. You realized your true identity, role, power, purpose, and might in this world, and your word was making you more perfect." I was mystified by his thoughts and asked him gently, "Again, what do you mean by 'your word was making you more perfect'?"" The pigeon just said, "That's all I know, and that's what I said. Believe in yourself, master, and become stronger, and your word will do it." He didn't say goodbye. He just got back on the eagle's back and sat. The eagle looked at me and said, "I was very proud of you, master. We are your friends and servants. Make us also live long. Send the lighting and thunder to Russia. Goodbye, master, for now." They flew away from me, and my first friends in this search world went far into the skies. I never saw them after that. I didn't know how they knew all the things they had told me. By sending the thunder and lightning, is that the way I would prevent this hacking from Russia? I did send the thunder and lightning to Russia, but I couldn't strongly believe it.

I was promoted to CIO of the company. My dream through my word was fulfilled that day. I wanted to thank Dan, and I remembered to wake my father up from the dead. I really killed him in the search world because of the notion that if I grew up fatherless, with crudeness from society and people, I would be more aggressive and somehow I could find an answer. Because I killed my own blood, the man who gave me life, I couldn't wake him up, and that was the very first time I lost my control and power over the search world I had created. It took me a month to do it, and I even went to the cemetery and opened up the grave and saw his bones, but when I touched them, they turned into powder and dust. Yes, when the building blew, he was burned, and I was in terrible pain, and all the ashes and bones were collected by themselves and settled down in and buried in an anonymous cemetery in Iraq. He was my father, and I killed my own blood, and the universe sent angels from the sky, and they did wake him, because he was my father, the God of this world. This time, I had no choice. My final chance to believe in the Science of Verbum Victus provided me with the true answer. For a month, I got headaches, and I said the same thing again and again: "Wake up, Father, from the ashes." I said it a billion times, and my mind was about to explode. Then I saw him through the window, and I realized I had woken up my father. In that moment, I felt that I had found the answer to the puzzle in that library. It was the Science of Verbum Victus. I rejoiced, and I went to see Dan Root, Edgar, and Nyah, but they were all missing. Salomeya was sitting on the wrong floor, Demonthin had left me, and even Madison, my dad, Fernando, Sandra, and Claudia—everybody—were missing. My mind was hurting me so bad, and my head was about to explode, and my search world was not working in the way that I expected. At that time, I felt the moment of truth that I had found the answer and was no more a creator here, my purpose was fulfilled and I had lost my power. I didn't want to drag myself anymore through that search world, still looking for better answers, so I left it as it was and came back to the real world with answers.

Was the search world a dream world? No, it was a world that I built through my mind and word, and it existed virtually somewhere. The dream was the one concept that was widely spoken of. Humans became so ignorant; they stopped all their thoughts at the first place they started, the dream. The dream was just an interface between body, mind, soul, and consciousness. It was just the beginning of a shadow of revelation, just by dreaming and changing the dream. As humans, we cannot do anything otherwise. The mind has to believe the dream, and the word has to be spoken, and then the dream kicks in. It is the word that takes the actions and fulfills all your desires. Without the word, dreams and the mind are nothing, but with your word, you can control your dream and mind. Everyone dreams every day, and there are a trillion dreams a day that travel to the roof of this universe and nothing happens. How many people dream of being rich? How many really make it? A handful. Why is that? Your dream should have great power to achieve it, but it has no effect unless you are opening your mouth to speak constructively: the Science of Verbum Victus.

Although I created a perfect world, I had all the problems of my real life. I built my life based upon what I read in this library, thanks to all the writers over the centuries who spent their time and dedicated their lives to writing on the subject of their expertise. I appreciated all their thoughts and the time they put in, their expressions, and their genius, but did they fix anything? Those were only the works of fallen men, though; from the wind tunnel that our forefathers built and the evolution story that Dan Root told us. This example leads us to ponder what sort of world we live in and what sort of lifestyle and thoughts we surf, day in and day out. From all the books that were in this secret library with all its knowledge and wisdom, imagine that we heard of a parallel world that was just the same as our galaxy, with a sun, a moon, an earth, eight planets, stars, the Milky Way, water on the earth for life, and everything the same as us. America, Russia, China, Japan, and all the superpowers would spend trillions of dollars to go there. In the name of exploration, colonization, and life extension, each one would fight like a dog, steal information, resources, and scientists, and even bomb the others to go there. Say that American astronauts went there first, and then the Russians soon after, followed by the Chinese and the Japanese. We would start to fight, and a war would happen to see who owns the land and how far the boundaries are set, and finally we would settle down with lots of blood lost. Americans would have one more Fourth of July and import people from poor Third World countries to go to the parallel world and build it. Then there would be a revolution for freedom and liberty, and we would have another Martin Luther King Jr., another Che Guevara, and other freedom fighters. Following this, we would give awards for books, TV shows, Broadway shows, entertainment in the form of comedy, and movies based upon the true story of *War in the Parallel World*. So what is the big deal with this space explorer story? It shows how the knowledge that we have gained through our entire time is a great folly, talking about the negativity and failures of life again and again.

You may wonder what point I am trying to make. Though we had infinite knowledge and wisdom spawned by intellectuals, geniuses, and legends, we still have chaos and problems in this world. Why? Everyone who has had a message to tell this world has had very good intentions, but they have failed to provide an answer to all the chaos and problems of humankind. Why? Did all of them race for intelligence or have selfish thoughts to make their names exalted, and miss the fundamental theory of everything? ***This is a message from Oliver Oscar to all living forces across all Universes.*** I have finally found the solution to all the problems in human life: it is the Science of Verbum Victus. The only reason I feel it is the strongest force is that once I found the answer, my own search world kicked me out and I couldn't go back. With the most powerful concept in my mind, I knew all the problems in this world. What could I say in one line about all these millions of books in the library? "All these books were written by fallen men, and their wisdom was based upon utmost ignorance, failures, alternate ideas, and weakness." The world is based upon the biggest lie of all time, good versus evil, which is a universal concept. "We do it for the betterment of humanity." Is that wrong? My answer is that there is only good, and the word *evil* should not escape from our mouths. I want to slap the first person who said there was evil. That was the beginning of the destruction of life in this system. If this basic theory and practice is broken, humanity will rule the world once again.

Where do I start? Who is responsible for the destruction of humanity? We all are, each and every one of us. Knowingly or unknowingly we all did it, and we cannot escape this responsibility. It started from the very words that we spoke day in and day out, whether those were lies, bedtime stories, or curses; whether it was about psychology, revolution, conceptual expression, religious rivalry, wisdom speech, freedom of speech, cultural values, the status quo, patriotism, philosophy, or equality. It multiplied in the name of literature, comprising epics, poetry, journals, biographies, drama, stage plays, folktales, ballads, books, encyclopedias, and all letters ever printed. I want to ask one question of all the writers who came before me and who will come after me: in that perfect world —without pain, suffering, and death—which is in complete peace and harmony, what would you write or talk about? I know what my own book would be about. It would contain just one line: "We were happy, we are happy, and we will be happy." That word *happy* could be replaced by, for instance, *blessed, blissful, cheerful, delighted, ecstatic, joyful, merry, peaceful*, and many others. We didn't know death or pain in the beginning, but we started to talk about it again and again and to think differently, and finally, as a consequence, death became our destiny. All of the ideas and concepts about it were invented or discovered after the word fell from our mouths.

To add more fuel to the suffering, men came up with the concept of philosophy and called themselves philosophers. They are called wise men filled with wisdom, but what wisdom did they have? Go through history to see how Alexander the Great was tutored by Aristotle. What did he do? He became nasty and ignorant enough in his wisdom and in his philosophy to conquer the world. Is that what philosophy teaches? During World War II, Martin Heidegger, who spawned the theory of Philosophy of Modern Technology (PMT), joined the Nazis. Is that what philosophy teaches? To go kill one another?

Wisdom without words is nothing. I know there are philosophers *who spoke* about the WORD. The message of the WORD was spoken in all subjects, but no one ever stressed it or found the truth of it. Again, in a perfect world, what would the philosopher's role be? I have one philosophy: we are always doing the best. But with chaos all that we have now, we have lost our identity. We didn't know how powerful we were, and people came up with random answers, talked a lot of negativity, and made our lives worse.

If philosophers have wisdom in their answers, then why does one philosopher try to prove the other one wrong? For instance, some philosophers said the world was flat. Galileo proved the world was a sphere. Where did the wisdom of those earlier, misguided philosophers then go? That is not my actual question, though. We were once flying across the universe and even became ignorant of the fact that Earth is a sphere. How did we become so ignorant? Through cycles and trains of negative and false thoughts that we thought again and again, and through words we spoke again and again. Did philosophers have wisdom? They did, but they didn't have eternal or true wisdom—just big mouths to say whatever came into their minds. My entire life I've pondered, what is wisdom? I now know the answer: wisdom is good memory, and Aristotle definitely knew the world was a sphere. All he had was good memory—in the name of wisdom. That's why the Greeks built stages to debate the question that boils down to this: does a bullet, a knife, cyanide, a rope, or a microwave kill faster? My answer to all the Greeks and to the philosophical world is "We will live longer and forever." I don't even want to answer with "I never heard the word *death*," or "Humans can't die; they are eternal." I will never open my own mouth to say the word *death*.

There are books based on positive thinking and positive talking, and I sincerely appreciate their thoughts and contributions. All such writers teach how to be positive in life, work, family, and situations, and at the end of the day, I'll bet they go watch a thriller movie or see a depressing movie about a true story or listen to opera and then go to bed. Where did the positive thinking go? In the name of art and entertainment we have lost ourselves and made fools of ourselves. The worst things we give awards for are "best performance" and "best story," because generally the message of these winning writers is that there is evil, and they advise or show how to overcome it. My response to that is "To see radical change in our lives, let us not speak negatively."

The vast majority of writings and teachings are based on success stories, religious practices, myths, and sections in philosophy or science books. They are not based on evolution, the strings of a symphony at the advent of the big bang, universal consciousness, nature's law, and the purpose of life. Most religions simply file away these kinds of things as matters of faith and don't carry them further. I don't blame anyone, because all of us have been programmed from the day we were born. Certainly, you've heard such well-known sayings as "Life is short," "Shit happens," "Always expect the worst," "Through pain we seek wisdom," "Life is a journey," "Death is inevitable," and a million more. At the time you were born, the universe rested its arms for you to live long and forever. With all of those teachings that you've heard and yourself spoken, and based on which you build a life and become accomplished and successful, ultimately you breathe on this earth for less than a hundred years and then you die. To summarize our lives takes a combination of hundreds of books, movies, and experiences, and we apply our logic with our intellectual brains to create another set of books, movies, and experiences for the future generations. My question to all of those who came before me and will come after me is "How long did you teach, and will you be teaching these worn-out facts to your kids, friends, families, and society?"

An old man once said, "At the end of the day, we all are humans." That is true, and our traditions are that we are the supreme creatures created by the supernova. We have created two worlds, man's world and woman's world. Love and romance are natural instincts and feelings that are built into us, but we have complicated and twisted the true meaning of love and romance and blamed the natural characters of men and women. I felt myself disgusted to have to know from a book about how love and romance works, when they are already coded in our DNA and enfolded in the deepest knots of our brains. This is what happened in the romance literature world. I've read all the romance stories in the library, and all of them described love in all of its dimensions and in different situations, but only one thing was true in the end: the characters expressed how much they felt for each other. There are millions of stories of failed love, and after reading them, we comment about how well they told the truth. I myself remember how deeply I enjoyed my emotions with pain and recollected all my past romances and the love I felt for him or her or them and so on. A recollection of failures and pain is not the one that is going to change our lives. All these books are written to wake up emotions and feelings, but after that, you are the one to choose what to think of all these stories about how someone could fail and lose their loved one, when they loved someone beyond their imagined capacity. Their love was strong, but their word and mind was not with them. If you have your word, there is no one who can take away your loved ones. I made my choice, and no matter how many parallel universes I build and live in, Madison will be the only woman in my life.

Again, in a perfect world, with a perfect partner next to you, what will you do? I know what some are thinking: I don't want an angel putting grapes in my mouth; I need salsa and games. Well, that was how you evolved in knowledge and thinking, and that is the reason we are all dying. I would say to the one next to me, "I love you today more than yesterday." Love is the only thing that keeps expanding and expanding all the time, but the central idea remains the same: you love them.

The dilemma with love and romance also holds true for all the cultural and traditional values we have built up over the centuries, according to all the books I've read. It's been the biggest scam ever, and again and again for nothing. But we were blind. Though we made countless efforts to understand different cultural values, we didn't know the truth: that we are all one, and our commonality is our strongest heritage. Each culture and tradition is based on teachings and ideas, has opinions about idolatry, contains superstitions, draws boundaries, and inculcates customs you fit into, and they draw the equation for your life. My brothers and sisters, you are not a variable or a constant in an equation, but you are the equation of this universe. Please wake up and change your lives. Don't ignore my voice by thinking I am a radical preacher. You have loved me so far and came with me until this end, and your life has already changed.

In the name of defeating evil, we all became evil and grew worse and worse every day. It was the same with all the books that were written about what the future held in store, with war, pain, suffering, famine, hunger, depression, and all sorts of other problems. Such books just want to foretell the future as being chaotic. They assume themselves to be prophets of that era. We should have stoned all the prophets and writers who said the future would be chaotic. They were the biggest enemies of humans. You know why? It is not in how they portrayed it; it's that you believed it. And that makes me sad.

Yes, anyone can say anything about the future and its potential chaos, but it will never happen to you because your WORD—not others' words—will be your destiny. You are the master of your world, as I was the master of my search universe.

There are good scientific books about medicine, plants, nature, and geography; I am not against any of those books. They helped mankind progress, but the fundamental dilemma is that if we had been in our true state, everything would be exposed to everybody and not to only a select few. We are all born equal, where everyone could be the master of everything, and all it would take would be time and pressure to learn everything by ourselves. By pressure, I mean I don't need those medical books because I'm not sick yet.

We haven't seen aliens in our lives after the fall from the wind tunnel, but we classify them as a different species. We always looked for them, liked our forefathers did, to invite them to invade our lives and cause a mess. We spend so much money, time, and energy searching for ugly and envious creatures. I built my search world based upon what writers gave me and what the world fed me; I didn't cook up anything. I climbed the ladder and used books as my steps of knowledge and concepts as I built my life in the search world. A book always needs a plot, a character, tenses, grammar, content, language, but where is the true purpose and message of the book? And why am I so hard on the books and their authors? At the dusty dawn of human civilization after the fall from the heights of the universe from the wind tunnel, we were drawing and scribbling on the walls. Eventually we started to write on leaves, papyrus, clay, parchment, paper, and digital documents. Every time we wrote something false, we made humanity into folly, and in the name of message and story we pushed humanity into the abyss.

Everybody, when they put their pens and thoughts to paper, says, "This is a true story, or I have a gift or I have a message I want to show the world." We repeat our negative thoughts again and again and get caught in an endless loop. But did it change anything? No. The writers all changed something for a temporary moment. Do we know where we picked up all these crazy ideas? I used to think about controlled community, communist countries, and closed religions that denied freedom of speech. Somehow they were right in a way, because in the name of "freedom of expression and speech," the rest of us have blabbered so much that the universe itself hated us and turned its face from us.

What about the music world? I love music a lot, but we've turned this noble pursuit into an emotional toy. Who is the greatest musician in the world? The universe and its strings of symphony are. The ears of the universe would love to hear positive things from us, but we triggered the universal sound to move away from us. The universe always plays the most melodious music, but we've gone so far from it, we can't hear anymore. One of our powers was to uplift ourselves through music, but we rotted it with words and notes. I want the universe back to play it for me, and I am preparing every day for the universe to shine its face like that again.

I didn't bring Bickey to my search world because Purdhil's mother said, "Dogs don't go to heaven." I don't want to explore AI, because there are so many dummy books that speak about machine intelligence but not human intelligence. I have seen far beyond it from R Smith and learned from him. So, in my search world, I was not much concerned about robots, because they were built with the evilness and negativity from us.

There are no midgets, because I cured all of those who had dwarfism. But there were homosexuals, bisexuals, and transsexuals in my world. Yes, I supported them, and they lived peacefully according to their choices. When I went through all the theories of antigay protest based on moral and religious values, I found answers different from those of others and came to different conclusions about them. My theory is that everyone is gay. Why do we deny it in the name of the opposite sex? What is the physical difference between a man and a woman? A woman has hairless cheeks, developed breasts, and a reproductive system different from a man's, and a man is the opposite of that in appearance and in reproductive system. But both are classified as humans, so we have relationships with our fellow humans. If that's right, then why do we deny gay sex? On the other side of that thought, there have been virgins—people who've never even masturbated and who lived like saints and died. I think about them: how is it possible that they could do that? They have one deepest wisdom in their mind: "To me everybody looks the same in both mind and body, a clear vision with no differences —men, women, and children—because we are all holy and we are all God." Then the question is If we all are made as an image of God, then what gender is God? If God has no gender, then why should he be concerned about the morality of our gender issues?

If we all were gods, then how could we reproduce? At a perfect stage like that, we can create new humans with no elements or matter; that is, we could create humans from nothing. Then what is sex? A state of not feeling loneliness, and not having the fear to multiply. With that theory, you could figure out the basic idea behind my theory. I am neither homosexual nor bisexual, so I already knew that the answer to the search is not there. What about the vampires, zombies, wizards, casters, and many of their kind? We have fantasized about them, pictured them in all their variations, and fed our thoughts with their dark natures. Oh, you mortal humans of this world, we have classified those as the banned and dark books. The question I have to all men and women of all times, with the true theory and standards of the Science of Verbum Victus, is this: shouldn't all the books be classified as banned and dark? We have always believed in a better and necessary evil, and my heart is troubled very much when I realize our true identity. With the madness of this world's knowledge, I was also a victim, and you made me think like you. I was not much concerned about vampires and their craziness, with their two crazy teeth and wanting eternity from the queen vampire. What a shame and how disgusting that we did this to ourselves in the name of self-expression, writing, and thinking differently. We love that stuff, don't we? If you don't like vampires, then move to zombies—also part of the pathetic arts-and-entertainment world we live in. Of all your books I read, I made my father—who was my role model and the one I loved the most—a vampire and a zombie, and I could live with that because he was an imaginary one. I loved Nathalie, and she is my true mother—the woman I owe my life to—and I made her a vampire, and she was about to kill me. We create and fool ourselves with so many funny, fantastic, and stupid stories. I never saw the biker kids in my world because they all have inheritances and are spoiled kids. And all of the fancy, rich men's and women's kids' stories I read made me think they all are useless, because I'm trying to create a world with singularity and with life forever.

If you honestly think about who the real enemies in this world are, it is not the government or a group or a religion. The real enemies are your mouth, your loved ones, and the role models you follow. Know why I say that? Because when you were a kid, you read in your bedtime story about a bean that rooted in the soil and grew so tall in the sky that it reached heaven. Then someone climbed up it to see what was at the top. This fantasy story has been different in all cultures in different forms. You are the loved one who is reading this story to your kids, your nieces, your nephews, your grandchildren. You are those children's biggest enemy. You raise all these questions—you know: How could someone climb into the sky without oxygen? How come a tree grew so fast? How much water is needed for this tree to grow so tall? And so on. Whereas the same kids you're reading the story to want to be doctors, astronauts, and scientists. When I bring this up with anyone, the only answer I get is, "They're just kids, and kids love to listen to stories." Don't you ever realize that you've actually fooled the kids? And who says kids don't know everything? But you have defined them as less than that for ages. There is this notion that as we grow, we gain wisdom. The biggest question is how much should we grow to gain wisdom? As tall as the beanstalk from the fairy tale? That is not just a story; it is a lie—a lie against universes—and how many unknowing lies do we perpetrate every day?

In my search world everyone was living forever, and death was necessary, but when I really want a life that the world talks about—Where is the bus stop? Where is the road to . . . ? Where is the cemetery? Where is the prison? Where is the hospital? Where are the law agents? and where and how in society will I live?—I have to build a cemetery, a prison, a hospital, and law agents for it. You could build a nation more or less like the one I built in the search world, with all the knowledge and wisdom you have gained from the words and letters of humankind.

At this point, if you are searching for a true answer, you should have already found it. I don't need to explain any further. Now, what do you think of me? A lunatic? A god? Satan? A maniac? Selfish? A finger-pointer? The chosen one? A messenger? After reading this, decide what you will call me, whatever that is, but I will tell you, I am the chosen one to stop World War III.

You may also wonder why I'm angry. Here it is: because I am fighting for your grandson and granddaughter, because you have pretty much messed it up for future generations, and I am here to fix it.

There are a few puzzles to the search world. Did the bank Harvest and Reap exist in the real world? The answer is no; I created this bank for my purpose. There are no banks in this real world, and on Wall Street, there are two, one of which is a boiler room—a fake bank—run by the government. Only ghosts hang out on Wall Street, with a few old dudes and smart but ignorant young folks with their blue suits and blue shirts. So, why did I create Harvest and Reap in the search world? After the war is over—because I stopped it—I want to open the first legal and global bank on Wall Street in the Fourth Dimension in the year 3500. It is the only bank this world needs, and I am the chairman and CEO. I should be rewarded for my work, and I will take a cut this time.

Who is Dan Root? I still don't know where he came from. He is not from the Fourth Dimension. All I know is that he is a man, and I wonder all the time who he is. I couldn't find anything about him and was the only one who saw him and interacted with him. Edgar and Nyah walked me in and then they left. They too never saw him. They only heard about him. In my search world, I didn't create him; he is a foreign energy who sneaked in. You know why? I built the first library in Chelsea in the search world, with my version of all of the books. They were all sources of knowledge, and every one of 7 billion people had free choice there. And I just imported all the books from the library from my real world to my holy and pure search world. Everyone read them and day by day became more evil, but not Dan Root. He is the mystery man and that is the only thing bothering me. Who is he? The God? I don't know. He called me a god, so don't get angry when I call myself god Oliver Oscar. I said I am *a* god, not *your* God. Dan Root said everyone is equal all the time, which means he was human. At this point, I could conclude that maybe he is my consciousness.

The last question in your puzzle is, why did Nathalie ask us to walk and not use technology? The answer is very simple: we are going to read the third-dimensional books, and we don't have any rockets or a GPS or an RFID or space shuttles to do it. If we walked in the Third Dimension, we would have a better understanding of the books in the library. I'm glad I surfed all the books in the library and found the puzzle. Will my answer stop the war? That is your choice to decide whether you want to make it or not, but I will practice and practice and come with my true power again. The only reason to believe in the Science of Verbum Victus is that once I found the truth of this universe, my own search world kicked me out. I cannot enter into that world again; the world has disappeared from my mind and has gone very far. From the dust to this day, everybody spoke about the mind and dreams, but I took a step ahead to the WORD. Always remember: mind will take you to infinity minus one dimension, and your WORD will take you to infinity plus one dimension. All the great works that have been created in the past and the one before my eyes are brilliant flaws of design for the fallen man. If we had been perfected from the time of the supernova, we wouldn't need any of the foolish knowledge and wisdom we have gained so far. All the answers that were built into the universe will work temporarily, but they'll never fix anything permanently. Your mind might be still wondering what this is all about and what Oliver is trying to say, and then wondering—after reading this—do I sincerely and truly believe in his concept, and will that make a radical change?

I will put you to a small test: you are holding this book in your hand, you take a deep breath, and you think, what concept is not in this book? It includes issues of philosophy, religion, culture, friendship, love, romance, evolution, corporate politics, fantasy, war, dreams, foster homes, escape, prison, parenting, child abuse, journeys, lesbians/gays/bisexuals/transsexuals, crime, courts of law, conspiracy, the future, prostitution, stripping, HIV, college life, school life, pirates, hacking, midgets, cults, encounters, mission, adventure, kids, zombies, patriotism, slavery, fear, ego, moral values, vampires, hallucinations, split personality, ghosts, revenge, friendship, cop stories, racism, Occupy Wall Street, cloning, robots, weddings, and adoption. If you're thinking there are concepts left over to challenge me, then you have not believed the Science of Verbum Victus, and your mind is still filled with the world's foolish knowledge and thoughts. It means you are in the Third Dimension if every word spoken, every letter written, and every work of art and creativity designed there is deep in your mind. If you want to go to infinite dimensions, the answers are with you. You are the author, the king, and the god of your future.

If you are blind and cannot read this text and you are listening to a loved one read it to you, then believe in the theory of truth, the Science of Verbum Victus, and keep speaking positively all the time to open your eyes, and one day you will get your sight back and see me. Till you get sighted, I will be in your memory and dwell in you. I will be there always, praying for you. If you can't speak because you have no voice, keep on thinking in your mind that you are going to be able to sing a song to me soon, and you will. Till then, keep writing down, "I will sing a song for Oliver"; I will be the first to dance to your song. If you are pregnant, always stay positive and keep saying, "My child will be the chosen one—like Oliver and his nine friends." I promise your baby I will send Nathalie the midwife, and she will bless it. If you are totally physically disabled and bedridden, without thought or bodily ability, my hands are on your shoulders, and I am talking on your behalf. You will soon wake up and make leaps of joy, and we will party in Milwaukee and take a road trip to New York City. If you are in prison or your hands are chained, just believe in hope and say every day, "I will be free and walk like a king." The day will come and it is close to you. The prison will break into two halves and your chains will be broken, and I will accompany you to your throne and the house of happiness. If you are homeless and have no hope in life, just believe in the Science of Verbum Victus, and you will be fed from the skies and clothed with the rich robes of the East, and your plate will overflow with wealth. If you are drowning in the ocean of problems, miseries and misfortune please keep thinking positive. The Universe will send you a dolphin or a whale, which will save your life and bring you to the land of hope and living.

If you're against this theory and generally destroy the universe's whole idea, you have that choice. But my only request is, please don't destroy the hopes of the people who believe in it, and always remember that this is the last chance we all have to survive this battle of existence. No matter what you do, I will fight for your children, your grandchildren, your family, and your other loved ones. And I thank you very much for being patient with me so far.

Niki is working on the chip that Professor Gavins gave us, and he found a machine to defeat everyone and bring down the war. Let's use his method, and I will use mine. Do I need to tell all my friends about the puzzle? Of course I will tell them. They will believe me because they trusted me from the beginning, and I have enough evidence to prove it. But one thing I am sure of, out of the nine: that no one will act in the same way and build a search world like me. Others will have their own stories and find their own answers. I also know that at this point, you don't want nine more books like this! I have given more than enough information about the eternal truth to change your lives, so let us extinguish all the old doctrines, the old knowledge, and the old wisdom. Remember that there is no big secret to any successful person in history. It is just the WORD—knowingly or unknowingly—through which they have made their lives like that. This means that whatever you do in your work, just be positive and begin by saying until the end that you will be in the hall of fame.

Last but not least, don't assume what all the geniuses have concluded —that the reason for the problems and chaos of this world is greed or selfishness. You are better than those people. Always remember that the source of all problems is your WORD. I have searched on behalf of everyone, but if you'd still like to search on your own to learn the single answer to all problems, you are of course welcome to do so like me, and I will be very glad when you find an answer. Now I must prepare myself to stop war and start my bank. I'm glad you're still alive and listening to me, and if you need to know how I'm going to stop the war, you need to understand how it began and why I am here.

To Begin . . .